FOR VANN!

MR.

TW...

BOYD MCCLOYD

AND THE

PERPETUAL MOTION MACHINE

BY RANDALL P. GIRDNER

 Acclimated Spooks, Light, & Power
Publishing Company

RPG 12-9-17

For Vana!

First published worldwide by Acclimated Spooks, Light, and Power Publishing

www.boydmccloyd.com

Cover design by Chris Canterbury & Randy Girdner.

Illustrations by Randy Girdner.

Girdner, Randy

Mr. Ping's Almanac of the Twisted and Weird presents Boyd McCloyd and the Perpetual Motion Machine

ISBN 978-0-615-25755-6

<u>First Edition</u>

<u>2008</u>

This book is emphatically and wholeheartedly dedicated
to the three stars at the epicenter of my galaxy:
Tracey
Harper
and
Abbey
If only everyone else was as lucky as I am.

A note to the reader:
Being that this is, more than likely, your first taste of *The Almanac of the Twisted and Weird*, the reader should note that important words have been highlighted and are followed by a number which will direct them to the appendix at the back of the book. The appendix has been created for scholars of Mr. Ping's work. There is *plenty* of information located in the appendix for those hearty souls interested in the Twisted and Weird, but the appendix IS NOT necessary to enjoy the book. Read the book first, then enjoy the "extra" information located in the back.

For internship inquiries and previous volumes of *Mr. Ping's Almanac of the Twisted and Weird*, please consult the address hidden within this book, and proceed with the instructions contained therein.

The opinions expressed in this book are that of the author only, and are not necessarily the views of *Acclimated Spooks, Light, and Power Limited, The Himalayan Outback Detective Agency, Serious and Earnest Incorporated* or any of their subsidiaries.

PART I

CHAPTER I
THE DAY THE YETI
KIDNAPPED
BOYD MCCLOYD
AND HIS SISTER, CINDY

The 3:15 bell was a welcome relief for Boyd McCloyd that afternoon, and he was eager to get home, far away from the troubles of school. It hadn't been a good day. From the minute Boyd slept through his alarm clock, to the moment when he realized his mother had forgotten the roast beef part of his roast beef sandwich, to the time when the ten-foot strip of toilet paper had stuck to his shoe during a bathroom break, Boyd had been having a terrible day. Now school was

out, and it was time for him to go home and forget that such a horrible day had ever happened.

His troubles were only beginning.

Boyd McCloyd was thirteen years old, and just like most thirteen year old boys, he loved comic books and video games and drawing pictures of giant robots destroying skyscrapers. Boyd wasn't the smartest kid in his class, but he was by far the most creative, and he used to take solace from the world in the elaborate comic books he would draw and strange stories he would write. However, Boyd was shy and because of this, he preferred to keep a low profile at school. That approach had served him well, but it was all about to change.

This particular day had been bad and Boyd was certainly glad it was over; but as he left class, he noticed something peculiar. All the students in the hall were staring at him as if he was a circus freak. A few even had their mouths wide-open when he walked by, as if there was some sort of ghost standing in front of them. As he continued walking, he began to think that the toilet paper might still be stuck to his shoe, or perhaps something was lurking in his nose. It was only when his little sister, Cindy, ran up to him that he realized something was really wrong, (because she would *never* acknowledge Boyd was her brother at school unless she absolutely *had to).*

"What are you doing?" she asked as they walked towards the exit.

"What do you mean, 'what am I doing?'" Boyd asked. "I'm going home."

"Have you looked behind you?" Cindy asked.

"At what?" Boyd asked, and just as he did, he saw that everyone was following him.

Some of them even smiled and began to chant, "Boyd! Boyd! Boyd!"

"What's going on?" he asked.

"You can do it!" one student told him.

"It's about time somebody stood up to him!" said another.

"Stood up to who?" Boyd asked.

Cindy spun him around and began walking Boyd towards the door. "Tucker Stevens!" she said. "That's who!"

"What about him?" Boyd asked. The large group of students followed them outside the school.

"He's been saying that he's going to fight you after school!"

"Fight me?"

"He said he was going to find you on the way home," she said, pulling him by the arm. "Come on! If we hurry, maybe we can get you safely hidden."

Tucker Stevens. This was bad.

Tucker was the school's biggest bully. He was twice as big as most seventh graders because he'd been held back a year to be the dominant player on the junior hockey team. It seemed that Boyd had the unfortunate luck to be involved in several minor incidents with Tucker that day.

It all started during gym class, when Boyd haphazardly launched a basketball into the air, which, by a sheer stroke of luck, happened to hit Tucker in the face. Strike one.

Then at lunch, as Boyd ate his roast beef-less roast beef sandwich, Tucker came over to pick on Boyd. As a gesture of strength, Tucker slammed his fist down on Boyd's sandwich. However, instead of intimidating Boyd, it simply squirted mustard out onto the front of Tucker's pants. Strike two.

The final straw was when Boyd bent over to tie his shoe between classes at the same time that Tucker was playing football with his buddies. Tucker had gone long to catch a pass, didn't see Boyd bent over, and went tumbling over him in front of everyone. Strike three.

Boyd could feel the butterflies in his stomach as he thought about how those three incidents could have angered Tucker enough that he'd want to fight. Surely Tucker was rational enough to realize that none of these incidents were Boyd's fault. Wasn't he?

"I'm not fighting Tucker," Boyd said to Cindy. "I'll talk to him about it and we'll work this out."

"You're talking like a wimp!" Cindy said, looking around to see if anyone had heard her brother. "Don't say that so loud. My *friends* are over there."

"Look, Cindy," Boyd said, as they left the school grounds followed by a throng of kids. "This is all just a big misunderstanding. When I see Tucker, I'll talk to him and everything will be fine."

"*Talk* to him?" Cindy asked. "*Talk* to him? Are you crazy? Guys like Tucker only talk with their fists. You're gonna get killed."

"I'm not going to get killed," he said.

Cindy stopped him in his tracks. "Trust me," she said, sounding grave. "You are."

"Go home, Cindy," Boyd said. She stood there as the crowd of students enveloped her.

Boyd paid no attention to the crowd and continued his walk home, yet with each step the group grew harder and harder to ignore. He could hear their laughs and chatter, their comments about what would happen and snickers about whether they should call the ambulance now or later. Though he tried to look strong, cracks began to form, and in his mind, he wanted to run away. He didn't want to fight Tucker at all.

"McCloyd!"

Boyd turned around to see the crowd part for Tucker and his friends. He looked angrier than Boyd had ever seen him as they stood on a street corner surrounded by most of the kids from school. Boyd tried to look like he wasn't intimidated, but it was all he could do to keep his hands from shaking.

"I wanna talk to you!" Tucker said, shouting right in Boyd's face.

For a split second, Boyd was relieved, thinking that Tucker actually wanted to talk. A quick shove to Boyd's chest soon vanquished that thought.

"I don't want to fight you, Tucker," he said, regaining his balance.

"I don't care what you want," he said, fists raised and ready to fight. "Now, drop your bag and let's go."

"Leave him alone!"

Like a bolt of lightning, Cindy shot through the crowd to stand between them, and with all of her pint-sized might, she shoved Tucker away from Boyd. After regaining his footing, Tucker's face grew red. "You're gonna let a *girl* do your fighting for you?" he asked.

"I could take you any day!" Cindy said.

"Cindy..." Boyd said, feeling awkward.

"Back off, Boyd," Cindy said over her shoulder. She turned back towards Tucker and shouted, "Bring it on, you big dumb jerk!"

Tucker was furious, and some of the students in the crowd made him even angrier when they snickered at Cindy's insult. "This is between you and me, Boyd," he snarled. "Get your sister out of here."

"Too scared to fight a girl, are you?" Cindy asked. Her brow was determined and her fists were squeezed tight. "You *are* as dumb as you look." Everyone laughed.

"You're lucky you're a girl," Tucker said.

"No, *you're* lucky I'm a girl," Cindy said, and more laughs erupted. Tucker could sense that he was losing the crowd, as the tension that had built up before the fight was now starting to disappear.

"Cindy," Boyd said. "Get out of the way."

"I'm trying to help you, Boyd," she said.

"I appreciate that," Boyd said. "But you should let me handle this."

"Yeah," Tucker said. "He doesn't need a girl to help."

Cindy stared at Boyd skeptically, as if she couldn't believe that he had made such a decision. Then she lowered her guard and gave Boyd a look that said she would miss him when he was dead. Tucker had rolled up his sleeves, and stood right in front of Boyd, ready to take it all the way.

"Come on, Boyd," he said, taunting him. "Let's go!"

"I'm not fighting you, Tucker," Boyd said.

"Oh, yes, you are," he replied.

"No, I'm not," Boyd said. "You're not the king of the school, and just because you're big, it doesn't mean that you can pick on anybody you want. I didn't do anything to you!"

"Man, I am going to wipe the floor with you, McCloyd," Tucker said. Even through all the fear and nervousness coursing through Boyd's body, he still couldn't help but notice that Tucker was talking like a third-rate professional wrestler.

"Can we talk about this?" Boyd said in one last attempt to diffuse the situation.

"Talk?" Tucker said with a sneer. "I only talk with my fists."

It was true, because with that, he swung a left at Boyd's head with all his might. What he failed to realize was that he gave every indication of what he was about to do and Boyd had plenty of time to dodge the blow. The force behind the punch sent Tucker flying forward with such momentum that he couldn't regain his balance, and when he tried, he tripped over Boyd's leg and fell to the ground, face first.

Laughter from the crowd ensued and Tucker stared up at Boyd with pure rage. Boyd just stood over him with an astonished look on his face. In that split second, Boyd knew that a) he had become a legend at Dave Karlskint Elementary, and b) he was about to receive the worst beating he had ever experienced.

Just as Tucker was about to jump for Boyd, the loud screech of skidding tires echoed behind the crowd. Everyone turned to see a large black limousine come to a halt behind them. The commotion was so distracting that even Boyd and Tucker looked over to see what was going on.

The back door of the limousine opened and a man dressed in a black business suit stepped out to survey the crowd. He wore mirrored sunglasses and his skin was olive and smooth. His hair was short and spiked straight up into the air and the look on his face was full of grim determination. He parted the crowd, walking right into the center of the chaos towards Boyd. "Boyd McCloyd?" he asked.

"Uh, yeah?" Boyd said.

"My name is Ho Yin," he said. "Where is your sister?"

There was a brief silence as the man scanned the crowd for Cindy. His target was obvious as almost everyone had craned their necks to find Cindy standing behind him. "Um, that's me," she said, raising her hand in a bashful manner.

"I need the two of you to come with me," Ho Yin said.

"Oh, that's typical," Tucker said as he rose to his feet. "Get this guy to help you out of a tight spot. You really *are* a chicken, McCloyd."

As Tucker dusted off his pants, Ho Yin looked over at him in confusion. "Who is this?" he asked Boyd.

"What do you mean, 'who is this?'" Boyd asked. "Who are *you*? If you think we're getting in that car with you, you're crazy."

"There's been trouble, Boyd," Ho Yin said. "I need both of you to come with me."

"Forget it, weirdo," Cindy yelled from her safe spot behind Boyd.

"You're good kids," Ho Yin smiled. "I figured this would happen." He reached into his pocket and pulled out a phone, dialing a number as he put it to his ear. "Yes," he said. "No, they don't want to come...Okay..."

He hung up the phone and the driver's side door of the limousine opened to reveal an eight-foot tall creature covered in long, white hair and wearing a black suit. As the creature stepped out onto the street, the car bobbed up and down in relief from its weight. The creature's eyes were obscured by its long hair, and its gnarled, sharp bottom teeth protruded from a mouth that looked like it could swallow a horse. The creature used its large, thick arms to flatten out the wrinkles from its suit and then surveyed the crowd before walking over to the center of the circle. Immediately, an audible gasp rang out from the crowd.

The yeti[1] had arrived.

Its breathing sounded like a mild earthquake, and its shoulders were so heavy that it had to walk hunched over, causing its extra-long arms to drag on the ground. It walked right up to Boyd as the crowd looked on, stunned at what was transpiring in front of them.

"This is him," Ho Yin said, nodding towards Boyd. He then looked over at Cindy and said, "And that's his sister."

The yeti looked at Boyd and Cindy through the thick hair hanging over its eyes and sniffed at them with its wide nose. It looked at Ho Yin for a second and then snatched Boyd and Cindy from the ground, stuffing them under its arm in a most uncomfortable position.

"Hey!" Boyd said. "Somebody help us!"

"Let me go!" Cindy yelled.

No one moved a muscle. All they could do was stand there and stare wide-eyed at the unbelievable situation unfolding before them. There were well-over a hundred kids watching the fight that afternoon and not a single one of them had any idea what to do to help Boyd and Cindy. They stood frozen, watching the pair being carried off to the limousine and thrown in the backseat with a thump.

However, there *was* one voice in the crowd that protested their kidnapping. Unfortunately, the voice was that of Tucker. "That's great," he said. "Just run away!" Although he was doing his best to sound brave, if one were to listen closely to Tucker's voice, one could have detected a hint of fear. "You're sure going through a lot of work to get out of a fight, Boyd! What a wimp." He continued to taunt Boyd all the way to the car until Ho Yin blocked his path.

"You know," Ho Yin said with a smile, "the Koran says, 'He who forgiveth, and is reconciled unto his enemy, shall receive his reward from God; for he loveth not the unjust doers.'"

"Get out of my way, jerk," Tucker said. He yelled over Ho Yin's shoulder towards Boyd, "It must be nice to be saved from a beating by a giant monkey!"

The silence that swept over the crowd was the surest indication that Tucker had gone too far. The yeti slammed the door of the limousine and stood there with its back towards the group of students. A sound like rolling thunder slowly filled the air and the creature turned towards Tucker. The yeti's top lip was quivering with anger, revealing its horrible fangs. Then it began to make its hands into fists over and over again, knuckles cracking like pieces of dried firewood.

"Uh-oh," Ho Yin said over his shoulder as he walked back to the limousine. "I believe you've made a grave error."

The yeti walked over to Tucker with its chest heaving in and out, taking deep breaths as it tried to control its incredible rage. It breathed through its nose, which sounded like the pistons of a freight train trying to pull away from a rail yard, and it rolled its head around as if loosening up for a fight.

Tucker looked for an escape route, but saw none. For the first time in his life, the bully had found a bigger adversary and he was scared. All the students began to run away, screaming bloody murder in fear of being gobbled up by the yeti. Tucker, however, simply fell to the ground, quaking in his shoes at the gigantic angry monster that stood over him. The creature looked at Tucker, and its eyes immediately filled with furious rage. Drool was hanging from its black lips, and its claws were extended, ready to swipe at any moment. Through its laborious growls, it howled, "DON'T…EVER…CALL…ME…A…MONKEY!"

Upon hearing this, Tucker burst into tears and said, "Please don't hurt me! I'm the star of the hockey team!" To make matters worse, the yeti unleashed a roar that sounded most akin to that of an elephant, lion, and cougar combined, and the force of its breath parted Tucker's hair.

With that, Tucker's eyes rolled back into his head and he flopped over onto the grass, fear having robbed him of consciousness. The creature stood there for a second or two, still in its attack position, and observed Tucker's soundly sleeping frame. It then stood up, no longer hunching its shoulders or dragging its arms. It wiped the drool from its chin and brushed the hair from its face to reveal two large, blue eyes. It straightened its suit and tie, and spun around to walk back to the limousine not like a hideous, man-eating beast, but more like a refined Englishman. It climbed into the car, shut the door, and pulled away with Boyd and Cindy in the backseat.

CHAPTER 2
THERE'S NO PLACE LIKE HOME...

...EXCEPT WHEN IT HAS BEEN DESTROYED

From inside the limousine, Boyd and Cindy watched in awe at what had transpired. Their mouths and eyes were wide open as they stared out the window to see what the yeti did to Tucker and they were entirely unsure of what might happen next. Where were they being taken? Who was this man named Ho Yin? Was the yeti going to eat them? There were so many questions.

After Ho Yin and the yeti returned to the car, they drove off, leaving behind the cookie-cutter houses, heading for a destination unknown to either Boyd or Cindy. Although they felt as if they were being kidnapped, Boyd and Cindy also knew that there was something more behind their abduction. It was that suspicion which told them not to put up a fight and so they remained placid, as if waiting for the next turn of events. They both settled into their seats and stared at the stoic fellow sitting across from them.

"You're in big trouble, mister," Boyd said, trying to act brave. "Although I appreciate the fact that you saved me from getting a couple of black eyes, kidnapping is a *serious* offense."

"Yeah, you big kidnapping kidnapper!" Cindy added.

Ho Yin smiled at them, and looked amused. "I'm not kidnapping you," he said. "We're going to your house."

"Huh?" Boyd asked.

"Something has happened," Ho Yin said, growing serious. "You're both in terrible danger and we must get you to safety. But in order to do that, we need to check something."

Boyd and Cindy grew quiet as he spoke. They stared out the windows at their neighborhood, a place that once felt familiar and safe, but now seemed menacing because of the strange turn of events on that dreary afternoon. Boyd felt a bit uncomfortable, for although Ho Yin was wearing sunglasses, it was obvious that he was staring at them. "Who *are* you?" he asked.

"A friend," Ho Yin said, "And you're going to have to trust me. Otherwise, this could become very unfortunate, very quickly."

"I don't trust kidnapping liars like you," Cindy said, her arms folded across her chest.

"I understand your skepticism," Ho Yin said. "I can't ask you to do anything but have faith in what I say."

"I won't do that," she said.

"She's always like this," Boyd said, embarrassed at Cindy's antics.

The limousine pulled up in front of Boyd's house and the glass divider between the driver and the backseat lowered. The yeti in the front turned around, waiting for orders. "We're going to go in," Ho Yin said, getting out of the car. "Keep an eye on things."

The creature grunted once to acknowledge the orders and raised the divider again.

As Boyd and Cindy emerged from the limousine, both of them noticed something odd about their house. There wasn't anything visibly different; it was the atmosphere. A strange electricity was in the air, like they had been transported to another dimension where everything was just a little bit off. It was their house, but it didn't *feel* like their house. Upon walking in the front door, Boyd found that the reality was much stranger than anything he could have imagined.

The house looked like a tornado had rolled through it. The couch had been ripped to shreds, holes had been punched in the walls, pictures were strewn across the floor, and glass was everywhere. "Boyd," Cindy said, "what happened?"

"I don't know," he said.

"We're too late," Ho Yin said. He looked very grim.

"Mom...? Dad...?" Boyd yelled, but his calls were met with silence.

"Boyd, where are they?" Cindy asked.

Boyd said nothing as he started to walk towards the bedrooms. Ho Yin placed a hand on his shoulder to stop him.

"Stay close," he said. "They could still be here."

"Who?" Boyd asked, but even as he did, he noticed the papery substance on the floor. It was long, like a giant tube of brittle wax paper, and it stretched across the floor of the living room, around the corner, and into the hallway. It looked like it had scales. "What's this?" he asked, pointing at the floor. He felt Cindy latch onto his arm for protection and they both stayed close to Ho Yin, who said nothing. He just kept searching the room, looking for any signs of danger. For some reason, this stranger felt safe to them, and judging by the defensive stance he took and the way his eyes scanned the room, they realized that if something *were* lurking in the shadows, he would do everything within his power to defend them.

They rounded the corner to see a man dressed in black from head-to-toe, standing in the bedroom hallway. "Well, well, well," said the intruder with a hiss. "If it isn't Ping's lapdog."

Ho Yin stood in front of Boyd and Cindy, his hands open and ready, his gaze as steady as a tiger. In contrast, the intruder had a nonchalance about him that gave Boyd the impression that he didn't perceive Ho Yin to be much of a threat.

"You shouldn't be nosing about this place," Ho Yin said.

"Oh, really?" the intruder said, his voice dripping with sarcasm.

"The Buddha says that he who looks for happiness by hurting those who seek happiness will never find it," Ho Yin said.

"Spare me your philosophy," the intruder said with a laugh. "Give me those kids and I'll let you live."

"A thorn defends the rose, harming only those who would steal the blossom," Ho Yin said.

"Very poetic," the intruder said, and in a flash, he dove for Ho Yin. Both of them seemed to be Kung Fu experts and Boyd was amazed at how quickly they were moving. The intruder could throw three punches so fast that Boyd's eyes could barely keep up, and in return, Ho Yin would block them countering with three punches of his own. The intruder ducked to the ground and tried to kick Ho Yin's legs out from under him, but Ho Yin did an effortless back flip to avoid him, landing like a cat on his hands and feet.

"I'm sorry," Ho Yin said, "But have you gotten slower since the last time we met?"

"Shut up!" the intruder yelled.

Then Ho Yin came at him with a series of roundhouse kicks, spinning around with such speed that his victim could barely dodge the blows. The intruder found himself backed up against the wall as Ho Yin's hands whirled about, and in the blink of an eye he extended his arm so that his fingers were stiff against the intruder's throat. If he moved even slightly, Ho Yin could have cut off his air supply.

He looked at the intruder grimly. "Who sent you?" he asked.

"Your mother," the intruder said, but a slight bit of pressure on this throat made him gasp for air.

"Shall I make the situation worse for you?" Ho Yin asked.

Boyd and Cindy were so awestruck with what was happening that they failed to see the shadow that was slithering beneath them. In a flash, their legs were taken out from under them and they were being dragged across the floor. Cindy emitted a high-pitched wail that could have shattered glass were it just a bit louder.

Boyd realized they had been captured by a giant snake, its scaly skin squirming its way around his throat as it lifted his entire body off the floor.

Ho Yin spun around to see Boyd and Cindy being taken, as the man he held captive started to melt, his skin changing to scales and his skull growing long and narrow. When Ho Yin saw the intruder's eyes turn reptilian and his forked tongue dart out of his mouth, he jumped backwards just in time to avoid the snapping jaws of his captive party.

The intruder had transformed into a snake.

"Ho Yin!" Boyd said, barely able to breathe as the other snake wrapped itself around his throat. Cindy was still screaming and being held in much the same position as Boyd.

"Yessss," said the snake holding Boyd. "Sssssee iff you cannn help himmm, lapdog." Neither of the snakes looked impressive, with colorful patterns or long, elegant bodies. They were both brown and ugly, and looked more like ravenous, scavenging beasts than actual reptiles.

Ho Yin was now cornered by the two snakes, one of which held Boyd and Cindy. They began curling and squirming and thrusting their way towards him, their forked tongues tasting the air. "Tell usss, Ho Yin," said the snake he had captured as a man mere seconds ago. "Tell usss and we'll let them live."

"Tell you what?" Ho Yin asked, steeling his gaze towards his captors.

"Pinggg," said the snake. "He'sss dead, isssn't he?"

"Mr. Ping is very much alive and well," Ho Yin said. "Which will not be something we can say about you when this is all over, unless you give yourselves up."

One snake turned to the other and smiled (if one could call it a smile). "He'sss quite funny, isssn't he?" it said.

"I think he'sss hilariousss," said the other.

"Tell usss, the truthhh, Ho Yin," said the snake. "We jussst need to know. If you tell usss now, we'll kill you quickly."

"You've got three-seconds to put them down and give up," Ho Yin said.

"You ssssee fit to threaten usss, do you?" said the snake.

"Three," Ho Yin said.

"Tell usss where Ping isss or we'll kill them," said the other snake.

"Two," Ho Yin said.

"I've waited a long time to do thissss," one said, coiling as if he were about to strike.

"One," Ho Yin said.

The snakes prepared to strike, but they stopped midway, as an unearthly, subhuman roar filled the hallways of the house. The floors vibrated and the windows shook, which filled the two snakes with so much fear that one dropped Boyd and Cindy almost instantly, and the other bit its own forked tongue.

They turned to see a horrifying sight, as the yeti was now standing in the hallway behind them. Boyd couldn't believe what he was seeing. The yeti's eyes were wild and angry, and its sharp, yellow fangs made the snakes writhe to escape. Regardless of the creature's size, it moved like a jackrabbit, snatching the two large snakes by their throats before they could escape.

Although he was far away from the hairy beast, Boyd could feel its hot breath. It looked at Ho Yin as though it was just *waiting* for permission to eat those snakes right then and there. Boyd noticed that the snakes were now changing shape, their long, squirming bodies formed arms and legs, their fangs receded back into their mouths, and their skulls grew hair.

"This is all a big mistake!" one said, having reverted to human form.

"Please," said the other. "We thought you were someone else..."

"Spare us your lies," Ho Yin said. Much to Boyd's surprise, Ho Yin still seemed unfazed about the fact that the men had just changed from snakes to humans. "I know both of you," he said, pointing at them. "You're Nick Lai and you're Ray Wong[2]. You both work for Fang."

Boyd could hear the yeti's menacing growl amidst the conversation. "He forced us to come here," said Ray, looking pitiful.

"Haven't you learned about the consequences of Mr. Wu's snake potion[3]?" Ho Yin asked them. "Stick out your tongues."

Both men stuck their tongues out to reveal that they were still forked like the snakes they were.

"You never fully change back, boys," Ho Yin said. "Each time you change in to a snake, a little bit of the reptile starts to take over."

"We had no choice," cried Nick. "He *made* us drink the potion."

"Let us go," Ray said. "We'll tell you everything."

"Yes, yes," Nick said. "We're good men. We have to feed our families. That's why we work for Fang."

"He's right," added Ray.

"We were poor…"

"We had no money…"

"He offered us work…"

"Threatened our families…"

"We had no choice!"

"No choice!"

Ho Yin looked at the two of them, lost in thought. He moved over toward the big picture window in the living room, and opened it up for fresh air. "So all you need is forgiveness and you'll stop being criminals?"

"Yes, yes," said Ray.

"This pathetic life of crime will be history," said Nick

"Finished!"

"Ended!"

"We need your compassion!" said Ray.

"We need your forgiveness!" said Nick.

"Two of the biggest lowlifes in Hong Kong want compassion and forgiveness?" Ho Yin asked. "I think you're both forgetting that I know who you are, and what I know tells me that you're not to be trusted." He looked at the yeti and said, "If you would be so kind…"

The yeti grunted its approval and drop-kicked both Ray and Nick straight out the picture window, one after the other. Their screams disappeared into the distance and ended with a thump and a roll much further down the street. Boyd and Cindy ran to the window to see them struggle to their feet and run off. "We'll get you for this, lapdog!" they yelled, shaking their fists in the air. "You'll pay!"

Boyd looked up at the yeti, just as the yeti looked down at him, its long, white hair obscuring its eyes like a sheep dog. "English Spectacular Football League[4]," it said to Boyd with an unmistakable British accent. "Of course, I'm much more used to kicking soccer balls than riffraff like that. Still, I got some good distance on them, if I do say so myself."

"You *talk*!" Cindy said, still trying to catch her breath.

"Of course I talk," the yeti said. "What did you take me for? A mindless, savage beast with brute strength and razor-sharp fangs? Pish-posh, old girl. I'm as sophisticated as the next person."

"It can talk," Cindy said again, almost to herself.

After checking to make sure the intruders were gone, Ho Yin walked over to everyone and said, "I don't think any of you have been formally introduced. Boyd, Cindy, this is Reggie. He's a yeti."

"Reggie?" Boyd asked.

"Yeti?" Cindy asked. "You mean like Bigfoot[5]?"

Reggie rolled his eyes. "Blimey, don't mention that name around me, please! Those blasted yahoos have set our cause back fifty years gallivanting down in the States like they were leprechauns."

"What just happened?" Boyd asked, his mouth still gaping as he pointed out the front window of his house at the two assailants running down the street.

"That's what we're up against, Boyd," Ho Yin said.

"Where are our parents?" Cindy asked.

Ho Yin sighed. "Kidnapped," he said.

Reggie sniffed the air a couple of times with his large, wide nose. "Taken this morning," he said. "A big group of fellows. I can smell at least ten or so."

"Then those two guys must have been the cleanup crew," Ho Yin said.

"Our parents were **kidnapped**?" Boyd asked.

"Unfortunately, yes," Ho Yin said. "We got here too late."

"It's a bloomin' shame," Reggie said, smacking his large fist into his hand. "I would have liked to grab ahold of any one of those rubes and give them a taste of yeti power."

"Why would our parents get kidnapped? They don't have anything worth ransoming. They're nobodies"

"Your parents weren't the ones they were looking for, Boyd," Ho Yin said.

"Well, then who **were** they looking for?" Boyd asked.

"They were looking for **you**," Reggie said.

"Looking for me?" Boyd asked, and he began running through the list of risky things he'd done recently that might have gotten him in trouble. The only thing he could think of was when he tossed a half-eaten apple into the bushes behind the school a couple of days ago, but he was sure it was biodegradable...wasn't it? "Why in the world were they looking for **me?**"

"Actually, they were looking for Boyd McCloyd," Ho Yin said. "What's your name?"

"What do you mean?" Boyd asked. "I'm Boyd McCloyd."

"What's your **whole** name?"

Boyd rolled his eyes and said, "Boyd McCloyd, Jr."

"So your father is Boyd McCloyd, **Senior**."

"They got mixed up," Reggie said, snapping his fingers at the realization. "They were looking for **Boyd McCloyd**. They never would have expected the Boyd McCloyd they were looking for to be a **kid**. No wonder they took your father."

"Right," Ho Yin said.

"They took my dad because they thought he was **Boyd**?" Cindy asked. "Why would they want Boyd?"

"That's complicated," Ho Yin said.

"Well," Reggie said, rubbing his furry chin. "Once those idiots realize they got the wrong chap, they're going to come back to try to find the real Boyd McCloyd. This place isn't safe."

"Right," Ho Yin said. "We'd best make a hasty exit and get to a secure location."

"Whoa, whoa, whoa," Boyd said, stopping them. "You guys expect Cindy and me to just pick up and leave? With some strange Japanese guy and a giant werewolf[6]?"

"Actually, I'm Cantonese[7]," Ho Yin said, clearing his throat.

"And I am *hardly* one of those nasty werewolves," Reggie said with a huff.

"Everything you think you know about the world is about to change," Ho Yin said. "The fact is you're in great danger. Your parents were kidnapped, you were just attacked by two shape-shifters, and you're in the room with an eight-foot-tall yeti. Now, you can either accept this and come with us, or you can refuse to accept it and I can have Reggie take you out by force. Either way, our job is to protect both you and Cindy, and we're going to do whatever it takes to ensure that happens."

Boyd paused for a second, trying to absorb what Ho Yin had just said. He searched his eyes for that one bit of trust that would convince him that everything was okay. He felt that Ho Yin was telling the truth, and the eight-foot-tall yeti was a convincing argument in favor of trusting him. Regardless of his instincts, he pretended he had a back-up plan. "Okay," he said. "Let's go."

Cindy began to protest almost immediately. "You *trust* this guy?" she yelled. "You can't trust him!"

"We don't have a choice, Cindy," Boyd said, "we don't have anywhere else to go." He winked at her, but she didn't see his signal and continued to complain.

"Sure we do," she said. "We could go to Aunt Thelma's house."

"Aunt Thelma's in Manitoba[8]," Boyd said.

"Well, maybe we could stay at her house," Cindy pleaded.

"We're going with them, Cindy. End of story." Boyd tried his best to indicate that he had a plan, but Cindy wasn't taking the hint.

"I'm not going," she said, planting her feet on the ground.

"Reggie," Ho Yin said, looking up at his large comrade, "Do you think you could help her out?"

"Absolutely, chum," he said, his smile revealing two rows of threatening, yellow teeth. He reached down, picked up Cindy with one hand and began carrying her to the limousine.

"What are you doing?" she yelled. "Put me down, you big monkey!"

"Now, let's not go saying anything we might regret, little princess," Reggie said as he left the house.

As they followed along, Boyd looked up and asked, "Where are we going?"

"To the safest place I know," Ho Yin said. "We're going to Ping Manor."

"Where's that?" Boyd asked.

"Hong Kong."

"In *Japan?*" Boyd asked, shocked.

"Actually, it's a part of China," Ho Yin said, clearing his throat.

"Oh," Boyd said, and they disappeared into the limousine.

CHAPTER 3

FAT, LAZY, RICH, AND DELICIOUSLY EVIL

In his fifty-two years on the planet Earth, Mr. Fang had built a grand empire that ruled Southeast Asia. Mr. Fang was a shipping tycoon who controlled the goods and products that were manufactured on the Chinese mainland and transported them to places around the world, all so that people from countries everywhere could enjoy those cheap, plastic toys and trinkets that sold for one hundred times the price they cost to make. Of course, he didn't acquire such a successful business without stepping on a few toes along the way. In fact, Mr. Fang had the reputation of being the most ruthless, arrogant, manipulative, cold, ferocious, evil man in the whole of Asia, and he wore this reputation like a badge of honor.

If there was a back to be stabbed, he'd do it; if there was a person he could fire to save money, he'd do it; if there was a politician to bribe, he'd do it; and if there was an enemy out to thwart his business dealings or muscle in on his empire, he would do everything in his power to squash that person like a pathetic little bug.

Even though Mr. Fang owned twelve hotels, twenty restaurants, a dozen houses and seven office buildings, he insisted on continuing to do business out of the back of the same little noodle shop that his wife had run since he began his wicked ways. Nestled in one of the grimy back alleys of Hong Kong was *Fang's Good Fortune Noodle Emporium⁹*, a dingy little restaurant with three tables, steamed up windows, and moldy tile walls, all lit by a few flickering lights that gave everyone inside a sickly glow on their faces.

Noodles were a Fang family specialty, and because of the constant cooking going on inside, the place smelled like old, wet socks and there was a bizarre rumor that Mrs. Fang (who did all the cooking herself) tended to use whatever animal she found in the alley to make the daily "special." Although it might have been a coincidence, it should be noted that there weren't very many rats in the alleys around Mr. Fang's shop in comparison to other parts of Hong Kong.

Behind the humid kitchen, there was a dark office that had never been cleaned and smelled like sweat. From this cramped little space, Mr. Fang ran his vast empire with the power of three phones that he kept attached to his belt at all times. He didn't need a computer; he didn't need a pencil and paper. All he needed was these three phones and his brain, because when it came to numbers, his dirty businesses, or any type of money, he had a perfect photographic memory. He always knew exactly how much money he had in his hundreds of bank accounts scattered around the world. He always knew the exact amount he used to bribe corrupt (and not so corrupt) politicians. He always knew, down to the last penny, how much profit he made by walking all over his customers and competitors. When it came to shady business dealings, there was no one better.

On this particular day, Mr. Fang was sitting in his office, leaning back in his chair, sipping a steaming hot cup of tea, and slurping down (with an emphasis on the world "slurp") a large, smelly bowl of noodles that his wife had just brought him, all while talking relentlessly on the phone. Because his wife was constantly bringing him noodles to eat, Mr. Fang was now the fattest man in Hong Kong; his large belly bulged over the waist of his trousers, his double-chin flapped away as he spoke. He was always sweating, and not just from the humidity of the restaurant.

One routine in Mr. Fang's life was the frequent appearances of his lackeys as they came in to provide him with up-to-date information and receive orders for whichever dastardly deed they were required to complete next. This day was no different, as he could barely take two slurps of his noodles without someone coming in to interrupt him.

"What do you want, Xiao?" he asked as a younger man in a business suit and mirrored sunglasses came into the little office. His mouth was full of slimy noodles and his pronunciation of *Xiao* (which should have sounded like *Shaow*) sounded more like *Schlgllllaow*.

"Mrs. Lee refuses to pay," Xiao said, his face stoic and harsh.

"Did she say why?" Mr. Fang asked, swallowing the rest of his mouthful.

"She says you're corrupt," Xiao said with an ironic giggle.

"Tell me something I don't know," Mr. Fang laughed, sending flecks of noodles flying everywhere. "Tell you what. Go get that expensive cat she likes so much and put it in Mrs. Fang's hot pot and tell her that if she doesn't pay next time, we'll get her dog, too."

"Yes, sir," Xiao said as he walked out.

Mr. Fang rubbed his hands together with glee, saying, "We're going to eat well tonight!" Just as he got another spoonful of noodles in his mouth, one of his cell phones rang. "This is Fang," he answered, and an annoyed look passed over his face. "Sink it! I don't care! They have life jackets. It's not my fault if they don't know how to use them.

Don't call me back until that boat is sunk!" And with that, he turned off the phone, muttering, "Idiots!"

"Do you want more noodles, honey?" Mrs. Fang asked from the kitchen.

"No, my little dumpling," he said. "I still haven't finished this bowl."

As she disappeared back into the kitchen, another cell phone rang. "Fang here," he said.

"Mr. Fang, it's Li," said the voice on the other end.

A serious look passed over Mr. Fang's face. "Go ahead, Li," he said.

"We've got the cargo," he said. "We're leaving Ontario now. Should be there tomorrow."

"Good, good," Mr. Fang said. "You've got both of them?"

"Yes," Li said. "We couldn't find their kids, though."

"Eh," Mr. Fang said. "Their kids aren't important. They can go to an orphanage and get adopted by a nice Asian family. That would be good for them."

"There's one more thing," Li said.

"What's that?" asked Mr. Fang.

"Ho Yin was there with the yeti," Li said. "They're the ones that stopped us from getting the kids."

"Ho Yin!" Mr. Fang said, slamming his fist down on the table and sending noodles everywhere. "One day, I'm gonna get that guy and make soup out of him. The yeti, too."

"What should we do?" Li asked.

"Don't worry," he said. "We've got the parents; that's what's important. I don't care about those kids. Bring the parents here and we'll see what they know. Good work, Li."

"Thank you, sir," he said.

"Did they get Boyd McCloyd?" Mrs. Fang asked, popping her head in from the kitchen.

"Yes, they got him," Mr. Fang said. "Now that Mr. Ping is dead and we've got Boyd McCloyd, nothing is going to stop us from being the most powerful people in world!"

"That calls for a special dim sum," Mrs. Fang said as she walked back to the kitchen, filled with joy.

Mr. Fang smiled and began, once again, to stuff his face with noodles.

CHAPTER 4

THE LONGEST AIRPLANE FLIGHT... ...EVER!

As they waited in the Toronto airport that evening, Boyd discovered that transporting an eight-foot-tall yeti from Canada to Hong Kong was not the easiest thing to do. Before they walked into the building, Ho Yin and Reggie went through an elaborate hat and sunglasses routine, combing his fur in just the right way so that it looked like a beard, sticking in a set of false teeth to cover his real ones and putting on a set of glasses with fake eyes hidden behind a pair of lenses that looked like the bottoms of soda bottles. On top of that, he had to suffer through the claustrophobic, polyester business suit and gloves he wore to cover his fur.

"I'm burning up," he muttered as they waited in line for their boarding passes. "I'm suffocating here! I may pass out!"

"Don't pass out, Reggie," Ho Yin said. "The last thing we need is a team of paramedics trying to resuscitate a yeti in the middle of the airport."

Soon, they were in the air, leaving Canada behind. As they flew off over the horizon, and Boyd stared out at the ugly, gray buildings of Toronto disappearing beneath him; there was a feeling in the pit of his stomach that told him it would be a very long time before he returned. It was as if he was leaving his old life behind him and would never experience anything like it again.

However, he couldn't say that he found such a thing depressing. The thought of leaving behind the bullies, the lack of popularity, the indifferent teachers, and the everyday monotony of school in Frankfurter was something that he found appealing. The possibilities, although a bit frightening, were also exciting. What would Hong Kong be like? Where would they stay? What would he eat?

Still, the excitement was tempered somewhat by the thought of his parent's predicament. It was a horrible thing that they'd been kidnapped. He hoped that they were being treated well, but there was something there that was nagging him.

"Boyd," Cindy said a few minutes into the flight, "can I ask you something?"

"What is it?" he asked.

"It's about mom and dad," she said. "Do you feel...like...?"

"Like what?"

"Like you're happy they're kidnapped?" she said.

"What do you mean?" he asked, staring at the seat in front of him.

"I know it's bad and all," she said, "But somehow I feel better that they're gone. Do you feel it? It's like I'm glad it's just me and you."

"I feel it, too," he said. "They were fighting so much lately that it's kind of a relief that we don't have to hear it anymore."

"I know," she said, pausing for a couple of seconds. "Does that make me a bad person?"

"No," Boyd said. "You're not a bad person if you don't want to hear your parents fight all the time. It's nice to have a break."

"Just asking," she said, before turning the other way. Boyd had been reassuring to Cindy, but he couldn't help but feel guilty about his own thoughts. His conscience told him that it wasn't right to think such things; that he should miss his parents, despite their flaws. However, the feeling of relief was just as strong as any feelings of guilt, and it plagued him for the entirety of the long flight over the Pacific.

He tried to sleep, but couldn't. What made it worse was the fact that every so often, he would look over to see Reggie, wearing his uncomfortable disguise, crammed into his seat, trying to look human. Reggie would glance over at him and give him a smile with those gigantic, fake teeth, which only served to make Boyd feel a bit uneasy, when it should have been reassuring.

"Can't sleep, Boyd?" Ho Yin asked as he looked up from a massive book he was reading.

"Not really," Boyd said.

"That's understandable," Ho Yin said. "You've probably got a million questions running through your mind."

A flight attendant interrupted their conversation, asking, "Can I get either of you something to drink?"

"No, thanks," Ho Yin said.

"What about you, sir?" she asked Reggie.

"You wouldn't perhaps have a head of lettuce, would you?" he asked. "Really, any lettuce would do. Romaine? Field greens?"

"Um, I don't think we have any lettuce besides what's in our in-flight meal, sir," she said. Reggie made her very uncomfortable. "Would you like another salad?"

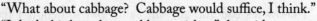

"What about cabbage? Cabbage would suffice, I think."

"I don't think we have cabbage, either," she said.

"And you call this first class?" Reggie muttered in his impeccable accent. "Fine, fine, just go away."

The flight attendant shuffled off back to the front of the plane, stealing nervous glances over her shoulder at Reggie. Reggie muttered a few more things under his breath before looking over at Ho Yin and Boyd, who were staring at him. "Well, a bloke has a craving for leafy greens every once in a while!" he said, perturbed. "Stop looking at me like I'm a bloomin' leper!"

CHAPTER 5
A MEETING OF EVIL MINDS

Although Mr. Fang usually had a lunch of noodles or hot pot in the shop every day, this Tuesday afternoon was different. He had an appointment to meet someone of great importance for dim sum at one of his restaurants located in the vast alleys of Kowloon[10], just across the water from Hong Kong. The meeting was to take place at ***Good Fortune Duck House,*** which was one of the first places that Mr. Fang had bought with the profits from his earlier criminal days.

Mr. Fang was nervous. He hadn't felt nervous in a long time, so the feeling made him even more nervous. He had eaten dinner with

Mafia bosses from around the world, shared cocktails with politicians, gobbled appetizers with famous actors, and brunched with many heads of state, but this meeting was different. This meeting was *important*.

Almost everyone in Hong Kong had eaten at **Good Fortune Duck House** at some point in their lives because of both its location and its fine food. The restaurant was always busy, and its many round tables were always filled with happy families, business delegates, and food-savvy locals.

But there were two distinct classes of people at **Good Fortune Duck House.** One was the average folk who came in once a month, once a week, or once a year, who were intent on having an excellent meal for a reasonable price. But there was another group of people, a different sort of breed, that made their way to the restaurant on a regular basis. These people knew that **Good Fortune Duck House's** menu was more than what was presented to the general public.

If one had the right connections, then they might be granted the privilege of a table in one of the prestigious back rooms of the restaurant. These luxurious spaces were for private guests, shady folks, and business acquaintances of Mr. Fang, and it was in these rooms that a "different" menu was served.

In these elite circles of the wealthy and powerful, it was widely known that **Good Fortune Duck House** was the place to go if you wanted to eat something a bit out of the ordinary. It seemed that the wealthy and powerful were always looking for something more to distinguish how eminently prestigious they actually were, so they would come to the restaurant looking to prove their prestigious mettle by engaging in some bizarre gastrointestinal concoction. Sure, one could find "exotic" foods on the main menu, like Number 112, the **Tibetan Yak Butter Tea** or Number 75 **Snake Soup**, but it was only in the back rooms that one could find such delicacies as **Dolphin Steaks with Roasted Monkey Finger Kebabs** or **Seared Rhinoceros Kidneys with Elephant Ivory Shavings and Tiger Claw Sauce**, or the ever popular **Orangutan Innards Stir Fry with Three-Toed Sloth Sausage and Beluga Blubber Appetizers.** If an animal was endangered, it was on the menu, and the more endangered it was, the higher the menu price (although price was never a factor for this type of clientele).

Hoping to impress his guest with lunch, Mr. Fang pulled out all the stops, preparing his most lavish back room and literally putting together a smörgåsbord of food. As he sat all alone in the red carpeted room, he could smell the delectable aroma of **Siberian Tiger Sausage** and the **Walrus Blubber Soup** he'd ordered. The food smelled so wonderful that his mouth began to water, and he wasn't sure he could keep from sampling the goods. To his fortune, Mr. Davis arrived on time.

Mr. Davis was a short man in his early forties, a little chubby in the face and around the gut, but overall a fine looking fellow. He was very clean cut. His hair was neatly combed which, combined with his fashionable glasses, gave him an air of an East Coast American Aristocrat. He carried a black briefcase and sat down across from Mr. Fang in a very businesslike manner, much like two politicians might meet during negotiations.

"Mr. Davis!" Mr. Fang said, extending his sweaty hand. "I'm so glad we're getting the opportunity to talk."

"Fang," Mr. Davis said. He neither smiled nor shook Mr. Fang's hand as he took his seat at the table.

"I was wondering whether you were going to make it," Fang said and he laughed.

"Let's cut to the chase, Mr. Fang," Mr. Davis said. "You're interested in joining our organization, are you not?"

"Yes, yes," he replied. "Very much."

"Can you tell me why?" Mr. Davis asked.

"Because everything I've worked to achieve over last twenty years has brought me to this moment," he said. "If I join your club, then I will know I am one of the best."

"First," Mr. Davis said, "it's not a club. It's an **organization**."

"My apologies."

"And second, we're not sure you have what it takes to be a member."

"Oh, but I do," he said

"We'll be the judge of that, Mr. Fang," Mr. Davis said, taking a sip from his tea and pulling out his briefcase. "Shall we begin?"

"Absolutely," Mr. Fang said. "Would you like to eat first?"

"I'm sorry," Mr. Davis said, failing to look up from his papers, "I only eat food prepared by my personal chef. Let's just get started, okay?"

"Sure, sure," Mr. Fang said, feeling a bit disappointed. He was very hungry, for it had been a whole hour since he last ate.

"I'm not sure if you're familiar with the way this works or not," Mr. Davis said, "but what I'm going to do is ask you three questions, which I'd like for you to answer as honestly as possible."

"All right," Mr. Fang said.

"Good," he said. "My first question is this: Name one time that you've cheated and it profited you."

"Do you mean when I've cheated and something good happened?" Mr. Fang asked.

"That's right."

Mr. Fang looked at the ceiling, reminiscing about the good times in his life. "Okay, when I was in grade school, I poisoned my main competition in a spelling contest. I didn't kill him. Just food poisoning."

"And how did that benefit you?" Mr. Davis asked.

"Well, he got sick, and had to drop out. I won. But that isn't what's important. What's important is that I realized for the first time that I could cheat and get away with it."

Mr. Davis wrote down his answer on the paper. "My next question is this: If you were driving and an adorable little puppy was crossing the road in front of you, what would you do?"

Mr. Fang put his fingers to his chin and thought about it. "This isn't multiple choice?" he asked.

"I'm sorry. No."

"Okay, it all depends on which city I'm in. If I'm in Hong Kong, I would stop to pick that puppy up and take it home."

"Take it home, you say?" Mr. Davis asked, as he wrote down the answer with a frown on his face.

"Oh, yes," he said. "Puppy meat is better in a stir fry when it's freshly killed. If I ran over it, it would be dead too long before I got home to cook it."

"Very good," Mr. Davis said, looking relieved as he continued to write. "Last, what's the most evil thing you've done in your career?"

"I poisoned my mother so I could take over her shipping business," he said. "She was a mean woman, so I didn't feel very bad about it. Is that enough?"

"Well, I don't know," Mr. Davis said. "You'd be surprised at the amount of applicants we get that have killed their parents. It's really quite passe nowadays. Regardless, we should move on. Part of the application process is the application fee. Usually, the fee is a billion dollars, but you say you have something else to offer us?"

"I have something you'll be very interested in," Mr. Fang said.

"And what would that be?" Mr. Davis said, rolling his eyes.

Mr. Fang knew that he really did have something Mr. Davis would want, and in knowing that, he had the upper hand. "I'd be more than happy to share that information with you, but first I would like to know the status of my membership," he said, full of arrogance.

"You know the process, Mr. Fang," Mr. Davis said, sounding annoyed. "I take the questions back to the organization, and we vote on it."

"Well, you'd better call a special vote, because I've got something good."

"And what exactly might that be?"

"You are familiar with Confucius Ping?"

Mr. Davis' eyes perked up. "Yes?" he said.

"I know who his successor is," Mr. Fang said.

Mr. Davis' mouth dropped open in shock. "You know who is replacing **Confucius Ping**?" he asked.

"Not only do I know who it is," Mr. Fang said, "But I kidnapped him yesterday."

"And you're willing to offer him up for your **membership fee?**" Mr. Davis asked. He was visibly excited.

"Of course," Mr. Fang said. "But before I give him to you, I want confirmation of my membership."

Mr. Davis took the sheets of paper he'd been writing on, wadded them up, and tossed them over his shoulder. He then extended his hand out to Mr. Fang. "Let me be the first to welcome you to the Conspiricetti[11]," he said. "We'd *love* to have you in our organization."

Mr. Fang shook his hand and then leaned back in his chair. "Let's eat," he said.

CHAPTER 6
THE ENCOUNTER WITH THE HORRIBLE SNOWMONSTER OF TIBET

A flight from Toronto to Hong Kong is approximately seventeen hours. Prior to this trip, the longest flight that Boyd had ever been on was the flight to his Aunt Margaret's house in Regina, and even *that* one was too long. "The flight's pretty rough, isn't it?" Ho Yin asked, looking up from his book.

"I'm so ***bored***," Boyd said. "Can't you tell me anything else about what's going on with this whole thing? I'm starting to get anxious."

Ho Yin smiled. He reached into his leather bag and pulled out an old, leather-bound book. "You know, Boyd," he said. "I don't expect you to understand what is happening. I'm only going to say this: you've been chosen to do something that is very important." He carefully examined the old volume in his hands before handing it to Boyd. "Mr. Ping prepared this especially for you. Have a look at it."

"Who's Mr. Ping?" Boyd asked, but Ho Yin didn't answer.

Boyd took the heavy book in his hands and looked at it. It was like an old encyclopedia with gold trim on the pages and fancy, embossed letters on the front. The letters said, ***Mr. Ping's Almanac of the Twisted and Weird, Volume 41.*** There was a portrait of this man named Mr. Ping smiling in a tiny picture above the title, and below, in a bigger frame, was a painting of a large, white-furred creature that bore a striking resemblance to Reggie. Its arms were raised in an attack position above its head during what appeared to be a blizzard. In front of the creature stood a small man with a lantern and a large stick.

When Boyd opened the book, an envelope fell out onto his lap with his name written on the front. He opened the envelope to see a letter written for him in the most exquisite handwriting.

Hello Boyd,

I'm Mr. Ping, but I'm sure you realize that. I'm writing this letter to answer a few questions for you, because by now, I'm sure you have more than a few of them. Although considering I won't be *hearing* your questions, (because I'll be dead when you read this), I can't really imagine how I'd begin to answer *any* of your questions, especially without a Ouija board[12] or some sort of crystal ball[13]...Oh, never mind! If I were to try to speak to you from beyond the grave, it would just... how do you kids say it now? Freak you out.

Boyd, you were born exactly one hundred years to the day after I was born, just as *I* was born one hundred years to the day after *my* predecessor. I've done my research. I've scoured the records and in all the world, not a *single person* was born within twenty-four hours of you. When I realized the significance of this amazing fact, I knew that you were the only person in the world who could take over my duties.

I have bequeathed my fortune to you, Boyd. You are now worth more than you would ever imagine. I've lived well over a hundred years and in that time, not only have I been lucky enough to be at the right place at the right time, I've also been lucky enough to be a collector of artifacts that are so numerous and valuable that the contents of my home would be worth more than all the museums of the world combined.

But keep in mind, part of the provisions of you keeping this fortune is for you to continue with the publication of my almanacs.

This planet is a vast and wonderful place, Boyd, full of things so magnificent and numerous that one could never expect to see it all in one lifetime. But then, that's just the world that one sees with their *eyes*. It was *my* job to investigate the things that people *couldn't* see; the things that could not be easily explained.

That's the key. Everything that I've seen, I've written about in my almanacs. From the Barbaric Camel Men of the Sahara[14] to the Bottomless Pit of Death in Peru[15]; from the Last Living T-Rex in Cleveland[16] to my bizarre encounters with Lieutenant Cyanide[17], I've seen many things over the years and written about every one of them. Now, it's your turn.

If you see something strange, you'll write about it in the almanac. If you meet an interesting person, you'll write about it in the almanac. Whether it's the Moon Men of Patagonia[18], or the Terror Paddle of Ms. Evelyn Crabtree[19], or the Three-Eyed, Bloodsucking Turtles of Mali[20], you'll have to find and document the things that other people in the world might never get a chance to see.

To help get this done, I've created an organization called Acclimated Spooks, Light, and Power[21]. For over one hundred years, I've traveled the world, keeping a record of what I've seen and Acclimated Spooks has helped me do this.

Boyd, I am asking you to continue with my work. The truth is that the choice is yours. I've instructed Ho Yin to give you a bit of time to make your decision. Whatever you decide will be for the best.

Sincerely,

Confucius Ping

Boyd put down the letter and began to thumb through the volume he held in his hands. He soon discovered that it was full of what appeared to be journal entries from Mr. Ping as he traveled around the world during the year 1934. The book was full of odd and unusual black and white pictures, some of which were benign landscape shots (such as one picture of a mountain range called The Annapurnas[22] in Nepal), while others were drawings that looked as if they were made in great haste, with captions that read, *The woolly mammoth of Lake Bakal just before the attack[23]*.

Some entries in the book were pages long, while others were as short as one sentence, yet all of them had titles, dates, and historical locations to give some sort of context to what the reader was looking at. Sometimes the pages were filled with elaborate floor plans of what seemed to be ancient temples, while others would offer detailed maps of exotic locales, with names that Boyd had no chance of being able to pronounce, like *Luklaboomaph[24]* or *Stagopktok[25]*.

"What is this, Ho Yin?" Boyd asked. "And who is this 'Mr. Ping' guy?"

Ho Yin smiled. "I bookmarked a page in there for you to read. Have a look at it."

A red ribbon was stuck in the middle of the volume, leading Boyd to a page titled, *The Encounter with the Horrible Snowmonster of Tibet, March 10, 1934.* The entry read:

> ...While traveling from Lhasa[26] on my way to Kathmandu[27], I heard some reports regarding a mysterious creature that lurked in a place near Gyantse, just southeast of my current location. Being relaxed from my visit with the young and quite charming Da'lai Lama, and having no particular timetable in regard to arriving in Kathmandu, I decided to enlist a guide

who would take me to see this dreaded creature that the locals spoke of with such fear.

"It ate an entire village in one night!' said a lone traveler on the rugged road just outside Gyantse. "It didn't even leave bones. It ate everything!"

Of course, it didn't help that my wide-eyed, fearful guide listened to these stories with rapt attention. His fear only made me want to move onward. We traveled through the rugged Tibetan landscape, a land of barren plains and valleys wedged between gargantuan mountains, and upward into the crisp air of the Himalayas.

As we trudged onward, I knew we were getting closer to our destination because the stories about the creature became increasingly fantastic. Over the course of fifty miles, the creature grew from being human-sized, to bear-sized, to elephant-sized. It went from having two wolf-like fangs to having a mouth full of razor-sharp teeth that could bite through rock.

Then there was its roar; a horrible bellow that echoed through the valleys for miles and miles. It was rumored that if a person heard the creature's roar, then it wouldn't be long before they were being served as dinner. Of course, if that was true, I didn't understand how anyone would know what the creature sounded like in the first place, but even so...

As we made our way up a steep mountain path, we were met by a large group of people, their shoulders laden with possessions. I asked my guide to find out what was happening and he reported that the creature's roar had been heard during the night and that they were leaving their village.

It was at this point that my guide informed me of some previously unknown personal business, and he began his descent down the mountain with the villagers. I found myself all alone on the side of the mountain as a severe snowstorm moved in over the horizon. As the snow was beginning to fall, I reached the abandoned village and encamped in a deserted house.

Just as I drifted off to sleep, I heard a strange sound through the wind outside. It sounded like something was rooting around outside the hut. I could hear its lumbering paws as it padded through the snow, sniffing its way around the shelter.

I had come here to find the creature, but it seemed that the creature had found *me* instead.

I scrambled over to a small window that had been dug into the mud walls to catch a glimpse of the beast, but its white fur blended into the snowbound surroundings. Unfortunately, the creature heard my shuffling, which caused it to let out such a massive roar that all the courage and bravado left me in an instant.

The creature's bellows were worse than any of the stories the villagers had spoken. The closest approximation would be that it sounded like an angry elephant, if that elephant were four times bigger than normal and had the lungs of fifty angry cougars. I grabbed a piece of unburned firewood and my lantern, and backed up against the wall as the creature began to kick at the door. My heart was pounding in my chest and I thought that this might very well be the end of me.

The wooden door exploded from its hinges and a gale-force wind flooded into the room, blowing out both the fire and my lantern. I stood there in pitch black silence as I saw the vague silhouette of the creature lumber in through the door. I couldn't make out any details, only that its size was massive and that it had white fur. I could hear its giant lungs breathing in and out as it sniffed at the air, looking for its next meal: me.

Figuring I was doomed and thus had nothing left to lose, I decided that I had to face my final adversary like a man and not a cowering fool. I grabbed my matchbook and lit my lantern so that I might see the thing which was to have me for dinner. Just as I got the lantern lit, the creature turned towards me and it was a horrible sight to behold. It walked on its hind legs, and stood at least eight-feet-tall. Its eyes were fierce with anger and its massive mouth held what seemed to be hundreds of sharp, yellowed teeth. Its entire body was covered with fur and it raised its massive, ape-like arms above its head to strike me as it let out another one of its hideous roars. I shut my eyes and prayed for a quick death, when...

...It stopped.

It froze in position and began sniffing at the air, as if the sweet smell of some wonderful food had calmed it. It continued to sniff all around itself, ignoring me as it lowered its arms to its sides and turned away. I watched it make its way over to my pack. It ripped open the side and pulled out four potatoes and several carrots that the Dalai Lama had given me for my journey. The creature sat down like a refined gentleman and began to eat, first a nibble of a potato, then a nibble of carrot, eating each one in a dainty way, as if it savored the taste. Then, it turned to me to said, "Oh, I'm sorry. Are these yours?"

As Boyd read the last sentence, he had a sudden realization. He looked over at Reggie, who was sitting in a very refined manner across the aisle from him, and realized that the creature that Mr. Ping was writing about in the story was *him*. The horrible snowmonster of Tibet was Reggie!

"This is about you," he said, looking at Reggie.

Reggie took the volume from Boyd's hands and lifted up his fake spectacles to check out the lettering on the front of the book. "Hmm," he said, looking down his nose at it. "Yes, 1934. I believe this one *is* about me. Quite inaccurate, I must say, but then Confucius was never big on eliciting my opinion on the matter."

Boyd looked at the portrait on the front of the almanac. "This Mr. Ping guy...are we going to see him?" he asked.

"No," Ho Yin said. "I'm afraid Mr. Ping passed away a couple of weeks ago. He was, however, a friend of your family and did make several trips to your house over the years."

"And he's dead?" Boyd asked.

"I'm afraid so," Ho Yin said.

"Well, what's this book?"

"A fabrication is what it is," Reggie muttered. "Paints me as some sort of brutal, savage beast. Like I'm going to eat his innards or something and have his eyeballs for dessert."

"You weren't?" Cindy asked. She'd awoken at some point and had been listening to the conversation the entire time.

"I beg your pardon, dear missy," Reggie said.

"Sorry," Cindy said. "It's the fangs that give me that impression."

"The book you hold in your hands," Ho Yin said, "is *Mr. Ping's Almanac of the Twisted and Weird, Vol. 41.* It's one of his very rare, but much sought after books in a series that he was working on right until his death. Each volume documents Mr. Ping's own, personal recollections of the strange and unusual things that he experienced in his very long life. On average, he published one every year or so, but sometimes he would produce two in a year and in some years none at all."

"And each one tells about his weird adventures?" Cindy asked.

"Yes," Ho Yin said.

"Except when he was making up lies about yetis," Reggie added.

"You see, Boyd," Ho Yin continued, "there's a whole world out there that no one knows about. One full of shape shifting snakes, yetis, ghosts, you name it. Mr. Ping thought it his job to document these things so that others might know of the secret world that thrives just out of sight from normal human beings."

"So he just wrote down what he observed?" Boyd asked.

"Yes," Ho Yin said. "Some of it is fantastic, some of it mundane, but each one is of great importance."

"And I'm supposed to continue writing these things?" Boyd asked. "I don't get a choice?"

"Of course you get a choice, Boyd," Ho Yin added. "There's nothing here that *has* to happen. We'd originally intended for you to make this decision when you were a bit older. The plan was for us to start talking about it when you were in university, not when you were thirteen-years old. But then again, we never expected to lose Mr. Ping so quickly, and we certainly never expected our enemies to act with such haste."

"Our enemies?" Boyd asked.

"Cool," Cindy said. "Boyd has *enemies.*"

"You mean I inherited a job that comes with people that *hate* me? If these guys are bad enough to kidnap my parents and turn from humans to snakes, then maybe I should take my chances with bullies in middle school."

"The bullies in adolescence are no less dangerous than the bullies in adulthood, Boyd," Ho Yin said.

"That's very profound," Reggie said, rolling his eyes and turning away.

"Okay, so why me?" Boyd asked. "What's so special about me that everyone is making such a big deal over?"

"Yeah!" Cindy said. "What's so special about Boyd?"

"When is your birthday?" Ho Yin asked.

"August 21st," Boyd said.

"No, it's not," Ho Yin said. "It's August 20th."

"No, it's not," Cindy said, interrupting them. "It's August 21st."

"No, it's not. It's August 20th."

"I'm sorry, Ho Yin," Boyd said, "But I think I know my own birthday."

"Do you?" he asked.

"Yes, I do," Boyd said, sure of himself.

"So you remember the *day you were born?*" Ho Yin asked.

"Well, no," Boyd said, feeling confused. "But I know when my birthday is."

"No, you don't," Ho Yin said.

"Would you two stop?" Reggie said, slapping Ho Yin with a magazine. "This is driving me utterly insane."

"It's driving me insane, too," Cindy said.

"This gets us to the point of why you've been chosen to take over Mr. Ping's job," Ho Yin said. "Boyd, you were born on August 20th at 8:20 PM, during the eighth full moon of the year, exactly eight years and twenty days from the day your parents met."

"Huh?" Boyd said.

"If you need further clarification," Ho Yin continued, "your birthday is exactly one hundred years to the hour after Mr. Ping's date of birth, thus the significance of your birthday. Mr. Ping searched long and hard to find you and when you were finally located, we had your parents change the date of your birth so as to not attract any attention in your direction."

"So they moved my birthday back a day?" Boyd asked.

"Yes," he said.

"This is too weird," Cindy said.

Ho Yin continued, "The date is very significant. There were lots of people looking for you, not all of them good. Mr. Ping knew of the significance of your birth date and went to great pains to hide your existence."

"And my mother and father knew all about this?" Boyd asked.

"Oh, yes," Ho Yin said. "Mr. Ping kept them well-informed of the significance of everything. That's why Mr. Ping occasionally made appearances at your home. At first, they were reluctant, but then a few things happened[28] and they were quickly convinced."

"What things?" Boyd asked.

"When we get to Hong Kong, you can read about it," Ho Yin said. "We've got a lot to do when we get there and we're going to need plenty of energy. So get some sleep and we'll talk about it later."

"But…"

"Later," Ho Yin said, leaning back in his seat and burying his head in his book. Boyd looked to Reggie for some answers, but saw that he, too, was asleep. Finally, he looked over at his sister, who just shrugged.

"Look," she said, "I wanted to go to Aunt Thelma's house. You're the one who wanted to hang out with these crazies." Then she turned away from him and tried to sleep.

When Boyd awoke towards the end of the flight, he found Ho Yin and Reggie deep in a private conversation next to him regarding a very serious matter. He looked over to see Cindy reading. "It's about time you woke up," she said without looking up from her reading material.

"Are we almost there?" Boyd asked, rubbing his eyes and trying to regain consciousness. The hair on the right side of his head was sticking straight up.

Cindy looked at him, perturbed. "I'm reading, Boyd," she said.

Boyd noticed that she was reading the almanac that Ho Yin had given him. "Hey, that's mine!" he said, trying to grab it from her hands. "Ho Yin gave that to *me*, not you."

"Oh, don't get your knickers in a bunch, Boyd," Reggie said, looking up from his in-flight magazine. "It's just a book."

"Yeah, but it's *my* book," Boyd said.

"See?" Cindy asked. "He gets like this."

"Here you go, mate," Reggie said, tossing him a book of crossword puzzles. "Have a gander at that and improve your vocabulary."

Boyd quickly flipped through it. "They're already done," he said.

"What?" Reggie said, taking the book back from him. "Blimey, they are! But I just bought that yesterday. Ho Yin, did you do all of my crosswords?"

"I can assure you that I did not," Ho Yin said, failing to look up from his book.

"Well, who did?" Reggie asked, looking around.

Cindy giggled under her breath.

"Can I have my book back, please?" Boyd asked, turning back to Cindy.

"I'm almost done," she said, and indeed, she was near the back of the book.

"Give it back," Boyd said, and he snatched the book from her hands in a forceful manner to signal to her that it was *his*, and she would *not* get it back.

"You're a jerk," she said, sulking in her chair.

"Who in the world could have done my crosswords?" Reggie said to himself. Cindy slowly snapped out of her pout and giggled again.

"Boyd; Cindy," Ho Yin said, "we're going to be landing soon. We need to prepare you for a few things."

"Prepare us?" Cindy asked. "Prepare us for what?"

"Well, as I've expressed several times," he said, "Boyd now has enemies, and they are numerous. When the people who kidnapped your parents find out that they've captured the wrong people, they're going to try to rectify that situation."

"So you think they'll come after me here?" Boyd asked.

"Well, if they do, I'll certainly give them a spanner they won't believe," Reggie said, pounding his fist into the palm of his hand. "They'll rue the day they messed with Boyd McCloyd."

"The truth," Ho Yin said, "is that we need to proceed through the airport with great caution. Remember that the world you think you know isn't always the world that is there. A good portion of it is quite dangerous."

Boyd looked over at Cindy to see if she understood and the fear in her eyes told him that she did. He got the feeling that they were in for quite an adventure.

CHAPTER 7
MISUNDERSTANDING
A LEPRECHAUN

Mr. Fang was giddy with excitement all evening. Being a shoo-in for membership in the Conspiricetti was enough to make him as excited as the first time he'd tortured a small animal. One of his planes was scheduled to arrive that evening, so he waited for the phone call that would signal its arrival. Sure enough, he soon received a call telling him that his "shipment" was arriving at eight-thirty. He called his driver and both he and Mrs. Fang left the noodle shop and headed toward the airport.

As the oppressive heat of the afternoon was settling in, a *Fang Industries* cargo plane pulled into a *Fang Industries* hangar populated by employees of **Fang Industries**. Wanting to get a firsthand look at the goods, Mr. Fang waddled over to the unloading bay to watch members of his crew toiling away at the plane's cargo ramp, unloading giant crates and containers from the back of the plane with forklifts and other types of heavy equipment.

From the back of the plane emerged a stern fellow by the name of Li, Mr. Fang's right-hand man. He directed a group of men in orange hardhats to bring out the final container. It had holes punched into the sides and seemed lighter than all the others. They wheeled the cargo down the unloading ramp and brought it over to where Mr. Fang was standing.

"Is this it?" he asked, with a sweaty smile plastered across his flabby face.

"This is it," Li said with confidence.

With a nod from Li, two of the workers opened up the large box to reveal its contents. There at the bottom of the container were two people, bound by their hands and feet, lying on the floor. The man and the woman had gags in their mouths and looked exhausted. The workers dragged them to their feet and brought them over to Mr. Fang so that he might get a better look.

"Well, well, well," Mr. Fang said. "Boyd McCloyd and his wife, Martha. Welcome to Hong Kong."

Mr. McCloyd was a man in his late thirties with a graying beard and a bald head. His glasses were sitting skewed on his face because of the cloth tied around his mouth. Mrs. McCloyd was around the same age, a brunette with short hair and a tired look about her. Mr. Fang gave his men a cue to take off their gags.

"Kidnapping is illegal, mister!" was the first thing out of Mr. McCloyd's mouth. "You'll never get away with this!"

"Oh, shut up, Boyd," Mrs. McCloyd said. "Do you think he really **cares?** We're on **his** turf now!"

"Not now, **Martha,**" Mr. McCloyd said, gritting his teeth. "I need you to stick with me on this."

"I would if you didn't say such stupid things," she muttered.

Mr. Fang leaned over to his wife and whispered, "He doesn't look like the hero-type, does he?"

Mrs. Fang nodded her head in agreement and said, "He looks like a nerd!"

"What do you want with us?" Mr. McCloyd said, trying to take control of the situation. "When the cops find out we're missing, you're going straight to jail!"

"I've already missed one day of work over this," Mrs. McCloyd said, looking flustered. "Is there any way I could phone the office to let them know I won't be coming in?"

"Would you be so kind as to shut up?" Mr. Fang said.

"How dare you treat me like that!" Mr. McCloyd said. "I'm a **Canadian citizen.** I have rights! This totally goes against the Geneva convention."

Mr. Fang gave Li a look, whereupon Li took a small, black plastic wand from his jacket pocket and zapped Mr. McCloyd with about ten thousand volts. He fell to the ground, unconscious from the shock. Mrs. McCloyd looked up at Mr. Fang in terror.

"Do you want to keep talking?" Mr. Fang asked. Mrs. McCloyd shook her head to say no. "Good," he said. "Li, bring the box over here."

Li walked over to the back of the limousine and pulled out a tiny, cloth-covered cage from the trunk, holding it far away from his body as he brought it over to Mr. Fang. The cage rattled and shook as if some bizarre wild animal was inside, just waiting to get out.

He sat the cage down in front of Mr. and Mrs. McCloyd, pulled off the cloth covering its contents, and then backed away.

Mrs. McCloyd looked puzzled. "Is that a…?"

"A Leprechaun[29]?" Mr. Fang asked. "That's right."

Inside the cage was a miniature, redheaded man about the size of a Chihuahua. He wore a green suit, a green bowler hat with a four-leaf clover pinned to the top, and a red plaid vest under his green sports coat. And yet, even though his features were human, there was a fierceness in his tiny, beady eyes that gave everyone the impression that there might just as well be a rabid Chihuahua locked in the cage. The way he shook the bars of his tiny prison with his miniature hands lent credence to the Chihuahua theory.

"Hello, little Leprechaun," Mr. Fang said, leaning down to peer in the cage. Unfortunately, he was a bit too close, as the Leprechaun shot his arm through the bars to grab at his face. Mr. Fang jumped away in fear, then turned back to Mrs. McCloyd. "I won him playing high stakes poker in Macao," he said. "He's a little feisty."

A tiny voice burst forth from the cage. "Ooozee justwayt ferde dey wenee geddoota these caj ya bonnycheenamen! Ten eel tair ya leem frum leem!" said the Leprechaun. "Eee get reevenj qwicker than ya knew!"

"He talks too fast," Mr. Fang laughed. "I can't understand a word he's saying." He leaned down again towards the Leprechaun, this time remaining a safe distance from the cage. "Okay, green man," he said. "You help me this time and you're one step closer to freedom."

"Eeel shohya freedom ya bonnybruce wheneee gedowdda thees caj!" it said.

"He's so cute," Mr. Fang said, smiling at the leprechaun like it was a puppy. "Okay now, I want you to tell me what I need to do with Boyd McCloyd now that I've captured him."

The Leprechaun moved like it had had a bit too much caffeine, but then it stopped moving and began to look at Mr. and Mrs. McCloyd intently, as if it was trying to figure out who they were. Then it began to laugh with its wee little voice. "Ooo," it said. "Yereen fer trubble new."

"What?" Mr. Fang asked. "What did he say? Why is he laughing?"

Li kicked the cage to get the Leprechaun's attention. "Why are you laughing, you little rat?"

"Year booncha eejets!" the Leprechaun said, laughing. "Ehrayt booncha eejets!"

"What's he saying?" Mr. Fang asked, looking at Li with an angry panic on his face.

"Thas nut baydmcclayd," it said.

"What?" Li asked. "We don't understand!"

"Thas nut baydmcclayd," it repeated.

"It speaks too fast," Mr. Fang said. "Tell it to talk slower!"

The Leprechaun looked at the two of them, laughing, and said, "Thas...nut...bayd...mac...clayd."

"It's not **Boyd McCloyd?**" Mr. Fang said. "Of course that's Boyd McCloyd!"

"Esnoot," said the Leprechaun, folding his arms across his chest and shaking his head.

"It is too! We've got his passport to prove it!" Mr. Fang yelled.

"Esnoot tha BaydMcClayd eh toldya aboot," it said. "Es justuh mannamed baydmclayd noottha one eh tolya aboot."

"Li," Mr. Fang said, looking furious. "What is this thing saying?"

"I don't know, sir," he said, squirming in place. "I checked all the records. This is Boyd McCloyd."

"Es Bayd McClayd *senior*," the Leprechaun laughed. "Ya won Bayd McClayd *junior*."

"Oh, no," Mr. Fang said, a look of panic settling in over his chubby cheeks. "What's this guy's kid's name?"

"I don't know," Li said, looking terrified.

"Oh, no!" Mr. Fang continued. "We've got the wrong Boyd McCloyd! We wanted his **kid**, not him!"

"Are you sure?" Li said in desperation.

This was enough to send Mr. Fang over the edge and he began to swat at Li for his stupidity. "You're such a chickenhead!" he yelled as he beat at Li. "You left the kid. You got the wrong Boyd McCloyd!"

"Ah yera booncha eejets!" the Leprechaun laughed.

"Shut up, you," Mr. Fang said, kicking the cage. "Now we don't have the kid. Ho Yin was there and got the kid. You've ruined me! Li, how many wishes do we have left?"

"We've used all three, sir," Li said.

"Argh!" Mr. Fang yelled. "That means he doesn't have to tell us anything else, right?"

"We can still get the kid," Li said. "We'll get him from Ho Yin."

Mr. Fang grabbed Li by the shirt and looked him over in anger. "You'd better get that, kid," he said. "or you're gonna end up like Mr. Fu at the bottom of Hong Kong Harbor! Got it?"

He stormed back over to his car, followed by Mrs. Fang. "What about the parents?" Li asked.

"Take them and leave them at the warehouse," Mr. Fang said over his shoulder. "Make sure you put your best guards on them. They might still be valuable."

As Mr. Fang drove out of the hanger, Li stood there, wondering about his fate. All the while, the Leprechaun just laughed and laughed, enjoying the stupidity of his captors to no end. He knew that, eventually, he'd be free again. He just had to wait.

CHAPTER 8
PANJA AMBUSH

Flying into Hong Kong's Chek Lap Kok[30] airport was an amazing sight for both Boyd and Cindy. The deep blue of the ocean below was dotted with several uninhabited, mountainous islands that were covered with lush greenery, and as the sun went down over the horizon, the islands' long shadows were cast out over the surrounding waters.

Chek Lap Kok airport was a magnificent structure built on a man-made island several kilometers from the most populated areas of Hong Kong. It was an amazing glass and steel building that looked like it was designed more for visiting spaceships than airplanes. It was clean inside and full of metallic angles and shiny surfaces.

As far as both Boyd and Cindy were concerned, they might as well have been in some sort of space station, as the jamboree of different cultures in transit was unlike anything they'd ever seen. Faces that had blended on a television screen or in a magazine now all looked unique, each one telling a different story about where they were from or where they were going. There was the Japanese executive running through the airport, yammering away on his phone and looking late. There was the African family, all in colorful, matching clothes, smiling and making their way to some happy destination far away. There was the Sikh fellow with his long, black, curly beard and immaculately wrapped turban, eating an exotic curry dish at the food court. Everything was rich and spectacular, like a tasty stew of individuals that one was meant to savor and enjoy.

"Gads, the weather here is boiling!" Reggie said. " I don't know why I even consider making this my home."

"You complain a lot," Cindy said.

"So do you," Reggie said. "Don't think I didn't hear you when you got that in-flight meal."

"It was gross," Cindy said.

"My sentiments exactly," Reggie said.

"We're going to head into the city," Ho Yin said as they continued onwards. "I've got a car waiting on us out front and then we'll be off."

Boyd and Cindy were trying to keep up with Ho Yin's quick pace and Reggie's great strides. Reggie had everyone's luggage in his hands, carrying the tremendously heavy bags with remarkable ease, all the while keeping a wary eye on what was around them, looking for suspicious people.

"Mom told me she came here once," Boyd said to Cindy. "Her and Dad; when they were younger."

"Really?" Cindy asked. "She never told me that."

"She told me once," Boyd said. "It was a long time ago. She said the planes used to land in the middle of the city and that it was scary."

"What were they doing in Hong Kong?" she asked.

"After they got married, they took a year off work and went backpacking around the world," Boyd said. "They started here."

"They backpacked around the world?" Cindy asked. "That doesn't sound like Mom and Dad. All Mom and Dad do is work," Cindy said. "I can't imagine Dad taking a week for a vacation, let alone a year."

"I know," Boyd said. "Can you imagine Mom traveling around with everything she owns in a backpack? She can't even leave for work without three bags. Sometimes I think she was making it up."

They trotted along in silence for a couple of seconds before Cindy said, "I miss Mom and Dad."

"Me, too," Boyd said, and he felt like the airport wasn't so extraordinary anymore without his parents being there to share it with him.

Reggie stopped in his tracks in front of them, sniffing all around at the air. "What's wrong?" Ho Yin asked, looking around at the terminal.

"Something's not right," Reggie said.

Suddenly, Boyd felt aware of his surroundings. His eyes began to dart through the crowd, scanning faces and looking for some sort of danger that might be lurking nearby. The Chinese family waiting for their flight were harmless. The Thai executives walking toward them on the way to their plane weren't a threat either. The crying Indian baby was distracting, but a benign presence, as its mother was doing her best to soothe it. Everywhere he looked, he saw nothing out of the ordinary.

But something was wrong.

Like lightning, Ho Yin and Reggie dropped their things right there and assumed defensive stances, scanning the room for danger. It was then that Boyd realized that the danger did not lurk on the concourse upon which they were walking, but above them in the rafters. High above Cindy's head, on the arrivals and departures board, was some sort of creature dressed in black, and it crouched as if it was about to jump. "Cindy, look out!" Boyd yelled, but it was too late.

The creature dove for Cindy, doing an elegant flip and forward roll on the ground, whereupon it snatched her into its arms, threw her over its shoulder, and began a mad dash for the exit. Cindy's ear-piercing scream destroyed any semblance of stealth that the creature hoped to have.

"PANJAS[31]!" Reggie yelled as he took off after Cindy's abductor.

Boyd looked up in the rafters and could see at least five more of the creatures crawling around, each one short, stubby, and dressed head to toe in black. They dropped from the ceiling and surrounded Ho Yin and Boyd, pulling out shiny, silver swords from the wooden sheaths attached to their belts.

"Stay close, Boyd," Ho Yin said. "Whatever happens, I promise you that you won't be hurt."

Ho Yin unbuckled the belt that was wrapped around his waist and began to crack it back and forth around him like a whip, threatening their assailants with each crack. One of them thrust its sword just inches from Ho Yin's face, but with catlike speed, Ho Yin whipped the belt around his adversary's neck and jerked backwards, sending his foe to the ground, head first and unconscious.

Ho Yin did a forward roll on the ground and snatched his opponent's sword from its hand and then stood up with a determined look in his eye. "I thought that you panjas would have learned your lesson the first time we met," he said. The ninja-suited strangers paused for a second, looking at each other for some sort of reassurance, before they all turned to Ho Yin and rushed him, swords drawn.

Meanwhile, Reggie was huffing and puffing down the airport corridor, trying to keep up with Cindy's abductor. "Crikey," he said between breaths, "might I ask you to be a gentleman and put her down? This running business is for the birds!"

"He's not stopping!" Cindy yelled.

"All right," Reggie said with a sigh, and he snatched a rather large grapefruit from a juice stand in a nearby food court. "I guess I'm going to have to get rough with you," he said.

He made a run, spun his arm forward and around, and threw the grapefruit with such velocity that it bounced off the ground straight into the air, hitting Cindy's captor squarely in the back of the head and exploding with juice and pulp. The black-clad assailant fell to the ground with a thud. Cindy scrambled to her feet and ran to the safety of Reggie's arms. "Good shot," she said.

"I was quite the cricket player in my day," Reggie said, somewhat proud of himself.

But their ordeal wasn't over, as the creature jumped back to its feet and pulled out a pair of knum-chucks, spinning them back and forth over its arms so fast that they were a blur of motion. "Who is that?" Cindy asked.

"A panja," Reggie said. "It's a panda from China, schooled in the Japanese martial arts. Basically, a ninja panda, thus panja. Quite vicious and very dangerous. You'd best stand to one side, old girl. This might get ugly."

Cindy ran over and hid behind a chair as Reggie prepared to face the panja. He grabbed a heavy steel chair from the waiting area as if it was light as a feather, and held it up in front of him as a shield. Sparks flew as the panja attacked him with his weapon and the clang of metal on metal echoed through the terminal as Reggie deflected each blow from the panja with the chair. The panja moved with incredible speed, doing rolls, back flips and spins, all in an attempt to get at Reggie, and eventually Cindy.

Reggie, too, was quite nimble and although he couldn't keep up with the panja in a foot race, he could dodge the creature's blows. The panja did a flip, trying to jump over Reggie's head, but it was too slow, and Reggie snatched the poor creature's leg in his hand. "This is going to hurt," he said with a smile, as he swung the panja around and down onto the ground, leaving it unconscious on the carpet. He pulled off its black mask to see the creature's face. The panja looked like your average, everyday panda, with cute, black and white fur and a short little snout.

"Aw," Cindy said. "He's so cute!"

"*And* he's a killing machine," Reggie said. "That's Po. He's one of Fang's men."

"Fang?" Cindy asked.

"Our enemy," Reggie said as he snatched her up in his arms. "Let's go."

Just around the corner, Ho Yin was still caught up in battle with the other panjas, whirling and twirling back and forth to protect Boyd from their every jab, poke and swipe. Boyd, meanwhile, was scared to even breathe, as it seemed that every direction in which he turned held some sort of danger, be it the gleaming blade of a panja sword, or the whizzing blur of a pair of nun-chucks. The panjas were fierce and relentless in their efforts to get at Boyd and it was taking everything within Ho Yin's power to keep them back.

Boyd couldn't help but be impressed with Ho Yin's martial arts skills. He seemed to be moving a hundred times faster than humanly possible, and he anticipated the panjas moves with great ease. Still, try as he might, every move he made was one of defense, and although he held the panjas at bay with a dizzying array of punches, jabs and kicks, Boyd was sure that one man fighting five incredibly agile and threatening panjas couldn't last forever.

"Tally ho, chaps!" Reggie yelled as he ran right into the fray, the swing of his large arms sending panjas flying across the airport lobby.

This was all the advantage Ho Yin needed as he began to go after two panjas at once with such aggression that they soon found themselves backed into a corner. With a great leap, he swung his leg around with a roundhouse kick that landed squarely on their jaws.

"They're Fang's men," Reggie said as he threw one through a souvenir stand. "The one that tried to nab Cindy was Po."

"Fang," Ho Yin said as a grim look passed over his face.

The final panja stood in front of both Reggie and Ho Yin defensively, waiting for them to strike. "Which one are you?" Reggie asked, baring his fangs. "Larry? Deng? Fess up, chap, or you're in for a world of hurt."

The panja said nothing as it rolled backwards, jumped to its feet and disappeared down the corridor. Boyd looked around to see that all the panjas had vanished into thin air just as quickly as they'd appeared.

"Better get a move on, kids," Reggie said, quickly picking up their belongings and making a hasty exit. "We've got company."

Boyd and Cindy looked over to see several police officers running towards them through the crowd. Boyd started to trot away with Cindy behind him. They exited through the front door where a car was waiting, and jumped in the back before the officers could get to them.

We're fugitives, Boyd thought.

His heart was racing and there was a sick feeling in the pit of his stomach as he remembered the panjas crawling through the rafters of the terminal. He looked down to see his hands trembling from all the danger and one thought kept running through his head: Maybe he wasn't cut out for this job after all.

CHAPTER 9

THE MYSTERIOUS HALLS OF PING MANOR

The car that took Boyd and Cindy through Hong Kong looked like a bullet, ready to rocket them to their next space age destination. It was an effort for Ho Yin just to get Boyd and Cindy *into* the car, because both of them kept gawking at their surroundings like country-folk that had been dropped off in the big city.

Once inside, Ho Yin allowed himself to relax and they jetted down the curvy highway that wound its way along the coast of the island towards the city. As they drove towards the heart of the territory, the green landscape was occasionally interrupted by a gathering of massive high rises, the likes of which Boyd had never

Manor. They climbed and climbed, back and forth, past giant, narrow buildings and through dense growth of tropical trees that lined the lanes, speeding along on the wrong side of the road, past crazy drivers and gated houses tucked in corners and ravines.

Occasionally, Boyd got a glimpse through the trees of the city below getting smaller, but no less dynamic. It was dark now and the orange lights of the metropolis below filled the night sky.

Mr. Ping's mansion sat at the top of Hong Kong Island, high above the city center, where things were still lush and green, but there was a bit more space to stretch out. Towards the water, things seemed to be so crammed together that the only place to build anything was straight up into the air, which most buildings did without hesitation. The higher up they went, the more private gates were visible, little compounds hidden behind fences of exclusivity, places the ultra-rich called home.

As they rounded the last corner, they came to a large, ten foot high stone gate that surrounded what looked to be a very prestigious house overlooking the city. "This is it," Ho Yin said.

"Thank the stars," Reggie said. "It will be quite pleasant to sleep in my own bed tonight."

"This is it?" Boyd asked, as the large, iron gates of the front entrance opened to let the limousine inside.

"This is where you're going to live," Ho Yin said.

The gates shut behind them and they drove through a series of large, tropical trees that lined a long, straight driveway and opened onto a rather large (by Hong Kong standards) front yard with a circular driveway. At the far end of the yard stood a massive, old mansion. It was straight out of a fairy tale and seemed to be perfectly suited for a king or queen. It was long, its two stories stretched from end to end of the property, and its walls were made of elegant stonework. There was a large, marble fountain in the front yard that they circled around, and the limousine made its way to the staircase leading to the large, mahogany front doors.

Boyd and Cindy were speechless as they stepped from the limousine, looking up at the glory of the place they were now going to call home.

"This is *ours?*" Cindy asked.

"Oh, yes," Ho Yin said.

"And this isn't one of those cruel television shows where they bring out cameras and say, 'Suckers!' is it?" she asked.

"No," Ho Yin said.

"This isn't one of those awful dreams where we'll get inside, fall asleep and then have our mom wake us up, saying, 'You're late for school!'?"

"No," Ho Yin said.

"And you're not some evil demon who will…"

"Cripes, old girl," Reggie said, throwing up his arms in exasperation. "It's as real as I am! Get with the program!"

Cindy looked at Reggie and said, "I'm still debating whether *you're* real."

They walked up the front step and into the grand foyer of the mansion. From the front door, they could see down the main hallway, all the way to the other side of the house. It was at least fifty yards from one end to the other, practically as big as the entire block that Boyd and Cindy had lived on in Frankfurter. The interior of the mansion was filled with dark wood that was carved with elaborate patterns one might find in Buckingham Palace, and polished floors so clean that their reflections were mirror perfect.

On the left side of the foyer was a coat closet and on the right side was a giant, stuffed polar bear on a pedestal placed in a small alcove. The bear was frozen in time with a snarl on its face and its paws raised to strike its victim. Ho Yin looked up at the polar bear and said, "Okay, Bjorn, you're relieved."

The polar bear lowered its paws and looked down at everyone. It plopped down on the pedestal, sitting with its large legs dangling off the sides under its round belly. "Jolly good job you've done while we were gone, Bjorn," Reggie said, setting the luggage down in the hall. "We still on for that chess game later?"

The polar bear grunted, which seemed to indicate that he was, indeed, ready for that game. He lumbered off the pedestal and down on all fours. This massive creature, who was apparently named Bjorn, walked from Boyd to Cindy and back to Boyd again, sniffing at both of them and issuing a few grunts in the process, all while Ho Yin and Reggie took off their coats and hung them in the closet.

Boyd didn't know whether he should treat Bjorn like a giant puppy or like the threatening creature he was. "Does he bite?" he asked. Bjorn huffed his terrible bear-breath in his face as a response.

"Only when he's hungry," Ho Yin said. "Are you hungry, Bjorn?"

Bjorn huffed at them, again, to signal yes, and then padded around the corner and out of sight.

"That was a polar bear!" Cindy whispered into Boyd's ear. She was as excited as Boyd had ever seen her.

The interior of the mansion was like a trip back in time. It looked like an old school adventurer's club, with strange and unusual artifacts from around the globe adorning every available space. There was a wide assortment of voodoo masks that looked as if they were from the deepest, darkest recesses of Africa, where only hearty souls dared to travel. There were strange helmets encased in glass and a large, Egyptian casket cast in solid gold. There were bizarre weapons hanging on the walls. There were odd and unusual paintings of macabre people and scenes that seemed to add to the weird atmosphere. Because it was night time, the mansion seemed dark and creepy, as if there were things inside that no one dared to talk about, a feeling perpetuated by the collection of alien-looking insects under glass in a display case in the living room and the shrunken heads that were kept in formaldehyde jars in the study.

"Here's your room, Cindy," Ho Yin said, opening the door to a cavernous suite with a large, four-poster bed in the center. The décor was opulent, but the problem was that the room was just as creepy, if not more, as the rest of the house.

"Uh-uh," Cindy said between yawns. "No way. Not a chance on Earth."

"What are you talking about?" Boyd asked. "Just get in your room."

"Are you kidding me?" Cindy asked. "Look at this room! It's *haunted*, for crying out loud."

"What?" Boyd asked.

"Look at it," she said, throwing her bags on the floor and walking around the space. "Over there in the corner, where that nice chest sits? That's where the ax murder happened. And over there? Behind those window curtains? That's where the masked madman hides before he comes out to kill me. And that chest at the foot of the bed? That's where the body parts are kept."

"I think you've watched too many of those detective shows on that idiot box people call a television," Reggie said, leading her to the bed and pulling the blankets up to her chin.

"But I'm telling you," Cindy said, trying to protest. Her efforts were futile, as sleep was beginning to overtake her. "This room has bad karma."

"Actually, this room has some of the best karma in the joint," Reggie said, smiling at her.

"But..." she said as her eyes closed. "Ax murderers. Body parts."

"Rubbish," Reggie said, but before the last syllable came out of her mouth, Cindy was fast asleep.

Once they were back out in the hall, Reggie and Ho Yin led Boyd to his room next door. "She's got quite an imagination on her," Ho Yin said.

"Yeah," Boyd said, sucking in a massive yawn. "Mom lets her read anything she wants. She's weird."

"She's certainly unique," Reggie said.

"Ho Yin," Boyd said, "what about Mom and Dad? Shouldn't we be out there looking for them?"

"There's not a lot we can do this late, Boyd," Ho Yin said. "Besides, I think we all need to get some rest."

Boyd's room was large and dark, with a giant, four-poster bed in the middle and a grandfather clock ticking away on the far wall. The biggest fireplace he'd ever seen took up one entire side of the room. The room felt safe, even if it was a bit drafty, and the bed looked to be the most comfortable Boyd had ever seen.

"Get some rest, Boyd," Ho Yin said, walking towards the door. "Tomorrow is going to be a very busy day for you."

"Okay," Boyd said, already drifting.

"Oh, and I should warn you," he added, popping back into the room right before he shut the door. "Ignore the clock."

"What do you mean?" Boyd asked.

"It didn't want to move, so it's been a bit belligerent," he said.

"Huh?"

"Never mind," he said. "Just remember. Ignore it. Good night."

Boyd was just too tired to try to figure out what Ho Yin was saying, and with record speed, he fell asleep on the immense, overstuffed, soft pillows. He was so tired, in fact, that he failed to hear the clock mutter something as he drifted off, thinking it was but a dream. If he hadn't been so tired, he would have heard it say, "Spoiled runt!" in a thick, British accent that was unmistakably belligerent.

Exactly two hours after he fell asleep, Boyd was awoken by a poke at his side. Actually, it was several pokes to his side, as it took Cindy a fair number of jabs to rouse her deeply sleeping brother. "Wake up, you dimwit!" she hissed as she thrust her fingers into his ribs. It had always been difficult to wake Boyd, no matter how tired he was.

"What do you want?" Boyd asked, blinking hundreds of times as he made out his sister's silhouette in the darkness.

"I need you," she said. It was the first time Cindy had ever said anything like that to him. However, Boyd was much too tired to appreciate the significance of the moment.

"Go to bed," he said, turning away from her. "I'm sleeping."

She poked him in the ribs again, only this time much harder. "Wake up!"

"Argh!" Boyd said, throwing his blankets off his body. "What is it?"

"I need your help," Cindy whispered.

"With what?" Boyd asked, exasperated with his sister.

"I'm thirsty," she said.

Boyd couldn't believe that those words had just come from his sister's mouth. "Well, get a glass of water," he said.

"There's no glass in my room," she said. "And I don't know where the kitchen is."

"Well, look for it," Boyd said.

"I'm scared to walk around here by myself," she said. "This place gives me the creeps."

As much as he hated to admit it, Ping Manor gave Boyd the creeps, too. He wasn't completely sure that he would be brave enough to go looking for water by himself in the middle of the night either. "Do you really want me to go?" he asked.

"Yes," she said, pulling him out of bed.

"All right, all right," he said, dragging himself to his feet.

Ping Manor was silent and dark, with only a few stray, dim lamps illuminating its vast hallways. The darkness of the Manor made the strange and unusual displays all the more ominous as they walked down the large staircase at the front, down onto the main floor. Boyd pretended to be brave, leading the way as he padded barefoot across the cold, wooden floor, while Cindy kept a tight clutch on his arm, never straying too far from his side.

All the doors on the lower level of the mansion were shut, forcing Boyd and Cindy to go through the hair-raising process of opening each one as they held their breath in fear of what horrors might lay behind them. Some of the doors were innocuous, leading to small bedrooms or closets, but others were creepy. In one particular instance, they opened the door to the large dining room and the blue light from the tall, open windows, coupled with the stillness of the room and the Victorian furniture, gave it a haunted quality and they couldn't shut the door fast enough.

"I don't know if I'm going to like living here," Cindy said.

"Well, I certainly won't like living here if you keep dragging me out of bed just to get you water every night," Boyd said.

"Oh, I'd like to see you walk around here at night by yourself, chicken," she said. "You're just as creeped out as I am."

All of a sudden, Boyd froze in his tracks and peered into the darkness down the hallway. "What's that?" he said. His voice was filled with worry.

"What's *what*?" Cindy asked, tensing her body.

"*That,*" Boyd said, still staring, wide-eyed into the darkness.

"What?" Cindy asked. "What do you see? What is it?" She was starting to panic.

Filled with fear, Boyd said, "I think it's...it's...nothing." He began to laugh and slap his knee as if he was the funniest kid on the planet.

"You're a jerk," Cindy said, hitting him on the arm.

"Here's the kitchen," Boyd said, opening the last door and flipping on the light.

The kitchen was large, but homey, with gleaming silver pots and pans hanging from the walls, and large ovens and sinks that looked big enough to feed hundreds of guests. Boyd walked around the room, surveying the wide variety of cooking utensils as Cindy got her water.

"What do you think of this place?" Boyd asked, examining a strange, multi-armed machine whose purpose he couldn't discern.

"I think it's creepy," she said. "I think that yeti is weird. I think my bed is lumpy. I want to go back home."

"Well, don't mince words, Cindy," Boyd said, being sarcastic. "Tell me how you *really* feel."

"Do you really think this place is ours?" Cindy asked. "I mean, this mansion and everything?"

"I guess."

"I wish mom was here," she said. She looked at the clock on the wall and sighed. "If we were at home right now, we'd be at school eating lunch."

Boyd looked at the clock and realized Cindy was right. "Yeah," he said, trailing off.

"Just think," she said, "two days ago at this time, you were about to get in a fight with Tucker."

"Yeah," Boyd said, feeling reluctant to dredge up those memories.

"Why did you do that, Boyd?" Cindy asked.

"Do what?"

"Stand up to Tucker," she said. "I don't know of anybody who ever did something like that. Why did you do it?"

"Because I hate bullies," he said. "And he's a bully. He picks on everybody in school and someone needs to say something."

"But he was going to beat you up," she said.

"Yeah," Boyd said, "But big deal. Nobody should have to be afraid all the time and Tucker made it so that everyone was always scared of him. I was just tired of being afraid."

"The Dalai Lama says that to conquer your fears, you must face them every day," Cindy said, looking off into the distance.

"What did you just say?" Boyd asked. "The Dolly-who?"

Cindy snapped out of her tiny trance and said, "Nothing. I'm going back to bed."

Sometimes Cindy could be quite strange and this was one of those moments, so Boyd just shrugged his shoulders and followed her out the door. The minute he walked outside, he froze. His eyes grew wide and his jaw dropped open as he stood there, filled with fear.

Cindy continued talking but then noticed that Boyd was no longer following her. She turned and stared at him, her hands on her hips. "Are you trying to scare me again?" she asked. "I can't believe you'd try the same trick again. You're such an idiot."

"Cindy," Boyd said, his voice barely above a whisper. "Behind you."

"Shut up!" Cindy said, full of anger. "You're such a jerk! I'm going to bed." She turned back towards the stairs, whereupon she ran smack dab into the very thing that had paralyzed Boyd with fear. Cindy looked up to see that she'd run into a person, but not your average, every day person. Standing before her was a dusty, decrepit, raggedy, zombie-like individual that was more of a rotting corpse than anything else. Everything suddenly clicked in her mind and she realized that she was standing in front of a mummy.

"EEEEEEEEE!"

Cindy's high-pitched scream at the sight of the mummy could have shattered glass and she had every reason to be frightened at the skeletal remains that stood in front of her. What made things worse was the fact that her scream seemed to enrage the mummy. It began to flail its arms back and forth and emit a low, raspy moan that sounded like it was out for blood.

It seemed that Cindy could have stood there and screamed for fifteen minutes straight had Boyd not pulled her away from the creature. They backed away, but the mummy was now walking towards them, howling in its frightening way, staggering along on its brittle legs.

"What *is* that?" Cindy yelled as they slowly backed down the hall.

"You tell me," Boyd said, starting to panic.

They had backed themselves into a corner and the mummy was slowly making its way toward them. Cindy squeezed her eyes shut in terror, but Boyd couldn't look away in terrified awe at what was in front of him. *This is how I'm going to die*, he thought. *Eaten raw by a mummy.*

"What in the blue blazes is going on down here?"

Boyd and Cindy looked over to see Reggie standing in the hallway in a silk robe, his hands on his hips as if he were perturbed. "Help!" Boyd said, for the mummy was now but inches from them.

"My goodness, lad, you've frightened poor Rama right out of his wits," Reggie said. He walked over to the mummy and put a reassuring arm around its shoulder. "There, there, old chap," he said to the mummy. "It's just the guests, mate. No need to get yourself in a tizzy."

The mummy seemed to be grunting and moaning something as Reggie turned it back down the hall in the opposite direction. Its hands jerked toward Boyd and Cindy as if it was speaking about them. "Yes, yes," Reggie said, sounding as if he was comforting the creature. "They meant no harm. You really can't blame them, can you? You look a fright."

Reggie motioned for Boyd and Cindy to follow as he led the mummy around the corner, towards the giant Egyptian coffin that they'd seen earlier. The coffin door was wide open as he directed the mummy back inside with a calm hand.

"I completely understand," Reggie said as the mummy continued to moan and grunt while it got back in the coffin. "You don't need to be wandering around like that anyway. You need your rest. Get some sleep, old bean."

Reggie closed the heavy coffin door with a quiet thud and slapped his large hands together to get rid of the dust that the mummy's rags had left on him. He turned to Boyd and Cindy and said, "Why in the world would you want to get Rama all stirred up like that?"

"It tried to *kill* us," Cindy said.

"Rama?" Reggie asked with a laugh. "Please! Rama wouldn't hurt a fly. For goodness' sake, he's a *mummy*. If you even *breathe* on him too hard, he'll fall apart. Believe me, I know. I've had to put him back together before."

"Why was there a mummy walking around the house?" Boyd asked as Reggie led them back upstairs to their bedrooms.

"Well, when you've been in a gold coffin for three-thousand years, you need a little excitement," Reggie said. "He probably heard the two of you thumping around down here and wanted to see what the action was."

"He tried to kill us," Cindy said, still traumatized.

Reggie knelt down beside her to look her in the eye when they reached her door. "Look, old girl," he said, "nothing's going to hurt you on Reggie's watch, okay? Especially old chaps like Rama. You just go on in there and get some rest."

"But..."

"None of that," Reggie said. "Get some sleep."

Reggie left Cindy standing in the middle of her room, speechless, as he shut the door and turned towards Boyd. "Well, now that we've settled Miss Candycakes in her room, I'm off to bed. Goodnight, old bean."

"You're not gonna walk me to *my* room?" Boyd asked, still frightened.

Reggie began to laugh, slapping his knee as if Boyd had just told a good joke. "That's funny," he said. "You've got a great sense of humor, Boyd. See you in the morning."

Boyd wasn't kidding. He really wanted the safety of Reggie's company. After Reggie had disappeared back down the stairs, Boyd made it back to his room and dove under the blankets, pulling them up to his nose to keep the bad things away.

It would take him a while to fall asleep.

CHAPTER 10

THE EGREGIOUS MR. PU

Sitting on the fourth floor of a nondescript office building in Wan Chai was an establishment well-known throughout Hong Kong called *Mr. Pu's Auction House*[35]. It was there that Mr. Fang, Mrs. Fang, and Li pulled up in a large, silver car, followed by three more cars containing Mr. Fang's bodyguards. Mr. Fang already had a healthy sweat covering his body from the humidity of the Hong Kong evening, but with the stress of failing to capture Boyd McCloyd and his impending debt to the Conspiricetti, his clothes were virtually soaked as he struggled to get his fat body out of the back of his car.

"Can I help you out, sir?" Li asked, offering him a hand.

Mr. Fang slapped his hand away. "Don't touch me, dog," he said between pants as he pulled himself to his feet. "You've caused enough problems already."

"Honey, do you want me to run home and make you some noodles before we see Pu?" Mrs. Fang asked.

"No, no, I want to get this over with," Mr. Fang said.

Mr. Pu's Auction House was the premier auction house in all of Hong Kong, selling luxury goods to the highest bidders from all over the world. From gold-plated toasters to leopard skin toilet brushes, Mr. Pu's Auction House sold items only for the wealthy and extravagant; nothing was too gaudy, nothing too ridiculous, and as long as it was worth a small fortune, it was up for sale.

The place was run by the ever-charming Mr. Pu[36]. Mr. Pu was a local celebrity in Hong Kong, known for his expensive parties, garish clothes, and lavish home. Mr. Pu prided himself on having one of the finest antiques collections in all of Asia, acquired by one of the finest businesses in all of Asia, and housed in one of the finest mansions in all of Asia. Mr. Pu's Auction House was an invitation-only affair.

Mr. Pu, himself, was a slight, older man with salt and pepper hair and black-rimmed glasses an inch thick. He was quite short and very well groomed, his hair always neatly slicked back to the side and his colorful suits without a wrinkle in sight. He looked harmless enough, but one was not to judge Mr. Pu by his looks.

"Mr. Fang," Mr. Pu said, meeting the entourage at the door. "What a pleasure it is to have you here."

Mr. Fang was breathing heavily as he walked into Mr. Pu's office. It was filled with paintings and antique lamps and regal chairs, and probably contained more treasures than was found in most world-renowned museums. "Good to see you, Pu," Mr. Fang said between huffs.

"I hope you don't mind if I avoid shaking your puffy, sweat-soaked hand," Mr. Pu said.

"Not at all," Mr. Fang said, surveying the room. "Where shall I sit?"

"Just one second," Mr. Pu said, and he turned to the open door. "Charles?"

"Yes, Mr. Pu?" said a man peeking in the door.

"Charles could you please drape a towel over the chair here?" Mr. Pu asked. "I'd like to avoid Mr. Fang's sweat staining my antique chairs." Charles disappeared and quickly returned, draping a towel over the chair as Mr. Fang sat. Mrs. Fang sat beside him and Li hovered in the background. "Now, Mr. Fang, what might I do for you?"

"Look, I've got a problem," Mr. Fang said, pulling a dumpling from a cloth in his pocket and stuffing it into his mouth. "A big problem. I think you can help."

"I'm all ears," Mr. Pu said, settling in behind the ornate Chinese desk between them.

Mr. Fang gave Mr. Pu a deliciously evil grin and said, "Who do you hate most in the world?"

"Excuse me?" Mr. Pu asked.

"I asked you who you hate most in the world," Mr. Fang said. "It's an easy question."

Mr. Pu laughed graciously and said, "I don't know what you're getting at, Mr. Fang, but I don't hate anyone."

"Oh really?" Mr. Fang said. "I think you're lying."

"Mr. Fang, what in the world are you talking about?"

With great effort, Mr. Fang rose to his feet and began to wander about the room, observing the antiques on display. He wandered over to a beautifully sculpted jade dragon sitting on a glass shelf on the far side of the office. "You have a very nice collection here, Mr. Pu," he said. "These antiques must be very valuable."

"It's the finest collection in the world," Mr. Pu said, his face full of pride.

"The finest?" Mr. Fang asked. "Oh, Mr. Pu, this isn't the finest. *Confucius Ping* has the finest antique collection in the world."

A tick began to form in Mr. Pu's eye and his face grew dark. "Mr. Fang, I assure you that this collection is..."

"...is second place to Mr. Ping's," Mr. Fang said. "You know, I think you've got nice antiques, but they're only so-so compared to Mr. Ping."

"Well, I'm sure Mr. Ping..."

"In fact, Mr. Ping makes you look like a second-rate junk store owner," Mr. Fang laughed.

"Shut up!" Mr. Pu yelled, his eyes seething with anger behind his thick glasses. His fists shook with rage. "That *fraud*! That *phony*! Confucius Ping is a two-bit, illiterate fool! His collection is *nothing* compared to mine. *Nothing*!"

"Calm down, Mr. Pu," Mr. Fang said, laughing at him.

"Calm down?" Mr. Pu asked. "You insult my life's collection by comparing it to that hack, Confucius Ping? That man has made a mockery of the antique business!"

"So you *do* hate somebody?" Mr. Fang asked.

"I do," Mr. Pu said. "I hate him with *every fiber of my being*."

"How *dare* you talk about a dead man like that," Mr. Fang said, smiling.

Mr. Pu froze in his tracks. He looked up at Mr. Fang with shock in his eyes. "He's dead?" he asked.

"Unfortunately, yes," Mr. Fang said. "Just the other day."

"My goodness," Mr. Pu said, almost to himself. "How I've *waited* for this day to come. What a joyous, wonderful, exciting day."

"And guess who has his things," Mr. Fang said.

"You?" Mr. Pu asked, his voice barely above a whisper.

"Yes," Mr. Fang said. "I've got his house, his land, and all those stupid little things he's got on display. I've got it *all*."

Mr. Pu looked like he was about to have a heart attack. "You've inherited Mr. Ping's collection?"

"Oh, yes," Mr. Fang said. "It's mine...as soon as I take care of one, little thing."

"What do you mean?"

Mr. Fang smacked his fist into his hand and stared out the window. "There's this thirteen-year old kid named Boyd McCloyd. This child says it's his. He won't give it to me."

"I don't understand," Mr. Pu said.

"Look, let me say this," Mr. Fang said, sitting down again. "I told some people I was going to give them Boyd McCloyd, but then I got the wrong person. It's very complicated."

"Well, how do *I* fit into all of this?" Mr. Pu asked.

"Here's the deal," Mr. Fang said. "I need to know what the most valuable thing in Mr. Ping's collection of antiques is. I'm gonna hold this kid's parents ransom until he gives me something worth as much as him. So what I want *you* to do is tell me what is the most valuable thing Mr. Ping has. Then, I'll make that kid give it to me."

"What's in it for me?" Mr. Pu asked.

"If you come up with something valuable for me to ransom...something really valuable...I'll give you everything else in his house."

"Why would you come to me?" Mr. Pu asked. "Why not Lu's Antiques? Or Xu's Sales of Fine Goods?"

"Because I *know* you," Mr. Fang said. "And I know how much you *hate* Mr. Ping. You don't like him, right?"

"Not like him?" Mr. Pu asked. "Why would I not like him? He only stole countless artifacts, gold, jewels, and ancient treasures out from under me all of my life. He only made me look like an utter and complete fool every chance he got. He only kept me from having the most incredible collection of antiquities and artifacts in the world. Not like him? Oh, no, Mr. Fang. I *hate* him. I hate him with every fiber of my being and I wish a pox on his soul and every soul that has anything to do with him."

"So are you going to help me?" Mr. Fang asked.

"You want something of immeasurable value from Mr. Ping's collection?" Mr. Pu asked, rubbing his hands together with glee. "Mr. Fang, I know just the thing."

CHAPTER 11

THE WEIRD AND WONDERFUL WORLD OF PING MANOR

That night, Boyd's dreams were filled with unusual sights and sounds. They were all about the mansion, as if the very place was alive and abuzz at his arrival. In the dream, he wandered through the dark halls, hearing excited whispers about his arrival from unknown sources. Whenever he would search for the mysterious voice, it would lead him to a dead end, a hallway that ended abruptly or a locked door. When he tried to make out what the voice was saying, it sounded like the Cantonese he'd heard in the airport upon his arrival.

It was then that he heard a creaking sound, as if a large piece of wood was being bent at an awkward angle. CREEEEEAK! The sound was getting louder and louder as it got closer to him and Boyd was ripped from his dreamworld and plunged back into reality when he realized that he wasn't dreaming. The sound was coming from his own room.

He dared not move. He had felt this place had horrible things inside of it and now one of those horrible things was in his room, getting closer and closer to him. The sounds emanating from just to the right of the bed were of something bulky and mysterious. There was a scraping across the floor and the occasional tinkle of metal scraping against wood. It sounded so horrible that Boyd couldn't open his eyes. But he would have no choice, because even as he squinted them shut, he heard the groan of something heavy leaning over the bed and the air grew cooler.

He opened his eyes to see that the grandfather clock was leaning over his bed.

"Yes, just as I suspected," it said. "A spoiled runt."

"AAAAAAAAAAAH!"

Boyd let out a howl unlike anything he'd let out in his life; a scream so deep and full of fear that it scared the clock back over to its place on the wall. As it shuffled across the floor, it made a sound like furniture being moved and the chiming of church bells. In fact, the clock moved so fast that it tick-tocked itself ahead by almost a minute and a half.

"So sorry, so sorry," it said with a British accent. "Never mind me. Go on about your business…"

Boyd stared in horror as the clock froze in its position, looking no more threatening than it did before, and as the seconds ticked away on its face, Boyd just sat in bed with the blankets pulled up to his nose, staring at it. The tick-tock of the old fellow provided a soothing rhythm that started lulling him back to sleep again. Tick, tock, tick, tock, tick, tock, tick…

Did the clock just stop ticking? Boyd thought.

His eyes shot back open, looking at the clock. It was still there. It hadn't moved, but it had stopped ticking. Now, the blankets were just below his eyes as he stared at it.

Shuffle!

Did the clock just move?

Shuffle!

It did it again!

Shuffle, shuffle, shuffle!

The clock was now waddling its way toward Boyd. "Don't hurt me!" Boyd yelled, putting his hands in front of his face.

"Hurt you?" the clock asked, its voice a deep baritone. "What a young fool you are. How on *Earth* could I hurt you? I'm a clock for pity's sake!"

By now, Boyd's face was buried deep beneath the blankets, as he muttered over and over to himself, "It's only a dream. It's only a dream…"

"Pah!" the clock said. Boyd couldn't see it, but it sounded like it was standing over the bed again. "A dream? I don't think so."

His hands were trembling with fear as Boyd pulled the blankets down just enough to get a glimpse of the mammoth figure looming over him. The face of the clock had two, smaller faces inside of it that told the seconds and the date, both of which served as the hulking beast's eyes. They seemed to blink as it looked at him. "So you're the new one, eh?" it asked.

"P-pardon?" Boyd said.

"The new one," the clock said. "Don't tell me you're as daft as you are ugly." The clock creaked as it leaned in closer to him. "You need a haircut, lad."

"What do you mean, 'the new one?'" Boyd asked.

"We've certainly heard a lot about you," the clock said. "Have to say I expected more. A *lot* more."

"Stephens!"

With the roar of wood, metal, and glass scraping across the hardwood floor, the clock turned towards the door to see Ho Yin standing with his hands on his hips, looking perturbed. "Stephens, what are you doing?"

Dropping its face in shame, it began scraping its way back over towards its space on the wall. "Won't happen again," it said. "I promise."

Boyd didn't know what he should be more shocked about, the fact that a giant clock could speak and move, or the fact that Ho Yin was now scolding it. "Are you okay, Boyd?" he asked.

"I think so," Boyd said, still a bit flustered.

Despite the early hour, Ho Yin was wearing the same thing he wore yesterday, a black suit with a black tie; it was his usual attire. As he walked over towards Stephens, he looked perturbed. "Didn't we talk about this, Stephens?" he asked.

The clock muttered something apologetic.

"Stephens!" Ho Yin said.

"Yes, yes, yes," the clock said. "You told me quite clearly, sir."

"And yet, you still did it?"

"Well, I, uh…"

"Stephens…"

"Yes, sir, I believe I did. It's true. And for that, I apologize with utmost sincerity."

"Would you prefer to be put in storage, Stephens?" Ho Yin asked.

"No!" the clock said, shuddering. "No, no, no, that would be dreadful."

"Well, you've almost left me with no choice."

"I swear, sir, on my great, great grandfather, Pocketwatch Stephens, that it shan't happen again," the clock said. "There's no need for any of that storage talk, sir. No need at all. I've learned my lesson, honestly, done and done. No storage for me!"

Ho Yin acted as though he was making a very hard decision, shifting back and forth as he gave the big, hulking beast the Staredown[37]. "All right, Stephens," he said, sighing. "I'll let you stay."

"Oh, thank you, sir," Stephens said. "Thank you, thank you, thank you! I won't forget this, sir."

"But if it happens again," he said, "you'll be boxed up, rolled out of here, and stuck down at the shipyards for longer than even *you* can keep track of. Understood?"

"Right-o, sir," Stephens said. "Won't happen again, sir."

"Good," Ho Yin said, turning his attention to Boyd, who was so enraptured with what was happening before his eyes that his mouth was wide open and a slight string of drool dangled from his lips. "Now, Boyd," he said, "I guess there's a little bit of explanation that needs to happen here."

"Certainly is, sir," said the clock. "The daft lad has no clue why he's here."

"I believe I can handle this, Stephens," Ho Yin said.

"Right you are, sir," Stephens said.

"Did you get any rest?" Ho Yin asked, turning back to Boyd.

"A little," Boyd said. He still felt groggy.

"Well, why don't you get yourself cleaned up and come down to get something to eat?" he said.

Later, after getting a bit disoriented trying to find the kitchen, Boyd found Cindy, Ho Yin, and Bjorn already seated at a rectangular wooden table. Reggie was at the stove in a white apron and cook's hat making what smelled like a delicious concoction. "Well, well, well," he said. "Look who's finally up and about!"

"It's about time," Cindy said. "We thought you were going to sleep all day."

"What time is it?" Boyd asked.

"Eleven," Ho Yin said without looking up from his newspaper.

"What's for breakfast?" Boyd asked.

"Breakfast?" Reggie said. "That's a laugh, mate. We're having lunch. You missed breakfast."

"Okay," Boyd said. "What's for lunch?"

"Pesto, Gnocchi, and Tomato sandwiches on Focaccia bread[38], with a small spinach salad and lentil soup," Reggie said, speaking as if he could taste his glorious creation simply by speaking about it.

"What's pesto?" Boyd asked.

"Pesto is a green sauce used for pastas and other Italian dishes," he said.

"I don't like pesto," Boyd said.

"Well, that's unfortunate," he said. "Look's like you're going to be out of luck because I'm not cooking anything else."

He sat down a plate of food in front of Bjorn, who began to nose around the plate with his large snout. "Ah-ah," Reggie said, wagging his finger. "You know the rules, Bjorn. At the table, we use cutlery."

Bjorn grunted his disapproval.

"I don't care how much you whine," Reggie said, turning away. ***Cutlery.***

Bjorn roared at Ho Yin, who failed to look up from his newspaper.

"Sorry, chum," Ho Yin said. "You know the rules."

Bjorn huffed a few more times, and then, with more grace and precision than most humans, he began to cut his sandwich apart with his silverware and to eat his food in a civilized manner. Boyd watched with fascination as the large polar bear seemed to be the model of etiquette at the table, having better table manners than most people he knew, including himself.

"Bjorn's always demanding equal rights," Reggie said, as Bjorn, once again, huffed at him. "I say if he wants to enjoy the same privileges as us, then in certain situations, he has to follow the rules of a civilized society." Bjorn growled at Reggie, but continued to eat his meal in a dignified manner.

"Boyd's a picky eater," Cindy said as she observed Boyd's untouched plate. "Mom always made him special meals because he wouldn't eat anything. It was so unfair."

"She did not," Boyd said, horribly embarrassed.

"Well, Uncle Reggie doesn't play those games," Reggie said, as he sat down with, not a plate, but a ***platter*** full of food. There had to have been at least ten large sandwiches on his plate and he had a salad bowl full of soup.

It was decided that Boyd and Cindy needed to see the place in which they'd be living and after they'd eaten, Ho Yin took them on a grand tour of the mansion. "So, Ho Yin," Boyd said as they walked down the long hallway that connected both wings of the manor, "what is all this stuff on display through here?" He paused in front of a large set of teeth with very sharp fangs displayed in a glass case, below which was a bronze plaque that read Bhoktapur, Nepal 1967[39].

"These are all the things that Mr. Ping collected over the years," Ho Yin said.

"It's like a museum or something," Boyd said.

"Holy cow!" Cindy yelled. She was standing in front of a colorful, abstract painting framed on the wall in front of her. "Is that a *Picasso?*"

"It certainly is," Ho Yin said, looking at the painting with her. "You have an excellent eye for artwork."

"How did you know it was a Picasso?" Boyd asked, his voice full of skepticism.

"She knew because she saw the autograph at the bottom," Ho Yin said, butting in on the exchange.

Boyd looked at the lower corner of the painting and saw the words, *Happy Birthday, Confucius! Your Friend, Picasso* written on the canvas. "Oh, right," he said.

"What are the wristbands?" Cindy asked, pointing to a shining pair of silver bracelets in another display case. "Is that real silver?"

"They're called Armicons," Ho Yin said. "And yes, that's real silver."

"Cool," Cindy said. Boyd failed to really see her wonder in the silver bracelets or anything else for that matter, and they ended up following her around like she was a puppy that had too much sugar for breakfast. She just kept running from object to object, trying to take in everything she saw and asking whatever came to her mind.

Eventually Boyd came around and started to observe things himself. The item that held his attention the most was a large, iron robot that sat in a dark corner near the dining room. It had to be one of the coolest things he had ever seen. It looked like some sort of robot from a science fiction movie in the fifties, but was in perfectly fine condition.

"This is awesome," Boyd said. He leaned up close to the expressionless, metal face and stared into its gold, taillight eyes. "Hey, Ho Yin," he asked, "what is this thing?"

"That's Dr. Frankenstein's SPU-BOT 2460," Ho Yin said, approaching Boyd quickly and pulling him away from the machine. "Don't touch it, please," he said.

"Why?" Boyd asked.

"It's a very sensitive robot," he said. "I've been meaning to put it in storage, but I just never got around to it. Moving on..."

"Well, what does the SPU-BOT 2460 do?" Boyd asked.

"It's a killing machine," he said. "Dr. Frankenstein sent it on a rampage in the 50's, but it malfunctioned before it could do any damage."

"Well, it looks awesome," Boyd said, and at that exact moment, he made the mistake of touching the robot's shiny, silver arm. The machine's eyes came to life, shining a bright yellow and scanning the horizon. "Uh-oh," Boyd said.

"Kill-*bzzt*-All-*click-breet*-Humans!" it spoke with its metallic voice. With remarkable speed for its bulky frame, it reached out to grab Boyd. Luckily, Ho Yin realized Boyd's danger and jerked him backwards by the shirt collar as they fell to the floor on top of each other. "Kill-*bzzt*-All-*breep*-Humans!"

"Whoa," Boyd said, his eyes filled with wonder.

"Way to go, Boyd," Cindy said from down the hallway, her hands perched on her hips in a know-it-all fashion.

The robot moved in a lanky, awkward way, as if each step was a painful process. "Not much in the speed department, is it?" Boyd laughed.

"Run, Boyd!" Ho Yin said, pulling him across the floor.

"What?" Boyd asked, moving in a lackadaisical manner. "Why?"

Before he could even get to his feet, Ho Yin shoved him to the ground again. However this time, the reason was obvious. With a click and whir, a compartment opened up on the arm of the robot to reveal a futuristic gun, which locked and loaded itself and quickly opened fire in Boyd's direction, blasting a volley of loud laser beams through the mahogany walls, sending shards of wood flying everywhere.

Boyd and Ho Yin turned to run from the robot, only inches ahead of its laser blasts. It wasn't fast enough to pursue them, so it locked into place and spun around on its hip, turning towards Cindy, who was frozen in wonder at the other end of the hall. "Cindy, get out of here!" Ho Yin yelled, but Cindy was too caught up in a terrified rapture with the SPU-BOT. The robot lifted its other arm and yet another device protruded from its forearm. Within seconds, a wall of flame burst forth from the nozzle and Cindy jumped backwards to avoid the blistering fire.

"*Bzzt! Click!* Kill all...*Bzzt! Click!* Humans!" the robot repeated as it began its awkward march towards Boyd's little sister.

Cindy scrambled backwards like a crab, but couldn't regain her footing. The robot moved closer and closer until...

...a large statue crashed down on top of its head, crushing its top like a pop can.

Smoke rose from the mangled mess at its top and the buzzes and whirs of its innards stopped. Behind the robot was Reggie, lifting a large, marble statue of a lion's head from the crevice it had created in its shoulders. "I hate to use Pappaw's memorial[40] for such nasty work," Reggie said, "but that bloke needed to be put out of its misery."

"That robot was trying to kill us!" Boyd said, running back down the hall to examine the wreckage of the machine.

"Ho Yin, why wasn't this stupid thing taken apart a long time ago?" Reggie asked.

"You *know* how I feel about taking robots apart," Ho Yin said. "I was going to put him in storage."

"Well, it's too late now," Reggie said, shrugging his shoulders. "Don't touch this thing, kiddos. His insides could be radioactive."

Ho Yin was surveying the damage to the walls of the mansion. "Looks like Boyd's got some repair work to do," he said.

"Me?" Boyd asked. "Why me?"

"The first rule of Ping Manor is **Don't touch anything!**" Reggie said. "There's lots of nifty things in here. Some of them are dangerous. You have to be very careful."

"All right, already," Boyd muttered and they continued the tour, leaving the robot to smolder quietly in the hall.

Boyd and Cindy enjoyed exploring Ping Manor. It was like being in a museum that was actually interesting; a place that was dense with artifacts, pictures, and strange and unusual curios that did nothing but intrigue. "Mom and Dad would love it here," Cindy said, as they walked down the vast hallway that connected the front of the mansion to the back.

"I wonder if they've been here," Boyd said. "It's weird to think that they knew Mr. Ping."

"That's for sure," Cindy said, staring at the wooden floor as she shuffled down the hall. "It's weird to think that Mom and Dad had a life. I always thought that they didn't exist before we were around."

They came to a room where there were twelve wax figures standing on pedestals, each of them dastardly and sinister in their own, unique way. A man named Lieutenant Cyanide was at the center of the room and he was surrounded by some grotesque people and some that didn't look like they could harm a hair on anyone's head. Yet all of them had elaborate costumes or a look that made them unique, ranging from the fearsome-looking Colonel Savage[41], who held his sword up to the sky in his outfit from the American Civil War, to the dark and brooding fellow in a pitch black mask and long cape, whose plaque bore the name, The Mysterious Man-Bat of New York City[42]. There was the confident, well-dressed fellow in a business suit over in the corner, whose plaque named him Tiberius Caesar[43], who could very well have simply been a banker and not some sort of evil villain.

"These people are your enemies now, Boyd," Cindy said with a laugh. "Scared yet?"

"They're not my enemies," Boyd said.

"Oh, yeah, they are," Cindy said. "You heard Ho Yin. His enemies are now your enemies. If you take the job, you've got a whole mess of trouble." She looked at a pale, thin wax woman in the corner with blackened eyeballs and visible veins all over her body, whose name read, Madame Hookworm[44]. "For your sake," she said, "I hope this lady doesn't come after you. She's the creepiest of them all."

Bored with the room, Cindy walked out, leaving Boyd by himself to observe the gallery of weirdos and creeps. Mr. Ping said Boyd would have questions, but Boyd never expected to have this many. The mansion was filled with thousands of bizarre things and every one of them filled his brain with questions too numerous to even start answering. What were they? How did Mr. Ping get them? What kinds of things would Boyd acquire if he took over the job?

For instance, there was one glass display case about midway down the hall that contained some of the most colorful butterflies that Boyd had ever seen, all in neat rows on a nice, red-velvet board. Boyd had never seen any butterflies as beautiful or as big as these, or with so many striking colors. Yet, the plaque below read, ***Carnivorous Butterbeasts of Bolivia, 1927***. What in the world did ***that*** mean? Boyd knew from Mr. Dullong's sixth grade science class that carnivorous creatures were animals that ate meat, but he'd never heard of a ***butterfly*** that ate meat, nor had he heard of butterflies ever being referred to as ***butterbeasts***. It was bizarre.

If those things weren't bizarre enough, there were several others which defied explanation as well. In one corner of the library, there was a giant glass ball which held another deep black ball in the center of it that reflected no light and hurt Boyd's eyes if he looked at it for too long. The label at the base of the pedestal read, ***Professor Blank's Man-Made Black Hole (Do Not Touch or Stare)[45]***. In one of the hallways towards the back was a three foot tall pyramid[46] (which looked like the pyramid with an eyeball floating in midair at the top on the U.S. dollar bill). It didn't have a plaque, but whenever Boyd walked by it, the eye watched him walk down the hall, never breaking its gaze. This left him a bit unsettled. There were paintings whose pictures seemed to change every time Boyd looked at them, a mirror[47] that gave a reflection of Boyd ten years older than he actually was, and a marble water fountain[48] in the ballroom that sprayed Cindy from the minute she walked into the room until the second she scrambled out in a panic.

As the day progressed, Boyd noticed that everything in the mansion, design-wise, seemed to have been unchanged since the 1920s. "Don't you find this place creepy?" Boyd asked Cindy as they stood in front of a large, Tahitian longboat[49] that had been nailed to the wall of the dining room. It hung just above a portrait of an electrified skeleton with a plaque under it that read **Powered Jack**.

"Actually, I think it's awesome," Cindy said.

"Well, you were scared last night," Boyd said, taunting his sister. "What? Have you suddenly changed your mind?"

"Night is a different story," Cindy said, looking at him gravely. "At night, you can feel the weird things come to life in this place. I don't like it here at night."

"Oh, you're just a chicken," Boyd said. He turned and sat down in the leather chair underneath the painting when he heard a snap and pop, and suddenly found the chair tipping backwards. "Whoa!" he yelled, trying to regain his balance.

Cindy reached out to try to prevent his fall, but failed. As she watched her brother flail and flop backwards in the chair, her eyes grew wide and she realized that sitting in the chair was the trigger to open a secret door in the wall. The painting of "Powered Jack" was the entrance to a secret passage.

Boyd, meanwhile, had rolled backwards into the passage and found himself lying on the cold, concrete floor of a dark tunnel that ran between the walls. "What in the world is this?" Cindy asked.

Boyd looked off down the narrow corridor on each side, trying to see what was further up the passage, but it was too dark. "It's some sort of secret tunnel," he said, struggling to get to his feet so that he could get out of there. His efforts were made harder by his perpetually curious sister, who struggled just as hard to get *into* the passage as he tried to get out of the passage. "What are you doing?" he asked.

"Exploring," she said, evaluating her surroundings with glee. "Come on!"

"I'm not going in there," Boyd said.

"Oh, who's the chicken now?" she said, taunting him. "Come on. We won't go very far. It's too dark to see anyway."

As much as Boyd reveled in his wimpiness, he was still too macho to let a taunt from his younger sister keep him from doing something dangerous, so he shoved her to the side and walked further into the tunnel. "Get out of the way," he said.

At that precise moment, a most unexpected thing happened. The minute they were both in the tunnel, the secret entrance swung closed, leaving Boyd and his sister in pitch darkness.

"Do I scream now or later?" Cindy asked, but even as she did, a series of dim lights popped to life above them and the hallway was illuminated. Boyd quickly walked over to the secret door, looking for some sort of latch or handle that would open it up again, but wasn't having much luck.

"If it opens that easily from the outside," he said, "then it should be just as easy from the inside."

"Cool! Boyd, look at this." Boyd looked over to see Cindy standing further down the hallway, observing something in the wall quite closely.

"Cindy, what are you doing?" he asked. "We need to get out of here."

"Seriously," she said. "Come look at this."

Boyd wasn't as rambunctious as his sister and his desire to explore was pretty minimal, but since he couldn't find the door handle, he walked down to where Cindy was standing. As he got closer, he realized that she was looking through what appeared to be a two-way mirror. The mirror looked out into the kitchen area, and there, in what he thought was a private moment, was Reggie, washing up the dishes from lunch. Washing dishes, however, wasn't the embarrassing part. The embarrassing part was that Reggie looked to be singing and singing quite passionately at that.

"Why can't we hear him?" Cindy asked.

"This place must be soundproofed," Boyd said. "Look." He pointed to a red button that was built into a small speaker in the wall and then pressed it. Reggie's voice came barreling through the speaker above them, booming yeti-tones filling the narrow passageway.

"I LOOOVE THE CHEEEESE," he sang. "FLAAAAAAVORFUUUUL GOOOOOOOUDA! GO-OH-OH-OAT CHEESE! CHEDDAR! AND MOZZA-RELLLLLL-AAAAAAAA!"

"Having fun?"

Boyd and Cindy practically jumped through the wall when they turned to see Ho Yin standing behind them. They were both nervous because they'd been caught. "We were...uh..." Cindy said.

"We thought...uh...we might..." Boyd said.

"I see you've discovered the secret passage," Ho Yin said, smiling.

"Boyd did it!" Cindy said, pointing at her brother.

"It was an accident," Boyd said, pleading his case. "I swear."

"Don't panic," Ho Yin said. "You're not in trouble. There's nothing dangerous about these passages. And sometimes it's faster to go through here to get to other parts of the house."

"These things go all the way through the house?" Boyd asked.

"From end to end," Ho Yin said. "Past every room."

"What in the world did he use them for?" Boyd asked.

"They were originally built as an escape route," Ho Yin said. "They lead directly to the underground garage."

"Escape?" Boyd asked. "Escape from what?"

Ho Yin put his finger to his chin and thought about it. "Where to begin? Because Mr. Ping did good things in his life and thwarted evil at every turn, he made a long list of enemies, most of whom will be glad to call you an enemy as well, but be that as it may, a partial listing would be Black Barry of Baltimore[50]...he's pretty dangerous...The Vengeful Fire Ants of Madrid[51], Dr. Absolute Zero[52], The Wicked Weather King[53], Baroness Von Stronheim[54], Helmut Frankenstein[55], The Taj Mahal Bandit[56], The Amazon Pirates[57]...Shall I go on?"

"Wow!" Cindy said. "That's a lot of people that hate you, Boyd."

"How can all those people hate *me?*" Boyd said, feeling ill. "I've never even *met* them."

"Oh, they don't hate you, Boyd," Ho Yin said. "They hate Mr. Ping. But because if you're taking over Mr. Ping's work, you're target number one now."

He shuffled everyone back into the dining room, leaving Boyd sitting on a chair under the portrait of Powered Jack, feeling the weight of the world on his thirteen-year old shoulders. He would remain there for more than an hour.

CHAPTER 12 CHOOSING NOT TO CHOOSE

After Cindy abandoned him to do whatever it was that Cindy found interesting, Boyd found Mr. Ping's office, a softly lit room with walls lined with books of all sorts of ages, colors, shapes, and sizes. In the very center of the room was a large, antique Chinese desk with intricate carvings on the front and around the edges. Behind the desk was a big, comfortable red leather chair on wheels. The light from the room came from a single, lawyer's lamp with an emerald green shade that sat upon the desk.

"Hello?" Boyd asked into the empty room. "Ho Yin?"

No one answered his call. He walked into the room to explore. There were two, matching blue leather chairs set on either side of the door as he made his way in and Boyd soon realized that the books on the shelves all seemed to be antiques, books that were from years, if not centuries, ago. Very few of them had writing on the spines to signify what they were, and almost all of them had old, yellowed papers stuffed inside them that seemed to be notes written in Mandarin.

On the right hand side of the room was a long, flat table that was piled high with maps. Boyd walked over and looked through a couple of them and realized that most of them were hand drawn and labeled in Mandarin, and that none of them seemed to be of any place he'd ever known. However, there was one map that he *did* recognize, if only because it was the most modern of all of them. It happened to be a road map of Frankfurter, Ontario, with a giant, red circle hovering over his very house on Dreary Lane.

The next thing he noticed was a series of identical books that were sitting upon the shelf directly behind Mr. Ping's desk. They were significant for the fact that there seemed to be well-over a hundred of them, each one of the same size, shape, and color, and each one labeled with a number, one to one hundred and three. He edged his way closer and saw that the thick spines contained the title of the book, which read, *Mr. Ping's Almanac of the Twisted and Weird.* He'd finally found the complete collection.

Taking one from the shelf (number seventeen, to be precise), Boyd began to thumb through the massive volume, trying to figure out what it was. Inside, he found pages upon pages of information, pictures, and statistics that seemed trivial. That is, it all seemed trivial until he stumbled upon an old drawing of what looked to be a twenty-foot tall man with one eye, raising a long stick of wood in rage at whoever the artist was. Below the picture was a caption that read, *The Cyclops of Western Borneo, 1916, drawing by Confucius Ping*[58].

On the opposite page was an article that accompanied the picture with the title, *The Perilous Encounter with the Cyclops of Western Borneo (Or Bruno Gets Angry at Me),* and it seemed to be about Mr. Ping, who happened to be on an expedition to find this Cyclops in the wilds of the Southeast Asian rainforest. It was fascinating to read, and as he flipped through the book, Boyd saw that every article had to do with something fantastic that happened in the year 1916. This led Boyd to realize that each of the books on the shelf had to do with a specific year of the twentieth century.

"Interesting reading?"

Boyd slammed the book shut and spun around to see Ho Yin standing in the doorway, smiling. "I was just…I, uh…I think…"

"Don't worry, Boyd," Ho Yin said. "I would hope that you would explore the office. There are probably things in here that we've all forgotten about."

"Are these the almanacs?" Boyd asked.

"Yes," Ho Yin said. He walked over to the shelf beside Boyd and pulled out one of the volumes, absentmindedly thumbing through it. He said, "Each year, Mr. Ping would scour the globe, looking for tales of the strange and unusual so that he might write them down."

"What's so special about these things?" Boyd asked.

Ho Yin looked at him seriously and said, "Do you think that the history books you have at school tell you everything that happened? I mean, think of the short life that you've led up to now. All the things you've done, the places you've seen, the people you know. Do you think one book could sum up all of that? History books only give you a part of the story, a part that has been twisted and manipulated and changed to fit what certain people want the average person to know. Mr. Ping's job was to write down the information that would never make it into a history book. He wanted to document the fantastic stories that might have been forgotten if someone hadn't written them down. That's how Mr. Ping spent his time, and that is why his books are so important."

"So that's what all the displays and statues and stuff are?" Boyd said, the light coming into his eyes. "It's all evidence of the things he's found and written down in his books over the years."

"We live in an amazing world," Ho Yin said. "You should really take some time and read some of these almanacs. Mr. Ping lived an incredible life, as will you, if you decide to follow in his footsteps."

"I'm not interested in living an incredible life," Boyd said. "All I want is to get my parents back."

"As we all do," Ho Yin said, putting his hand on Boyd's shoulder to offer him some reassurance.

AN UNEXPECTED VISITOR CALLS...

CHAPTER 13

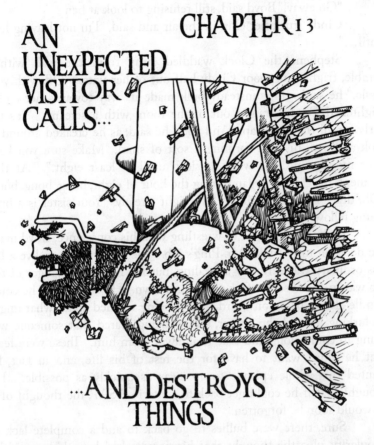

...AND DESTROYS THINGS

Boyd didn't sleep well that night. He was awoken the next morning by Cindy, standing fully dressed by the bed and staring at him. "Well?" she asked.

He rolled over away from her, trying to get a few more minutes of sleep. "Shouldn't you be annoying someone else right now?" he muttered into his pillow.

"Have you made your decision?" she asked.

"Go away," Boyd said.

"I want to know what your decision is going to be," Cindy said, her arms folded across her chest in an impatient manner.

"Go away!" Boyd said, still refusing to look at her.

Cindy stuck her chin in the air and said, "I'm not leaving here until…"

Stephens the Clock waddled away from the wall with a rumble, frightening poor Cindy half out of her wits. "Off with you, lassie," he said. His unsteady bulk made its way towards her and it frightened Cindy straight out of the room with a scream. "It's too early for all that claptrap. And you," he said, as he creaked around to look at Boyd, his face forming a sort of snarl, "Make sure you keep your mouth shut! I want to sleep until at least eight." At that moment, his chimes began to ring the hour of eight, bong, bong, bong. "Oh, drat!" Stephens yelled. "It's eight already. Your sister is a brat, young fellow."

After a long night of wrestling with his conscience, Boyd made the decision to not take Mr. Ping's job. The opportunity to live a life less ordinary was certainly appealing, but for Boyd, the danger of the job was in the absolute fear of the unknown. He wasn't sure he could handle always being on guard, always being worried about what might be lurking around the corner, always being scared that someone was going to come along and take it all away from him. These were fears that he didn't want to have for the rest of his life, and in fact, he wanted this whole episode to go away as quickly as possible. He thought that if he could get back to Ontario ASAP, the thought of it all would soon be forgotten.

Sure, there were bullies to go back to and a complete lack of popularity, plus the thought that his parents had been kidnapped by some unknown assailant, but he thought that these problems would be worked out eventually and all would be well and good, so he could go back to his normal little life without any real highs and lows. He tried to ignore the fact that Cindy would be disappointed, that he would never be rich, and that a life of high adventure would never be his.

Shame and cowardice are never pretty sights to see, so Boyd did his best to put on his game face as he walked through the hallway to tell Ho Yin the news. Ho Yin was in the back of the mansion in the grand ballroom that overlooked the city, where he was reading a newspaper and having a cup of tea in the early sun. The vista through the giant glass wall behind him was breathtaking, the very embodiment of the opulence and glamour that Boyd was throwing away.

"Ho Yin," Boyd said, "do you have a minute?"

"Absolutely," Ho Yin said, putting down his newspaper and devoting his full attention to him. "Do you have a question for me?"

"Well, not exactly," Boyd said, squirming.

It was then that Reggie led Cindy and Bjorn into the ballroom, purely by coincidence. "And really," he was saying, "the décor would have been almost entirely different had I been in charge, but unfortunately, no one looks to a yeti for interior design advice. Oh, look who's here!" They marched over by Boyd and Ho Yin, looking interested in what was going on. "We haven't interrupted, have we?"

"Well, actually…" Boyd said.

"Boyd had a question," Ho Yin said.

"Well, maybe I can answer it," Reggie said.

"Could Reggie help?" Ho Yin asked.

"Well…" Boyd said.

"You look sick," Cindy said to Boyd. "Are you gonna barf?"

"Well…" Boyd said.

Reggie looked surprised. "He's going to give the answer!" he said.

"You are?" Ho Yin asked, smiling.

Bjorn grunted.

"Finally," Cindy said, even though she hadn't been waiting for any significant amount of time.

"Well, what will it be?" Reggie asked.

Boyd smiled at them, but it looked more like a grimace than a smile, and his throat began to swell as he tried to speak. Just as he was about to tell them, he noticed something just out the window over the horizon, and it stopped him in his tracks. It was a streak of cloud that formed a large arc over the far green mountains, almost like it was the exhaust from a missile. Only there was no missile that formed the trail. As the white smoke came closer and closer, Boyd saw that at the head of the streak was a man!

"What in the world is that?" he asked.

Everyone turned to see what was a rather large man, traveling at a very high rate of speed, straight for the mansion. "Bjorn! Reggie!" Ho Yin shouted as he jumped up from his chair. "Get Boyd and Cindy to safety!"

Like lightning, Bjorn snatched Cindy, dragging her along by the shirt with his fearsome jaws. "You're ripping my shirt!" she yelled as they disappeared into the mansion.

Reggie picked Boyd up, but wasn't quite as fast as Bjorn, and just as he turned to run, the "missile" man burst through the large window, shattering the clear barrier into a million pieces, all of which fell to the ground with a clamor. Glass went everywhere, as both Reggie and Ho Yin scrambled to the safety of the outer reaches of the ballroom.

The man who crashed through the window was wearing some sort of jet pack, which propelled him straight through the ballroom and deep into the far wall, sending paintings and furniture and plaster flying in all directions. The noise began to settle as the remaining pieces of glass fell from the giant window with a crash, and the last of the papers and molding from the wall dropped into the smoke that was wafting out from the hole where this mysterious figure crashed.

Reggie was on top of Boyd, protecting him from any debris that might have flown his way. Meanwhile, Boyd was peeking out from the Reggie's strands of white fur hanging in his face, trying to see what was lurking in the smoke and chaos.

"Are you okay, Boyd?" Reggie asked.

"Uh, yeah," Boyd said.

Reggie looked down at him and said, "This could get ugly. I want you to do what I say, when I say it. Okay?"

"No problem," Boyd said. He could feel his hands shaking uncontrollably as Reggie stood up in a defensive position.

"Ho Yin?" Reggie yelled. "Are you okay?" He couldn't see Ho Yin through the smoke.

"I'm okay," Ho Yin yelled from somewhere off in the distance.

A clatter was heard in the general direction of the smoke, as if whatever was in there was shrugging off half the wall that had fallen upon it. A grunt was heard, and then it sounded as if a rather large man was shaking his head around, his jowls flapping as he growled. "ARR!" he yelled.

It was a man, and from what Boyd could see as he emerged from the smoke, it was a man who had to be at least ten feet tall and twice as wide. He was abnormally muscular, with long, black hair and a beard that hung down his chest. He wore what looked to be a jet engine on his back, which had been torn from an actual plane (and still had the airline's logo painted on its side). His brow was large and his eyes dark, and he wore clothes that were made of leather an inch thick.

"WHERE'S PING?" the man yelled, his voice so loud that it rattled the remaining windows.

Ho Yin stepped out from his hiding place, looking confident, yet defensive, as if he was dealing with a very dangerous individual. "Mr. Ping's dead, Barry," he said.

"THAT'S WHAT I THOUGHT!" Barry said, with a smile. "THEN I CAN FINALLY TAKE WHAT'S MINE!"

"And what's that?" Reggie asked, also emerging from the smoke.

"*EVERYTHING HE OWNED!*" Barry said with a laugh. Once again, the laughter shook the windows.

"You know we can't let you do that," Ho Yin said.

Reggie leaned over his shoulder to Boyd, who was now hiding behind a staircase, and said, "It's Black Barry of Baltimore. Indestructible, except for his armpits. We're in a bit of a pickle here." Boyd nodded as Reggie turned back. His hands would not stop shaking.

"YOU CAN'T LET ME?" Black Barry yelled. "I DON'T THINK YOU HAVE A CHOICE, LITTLE MAN!"

Reggie appeared with rabbit-like quickness, swinging a giant, brass coat rack that he'd snatched from a corner straight at Black Barry's head, trying to get the jump on him. The coat rack bent like rubber, barely even causing him to flinch. Barry grabbed Reggie's arm, swung him around like he was a rag doll and tossed him through the upstairs wall with a thud.

Meanwhile, using Reggie's surprise attack as a distraction, Ho Yin jumped onto Black Barry's head, latching onto his hair like a dog latches onto a sock. Barry flung him around like a cowboy riding a bull, but though he was being wildly tossed around, Ho Yin held on. "Give it up, Barry!" he yelled. "We've beaten you a hundred times before. Today will be no different."

"ARR! YOU LITTLE RUNT!" Barry yelled. "I'M GONNA EAT YOU FOR DINNER!"

Barry reached over his head and grabbed Ho Yin, flinging him across the room, right into the marble banister of the grand staircase, leaving him unconscious on the floor. This large man let out a huff, as if he was glad to be rid of such pests and he dropped the jet from his back, where it clanked on the floor and slowly fell over on its side.

Boyd watched as he began to survey his surroundings, sniffing at the air like a giant from an old fairy tale that smelled a foreigner in his castle. "WHO'S THERE?" he yelled. "I CAN SMELL YOU LIKE AN OLD, MANGY DOG!"

He began to walk around the room, trying to get a bead on where the smell was coming from and Boyd realized that he now had two options. One was to wait where he was until this gargantuan creature found him and ate him in one large gulp, and the other was to run for his life and hope that Black Barry had a small attention span so that he would forget what he was chasing.

With fear filling his chest, Boyd burst from his hiding space, running full speed for the main hallway, trying to flee from Barry. "A RODENT!" Barry yelled, a wicked smile crossing his face. "THIS MANSION IS INFESTED WITH VERMIN!" He began to lumber after Boyd, moving with surprising speed for a man of his size. "I MUST RID MY NEW HOME OF SUCH CREATURES."

Boyd ran so fast it felt like his lungs were going to burst, but no matter how quickly he moved, Barry kept up with him. Finally, Barry pulled a large, leather whip from his belt and with a hard crack, he snapped it in Boyd's direction, its end whipping around his feet, sending him sprawling on the hardwood floors at the end of the long hall. As he scrambled and struggled to break free, Barry dragged him all the way back down to where he was, picking Boyd up with one thick hand and holding him in front of his face.

"ARR," he said. "I'VE NEVER SEEN A RUNT LIKE YOU AROUND THESE PARTS." He turned Boyd from side to side as if he'd never seen a kid before. "ARE YOU WHITE MEAT OR DARK MEAT? OH, NEVER MIND. YOU'LL MAKE A RIGHT NICE APPETIZER. NOW, WHERE'S THE KITCHEN?"

Black Barry threw Boyd under his arm and began to explore the mansion, causing a general commotion everywhere he went, slinging Boyd every which way and knocking over everything in his path. Although he was terrified of this large, loud, smelly man, Boyd managed to make an assessment of the situation. Reggie said that Black Barry's only weakness was his armpits, and at that moment, that's where Boyd was caught, and man, oh, man, did it ever stink.

He looked at Barry's thick, leather shirt and saw that it was sewn together at the shoulder with some type of cord. Seizing the opportunity, he reached into his pocket and fished out his Swiss army knife. While Black Barry was distracted with his search for the kitchen, Boyd began to saw the thick cord in half, making a hole in the armpit.

"ARR," Barry said, "I CAN'T FIND ANYTHING IN THIS STUPID PLACE!"

As soon as he got a hole big enough for his hand, a putrid, foul odor burst forth from the seam, as if an old, airtight coffin had been opened after hundreds of years. Barry must have felt the cool breeze in his weak area, as he glanced down at Boyd. "WHA..?" he said.

But it was too late! Boyd had already rammed his hand into the gooey, wet, grossness of the hole and grabbed onto a large wad of Barry's armpit hair. The hairs were like wet straw and Boyd pulled on them with all of his might, trying to fell his captor.

Barry let out a howl of pain unlike anything that Boyd had ever heard before and as he flailed around, Boyd held on for dear life, knowing he had the advantage. Barry fell to the ground, his ten-foot frame unable to move under Boyd's death grip.

"ARR!" Barry yelled. "MERCY! MERCY!"

Boyd had regained his footing beside Barry, but was caught at an awkward angle, as his hand was still buried in the big man's armpit. The fact that Barry's gooey sweat was now running down Boyd's arm didn't help matters either.

"Reggie?" Boyd yelled. "Ho Yin? I think I need some help here."

Boyd had Barry at his mercy, but they were at a standstill. Like a classic game of chicken, if Boyd were to remove his hand from Barry's armpit, then he was sure that Barry would not make the same mistake twice and eat him right then and there. However, if Boyd were to have pulled the armpit hair any harder, Barry would lose all control and come barreling down on top of him. He wasn't sure that having a ten-foot tall, five foot wide lunkhead on top of him was the best idea.

"LET GO OF ME PIT HAIR, SON, AND I'LL PROMISE YA HALF O' EVERYTHING I GOT!" Barry said, wincing from the pain under his arm.

"You don't seem like the trustworthy type," Boyd said. "I'll take my chances with what I'm doing."

"ARR! YA LITTLE RUNT!" Barry spat. "IF I GET OUTTA THIS MESS, I'M GONNA EAT YA, THEN PUKE YA UP, THEN EAT YA AGAIN!"

"That's a charming thought," Boyd said, tugging at the hair in his hand to prevent this tough guy from any more tough guy talk.

"OW!" he yelled. "I WAS JUST KIDDIN'!"

They stood there for a few seconds, Boyd trapped in Barry's armpit, and Barry unable to move from his position. "Who are you?" Boyd asked.

"I'M YOUR WORST NIGHTMARE! I'M...OW! SORRY, SORRY! I'M AN ENEMY OF PING'S. HIS BIGGEST, TOUGHEST, MOST WORTHY OPPONENT. EXCEPT, OF COURSE, FOR THIS HERE ARMPIT THING."

"Mr. Ping's dead," Boyd said, feeling queasy from the stench of Barry's armpits. "Isn't it time for you to move on?"

"PING'S DEAD! WE *KNOW* THAT! THAT MEANS IT'S FREE REIGN, RUNT! THE CONSPIRICETTI WILL FINALLY HAVE THEIR WAY."

"The what?" Boyd asked. Little did he know that Barry had maneuvered his other hand around the handle of the ax on his belt and quietly unlatched the hook.

"YOU DON'T KNOW THE CONSPIRICETTI?" Barry asked, and just as he did, Boyd could feel him shifting his weight around. He knew that he had mere seconds.

Barry swung his ax around at Boyd in an attempt to chop off his arm, but Boyd pulled away just in time, but not before taking a fair amount of the pit hair with him, the sticky, gooey wad like a scouring pad in his hand.

Barry let out a howl and he spun around as if he'd been shot by a hundred bullets at once, before falling to the ground, unconscious. Boyd looked at the hair in his hands and saw that it was squirming around like worms poking their head out of the ground. He quickly dropped the foul handful, watching all of it wriggle off in different directions into the outer reaches of the mansion.

He walked over and saw that, sure enough, Barry was as unconscious as he could ever have been. Just as he breathed a major sigh of relief, Ho Yin and Reggie came limping into the room. "Boyd!" Ho Yin said. "Are you okay?"

"Look at this, Ho Yin," Reggie said, standing over Barry. "The bloomin' bounder's out cold!"

"What?" Ho Yin asked, running over. He turned to Boyd with a shocked look on his face. "How did you do this?" he asked.

"Reggie said his armpits were his weak point," Boyd said. "I pulled out his armpit hair."

"Oooo," Reggie said, looking concerned. "Let me see that hand, mate."

Boyd raised his hand, which was now purple and black from having been under Barry's arm. "We'd best get you something for that hand," Reggie said. "Sticking your hand in his pits is like sticking your hand on radioactive plutonium. Come with me, mate."

As it turns out, Reggie, Ho Yin, and Mr. Ping had dealt with Black Barry of Baltimore several times in the past, always having to find some cunning way in which to deal with him. He was indestructible, except for his armpits, and in their last few battles over the years, he'd made it harder and harder to reach them. One time, they had to drop him in a giant vat of concrete, another they had to leave him on an island in the South Pacific, far enough away from land so that he had no hope of swimming. Yet, never before had anyone rendered Black Barry unconscious by removal of the hair from under his arm.

"It must have been horribly painful," Reggie said.

Cindy and Bjorn joined the three of them in Mr. Ping's secret laboratories that were located just behind the greenhouse. Black Barry of Baltimore had been taken away by a team of Hong Kong police officers that were used to dealing with people like him, and Ho Yin was busy examining one of Barry's hairs that they'd managed to capture before it crawled away. Boyd sat in the corner of the lab, trying to regain the feeling in his hand, as some strange chemical in Barry's sweat had left it numb.

"Amazing," Ho Yin said, looking through a microscope at the hair. "It's alive!"

"Let me see, let me see," Cindy said, squirming to get in front of him. She looked in and said, "Whoa! It seems to be multiplying in a classic, mitochondrial pattern..."

Everyone looked at her as if she'd just spoken Chinese.

"Uh, I just made that up..." she said, smiling in an embarrassed way.

"Did you say that there were a handful of these that got loose in here?" Ho Yin asked.

"Yeah," Boyd said.

Ho Yin put his hand to his chin, looking concerned. "Hmm," he said. "There's no telling what those things will turn into. Snakes, lizards, floating skeletons. It can't be good. Bjorn, will you get your X-500[59] for me?"

Bjorn grunted and walked over to a box, whereupon he pulled out a tiny robot that was about the size of a box of matches. Using his large paws, he daintily set it down on the counter, then pulled out a remote control from the same box and pressed a button that made the tiny robot sprout legs like a spider and walk around.

Pressing more buttons, Bjorn made the robot go over and "sniff" Black Barry's armpit hair, and then it took off, crawling down the side of the table and out the door. "That should take care of that," Ho Yin said. "Thanks, Bjorn."

Bjorn grunted.

Ho Yin came over and sat beside Boyd. "That was excellent work you did in there, Boyd," he said. "Mr. Ping would be proud that you are his successor."

"Well," Boyd said, squirming, "I don't know if I'm the right person for the job."

Ho Yin smiled. "Having doubts?" he asked.

"Well, it's just that there are probably better people for the job than me. I mean, I'm just a kid. There's nothing brave or special about me. I got lucky. That's all."

"Luck is simply how you react when an opportunity presents itself," Ho Yin said. "Personally, I think you're the perfect person for this job. Do you know why? It's not because you're the strongest or the bravest or the fastest. It's not because you're the smartest or most popular or had the best grades in school. It's because you, more than anyone else I've known, know the difference between right and wrong.

"We've watched you for years, Boyd, just to make sure that you were the right person for such an important task, and in every choice you've made, you've chosen the right way. You've made moral decisions that didn't just benefit you, they also benefit others. It could have been little things, like when the lunch lady forgot to charge you for your lunch, but you paid her anyway. Or when you let your friend, Billy, have the last ice cream sandwich that day at your house. Or it could be something big, like when you stood up to Tucker Stevens the day we came for you. Either way, these aren't the everyday decisions of your average person. These are the decisions of a person with a good heart, and that good heart is the reason we want you to take over this special task. We're just giving you the opportunity to spread your influence.

You could change the world, Boyd, but only if you want to. It all rests on your shoulders."

Boyd let the words sink into his head. Ho Yin was right. It wasn't about the money or the adventure. It was about doing the right thing, and in that moment, he realized that if there were people out there who were willing to kidnap his parents, like Mr. Fang was, or hurt innocent people, like those panjas at the airport, or even if there was someone like Black Barry of Baltimore out there, who would have eaten Boyd whole if he'd had the chance, then those people needed someone to stand up to them. They were the Tuckers of the real world, and if Mr. Ping was no longer around to protect us, then who would that person be? In that moment, he knew what he had to do.

"Okay," Boyd said to Ho Yin. "I'll do it."

PART II

CHAPTER 14

ACROSS THE HARBOUR INTO THE NEXUS OF THE STRANGE AND UNUSUAL

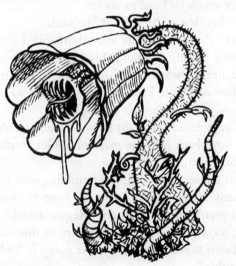

"AAAAAAAA!"

The scream echoed through the whole mansion that afternoon, causing Ho Yin, Reggie, and Boyd to drop whatever tasks they'd been doing and run for the source. The source of the scream was Cindy and hearing her high-pitched, siren-wail echo through the halls of the mansion had become a common occurrence over the last three weeks.

On this day, they found her in the greenhouse, where she'd been wrapped up in several, snakelike vines that held her in place as she was examined, head-to-toe, by what appeared to be a giant, yellow flower. The flower moved as if it was trying to figure out how to digest her properly at meal time. Ho Yin, Reggie, and Boyd all burst into the greenhouse at the same time, which startled the flower.

"Pascal[60]!" Ho Yin said. "What do you think you're doing? Put her down!"

The large flower that went by the name of Pascal looked at Ho Yin sheepishly, its body language conveying the fact that it knew it had done something wrong. Yet it still held on to Cindy.

"*Pascal,*" Ho Yin said again, this time a bit more threatening. "Do you want me to prune your leaves *again* this week?"

The flower shook its head to say no.

"Then put her down, this instant," he said.

Reluctantly, Pascal let slip its leafy, thorn-filled vines and Cindy was free. Breathing heavily, she ran behind Ho Yin for safety, peeking out from behind him to watch the killer plant. Ho Yin scolded the plant, saying, "How *dare* you, Pascal! We have been so generous with you and this is how you repay us? It just isn't fair…"

As Ho Yin lectured the giant flower in the greenhouse, Reggie took Cindy and Boyd back into the mansion. "Got yourself in a bit of a pickle, there, didn't you, lass," he said.

"It tried to kill me," she said, still trembling with fear.

"How many times are we going to have to warn you about going places you aren't supposed to go?" Reggie asked. "There are a million different ways for you to get hurt here in this mansion, Miss, and if you don't listen to our warnings, you're going to find yourself in a whole heap of trouble."

"I'm naturally curious," Cindy pleaded.

"That's what you said when the antigravity marbles[61] got loose," Boyd said.

"And when you used the laser to shoot a hole in the wall," Reggie said.

"So?" Cindy said.

"She doesn't listen very well," Boyd said.

At that moment, Bjorn walked out of one of the offices and Cindy grew excited, running over towards him. "They're picking on me, Bjorn," she said, looking at Boyd and Reggie as if they were somewhat evil. Bjorn huffed at the two of them as Cindy ran off down the other hallway.

Ho Yin appeared from the greenhouse just as they left, saying, "Boyd, I hope you're prepared for the day when your little sister suffers a gruesome fate in this mansion. I fear that, one day, we might not save her in time."

"Well," Boyd said, shrugging his shoulders, "I guess we'll just have to do our best."

He turned to walk back down the opposite hallway, but Ho Yin stopped him and led him back towards Mr. Ping's office. "Have you read volume thirteen yet?" he asked.

Boyd sighed and said, "I finished it this morning. Can't I have a break, Ho Yin? I've already read more in the last three weeks than I have in my whole life. Plus, I haven't even left the mansion."

"There are one hundred and three almanacs, Boyd," he said. "You have to read them all. And anyway, it's too dangerous to leave the mansion. Just continue to read the almanacs and we'll go from there. Okay?"

"All right," Boyd said. He settled into the chair and casually began thumbing through Volume 14.

"Mail's in," Reggie said as he walked past Ho Yin with a stack of envelopes and packages piled high in his arms.

"Look for my bill from the Book Society," Ho Yin said as he left the room. "I believe I owe them for this month's edition of **Chester's Quarterly**." Boyd was relaxed back in the old, rolling leather chair behind the desk with his feet propped up on the corner. When Reggie came into the room, Boyd jerked his feet off of the table as if he'd been caught doing something horribly wrong and he subtly wiped the surface of the desk with his elbow to hide the scuffs his shoes had made.

Reggie dropped the mail on the table and began to sort through it as Boyd casually wandered over to see what had been delivered, peeking around Reggie at the bounty on the table. "Bills, bills, bills," Reggie muttered, carefully sorting through the envelopes. "Never get a credit card, Boyd. They were invented by the devil himself."

"You have a credit card?" Boyd asked.

"I have *forty-seven* credit cards," Reggie said with a sigh.

Boyd picked up one of the packages and looked at the front. "Lettuce of the Month Club?" he asked.

Reggie swiped the box from his hands and quickly opened it. "Blimey, it's here!" he said. He pulled out a wad of Styrofoam stuffing and then removed a pristine head of leafy green lettuce from a plastic bag, observing it as though it was a fine work of art. "Will you look at that?" he said. "Perfection."

"It's lettuce," Boyd said, unable to see the vegetable in quite the same way as Reggie.

"Not just *any* lettuce, Boyd," Reggie said. "It's a Winchester Laroux Third Generation head of iceberg lettuce from the south of France. It's the best of the best."

"It still looks like lettuce to me," Boyd said. "Lettuce is lettuce. You put it on burgers."

"Au contraire," Reggie said.

"I can't believe there's such a thing as the Lettuce of the Month Club," Boyd said as he began nosing through the boxes and envelopes again. A small, white box heavily wrapped in tape caught his eye and he pulled it from the pile. He looked at the address and saw his name. "Hey," he said, looking at it. "This one's for me."

In the blink of an eye, Reggie slapped the package out of Boyd's hands, across the room, and then jumped on top of Boyd as though he was protecting him. "Can't...breathe," Boyd wheezed, feeling the full weight of Reggie's bulk on top of him. Reggie gave Boyd a bit of air, but stayed over him, sniffing in the direction of the package that he'd knocked out of his hands. "What did you do *that* for?" he asked.

"Just playing it safe," Reggie said.

"By *tackling* me?" Boyd asked.

"That package," he said. His eyes narrowed as they examined the seemingly innocuous white box on the floor. "That's a *bad package*."

"It's just a box," Boyd said.

"*From who* is the question," Reggie said. "Nobody knows you're here."

"Oh," Boyd said, and he saw the small package in a whole new way. It seemed a lot more menacing now. "Do you think it's a bomb?"

"Bomb?" Reggie asked, slowly getting off the floor. "No, it's not a bomb. Bombs are for stupid people. The people we're up against aren't stupid. Besides, I can smell bombs."

"Well, what could it be?"

"Lots of things," Reggie said, helping Boyd to his feet. "A piranha-bird; a pox on your firstborn; Mexican, flesh-eating jumping worms; you name it." He began to lead Boyd out of the room, watching the box over his shoulder along the way. "Let's keep a safe distance from it, okay? I don't trust that thing."

The sight of Bjorn in a bomb-disposal suit, awkwardly making his way into Mr. Ping's office to retrieve the white package was yet another bit of the strange and unusual in a series of ever-increasing strange and unusual events that Boyd had witnessed. Bjorn looked like a giant, stiff robot when covered in the black disposal suit, which was all odd angles and sharp points, due to the protective metal plates inside the fabric. He moved like a robot as well. Boyd and Cindy watched from a safe distance down the hall behind a protective plastic shield as Reggie directed Bjorn into the office like a construction manager.

"Bjorn takes care of the dangerous objects," Ho Yin said, holding the shield in front of Boyd and Cindy. "He's something of a demolitions expert."

"I don't know what's weirder," Boyd said, "the fact that Bjorn is a demolitions expert or the fact that you found a bomb-disposal suit big enough to fit a polar bear."

"He's going to be okay, isn't he?" Cindy asked. "He won't get hurt, will he?"

"He's done this hundreds of times," Ho Yin said, an air of reassurance in his voice.

"He's coming out, chaps," Reggie yelled, marching down the hall with purpose to shoo Boyd and Cindy out of the way. "Back! Back!"

Bjorn emerged from the office holding giant, six-foot steel tongs, the end of which held the infamous white package. He walked slowly, trying not to rattle the package or make any wrong moves as he took it to the laboratory at the far end of the building. As Bjorn moved on to the lab, Reggie stopped by the three of them and sighed. "Don't rightly know why that bear enjoys doing things like that, but he does," he said.

"A bomb-disposing bear," Boyd said, trying to get a handle on the situation. "What's next? Mine-detecting monkeys?"

"Actually, yes," Reggie said. "The Battling Baboons of the Eighteenth Armored Division in Britain has been doing some fine work in Angola. Have I told you their story?"

"Forget I even asked," Boyd said, shaking his head in disbelief and walking away. "This place is just too weird."

Bjorn had taken the mysterious package to a special room in the lab for dealing with volatile and dangerous items, and Cindy, Reggie, Boyd, and Ho Yin observed him through a thick window as he carefully opened up the package to examine the contents. "Now, if a horrible, green, gelatinous blob emerges from the package and starts to get bigger and bigger quite quickly, run for the car," Ho Yin said. "Those blobs can be dangerous."

"Are you joking?" Cindy asked.

"Um, no," Ho Yin said. "Don't worry, though. It's just a precaution. We haven't seen one of those in years."

Boyd and Cindy exchanged a look and continued to watch Bjorn at work. After meticulously removing the tape and cutting open the box, he slowly pulled back the sides to reveal the contents. "What is it?" Cindy asked. "I can't see it."

Boyd was standing on his toes to try to get a better look. He said, "I think it's a..."

"It's a phone," Reggie said.

They saw Bjorn lift up his protective mask, sniff the phone a couple of times, and then turn to them. He gave a "thumbs-up" sign and motioned for them to come inside the special room.

No one really knew what to make of the sleek little phone that sat on the table in front of them. It seemed innocuous enough, but then in this new world that Boyd had found himself, nothing was really harmless and he never knew when things could go awry. "So it's a phone," he said.

"Perhaps," Reggie said.

"Perhaps not," Ho Yin said.

"Well, it's not a *bomb*, right?" Boyd asked.

Reggie gave it a couple of sniffs. "No," he said. "It's not a bomb. It's definitely a phone."

Bjorn grunted a few times and nudged the phone.

"You're right, old bean," Reggie said, examining the device.

"What did he say?" Cindy asked.

"It's got some writing on the side," Reggie said. He picked it up to read it. "It says, *Property of Fang Industries.*"

"So it's from that Fang guy," Boyd said. "The one who took my parents?"

"It would seem so."

With an alarming beep, the phone rang. It's electronic tone was so loud and sharp, and everyone was so tense, that it caused them all to jump three feet off the ground. In the blink of an eye, Boyd and Cindy found themselves surrounded on all sides by Reggie, Bjorn, and Ho Yin, each one in a defensive position, ready to protect them. When they saw that there was no danger, everyone relaxed and they resumed their gaze at the ringing phone. It rang at least ten times before anyone said a word.

"Well?" Cindy asked. "Are we going to answer it?"

"It could be a trap," Reggie said.

"A trap?" Cindy asked. "It's just a phone. I think you guys are being too paranoid."

"These people are quite dangerous, Cindy," Ho Yin said. "We have to take precautions."

They stared at the phone a while longer. Finally, Cindy had enough. "Argh!" she said, grabbing the phone from the table. "It's driving me insane!"

"Cindy, wait!" Ho Yin said, but it was too late.

"Hello?" she asked. "Who is this?"

"Cindy?" asked a familiar voice on the other end of the line. "Cindy is that you?"

"Mom?" Cindy asked, shocked at the sound of her mother's voice.

"Cindy, oh, darling," her mother said. "Are you okay?"

"Mom, where are you?" Cindy asked.

Ho Yin quickly grabbed a cord and plugged the phone into a speaker so they could all hear the conversation. "Mom?" Boyd asked.

"Oh, Boyd," she said, her voice echoing through the room. "I've been so worried."

"They're in good hands, Mrs. McCloyd," Ho Yin said.

"Ho Yin!" she said. "Keep them safe."

"Mom, where are you?" Boyd asked. "Are you okay?"

"They're fine," said a voice in the room with their mother. "They're being treated quite well. I haven't hit them or anything."

"Fang," Reggie said under his breath. Boyd could hear a growl rumbling in the big yeti's chest.

"Is that the yeti?" Mr. Fang said. "Hello, you big, stupid monkey!"

"Well, it's better than being a rat like you," Reggie said.

"Hey, at least rats *taste* good," Mr. Fang laughed.

"Boyd, Cindy, everything's going to be okay," Mrs. McCloyd said into the phone. "Your father and I are fine. Don't let him..."

"Hey, Li," Mr. Fang said, interrupting Boyd's mother, "Get her out of here. She's served her purpose."

"Keep them safe, Ho Yin!" Mrs. McCloyd yelled over the sound of Li dragging her out of the room.

"Mom!" Cindy yelled, a hint of desperation in her voice.

"What do you want, Fang?" Ho Yin asked.

"You stupid man!" Cindy yelled. "Give me my Mom back!"

"Ugh!" Mr. Fang said. "That girl screeches like a boiling cat. Tell her to shut up."

"What do you want?" Ho Yin asked again.

"Look, we're at an impasse," Mr. Fang said. "I want Boyd McCloyd. It's pretty obvious I'm not going to get him with that big, ugly monkey around."

"Rat!" Reggie said.

"Monkey!" Mr. Fang said, taunting him.

"Get to the point, Fang," Ho Yin said.

"The point is," Fang continued, "that I've got something *you* want and *you've* got something *I* want. Hey Boyd...do you want your parents back? You've got to do something for me."

"What's that?" Boyd asked, trying not to sound sheepish.

"Mr. Ping has lot of valuable things in his place," Mr. Fang said. "And I want the most valuable thing in Ping Manor. The Perpetual Motion Machine."

"What?" Boyd asked.

"Fang, you're as crazy as you are ugly," Reggie said. "We're not going to give you the Perpetual Motion Machine. We don't have it."

"Oh, you're lying," Mr. Fang said. "I know you've got it. Mr. Pu told me you've got it."

"Wang Pu has no idea what he's talking about," Ho Yin said. "The Perpetual Motion Machine is a myth."

"What's a Perpetual Motion Machine?" Boyd whispered to Reggie.

"Tell you later," Reggie said.

"Look, you can lie to me all day long," Mr. Fang said. "It won't do you any good. If that stupid kid wants to see his stupid parents alive again, then he'd better get me that machine. He's got one week to do it. If it's not in my hands by the end of the week, his mommy and daddy are going to be on the menu at my restaurant. Got it?"

"But Fang..." Ho Yin said.

"This conversation is over," Fang yelled. "Goodbye!"

And with that, the line went dead, filling the room with silence. "That bloomin' idgit!" Reggie said, waving his arms around with anger. "The Perpetual Motion Machine! I've a right mind to go slap that Mr. Pu fellow around to teach him a lesson."

"What's the Perpetual Motion Machine?" Boyd asked.

Ho Yin looked at Reggie seriously. "We should get down to Tony Tang's. They might know what to do down there."

"Good idea, mate," Reggie said, and he quickly left the room.

"Do you think Mom and Dad are going to be okay?" Cindy asked. "Can't we just give them the machine and be done with it?

"Well, we could if we **had** all of it," Ho Yin said. "We have several of the pieces, but we don't know if we have them all, or even how to put it together."

"Well, let's just give them what we have," Boyd said.

"I'm afraid it's not that simple," Ho Yin said.

Reggie walked back into the room with a set of car keys and said, "Get your things, Boyd. We've got to go downtown to meet some people."

"What? Why?" Boyd asked. "What about my parents?"

Ho Yin looked at Boyd and Cindy and said, "Trust us. We're going to do everything we can to get your parents back, but we'll need your help."

Ho Yin ran out of the room and Reggie left to bring the car around to the front of the house, leaving Boyd and Cindy in the labs with Bjorn. "I'm scared, Boyd," Cindy said. "I don't want anything to happen to Mom and Dad."

"Me neither," Boyd said. "We'll figure this out."

Bjorn could see that Cindy was frightened as he walked over and gave her a gentle, reassuring nudge. Cindy walked out of the room in silence with the big bear, leaving Boyd all by himself in the lab, scared, confused, and full of anxiety. It was going to be a long night.

CHAPTER 15

DEEP, MEANINGFUL CONVERSATION WITH A YETI

Boyd was very nervous to be going out that night with Reggie and kept watching Stephens the Clock, waiting for six o'clock. Being the rambunctious fellow he was, Stephens made Boyd the subject of a cruel trick by forcing his hands to go backwards every other second. Eventually, Boyd figured out what was happening and threatened to put fingerprints on him if he didn't set the time back. Stephens quickly relented, as it is widely known that grandfather clocks cannot stand dust or fingerprints on their finely crafted exteriors.

"Ready to go, old bean?" Reggie asked, popping into his room wearing a plaid sweater vest and khaki knickers. He looked like he was prepared for a round of golf.

"What are you wearing?" Boyd asked.

"Stylish clothes," Reggie said. "What? Is there something wrong with them?"

"Uh, no," Boyd said.

"A chap likes to look sharp when he goes out on the town," he said, straightening his sweater.

They walked out into the humid air of the Hong Kong evening when they were stopped by Ho Yin on the gravel path just before they reached the garage. "Reggie, I don't think it's such a good idea for the two of you to go out tonight," he said. "The dangers are just…"

Reggie interrupted him by shooing him away with his large hand. "Tut-tut," he said. "If it was up to you, the boy would be living in a plastic vacuum tube and eating genetically enhanced French fries. He's not a museum piece. He's a kid and he's probably about to go mad-crazy sitting in this stuffy mansion all the day. Am I right, Boyd?"

"He's right," Boyd said. "Mad-crazy."

Ho Yin looked as if he was swallowing a bitter pill. "Fine," he said. "You're right. There and back, though."

"There and back," Reggie said, putting on a cap that matched his knickers.

"Boyd," Ho Yin said, turning towards him, "I want to tell you a few things before you go down there. The Temple Street Night Market[62] is unlike anything you've ever seen, not just from a weird aspect, but also from a foreign aspect as well. Some people say it's the center of gravity for the whole of these islands, and that's because strange and unusual things happen down there. It also means that peculiar things are drawn there as well. You'll need to be on the lookout."

"Cripes, Ho Yin, you're going to give him nightmares," Reggie said. He looked at Boyd and winked, saying, "It's a weird place, chap, so you'd best watch your back."

"All I'm saying," Ho Yin added, "is that you should be careful. It can be dangerous down there."

"Got it," Boyd said. "Safety is my middle name."

As they drove away, Boyd watched as Ho Yin stood in the driveway, observing them cruise off into the distance like a mother hen. "Sheesh!" Reggie muttered as he maneuvered their large, black car down the twisting roads into the city. "He's really being protective of you, old chum. You'd think there was danger lurking around every corner the way he talks."

"Well, he's quite convincing," Boyd said.

"Eh, he's mostly full of hot air," Reggie added. "Sure, there's a couple of really dangerous cats lurking down there, and that Mr. Fang fellow is one of them, but the way Ho Yin acts, you'd think they have nothing better to do than watch for you all day. That isn't the case. As long as we're not too daft, we'll be fine."

Ho Yin watched Reggie and Boyd drive off, out the front gate of the mansion, and when they were out of sight, he pulled a phone from his pocket and dialed a number. "It's me," he said. "They're headed there now. Stay close." He tucked the phone in his pocket and went back inside.

The streets from the Peak down towards the waters of Hong Kong harbor were magnificent, not only for the views they afforded as they drove into the city, but also for their lush greenery and hidden alcoves. All along the road, there were trees, shrubs, and bushes that looked like they'd creep out onto the road and take their space back from the concrete that had been laid over them if someone wasn't careful. Breaking up the greenery were magnificent houses for the extremely wealthy, some out in the open for all to see, while others were hidden behind security gates that only seemed to deepen the mystery of what lay behind them.

Punctuating the view was the Hong Kong skyline, emerging in all its magnificent glory as evening fell. Buildings of all different shapes and sizes lay below them as they descended into the valleys of the city, each so crammed together that it looked as if there weren't even roads between them. Some were huge, like Central Plaza, while others were just striking in their shape and design, like the Bank of China building, which was all angles and corners, or the Lippo

Building, a huge glass structure that, if one were to look at it in just the right way, they would see a pair of koala bears built into the side.

In between all of these massive buildings were hundreds of smaller ones. Some were boxy and bland, while others were as grand as the island that they sat upon with stately grace. Most of the buildings had office lights, creating a sea of bluish, white stars across the landscape. Yet those tiny universes were regularly interrupted by massive, well-lit structures that looked like they were straight out of a science fiction film.

As Boyd and Reggie rounded the corner, they could see the biggest building on the island, a massive beast, full of strange angles, tons of steel, and more glass than all the buildings it surrounded. It was lit up with a glare that was blinding as it casted jets of light and shadows over all the buildings around it, yet it's structure had none of the flair of its companions. It was just a giant, steel and glass monstrosity.

"See that blight on the horizon?" Reggie said, pointing at the building as he drove down the road. "That's Fang Tower[63]. It's the newest building in Hong Kong and the biggest in the world. Guess who built it."

"Mr. Fang?" Boyd asked, staring at it.

"Bingo," Reggie said. "Everyone in Hong Kong hates it because of its Feng Shui. Have you ever heard of Feng Shui?"

"No," Boyd said. "Is that some kind of food?"

"No," Reggie said, rolling his eyes. "It's the Chinese art of spatial arrangement. Some people believe that if you arrange things a certain way, either inside your house or outside your house, then it will bring you good fortune or bad fortune, depending on the placement of your possessions. For instance, there are certain sections of your house for career and family and wealth, and if your furniture is arranged in the right way in those sections, then you may get lucky."

"So if I put my comic books neatly in the money section of my room, then I'll make money off of them?" Boyd asked.

"Close, but not quite," he said. "It's a little more complicated than that. If you put all of your comics in your wealth section, it might mean that you spend all of your money on comic books. However, it could also mean that, perhaps in the future, you might make some money from comics. It just depends."

"Are you sure this isn't just a ruse to get me to clean my room?" Boyd asked.

"If it is, then the Chinese have been practicing it for thousands of years, so it must be pretty elaborate," Reggie chuckled. "Anyway, Fang Tower has really bad Feng Shui."

When they arrived downtown, there were neon signs in all directions, lighting up the streets like it was daytime. It was everything that Boyd had ever wanted to experience: being in a foreign city under these extraordinary circumstances; seeing so many people with unique faces and clothing; absorbing all the sights, sounds, and smells of a new place, with a hint of adventure lurking behind it all. This was so much more than Frankfurter, a place whose main neon sign was the bright orange "M" of the local McDougal's[64] restaurant. In Hong Kong, there were many tall buildings, all of them unique and brimming with life, while in Frankfurter, the tallest building wasn't a building at all, but a large, robin's egg blue, water tower that said, *Frankfurter, Home of the World's Largest Hay Bale*[65].

Hong Kong filled him with joy, even if it was a joy that produced a temporary amnesia, for in those moments Boyd forgot about the precarious situation that was his life. Riding through the streets of Hong Kong, it was easy to forget that everything had changed so dramatically and his parent had been kidnapped.

"Do you have parents, Reggie?" he asked as they cruised down the highway, into the tunnel that ran beneath the harbor.

"Yes," Reggie said. "But I don't really speak to them anymore." Reggie stared at the road ahead, lost in thought for a few seconds. "They didn't really take to my coming into the human world like I did. They thought humans were foolish and dangerous. Of course, they were right, but that doesn't matter. They wanted me to stay and live in the mountains forever, just like they did. But I couldn't do it. I had to see the world."

As they cruised through the tunnel under Hong Kong harbor, Reggie's words sank into Boyd's head. Though they were spoken by an eight-foot tall yeti, they still had the same effect. He'd been so worried about how he felt as his parents fought, he was unable to think about how they had to have felt. Was it lonely for his father to sleep on the couch night after night? His parents had spent so many years together, so was fighting between the two of them like being betrayed by your best friend? When Boyd had troubles, he sometimes went to his mother or father to talk about it and occasionally have a good cry. Who did his mother go to to console herself? And what about his father?

He didn't know the answer to these questions, but it did make him determined to give his parents a second chance. If he ever saw them again, he was going to be a better son. The only problem was finding them.

CHAPTER 16

GETTING A GOOD CASE OF THE CREEPS WHILE SURROUNDED BY JUNK

Reggie parked the black car on a busy street in a section of Hong Kong called Kowloon, just off of an area known as the Golden Mile[66]. It was nighttime, but one would never know it by the amount of lights shining overhead from the neon signs of various shops and stores. The main street was Nathan Road, but shops and restaurants were packed into every available corner, and each one of them was busy with both locals and foreigners, all jabbering away on their phones or yelling to be heard over the pounding dance music of the clothing stores.

More than a few people stopped in their tracks when Reggie got out of the car. It wasn't a common occurrence for an eight-foot tall yeti in a plaid sweater vest, knickers, and golf shoes to get out of a car on the street in this city, no matter how many strange and unusual things they'd seen over the years. Cigarettes dropped from mouths, people on the other end of phones were left chattering to mute zombies, and Boyd saw at least one car accident (although he wasn't sure that the sight of Reggie caused it). Everyone stopped what they were doing to stare at Reggie.

However, a benefit to walking down an incredibly crowded sidewalk with a yeti was that one didn't have to fight the crowds. The crowds just parted without saying a word, afraid to get too close to this hulking creature, for fear he might lash out at them. "Yeti prejudice," Reggie muttered. "It's everywhere."

"Yeti prejudice?" Boyd asked, trying to keep up with Reggie's long steps.

"Look at all of these blokes," he said, motioning around to the staring crowd. "All of 'em looking at me like I'm a bloomin' freak show."

"Well, maybe they've never seen a yeti before," Boyd said.

"That doesn't matter," he said. "If you see some bloke looking like he's just been in a car accident, with his nose on the wrong side of his face and missing an ear or something, you don't stare at him, do you? No, because it's *rude!* You might hurt his feelings. But along comes a yeti and everybody forgets the simple rules of etiquette and starts starin' away. It's a double-standard, I'll tell you."

Reggie was leading Boyd back away from the crowds of Nathan Road to less trendy, though no less busy, streets and all around him were the sights and smells of life in the city. There were Indian and Pakistani tailors standing in front of their shops, offering custom-made suits in twenty-four hours. There were steamy restaurants with chicken parts hanging in the windows, trying to lure in customers. There were jewelry shops with heavy, steel doors and peep holes for the owners to see who was on the outside. And there was, of course, the hundreds of electronic stores, all selling the latest computer, television, or audio devices for prices so low that a person would have to be crazy to buy from anyone else (unless they were going to the guy next door).

"Where are we going, Reggie?" Boyd asked.

"We're going to get some advice from a couple of friends," Reggie said. "They own a little tea shop down near the night market. A man named Tony Tang runs the place."

"Is this the Temple Street Night Market that Ho Yin was talking about?"

"It is," Reggie said. "It's like a bazaar. You can buy all sorts of things here, like clothes and movies and little, plastic, junky toys that have absolutely no value. They sell everything down here, as long as it's cheap."

"Why is it so dangerous?" Boyd asked.

"It's not dangerous," Reggie laughed. "Maybe a pickpocket or two, and a stall seller who might want to rip you off, but it's not dangerous. Ho Yin was just being paranoid. However, once we get near the fortune tellers, it's a different story."

"Fortune tellers?"

"There's a whole section of the market with fortune tellers. Magic people. Weird folk. They always give me the creeps. Anyway, they do things like palm reading, face reading, and they have little birds who will tell your fortune."

"Birds?" Boyd asked.

"Yeah. They come out of their cage and pick a card from a deck. It tells your fortune. It's a scam, if you ask me. Anyway, since there's a lot of magic down here, some weird things can happen, so stay close."

"This is so cool," Boyd said, his eyes wide open at the vast array of kiosks and tents that sold all the junk, clothing, and bootlegged merchandise one could imagine. The flash and shine of useless items immediately clouded Boyd's judgment and he could barely keep from leaving Reggie's side to examine the bizarre knickknacks that were piled high on tables.

As they made their way further down into the market, under the startled gaze of visitors and shopkeepers, Boyd couldn't help but be amazed at what he saw, and it wasn't just the amount of things being sold that filled him with fascination. Throughout the Night Market was a proliferation of Cantonese opera singers performing in various places. The Cantonese opera singers were unlike anything Boyd had seen before, as they didn't perform in any way similar to the western opera that he'd seen in North America. It was very stylized and elaborate, and their voices sounded quite strange, not just from the fact that they were speaking another language, but also because the style in which they sang was distinctly different. "I've never seen anything like this before, Reggie," Boyd said as they drew nearer to the fortune tellers.

"Well, then," Reggie said, "this will be an interesting little experience for a chap such as yourself."

"What's this Tony Tang fellow like?" Boyd asked. "He's the guy who runs the shop, right?"

"Yes, but I never really deal with Mr. Tang. Can't say I know him all that well," Reggie said. "Can't say I like coming down *here* too much, either. I don't particularly like to be around these fortune tellers."

"Why is that?" Boyd asked.

"Well," Reggie said, "first, there's an air of superstition that hovers around those cats that gives me a big, fat case of the creeps. They've been doing this stuff for so long that there's a weird energy here. A bad energy. And this place has got it in spades."

"What's the other reason you don't like coming down here?" Boyd asked, just as they came around the corner to see the fortune tellers.

One of the fortune tellers looked up to see Reggie coming his way and yelled, "YETI!" before throwing all his stuff in a bag and running off down the street. He was soon followed by everyone else.

"The other reason is because I scare the pants off them," Reggie said. "Call me sensitive, but the sight of people running away in fear at the sight of me just kind of gets me down, you know?"

The fortune tellers' unexplained fear of Reggie set off a panic, and everyone began rushing to clear the area and get as far away from the yeti as possible. Vendors, fortune tellers, and opera singers alike were closing up shop to get away, and soon, everyone was scrambling all over each other, causing a chaotic melee.

"Blast!" Reggie said. "This happens to me every time I come down here."

Boyd was so enamored with the chaos and confusion that he wasn't paying attention to where Reggie was, and just as he turned back towards him, a surge of panicked people pushed him out of the way and down a back alley. "Reggie!" he yelled, but there was no way that Reggie would have been able to hear him, what with the screams and shouts from the crowd. Try as he might to resist, the crowd kept pushing him farther and farther away, and he felt as if he was trying to swim upstream in a raging river.

Finally, he managed to work his way to the side of the street, where he could stop moving and take in the whole scene. Utter and complete chaos had broken out before him as crowds of people were now running every which way through the cramped stalls of the market, most of them unsure as to even why they were running. One group ran headlong into a kiosk of tiny rubber doll heads, sending them flying everywhere, while another group ran one direction until they reached a dead end, whereupon they would turn around as a group and run until they reached another dead end. Boyd noticed that each group of panicked passersby had at least three to four people who were still gabbing away on their phones amidst all the confusion.

He watched with fascination as the market began to clear of people, and a subtle wave of panic swept over him at the thought that he'd lost Reggie. He had no clue as to how to get around Hong Kong, and what made matters worse was the fact that he felt like the whole world was out to get him; as if every person he saw on the street worked for Mr. Fang.

Then he heard Reggie's voice booming through the chaos. "Boyd?" he yelled. "Boyd?"

It should have been easy to spot a giant, white yeti in the middle of a rapidly clearing market, but try as he might, Boyd couldn't find him. "Boyd?" he heard. "Boyd?" It was strange. One minute, Reggie's voice came from one direction, while the next minute, it came from the exact opposite direction.

"Reggie?" Boyd asked. "Reggie, where are you?"

"Boyd?" he heard, but still he couldn't see him.

Boyd began to wander through the now-empty stalls, trying to see around the clutter and chaos, but he couldn't find Reggie. He walked by a darkened alley and heard, "Boyd?" He looked just off the main street to see that the sound came from the only poorly lit alley in Hong Kong. There was a single yellow streetlight at the far end, but most of the alley was obscured by the steam rising from the pipes of a nearby restaurant. "Boyd?" he heard.

"Reggie, is that you?" he asked. It sure didn't seem like Reggie. Why would he have gone down that alley?

"Boyd?"

Boyd took a few steps towards the alley and a chill fell over him, as if some unseen force had just walked in front of him. He edged his way into the alley, closer and closer to the source of the sound, trying to peer through the haze to see what lay at the dark end of the street. As he passed through the thick steam that came from the pipes, he found the alley to be empty, save for a lone man dressed in traditional Chinese imperial silk robes, with a tall, square hat that matched its fabric. He sat under the sole street light with a small table in front of him that had cards laid out upon it. Behind him were hundreds of tiny, bamboo cages that sang out with a cricket symphony. The man had dark eyes and a cagey smile as he turned to Boyd, acknowledging his presence. "Hello, young man," he said.

"Uh, have you, perhaps, seen a large, white yeti around here?" Boyd asked.

"Indeed, I have not," the man said. "You look like a curious fellow. Would you like your fortune told?"

"Uh, no thanks," Boyd said. "I'm looking for a yeti."

"I'm sure the yeti will be along any minute now," the man said. "If you wander around looking for him, you could be wandering all night long. If you stay here, he'll probably find you before you know it."

One of Boyd's growing attributes was his ability to smell trouble, and he knew that this fortune teller and his thousands of crickets were bad news. He had always hated crickets from his days when the farming season would come to Ontario. Just as the corn was at its height, the crickets would descend upon the area, and soon infest everything. He didn't care until he'd left his window open one night and was soon joined by four of the little beasts, crawling all over him as he slept. It was a rude awakening and he struggled and jerked his way out of bed that night to avoid their creepy, crawly, sticky legs. He knew then that he would forever hate crickets.

"The look on your face tells me you're not a fan of crickets," the fortune teller said.

"Not really," Boyd said.

"Ah, but crickets make wonderful pets," he said. "And sometimes, they bring good luck. Let me show you mine." He reached back and pulled out a rather large, bamboo cage, opening the door to let out what looked to be the world's biggest cricket. It was the size of a guinea pig and crawled out of the cage, onto his hand. "This is Ming," he said. "I've had him for over thirty years."

Boyd could not hide his disgust at the hideous creature that sat on the fortuneteller's hand. Crickets were tolerable when they were small, as all the different pieces and mechanisms that made them work were too tiny to see. But Ming was huge and Boyd had a full view of his menacing black eyes, his long, waving antennas, and his claw-like front legs that he used to wipe his face, over and over.

"I, uh, didn't know crickets could live thirty years," Boyd said, glancing over his shoulder to see if Reggie was making his way down the alley yet.

"This is no ordinary cricket," the fortuneteller said, a creepy smile passing over his face. "He eats mice. His love of mouse flesh has kept him alive for a very long time. Sometimes, he'll eat the occasional bird or frog, but most of the time, he prefers mice."

The cricket turned its odd little head in a clockwise motion towards Boyd and hissed like a tiny cat. A shiver ran down Boyd's spine.

"He likes you," the fortune teller said, still smiling in a malicious manner. "Now, would you like for Ming to tell your fortune?"

"No, thanks," Boyd said, preparing to walk away.

"You wouldn't want to know your future?" the fortuneteller asked. "Whether your hopes and dreams will come true? What riches await you? What happens to your parents?"

Another chill ran down Boyd's spine as he looked at the fortune teller with wide eyes. "How do you know about my parents?" he asked.

The fortune teller began to shuffle the deck of cards in front of him, smiling to himself with Ming perched on his shoulder. "I would not be able to make my living as a fortune teller if I did not have some sort of skill," he said. "Now, let's let Ming pick out a card for you, shall we, Boyd?"

Boyd didn't move as he said, "How do you know my name?"

"You don't need to know anything about *me*," the fortuneteller said. "You only need to know things about *yourself*. Ming?"

On cue, the cricket crawled off the fortune teller's shoulder and down to the table. It circulated its large head over to look at Boyd, then hissed, before turning back to the cards stacked neatly in front of it. It then began to use its large, hind legs to spread the cards out on the table like a fan.

The cricket crawled back and forth across the table, as if it was looking for the very best card to choose, before finally settling on one. With great dexterity, it picked up the card with its front legs and brought it over to the fortuneteller. "Very good, Ming," he said. "Look what I have for you!"

The fortune teller reached into a box at his feet and pulled out a squirming mouse by its tail, gently lowering it into Ming's cage. The cricket hissed its approval and crawled back into the cage. The fortune teller shut the door behind it and put it back on the shelf behind him. Boyd could hear the squeals coming from the mouse, and an occasional hiss from the cricket, but was glad he couldn't see the gruesome affair.

"Now, let's have a look at your card," said the fortune teller. He turned the card over and he let slip a quick grin, but then grew serious again. "Oh, my," he said. "This is certainly grim news."

"What is it?" Boyd asked.

He looked surprised at Boyd. "Well, I thought you didn't **want** your fortune told," he said. "Now you want the answers to all of your questions?" Boyd had no response. The fortune teller held up the card to Boyd's face. It contained a single, Chinese character on it, **suh**. "Here is the answer to your question."

"What is it?" Boyd asked.

The fortune teller smiled. He handed the card to Boyd, telling him, "This is the number four. The number four in Chinese is pronounced 'suh.' This is the same character we have for the word death."

"Death?" Boyd asked, swallowing hard.

The fortune teller picked up another card. "Oh, this is very interesting," he said.

"What?" Boyd asked.

"I see the long, sharp nose of an evil creature," he said. "It's looking for you and will do everything within its power to make sure that you don't live to see tomorrow." Boyd looked confused and the hairs on his forearms began to stand on end. The fortune teller continued to examine the card and said, "I see snarling fangs in your future, drool dangling to the ground, and the lost souls of the dead counting you as one of their own."

Boyd gulped. "What does that mean?" he asked.

The fortune teller shrugged him off. "Be observant of your sister," he said. "She's more than what she seems."

"What are you talking about?" Boyd asked. "This doesn't make any sense."

"Someday, it will make sense," he said with a smile. "But even so, there is one last piece of advice that I can give you."

"What's that?" Boyd asked.

"Pay me money," he said.

"What?"

"I read your fortune, now pay me money," the fortune teller said.

"But I don't have any money," he said.

"Boyd?"

Boyd turned back down the alley as he heard Reggie yelling for him.

"Boyd, where are you?"

He turned to the fortune teller, who leaned back comfortably against his cages as his cricket emerged from its tiny cell to crawl on his shoulder, mouse fur covering its body. "I'll tell you what," the fortune teller said, "you can have this one for free, but next time, I'm charging you. Run along now. Your yeti is waiting."

Boyd looked at the him as if he wasn't sure he should turn his back on him and he backed out of the alley, through the steam, and onto the main street. "Oh, and Boyd," the fortune teller added, "if I might give you one last piece of advice: Calamitous dragons know more than they'll tell you."

Boyd was perplexed as he left, unsure of what to think about what the fortune teller had said. Sharp noses? Drool? Dragons? It didn't make any sense. Boyd looked down the street to see Reggie searching high and low for him, running back and forth, peeking in each of the alleys. Finally, Reggie turned to see him, breathing a great sigh of relief.

"There you are," he said. "I've been looking all over hill and dale for you, lad. I was getting quite chaffed."

"I got lost," Boyd said, looking into the steam behind him for the fortune teller. "There was a…"

"Come on, mate," Reggie said, pulling him along. "We've got to get to Tony Tang's before word gets out that a yeti was in the market."

As they walked along the line of abandoned benches and tables that the fortune tellers and shop owners had set up on the sidewalk, Boyd could not hold back his questions. "Reggie," he said, "why did the fortune tellers freak out when they saw you?"

"Well," Reggie said, in an embarrassed manner, "They know what a yeti is."

"So?" Boyd asked.

"Let's just say that yetis don't exactly have the best reputations," he said. "Sure, I'm all nice and cuddly, but I have more than one cousin, and even a sister, who would just as soon eat you as look at you. Why do you think that so few people have ever seen a yeti?"

"I don't know," Boyd said. "Why?"

Reggie looked at him with a devilish grin, smiling in a manner that showed off every one of his yellow fangs. "Because those that have seen a yeti don't normally live to tell about it," he said.

"Gotcha," Boyd said as he wondered whether Reggie was really as trustworthy as he claimed to be.

"But seriously," Reggie said, as if he could read Boyd's mind by looking at his face, "Those days are long gone. An ancient memory. Heck, I can't even remember what humans taste like anymore. Ah, here we are!"

As Boyd tried to absorb what Reggie had just said to him, they found themselves standing at the far end of an alley, where an old shop stood in the side of a building. Its facade was made of wood, decorated in a manner that made it look like it was from ancient China, with ornate carvings surrounding the smoked glass of the windows and two red lanterns with long tassels hanging from the awning on each side. The wood of the building looked old and the worn red paint was peeling away in large flecks.

At first, when Boyd looked at the window, all he saw was Chinese writing, but he glanced away and when he looked back, the writing was in English. He was a bit surprised to see that it read, *Tony Tang's Teas*[67] in bold, black letters. Now, there was no Chinese writing anywhere in sight.

"Did you see that?" Boyd said.

"See what?" Reggie asked.

Boyd thought his eyes were playing tricks on him, so he muttered, "Never mind," as they entered the shop.

Inside, Reggie could barely move in any direction due to the shop's small size and his incredible bulk. He just kind of hovered by the door with his head stooped towards the ground. The shop's walls were lined with shelves packed full of jars, and each jar contained some sort of interesting liquid or powder, labeled with a little, white sticker that had a series of Chinese characters on them. Some of the jars were a bit grotesque, and contained dead animals, like snakes and rats and the heads of chickens or the paws of unknown creatures. It all gave Boyd the willies.

A young boy sat at the counter and as they came in, he looked at Reggie and yelled, "Dad! There's a big yeti here for you." He never moved from his place at the counter and never took his eyes off Reggie, as though he didn't trust such a creature.

An older fellow in shirtsleeves and gray slacks emerged from the back of the shop and spotted Reggie. "I thought I put the word out that yetis aren't welcome in my shop anymore," he said, a look of contempt on his face. "I think the two of you should leave."

"You know," Reggie said, sounding miffed, "I don't feel that this kind of discrimination against yetis is an appropriate way to greet a customer."

"You tell that to my cousin!" the man said. "Thanks to you yetis, he's got no arms and legs! Why? Cause you yetis *ate* his arms and legs! Now, get out of my shop!"

"I know about your cousin, Tony," Reggie said. "He was hunting yeti to put in his youth powder, wasn't he?"

"I don't know anything about that," the man said, looking away.

"Oh, I think you do," said Reggie. "You know, good and well, that yeti powder[68] is very popular down here, and your cousin was hunting yeti. In fact," he said, as he swiped a jar full of blue powder off the shelf, "*This* is yeti powder, if I'm not mistaken."

The man looked a bit nervous. "No, no," he said. "That's duck wart[69]. Good for the liver!"

"Yeah, right," Reggie said, putting the jar back on the shelf. "Anyway, we're here on business. We need to see Bird and Goldfish. I've got Boyd McCloyd here."

The man looked at Boyd and said, "You mean this is Mr. Ping's protégé?"

"Yes," Reggie said. "Boyd, I'd like you to meet Tony Tang. Tony Tang, this is Boyd McCloyd."

Tony shook Boyd's hand in a reverent fashion. "It's so nice to meet you," he said. "Finally, we get to see you in person."

"Thanks," Boyd said, unable to think of a response.

"Come, come," Tony said. "Let me make you some tea." He turned to Reggie as he led Boyd to the back, giving him the evil eye. "Keep an eye on that one," he said to his son. "Yetis can't be trusted."

"Yap, yap," Reggie said, dismissing him. "You're all talk."

Tony led Boyd to a small table in the cramped quarters at the back of the shop and offered him a chair. Boxes and jars were stacked in every corner as he sat under the naked bulb of the overhead light. Tony began to pour some tea into a nice, blue and white mug as he sat down across from him. "We've been waiting on you for a long time," he said.

"Me?" Boyd asked.

"Oh, yes," he said. "Of course, I didn't expect you to show up with the yeti, but we're not all perfect, are we?"

"Reggie's not so bad," Boyd said. "I don't think you should talk about him like that."

"Right, you are," Tony said. He looked around nervously for a couple of seconds, trying to get his bearings. "Well, if you'll just wait here, I'll go get them."

"Huh?" Boyd asked.

"I have to get them," Tony said, getting up to leave.

"Get who?" Boyd asked. "I though we were here to see *you.*"

"Me?" Tony laughed. "Oh, that's a good one. I'm not important. You're here to see Bird and Goldfish[70]."

"Bird and who?"

"They can explain a lot better than me," he said, leaving. "You wait here."

As Tony left, Boyd had a chance to examine the back room of the shop, which failed to put him at ease. The walls in the back were filled with sinister-looking jars that somehow appeared worse than the ones out front. There was also a work table that had strange, multicolored powders piled on top of it, odd bottles of motley-looking potions, one or two dead animal skulls, and even the paw of some sort of bear or tiger.

After a couple of minutes, Tony reappeared in the room, carrying a bamboo bird cage, with a purple towel draped over it. "Here you go," he said, smiling. He pulled away the cloth to reveal a yellow canary in the birdcage and he pulled away another cloth on the wall to reveal a gargantuan fish tank with a large, orange goldfish swimming around inside. "I'll give you guys some privacy while you chat," he said and he exited the room to the front of the shop, closing the door behind him.

Boyd didn't know what to do as he sat across from the bird and the goldfish, and he began to feel as if he was being set up by one of those practical joke television shows. His eyes began to wander around the room, and he was trying his best to pretend he wasn't uncomfortable. He kept glancing over at both the bird and the goldfish, wondering what in the world was going on here. It was then that he noticed something really strange.

Both the bird and the goldfish were staring at him.

CHAPTER 17

THE BIGGEST BRAIN A FIFTH GRADER COULD EVER HAVE

Ping Manor could be a forbidding place at night, what with its myriad of strange and unusual artifacts. If someone were interested in things of this nature, then the mansion might have been a fascinating place, but that wasn't the case for its current occupant. Its current occupant wanted to be anywhere but where she was at the moment.

Cindy had been wandering around the mansion for the last hour with two things on her mind: one was to find a television, and the other was to wait on Ho Yin, who had taken off earlier to take care of some unknown business. The house was empty except for Cindy and Bjorn the Polar Bear. Bjorn had been following her on her entire trip through the mansion, quietly shuffling along behind, but maintaining a distance so that Cindy might not think she was being followed (although it was hard not to hear him breathing heavily or hear his grunts as he walked up the stairs).

"I know you're following me," she said as she turned towards him from one end of the hallway. "Why don't you just come out?"

It took a couple of seconds for Bjorn to pop his silvery head around the corner. He had a tentative look on his face that gave the impression that he was a bit shy.

"Come down here and join me, Bjorn," she said, smiling. "It's okay."

With a hint of hesitation, Bjorn began to walk down the hall towards Cindy, ducking his head down in deference to her when he arrived. He grunted a couple of times and sniffed at the air with his long snout.

"Were you lonely?" she asked.

Bjorn gave a sniff of acknowledgment.

"I'm lonely, too," she said, scratching his neck. If she ever before wanted to get in this big, cuddly bear's good graces, this was the way to do it. In fact, he liked the scratching so much that he kept moving closer and closer to her to get more, until he had her pinned against the wall. "Okay, okay," she giggled. "Let's go explore some more, shall we?"

Bjorn nodded and slowly walked beside Cindy in the hall as they made their way through the house.

"Are you from the North Pole?" she asked,

Bjorn grunted.

"This place sure is different from where you're from, I'll bet."

Bjorn grunted again.

"I guess you make due, don't you? This place is different from Ontario, too. It's fun and interesting and everything, but sometimes you miss home, don't you?"

Bjorn rubbed his head up against Cindy to reassure her.

"It's weird how you can miss home. Sometimes the place you're from can be pretty comfortable, I guess. I always wanted to travel around the world, but I guess I wanted to do it on my terms, not just as the little sister who always has to be dragged around by her brother. I wanted to do it all on my own."

"There will be plenty of time for that," Ho Yin said. He'd startled Cindy and Bjorn by appearing in one of the doorways as he waited on the two of them. "You'll get your time, Cindy."

"That's what they always say, Ho Yin," she said.

"I'll tell you what," he said. "It might take less time than you ever imagined. Come with me."

Ho Yin led Bjorn and Cindy down the hall to a secret door that was hidden in the wooden paneling. He lifted a hidden latch, pulled out a skeleton key, and opened the door, leading the two of them through a secret entrance into the science lab.

"I have such fond memories of this lab," Ho Yin said. "This is where Mr. Ping used to do all of his experiments."

"Experiments?" asked Cindy, as she continued to scratch Bjorn's neck. "I thought Mr. Ping was a writer."

"Perhaps science and writing go hand in hand," Ho Yin said.

"Perhaps," Cindy said, looking at him out of the corner of her eye. "Perhaps not."

"You're skeptical," Ho Yin said. "That's an excellent trait to have."

"Perhaps," Cindy said, looking at him out of the corner of her eye. "Perhaps not."

"Come here," he said, motioning her over to a computer screen. "I want you to look at this and tell me what you see."

Cindy made her way over to where he was standing and began to look at the screen. There, before her eyes, were thousands upon thousands of white numbers and letters, all pouring down a black screen like rain, some bright, some dull, as if they were on different layers. Occasionally, sets of numbers would glow, as if they were important, while others would simply drift down, cascading across the screen in an even flow.

Ho Yin was observing Cindy's face to gage her reaction. "Notice anything?" he asked. For a few seconds, she was in awe of the screen, looking at it as if it was the most beautiful thing she'd ever seen. Her eyes lit up and it seemed as though she was absorbing every number that appeared before her, but just as she realized she was enraptured with what was happening on the screen, she snapped herself out of it and focused back on Ho Yin.

"What did you say?" she asked.

"I asked if you noticed anything," he said.

"It's just a bunch of numbers," she said, sounding bored.

"That's all you see?" Ho Yin asked, smirking at her. "Just a bunch of numbers?"

Cindy paused for the briefest of seconds. "Yeah," she said. "Just a bunch of stupid numbers and letters."

Ho Yin acted convinced. "Hmm," he said. "I guess you're right. That's all it is. Just a bunch of numbers." He began to walk away from Cindy and Bjorn, towards the door. "I guess we were wrong."

"What do you mean?" Cindy asked, walking after him. "Wrong about what?"

"About *you*," he said. "Sometimes these things happen."

"Well, what did you think I was going to do?" she asked.

"It's not important," he said. "Let's go have a snack and watch some TV, shall we?"

"Wait," she said. "I want to know what you thought I could do."

Ho Yin turned back to her, looking serious. "You don't have to pretend, Cindy. I *know* what you can do."

"What do you mean?" she asked.

"You tell me what you can see on that computer screen," Ho Yin said, narrowing his eyes, "And I'll tell you what I think you can do."

"All I see are numbers and letters," she said.

"Wrong answer," Ho Yin said, walking out the door. "Let's go have dinner."

"Okay, okay," Cindy said, stopping him. She looked at the ground as if she had done something wrong. "It's a message."

"What kind of message?" Ho Yin asked.

"A message for me," she said.

"And what does it say?" he asked.

"It says..." she paused for a second, "it says, *Cindy is a lot smarter than anyone knows.*"

Ho Yin smiled. "You mean to tell me that all of those letters and numbers on that computer screen give a *message?*" he asked. "That's impossible."

"It's not impossible," she said, looking at him seriously. "It's ridiculously easy. You used such a simple form of encryption that you'd have to be an idiot not to figure it out."

"Well, most of us idiots can't figure it out," Ho Yin said. "Especially in less than three seconds." Cindy started staring at the floor again. "You don't have to pretend anymore, Cindy," he said. "I know how smart you are. And I know you've been trying to hide it for a long, long time."

"No, I haven't," she said.

"Yes, you have," he said. "You don't have to do that anymore. You don't have to pretend to be Little-Miss-Popular anymore. You don't have to try to fit in anymore. You don't have to play with Barbies or hide the computer code that you write when you say you're chatting on the internet. Around here, it's okay to be smart."

Cindy had started to cry, sniffling as she said, "But no one understands an eleven-year old who can do quantum physics."

"I do," Ho Yin said. "It's not your fault you're smart, Cindy. It *is* your fault, though, if you think it's something you should hide. I don't want you to hide it anymore."

At that moment, Cindy looked up into Ho Yin's eyes and knew that she could trust him with her secret; the secret that she was probably the smartest fifth-grader in the world, who had been keeping her gifts hidden for years. Now someone knew. She felt a massive weight lift off of her shoulders because for the longest time she felt like she couldn't trust anyone with the truth, not her friends, not Boyd, not even her mother and father. Now, Ho Yin made it seem okay that she was a genius and she felt free for the first time in her life.

"Now," Ho Yin said. "We've got some work to do."

"Work?" Cindy asked. "What kind of work?"

"Well, nothing all that hard, really," Ho Yin said. "Just something none of us have been able to figure out for the last thirty years. It should be no problem for you."

Cindy couldn't help but smile at the thought of what she was about to do.

CHAPTER 18

THE STRANGE BIRD

AND THE SMART GOLDFISH

Back at Tony Tang's Teashop the goldfish was turned in a position in the water where it could get a good look at Boyd, twisting back and forth, just as the bird was *twitching* back and forth. They both did the exact, same thing, examining Boyd with one eye, then the other, then back again. To be stared at by a bird and a goldfish was unnerving, and the wimpier side of Boyd's personality made him want to get out of there as quickly as possible.

Then, another strange thing happened. The bird, who had been watching him, hopped down from its perch, grabbing onto the walls of its cage beside the door. It carefully lowered its head down, and with its beak, lifted a latch that opened the door. Slowly, the door swung open. It flew out of the cage and landed on the table beside Boyd's tea where, for a few seconds, it began to examine Boyd again. Then, it hopped up on top of the goldfish's tank and perched itself on the side. The goldfish casually swam to the top and extended its head over the side of the bowl completely out of the water, so that it could look at Boyd as well.

"He looks a bit puny to be a hero, doesn't he?" the goldfish said.

"I'd say he's excellent material," the bird said.

"Oh, you're *too* generous," the goldfish said.

Boyd was speechless, staring at the talking bird and goldfish as if he'd just gone insane. "Not a talkative one, is he?" said the goldfish.

"As it is with all great ones, Goldfish," the bird said. "They need not say much. The language of their bodies speaks volumes."

Boyd absentmindedly straightened his posture, before saying, "What's going on here?"

"Oh, I spoke too soon," the goldfish said. "I thought they'd send us some nice Cantonese boy, or a Brit if worse came to worse, but this is a Yank!"

"I resent that," Boyd said. "I'm Canadian, not American."

"Same difference," the goldfish said.

"No, no, Goldfish," said the bird. "The Canadians still have the Queen as their benefactor. It's a far cry from those Yanks."

"Ah, right you are. Right you are," said the Goldfish.

"I was supposed to meet Tony," Boyd said. "But then Tony told me I was supposed to meet the two of you."

"And right, he was," said the bird. "Please forgive us. I know that this must be somewhat disconcerting for you. We sometimes forget how utterly bizarre this must be for people who are only beginning to open their eyes."

"Yes, yes," said the goldfish, lazily flapping its tail in the water. "Your world must seem so flat and stale at the moment."

"My world?" Boyd asked.

"When he says, your world," added the bird. "He's mainly thinking of the life that you lived before experiencing all of these strange things that you're seeing right now. For instance, did you expect to meet a talking bird and goldfish when you came in here? Absolutely not. But you did, so now your world has been expanded a bit more. Does that make sense?"

"Absolutely, it makes sense," said the goldfish. "Why wouldn't it?"

"I'm not talking to you," the bird said, looking at the goldfish as if he was stupid. "I'm talking to him."

"Oh, right you are. Right you are."

"First," the bird continued, "let me just introduce myself to you. I am Bird. And he is Goldfish."

"And we are Bird and Goldfish," said Goldfish. "But please, abandon all formalities and call me Goldfish."

"And me, Bird."

"Bird and Goldfish," Boyd repeated. "I'm Boyd McCloyd."

"Oh, we most certainly have heard of *you,*" Bird said. "Mr. Ping started filling us in on you long ago."

"It can't have been that long ago," said Goldfish. "The bugger only looks to be nine or ten years old."

"I'm thirteen," Boyd said, somewhat offended.

"Oh, all apologies, sir," said Goldfish, filled with affected embarrassment. "Would it have been better if I referred to you as an **adolescent?**"

"Maybe," Boyd said, unsure as to whether or not he'd just been insulted.

"The two of you should stop your bickering so that we can get on with it," Bird said. "Ho Yin informed us of your dilemma. That cad, Fang, wants the Perpetual Motion Machine, doesn't he?"

"Yes, I believe so," Boyd said. "But we don't have all the pieces. That's all I know. We were hoping you could help."

Bird flew off to another room and came back with a small, dusty box, tied with a rope string, which she held in her mouth. "Do you know what perpetual motion[71] is, Boyd?" Goldfish asked.

"Not really," Boyd said.

"Coming into this blind, I see," Goldfish said, doing some figuring in his head. "Okay, cars. What do they run on?"

"Gasoline," Boyd said.

"What do trains run on?" Goldfish asked.

"Coal, I guess?"

"Airplanes?"

"Jet fuel."

"Right-o," said Goldfish, flapping his tail in the water. "So, the truth is that if you want to run a machine, then you have to have some sort of fuel, don't you?

"Sure," Boyd said.

"Could you imagine a machine that takes no fuel to make it work?" Bird asked. "What we mean is that once you got it started, it would run forever and never need fuel. It powers itself."

"Sure, I can imagine that," Boyd said. "It would just keep going and going."

"No more gas," Goldfish said.

"No more coal," Bird said.

"No more jet fuel," Goldfish said.

"No more pollution," Bird said.

"No more worry," Goldfish said, "because you could have a machine that powers itself and creates energy for the whole world."

"That's what a perpetual motion machine would do," Bird said. "It would change the world. As much energy as you needed and not only is it pollution free, it's also free itself."

"Sounds great, doesn't it?" asked Goldfish.

"Sure," said Boyd.

"Bet you'd like to have one, wouldn't you?"

"Sure."

"Well, you can't," Goldfish said. "Because it's impossible."

"Huh?"

"It's impossible to create a perpetual motion machine. They don't exist. Zip. Nada. Nobody has one. Nobody can invent one. It's scientifically impossible."

"Science can't create one," Bird said. "But *you* already *have* one."

"How can I have a perpetual motion machine if it's scientifically impossible?" Boyd asked.

"Let me explain this to you, Boyd," said Bird. "For years, Mr. Ping has been looking for clues regarding the mythical perpetual motion machine that was created by a Chinese emperor thousands of years ago. This emperor was a genius, wise beyond his years, and he spent all of his free time inventing things. One of the things he invented was a perpetual motion machine. That is, a machine that required no fuel, that powered itself, and would continue to run forever and ever. It was a machine that could have changed the world. But things went awry."

"Okay, okay," said Goldfish. "Don't hog the story all for yourself. Let me finish." Goldfish turned to Boyd and continued, "Along came the Mongols[72]."

"The Mongols?" Boyd asked. "You mean like dogs?"

"No! It's *Mongols!* Not *Mongrels,*" Goldfish said. He then looked at Bird, saying, "Is this boy for real? The lights in his head seem very dull."

"Continue the story," Bird said.

"All right, all right," said Goldfish. "The Mongols are a race of people. Have you ever heard of Mongolia[73]? It's where they are from."

"In South America?" Boyd asked.

Goldfish just rolled his eyes and continued. "The most famous of the Mongols was a man named Genghis Khan[74]. He conquered lands throughout Asia and as far west as Europe. Do you know of him? Anyway, the Mongols got word of this emperor's invention and went to China to conquer the land and steal the riches, including the Emperor's perpetual motion machine."

"My turn," said Bird. Goldfish relented with a huff. "The Emperor knew that if this machine were to get in the hands of the Mongols, it would spell doom for all of China. So, before the Mongols marched through China, he took the machine apart and scattered the pieces all over the region. Thousands of pieces, and only *he* knew where they were."

"Mr. Ping stumbled across the first piece in 1919[75], and soon found many more after that," added Goldfish. "Once he'd realized what they were, he went on a lifelong quest to gather all 1037 pieces from all over China. Each time he would come across a piece, he would take it back to the mansion. When he died, he thought he had all the pieces of the machine, but he didn't know how to put it together. You see, the parts are so intricate and complex that he wasn't sure how they fit. Try as he might, he couldn't make it work. What he needed was instructions that told him how."

"Is this story going anywhere?" Boyd asked, feeling bored.

"Yes!" cried Bird. "We've found them." Bird hovered over the table and unraveled the string on the package she'd brought into the room earlier. The wrapping fell off to reveal a rolled-up scroll that looked like it had seen better days. "These are the instructions," she said.

"The instructions will tell you how to put the machine together," Goldfish said. "You'll be able to finish Mr. Ping's work. If completed, the Machine could be the greatest thing to ever happen to humanity, Boyd. It could end poverty, pollution. It could stop wars or provide heat to those who have never had it before. The benefits that the Machine could bring to the world are enormous."

Boyd unrolled the scroll and began to examine it. Everything was written in virtually microscopic Chinese characters, like a diagram, pointing to the bizarre-looking pieces of some fantastic machine. "I don't understand any of this," Boyd said.

"Get your sister to help you out," said Bird. "She likes things like this."

"My sister?" Boyd asked. "Why her?"

"He doesn't know yet," Goldfish snickered in Bird's direction.

"What about my sister?" Boyd asked again.

"It was wonderful chatting with you, Boyd," said Goldfish. "We'd love to talk more, but we have an engagement soon and we really must part."

"It is to be hoped that this scroll will be of some help," said Bird.

"Wait!" Boyd said. "You're gonna throw all this stuff at me and then just leave?"

"It's all we have to offer," Bird said. "We never said we were going to make things easy for you. Anyway, this won't be our last visit, so don't fret."

"Well, where did you get these instructions?" Boyd asked. "How did you know about me? You can't just leave me like this!"

"Ah, but we can," said Bird, flying off to another room.

"Ta," said Goldfish and he swam towards the murky depths of the back of the fish tank, leaving Boyd looking at the map, all by himself, in the shop. He stared at it for a couple of seconds, but he couldn't tell which side of the map was the top. He finally gave up trying to understand anything on it, and put it in his pocket.

Outside, he found Tony Tang and his son still engaged in a fierce staredown with Reggie, who also had not moved from his position. "Let's go, Reggie," Boyd said.

The sound of Boyd's voice snapped Tony out of his stupor. He looked at Boyd and said, "Did you take care of your business?"

"Yeah," Boyd said. "I think so."

Tony climbed off of his stool behind the counter and retrieved a small vile which contained a pink powder from one of the shelves. "This is for you," he said. "Only use it when you find yourself in a tight spot. Okay?"

"Sure," Boyd said, examining the bottle. It's label was in Chinese, so he was unsure what it was.

Reggie quickly swiped it out of his hands and examined it between his long, black claws. "Be careful, Boyd," he said. "I'm not sure this guy can be trusted." He turned to Tony and narrowed his eyes. "What's this made of?"

Tony narrowed his eyes back at Reggie and said, "None of your business, furbrain!"

"Furbrain?" Reggie asked. "How dare you!"

"Get out of my store!" Tony yelled. "You're not welcome here anymore!"

"Fine," Reggie said. "I'll meet you outside, Boyd." He tossed the vial back to Boyd and squeezed his way out the door in a huff.

"Seriously," Tony said to Boyd," You'd better watch who you hang out with."

"Thanks for the gift," Boyd said. "I appreciate it."

"I hope it will come in useful," Tony said. "I'll see you around."

Boyd looked over at Tony's son sitting behind the counter and smiled. He took one last look at the bizarre little tea shop and walked out the door.

CHAPTER 19

SWORDFISH!

Boyd could tell that Reggie was upset by the way Tony had behaved in the store, especially considering that he started spouting off an unending monologue the minute Boyd came outside. "The way people behave nowadays *astounds* me! It literally *astounds* me!" he said, waving his arms around passionately. "Oh, *sure,* someone hears that a yeti munches down on a few people and suddenly every yeti in the world is *bad*? I don't think so. And let's not even get into what some *human beings* have done. But do we yetis blame *all* human beings for the shortcomings of a *few*? No! We're a tolerant race, we yetis. Not judgmental. **Humans** are judgmental and that's not a very endearing quality if I might say so myself."

"Sometimes people's feelings take a long time to get rid of, Reggie," Boyd said. "Maybe the fact that he saw me with you might change his mind."

"Yeah, maybe," Reggie said, grumbling under his breath.

"Did your cousin really eat his cousin's arms and legs?' Boyd asked.

"Of **course** not!" Reggie said. "We're **vegetarians!**" Reggie took a deep breath, trying to calm himself. He looked like he was about to explain something he'd explained a hundred times over and said, "Look, the reason we yetis have such a fierce reputation is just because all we want is to be left alone. We roar and growl and do our best to scare people off, but we don't **eat** them. Pah! The taste would just be horrible. Meat? Just the thought of it turns my stomach."

As they continued their conversation, they made their way through the empty market until Boyd froze in his tracks. He began to focus on his surroundings, looking for an imminent threat. "Something's wrong," he said.

Reggie puffed up his shoulders, sniffing the air. "I smell it, too," he said.

"Why would we be in danger now?" Boyd asked. "Nobody knows we're here."

"We're dealing with a crafty bunch," Reggie said. "They move fast."

Boyd continued looking around the area, but couldn't locate the danger. Then, far down the alley, he could see the wind whipping around the debris, as if something fast was moving towards them. "What's that?" Boyd asked.

"Stay close to me, Boyd," Reggie said.

When Boyd finally spotted movement, he saw a strange, wheel-like object moving towards them so fast it was like a green blur. It rolled with precision and stopped right in front of them, unfolding itself to reveal a large crocodile that was holding onto its own tail as it rolled. As it unfolded it popped up and stood on its hind legs, its long tail behind it. As if that wasn't strange enough, the crocodile was also wearing sunglasses, shorts, and a T-shirt.

"Aha!" it said.

"What do you want, **Smelts?**" Reggie asked, snarling.

"Is that any way to greet an old friend?" the crocodile asked. "Where's the love?"

"Things aren't so easily forgotten with yetis, Smelts," Reggie said.

"You know him?" Boyd asked.

"We used to work together," Reggie said.

"Until Reggie betrayed me," Smelts said.

"Betrayed **you?**" Reggie asked. "Ha! That's a laugh."

"You know the truth," Smelts said. His accent was unmistakably Australian. "Anyway, I don't have time to chitchat. I've come to warn you. You've got trouble just a few seconds away."

"You came to warn us?" Reggie asked.

"Of course, I came to warn you!" Smelts said.

"Oh, that's rich," Reggie said.

"Are you gonna be stubborn, you nitwit?" Smelts asked. "We don't have time for you to be hardheaded. We've gotta get outta here."

But it was too late. With a roar of engines, three sleek, black cars barreled their way through the alley, sending clothes and tents and worthless plastic knickknacks flying everywhere. The cars came to halt a short distance from Boyd, Reggie, and Smelts, and rumbled motionless at the end of the street. For the first time, Boyd began to get scared, especially as he noticed that the streets were now entirely without people, almost as if they were anticipating something big to happen.

"Drat!" Smelts said. "I'm always just a hair too late."

"The story of your life," Reggie muttered.

Both Reggie and Smelts assumed a defensive stance as the cars sat there with their tinted black windows reflecting the colorful lights of the alley around them. Boyd, too, found himself in a defensive posture, if defensive meant that he was ready to run as fast as he could at the first sign of danger.

After a quiet face off that seemed to go on for an eternity, one of the car doors opened and out stepped a large swordfish, walking on its tail fins with a cane and wearing a black turtleneck and cargo pants. It looked menacing and angry, its skin gleaming in the light of the alley, and it was followed by at least twenty men who got out of the other cars wearing black sunglasses and suits. "Well, well, well," the swordfish said. Its voice was garbled and its throat sounded like it was full of phlegm. "Reggie the yeti and that lowlife Smelts. What a lovely surprise!"

"You're looking good, mate," Smelts said. "But your smell is another story."

"What do you want, Hedley?" Reggie asked.

"I guess the more appropriate question is what do you have to offer," Hedley said.

"We don't have anything to offer you," Reggie said. "I think you and your boys there had better just pack up and leave."

"Yeah!" Smelts said. "Pack your slimy butt up and leave!"

"I'll handle this, Smelts," Reggie said, under his breath.

"Everyone needs a smart-aleck sidekick," Smelts replied. "I'm yours."

"Those days are long gone," Reggie replied, still whispering.

"If you two are done with your bickering," Hedley yelled across the alley, "I would like to get on with my evil demands. I don't have all night."

"All right tuna-breath," Smelts said. "Whaddya want?"

"I want the boy," he said. "And I'm going to take him, dead or alive."

Boyd's skin turned to ice as he heard those words. It immediately took him back to the sick feeling he'd get when Tucker would threaten him if he showed his face after school. Still, he felt confident, as if Hedley had no chance against Reggie and Smelts. Something told Boyd that they'd been in this kind of situation together several times in their lives.

"Well, let us make you a deal," Reggie said, snarling. "You let us go without anybody getting hurt, or you try to take this kid and everybody gets hurt. Which do you choose?"

"You leave us no choice, then," Hedley said, and from his cane, he pulled a shining, silver sword. "I guess we'll just have to kill you all. Come on out, boys!"

The doors to the other vehicles opened up and out stepped at least thirty panjas. They all carried bizarre, martial arts weapons that gleamed in the light and looked like they might disembowel a person in a variety of ways.

"Panjas!" Boyd said.

"Bring it on, suckers!" Smelts yelled, itching for a fight as he raised his fists. "Reggie and Smelts are back in action!"

Reggie sniffed at him over his shoulder, saying, "Will you tone it down a notch?"

Two panjas started doing somersaults towards them at lightning speed. "Here we go," Smelts smiled. "That's the way I like it."

Moving with a speed that betrayed his gargantuan bulk, Reggie raised his huge leg and kicked one of the panjas fifty feet away into a tent full of clothes. Smelts moved with a burst of crocodilian precision and took the other panja's legs out from under it with a whip of his tail. Both panjas howled with anger and more of them began running towards them.

One of the panjas sent a series of throwing stars directly towards Boyd's face, but Smelts dispatched each of them with a flip of his tail, their silvery blurs redirected with a clang against the walls. Then he dropped to all fours and weaved his way through the cars to take on the panjas. "I hate panjas!" he yelled as he charged forth.

Meanwhile, Reggie had grabbed one of the panjas by the leg and began swinging it back and forth like a club, knocking his adversaries first to the left, then to the right, all as the panja in his hands screamed with frustration. "You...guys...should...never... have...messed...with...us!" he yelled, swinging the beast back and forth.

Boyd was somewhat enraptured with the battle but soon noticed that he was surrounded on three sides by men who looked large and dull-witted, but also extremely dangerous. Immediately, he thought of the pink powder in his hands that Tony Tang had given him just minutes earlier. He looked at the label, which was previously written in Chinese, and saw that it was now written in English and said, *Throw on the ground for best results.* Boyd figured, *Why not?* and tossed the vial of powder on the ground. He was suddenly enveloped in a pink mist and felt a surge of energy through his body.

One of the henchmen grabbed at him and without any effort at all, he jumped up into the air, delivering the heel of his right foot to the chin of one of his abductors with an exactness that he could barely believe. The kick was so hard that it sent the man flying backwards to the ground, unconscious.

"Whoa," Boyd said, staring wide-eyed at the man's motionless body. "Did I just do that?"

Boyd's sudden fly kick was so shocking that the other two men hesitated before they made their next move, but it was too late. Boyd felt another sudden surge of energy and he dropped to the ground, sending his leg out like a piece of wood and swinging it around to take one of the men off of his feet. He then flipped back to his feet to face off with the others, all so quickly that he was nothing but a blur.

Sensing an opportunity, one thug swung his fist at Boyd, but he dodged it and took the momentum of the fighter's arm and swung him forward into the hard shell of a dumpster, also knocking him unconscious. Then, with a sour look on his face, Boyd swung around towards Hedley and gave him the stare down. "Ready when you are," he said with a hint of menace.

Boyd's surprise abilities shocked Hedley so much that the toothpick he had in his mouth fell to the ground, but just as quickly, a look of grim resolve passed over his face and he yelled, "Take the kid, men!" The rest of his goons headed for Boyd.

With ease, Boyd began dispatching them, one by one; a roundhouse kick for one; double punches to the face for another; a perfectly swung elbow on one goon; a skilled head butt for his partner. With a speed and finesse that he'd never had before in his life and a set of kung-fu skills to rival the ancient masters, Boyd left every one of Hedley's henchmen down on the ground, if not unconscious, then in an extreme amount of pain. He felt like he had powers far beyond anything he'd ever imagined and he was now filled with confidence at his ability to handle himself.

Then in a flash, he could feel the power leave him. Every bit of extraordinary energy that filled his body vanished, as the pink powder's power diminished. Just as Boyd was immediately transformed into an incredible kung fu artist, he was instantly morphed back into the powerless teenager that he had been before the pink mist had appeared. *Uh-oh*, he thought.

At the same time, both Reggie and Smelts were fighting a losing battle against the panjas. One, two, even three at a time they could handle; but the panjas were relentless and no matter how many times they were knocked down, slung around, or pounded into the ground, they got back up, twice as angry. Reggie could throw one fifty yards away, and a few seconds later, it would come trotting back around the corner, as mad as ever. Smelts could whack one in the face with his tail a hundred times over and it would still fail to quell any of its anger.

"This isn't going so well," Reggie said to Smelts in the heat of battle.

"They take a lickin' but they keep on tickin,'" Smelts said, pounding one with his fists while smacking another one with his tail. "Should we try an oh-two-hundred?"

"That sounds good," Reggie said.

Boyd ran up to them to get away from Hedley's men, who were slowly regaining consciousness. "What's an oh-two-hundred?" he asked, standing behind them for safety.

"A code word," Reggie said as he swiped Boyd off his feet. "It means run!"

Reggie, Smelts, and Boyd went dashing through the streets of Kowloon as fast as they could, trying to zigzag back and forth through the maze of alleys and crowds of people so as to lose the panjas, but it did them little good. The panjas were fast and worked well in teams. Instead of running on two legs like Reggie and Smelts, they dropped down and zoomed along on four, which gave them a slight edge.

Boyd bounced around in Reggie's arms, watching the panjas over his shoulder. "Was that *really* a swordfish?" he asked.

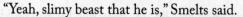

"Yeah, slimy beast that he is," Smelts said.

"Well, how can he be out of the water?" Boyd asked.

"He's an air-breather," Reggie said. "One of those oddball fish that can't live in the water. No time to explain."

Reggie knew that they couldn't outrun the panjas for long, so he motioned to Smelts and ducked into one of the residential buildings, ripping the large, black metal door from its frame. With Smelts following and Boyd under his arm, they ran up through the garbage room, into the living area of the building, and then through the carpeted hall into the stairwell. As Boyd flopped around in Reggie's arms, he could hear the snarls of the panjas close behind them, but he couldn't see them.

The three of them traveled up the stairs at a pace that could have won an Olympic medal, and kept it up for the entirety of the seventeen flights of stairs, until they got to the very top, where they were faced with a locked door. This presented no problem for Reggie, and he gave the door a kick, sending it flying across the roof. "Remind me to send them a check for the damages, would you, Smelts?" he asked.

"Will do," Smelts said as they ran out onto the roof.

"They're right behind us!" Boyd said, panicked. "We're gonna be trapped up here."

"That's what I'm hoping for," Reggie said. "Smelts?"

"Gotcha," Smelts said. He leaped forward, once again turning himself into a giant wheel, and began to roll towards the edge of the roof, increasing his speed until he was flung over the side, his body flattening out as he propelled himself across. He landed with a forward roll, gracefully stopping on all fours on the roof across the way. He popped back up and turned back to Reggie and Boyd.

"Ready?" Reggie yelled at him.

"Right-o!" Smelts yelled.

Without warning, Reggie tossed Boyd right over the edge to the other building, where Smelts was waiting to catch him. Boyd screamed as he sailed through the air. His arms flailed in every direction as the busy neon streets of Kowloon zipped by far below him. With a wallop that took his breath away, he landed in Smelts' arms.

"I reacted much the same way the first time he did that to me," Smelts said, smiling (or at least, as much as a crocodile could smile).

It took a second or two for Boyd to get his bearings. He looked across to the opposite building and saw Reggie standing his ground as a flood of panjas came out the rooftop door. "Meet me in the lobby!" he yelled at them. Before Smelts led him down the stairwell, Boyd saw a couple of panjas try and fail to make the leap across the buildings. They sailed through the air, but their momentum only carried them halfway and they fell down into the center of the chasm between the buildings.

"Don't worry about them, mate," Smelts said. "The fall is seventeen stories, but those stupid buggers are a lot more resilient than one would suspect, considering they're almost extinct." He laughed and they began to descend the staircase.

Meanwhile, Reggie was engaged in a face-off with sixteen angry panjas, who were each foaming at the mouth and scratching at the floor to get at him. Soon, Hedley waddled through the door, looking calm. "Well, well, well," he said. "Where's the boy, yeti?"

"Long gone," Reggie said. "I don't know what you're trying to pull here, Hedley, but you're wasting your time."

"Oh, the money's too good for me to be wasting my time, you furry buffoon," Hedley said, his voice filled with horrible phlegm. "I'll tell you what. You give us Boyd McCloyd and we'll let you join our organization and devote your life to evil. You want that deal?"

"No thanks," Reggie said, looking bored.

"Well, then," Hedley said. "I guess we've got no choice but to kill you and have yeti steaks for dinner. So it goes…"

One of the panjas stepped forward and growled, which was the signal that the others had been anticipating. They each began to move towards Reggie at the same time, stepping slowly as they snarled, drooled, and licked their panja chops.

As tough as yetis think they are, they're really no match for sixteen, semi-rabid panjas all at once, so Reggie knew that he was severely outmatched. Of course, this was no problem for him, for he'd always had a plan. Considering he was backed up against the edge of the building, he had no place to run, but running wasn't in the cards. He casually stepped up on the edge of the building and smiled. "It's really been a pleasure, this little ruckus of ours," he said, "but I fear I must be going."

"What? Are you going to fly away?" Hedley snickered. "Yetis have wings?"

"Uh, no," he said. "We've got brains. Which is more than I can say for swordfish."

And with that, Reggie stepped off the edge of the building, disappearing over the side.

"He jumped!" Hedley said, a look of shock passing over his face. "That stupid yeti just committed suicide!"

Alas, Hedley was wrong, as Reggie had seventeen stories of people's laundry to break his fall all the way down. He just fell from floor to floor, each time slowed by someone's blankets or T-shirts or underwear, never picking up enough speed to make a large splat on the ground.

Both Smelts and Boyd had taken the elevator down from the opposite building, and although they got the odd stare from the various tenants who refused to board an elevator in which there was a crocodile standing on its hind legs next to a thirteen-year-old boy, they made it to the lobby safely. Boyd was still trying to recover from the whirlwind of events that had unfolded over the preceding few minutes, but finally worked up the courage to talk to Smelts. "Thanks for your help," he said.

"No worries, mate," Smelts said. "You handled yourself pretty well out there."

"It was a potion that Tony Tang gave me," Boyd said.

"Hmm," Smelts said, looking skeptical. "You gotta watch Tang's potions. Some of them can be pretty dodgy. Still, we're just lucky that cat's on *our* side." Smelts looked around the lobby for a couple of seconds, saying, "Now where is that yeti?"

"I hope he's okay," Boyd said.

Smelts looked out the front doors of the building to see Reggie pull up in the black car and honk the horn. "I think he did just fine," he said, and the two of them walked outside to get in the car.

Reggie sped through the streets of Kowloon, on his way back to the mansion. "Is everyone okay?" he asked.

"The kid's a little shaken up," Smelts said, rubbing Boyd's head playfully. "But I think he's got a thirst for that kind of thing inside him."

"What are you doing here, Smelts?" Reggie asked, his large brow furrowed in annoyance.

"I just came back to pay my old buddy, Reggie, a visit," Smelts said, avoiding the subject by observing the scenery passing by outside the window.

"That's a lie," Reggie said. "You know I can smell a lie a mile away."

"All right, all right," Smelts said. "Ho Yin was worried about you bringing Boyd down here, so he called me and asked if I'd tail you guys to make sure nothing happened."

Reggie smacked the steering wheel in anger, bending it slightly. "Drat!" he yelled. "When is Ho Yin gonna learn to trust me?"

"Well, he wasn't wrong, was he?" Smelts said. "You'd have been in big trouble with Hedley and those panjas if I hadn't come along."

"Those panjas?" Reggie said, looking incredulous. "Those panjas were *nothing*. We would have been just fine."

"Oh, that's typical," Smelts said. "Mr. Ego thinks he can handle himself. Wonderful..."

"Don't start!" Reggie said.

"*You* started it," Smelts said.

"No, I didn't," Reggie said.

"Please forgive me, Boyd," Smelts said. "I'm sure that this is a poor introduction for me. It's just that Reggie tends to get me riled up sometimes."

"*Me?*" Reggie said. "It takes two to tango, mister."

"You see, we have a bit of history between us," Smelts said. "We used to be partners."

"And quite good partners," Reggie said, smiling as he remembered the good times. "We were the best detective agency in all of Europe. There wasn't a crime we couldn't solve, a person we couldn't find, or an evil plot we couldn't foil."

"We were even shortlisted for the Nobel Peace Prize," Smelts smiled, "but then Martin Luther King, Jr. won it." He looked at the ground shaking his head and reliving past glory. "Nobody ever remembers who finished second," he sighed.

"So what happened?" Boyd asked. "If you guys were so great, why'd you stop?"

"I don't want to talk about it," Reggie said, waving off Boyd's question.

"It's a subject best left unspoken," Smelts said, turning his head towards the window.

"How long have you two have been holding this grudge against each other?" Boyd asked.

"July 31st, 1970[76]," Reggie and Smelts said, simultaneously.

"What?" Boyd asked. "You've been holding a grudge against each other for over thirty years? That's crazy!"

"Betrayal can do that to a person," Reggie said, smoldering.

"Oh, get over it," Smelts said. "It was what you did afterward that caused the real problems."

"And can you blame me?" Reggie asked. "I was just reacting to what you'd done to me!"

"What you *allege* that I'd done to you," Smelts said. "You can't prove anything."

"The proof is in the pudding, Smelts," Reggie said. "The proof is in the pudding."

"What does that *mean?*" Smelts asked.

"It means never trust a crocodile," Reggie said.

"No, it means you're a big, smelly, fur brained monkey!" Smelts said.

"Enough!" Boyd said. "No more talking. It's bad enough that my parents fight all the time. I don't want to have to sit here, listening to you two squabble."

"Fine," Smelts said.

"Fine," Reggie said.

"Fine," Boyd said, and they rode along in silence all the way back to the mansion.

CHAPTER 20

PERMISSION TO DO WHAT AN AIR-BREATHING SWORDFISH IS GOOD AT

Mr. Fang had spent the evening in his luxury tower, watching his servants clean his guns, knives, and other weapons from his collection as he waited on word from Hedley regarding the capture of Boyd McCloyd. Occasionally, he would whack them over the head with a cane if they failed to do things to his liking. "You left a streak on my best sword!" he would yell before giving them a smack. "If you didn't work for me for thirty years, I'd toss you out that penthouse window!"

Mr. and Mrs. Fang lived in the very top of Fang Tower in the center of Hong Kong. Reggie had been correct about the bad energy of the tower for Mr. Fang had the building constructed specifically to project negative vibrations at all the buildings around it. Mr. Fang wanted to be the most powerful man in Asia, and the construction of Fang Tower, what with its terrible Feng Shui, was part of the process.

Their penthouse was like a giant monument to greed and evil. The gun and knife display was one example, and another would have been Mr. Fang's "trophy" room, where he displayed all the endangered animals he'd killed and stuffed from his hunting trips. He also had a picture frame that held the first hundred dollar bill he'd ever made from his evil exploits, as well as his first thousand dollar bill and his first hundred thousand dollar bill. He'd even tried to get the government of Hong Kong to make a million dollar bill so that he could have that framed as well, but they wouldn't do it, even if he bribed them.

Mrs. Fang knew that Mr. Fang was upset because whenever he was upset, he always made his servants clean his weapons. She watched as he paced back and forth in front of the massive picture window that looked out over the nighttime Hong Kong skyline. "Have some noodles," she said. "It will make you feel better."

"I can't eat noodles right now!" he yelled. "This is a big moment for me. If we don't get Boyd McCloyd, the Conspiricetti is going to kill me." He paced back and forth a couple of times before he turned to her and said, "Maybe noodles aren't such a bad idea. Hey, servant! Go get me a bowl of noodles."

"Right away, Mr. Fang," said the servant, relieved to be getting out of the room.

At precisely that moment, one of the phones on Mr. Fang's belt rang and he whipped it up to his ear. "Fang here!" he said.

"No wonder you're a two-bit player in international evil circles," gargled Hedley on the other end of the line. "What's with these worthless panjas you've got working for you?"

"Did you get him?" Mr. Fang asked.

"No," Hedley said. "He got away. That crocodile was with the yeti and your worthless hired guys couldn't take them out."

"What are you talking about? Those panjas are the best in the business!"

"Not where I come from," Hedley said. "Now, look...Do you want me to do this right or what?"

"Yes! Yes! I want you to do it right!" Mr. Fang pleaded.

"Well, if you want me to do it right, then you're going to have to let me do it *my* way. And *my* way costs money!"

"Money isn't a problem," Mr. Fang said. "You get that ugly kid Boyd McCloyd for me and I'll give you whatever you want."

"Whatever," Hedley said. "But you've got to go along with me all the way. Do you understand? And my way isn't pretty."

"Just do it, you stupid fish!" Mr. Fang yelled. "I'll pay you the money."

"Done," Hedley said. "Give me twenty-four hours to get my crew together and before you know it, Boyd McCloyd will be all yours."

Hedley hung up on a breathless Mr. Fang, who stood there, trying not to cry. All the money in the world and he couldn't kidnap a ·stupid kid. It was enough to make him hungry. "Where are my noodles?" he yelled. "Someone had better get me my noodles or I'll fire you all!"

CHAPTER 21

SETTLING OLD SCORES AT THE HIMALAYAN OUTBACK DETECTIVE AGENCY

Back at the mansion, Cindy was enjoying the splendor of her newfound freedom as Ho Yin had given her free reign in the laboratory. She had never had the chance to explore what she was capable of doing and she made the most of her time since Boyd had been gone. In that brief period, she'd synthesized a form of bacteria that, when sprinkled on food, produced wonderful tastes in a person's mouth no matter what they were eating, developed a metal that never got hot and never got cold, even at temperature extremes, and created a swarm of tiny, molecular-sized robots that she was able to control using a hand-built, portable computer that she carried on her wrist (another device she'd created).

All the while, Bjorn, who had designated himself Cindy's new personal assistant, took copious notes, constantly following her around with a little clipboard, writing meticulous observations regarding what she was doing (even if it was in his terrible, polar bear handwriting). "Did you get that last part, Bjorn?" she asked, as she typed in the finishing flourishes on the computer. Bjorn grunted an acknowledgment. "Okay," she said. "Let's try it out."

She typed in a series of commands into her wristwatch (on a four-button keyboard that worked in a binary language that she'd invented back in Ontario), and the two of them began to stare off into the empty space before them. For a few seconds, nothing happened, but then a strange, dark cloud began to form in front of them that seemed to be rectangular in shape, like a television screen. Glowing green letters began to flash on the screen that said, *Hello, Bjorn!*

Bjorn, of course, was delighted and began to roar with excitement, clapping his paws together in an appreciative fashion.

"It's a work in progress," she said. "I synthesized the chemical found in the tails of lightning bugs and had the nanobots create that in a pattern that was visible in this light spectrum. Cool, eh?"

Bjorn grunted approval once again.

"I'll make you your very own set of nanobots," Cindy said. She smiled at Bjorn, lost in thought. "You know, it sure is nice having someone to hang around with like this. When you're smart, it seems like no one gets you. Even though you've got all these skills, no one sees the benefits of that. When I was back in Ontario, all the fifth grade girls used to pretend they had cell phones. If they'd only known, I would have *made* them cell phones. But they didn't know, and if they *did* know, they would have made fun of me."

Bjorn let loose with a big, bear sigh, as if he was thinking abut his own problems.

"Yeah, I know," Cindy continued. "It must have been hard for you, too."

Bjorn nodded.

"That's why we're going to work well together, Bjorn. We were outsiders before, but now we have each other." Cindy perked up as if she remembered something exciting she'd forgotten. "By the way, I have something for you!" She ran off to the other side of the lab and pulled a small machine out of a cabinet. Bjorn was curious, as bears usually are, and began to edge his way over towards her, but Cindy quickly turned away from him. "No, no," she said. "It's a secret!"

Bjorn huffed his disapproval and plopped down on his behind to sniff at the air for clues.

After a few minutes, Cindy came back over, carrying something behind her back. "Now, close your eyes," she said. As Bjorn closed his eyes, she began to attach several straps around his chest, pulling and twisting and tightening them until she was satisfied. "Okay," she said. "Open your eyes."

Bjorn looked down to see a metallic device strapped to his chest with a small, red button in the center. "Go on," she said. "Push the button!" Bjorn examined it for a couple of seconds, then pushed it, which caused several motors and gears and belts to whirl into action, and a metallic arm to extend out in front of him that contained a small, gray keyboard. "Type something," she said.

With a bit of hesitation, he tapped out the word "hello" on the keyboard. When he pressed the enter key, a metallic voice rang out from his chest and said, "Hello."

A look of sheer delight passed over Bjorn's furry face and he let out a huge growl of happiness. He quickly typed in another phrase and pressed enter, whereupon the computer said, "Me can communicate!"

"You sure can," Cindy said. "It's very rough, but I've only had a couple of hours to work on it. We'll make a better one over time, but this one will do for now."

Bjorn began to type again. "I am owing you big for this, Cindy," the metallic voice said.

"No, no, no," Cindy said. "You don't owe me anything. I did it because you're my friend."

"Me am your friend," Bjorn's computer said. "This is the nicestest thing somebody ever done for me. Thank you much."

"Well, we're just lucky you can type," Cindy giggled. "It's not every polar bear that knows how to type."

"Me amm a bear of mmany talents," the computer said.

Just as Cindy and Bjorn were having their wonderful little moment of bonding, Ho Yin entered the room yammering away on a phone in Cantonese and pacing back and forth. Although Cindy didn't know what he was talking about, she was sure that whatever was happening wasn't good. "We've got trouble," he said as he hung up the phone. "Boyd and Reggie were ambushed at the market. They believe it was Fang's men."

Bjorn quickly typed into his computer, which said, "Me hate thatt man."

Ho Yin was stunned at Bjorn's newfound communication device and despite the imminent emergency, a smile passed over his face. "Bjorn can speak!" he said, turning to Cindy. "Did you build that?"

"Yes," Cindy said with pride.

"Impressive," he said. "You're much more skilled than I ever anticipated." He grew serious again.

At that moment, Boyd, Reggie, and Smelts burst into the labs, full of excitement and joy. "We've got the instructions," Boyd said, waving them in his hand. "You should have seen what we had to go through to get them."

He stopped dead in his tracks, shocked at the sight that lay in front of him. There, on the floor, was Cindy, with wires and equipment and tools strung out all around her, with Bjorn right beside her, wearing the computer on his chest. "What in the world is going on, here?" Boyd asked.

"It looks as though she's been workin' on somethin,' mate," Smelts said.

Cindy had failed to hear Boyd and the gang come into the labs, and when she looked up, she was surprised to see her brother. "You're back," she said.

"What in the world is going on, Cindy?" Boyd asked.

"I've been working," she said.

"Working?" Boyd asked.

"That's what the gal said, mate," Smelts added. "Are you deaf or something?"

"Cindy has many more talents than you would expect, Boyd," Ho Yin said, walking over to him. "More than you would even think to ask about."

"Talents? Cindy?" he asked. "Ha!"

"See?" Cindy said to Ho Yin. "I told you he'd be weird about it."

"Cindy has an IQ of two hundred and twelve, Boyd," Ho Yin said. "She can process information much faster than the average human being, yourself included. She can do quantum physics, create languages, and build things that you might concoct only in your dreams. To put it simply, she's a genius. You just never knew, because you never asked."

"Who would have thought to ask something like *that?*" Boyd said.

"You should have," Bjorn said, through his computer.

"Bjorn can talk!" Reggie said. "Holy moly, Bjorn can talk!"

"Me sure can," Bjorn said. "Thanks to Cindy."

"Wait, wait, wait," Boyd said. "A yeti, I can handle. A crocodile that walks upright, I can handle. Ninja pandas and a polar bear with a computerized voice, I can handle. But my fifth grade sister being a super genius? I'm having trouble with this one."

"You would," Cindy said.

"Believe it or not, it's true," Ho Yin said, taking the scroll from Boyd's hands. "She's also got some work to do."

"What kind of work?" Smelts asked. "Is super-genius-girl, there, gonna figure out what those instructions tell us?"

"Absolutely," Ho Yin said.

Ho Yin brought the scroll over to Cindy to let her examine it. Looking at it as if it was the most interesting thing she'd ever seen, she began to turn it sideways, upside-down, and back again, all in an attempt to decipher the clues hidden upon it. "Wow," she said. "This one's tough."

"Do you think you'll be able to figure it out?" Ho Yin asked.

"With time," she said. She then started shooing everyone out of the room. "Go! All of you. I need time to think. I need silence. Your brain waves might interrupt my brain waves."

"How's she gonna understand these instructions?" Boyd asked. "They're in Chinese!"

"I know Mandarin," Cindy said. "Now, get out of here."

"Mandarin? It's in *Chinese*, Cindy," Boyd said.

"Bjorn, will you get rid of them?" Cindy asked, still staring at the scroll.

Bjorn nudged Boyd and the rest of the gang out of the labs, leaving the two of them hunkered down with the instructions and a myriad of computers, scanners, wires, and electrodes all at their disposal. Once Boyd, Reggie, and Smelts were out in the hallway, Ho Yin said, "The three of you look hungry. Why don't you go wait in the study and I'll bring something to you."

"Sounds brilliant," Smelts said, licking his lips. "If it's a meat-based meal, please make mine raw."

"Smelts was just leaving," Reggie interrupted.

"I was not," Smelts said.

"Yes, you *were*," Reggie replied. "You weren't invited here in the first place."

"So?" Smelts said. "If it hadn't been for *me*, you'd be yeti soup right now."

Ho Yin calmly came between the two of them, as if he'd seen this a hundred times. "Smelts can stay, Reggie," he said. "I think it's time the two of you buried the hatchet. This feuding has gone on long enough."

"*He* started it," Reggie said.

"There he goes again," Smelts said. "*He's* the one that always starts it."

"I do not!"

"Do, *too!*"

"Look, I've had enough from both of you," Ho Yin said. "Fighting over the past and carrying this feud on for thirty years...is that what you two should be doing? Do you remember what the Buddha said?"

Reggie and Smelts stopped squabbling and looked at the floor as if they'd suffered some horrible shame. "Yes," they said, simultaneously.

"Do you remember page seventy-two of the 'Dhammapada'?" Ho Yin asked.

"Yes," they said, simultaneously.

"What did page seventy-two of the 'Dhammapada' say?" Ho Yin asked, adopting the look of an impatient instructor with each sentence. "Reggie?"

Reggie sighed, continuing to stare at the ground as he recited the poem from the Dhammapada. *"Look how he abused me and beat me,"* he said. *"How he threw me down and robbed me. Live with such thoughts and you live in hate."*

"Smelts?" Ho Yin asked.

"Look how he abused me and beat me," Smelts continued. *"How he threw me down and robbed me. Abandon such thoughts and live in love."*

Ho Yin looked at both of them and continued the poem. *"In this world, hate never yet dispelled hate. Only love dispels hate. This is the law, ancient and inexhaustible. You, too, shall pass away. Knowing this, how can you quarrel?"* He looked at both of them sternly. "Thirty years," he said. "Thirty years the two of you have kept up this ridiculous argument. That's thirty years of missed opportunities with each other. Thirty years of laughter gone, adventures unattended, love and kindness wasted. Mr. Ping was very distraught that the two of you failed to settle your differences before he died, because he thought he'd failed. If this is the way you want to continue to act, fine. But I suggest you both go off and think about the poem you just recited before you go back to your petty, little quarrel."

Ho Yin stood there in silence, looking at both Reggie and Smelts as the two of them shuffled back and forth in place, like children who had gotten in trouble on the playground. "So, uh, Smelts?" Reggie said. "Would you, uh, like to get a cup of tea?"

Smelts looked at the ground and said, "Sure."

Without saying a word, the two of them walked off down the hall together to make tea in the kitchen. Boyd stood in awe of what had just transpired in front of him. "That's it?" he asked. "Thirty years of feuding and one little poem solves it all?"

"Sure," Ho Yin said, standing beside him. "They both know the way. It's just that over time, their minds get clouded. Buddhism is an every day activity, like exercise. You must think about it at all times or you'll lose practice and end up like these two."

"What is Buddhism?" Boyd asked. "Is it a religion?"

"Kind of," Ho Yin said. "But not a religion in a western sense, like Christianity or Islam. In a nutshell, it's a belief that the mind can be clouded by the physical pleasures and emotions of the real world and that the only way to conquer the negative energy that lives in this world is to be in constant practice of loving kindness. Once a person brings unconditional love into the world, they will, in a sense, be one step closer to Nirvana."

"What's Nirvana?" Boyd asked.

"Nirvana is similar to what you call heaven."

"Okay, okay," Boyd said, waving him off. "That's too much to understand right now. Can we just talk about what's going on? I mean, with that swordfish and Smelts and the whole scroll and perpetual motion machine thing?"

"What would you like to know?" Ho Yin asked.

"*Why,*" Boyd said. "*Why* does Smelts exist? *Why* are there ninja pandas chasing after me? *Why* was I talking to a bird and a goldfish? I mean, these things are amazing! I'd figure I would have read about them somewhere or seen them on TV, but I haven't. And you guys just act like it's no big deal."

Ho Yin laughed as he sat down in one of the red leather chairs in the hallway. "Boyd, the world's full of fantastic things. There are, literally, thousands upon thousands of things that would make your jaw drop open in wonder if you knew about them. Amazing buildings, amazing places, amazing people, and amazing creatures. The problem is that nobody even bothers to scratch the surface anymore. They don't go out and explore the world, look beneath the rocks, or see what life's like outside their neighborhood. They get distracted by things like paying bills, or nice cars, or their favorite television shows. They're spoon fed what their lives should be and they accept it, and because of that, they lose their imaginations.

"And that is exactly what we're trying to battle here. These people that we're up against, they want to keep people from thinking, from using their imaginations, because if they can do that, then they have total and complete control over the world, and they become rich off of it. And they'll continue to do so until somebody stops them. That's why they want you, Boyd, because you're the one who has been chosen to stop them. They see you as a threat and they don't want to lose control, so they're willing to lie, cheat, or steal to stop you. We have to stop them first."

Boyd sighed and looked at the floor, saying, "I've got a lot of learning to do, don't I?"

"You certainly do," Ho Yin said.

"Okay," Boyd said. "Now, what is Cindy doing in that lab? Working on some sort of machine?"

"She's translating the instructions so that she can put the Perpetual Motion Machine together," Ho Yin said. "Mr. Ping had collected all the pieces. He just never knew how to put it all together. After all, there are over a thousand pieces to it. When I first showed all the pieces to Cindy, she put more of it together in five minutes than Mr. Ping and I had in thirty years, but it's still not complete."

"So she's a genius?" Boyd said.

"It's true," Ho Yin said.

"Well, why didn't she *tell* anyone she was a genius?" Boyd asked. "I mean, that's a great thing, right? To be as smart as her? Why would she keep it a secret?"

"Your's wasn't the happiest of households, Boyd," Ho Yin said. "Your mother and father fought quite often. Cindy, for some reason, felt like it was her fault and that explaining her genius would only cause more problems."

"But that's not true," Boyd said. "None of that was her fault. If she's so smart, why didn't she know that?"

"Because emotions and intellect are two different things entirely," Ho Yin said. He looked at his watch and then turned down the hall. "I have to make a couple of phone calls, Boyd. Try to keep yourself occupied while I run to the office. I'd suggest starting with Volume Fourteen…"

He winked and smiled, and made his way off further into the mansion, leaving Boyd to ponder everything he'd absorbed over the course of the evening.

CHAPTER 22

SOLVING A THOUSAND YEAR OLD RIDDLE

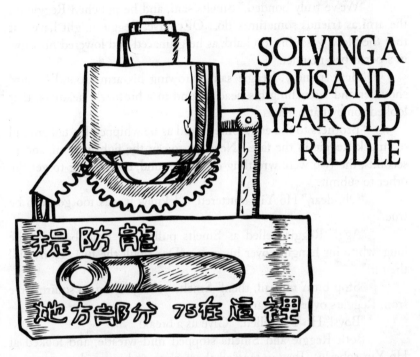

Later that night, voices were heard in the hallway, laughing and carrying on about something as they spoke, and Boyd instantly recognized the familiar, deep tones of Reggie and the crocodilian rasp of Smelts. *Sounds like they're on good terms now*, he thought, and he wandered out in the hallway to see them bent over, laughing as hard as they could. It was obvious that they had worked out their differences, for all the animosity that they had towards each other prior to that moment seemed to have vanished without a trace.

"Looks like things seem to be on firmer ground with the two of you," Ho Yin said, smiling as he approached.

"We've mended fences," Reggie said.

"Licked out wounds," added Smelts.

"We're buddies again," Reggie said, and he slapped Smelts on the back in a good-natured way. Smelts was startled by the force of Reggie's blow and gave him a look out of the corner of his eye.

"We've truly bonded," Smelts said, and he punched Reggie on the arm as friends sometimes do. Of course, Reggie might have felt that the blow was a bit too hard, as he grimaced and lowered his brow in a perturbed manner.

"Best friends," Reggie said, throwing his arm around Smelts' shoulder and wrenching his head around in a brotherly headlock that looked somewhat harsh.

"Brothers to the end," Smelts said as he whipped his tail around to smack Reggie in the face. Needless to say, the fight was on, and in seconds, the two were wrestling on the ground, each trying to get the other to submit.

"Oh, dear," Ho Yin muttered. "I knew it was too good to be true."

"Agg!" Reggie yelled as Smelts pulled his head back by the long, white fur hanging over his eyes. "Don't pull the fur! Don't pull the fur!"

"Stop bitin' my tail, then!" Smelts yelled, trying to squirm free from Reggie's oversized hands.

"Boys!" Ho Yin yelled. "Give us a break!"

Both Reggie and Smelts stopped mid-wrestle, and looked at Ho Yin soberly. They untangled themselves and jumped to attention in front of him. "Best friends," Smelts said, looking at Reggie out of the corner of his eye. "Right, mate?"

"The very best," Reggie said with a smile that was one step away from a sneer.

"Guys! Guys!"

Cindy's voice echoed through the halls of the mansion, her running shoes slapping the hardwood floor. Everyone saw her round the corner, waving the scroll over her head, as if she was tremendously excited. "I've got it!"

The group reassembled back in the labs, where Bjorn was preparing an overhead presentation, tapping away on a laptop connected to a projector. Cindy grabbed a pointer, gave Bjorn a signal, and then instructed everyone to look at a picture of the scroll generated on the screen. "When did she have time to do all this?" Boyd asked. "She *must* be a genius."

"I think I've figured out how to put the Machine together," she said. "It was difficult, considering my limited Chinese skills, but I've never been one to shrink away from a challenge."

"Yeah, whatever," Boyd said, giggling.

"Anyway," Cindy said, ignoring her brother, "The instructions are full of riddles to be solved. The thing is," she said, "we're not finished getting all the pieces. There's one piece missing and I can't quite figure out what it is."

"What?" Ho Yin said. "But that doesn't correspond to what all the historical texts say."

"What do the historical texts say?" Reggie asked.

"Most people believe the Machine is a myth," Ho Yin said. "No one has ever believed that a machine such as this could ever exist, so everyone just assumed that all of this was fiction. Yet just as Mr. Ping collected all the pieces, he collected information about the machine as well, most of it in the form of ancient scrolls. And those scrolls say there are only one thousand thirty-seven pieces of the Machine."

"Can I have a look at these scrolls?" Cindy asked. "They might give me a clue as to how to figure out this last riddle."

"Sure," Ho Yin said.

They walked down the main hallway to the library at the back of the mansion, where Ho Yin pulled out a large drawer at the base of an oak bookshelf, inside of which were thousands of photocopied pieces of paper, each one meticulously stacked and ordered. "Mr. Ping searched through the archives in Beijing, Xian, Taipei, and Shanghai, collecting as much information as he could. Most of these photocopied writings were from the Qin Dynasty from around 221 BC."

"And he took notes?" Cindy asked.

"Yes," he said. "There are notes scrawled in the margins here." Ho Yin began to look through some of the writings, examining each piece of paper.

"Uh, Ho Yin," Boyd said, "what was the Qin Dynasty?"

"Good question, mate," Smelts said. "I'm listenin' to those two, but I don't understand a word they're sayin.'"

"The Qin Dynasty was the period when China was first unified," Ho Yin said. "It was, basically, the organization of the country, meaning it was the first time they had a monetary system and a unified, written language, plus the first time they had local governments that reported to a larger body. It was all organized by Qin Shihuangdi, the first emperor of China."

"He's the bloke who built the Great Wall of China," Reggie said, puffing out his chest as if he was proud of the fact that he could contribute to the conversation.

"He must have been a great man," Boyd said.

"Not really," Ho Yin said. "He was a tyrant. He used slave labor to build the Great Wall. Millions of people died on his 'projects.' He was also obsessed with immortality and constructed a massive tomb for himself, with thousands of terra cotta statues, each with their own design, to protect him in the afterlife."

"Huh?" Boyd asked.

"Have you ever heard of the Terra Cotta Warriors in Xian, China?" Ho Yin asked.

"No," Boyd said.

"They were discovered by some farmers digging a well," he said. "Thousands of life-sized statues, each one based on a real soldier, so that they were all different. Qin Shihuangdi had thousands of these made to protect him in the afterlife. They were all buried underground until the farmers discovered them."

"That sounds cool," Boyd said.

"Here it is," Ho Yin said, flicking the page he was holding. "It says, 'The significance of the Machine is that each piece represents a person of my cabinet.'"

"So when the Machine is taken apart," Cindy said, "each piece represents a person that worked for him?"

"Yes," Ho Yin said. "He thought that his government and his leadership was perfect. A flawless government that ran much like a machine. And if we look at the further records, it says...here it is...it says that in his bureaucracy, there were one thousand, thirty-seven ministers."

"And there are one thousand, thirty-seven pieces," Cindy said.

"So why do you think that there's another piece, Cindy?" Reggie asked.

"Because of this," Cindy said, holding up the instructions to the Machine to read them. "It says, *A plow without an ox tills no land/Useless is the arm without hand/A warrior without a sword cannot fight/The Earth without the sun is just night/Like a genius that's missing a brain/Without this, the Machine is just plain.'*"

"Without what?" Boyd asked.

"He's talking about himself," Cindy said, snapping her fingers at the revelation. *"A plow without an ox tills no land...Useless is the arm without hand...'* There are one thousand thirty-seven pieces of the Machine, just as there are one thousand thirty-seven members of his government. But those one thousand thirty-seven members are useless without a leader. He's the final piece of the puzzle. One thousand thirty-seven members of the government and one leader of them all."

"You're right," Ho Yin said. "Mr. Ping was only counting the members of his government and not him. Then there *is* one last piece."

"Okay, that's great and all, if you understand anything of what the two of you are talking about, but let's help out the non-genius folk here, like me," Boyd said. "I thought we had all the pieces of the machine."

"We do," Cindy said, "but we're lacking the one thing that makes it all work, just like the government can't work without a leader."

"So, we've gotta get one more piece?" Smelts asked.

"Yes," Ho Yin said.

"But we don't know what it is or where it is," Reggie said.

"Right," Cindy said.

"Oh, that's great," Boyd said. "It could only be anywhere in the world!"

"No, it's not," Cindy said. "If he considered himself the piece that made the machine of his government work, then the last piece of the Machine must be with him. Wherever Qin Shihuangdi is buried, the last piece of the Machine is buried."

"Then that must be Xian," Ho Yin said. "That is where his tomb is located."

"Ah, but that's where you're wrong," Reggie said. "His body has not been found at Xian. They cannot find the place where he was buried. Everyone *thinks* they know where it is, but it's never been proven."

"Right," Cindy said. "And the instructions for the Machine say differently as well." She pulled out the instructions again and read, *"The wise emperor knows the truth/Of the base nature of man in his darkest hour/So in order to preserve the tomb's youth/And prevent it's wither, like a sickly flower/There will be two tombs to house this shell/One that is clear, one hidden away/One they will say, "This is where he fell"/While the other shall be hidden for another day."*

"Ingenious," Reggie said. "He made *two* tombs!"

"Why would he do that?" Boyd asked.

"Because of grave robbers," Ho Yin said. "Ancient emperors and kings were usually buried with their riches so that they could take them with them to the afterlife, but in most cases, their tombs were robbed. People would sneak in and take the gold and jewels."

"So he built two graves for himself?" Boyd asked.

"Yes," Ho Yin said. "One to trick people."

"Which is the one in Xian," Reggie said.

"And one someplace else," Ho Yin said. "The hidden one is the one we want."

"Is there any more information?" Smelts asked Cindy. "Something that might give us a clue as to where this other tomb might be?"

"Only this," she said, reading again. *"To find the hidden secrets, to finish the quest/One needs only to find the scroll that looks like the rest/The paper is white, the writing the same/It will look like the others, the script will be plain/Yet on this nondescript scroll is a purple wax seal/And observing by candle will reveal/The map to the place where the Emperor lies/And where lies the key under the dragon's eyes.'"*

"Could that be any more confusing?" Boyd asked. "What did that mean?"

"It means we're looking for a special scroll," Cindy said. "It looks the same as all the others, only instead of a red wax seal, it's got a purple wax seal. And when you look at it by candlelight, it will show you where the Emperor's tomb is located."

"Well, were are we gonna find a scroll from 221 B.C.?" Boyd asked. "It's probably lost."

"Actually, no," Ho Yin said. "Qin burned all books in China, but kept one copy for the state library."

"A book burner, eh?" Smelts said, rubbing his chin, as if he knew the sort. "He really *wasn't* a good man."

"Several of the scrolls from the Qin Dynasty are kept right here in Hong Kong at the Museum of Antiquities."

"We could go there and look for it," Reggie said.

"It's not that easy," Ho Yin said. "The government is very protective of its antiques. All the scrolls and other artifacts are located in a vault in the basement of the museum. Security is very tight and you'll need a special pass to even look at them."

"Oh, that won't be a problem," Smelts said, winking at Ho Yin. "You see, Reggie and Smelts always have a special pass."

"Oh, no," Ho Yin said. "You're not breaking into the museum."

"Come on," Reggie said. "It'll be just like old times. Back when the Himalayan Outback Detective Agency[77] was in full force."

"No," Ho Yin said. "You'll tear the place apart like you did that apartment building."

"We'll be careful," Reggie said, patting Ho Yin on the back.

"Do I get to eat before I go?" Smelts asked. "Seriously, mate, I ain't ate since about four this afternoon and I'm feelin' a bit peckish."

"We're in a hurry, Smelts," Reggie said.

"Well, blame it on that stupid, worthless, swordfish," Smelts said. "All that slappin' around got me famished. Look, what say I go and get me somethin' to eat really quickly and meet you all at the car? Okay? Okay!" He ran off in his odd, crocodile-like fashion, as Boyd, Reggie, and Ho Yin left Cindy and Bjorn alone to put the Machine together in the lab. Reggie led them through a secret door in the main foyer of the front hallway to a small, underground parking garage, where the limousine was waiting.

"I should warn you," Ho Yin said, "every single thing from the machine that Mr. Ping has found over the years has had some sort of booby-trap on it."

"Like what?" Boyd asked. "A bomb?"

"No," Ho Yin said, sounding concerned. "They've all been rather unusual. Mr. Ping suspected that this emperor used some sort of black magic to aid him in the creation of the machine, so there's really no telling what might happen. One time, after finding a piece, his fingers fell off."

Reggie and Boyd looked at Ho Yin as if he was crazy.

"They grew back," he said. "Another time, all of his hair fell out. And those times were with the *smaller* pieces."

"And the bigger pieces?" Boyd asked.

"Earthquakes, tsunamis, thunderstorms, the works."

"Wait, wait, wait," Boyd said. "Wasn't this just a *hobby* of Mr. Ping's? If we're risking earthquakes and lightning and that kind of stuff, why do we really need to do this?"

"Because this machine could get your parents back," Ho Yin said.

"Yeah, it's always gotta be something like that, doesn't it?" Boyd muttered.

Smelts ran down the stairs carrying a tray full of roasted chickens, which he began swallowing whole. "I'm ready," he said between swallows.

"Oh, do you have to do that in front of us?" Reggie asked, looking disgusted.

"No time," Smelts said, his mouth full as he chomped a chicken down, bones and all.

"Don't dally in there," Ho Yin said. "Try to find the scroll and get out. And remember that Fang's men have been looking out for you. You want to make sure and avoid trouble."

"Aw," Smelts said, licking his fingers clean. "Trouble's so much fun!"

"I'm serious."

"Will do, chief," Reggie said. "Come on, gang." The three of them jumped in the limo and drove off.

Mr. Ping had always known people kept a close watch on him so he established a hidden exit for his cars, whose door looked like a giant rock wall on the side of an ivy-covered hill. It enabled him to come and go without paying any mind as to who was watching. However over time, word spread of the secret entrance, and soon a select few of the dastardly, vile villains in his life had figured out the door's location, and as Boyd, Reggie, and Smelts left the grounds of the estate, there were two, beady eyes watching, and waiting in anticipation for any sign of life. This mysterious individual heard the cold, granite sound of the door slowly opening and observed as the headlights came on and the limousine began to wind its way down the hill.

He flipped a switch and dialed a number on his phone. As soon as his call was answered, he spoke in a low, guttural voice that sounded like thick wads of slime and mucus had permanently lodged themselves in his throat. "They're leaving," he said over the line. "Get ready."

CHAPTER 23

WHAT SORT OF EVIL THINGS ARE FOLLOWING US?

As evening settled in, Reggie was behind the wheel of the limousine as it made its way down the hill towards the center of Hong Kong, where the Museum of Antiquities was located. Coming down from the mansion into the city was breathtaking for Boyd. To be on a road that wound its way down from above the gargantuan skyscrapers was awe-inspiring. He stared out the window, fascinated at what lay below.

"Great views, eh?" Smelts asked. He was riding in the back of the limo with Boyd, his long tail curled up beside him.

"I've never seen anything like this city," Boyd said, staring out the window.

"Yeah, it ain't bad, is it?" Smelts said. "But if you want beautiful cities, might I suggest Buenos Aires. And, of course, my home turf,

Sydney. Although there's a lot of anti-crocodile sentiment down there, thanks to that bloke from the zoo who was always wrestlin' my mates on TV. Man, that guy was annoying."

They rode along in silence for a couple of minutes and Boyd had his first chance to really observe Smelts. He had the cool, remorseless look of a reptile, his skin craggy, his teeth jutting out from his mouth, his clawed hands and feet clicking when he walked, and yet there was one part of Smelts that made him different. His eyes. His eyes had a warmth about them that betrayed his reptilian origins. They were soft and expressive, where a snake or a lizard, or even another crocodile, might be cold and impassive.

"Seat belts on, boys," Reggie said over his shoulder from the driver's seat. "We've got trouble."

"What's up, Reg?" Smelts asked.

"Somebody's following us," Reggie said. "Can't tell who it is yet."

Smelts leaned over Boyd's shoulder to peer out the back window. "Ack!" he said. "It's that stupid swordfish!"

Boyd turned around to peer out the back window as well, and saw that there was a small, black car following them down the road. "Nobody's explained this whole 'swordfish' thing to me," Boyd said. "Shouldn't he be in the water?"

"He's a genetic anomaly," Reggie said from the front. "He was born without the ability to breathe in water, so he had to make his home outside of the ocean. It's kind of creepy, actually."

"Yeah," Smelts said. "He's a work-for-hire type. A freelancer. Really dangerous cat. I bet Mr. Fang is payin' his wages."

"This gets weirder by the second," Boyd said. "What do we do now?"

"Well, we lose him," Reggie said, and just as Boyd got his seatbelt snapped into place, he felt his center of gravity sink into the seat as Reggie floored it. Smelts, who hadn't buckled himself in yet went flying into the back window, nose-first.

"Thanks a lot, mate," he yelled up towards Reggie.

"I *told* you to buckle up," Reggie yelled.

Hedley was right behind and increased his speed to keep up with them. While he had one flipper on the steering wheel, he used his other flipper to dial his phone. "They're trying to get rid of me," he yelled over the roar of his engine. "You guys stand back. I'm going take them out myself!"

The road down from the Peak was like a giant roller coaster, curving back and forth, its large rock walls giving way to thick patches of trees and bushes, with the occasional apartment building sitting just below the cliffs. Reggie was driving as fast as he could, zipping back and forth, sending both Boyd and Smelts whipping to and fro in the backseat. "Cripes!" Smelts yelled. "Are ya' tryin' to kill us, man?"

"He's pretty crafty," Reggie yelled. "I can't seem to lose him and there's not a lot of detours I can take until we get into the city."

Boyd noticed that Smelts' naturally evergreen reptile skin was beginning to take on a lighter tint. "Are you okay?" he asked.

"Shouldn't have eaten that last chicken," Smelts said, holding his stomach. "I'm feelin' a bit carsick."

Boyd went silent as he envisioned what kind of horrible things a carsick crocodile might barf up everywhere. "Focus on the horizon," he said.

"He's gaining on us," Reggie said.

Boyd spun around to see Hedley's black car almost close enough to drive beside them. He darted back and forth across the road, working desperately to get beside the limo, but just as he would inch his way up beside the car, another car would come flying around the corner in the opposite direction, forcing him to whip back behind them.

After playing this game of cat and mouse for a few kilometers, Hedley caught up with them and pulled up beside the car with his window down. Boyd couldn't help but look out the window and was so fascinated with Hedley that he failed to realize that the swordfish was a threat no matter where he was. Hedley whipped his head around towards the window and smashed the glass with his long, sharp nose, narrowly missing Boyd's face.

"Give up the brat and nobody gets hurt!" he yelled, his head sticking out the window.

Being the hothead that he was, Smelts shoved his head out the window and snapped his long, iron-like jaws at Hedley, causing him to swerve the car to the left to avoid Smelts' choppers. In his attempt to dodge Smelts' snapping jaws, he almost went crashing into the hard, rock face of the cliff. Smelts laughed as he watched Hedley fall behind and attempt to regain control of the car. "You're lucky I missed!" Smelts yelled, still hanging out the window.

The flash of a small explosion erupted from the front of Hedley's car, and a large, slimy projectile went flying into Smelts' face, temporarily blinding him. He would have fallen out of the window had Boyd not grabbed him in time. "My eyes!" Smelts yelled, clawing at the black, slimy substance that covered his face. "I'm blind!"

"You're not blind," Boyd yelled, trying his best to pull the crocodile back into the car. "He shot you with some sort of..."

"Fish eggs!" Reggie yelled from the front. "He shot him with fish eggs. Now get in the car. He's dangerous."

Boyd finally pulled Smelts inside, just as he heard the gush of another volley of fish eggs go flying past his face. Smelts kept clawing the gooey, black eggs out of his eyes in the seat, trying to see again as his tail whipped back and forth. "They sting!" he yelled. "Ow, ow, ow!"

"You're going to be fine," Boyd said, disgusted with the eggs as they stuck to his hand. "I think you're overreacting."

"Easy for you to say," Smelts said, getting the last of the goo out of his eyes. At that moment, they heard the whoosh of a small missile whip past their window and explode on the sheer, rock face of the cliff in front of them with a loud boom.

"What was that?" Boyd asked. But he needn't ask, for he heard a large portion of rocks tumble down on the car, narrowly missing them in the avalanche.

"He's got missiles!" Reggie said. "This isn't good."

Reggie looked ahead on the road and saw that there were three, large, black SUVs approaching up the hill in front of them. They spun across the road, forming a road block in the narrow part of the lane. Hedley was still behind them and the path in front of them was blocked. "Uh-oh," he said. "Hold on to your hats, gang."

Reggie did a hard right and the limousine went crashing through a guardrail and down the grassy side of the hill. "What are you doing?" Smelts yelled. As the limousine bounced and careened down the side of the mountain, Reggie could see that they were headed straight for a cliff.

"This is gonna be rough," he said.

As the car sailed out into thin air, for a split second, Boyd looked out the window to see over a hundred feet between the car and the ground, and he felt, for the briefest of moments, a pang of regret as he thought about how unfair it was that he was going to die so soon in his young life. However, the thought was interrupted by the loud crash and clatter of the limo hitting solid ground. After righting himself in his seat, he realized that the limo was speeding across the roof of an apartment building.

"What in the world are you doing?" Smelts yelled. "Are you crazy?"

Reggie had driven the limousine off the side of a cliff, onto the roof of a long, narrow, eighteen-story apartment building. Boyd looked back to see Hedley's tiny black car follow along, jumping from the cliff to the roof of the building as well. "He's still behind us," Boyd yelled.

"Aw, no," Smelts said. "How are we gonna get off this roof?"

The car was still speeding along, getting closer and closer to the edge of the building. "It gets worse," Reggie said. "The brakes are out."

"What?" Boyd yelled, but even as he did, he felt the car crash through the edge of the roof, sailing through the air. But again, the limo would not be hitting the ground anytime soon, for it crashed right into the twin apartment building right beside the one from which they'd just left.

With a tremendous roar and the sound of crumbling concrete and breaking glass, the limousine crashed into the fifteenth floor apartment of an old Cantonese couple. The couple sat there, looking at the front half of the limousine that had just come through the wall of their living room. Reggie opened the door and stepped out of the car, brushing the dust from his fur.

"Hello," he said, smiling at the couple and pulling a card from his wallet. "We're sort of in a hurry right now, but here's my number. We'll be glad to pay for the damages." He then casually strolled around the limousine, observing that the back half of the vehicle was sticking out the side of the building, dangling fifteen stories above the ground. He leaned in on the driver's side to look back and see Boyd and Smelts looking somewhat shell-shocked.

"You guys okay?" he asked.

"That was awesome, Reg," Smelts said. "You okay, Boyd?"

"Yeah," Boyd said. "Just a little sore, is all."

A loud thump came from behind them and they looked out the back window to see that Hedley had jumped from the opposite building and landed on the back half of the car. With lightning speed, he used his sharp snout to shatter the glass of the back window and he started grabbing at Boyd. "Come here you ugly runt!" he yelled inside at him.

Smelts grabbed Boyd by the shirt and dragged him out through the front seat. "We should be going, mate," he said.

"You're dead meat, you little runt!" Hedley yelled, working his way in the back window.

Once Boyd was out, the three of them ran past the old couple and out the front door, into the hallway. "Elevator or stairs?" Reggie asked. He was answered by the familiar ding of the elevator door opening on their floor.

"That was easy," Smelts said.

They hopped into the elevator as they heard Hedley's gurgles of anger emanating from the apartment. As the doors of the elevator closed, there was an awkward silence, as the yeti, the crocodile, and the thirteen-year-old boy traveled down to the lobby, listening to the soothing strains of Cantonese muzak echoing though the cramped quarters.

"We're being chased by a swordfish," Boyd said.

"Yep," Reggie replied.

"That's true," said Smelts.

More silence.

"We just crashed the limousine into the fifteenth floor apartment of an old couple."

"Yep," Reggie replied.

"That was a good one," Smelts said.

More silence.

"This is turning into a very weird day," Boyd said.

"Yep," Reggie replied.

"Ain't it, though?" Smelts said.

A loud crash dented in the ceiling of the elevator as Hedley jumped on the roof. His sharp nose came jutting into the compartment as he began to cut his way into the elevator. "You're all going to be fish food tonight!" he yelled.

Reggie reached up and grabbed his nose, pulling his face into the roof of the elevator several times. Despite Hedley's howls of rage, Reggie held onto his nose, bending it sideways so that he couldn't free himself. Hedley struggled and strained, but could not pull his nose out. "Feel good, you worthless bottom feeder?" Reggie asked, looking at Hedley through a hole in the roof.

Hedley looked at him with his beady eyes and said, "If there's one thing you oughtta know, yeti, it's to never mess with a swordfish's nose!" He was so full of hate and anger that Boyd could barely understand him through his bile-filled throat.

A strange click and snap was heard, followed by the sound of some sort of metal object rolling across the roof of the elevator, towards one of the holes Hedley had made. "Say your prayers!" Hedley laughed as a hand grenade came falling through the ceiling. With an effort, he jerked his head upwards with all of his might, freeing his nose from Reggie's strong grasp.

Boyd looked at the tiny, black pineapple that was smoking on the floor in front of them and asked, "Is that what I think it is?"

Smelts whipped Boyd into his arms as Reggie used his mammoth, yeti strength to rip open the door of the elevator, and with incredible speed, they jumped to freedom into the hallway, narrowly avoiding an explosion that sent pieces of the elevator flying in all directions. Dust and debris began to settle on the ground as Boyd tried to catch his breath from the weight of Smelts landing on top of him. "You okay, mate?" Smelts asked him.

"Yeah," Boyd said between wheezes. "My ears are ringing."

"What floor are we on?" Smelts asked.

"Three," Reggie said, as he stared at the blackened, smoke-filled doorway to the elevator shaft. "Smelts," he said, "I want you to get Boyd out of here, now."

"What about you?" Smelts asked.

Through the smoke, Boyd could see the silhouette of Hedley appear in the hallway, waddling his way towards them on his tail, his head tilted downward in a threatening manner. "I'm having a little swordfish for dinner tonight," Reggie said, preparing for battle.

Smelts grabbed Boyd by the hand and dragged him towards the stairwell. "Come on, kiddo," he said. "We gotta get outta here."

"But what about Reggie?" Boyd asked.

"He'll be fine," Smelts said, and they disappeared down the stairs.

"You know I'm going to get that kid and have him for breakfast, right?" Hedley asked, licking his lips.

"Over my dead body," Reggie said, growling and bearing his huge, yellow fangs.

"I wouldn't have it any other way," Hedley said as he charged Reggie with his sharp nose. With unnatural quickness, Reggie dodged the swordfish like a bullfighter, stepping out of the way as his enemy charged past him.

Hedley spun around and assumed a defensive position, but Reggie just watched him, calmly. He noticed that Hedley had some sort of utility belt around his waist, from which he pulled a small, black ball. He threw it into the air and it exploded in a bright flash, leaving Reggie temporarily blinded, which was enough time for Hedley to whip around and pound Reggie in the stomach with his strong, thick tail. Reggie fell to the ground, dazed, and struggling to catch his breath as he tried to recover from the heavy blow.

Hedley was fast, and while Reggie was still blinded, he spun around behind him and tied his arms and legs together with a black cord. "One thing I've learned," he said, "is that in order to defeat a yeti, one cannot fight fair."

"Dirty tricks," Reggie said, struggling to free himself from the cord. "I should have expected as much from a swordfish."

Hedley casually waddled around to look Reggie in the eye. "You just remember that it was a lowly swordfish that took you down, yeti," he said. He began to walk away, speaking over his shoulder. "I'm going to let you live, just so you'll know that it was *you* who caused the death of that poor, innocent little boy."

"You'd best think again," Reggie said. Hedley turned around and saw that Reggie was now standing upright again, the black cord in pieces at his feet. "You're gonna have to do a lot better than that to take me down."

With a gurgle of rage, Hedley charged Reggie, stabbing at him repeatedly with his nose, but with the quickness of a cat, Reggie dodged all of his blows. On the last thrust, he grabbed him by the nose and swung his long, sleek body into the wall, leaving a giant indentation of a swordfish in the drywall.

Hedley fell to the ground, trying to catch his breath through his pulsing gills as Reggie stood over him. "Mercy," he said. "Please, offer me mercy..."

"Yeah," Reggie said. "You really deserve..."

Hedley cut him off as he whipped his tail against Reggie's legs, tripping him to the ground. He then jumped to his feet and stood over Reggie, jabbing his nose into the floor as he tried to stab his nemesis. "Arr!" he yelled, filled with glee in his attempts to maim Reggie.

Then, almost as if he sensed something amiss, Hedley looked down the hall to see the blur of what looked to be a giant wheel rolling straight towards him. The wheel unfolded itself and Smelts went flying into him. Smelts' dropkick sent Hedley tumbling backwards into the wall. He slid to the ground, rendered unconscious by the powerful blow. "That's what I think of swordfish," Smelts said, standing triumphantly in the hall. He offered a hand to help Reggie to his feet.

"I told you to get going!" Reggie said, glaring at both Smelts and Boyd. "I could have taken care of this guy."

"We don't leave our friends," Boyd said.

"Yeah," Smelts said. "We felt sorry for you."

"Felt sorry for *me?*" Reggie asked, a hint of annoyance in his voice.

"Don't start," Boyd said. "We've gotta get going. If that swordfish has been following us, then he's probably got more of his buddies on the way now. Not to mention the fact that the police are gonna be here any second to deal with the limo sticking out the side of the building. They might get a little freaked when they have to question a crocodile and a yeti."

"Good thinkin,'" Smelts said.

"The boy is smart," Reggie conceded.

So, the yeti, the crocodile, and the thirteen-year-old boy ran out of the building into the busy streets of Hong Kong, leaving the unconscious swordfish behind them in the hallway.

CHAPTER 24

DEAD ETIQUETTE

The afternoon began to creep across the city as Boyd, Reggie, and Smelts jogged down the sidewalks of Wan Chai, looking for a taxi to pick them up. Crowds on the street would part, panicked at the sight of the three of them, and this didn't help with the taxi situation. More than one taxi had sped away in a panic as Reggie approached them, frightened by the sight of a yeti with his arms waving in the air to get them to slow down and pick them up. One cab driver, who was cornered at a stoplight, burst from his taxi and fled down the street, screaming, "Yeti! Yeti! Yeti!"

As the last of the taxis sped away from them, Reggie stopped, tired and out of breath, on the sidewalk in front of a Thai food restaurant. "This is ridiculous," he said. "No taxi in this city is going to stop for the three of us. I, alone, look like their worst nightmares come true and that's not even including Smelts."

"Are you implying something about my looks, mate?" Smelts asked.

"No, no," Reggie said. "The bottom line is that we need someone reliable."

"Well, who could that be?" Boyd asked. "No taxi in this city will stop for us."

"Yeah," Smelts said. "And that stupid swordfish is gonna be comin' along any minute now."

"I have my connections," Reggie said, pulling a phone from his pocket and tapping in a number. "Hello, Xiao? It's Reggie...Yeah, it's been way too long...Listen, we're in a bit of a spot down here at Johnson's Road and Queen's Road East and we need a lift...Yeah... Yeah...Okay." Reggie turned to them and said, "We're in luck. He's in the area."

After a wait of around five minutes across from the prying eyes of a group of locals standing a safe distance across the street, Smelts said, "I think our ride is here."

Up to the curb pulled a taxi cab that in weight, shape and size looked very much like the thousands of taxis that circulated throughout the arteries of the city, only there was something a bit peculiar about this one. The main difference between this taxi and the ones Boyd was used to seeing was the fact that this one looked as if someone had rolled it off the side of a cliff. There were scrapes and dents and scratches all over it, and it looked as if it might fall apart at any time. It also had the usual markings of a taxi all over it, including the little sign on the roof and white writing on the doors. But upon closer inspection, it was obvious that all the writing on the cab was backwards and the windows were smoky, making it impossible to see inside. "That's our ride?" Smelts asked. "Why don't we just hop in the back of a garbage truck?"

"Garbage trucks aren't reliable," Reggie said. "*This* guy is reliable."

They ventured up to the cab and opened the back door, which was like opening the door to an ancient tomb as a major gust of white smoke burst forth from the cracks. It was as if the air inside the car had been trapped for centuries. Strange, creepy-crawly bugs began to make their way out from the inside, and Boyd saw several birds (although he was sure they were actually bats) flutter forth from the door to freedom.

"What kind of taxi is this?" Smelts asked.

"You're just going to have to trust me," Reggie said. "Get in."

"I'm not gettin' in there," Smelts said. "You go first."

"Fine," Reggie said. "Chicken!"

Reggie climbed into the taxi first, followed by Smelts and then Boyd. Once inside, Boyd could see that all the lurking suspicions he'd had about the interior were confirmed as he settled into his seat. The backseat was rotting away. In some places, the inside cushioning was exposed. In others, the very same cushioning was disintegrating away into a pulpy mess. Cobwebs hung from the ceiling and an eerie haze hung in the air that contained a putrid odor that was much worse than smoke. From beneath the seat in front of him, Boyd caught a glimpse of two, yellow eyes watching him from the shadows.

"Cor!" Smelts said as he shut the door. "I put my foot in something slimy!"

"Reggie! Good to see you!"

In all the time that Boyd spent examining the fragile and rotting interior, he failed to have a look at the driver. Had he done so, he would have been equally shocked. The driver was little more than a rotting skeleton dressed in ragged clothes and covered with dried, papery bits of flesh. As they settled into the taxi, he turned to stare at the three of them with a look that chilled Boyd's soul.

"Boys," Reggie said, "this is Xiao Ping. Xiao, this is Boyd and Smelts."

"Nice to meet you," Xiao said, his skeletal jaw clopping away. Boyd didn't really question how Xiao could speak to them with such sparse material for lips, but he'd accepted so much over the last few weeks, he figured it was only right to accept this as well. "Where to, Reg?" Xiao asked.

"The Museum of Antiquities," Reggie said. "And quick."

Because of his decaying skin, it was impossible to tell his ethnicity by looking at him, but Xiao's accent was unmistakably Cantonese. "In a hurry, are you?" Xiao asked.

"Yeah," Reggie said. "And keep an eye out. We don't want anyone to tail us."

"Right-o," Xiao said.

With a lurch and a crank and a rattle, the taxi took off and was quickly moving through the streets of Hong Kong, its horrible noise echoing the entire way. As they made their way through the city, Reggie rode along in content silence, staring out the window and watching the people on the street. Meanwhile, Smelts sat there petrified at the fact that there were now several creepy crawlies popping out from all sorts of holes and crevices of the backseat of the cab. Boyd just sat there examining Xiao, for he'd never seen the living dead before.

"So, uh, Xiao," he said, "you're dead, right?"

"Boyd!" Reggie said, scolding. "Don't pry."

"Really, it's okay, Reggie," Xiao said with a fractured smile. "It is true, Boyd. I am, in fact, dead."

Boyd paused for a couple of seconds before asking, "Uh, do you usually drive many people in your taxi?"

"Only the ones who can tolerate being driven around by the living dead," Xiao said in a cheery voice, "when I'm not cabbin' it through the city though, I'm sittin' at the bottom of a particularly steep gorge under a bridge on an abandoned road in the New Territories. Nobody's found me, yet."

"Oh," Boyd said. "That's too bad."

"Well," Xiao said, "it was my own stupidity. Anyway, I spend most of my time trying to get fares down here in the city, although no one really wants to give me any business. They're all too superstitious. Ha! Like they don't ride with other members of the walking dead and don't know about it!"

"Xiao and I knew each other when he was alive," Reggie said. "I went to his funeral. How long ago was that?"

"Beats me," Xiao said. "Twenty years or so? It was right around the time of your hundredth birthday party."

Boyd was a bit shocked at Reggie's age. "You're over a hundred years old?" he asked.

Reggie looked a little bit perturbed at the charge. "Boyd," he said, "don't you know *anything* about yetis?"

"Hey, lay off him," Smelts said. "I can think of much more important things to study in school than *yeti* history."

"Like what?" Reggie asked.

"English, math, science," Smelts said, counting off on his fingers. "He could study reptiles."

"Does every conversation we have need to be about you?" Reggie asked, before turning back to Boyd. "Yetis can live to be well-over three hundred years old, Boyd. Some live even longer than that. We don't really know why. We just know that they do."

"And how old are you?" Boyd asked.

"I'm one hundred and seventy-five," he said.

"I'm seventy-five years old," Smelts said.

"I would have been seventy years old last week," Xiao said. "But since I've been dead, I've started counting backwards. So now, I'm thirty years old."

"What's it like living so long, Reggie?" Boyd asked. "I mean, it seems like it would be great."

"It's got its pros and cons," Reggie said. "Time is relative, you know. What might seem like a long time to you isn't very long to me. It's amazing to live such a long life, but it can also be horrible. I guess the worst part about it is seeing people you love pass away. Having lived so long, I've seen many bright, shining people move on. Some of them were my best friends, including Mr. Ping. But then, I just kind of operate by the notion that you should really enjoy the life you lead now."

The three of them rode along in silence for the next few minutes, trying to absorb the wisdom that Reggie was trying to impart to them. However, all philosophical introspection was shattered when Xiao said, "Hey, I'm *dead,* you fools, and *I'm* still alive. Reggie's argument doesn't make any sense. Explain that!"

Needless to say, none of them could explain why Xiao still seemed to be alive, even though his body was, quite clearly, as dead as it could be at that moment.

"How was it you died again?" Boyd asked him

"Boyd," Reggie said, "you're really going to have to brush up on your dead etiquette."

"Dead etiquette?" Boyd asked.

"There are certain questions that are considered rude to ask the dead."

"Huh?"

"Think of it, Boyd," Smelts added. "It could be mighty embarrassing to a person if they died in a peculiar way. Like what if they were chopped in half on a Ferris wheel, or died because they ate too many cheese fries?"

Reggie looked at Smelts seriously and said, "Did you really just say that?" He turned back to Boyd and said, "Mr. Ping wrote extensively about etiquette with the dead[78]. It's in his almanac. Volume sixty-three, I believe."

"Ah, don't be too hard on the kid," Xiao said from the front. "I can't say I wouldn't be intrigued about how I might have died, had I been in his shoes."

"So how did you die?" Boyd asked.

Reggie and Smelts began squirming in their seats, as if Boyd had made a huge error in judgment. "Boyd," Reggie said. "Please stop."

"Why?" Boyd asked. "He said he didn't mind."

"There are...other reasons," Smelts said. "Just don't."

"Ah, ah, ah," Xiao said. "You guys know the rules. Pipe down." Reggie and Smelts sat there in perturbed silence, giving Xiao the Evil Eye. "Now," Xiao said. "What was it you wanted to ask me?"

"How did you die?" Boyd asked.

Thunder rolled across the horizon and the sky seemed to grow a bit darker. The clouds moved over the sun as Xiao ground the cab to a halt in the middle of the road. He turned around to Boyd and said, "*That's* three."

"Three what?" Boyd asked.

"*For everything ye know of me, you must now answer these questions three,*" he said.

"Questions three?" Boyd asked.

"We *told* you to stop!" Reggie said. "But did you listen? *No!*"

"What in the world are you guys talking about?" Boyd asked. All eyes in the car seemed to be upon him.

"If you'd followed Reggie's advice," Xiao said, "you would have discovered that to ask a dead person how they died three times gives the dead person the opportunity to switch bodies with the asker of the question."

"You're gonna switch bodies with me?" Boyd asked, swallowing hard.

"If you get any of the following three questions wrong, your body is *mine!*" Xiao cackled.

"Wonderful," Smelts said to Reggie. "I thought this guy was on *our* side."

"How was I supposed to know Boyd was going to break the rules?" Reggie said.

"Silence in my cab!" Xiao yelled, and thunder roared through the glass and steel canyons of the city. He turned around in his seat and raised his bony index finger to signify the first question for Boyd. "All right," he said. "Question number one: What is your father's middle name?"

"Oh, man," Smelts said, looking defeated. "I could *never* answer that question."

"Cooper," Boyd said.

"Argh!" Xiao said, slamming his fist on the seat in anger. "That one usually gets them."

"My father and I have the same middle name," Boyd said. "If you want to switch souls with me, you're going to have to do better than that."

"Fine, fine," Xiao said. He put his finger to his chin to think.

"You know," Reggie said, "we're kind of in a hurry, Xiao."

"Pipe down, you!" Xiao said, annoyed. "You think these opportunities come along every day? I need time to think!" He paused for a few seconds, as if he were examining his surroundings for inspiration. "Okay, okay," he said, turning to Boyd. "Name the capital of Canada."

"Ottawa," Boyd said, looking at Xiao as if he were crazy. "Are these questions for real? I'm Canadian!"

"You are?" Xiao asked. "Ai yo! I thought you were American! Americans never know a thing about Canada."

"That's two," Smelts said. "Make this last one quick."

"Okay," Xiao said, "but if he fails on this last question, then his soul is forever doomed to this decrepit, rotting flesh that is mine. Got it?"

"Hey," Boyd said, turning to Smelts and Reggie in a perturbed manner. "Why didn't you guys warn me about this?"

"If we warned you," Reggie said, "then the dead person can take the soul of the person who warned you. We couldn't risk it. There are rules, you know. You can't break the rules."

"Thanks a lot," Boyd said.

"All right," Xiao proclaimed. "Now comes question three! A question so simple, yet so astoundingly hard, it's like a riddle, wrapped up in some sort of enigmatic puzzle that can't be conjured…or something like that."

"JUST ASK THE QUESTION!" Boyd, Smelts and Reggie yelled at the same time.

Looking a bit taken aback, Xiao composed himself and said, "What is your *father's middle name?*"

"Cooper," Boyd said. "Let's go."

"You already asked that question," Smelts said.

"I did?" Xiao asked, genuinely shocked. "Oh, no! I *did!*"

"Way to go," Reggie said.

"No!" Xiao said. "That's not fair! I deserve another question."

"Forget it," Reggie said.

"And you know the rules now, Xiao," Smelts said.

"No!" Xiao said. "Give me another chance!"

"I'm sorry, but that's not in the rule book," Reggie said. "You know what you've got to do."

"Okay," Xiao said.

"What does he have to do?" Boyd asked.

"If he can't stump you with a question," Reggie said, "then he has to pledge his undying loyalty to you for one year and no longer."

Xiao threw up his hands in defeat. "You got me, kid," he said. He raised his skeletal hand and said, "I hereby pledge my undying loyalty to you for the next year, blah, blah, blah."

"Does this mean we don't have to pay the fare?" Smelts asked.

"Don't rub it in," Xiao said to himself as he headed on down the road, filled with depression. The chance of the century had slipped by him. It wasn't every day that a dead person found a gullible thirteen-year-old to trick out of their body. Now, he was forced to wait even longer to end his torment.

They arrived at the museum just before closing time. The museum was in a large, modern building tucked next to a small park. It looked as if some avant-garde architect had spent way too much time designing it, for it was full of strange and unusual angles, with bizarre sculptures in a fountain in the front, and large, glass windows that seemed to be in odd places. They bought tickets just before closing time from a stunned ticket-taker and continued to make their way inside.

"So what now?" Boyd asked as they strolled down the marble foyer, past the watchful eyes of the tourists and employees.

"Now," Smelts said, rubbing his leathery paws together, "We scope the place out. Or, as we refer to it in the cat-burgling business, we *case the joint.*"

"You were never a cat burglar," Reggie said.

"No, but I've burgled some," Smelts said. "Cats sure are tasty."

"What Smelts is talking about," Reggie told Boyd, "is that we need to go in and see what kind of security system the building has. If we're going to get the scroll, then we have to know what we're dealing with."

"Yeah," Smelts said. "So we *case the joint.*"

"Would you stop?"

They began to wander through the building like tourists. To Boyd, it felt like Reggie and Smelts were just checking out the exhibits and he began to get a little bit bored, wondering if this was just an excuse for the two of them to go to a boring museum. Occasionally, they would walk over and whisper something to each other, but otherwise, they simply seemed to be enjoying an evening stroll.

Finally, they converged in a small hallway beside a very non-nondescript door with a keypad on the wall beside it. "This is it," Smelts said.

"This is what?" Boyd asked.

"This is where the entrance to the warehouse is," Reggie said.

"It's just a door," Boyd said.

"It's a door," Smelts said, somewhat exasperated, "that leads to a basement, inside of which is a vault, that contains the scrolls."

"Oh," Boyd said. "Well, why didn't you just say so?"

"Excuse me," said a voice.

Reggie and Smelts immediately spun around into a defensive stance, but were quite embarrassed to see that it was only a security guard. The guard looked stunned, not only from their defensive postures, but also because he was now face to face with a yeti and a crocodile. "Uh...the...uh...museum is now closed," he stammered. "You'll have to be leaving now."

"Oh, right," Smelts said, walking by the guard as he patted him on the back. "No worries, mate. We were just going."

As they walked out of the museum, Reggie and Smelts began to pick apart the security system, using technical terms that made Boyd feel as if they were speaking another language. "They had an open source system running the security," Smelts said. "Probably

'Whaletooth[79]' or 'Wirecage[80].' Did you see the interface at the workstation?"

"It was 'Whaletooth,'" Reggie said. "It'll be easy to hack. The problem is those H-71s[81]. We've got to hope they're not heat sensitive."

"Or that they've got a two-twenty aural recognition and attack neutralizer trigger."

"Oh, I'm sure they don't have that, or this place would be a walking tomb."

They exited the museum and stood on the front steps as a storm began to blow in over the horizon, whipping up the trees on the sidewalk entrance around them. There was a sick feeling in the pit of Boyd's stomach, as if he could feel that something dreadful was waiting on them in the basement of that museum. Reggie and Smelts seemed very nonplussed about the whole affair, but Boyd didn't. He felt like this was going to be much harder than it seemed. Still, he knew that he and Cindy were his parents' only hope.

They walked down into the village and bought some noodles as they waited for the sun to go down and their work to begin.

CHAPTER 25

YOUR AVERAGE, REFINED, CULTURED WEREWOLF

Hedley was angry that he had lost Boyd on the road down from the mansion. Mr. Fang had given him a large amount of money to hire his crew and he had hoped to capture Boyd himself, keep all the money, and then send his crew back home. Alas, he couldn't capture Boyd and he now found himself waiting in a warehouse at the dockyards for his "special" handlers to arrive.

He waddled back and forth in the vast, empty warehouse, feeling bitter that a thirteen-year-old kid and his cronies had outsmarted him. After all, he was the world's greatest hit-man, the person that hundreds of the most evil people in the world relied upon to do their dirty deeds, the most deadly, skilled, vile, disgusting, air-breathing swordfish on the planet. The more Hedley thought about Boyd McCloyd, the angrier he got, and he knew that strangling this thirteen-year-old boy was going to be sweeter than any of the thousands of people he'd strangled before in his life.

The buzz of an alarm echoed through the empty space, and immediately, the garage doors at the far end of the building opened to let four black SUVs cruise inside. Hedley waited patiently at the far end as they rolled to a stop near him and shut off their engines. The doors opened and twelve large, ferocious, wolf-like creatures, all dressed in classy business suits, emerged from the vehicles.

They were hideous, with beady, yellow eyes, long snouts, and imposing fangs protruding from their mouths. Yet unlike real wolves, they walked on their hind legs, like humans. Their shoulders were wide, giving them the look of a creature that was very strong, and yet as agile as a tiger.

A particularly fierce-looking creature in a blue, pinstriped suit and red tie, walked up to Hedley with a large cigar in his mouth. "Well, well, well," he said, his voice low and raspy. "Haven't heard from you in a while, Hedley."

"I'm usually a one man job, Neville," Hedley said, giving him a smarmy smile. "But this one's big."

"Big, eh?" Neville said. "It must be if you brought me and my whole crew here. I guess when the going gets rough, you've gotta call in the big boys, don't you?"

"Now, look," Hedley said, angrily pointing a flipper at him. "I don't like working with you werewolves. Never have. So, don't start pulling that macho stuff with me. Got it? You work for me! I write the checks."

"Fine, fine," the werewolf said. "But just so you know, we don't accept checks. Only cash or major credit cards. But we prefer cash."

"Whatever," Hedley said, rolling his eyes.

"So what's the plan?" Neville asked.

"Ever heard of Confucius Ping?" he asked.

"Yeah, why?"

"We've got a little kidnapping job that's gonna happen. Kid named Boyd McCloyd."

"You want us to kill him?" Neville asked, licking his lips.

"Did you not listen to me?" Hedley asked, annoyed. "I want you to *kidnap* him. Kidnap! That means *alive,* not dead. Crimony, you werewolves can be idiots."

"Look," Neville said, trying to explain things calmly. "Sometimes in the frenzy of the hunt, my boys can get a little bit overeager. I just want you to know in case something happens."

"Unacceptable," Hedley said, shaking his head back and forth. "You kill that kid, you don't get paid. Understand? You can kill only when I *say* you can kill."

"I'm just telling you," Neville said, still trying to get his point across. "Accidents happen."

"If anybody kills the kid, it's gonna be me," Hedley said.

"Excuse me," one of the other werewolves said, raising his hand to speak. "What if we just maim him? Nothin' deadly, but I think a swift claw stroke across the face might be nice."

"Yeah, or perhaps rippin' off an arm or a hand," said the one beside him. "He'd be all right w'out a hand."

"Well, if you reep off one 'and, you might as well reep off the othah," added a third. "You gots to retain the balance, you see…"

"None of that," Hedley said. "No ripping off of the hands."

"Well, what about blunt trauma to the head?" said the first werewolf again. "You know, like smashin' his head with a brick or a large rock?"

"Yeah," piped in a fourth. "Not necessarily to kill the little chap or anything. Just a little brain damage."

"And then maybe a claw stroke across the face," said another one.

"Yeah," one said.

"That would be swell," said another.

"No!" Hedley yelled. "No claw strokes, no blunt traumas, no injuries! Your job is to bring the boy in alive and unharmed! Do you understand?"

"You hear that boys?" Neville said, turning to his other werewolves. "It's a flower job. Treat the kid like a delicate flower."

"An edible delicate flower?" one asked.

"No," Neville said. "A pretty flower you'd like to give to your mother or girlfriend. That's how you treat the kid."

"Me mum would have preferred a hand more than a flower," said one werewolf.

"Or blunt trauma," said a second.

"Are you gonna be able to control these guys?" Hedley asked, extremely annoyed.

"We're professionals," Neville said. "You just tell us what to do and we'll do it."

"Then pack up," Hedley said. "We're leaving in an hour."

As they got into their cars, one of the werewolves said to another, "Did he say yes to the blunt trauma? I forget…"

CHAPTER 26

THE STINK, THE SUBWAY, AND THE NEAR-DEATH EXPERIENCE

As evening settled in on Hong Kong and a violent storm rolled over the horizon, Boyd found himself sneaking down an alley as Reggie pulled three black suits from his backpack. He handed one to each of them and they slipped into their suits while approaching a storm grate that sat next to the building. Boyd began to feel hip and stealthy, like a ninja or some sort of special operations agent, but all of those feelings vanished when he saw exactly what Reggie and Smelts were doing.

Reggie bent down and ripped the heavy iron grating from the drain tossing it over to the side. "What's going on?" Boyd asked.

"Climb in," Reggie said, motioning for Boyd to hop into the drain.

"*What?*"

"How do you expect us to get in the museum?" Smelts asked, patting him on the back in a good-natured way. "Knock on the front door?"

"Well, no," Boyd said. "But couldn't we try the roof?"

"Not with the Extrapolating P-92 sensors[82] they've got up there," Reggie said, strapping on a belt full of tools. "No way would we get by those."

"It's a pretty sophisticated museum," Smelts said. "We've got to go in *this* way."

Boyd looked at the slimy, gunk-encrusted, trash-ridden hole that Reggie stood over and felt a wave of anxiety wash over him. "I've never been in a sewer before," he said.

"Well, then, this should be fun," Smelts said, disappearing down into the hole.

"After you, Boyd," Reggie said with a smile, delighting in Boyd's squeamishness.

"But...look at it," Boyd said.

"You think it *looks* bad," Smelts yelled from below, "You should *smell* it."

"Maybe you guys should go without me," Boyd said.

Reggie sighed and said, "I figured I'd have to do this."

He reached over and picked Boyd up by the shirt, carrying him over his shoulder as he descended the metal ladder down into the storm drain. Boyd held his breath in the darkness as long as he could, but he soon had no choice but to take the foul air into his lungs, and when the stench of the tunnels below the street hit his nose, he began to wish he didn't have to breathe at all. All the horrible smells that had ever visited his nose seemed to have formed a team and bombarded him all at once.

"Sheesh!" Reggie said, taking a deep breath. "That's some putrid stench!"

"Paris was worse," Smelts said, shining his flashlight around on the moldy walls.

"Paris was pretty bad," Reggie said. "But London tops my list."

"Ooo, right," Smelts said. "London was pretty bad."

"Do you guys travel the world to smell the sewers or something?" Boyd asked, holding his nose.

"Ha, ha," Reggie said. "Very funny. Let's get going."

They walked down the tunnel, their rubber boots splishing and splashing in the water. Smelts led the way, meticulously counting the shafts that darted off in all directions from the main tunnel. On occasion, Boyd would step in something in which his foot would softly sink a couple of inches, and he prayed that he would never know what horrible thing it was. However, as much as Boyd had no desire to be walking through the Hong Kong sewers, the rats in the tunnel were delighted by their arrival and were chattering away the whole time, welcoming Boyd by scattering over his feet every chance they got.

It was so dark in the tunnels and they made so many twists and turns, Boyd felt sure that he could stay lost down there for several days. He elected that his safest bet was to stay close to Reggie, and he kept a white knuckle grip on the tail of his shirt (a grip that also kept him from taking a dip in the muck below when he would occasionally slip).

Finally, they arrived at a metal door with a large, round handle, like the door on the inside of a submarine. Smelts checked the number above the door with his flashlight. "Thirty-eight B," he said. "This is it."

He wrapped his reptilian paws around the handle and pulled with all of his might, but it failed to budge. He glanced at Boyd and Reggie out of the corner of his eye, a little bit embarrassed at his inability to open the door, before attacking the handle a bit more fiercely. Still, it wouldn't move.

"Well," Boyd said, "looks like we're out of luck. We'd best get back to the mansion."

Reggie edged past him with an annoyed look on his face. "Let me see that," he said. He wrapped his massive hands around the handle and it spun open.

"Show off," Smelts muttered.

As Smelts shined his flashlight in the hole, it looked like just another tunnel to Boyd. It was a bit more dry and the air seemed fresher, but a tunnel, nonetheless. Then a high-pitched wail burst forth and bright light filled the passage. Smelts jerked his head from the doorway just in time to keep it from getting whacked by the subway train that roared past them. The noise was deafening, but it was quickly over and the dust began to settle in its aftermath.

"That was close," Smelts said.

"We should watch out for trains," Reggie said.

"Wow!" Smelts said. "What a *brilliant* deduction!"

"Don't start, you two," Boyd said. "I want to get out of this sewer before I turn fourteen."

"Good call," Smelts said, and he climbed into the subway tunnel. There was a walkway on the side of the tunnel for the first twenty meters, but then it got narrow and their only choice was to walk along the tracks.

"How much further do we have to go, Smelts?" Reggie asked. "This is pretty dangerous."

"About fifty meters," Smelts said. "That's where the service entrance is."

"Well, when do you expect the next train through?" Boyd asked.

"The trains run about every five minutes," he said, checking his watch. He shined his flashlight into the darkness ahead and looked around. "This tunnel looks pretty straight, but you never know. I'll run ahead to find the door and when you hear me yell, you guys can come along. I'll watch for trains."

Boyd and Reggie looked at each other as though it wasn't such a good idea, but they said nothing. "Be careful," Reggie said. "Sometimes you do stupid things and I don't want this to be one of those times."

"No worries, mate," Smelts said. "If there's a train comin,' you can feel the wind being pushed toward you. There'll be plenty of time to duck out of the way."

He smiled and saluted the two of them, then took off down the subway tunnel. They listened as he padded his way off into the distance, and eventually the sound and light disappeared and they were forced to sit in silence, listening for him. They heard nothing for the longest time.

"How long do we wait?" Boyd asked.

"I don't know," Reggie said. The two of them were starting to get impatient as the minutes dragged. In the silence of the subway tunnel, Boyd lost track of how long they'd actually been waiting. It felt like an eternity.

"What has that stupid croc got himself into this time?" Reggie muttered. He waited a couple more minutes before sighing and rising to his feet. "I guess I've gotta go get him," he said.

"Wait!" Boyd said, stopping him from going deeper into the tunnel. "You're not leaving me here."

"It's safer here," Reggie said.

"No way, uh-uh," Boyd said, following him onto the tracks. "No way am I getting left down in these tunnels alone. No, sir."

"Fine," Reggie said with a sigh. "I'm supposed to be looking out for you and this is what I have to deal with."

"Oh, complain, complain," Boyd said, dismissing his gripes.

"Stay close," Reggie said. "If a train comes, I don't know if we'll have time to get out of the way."

"Gotcha," Boyd said.

They creeped into the tunnel and onto the train tracks as slowly as possible, making a special effort to avoid the electrified steel of the rails. It was quiet in the tunnel, a bit too quiet for anyone to feel comfortable, and all they could hear was each other breathing. "Having fun yet?" Reggie asked as they walked along.

"This is fun?" Boyd asked. "I almost barfed from the smell back there. To me, that's not fun."

"Yeah, it'll do that sometimes," he laughed.

"You have such a strong sense of smell," Boyd said. "Why didn't it bother you?"

"To a yeti," Reggie said, "aromas are simply the everyday spices of the world. I find them to be neither good nor bad. The only thing that drives me bonkers is the smell of yak butter[83]. Can't stand it."

"What's yak butter?"

"It's Tibetan food," Reggie said. "My reasons for hating it are better left unsaid."

After what seemed to be an inordinately long amount of time, Boyd began to get nervous. They'd been walking along through the tunnel for a distance that seemed much further than the fifty meters that Smelts had spoken of and still they'd seen no door. "Where do you think this thing is?" he asked.

"I don't know," Reggie said, through clenched teeth. "This happens every time. I swear that crocodile doesn't have an ounce of common sense. If I…"

Reggie went silent as the breeze gently brushed up against his face. Boyd, too, got quiet, knowing what the breeze meant. "Do you feel that?" he asked.

"This doesn't bode well," Reggie said, turning around to go back the way they came. "Come on, Boyd."

They began to trot back down the tunnel as the wind picked up at their backs. "We sure walked a long way," Boyd said.

"I didn't realize how far we'd come," Reggie said, a hint of fear in his voice.

At that point, the only thing to warn them of any danger was the gentle breeze that wafted through the tunnel, but then they felt the vibrations from the tracks and they heard the roar of the train back behind them. "I guess it's getting close," Boyd said.

"We'd best quicken our pace, mate," Reggie said, and their gentle trot became an urgent jog. As the light from the subway rounded the corner in the distance, their urgent jog became a run, and as the train bridged the distance between them, their run became a desperate panic. "No time to dally," Reggie yelled over the roar of the train as he scooped Boyd up in his arms and ran as fast as he could.

Boyd kept bouncing on Reggie's shoulder and had a bird's eye view of the train as it soared down the tunnel towards them. "It's gaining on us," he yelled. "Go faster!"

"I'm trying! I'm trying!" Reggie said, huffing and puffing his way forward, desperately trying to get back to where they were.

Just as the train was on the verge of overtaking them, Smelts burst from the side of the tunnel, tackling both Reggie and Boyd into a doorway that stood on the side of the tracks, just out of sight. The subway cars roared past the open doorway, whipping up dust and wind all around them.

Reggie and Boyd sat on the floor, trying to catch their breath as Smelts stood over them, his hands perched on his hips as if he was annoyed at them both. "What in the world were you doing?" he yelled. "Are the two of you completely daft?"

"Where were you?" Reggie asked, struggling to get to his feet.

"Here!" Smelts said. "I told you I'd yell at you when I was ready."

"Well, we waited forever!" Reggie said.

"I had to get the door open to make sure it was safe," he cried. "Then I went inside to look things over real quick. You must have walked right past me. I didn't hear you."

"Well, you almost got us killed," Reggie said, folding his arms across his chest and turning away from him.

"*I* didn't almost get you killed," Smelts said. "*You* almost got you killed, because you didn't follow directions."

"Stop it!" Boyd yelled. "At first, I enjoyed your witty banter, but now I just find it exhausting. We've got a job to do while we're here and the longer you two keep bickering, the longer I have to stay down here in these stinky, dirty, smelly, slimy sewers, and to be quite honest, I'm not enjoying it. So, can we just get along?"

"Sure," Smelts said.

"Of course," Reggie said. The two of them looked a little bit embarrassed to have been reprimanded by a thirteen-year-old.

"Good," Boyd said. "Now what do we do?"

CHAPTER 27
UNWANTED, FURRY, DROOLING GUESTS

A large amount of time had passed since Boyd, Reggie and Smelts had left the mansion to look for the scrolls at the museum, and Ho Yin was getting worried. It was now well past midnight and he had heard nothing from them for hours. Thus, he had been pacing back and forth in the labs for an inordinate amount of time as Cindy and Bjorn worked to put the machine together.

"I'm sure they're fine, Ho Yin," Cindy said, trying to be reassuring.

"Me, too, think they're also," Bjorn said through his computer.

"Thinking and knowing are two different things," Ho Yin said. "There are so many ways they could get into trouble out there, so many dangers and enemies and traps and tricks. I should have never let them go out by themselves. I'm such a fool."

"You can't be everything to everybody all the time," Cindy said.

Try as she might, her words failed to calm Ho Yin and he kept pacing back and forth. Finally, an alarm signaling someone's arrival at the mansion snapped him out of his funk. "That must be them," Cindy said. "I can't wait to hear Boyd's story on this one. He probably complained the whole time."

Ho Yin said nothing as they walked through the mansion to the garage, listening to Cindy and Bjorn prattle on and on. "After all of this job, me need a ham sandwich," Bjorn said.

"A ham sandwich would be nice, wouldn't it?" Cindy said.

"Yes, it very would," Bjorn said. "With relish."

"Eeew!" Cindy said.

They came to the secret entrance into the garage and walked down the spiral staircase to where the cars were parked. The only problem was that there was no car parked where it should have been. "I thought you said they came in through the garage," Cindy said.

Ho Yin looked deadly serious. "That's where the sensors showed they entered," he said.

Cindy scanned the large garage, looking past the cars to see if anyone was there. "I don't see them," she said.

"And me no smell them," Bjorn said.

"That's because they're not here," Ho Yin said. His eyes were like a nervous cat, scanning his surroundings for danger. "Cindy, Bjorn," he said, "I want both of you to back out of here slowly and do exactly what I say."

"Why?" Cindy asked, a look of fear passing over her face.

"Because we're not alone in here," Ho Yin said.

As they began to back out of the large, underground garage, Cindy scanned the room with her eyes, looking for something wrong. It was the large shadow in the far corner of the room that caught her eye. "Ho Yin," she whispered. "What's that?"

He looked at her grimly and said, "A werewolf."

"Little pig, little pig, let me come in," came a voice.

As they reached the top of the stairs, they saw a ferocious werewolf walk out from behind a column at the far end of the garage.

It was Neville dressed in a very dapper business suit that betrayed the manic, crazed look in his glowing yellow eyes. "Shall I huff and puff for you?" he asked, drool dripping from his sharp, fanged mouth.

"You shouldn't be here," Ho Yin said. "I thought we put you werewolves in your place back in London. Do you really want to suffer the same humiliation[84]?"

"Ah, Ho Yin," Neville said, "the last time, you had Mr. Ping on your side. And the last time I checked, good, old Mr. Ping had kicked the bucket. True?" Neville began to walk towards them as several other werewolves emerged from the shadows.

"There's more than one," Cindy whispered, terrified.

"You need to do something," Ho Yin said, pulling a key from around his neck to give to Cindy. "Find crate 2368."

"What?" Cindy asked, confused.

"You'll see," he said.

"The thing is, Ho Yin," Neville continued, "we're here for Boyd McCloyd. Our job is to take him out." He flashed a wicked smile at the three of them and said, "Everyone else is just part of the dinner menu."

In a flash, all the werewolves were running for the stairs on all fours, moving towards them quickly. "Bjorn," Ho Yin yelled, "get Cindy out of here! Now!"

Bjorn snagged Cindy's shirt by the collar and dragged her out the door, down the hall, leaving Ho Yin behind on the stairs. As the werewolves began to ascend the stairs behind Neville, Ho Yin loosened a chain from the railing and whipped it around his shoulders like a weapon. "You've got to go through me to get to them," he said.

"I was hoping you'd say that," Neville said, charging after him. Just as quickly, Ho Yin whipped the chain around, sending a stinging blow to Neville's face. He yelped in pain and was distracted long enough for Ho Yin to whip around and kick him right off the balcony of the stairs, down onto the windshield of the car below.

The other werewolves paused for a second, each one shocked to see their leader taken out so soon. All the while, Ho Yin stood defiantly at the top of the stairs, the chain pulled tightly between his hands as he stared down his assailants. "Who's next?" he asked.

Meanwhile, Cindy was being dragged down the hallway by Bjorn, kicking and screaming the whole way. "Let me go, Bjorn," she yelled. "I can run on my own!" But Bjorn didn't listen to her. He continued dragging her all the way to the far end of the mansion and up the stairs to a small, guest bedroom. He then slapped his paw on the center of a painting of Mr. Ping that hung above the fireplace, and the back of that fireplace gave way, revealing a secret tunnel.

Bjorn released her and quickly typed, "In there! Go!"

"I'm not leaving you," Cindy said.

Bjorn huffed, and with his big head, he shoved her backwards into the fireplace. She fell into the tunnel with a thump. "Bjorn!" she yelled, but it was too late. Bjorn had already pressed the secret button in the painting and the door swung closed. "Bjorn!" she yelled, beating on the concrete.

She found herself in a long tunnel just big enough to walk through and lit by floodlights. She put her ear to the wall where Bjorn had been and called out his name several more times, but she heard nothing. For a second or two, she felt like she might burst into tears, but then her rational mind took over and she steeled herself.

Knowing that this was all part of Ho Yin's plan, she began to walk through the tunnel, down the narrow passage. At the far end, she came to a set of stairs that led downward, into the darkness. She realized that the tunnel must lead to someplace important.

She knew that Ho Yin would not have sent her here if there wasn't a purpose to what she was doing, and she assumed that something lay at the bottom of the stairs. Although she felt a great pang of regret at leaving both Ho Yin and Bjorn behind, she knew that she had a purpose. She took off down the ever descending stone staircase until she came to a door at the bottom. The door was made of thick wood and reinforced with steel joints, looking like the entrance to some sort of castle.

Assuming that the key that Ho Yin had given her was for the door, she used it on the lock and the large door swung open. Inside was something that Cindy wasn't expecting at all. There before her lay a vast, underground warehouse filled with thousands upon thousands of wooden crates. Like all the exhibits in the mansion upstairs, each of the wooden crates in front of her was labeled on the side with its contents. One large crate was labeled, ***Hamster Rations, 1958***[85]. Another said, ***Giant, Man-Eating Flying Lizard Repellent***[86], while the biggest one was labeled, ***Head of Japanese Man-o-Bot™, 1968***[87].

Cindy assumed that all the crates in this subterranean warehouse were things that Mr. Ping was unable to display in the mansion or extra supplies. Yet, there were thousands of crates here, and if Ho Yin expected her to find something with which she could deal with the werewolves, he sure had a lot of faith in her abilities.

Okay, she thought, ***Find crate 2368. It can't be that hard...can it?***

CHAPTER 28

YETI-HEIST

Boyd was standing with Reggie and Smelts in a small, stuffy, concrete room that they had entered from the subway tunnel. The lack of space filled him with a vague sense of claustrophobia, especially with two large individuals like Reggie and Smelts crammed inside with him. A couple of big pipes ran along the walls and a few cobwebs that looked as though they'd been abandoned a long time ago hung from the ceiling.

"There's a narrow service tunnel that runs right up into the museum just up there," Smelts said, pointing to a ladder that led upwards into the darkness. "I climbed a ways to see how far we could go, but they've got some metal grating about four meters into the tunnel and I couldn't get it open."

"No problem," Reggie said, climbing the ladder. "You might watch out below."

Sure enough, Boyd heard a grunt and growl and clang and crack, as the metal grating fell down the tunnel onto the floor in front of them. "Well, that's that," Smelts said, climbing after Reggie.

"Never underestimate the value of brute strength," Reggie said, looking down from the hole above them.

Through another metal door at the top of the ladder was the basement of the museum, where the electrical equipment that ran the lights and security was stored. Each machine in the room was humming with electricity and in one corner was a computer lighting up the dark room. "Presto!" Smelts said as he walked over to the computer screen. He began to type in a series of hacks on the system. "Maybe when all this is over, I can hire myself out as a security consultant at this place," he said. "This is too easy." A green light appeared on screen and he turned to Reggie and Boyd, to say, "System One and One-B are out."

"Now we just have to watch out for the lasers," Reggie said.

"You mean like motion detector lasers?" Boyd asked.

"Actually, no," Reggie said. "These are lasers that will slice through you like a hot knife through butter. They're the latest thing." He smiled at Boyd and then trotted up the stairs, whistling a happy tune.

Boyd turned to Smelts and asked, "Is it always like this with you two?"

Smelts put his finger to his chin to think about it. "Yes. Yes, I believe it is," he said.

Getting into the museum from the control room was easy, just a few doors ripped from their hinges and a few steel bars bent at awkward angles. Soon they found themselves on the main marble floor that they'd walked down just a few hours earlier. Boyd started to make his way through the open space, but Reggie grabbed him and jerked him backwards. "Not a good idea, chum," he said.

He pulled a small, black box from his utility belt and flipped a switch, which sent a black light emanating out in front of them. In the light, were hundreds of purple lasers crisscrossing the room. "Cool," Boyd said.

Reggie pulled a brochure from one of the kiosks and held it in front of a laser. It burst into flame as the laser burned a hole through it. "Not so cool," he said.

"This is why they don't need to pay for security guards," Smelts said.

"Well, how in the world do we get to the door?" Boyd asked.

"Do you always give up so quickly?" Smelts asked. "A little ingenuity goes a long way."

"What's ingenuity?" Boyd asked.

"Never mind," Smelts said. "Observe."

For the next few minutes, Smelts surveyed the lasers, doing mental calculations in his tiny, crocodilian brain, examining each one up and down. He then detached a small bag from his belt, inside of which were hundreds of tiny mirrors, each one about the size of a quarter. He began to slide the mirrors in front of the lasers, reflecting the deadly rays off in other directions, all of them meticulously aimed at other reflective surfaces, so as to keep them from burning holes in the walls. Soon, he had created a narrow little corridor through the lasers. It was big enough to walk through, but not without a little ducking and weaving along the way.

They each began to make their way through the tunnel of lasers, occasionally stepping over a stray, purple beam on the floor or ducking beneath one overhead. Reggie, being the biggest, had the hardest time and he occasionally singed his hair when he got too close. "Gonna need a trip to the beauty salon after this one," he muttered each time he heard the sizzle of burning hair.

Boyd was the last of the crew, just behind Smelts, and he was beginning to feel skilled as he weaved his way through the lasers. He felt that he might take an interest in this cat-burgling stuff and made a mental note to pick Smelts' brain about how he did what he did.

Just as Reggie and Smelts made it through the maze of lasers, Boyd let loose with a rip-roaring sneeze that startled everyone. The force of Boyd's sneeze blew one of the mirrors off-kilter, and suddenly all of Smelts' fine work shot off in different directions, trapping Boyd in the very center of a laser cage, unable to move.

"Help," Boyd said.

"What in my bloomin' knickers just happened?" Smelts asked.

"Don't move, Boyd!" Reggie said.

"Don't worry," Boyd said, quietly eying the laser reflected mere centimeters from the bridge of his nose.

"It was the sneeze!" Smelts said. "Something about the sneeze messed things up."

"Well, fix it!" Reggie said.

"I'm trying!" Smelts said. "But you keep interrupting my train of thought!" Smelts was doing thousands of mental calculations a second, trying to solve the mystery of the refracted laser. He kept muttering numbers and angles, all in an attempt to figure out which mirror was off its mark, while Reggie paced nervously back and forth behind him. Every few seconds, he would turn to Boyd and hold his hands up with caution to say, "Don't move, Boyd!"

Boyd had no plans to go anywhere.

"Um, Smelts," Reggie said, "I don't think we have all day."

"Not to worry," Smelts finally said. "I've figured it out!"

"Well, fix it," Reggie said.

"Only Boyd can fix it," he said. He turned to Boyd, pointing at a little mirror beside his right foot. "Apparently you knocked mirror 32-C off track."

"Mirror what?" Boyd asked.

"When you sneezed, it knocked Mirror 32-C off its mark. It's at your right foot. You need to put it back."

"How?" Boyd asked. "I thought those lasers would burn me."

Smelts shrugged his shoulders. "They will," he said, "which simply reiterates the fact that we're in a bit of a pickle." He turned again and paced back and forth for a couple of seconds, his arms folded across his chest, lost in thought.

Reggie, already bored with what was happening, sat down on a bench and sighed, "We're gonna be here all night."

"I've got it!" Smelts said. "I've got one mirror left, Boyd. I'll toss it to you and you slide it in front of 32-C."

"How am I going to bend over?" Boyd asked. "I can't even move."

"Well, it's try *this* or wait until the cops get here *tomorrow,*" Smelts said, once again shrugging his shoulders. "Of course, you could pass out from exhaustion from standing still for twelve hours before then, which would cause you to fall into the lasers anyway, but I guess we'll just have to take our chances."

"All right, all right," Boyd said. "See my hand?" He held his hand open at his side. "You've got to toss it right at my hand."

"No problem," Smelts said, rearing back to toss the tiny mirror.

"Wait!" Reggie said, jumping to his feet to stop him. "Let *me* do it! You're a terrible thrower."

"No, I'm not," Smelts said. "I can toss just fine."

Reggie swiped the mirror from Smelts' hand before he could react, then reared back. "Okay, one, two, three!"

He gently tossed the mirror and it landed perfectly in Boyd's hand. "Good shot," Boyd said.

Reggie turned to Smelts with a smarmy grin on his face. "He said it was a good shot."

"Lucky toss is more like it," Smelts muttered.

With sweat pouring down his face, Boyd ever so slowly squatted down, his knees pointing at an odd angle and shaking like mad. Finally, he was able to rest on the balls of his feet. With a laser mere centimeters from his throat, he leaned over, stretching out his arm as far as he could to place the mirror in front of the other one, but his reach was just short of where it needed to be. He stretched as far as he could, but he was too far away.

Finally, with a hint of grim determination, he stretched with all of his might, but in the process, went too far. "Ow!" he yelled as the laser singed his cheek. The pain was so intense that he dropped the mirror. It fell to the ground, rolling like a quarter on the floor, doing a long, lazy circle around the room, far away from where Boyd was standing.

Then slowly, it turned on itself and began rolling back towards him, and after a couple of loops, it rolled straight over to the mirror by Boyd's feet and came to a rest exactly where Boyd needed it to stop. Instantly, the lasers were all reflected back the way Smelts had originally intended.

Realizing he was now free, Boyd ran over to meet Smelts and Reggie at the end of the hall. "Holy guacamole was that ever lucky!" Smelts said, his large jaw wide open. "How'd you get so lucky?"

"Let's not question it," Boyd said, wiping a trickle of blood from his cheek. "That laser really hurt."

Reggie examined the wound and whipped out a Band-Aid from a pocket on his belt. "Just a scratch, there, my friend," he said.

"Okay," Boyd said. "Can we just go get that thing and be done with all of this? I'm tired of risking my life today."

"Sounds good," Reggie said, and they marched on down the hall, towards the door that led to the basement.

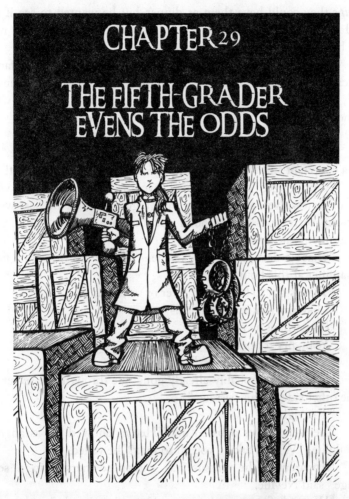

CHAPTER 29

THE FIFTH-GRADER EVENS THE ODDS

Although the werewolves were intent on making Bjorn and Ho Yin the main course at a succulent feast for the night, the late arrival of Hedley indicated that they were merely to cart them off to destinations unknown. "Come on," one of the werewolves pleaded. "Polar bear is a *delicacy* back in London. Let us eat 'im!"

Despite their pleas, Hedley refused. He told the werewolves that maybe when they'd fulfilled their jobs in their entirety, then *perhaps* they could have them as dinner, but he wanted to see if they could get Boyd first. "Besides," Hedley said, "these three will make good bargaining chips. Now, go get that girl."

Grumbling about their hunger, the werewolves quickly fanned out across the mansion in search of Cindy, and with their keen sense of smell, it wasn't long before they'd sniffed out the freshest scent, which led them directly to the fireplace in which Bjorn had stashed her.

"She's in there!" said one werewolf to another.

"How can she be in there?" said the other. "It's a fireplace." He took a couple of sniffs and said, "Blimey! You might well be right!"

A prolonged debate ensued, eventually attracting the whole team of werewolves, all of whom were arguing about the best way to enter the secret passage through the fireplace. "We could get a jackhammer," said one.

"That's a daft idea," said Neville. "Where are we gonna find a jackhammer at this hour?"

"There's got to be a secret lever or something."

"I like the jackhammer idea."

"Or perhaps a crow bar."

"Yeah, pry it open."

"We should just give up."

"Yeah, she's probably already gone out through the secret exit on the other side of this passage."

"Too right."

The werewolves debated until Hedley showed up, as angry as he could be. "What's taking you all so long?" he yelled.

"Apparently, the missus has ensconced herself in a secret passage," said Neville.

"We can't figure out how to get ourselves inside," said another werewolf.

"Ack!" Hedley said, throwing up his flippers in frustration. "You werewolves are idiots!" He began twisting and turning every knob, latch, or lever around the fireplace until he eventually slapped a flipper on Mr. Ping's face in the painting. The back wall of the fireplace swung inward, revealing the passage. "Now, see?" he asked. "That was pretty simple, wasn't it? Go get the girl!"

As the werewolves ran off down the secret passage, they were all commenting on Hedley's ingenuity. "Right brilliant, that fish is," said one.

"I'da never thought of doin' that meself," said another.

"I still think we shoulda used the jackhammer."

They ran down the dimly lit passage and all converged on the stairs, traveling down the narrow spiral one by one until they reached the heavy wooden door at the bottom. They quickly adopted the menacing, monstrous look that made them the popular hired hitmen that they were.

The door was slightly ajar and they used this advantage to fan out in the warehouse with military-like precision, each werewolf knowing exactly where to go in such a situation. The lead werewolf followed Cindy's scent trail around the room until he came upon an opened crate.

"That's funny," he said. "Her scent leads here and then disappears."

"What?" said another. "Nobody's scent just disappears."

"They do if they have this," said Neville. In his hand was an empty spray can, the side of which read, *Mr. Ping's No-Scent Werewolf Repellent*[88].

"She's got *No-Scent!*" one said.

"Oh, blimey!" said another.

They looked at the lid of the crate and saw that the words *WEREWOLF 2368* were written on the top of it. "Crimony!" Neville said. "This box was full of stuff to deal with *us!* Let's get outta here!"

"Not so fast, losers!"

The werewolves looked up to see Cindy standing on a stack of crates high above them. In her hands was something that looked like a rifle, except a bullhorn-like device was on the end of the barrel. She tossed down what looked to be large dog collars[89], big enough to fit around the werewolves' necks. "Put those on and nobody gets hurt," she said.

"I'm not puttin' on a collar!" one said, walking towards her with determination. Cindy aimed the device in her hands in his direction and pulled the trigger. Although no sound or explosion burst forth from the weapon, the werewolf fell to the ground, howling and covering his ears in horrible pain. "Ack!" he yelled. "Make it stop! Make it stop!"

"It's a ***Dog Whistle Gun***[90]!" shouted one werewolf.

"Run for your lives!" Neville shouted.

The werewolves began to scatter, each of them running for the exit, but Cindy was able to pick them off, one by one, sending each one to its knees with the gun, silent though it was to human ears. It was mere seconds before every werewolf in the room was cowering before her, pleading for mercy. "Now," she said, kicking the giant dog collars across the room at them. "Put those on or I'll zap you with this thing again."

The werewolves dutifully put on the collars, no longer looking like the dapper, yet intimidating creatures they were before as much as they looked like mangy mongrels that had been whacked with a switch one too many times. Not only were they frazzled by the Dog Whistle Gun, they were also mortally embarrassed at the fact that a mere fifth-grade girl had so easily dispatched twenty of the most ferocious werewolves in the world. If word of this moment got out, they'd become the laughing stocks of the organized crime world.

"See this?" Cindy asked, holding up what looked to be a small, black remote control. "You're each wearing electric shock collars. Get out of line and I zap you. Like this…"

She pressed a button and one of the werewolves began to writhe in pain for a couple of seconds as thousands of volts of electricity flowed through him. "Yow!" he yelled.

"Don't pull anything stupid," she said.

"Oh, this is pathetic!"

Everyone looked over to see Hedley standing by the door of the warehouse looking annoyed at the pitiful state in which his hired werewolves had found themselves. "This is absolutely ***ridiculous,***" he said.

"On your knees, buster," Cindy said, pointing the Dog Whistle Gun at him, "Or one zap will send you to the floor."

Hedley looked at her and smiled, saying, "They're so sweet at this age, aren't they?"

"I'm serious!" Cindy said. "Put the collar on, you...fish... thing...Whatever you are!"

"Look, sweetie," he said, walking towards her casually. "I don't know if you've noticed, but I'm not a werewolf. I'm a swordfish. So that nifty little gun of yours isn't gonna work on me."

Cindy pulled the trigger several times, and although it made the werewolves howl in pain, Hedley was unaffected. He just kept coming towards her, slowly waddling in the strange way in which a swordfish might walk on land. He kept backing her up, further and further away, until she found that she had no place else to go. Her back was now up against the wall.

"I must say," Hedley added, "you've certainly made a valiant effort." He jumped toward her and whipped his nose around, pinning his sharp proboscis through the shoulder of her shirt, into the wall, so that she couldn't move. "Cindy McCloyd, I presume?" he asked. His breath smelled of rotten fish. "Got yourself in a whole heap of trouble now, don't you?"

"My brother is gonna put a stop to you," Cindy said, unafraid as she looked Hedley in the eye.

"My dear," Hedley said. "I can't *wait* for him to try."

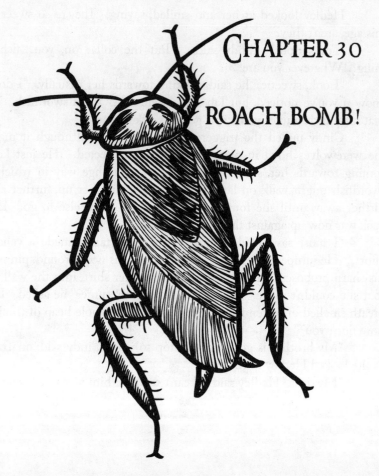

CHAPTER 30

ROACH BOMB!

Back at the museum, Boyd, Reggie, and Smelts were making their way down into the basement to look for the scroll. Again, Smelts had hacked into their computer system and disabled all the key codes along the way, effectively making it a cakewalk all the way down to the lower floors of the museum.

At the bottom of the non-nondescript concrete stairs was a long hallway with several large, steel doors on the sides, each one labeled with numbers painted on the front. "This is it," Reggie said.

"Which door is it?" Boyd asked.

"According to the database on the computer upstairs, the scroll archives are in door 3228-H," Smelts said. They walked down the hallway until they came to the right door, whereupon Smelts tried to open it. "It's locked," he said. "Go figure."

"Let a professional take care of this," Reggie said, puffing out his chest as he edged Boyd and Smelts out of the way. He latched on to the handle with his large hands and pulled with all of his strength. He struggled and strained, loosening and tightening his grip, adjusting his stance, sweating and grunting, but all of his yeti strength couldn't open the door.

"Nice work, Mr. Professional," Smelts laughed.

"I don't get it," Reggie said, breathing heavily. "That door should have popped off easily."

"I think this is the problem," Boyd said, pointing to the brand name of the door that had been etched into the sides. It read: **Yeti-Proof: Making Quality, Yeti-Proof Doors Since 1978**[91].

"Argh!" Reggie said, shaking his fist at the sky. "Curse that company! They've been a bane to my existence since the seventies."

"Well, what do we do now?" Smelts said, his hands perched on his hips in frustration.

"Hold on, hold on," Reggie said, pushing both Boyd and Smelts off to the side. "There's more than one way to peel a banana."

"There is?" Smelts asked. "What other ways are there to peel a banana?"

"Never mind," Reggie said, rolling his eyes. "Never mistake brute strength as being the only use of a yeti. We've got brains, too." Reggie reared back with his basketball-sized fist and punched right through the concrete beside the door like it was a piece of paper, his large arm sinking in up to his shoulder. "Brains and strength go hand in hand. If I can't rip the door off, then I'll go around the door."

"You've gotten much better at that since I last saw you," Smelts said, clapping his hands.

"Why, thank you," Reggie said. He was feeling his way around to the inside of the door through the hole, looking for some sort of handle. "Aha!"

A couple of clacks were heard and the large steel door popped open, slowly swinging outward. "Didn't that hurt your hand?" Boyd asked.

"Actually, no," Reggie said. "Through the process of evolution, we yetis have developed bones with the consistency of reinforced steel. You see, because we live in the mountains, we're used to pounding rocks and...Oh, what am I explaining this to you for? Read Mr. Ping's writings on yetis."

"And crocodiles," Smelts said.

They walked into what seemed to be a very large room lit by several overhead lights. The room was a long corridor, extending about ten meters to the far wall. On one side was what looked to be an elaborate wooden filing cabinet, with hundreds, if not thousands, of tiny drawers, each one numbered, with a handle on the front. On the other side was a giant, glass enclosure with a door at the far end, inside of which were several shelves, all filled with large, white, ceramic jars that had elaborate Chinese patterns and pictures painted in blue on the sides.

"What are those?" Boyd asked.

"Ginger jars[92]," Reggie said. "They were used for storing things like salt and spices. Qing dynasty."

"Huh?" Boyd asked.

"Never mind."

Smelts began to open a few of the tiny drawers on the other side of the room, pulling out brown, paper scrolls that were rolled up on deep mahogany rods inside of plastic bags. "Sheesh!" he said. "How many of these things are there?"

"Roughly one hundred thousand," Reggie said.

"And we've got to look at every one of them?" Boyd asked.

"Well, look at it this way," Smelts said, "you might get lucky and find it on your first try. That way, you wouldn't have to look through them all."

"Ever the optimist," Reggie muttered.

"*Somebody* has to be, especially around you two sourpusses," he said, and he cheerily began opening the drawers to pull out the scrolls.

"What are we looking for again?" Boyd asked.

"We're looking for the purple wax seal," Reggie said. "All the other seals should be red."

The task of opening the drawers, pulling out the scrolls, and then peering through the plastic bags proved to be an arduous one that took up most of the night. Sometimes, the scrolls had no wax seal, sometimes they were so old that they crumbled to dust inside the bags as soon as they were touched. Even when they thought they were making good progress, they would grow confused as to which drawers they'd actually looked through and end up looking at the same scroll several times. Finally, they devised a system of potential candidates and stacked them to one side, where Smelts would meticulously open each of them and observe by candlelight so as to discern whether or not it was "special."

After a few hours, the frustration amongst the three of them was beginning to take its toll. Smelts was no longer able to focus on the scrolls, Reggie was getting tired of hunching over from the low ceiling, and Boyd was just tired because he hadn't gotten any sleep.

"This is goin' nowhere, mates," Smelts said, throwing a scroll in a pile beside him. "If I look at another one of these, I'm gonna go bloomin' bonkers!"

"He's right," Reggie said. "It's only a couple of hours before the morning shift comes in to work and we've totally trashed the place."

"Well, what do we do if it's not here?" Boyd asked. "This is where it's supposed to be, right?"

"Yeah, but lookin' for a scroll with a special wax seal here is like lookin' for a extra-special piece of hay in a special haystack," Smelts said.

"Please don't create your own metaphors," Reggie said, waving Smelts away. "You're not very good at it."

"Oh, be quiet," Smelts said. "Besides, this here candle is runnin' out. We can't check the map by candlelight if we ain't got a candle."

"Boyd's got another one in his belt," Reggie said.

"I do?" Boyd asked. He reached in his belt pack and sure enough, there was a white candle inside. "I *do*," he said. He pulled the candle out and lit it with a pack of matches that Reggie tossed over.

As he walked over to hand Smelts the lit candle, he caught the most peculiar sight out of the corner of his eye. It was almost as if one of the drawers glowed a ghostly white on the inside as he walked past. At first, he thought it was just a trick of the eye and dismissed it, but the more he thought about it, the more he began to wonder. "Can I see that candle?' he asked Smelts.

"Sure," Smelts said, handing it to him.

Boyd took the candle and began to slowly move it in front of the drawers, looking at each one. He started to doubt himself, for none of the drawers glowed like he thought they did, until he came to one near the bottom. Sure enough, the inside of the drawer began to glow. The closer the candle came to the drawer, the more intense the glow.

"I think I've found it," Boyd said.

Reggie dropped a large pile of scrolls and followed Smelts over to where Boyd was standing. "By gum, I believe you have," he said.

Boyd opened the drawer to see a scroll inside that glowed as brightly as a lamp in the light of the candle. He pulled the scroll from the drawer and examined it. "There's the purple seal," he said.

"Nice work, Boyd," Smelts said.

"Why didn't you think of this earlier," Reggie asked.

"Why didn't *you?*" Boyd laughed.

They removed the scroll from the plastic bag and set it on a small table at the far end of the room. The purple wax seal had the markings of Qin Shihuangdi on the front, and the paper seemed slightly brittle with age. "What now?" Smelts asked.

"Well, we open it," Reggie said.

"I thought Ho Yin said these things were booby-trapped," Boyd said.

"It's a scroll, Boyd," Reggie said. "It's not like it's going to explode."

"Yeah, but…"

"Look, let's just open it and be done with it," Smelts said, perturbed. "I'd like to go back to the mansion and get a good night's rest, thank you very much."

"If you say so," Boyd said.

"Really, Boyd," Reggie said, "I don't think we have anything to worry about."

Boyd took a deep breath and peeled back the wax seal as Reggie and Smelts leaned over his shoulder to watch. They each unconsciously held their breaths until the seal was completely removed, for although they knew it was a ludicrous idea, they secretly did expect it to explode. Boyd unrolled the scroll and each of them took a deep breath at the sight that lay before them.

In front of them was a map that glowed a crystalline white over the black ink of the characters on the paper. It was gorgeous and detailed, depicting what seemed to be the southern part of China and a series of islands at the bottom, with one island in particular appearing as prominent.

"That's it, all right," Reggie said, completely in awe of the elaborate artwork that glowed in front of him.

"It's incredible," Smelts said.

"Yeah, it is," Boyd said, and he quickly rolled up the map, stuffing it in his pouch. "Let's get out of here."

"What's the rush?" Smelts said.

"The rush is that I'd like to get out of this museum as quickly as possible," Boyd said. "Ho Yin said this thing would be booby-trapped, and I feel a little bit like a sitting duck."

"Come on, mate," Smelts said. "Nothin' happened. We're in the clear."

"So you say," Boyd said. "But I'd still like to get out of here."

"All right, all right," Smelts said.

As they began to walk out to the hallway, Boyd noticed something peculiar. At first, he heard just a faint rattle coming from the direction of the ginger jars behind the glass. Then, the rattle grew louder and louder, as all the jars began to shake.

"It *was* booby-trapped," Smelts said. "It's an earthquake!"

"Let's get out of here before the building falls down," Reggie said, but Boyd stopped them.

"It's not an earthquake," he said. "The ground isn't shaking."

Boyd was right, and they began looking at the ginger jars on the far wall. They were still shaking, some more violently than the others. "This isn't good," Smelts said.

Just as he said it, one of the lids popped open and out crawled a single cockroach. It scurried around on the outside of the jar until it looked up to see Boyd, Reggie and Smelts. Then it made a b-line straight for them, crawling across the glass wall and out the door at the far end, straight for Boyd's feet. Its quest was ended when Smelts stamped on the poor creature with a splat. "And so ends his journey," he said.

"That's disgusting," Reggie said, examining the pulpy mess that Smelts had made of the roach.

"Uh, guys," Boyd said, still staring at the jars, "I think we've got a problem."

"Oh, my," Reggie said, looking up.

More roaches were trickling out of the jar, each of them crawling around for a second or two, just as the first, until they would spot Boyd, who was carrying the map. Once they spotted him, they would run straight for him. "Kill them all!" Smelts said, stomping on each of the roaches with glee as they came out of the glass door.

"That might be wishful thinking," Reggie said.

Hundreds of roaches were pouring out of the jar now, along with several who were popping out of the other jars. "They're going for the map!" Reggie said. "Shut the door!"

Smelts swung the glass door shut just in time to keep the roaches at bay, and he stomped on the unfortunate few who did escape. Through the door, they could see that the roaches were trapped as hundreds of them squirmed on the glass door.

"Vile creatures," Reggie said as the three of them stared at the ginger jar enclosure, each of them enraptured with the large roach farm that had sprung forth inside. By now, the lower half of the glass room could no longer be seen as the tide of roaches rose ever higher.

"That must have been the booby-trap," Boyd said.

"Kind of a lame one," Smelts said. "Just a bunch of roaches? That doesn't seem like it could do much damage."

"I don't know about that," Reggie said. The roaches were now waist high in the glass case, climbing, skittering, and crawling all over each other in a giant, pulsating mass of insects. In mere seconds, the roaches were piled up, reaching over Boyd's height, and soon, they were over Reggie's height, until the entire glass case, from floor to ceiling, was filled with millions of the beastly creatures.

"You know," Smelts said, "simple laws of physics tell me that the weight of all those roaches cannot be held by that glass wall."

"What do you mean?" Boyd asked.

As the sound of the wall joints was heard, the strain of its seams began to crack under the stress of the roaches' weight. "I mean," Smelts said, "that that glass wall is about to go boom-boom."

"It's gonna blow!" Reggie yelled. "It's a roach bomb!"

"We can't kill them all!" Smelts yelled. "Let's get out of here."

They ran for the exit, listening for the wall behind them to burst open. It wouldn't be until they ran up the concrete staircase and started to weave their way through the laser maze that they heard the crack and snap of the shattering glass in the basement below. The roaches poured out onto the floor like liquid, each of the creepy-crawlies making tracks up the stairs for Boyd.

"Holy cow!" Boyd cried, looking over his shoulder to see millions of roaches skittering towards him, their thousands of bodies covering every available surface of the museum, roof to floor. "Go! Go!" he said, terrified.

"Don't push me!" Smelts said, ducking and weaving his way through the lasers. "I'm moving as fast as I can!"

"Move faster!" Reggie said, bringing up the rear. He was just as terrified of the critters as anyone else was and they were almost upon him.

Smelts saw the last opening and dove for the hole, doing a perfect forward role to land on his feet. He then looked back to see Boyd making his way out of the maze as well. Last was Reggie, whose inordinate bulk caused him to move a bit slower through the lasers. "Go ahead!" he yelled. "I'll catch up!"

"Can't argue with that," Smelts said, taking off as the clicking sound of the oncoming roaches filled the marble hallway. He and Boyd ran for the front doors, but stopped when they reached them. Smelts beat and kicked at the door a few times, only managing to hurt his toe in the process. "It must be unbreakable glass!" he yelled. "I can't break through."

Boyd picked up a chair and hurled it at the door, but the chair just bounced off of it. "That always worked in the movies," he muttered. "What do we do now?"

"Coming through!"

The two of them spun around to see Reggie barreling down the hallway, the top of his furry white hair singed and smoking from coming too close to a laser. He was followed by the largest gathering of roaches that Boyd had ever seen, and in his attempt to evade the roaches, Reggie gave no thought to slowing down for the doors, for his speed propelled him straight through the glass and out into the predawn air.

"Go! Go!" Boyd yelled, and soon, they ran out of the building, its alarms blaring and bells ringing, alerting the world that someone had broken inside the museum. They ran around the corner, away from the sounds of the building alarms to find Xiao the Dead Taxi Driver parked and waiting for them. They crammed into the dusty taxi as Reggie yelled, "Go, Xiao, Go!"

"Right on," Xiao said, and he quickly sped off through the streets of Hong Kong.

"So…many…roaches…" Reggie said, trying to catch his breath. "So…many…roaches!"

"They were after the map," Boyd said.

"I hope they can't follow us," Smelts said.

"Where to, kids?" Xiao asked.

"Ping Manor," Smelts said.

They sped through the streets of Hong Kong, leaving the scene at the museum behind, and as they drove along, Boyd looked at the map in his hands. He couldn't understand how one piece of paper could cause so much chaos.

"Quite a fuss over something as simple as a map, isn't it Reggie?" Smelts asked. There was no answer. "Reggie?"

"So...many...roaches," Reggie muttered, still petrified with fear. It would be a while before he was able to calm himself again.

PART III

CHAPTER 31
ESCAPING
THE PACKHOUNDS

As Boyd, Reggie and Smelts wound their way up the hill towards the Mansion, the wind whipped all around them and the rain began to patter on the windshield. Branches both large and small now littered the lane ways and the higher they got, the fewer cars were on the road. Hong Kong had the feel of a city under siege and considering what had just happened, the next few hours looked to be chaotic. Boyd could feel the taxi sway back and forth with intense gusts of wind. It seemed to be a long ride back to the mansion.

Soon, the city below them disappeared into a haze of clouds and they rounded the curve to enter the private driveway of Ping Manor. In the wind and gloom, Boyd couldn't help but notice an air of foreboding surrounding the place. The sky had grown dark with the storm, which gave the building an eerie quality. It was the way it just sat there, its limp curtains, its foggy front yard, the drab, yet menacing, front door. Something was off about the place. Reggie noticed, too, as the cab pulled to a stop in the driveway.

"What's the matter, Reg?" Smelts asked, his gaze also fixed on the mansion.

"Something's not right here," he said, his brow furrowed down over his eyes. "I don't like it."

"Hey, you guys gettin' out or what?" Xiao asked from inside the taxi. "I got another call and I gotta get going."

"Here you go," Reggie said, giving him his fare. "There's a little extra for the disappointment over the whole switching souls thing."

"Hey, thanks," Xiao said. "Thanks for nothing!" He laughed and the three of them got out of the cab. He turned the taxi around and rolled down the window. "Hey, fellas?" he said.

"Yeah?" Reggie said, his face still gazing up at the house suspiciously.

"Look," he said, "I don't know if you've heard, but there's a lot of talk in the underworld[93] about big things happening this weekend, if you know what I mean."

"What are you saying?" Reggie asked.

"Well, it's like this," he said. "The dead…they can see the future sometimes, just the same as they see the past, you know? And the word is…amongst the dead I mean…is that something quite large is happening soon. Maybe this weekend. I'd be careful if I were you."

"Thanks," Reggie said.

"Yeah, no problem," Xiao said before speeding off into the fog, down the hill.

The rain began to patter all around them as a typhoon moved in over the island. Still, Boyd, Reggie, and Smelts refused to enter the house, preferring to stand in the rain. "So, do you think this weather has anything to do with us getting the map?" Boyd asked.

"Maybe," Smelts said.

"Probably," Reggie said.

They stood there in silence for a couple of seconds, before Boyd said, "So, I guess there's something wrong with this picture, isn't there?"

"Maybe," Smelts said.

"Probably," Reggie said.

Again, they stood in silence for a couple of seconds, before Boyd said, "So, do you think Cindy's okay?"

Reggie sighed and said, "This has been a really long night." He took a deep breath, puffed out his chest, and said, "Time to go in. Be prepared for a surprise attack."

"Yes!" Smelts said, rubbing his hands together. "They're my favorite."

They crept up to the front stairs and stood there as Reggie put his big, yeti ear to the front door as if he could hear the very heartbeat of whatever it was that lurked inside.

"What do you hear?" Smelts asked, his ear pressed against the other side of Reggie's head, as if he could hear through it.

"All I hear is your stinking breath in my ear," Reggie said.

"Ack! Hit me where it hurts, why don't you?" Smelts said.

Reggie opened the front door of the mansion and peeked inside. Almost on cue, a huge lightning bolt lit up the sky behind them, which scared Smelts so badly that he ruined any semblance of stealth and burst inside the foyer to escape the electrical onslaught, knocking both Boyd and Reggie to the ground in the process. "Ooo, sorry about that, fellas," he said as he helped them up from the ground. "I'm not a big fan of lightning."

"The electricity is off," Boyd said. He looked around to see that the entire mansion was dark and still, the vast hallways disappearing off into eerie silence.

"Aw, man," Smelts muttered, "that means my food in the fridge is going to go bad."

"Something's not right about this," Reggie said, peering back and forth. "The mansion has back-up generators. Technically, we shouldn't lose power."

"Then what's happening?" Boyd asked.

Reggie sniffed the air in a way that only yetis could and muttered, "Ambush."

On cue, two werewolves jumped out from nowhere to attack, fangs bared, claws out. With tremendous speed, they went for Reggie first, throwing him off balance and pinning him to the ground. At the same time, two more werewolves came running down the hallway towards Smelts, and even though he got in a few, lightning-quick blows on them, it was mere seconds before they had him pinned to the ground as well. In the chaos, Boyd was knocked to the ground and the map went rolling across the floor.

"Run, Boyd!" Reggie yelled as he struggled to escape his captors.

For a split second, Boyd was terrified. He'd never seen werewolves before and the ones that had confronted them were particularly frightening. Their eyes were yellow and angry, and their fangs were extended, as if somehow, these werewolves were even more bitter and vengeful than your usual lot.

Regaining his composure, he jumped to his feet and turned to run down the hallway. A sorrowful howl echoed throughout the mansion, signaling Boyd's escape. It sent a chill down his spine, and as he ran, he could see another werewolf running towards him on all fours from the opposite end of the hallway.

In a panic, he changed direction and turned towards the stairs, bounding up them in record time as he heard the clip of the werewolf's claws behind him on the hardwood floor, a growl echoing forth from its chest with every step it took. Once he'd reached the top of the stairs, Boyd peered down the dark hallway to see that at the opposite end, there was yet another pair of glowing eyes coming for him. Thinking quickly, he ducked into a bedroom and slammed the door shut, locking it behind him. Almost immediately, the werewolves outside began to shriek and growl, clawing at the door in an attempt to get inside.

With all of his strength, Boyd pushed a giant dresser in front of the doorway to keep the werewolves at bay. They were now pounding on the door in unison, trying to break it down. But just as quickly, the pounding stopped and a creepy silence fell over the room. Boyd was now backed up against the wall at the far corner, breathing hard and trying to calm his fears.

A low, guttural voice came from outside the door. "Boyd," it said in a singsong tone. "We know you're in there. Why don't you let us in before we hurt your friends?"

Choosing to avoid talking to them, Boyd scanned the room, trying to formulate a plan. There were no weapons anywhere that would have been effective against two werewolves. His only hope was the window. Being on the second floor, he looked outside to see that it was a long drop down to the ground below, but he could jump across to a large tree branch that came close to the building. That is, if he had the strength.

"Boyd," the voice spoke from outside. "I think it's time you let us in."

Just as Boyd opened the window, the werewolves began pounding on the door again, only this time much harder. Soon, cracks began to form in the heavy oak, splinters jutting out from the blows, until they were just large enough so that the beasts could dig through it.

With the horrible ferocity of their claws, the werewolves tore open the door, ripping the wood into a million pieces. Then, with their extra keen sense of smell, they began to scan the room for Boyd's scent. It didn't take much to detect that Boyd had gone out the window because the latch was undone and the curtains were whipping around from the powerful wind outside. One of the wolves ran over and peered out into the distance, but his sight was poor and the wind had stirred up too many smells in the air for him to get a good lead on where Boyd was.

"He's gone outside," he said to his partner. "We'd better start tracking him." The werewolves immediately bolted out of the room and back down the stairs, their eyes narrowed, their brows furrowed, and their long, cold noses lifted up to the air as they ran out of the mansion to search for their prey.

That night, the werewolves prowled the mansion and its grounds with fervor, using their incredibly powerful snouts to search high and low for their missing quarry. And yet, they found no trace of him. They assumed that from the bedroom, he'd managed to jump from the window to the tree outside, and then he must have shimmied down and run away. The problem was that Boyd's scent was nowhere to be found anywhere around the tree.

"The bloke must have some sort of magic spell goin' on," one of the wolves muttered as he reported back to Neville in the wake of a long and fruitless search.

"You can't find any trace of him?" asked Neville.

"Nothing," said the wolf. "We'll be on the lookout."

And so it was that because the werewolves were too boastful and full of pride to admit that they'd lost their prize, they all convinced themselves that it was no fault of their own. In their opinions, it had more to do with a magic spell that the boy had conjured to throw them off his scent. Throughout the evening, the wolves huffed and tut-tutted and sniffed about how it must have been a very powerful spell and that this was the first time ever that they could remember losing their prey.

If only the werewolves had used more of their brains than their noses, they would have discovered that Boyd had not actually left the house that evening. Boyd knew from skimming through Mr. Ping's almanacs that werewolves relied on scent to track their prey and had very poor eyesight, so in a bid to deter them from finding him, he made a great effort to leave his tracks all about the window area, as if he was scrambling in fear, unable to figure out what to do. He then retraced his steps over to the fireplace and slowly made his way up the blackened chimney.

He stayed there, suspended just above the entrance to the fireplace, covered in thick, black soot, for what seemed like several hours, although it was really only forty-five minutes. He waited for the hideous beasts to move on in their search and when they did, he finally allowed himself to flop down. He sat there for the longest time, listening to the wind howl outside and rip the trees back and forth as the day began to turn to night.

Boyd was now at a crossroads. Something about his nature made him want to stay right there in the fireplace until the entire situation resolved itself. After all, if he didn't try to solve the problem, he would never be a failure. Staying right there in the fireplace seemed like a great idea.

Something kept gnawing at his heart. They now had Cindy. He had done just that thing so many times in his life, waiting it out, ignoring the problem, hoping that whatever threat that was posed to his existence might somehow magically disappear.

As he sat there in the ash, thinking about how much his life had changed over the short span of time since he'd met Ho Yin and Reggie, he came to a realization. He realized that he was never going to be able to ignore the problem again. All of those times he'd been in such horrible situations at school or at home, be it from Tucker and the bully problem, to sitting in his room in silence while his mother and father argued in the living room, he realized that the problems in his life never went away when he ignored them. He could walk to the other side of school, completely out of his way, to avoid Tucker Stevens, but it still wouldn't mean that Tucker could not find him. He could go down to breakfast every day and pretend that he still lived in a happy family, but it wouldn't bring his mother and father closer together. Ignoring the problem was no longer an option for Boyd now. He had to take action.

So although there was a fear in his belly that made his limbs feel as heavy as concrete blocks and made his brain cloud over with fog, he knew that the fate of his family, friends, and possibly the world, rested on his shoulders. With a new determination, he rose from the ashes of the fireplace with a new mandate.

Knowing that the only way that he was going to save his friends and family was to take action, Boyd snuck out of the fireplace and peeked out the door of the room to see if there were any dangers lurking about in the hall. From his vantage point, he could see that the house was abuzz with activity, as it had been invaded by an army of what appeared to be moving men, all of whom were packing up the artifacts that Mr. Ping had collected over the years and taking them out of the house.

Boyd knew that there was no way that he was going to be able to walk around the house undiscovered, so he ran across the hall to where a fake flower pot stood on a pedestal. He twisted the flower pot, which was a mechanism to open a secret door on one of the wooden panels lining the wall. He ducked into the secret passageway and shut the door behind him.

Boyd ran down the passage from room to room, looking through the two-way mirrors for some sort of clue that would tell him where to begin his rescue attempt, but all he saw in each room were movers packing up the entire contents of the place. The living room, the dining room, the study, all of it was being crated and whisked away.

Just as he was about to give up hope, he heard a very familiar gurgle coming down the main hallway of the mansion. He ran to a two-way mirror and saw that it was Hedley doing his peculiar waddle, walking beside a well-dressed man who was writing in a rather large book.

"...People have tried to get in here for years," said the man. "How in the world did you manage to sneak in?"

"Easy," Hedley gurgled. "That idiot yeti left the garage door opener in the car and I had some of my boys hack the code."

"He just left it in the car?" the man asked.

"Well, the car was sticking out the window on the eighteenth floor of an apartment building," Hedley said. "But the circumstances aren't important. What is important is that I'm the first person to ever break into this mansion and now that I have, I'm taking what is rightfully mine."

They turned into a room down the hall and Boyd quickly followed, weaving his way through the maze of passages until he came to a see-through painting that hung just over a desk. Hedley was looking through the man's book and Boyd had an excellent view from his position. He saw that it was some sort of ledger. At the top of every page was a heading that read, ***Mr. Pu's Auction House*** and below that, everything that was found inside the mansion; the lamps, the carpets, and the artifacts that Mr. Ping had collected were meticulously cataloged.

Hedley and the man, whose name was apparently Mr. Pu, were still deep in conversation. "...And so," Mr. Pu said, "the contents of the upstairs bathroom alone are worth well over a quarter of a million dollars. The gold faucets, the jade counter top, the marble bathtub. I figure we can split it evenly."

"Sounds good," Hedley said. "What's the running total?"

"That's what I'm trying to tell you," Mr. Pu said. "The contents of this mansion are invaluable. We stand to make an excellent showing at the auction house when we sell all of these things."

"Fine, fine," Hedley said. "Just make me rich. That's all I care about. Let's go to the laboratory. That's the only place you haven't seen."

As they got up to leave, Boyd rushed back through the maze of the secret passages on his way to the laboratory. He got there just before Hedley and Mr. Pu, and as soon as they walked in, he saw Mr. Pu freeze in his tracks. He had seen the Perpetual Motion Machine.

"What's your problem?" Hedley asked.

"It truly exists," Mr. Pu said, moving with silent reverence through the room towards the machine.

"*This* contraption?" Hedley asked, looking it over. "What's the big deal?"

"The *big deal?*" Mr. Pu asked. "The big deal is that this is the most important artifact in the history of the world! *This* is what Mr. Fang was looking for."

"Yeah, but is it worth much?" Hedley asked.

Mr. Pu ignored him, walking around the machine in a circle, as if it was a work of art so beautiful that it made him dizzy. "This is the Perpetual Motion Machine," he said. "Invented by Emperor Qin Shihuangdi in the second century B.C. I've read books, articles, and research papers on this machine. I've heard rumors of its existence, but nothing has ever been confirmed before. I told Mr. Fang that Ping had it, but I wasn't convinced that he had all the pieces. Now, here it is!"

"That's great," Hedley said, rolling his eyes. "What's this hunk of junk worth?"

"Worth?" Mr. Pu asked. "Money means *nothing* with this. This machine could make whoever owns it the most powerful person on the planet. This machine could change the world! Revolutionize the energy industry, feed the hungry, clothe the poor. There's *no limit* to what this could accomplish."

"But it doesn't *do* anything!" Hedley said. "We tried to get it working, but it just sits there."

"Well, that's because there's a piece missing," Mr. Pu said as he examined it. He pointed at a keyhole on the front of the machine. "It won't work without the key."

"The key?" Hedley asked.

"Yes," Mr. Pu said, looking over his reading glasses. "A jade key. I've studied this machine all of my life. Mr. Ping and I were rivals in this business, but what I always knew that he didn't, was that the machine needed a jade key in order to work properly. I knew from certain documents that the key was the final piece. The Jade Key is the final test, and if one can recover the Jade Key, then the riches of the world will be theirs for the taking."

"Riches of the world, eh?" Hedley asked. "I'm in. Where's it at?"

"I don't know," Mr. Pu said. "Supposedly, there's a map somewhere that will lead to it, but it's never been found."

"That's it!" Hedley said, realizing the answer. "That bratty kid dropped something when we tried to get him." He dialed his phone and said, "Yeah, Basil, it's Hedley. You remember that thing the kid dropped when we got that yeti and crocodile? Yeah, bring it up here, would you? I'm upstairs." He hung up his phone and turned to Mr. Pu. "I've got your missing map."

Soon, a werewolf walked into the room, carrying the map from the museum that Boyd had dropped. As the werewolf entered the room, he paused for a second, sniffing the air and looking confused. He then got himself back in order and handed the map to Mr. Pu.

"My goodness," Mr. Pu said, holding the map with a reverence that one would reserve only for the Holy Grail.

"That doesn't look like a map to me," Hedley said.

"Of course not," Mr. Pu said. "And the reason it doesn't is to *trick* people like you. Qin Shihuangdi knew about your type and he worked to keep you away."

He walked over and turned out the laboratory's lights. "What in the world are you doing?" Hedley asked.

With a couple of swipes, Mr. Pu lit a match, and again, the map began to glow in the firelight. "Just as I suspected," he said.

"Whoa!" Hedley said. "Look at that!"

"*This* is the map that will lead us to the Jade Key," he said.

"Thanks to that brat Boyd McCloyd," Hedley said. "Where does it point to?"

Mr. Pu looked grim as he blew out the match and flipped on the lights. "Dragon Island," he said.

"Where's that?" Hedley asked, but just as he did, his phone rang. "Yeah, this is Hedley."

From the top of his luxury tower, Mr. Fang had called after having paced nervously almost all night, awaiting word on Boyd McCloyd's capture. "What took you so long?" he yelled. "I've been waiting forever for you to call!"

"I work on a different timetable than you," Hedley said. "Now, what do you want?"

"I want to know if you got Boyd McCloyd," Mr. Ping said. "I want to know if I can relax because all this waiting is making me tense."

"We lost the kid, Fang," Hedley said.

"You *lost the kid?*" Mr. Fang yelled. "What do I *pay* you for? You're *worthless!*" He began to clutch his heart as if he was in extreme pain. "Oh, I feel sick! I think I'm having a heart attack!"

"Would you calm down and listen to me, Fang?" Hedley asked. "I have something *better* than the kid."

"What's better than the kid?" Mr. Fang asked. "The Conspiricetti wants the kid and they'll kill me if I don't get him."

"Forget the Conspiricetti," Hedley said. "They're old news. You wanted the Perpetual Motion Machine? You got it."

And with that, Hedley walked out of the room. Mr. Pu turned to a couple of movers who were waiting by the door, pointed to the Machine, and said, "Box that up and put it in the lead van. Be *very* careful with it."

He rubbed his hands together in a gleeful manner and whistled a happy tune as he left the room.

CHAPTER 32

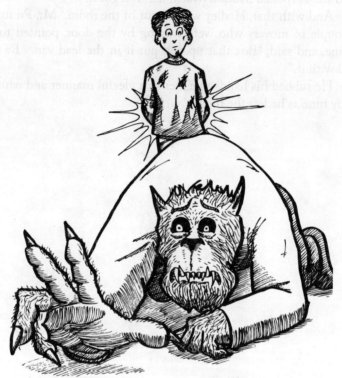

THE DELIGHTFUL INTERROGATION

Boyd tried to follow Hedley and Mr. Pu as they made their way to other parts of the house, but the maze of passageways was too complex and it wasn't long before he lost them in the sea of movers. Finally, he sat down in a small alcove between the dining room and the kitchen to formulate a plan.

He felt overwhelmed, wondering what he should do. Everything he thought he knew was changing. Yesterday, Mr. Fang was after him and he was running in fear for his life, but, the tables had turned and if he was to believe what Hedley was saying on the phone, Mr. Fang would now have no interest in him whatsoever. Normally, that would have filled him with joy, but the thought of Mr. Fang being in control of the Perpetual Motion Machine and having his parents and his sister was more than Boyd could stomach. Mr. Fang had upset his life, kidnapping his parents, sending strange, air-breathing swordfish and drooling werewolves to kill him, and now threatening to take over the world with a device that was stolen from *his* house. Things had gone far enough. Boyd knew he had to do something.

He just didn't know what that was.

He hid until the mansion was silent and the movers had gone for the day. With the howl of the wind outside rattling the windows, he slowly opened a secret door and peeked out into the dark hallway. It was late in the afternoon and the house was empty. There were no lights on in the mansion and the darkness from outside made the place foreboding, as if something was lurking around every corner.

He listened to see if there was any movement on the stairs or in the hallway, but heard nothing, so he made his way over to the balcony that overlooked the main part of the building. The great span of hallway that connected the two sections of the mansion was also eerily quiet. He was on the edge, aware of every snap, crack, or creak that he heard, listening intently for some sign of danger. A chill would go up his spine when the wind would blow a branch against the building or start to moan in a mournful way.

He made his way down the stairs, always on the lookout for the werewolves, but they were nowhere to be found. He assumed that they were out looking for him, or had taken Reggie and the others off to some unknown destination, and he realized that if he was going to get anything accomplished, the first thing he would have to do was to figure out how to stop them. Their massive size and brute strength was enough to lay Reggie and Smelts low, so what chance did he have against such powerful creatures? The answer lay in the Almanacs in Mr. Ping's office.

Because the office was at the far end of the hallway, it hadn't been packed up yet, so once inside, Boyd began to pull out the books, one by one, to search in the index for any sort of reference to werewolves. His search was short, for werewolves made their first appearance in Vol. 14, from 1921, as Mr. Ping was traveling through Russia:

> "...It was a fearsome creature that confronted me in the lobby of the Cormorant Hotel that evening. Wide and muscular at the top, with short, spry legs that seemed ideal for catching prey, be they a caribou desperately running for their lives across the tundra, or small, helpless school children desperately running for their lives across the playground. Its teeth were fierce, its molars long and sharp, perfect for tearing beastly, or dare I say, human limbs from the body. Most frightening of all, though, was that it could talk.
>
> Now, had I spoken even the smallest amount of Russian, the words this creature used would have let the icy fingers of fear take hold of my heart, as I was sure he muttered something about eating my liver raw and then picking his teeth clean with my bones. Thankfully, I spoke no Russian, so his intimidating words fell upon deaf ears. Still, with all of his bluster and thunder, growling and drooling, snorting and huffing, he did his best to intimidate me, but I was tired. I shrugged him off and said, "After dealing with what I've dealt with today, I have no time to waste on you!" and promptly walked by him to my room.   I assume that my

nonchalant attitude left him confused and
I failed to see him again for the rest of the
trip..."

There were only casual mentions of werewolves in the next few
volumes, mostly rumor and innuendo about what might have
mutilated the livestock of small towns or what might have caused
Little Louie to disappear down by the woods. Mr. Ping's first real
encounter with one of the ghastly creatures came in the north of
England in 1937:

"...Walking home after a few filling
pints at the local pub, the hairs on the
back of my neck began to stand on end,
for I had the distinct feeling that I was
being followed, and that whatever was
following me was not human. The most
telltale signs were the sound of not two
feet, but four paws padding along in
pursuit, plus the distinct, guttural growl
that was aimed in my direction. I
quickened my pace, and luckily made it
to my hotel before the dreadful beast
that followed me had the chance to
launch an attack..."

Mr. Ping later discovered that the town had been riddled with
werewolves. He also noted that there was no correlation between the
appearance of werewolves and full moons. They seemed to appear at
random, without warning or provocation. Begged by the people of the
town to do something about the problem, he quickly set about finding
a solution in his own, unorthodox way. Soon, he was on to something:

"...It seems that the myth of the silver
bullet is more grounded in reality than
what I had first assumed, although it's
not the *bullet* that does the damage to

the werewolf.   No, it seems that it's actually the *silver* that affects them with some sort of illness.   Considering my general and utter loathing for all firearms, I can't say I'm disappointed in this discovery.   Something about the molecular structure of silver, coupled with the genetic make-up of the werewolf, causes a reaction in said beasts that makes them wither and grow weak, like radioactive materials might be to humans.   Prolonged exposure to silver will kill a werewolf entirely.   I've never actually killed one of the creatures, though, as I would hope that I'd find a cure for their ailment before being forced to kill them.   In the meantime, I've developed *The Armicons* to help me deal with them until I can help them…"

The Armicons!   Boyd was sure that he'd seen a display in the mansion with the label *Armicons* at some point. He hoped he'd be able to find them, but unfortunately, the heavy breathing behind him made him realize that his luck may have finally run out.

"Look what I've found," said a low, growling voice. "Lunch."

Boyd turned around to see Basil, the fearsome looking werewolf that had delivered the map to Hedley. His eyes were glowing yellow in the darkness of the mansion and his heavy breathing echoed about the room. He was blocking the entrance, so Boyd had no chance of escape. Boyd wanted nothing more than to throw his hands over his head and yell, "Just eat me quickly!" until he was inspired by Mr. Ping's very own words from the almanac and his lack of intimidation regarding such creatures. So he did what Mr. Ping would do in such a situation: He bluffed.

"Where are my friends?" he asked, trying to puff out his chest in order to seem tough.

"Excuse me?" Basil asked. "You've got some nerve for an appetizer, chap."

"You're all by yourself, aren't you?" Boyd asked with a smirk, and for the first time, he saw a crack in the werewolf's tough-guy exterior as his evil smile seemed to melt.

"What do you mean?" the werewolf asked.

Boyd laughed. "Don't you know who I am?" he asked. "You're in mighty big trouble, wolfie. Why do you think they sent so many of you guys to get me?" He rose from his chair, trying his best to be intimidating. "I'll tell you why: Because *one…is…not…enough.*"

"You little runt!" Basil yelled. "I'm gonna make sausage out of you!"

For a split-second as Basil was ready to pounce, Boyd had the faint notion that all of his posturing had been a mistake and that he was on the verge of becoming wolf-meal. However, just as the wolf sprung for him, a most peculiar thing happened. A large grandfather clock appeared from nowhere, toppling over as it slammed the werewolf to the ground, trapping it underneath.

"Good show, old chap!" Stephens said. The werewolf was pinned beneath him and the awkward angle in which he was pinned, coupled with Stephens' tremendous weight, left him trapped. "Your bluffing gave me just enough time to nab him."

"Get off me, you piece of kindling!" Basil yelled, struggling in vain to break free.

Stephens maneuvered his weight around to grind one of his sharp corners into the werewolf's back, making him howl with pain. "My parts are from Europe's *finest* brass, you mangy mutt!" he said. "You're lucky I don't wallop you with my pendulum!"

"Stephens," Boyd said, "are there any more in here?"

"Not that I'm aware of," he said. "I've been searching the house, trying to avoid those pesky movers and haven't seen any."

"Good," Boyd said. "Can you hold him while I get something?"

Once again, Stephens ground one of his corners into the werewolf's back. "Not a problem," he said, as Basil let out a howl of pain.

Boyd dashed out of the room, towards the far end of the house. He rounded the corner to find a large, glass display case full of several gadget and gizmos that hadn't been moved yet. There he found two gleaming, silver bracelets with a small sign below them that read, *The Armicons.* Because he couldn't see a way into the case, he picked up a candlestick, ready to toss it and said, "Sorry, Mr. Ping." With a quick swing, he shattered the glass into a million pieces, picked up the large silver bracelets, and put them on his wrists.

Back in Mr. Ping's office, Stephens was continuing to be belligerent to the werewolf as Boyd came into the room. "It wouldn't hurt you werewolves to bathe every once in a while, would it?" he asked.

"Oh, be quiet!" Basil said, before shrieking in pain.

"Now, now," Stephens said. "Play nice."

"Where are my friends?" Boyd asked from the doorway.

"Your friends are probably being served in a nice buffet down in Wan Chai, you brat!" Basil said.

"This isn't the time for games," Boyd said. "Where are they?"

"We sold them on the black market," he snickered. "Couldn't get a good price for 'em, though."

Boyd looked at the werewolf squirming on the floor and smiled. "I'm going to let you up now," he said. "But before I do, you have to promise that you'll behave."

"Might I interject, Boyd, by saying he's quite dangerous," Stephens said with trepidation.

"He's nothing I can't handle," Boyd said. He turned back to the werewolf. "Do you promise not to make any sudden moves."

"Oh, yes," the werewolf said. "You and your clock have shown me the error of my ways." It was obvious that he was bluffing. The drool was already beginning to fall from his lips and though he looked subservient, his eyes had a ferocious quality about them.

"Let him up, Stephens," Boyd said.

The old grandfather clock paused for a couple of seconds before reluctantly shifting his heavy bulk. His stiff, oak body defied the laws of physics as it lifted upright. Basil started laughing as he got to his feet, turning towards Boyd as drool fell from his mouth. "That was your *last* mistake, runt. Rules or no rules, I'm eatin' you."

With the agility of a jaguar, Basil leapt for Boyd, his teeth bared, claws protruding, and a howl of anger emanating from his mouth that shook the windows. Just as quickly, Boyd brought his hands out from behind his back, crossing his forearms in front of him to display the Armicons to the beast, the silver seeming to glow in his presence.

The werewolf tumbled to the ground in a lump, as if all of his strength had vanished. He soon began to use what little energy he had to scurry towards the back of the room away from Boyd. "Please," he said. "P-please m-make it stop!"

"Well *done*, Boyd," Stephens said.

Boyd never shifted his gaze from the werewolf. "I asked you a question," he said. "Where are my friends?"

"I don't know," Basil said, shielding his eyes from him.

Boyd walked closer to him, holding out one of the silver bands in front of him. "Now is not a good time to lie," he said.

"Okay, okay," the werewolf said, in obvious pain. "Your friends are with Hedley!"

"I know that," Boyd said, shoving the Armicons in his face. "Where is he taking them?"

"Agh!" Basil screamed, cowering in the corner. "I *don't know* where he's taking them!"

"He's lying and he's being belligerent," Stephens said, tipping back and forth in his excitement. "Shove one of those silver things down his throat!"

"Be quiet, Stephens," Boyd said. He turned back to the werewolf. "Okay," he said, "this is your last chance before I start taking the clock's advice. Where are my friends?"

"Look, mate," Basil said, his paws shaking as he squirmed in pain. "I honestly don't know where they are, but I *do* know that Hedley told us to meet him at Fang's shipyards at four o'clock tomorrow afternoon. That's it! That's everything I know."

"He's still spinning falsehoods," Stephens said. "Werewolves only know how to tell lies and trick the innocent. Don't let him trick you, too, Boyd. Shove those bracelets down his throat!"

Boyd looked at Stephens calmly and said, "Thanks for the advice, Stephens, but I'm letting him go."

"What?" Stephens asked. "At least touch those things to his face or something to see what happens!"

Boyd turned back to Basil and said, "Get going! I'm going to rescue my friends, and if I see you anywhere in the area, you can be sure I won't be so nice to you next time."

Basil looked surprised as he slowly backed out of the room, away from Boyd, and then he was gone, quick as a flash. "What a mistake!" Stephens yelled. "That mangy mutt would just as soon eat you as look at you!"

"What was I supposed to do?" Boyd asked. "Kill him?"

"That would have been a *start!*" Stephens said.

"There are better things to do in life than go around killing," Boyd said. "Anyway, I need to get to Kowloon. Fast!"

CHAPTER 33

A LITTLE HELP FROM HIS FRIENDS (BOTH LIVING AND DEAD)

Tony Tang's teashop looked different in the daytime than at night, just like the whole of the Temple Street Market looked different. It was more run down, older and falling apart, and the door looked like it had been opened and closed one too many times. Having hitched a ride with one of Stephens' old buddies from an antique store in which he used to be housed, Boyd was now in Kowloon, searching for the only people that he knew that might be able to help him.

Ignoring the "closed" sign that hung in the front window, he checked the door to see if it was locked, and he found that it wasn't. He walked in as a small bell on the door rang and found that there was no one behind the counter. "Hello?" he asked. "Is anyone here?" A chill went up his spine as he listened to the oppressive silence of the shop. There was no sound from the howling storm outside filtering in at all, and the room seemed to grow even darker with the daylight being blocked by the storm.

Then Boyd heard a shuffling, and in the gloom, he saw a figure standing in the doorway to the back room. His heart jumped into his throat at the sight and it was everything he could do to keep from screaming in that adolescent, ear-piercing way when he saw that the figure standing in the doorway was a skeleton. It stood, tucked away under the cover of darkness, only an apparition that wore baggy clothes and had a vaguely menacing look about it.

"Go away," it said, its raspy voice sending a shiver up Boyd's spine. "We're closed."

"Tony?" Boyd asked, almost afraid to talk.

"Boyd?" the skeleton asked.

"Yes?" Boyd said.

The skeleton cleared its throat and walked out into the open, straight towards him. "What are you doing here?" it asked, its voice now as clear and pleasant as anybody else's. It dawned on Boyd that the skeleton had the voice of Tony Tang. "Oh, I'm sorry," Tony said, straightening his clothes as if he was horribly embarrassed. "I forget about my appearance sometimes. It must be a bit unnerving."

"A little," Boyd said, feeling wary that a skeleton was standing so close to him.

Tony sighed and said, "This is why business is so bad. It's this *curse!*"

"Curse?" Boyd asked.

"A witch's curse[94]," Tony said, scratching his skull with his bony fingers. "It's a long story, but there's a curse on me so that whenever the sun is up, I'm supposed to be exposed for what I really am. Why it's a skeleton, I don't know."

Boyd began to put it all together in his head, "So that's why the other night…"

"…I was human," Tony said. "Yes, that's right. Usually, I get my nephew to work the shop during the day, but he's at school. I must have forgot to lock the door. Curses are such a nuisance. Did you know that your average, run-of-the-mill curse can last up to fifteen years?"

"No, I didn't know that," Boyd said.

"Well, it's true," Tony said. "By the way, where is that yeti of yours?"

"Actually, that's what I wanted to speak to Bird and Goldfish about," Boyd said. "Are they in?"

"Of course, of course," Tony said. "Follow me."

For a moment, Boyd felt wary of going into the back of the teashop with a skeleton that clickety-clacked along the floor, but as with everything else he'd seen, he swallowed his fear and off he went. He soon realized that all of his fears were without merit when he saw Bird in the back.

"Boyd?" Bird was standing over a book, wearing tiny reading glasses and looking surprised to see him in the shop.

"Hi, Bird," he said.

"Is something wrong?" she asked, sounding concerned.

"Uh, yeah," Boyd said. "They've got the machine."

"Who?" she asked, flying over to stand in front of him.

"This Mr. Fang guy," he said. "They got in the mansion and kidnapped everyone and took everything."

"Oh, my," Bird said. She turned to Tony and said, "Can you bring Goldfish in here, please?"

"I was a little confused about what to do, so I came here," Boyd said.

"That's entirely understandable," Bird said. "This is a very dire situation. If they have the machine, they have quite an advantage."

"Well, that's the thing," Boyd said. "The machine doesn't work."

"I say," said Goldfish as Tony brought his large fishbowl into the room, "I was well into my evening constitutional when Tony interrupted me. What's the problem?" He looked up to see Boyd in the room and suddenly looked troubled. "Something's gone horribly wrong, hasn't it?"

"They've got the machine," Bird said.

"The Conspiricetti?" Goldfish asked.

"The Conspiri-who?" Boyd asked.

"Never mind," said Bird. "You were saying that the machine didn't work."

"Didn't work?" asked Goldfish. "But we'd heard that you had all the pieces!"

"All but one," Boyd said. "My sister assembled all the pieces, but she didn't get to finish it. That's when the swordfish…"

"Swordfish?" Bird asked.

"Hedley?" Goldfish asked.

"Yeah, Hedley," Boyd said.

"That annoying air-breather," Goldfish grumbled, sounding as if he had history with him. "We should have thrown him into that volcano[95] when we had the chance!"

"You *know* him?" Boyd asked.

"It's a long story," Bird said.

"What else happened?" Goldfish asked.

"Well," Boyd continued, "my sister figured out that we needed a map to find the final piece of the machine."

"A map?" Bird asked.

"A map," Boyd said.

"A map of what?" Goldfish said.

"A map that led to a key of some sort," Boyd said. "A jade key."

"A jade key?" Bird asked, shocked.

"*The* Jade Key?" Goldfish asked, shocked.

"Yeah, that's it" Boyd said.

"You say the map led to the key?" Goldfish asked.

"Yeah," Boyd said. "But Hedley got the map. They haven't left to get it, though, so I figured I should get the key before they do, and maybe then I could rescue my family."

Bird and Goldfish looked at each other in a knowing manner. "So the legends are true," Goldfish said.

"The legends are true," Bird said.

"What legends?" Boyd asked.

"Where did the map lead to?" Goldfish said.

"Well, I didn't get a good look at it," Boyd said, "but I heard them mention something about a place called Dragon Island. Do you know it?"

"Dragon Island," Goldfish said, a hint of concern in his voice.

"Dragon Island," Bird said, a hint of fear in her voice.

"So you *do* know it," Boyd said. "Hey, why does everyone have to be so cryptic? Give me some straight answers! I can handle it."

"You certainly did the right thing in coming to us," Goldfish said.

"He's going to be a worthy successor to Mr. Ping, isn't he?" Bird said.

"He certainly is," Goldfish said.

"Boyd," Bird said, "the Jade Key on Dragon Island is a legend that's been around for centuries. Only a few people know where, exactly, Dragon Island is. Many people have searched for it, but very few have returned. Legend has it that the Jade Key is on the island and is guarded by a very powerful being."

"What kind of powerful being?" Boyd asked, taking a big gulp.

"No one knows," Bird said, "because no one's lived to tell about it."

"It's much too dangerous, Boyd," Goldfish said, waving him off. "We can't let you go to Dragon Island. They won't survive, and neither will you. I'm afraid your friends are out of luck."

"We're talking about my sister!" Boyd said. "You mean if they go to that island, they're sure to die?"

"The odds are certainly stacked against them," Goldfish said.

"But what if Hedley and Mr. Fang get the Jade Key?" he asked.

"That would most definitely be a dire situation," Bird said. "If the Jade Key will make the Perpetual Motion Machine work and the Machine is in the wrong hands, the consequences could be disastrous."

"We're in a very grim predicament," Goldfish said.

"Look," Boyd said, "someone has to put an end to this mess. We can't let Mr. Fang and that swordfish get this thing. I'm going to Dragon Island, one way or another."

"Boyd, you can't go," Bird said. "It's much too dangerous."

"I'm going," Boyd said. "I need you guys to help me get there."

"But Boyd," Bird said.

"No, no, Bird," Goldfish piped in, "his mind is made up; after all, this is his family and friends we're talking about now; and if the boy is going to go there, we've got to help him." Goldfish began to swim in circles around his bowl, looking as if he was deep in thought. "We're probably going to have to call in a few favors for this one. There are only a few ways to get to Dragon Island safely. I think I know just the person to get you there."

"What kind of men does Hedley have working for him?" Bird asked.

"Werewolves and panjas," Boyd said. "Lots of them."

Bird and Goldfish looked at each other again, seeming to smile (or at least as much as a bird and goldfish could smile). "We're going to get you everything you need to beat those chaps," said Goldfish. "Just leave it to us."

And so, the two began conversing with each other, trying to devise a plan to get Boyd to Dragon Island. Although he was scared, Boyd was convinced he was in good hands, and there was no way that he was going to let Hedley and Mr. Fang win this round.

No way at all.

CHAPTER 34

LET'S HAVE A BAD-GUY-PARTY!

Reggie's mood was the sourest that Smelts had ever seen it. It was more sour than when yeti-hunting[96] became a popular sport for rich people in the 1950s, more sour than when his favorite football team lost the World Cup in overtime several years earlier, and even more sour than when Smelts accidentally spilled a drink[97] on his prized, first-edition copy of *To Kill a Mockingbird*. No, all of these moments paled in comparison to the sour grapes that he had pasted on his face at that moment. The reason wasn't just that he had failed in his mission to protect Boyd at all costs, but also because he had let down a new, valued, and trusted friend. The thought that both he and Smelts were unable to protect Boyd from the werewolves ate at his soul and he vowed that, were he ever given a second chance, no one with an evil intent would ever get within ten feet of Boyd McCloyd again. That was his promise.

However, at this moment, he was in no position to do anything about it, because his hands and feet were tied behind his back with some kind of industrial strength rope and he was lying face down on the cold metal floor of a van that was speeding through the streets of Hong Kong.

However, he was not alone in his predicament. Just as Reggie had been thrown into the back of the van, so, too, had Smelts, having been deposited right on top of him. This made Reggie uncomfortable and angry, a problem compounded by the fact that Smelts couldn't keep from squirming back and forth, trying to break free from his bindings. "Reg!" he said, just loud enough to keep from being heard by the drivers up front. "Reg, where we headed?"

"Don't know," Reggie whispered. "Boyd's gone."

"Yeah, I know," Smelts said. "What are we gonna do?"

"Well," Reggie said, "we're gonna get out of these ropes and get out of this van. Untie me!"

"I can't see your hands," Smelts said. "I'm blindfolded."

"Me, too," Reggie said. He began to feel sharp pains, as if several small knives were poking into his back.

"I'm going to try to get free," Smelts said. "Hold still!"

"Ow!" Reggie said. "That hurts! What are you doing?"

"Cutting myself loose with my claws!"

"That's not rope!" Reggie said. "That's the hair on my back! Stop cutting it!"

"That's not rope?" Smelts asked.

"No!" Reggie said. "You idiot! You've got a big wad of my hair in your hands."

"Then what do we do?" Smelts asked.

"Well," he said, "if I know these idiots like I think I do, then they're taking us straight to the place where we'll be able to rescue

Boyd and Cindy. And once they do that, I'm gonna open up a world of hurt on those blokes."

True to Reggie's word, the van arrived at some unknown destination, and both Reggie and Smelts were taken from the van and dragged to what seemed to be a cavernous building with a strange echo. Reggie gave the air a couple of sniffs and soon knew the other members of the party were there with him. One unmistakably fishy smell seemed to be a bit more putrid than the other smells around him and a grim look passed over his face.

"Hedley," he muttered.

His blindfold was yanked off the top of his head and he had a full view of the slimy swordfish standing in front of him. "Well, well, well," Hedley said. "If it isn't the stinky monkey and his gecko partner. What a horrible surprise!"

"What'd you do with Boyd?" Reggie asked, steeling his gaze.

"Gee, I wish I could say that I'd gutted and filleted the little brat, but alas, I have not. He took off like the little weasel he was and we haven't seen hide nor hair of the punter ever since."

As they were talking to Hedley, both Reggie and Smelts surveyed their surroundings. The smell of the ocean was strong and there was a dampness in the air that was more prevalent than what the typhoon would bring onto the island. It looked to be an empty shipping warehouse with a few black SUVs parked to the side. Several werewolves were loitering about, smoking cigarettes, playing cards, and chatting with each other.

"You do realize you're in over your head this time, don't you, Hedley?" Reggie asked.

"What?" Hedley asked. "Does that mean a little thirteen-year-old is gonna come rescue you all? Don't be stupid. That kid is long gone by now because he's a big sissy. And anyway, we've got bigger fish to fry, pardon my pun." He jerked his head over one way to attract their attention to the Perpetual Motion Machine, which was being carefully loaded into a van by the door. "Recognize that?" he asked.

"Oh, my goodness!" Smelts said, turning to Reggie in a panic. "They've stolen my toaster oven! Whatever shall I do?"

"It's just a toaster oven," Reggie said. "We can get a new one tomorrow."

"I already know what that thing does, you morons," Hedley said. "Mr. Fang has already promised me a hefty price for it. We're going to get the last piece right now."

"Last piece?" Reggie asked, an innocent look pasted on his face.

"The key!" Hedley said. "The Jade Key on Dragon Island!"

"See, Smelts?" Reggie said, looking smug. "If you lead these evil idiot villains on long enough, they'll always reveal their master plans."

"They do *so* love to talk, don't they?" Smelts said, looking up at the sky wistfully.

"They certainly do."

"Shut up!" Hedley said, filled with anger at being duped. "You're going to regret your choice of sides when this is all over, because guess what! Mr. Ping isn't here to bail you out anymore."

"Oh, I'm shaking in my boots!" Smelts said, pretending to be afraid. "Whatever will we do, Reggie?"

One of the large, bay doors at the far end of the warehouse opened and three black vans drove down to park in front of them. Two rather bitter-looking werewolves stepped out from one of the cabs and came over to Hedley. "What's up, fishy?" one said.

"Don't call me fishy!" Hedley said. "Do you have them?"

"Yeah," said the other werewolf, puffing on a cigar. "You want us to dump them out here?"

"Yes," Hedley said. "We're just waiting on the boat."

"It was a rough time trying to keep Simon, there, from chowing down on them, but we managed," said the first werewolf.

"They looked so tasty!" Simon, the other werewolf, said.

"Yes, well, we would have had to shoot you if you did eat them, so I guess it's your lucky day," Hedley said.

Another werewolf approached him, saying, "We got that machine loaded now. What would you like us to do with it?"

Hedley whipped out a piece of paper and wrote down an address. "Take it to the Penthouse at Fang Tower," he said. "They're waiting on it. When you drop it off, come straight back here."

Meanwhile, the other two werewolves were unloading the vans. Reggie and Smelts saw that Cindy was bound and blindfolded like they were, and Bjorn was stuffed inside a cage that was half his size. "Let go of me, you stupid jerks!" Cindy yelled, as feisty as ever.

"Ah, shaddup!" the werewolf said, throwing Cindy to the ground beside Reggie. They carted Bjorn's cage over beside them and then brought out a large potato sack stuffed to the brim. "What do we do with this?" it asked.

"Just dump it here," Hedley said. "But try to keep all the pieces together."

The werewolf dumped out the sack and its contents rolled to the ground.   Cindy let out such a high-pitched wail that the werewolves thought she'd found the Dog Whistle Gun again. "They *killed* him!" she yelled, staring at Ho Yin's head, which was lying at her feet.

"Cindy, I'm fine," Ho Yin's head said, looking up at her.

It was understandable how Cindy might have lost her cool in such a situation. After all, from her point of view, the werewolf had just dumped out a bag full of Ho Yin's body parts; an arm here, a torso there, a finger underneath, a foot on top. But upon closer examination, she saw that each part had wires and gears and motors that made Ho Yin function.

Ho Yin was a robot.

"You're a *robot?*" Cindy said.

"You didn't know?" Smelts asked, genuinely shocked.

"She didn't know," Reggie said over his shoulder.

"He's a *robot!*" Cindy said, turning to them.

"I'm sorry, Cindy," Ho Yin said.   "I should have told you earlier."

"Why didn't you tell me?" she asked.

"Because we wanted to make this transition as smooth as possible," Reggie said.   "And even if we'd told you he was a robot, would you have believed us?"

"Yes!" Cindy said.

"Well, it was a gamble," Reggie said, shrugging.

"Some people are very fickle about talking to a robot," Ho Yin said. "There's a lot of anti-machine prejudice out there, so we kind of keep it quiet."

A gaggle of werewolves approached them, causing Bjorn to struggle to get out of his cage in anger. The computerized voice that Cindy had built for him was smashed at his feet, so growling was his only means of communication. "That'll do," one of the werewolves said, pointing at Ho Yin's head lying on the ground.

"Too right," said another as he picked up the head and took it.

"Hey!" Cindy said. "Bring that back!"

"Did you hear something?" one of the werewolves asked, ignoring her.

"Nope," said another.

"Must be the wind," the first one said, and they all laughed.

"Goodbye, all," Ho Yin said as they carried him off. "I'll be back in a bit."

Cindy was struck by Ho Yin's consistently good-natured smile as the werewolves took him to the far end of the warehouse and continued to have an excellent soccer match using his head as the ball. "That's horrible!" she said, watching them kick the head back and forth.

"Yeah, their toes are gonna be sore tomorrow," Smelts said. "Ho Yin's head is *hard.*"

Hedley walked over to the werewolves in between phone calls and said, "We're leaving after dark. Don't run off anywhere."

Cindy looked over at Reggie and whispered, "We're leaving? Where are we going?"

"Dragon Island," Reggie said.

CHAPTER 35

ARE YOU CHARON'S COUSIN?

After his meeting at Tony Tang's Teas, Boyd found himself being driven to a secret destination in a car with no driver. Bird and Goldfish had told him to wait out in front of the tea shop so that their car could pick him up. Their car turned out to be an old, immaculately clean British diesel and as it pulled up to the curb, the door popped open automatically. Boyd was somewhat stunned to see that there was no driver in the front seat, but he simply shrugged and got inside. Although he said nothing, this mysterious vehicle knew exactly where to go, for when Boyd was in the backseat, the door slammed shut of its own accord and it took off down the road at an intense clip, weaving in and out of the cars and making its way through the streets of Hong Kong.

The car swerved through the windy streets until Boyd found himself cruising through less-populated areas where there were fewer streetlights and the surroundings disappeared into blackness. Night had fallen on Hong Kong, and as it did, an eerie darkness settled over the land. It had begun to pour and the heavy sheets of raindrops dimmed all the light from the surrounding buildings. Boyd realized they were going to the outer edges of the island.

Just over a large mountain pass, the car swerved down the curvy road and came to a stop in front of an old, concrete drainage tunnel carved into the side of the mountain. It slowly pulled to a stop and once again the door opened of its own accord. Goldfish had instructed Boyd to enter this tunnel and go to the very end of it, until he saw the lanterns, whereupon he would wait for the boat that would take him to Dragon Island.

"Take this bag with you," Goldfish said, handing him a small cloth sack filled with coins. "Give it to the driver of the boat as a toll. And whatever you do, don't look him in the eye!"

One thing that irked Boyd about this new world that he had found himself in was the fact that it was full of rules. *Don't look him in the eye! Only speak her name backwards! Knock three times, then turn a circle to enter the temple!* He couldn't understand why nothing was straightforward. It was all curses and terror and anxiety.

He hopped out of the car and it sped off into the darkness, leaving him all alone in the orange streetlight, standing in front of a gated drainage tunnel big enough to drive a truck through. The wind from the typhoon was whipping all around him, swaying the trees and bushes back and forth violently, giving the night a sense of foreboding.

Might as well get on with it, he thought. He climbed the fence and began to walk down the hole, into the blackness below. There were service lights along the walls that led into the tunnel, but then the concrete gave way to a large, black gorge. He looked back and forth to see if there was a way down the gorge, but saw nothing but a rickety set of wooden stairs that seemed to disappear off into the blackness below.

The stairway curved around the side of the rock, into the darkness, and he inched his way down as the light grew dimmer. He made it to the bottom of the stairs and dipped his foot right into a black puddle of water. The shock of stepping in the water panicked him and he fell to his knees as he stepped forward. He looked behind himself and couldn't see anything, including the stairs that he'd come down. A wave of anxiety rushed through his head at the thought of being trapped in a pitch black cave and he began to think that there was no hope until he saw a faint glow around a far corner, so dim that it was almost imperceptible. With his hands out in front of him as though he was blindfolded, he began to make his way toward the light. The closer he got, the brighter the light became. He rounded a corner and saw that he was standing in a giant cavern with a calm pool of water in the center. At the far end of the cave was a small, gravel beach with a single, white Chinese lantern hanging from a stick in the ground. The faint light of the lantern illuminated the entire cavern and it hung on a string between two poles that were stuck in the gravel bar. Three other lanterns hung on the string, but none of them were glowing.

Boyd waded through the still, black waters, towards the gravel bar and found himself standing under the lanterns. *These must be the lanterns to call the boat,* he thought. He looked at the glowing lantern and could not figure out how it was staying lit. There were no candles inside, only light, and whenever he would try to peek in the bottom, the light would grow so bright that he couldn't see.

When he touched the first one, he saw that the one beside it started to glow. It was dim at first, barely visible, but its intensity grew stronger, and soon it was as bright as the first. Then the next one started to glow, and then the one after that. Just as they were all glowing as brightly as the first, the wind began to pick up in the cave.

In the beginning, it was only a slight breeze, but soon it grew stronger. A ghostly, white fog rolled over the water towards Boyd, blanketing the dark waters of the cavern as it grew thicker and rose from his ankles, to his knees, to his chest, and finally, well above his head. Soon, the whole cavern was filled with fog and the wind subsided. He heard the parting of the water and the creak of an old ship, but the fog was so thick, he couldn't see anything. The distant clang of a bell echoed through the cave.

Then, almost as if it appeared from nowhere, a large ship emerged from the darkness, silently riding up beside the gravel bar where Boyd stood. It was gray and dull in the dim light of the lanterns, and craggy barnacles and seaweed had collected around the water line of its hull. Above the ship were three old, tattered, orange sails that hung limp in the stale air, their shape much more angular and sharp than the majestic, white sails that he was used to seeing in western culture. It was a Chinese "Junk" and looked like it could have been well-over a hundred years old. It also looked like it had been rotting away in some unknown cave for a very long time.

When the junk came to a stop, Boyd heard the slow knock of footsteps on the deck as someone made their way towards the side. A shuffling sound was heard and then a large plank rattled over the edge, as one end fell to the ground in front of him with a thud. Boyd looked up to see an ethereal figure standing at the top of the plank. It seemed to be a man, but in the darkness, only his silhouette could be seen as he stared at Boyd from on high.

"Hello?" Boyd asked. "I need some help." His statement was met with an eerie silence from the stranger. "I need to get to Dragon Island. Bird and Goldfish sent me."

The stranger began to make his way down the plank, towards Boyd. As he moved closer, Boyd could see that underneath his large, straw hat, where his eyes should have been, were large, black holes. His skin looked old, more wrinkled than normal, and the light, pajama-like clothes he wore were full of holes and seemed to be as old as he was. He said nothing to Boyd, only choosing to extend his hand towards him, as if he expected something in return for his help. "Oh!" Boyd said. "The toll!" He fished in his pockets and pulled out the bag of coins, giving it to the boatman.

The creepy boatman looked at the coins for a second, then looked back at Boyd.

"It...It's all I have," Boyd said.

The boatman led him up on deck and took the wheel of the ship. He pointed to the plank, and Boyd walked over, lifting it back up to the deck. Slowly, the junk started to drift away from the gravel bank, with only the occasional creaks from the hull breaking the calm silence of the cave. Boyd made his way back to the boatman, watching him steer his way into the fog. The mist grew more thick the further they went, and soon Boyd could barely see his hand in front of his face. "How can you see where you're going?" he asked.

The boatman said nothing, staring off into the distance with a grim look on his face.

Just as Boyd was unable to see much further than the edge of the ship, the wind began to pick up, shifting from a gentle breeze to gusts so strong they almost blew him off the boat. As the first spray of a wave jumped over the side railings, Boyd frantically grabbed onto a rope in the hopes of preventing himself from being washed off the deck.

With a mammoth flash of lightning, the fog cleared and Boyd realized that they were now floating out in the open ocean, and were being whipped back and forth by the typhoon that was lashing the island. Rain pounded his face so hard that it stung and the deck bobbed and weaved ferociously in the swells of water. The metropolis that was Hong Kong was nowhere to be seen, but even if it could be seen, the torrent of rain falling from the sky would have obscured its brightness. They had been transported to the middle of the ocean.

Just as Boyd began to feel queasy from the constant up and down motion of the boat, a flash of lightning revealed that they were only about a hundred yards from the coast of a large, black island whose steep cliffs loomed over the ship like a giant. The boatman looked at Boyd and pointed at the island.

"I don't see any lights," Boyd said, yelling over the din of the storm.

The boatman steered the ship straight towards one of the inky, black cliffs that looked like it would smash it into a thousand pieces. "Are you crazy?" Boyd yelled. "You might be dead, but *I* don't want to be!" The boatman ignored his pleas and stared at the rocks ahead. "We're going to be smashed to bits!" Boyd said.

Just as Boyd closed his eyes, certain that his death was imminent, the boat sailed up onto a large wave and then came crashing down past the rocks, into a large opening on the rock wall. Very soon, the thunder, lightning and crashing waves grew fainter as the ship moved on into the calm waters of the cave. It was now so dark that Boyd couldn't see, but further ahead, he noticed the dim glow of lights. They were traveling through some sort of tunnel and at the far end of the shaft, several expensive speedboats and fishing trawlers were moored at a stone dock. On the back of each boat was a logo that read, ***Fang Industries.***

Lenny was a werewolf from Kent, England. He'd been a werewolf for as long as he could remember, although it must be said that werewolves weren't really renowned for their memory skills as much as their ability to rip and tear the flesh off of living creatures. If it must be known, before Lenny became a werewolf (in the year 1963), he was a cab driver from Pakistan that made his home in London.

One night, he absentmindedly picked up a nervous, twitchy fellow who turned into a snarling, raving monster, all whilst in the backseat of his taxi. Lenny wasn't killed, but he did gain "the curse" and spent the next few years mangling late night pedestrians. In fact, Lenny was one of the pioneers of the British werewolf explosion of the early seventies.

As with all werewolves in the beginning Lenny (his original name was Sanjay) would spend his day being a normal human being and his nights ripping people to shreds, but soon, long explanations to his wife about where he'd been all night and why there were bloodstains and fur all over his clothes became too much of a hassle for him. He opted, as 99% of all werewolves usually do, to remain a werewolf full time and he gave up his life as a human being. The only reminder that he was once human was the white turban he wore on his furry head, for he was too proud of his Sikh heritage to give it up.

Lured by the lucrative money in the werewolf-for-hire business, Lenny soon found himself taking hired jobs and after a few years found himself as a member of the werewolf "elite." However, sometimes the hired work proved to be exceptionally boring, as most of the time it involved him sitting around, guarding things. This night was no exception, and Lenny now found himself sitting on a rock in a large cave, guarding speedboats while everyone else got to have all the real fun further in the cave.

He found himself struggling to stay awake as he sat on the dock. It's a little known fact that werewolves growl in their sleep instead of snoring, and when one of his own growls woke him from his slumber, he knew something was wrong. There was a smell in the air; something old, wet, and dead. He rose from the small stool that he'd been sitting on to peer off into the darkness of the tunnel in front of him, but he saw nothing. His nose told him otherwise.

A fog rolled into the cave, slowly filling the space in front of him, making visibility poor, and then like a ghost materializing from nowhere, an old, Chinese junk swept towards the docks, with a thirteen-year-old boy standing on the bow. The boy was clad in what looked to be an old, monk's outfit[98]. He wore a long shirt that looked like a dress and was colored maroon, with deep, gold trim. His pants matched the outfit and they waved in the wind as the boat moved towards him. It happened so fast that Lenny had no time to react as the boy jumped onto the dock, smacking his silver-clad wrists together in front of his head. The pain from the silver bracelets was so intense that he fell to the ground almost instantly.

"Now, you're going to be a good fellow, aren't you?" the boy asked.

The bracelets he wore on his wrists were silver and they made Lenny whimper. "Don't hurt me!" he said. "I've got a wife and puppies."

"Yeah, yeah," the boy said. "I'm Boyd McCloyd and I'm here to rescue my friends and family. Are you gonna help me, or is this going to get ugly?"

"I'll help! I'll help!" Lenny said. His loyalty was beholden to no one when his life was at stake. "What do you want me to do?"

"How many other werewolves are here?" Boyd asked.

"Almost forty," Lenny said. He kept shifting uncomfortably, squirming on the ground as he tried to inch further and further away from Boyd. "Look, friend," he said. "I don't know what you got on your hands, but it's killing me."

"Oh, yeah," Boyd said, sticking his hands behind his back. "Who else is here?"

"Panjas," Lenny said. "A whole mess of them. And Hedley. Mr. Fang, too."

Boyd looked up the trail to the canal that led further into the caves. A string of lights had been hung along the path to light the way. "Okay, puppy," he said. "I want you to get on that speedboat there, and get going. If I see you again, you're gonna be eating these silver bracelets. Got it?"

Lenny didn't even answer. He ran to the boat, turned it on, and drove out of the cave.

Boyd began to make his way up a trail that followed alongside a small canal that led deeper into the cave. As he made his way through the narrow tunnel, he saw that the small cave expanded into something much more elaborate. He walked into a much larger cave, which was divided by an ancient, marble wall and a gate that looked to be thousands of years old.

A river of ocean water flowed right through the gate, with two narrow paths running along each side. It looked like the entrance to a Chinese temple, with several steps leading down to the paths alongside the river. At the foot of the steps were two weathered statues of lions staring at Boyd, but no one was around to guard the gate.

Boyd made his way down the steps and through the door to find himself in another tunnel that ran along the canal, further into the cave. The walls were old and jagged, but the paths along the water were paved with polished marble stones. More torches and lanterns hung on the walls to light the way.

As he made his way through the tunnel, he heard talking further up the path. He ducked behind a large rock to listen in on what was being said. Peering around the edge, he saw two werewolves dressed in black, walking towards him. They were oblivious to his being there.

"...No, no, you're totally wrong," one of the werewolves said, "the meat off your average American is much too fatty. Sure, it *tastes* good, but if you eat too many of them, you start to put on the pounds, you know what I'm saying?"

"I disagree," said the other, licking his lips. "Where I'm from in Mayfair, we don't get many Americans roaming through the neighborhood, and when we do, it's a fight to see who gets to devour 'em first."

"I don't know if I can take eating another one of these Chinese blokes, though," said the first werewolf. "They're so lean. It's too much work for too little payoff."

"Too right," said the other. "It's almost like..." The werewolf perked up and began to sniff the air. Both of them snapped to attention, on guard as they scanned their surroundings. "You smell that?"

"That Yank kid is here," said the other.

The two of them dropped to all fours and began to sniff at their surroundings. "I've got 'im!" one of the wolves said and he rushed down the passage in pursuit. But his pursuit ended when Boyd stepped out from behind a wall. The werewolves started to growl.

"I'll have you know," Boyd said, "I'm *Canadian,* not American."

"Canadian, American," said one werewolf, "they both taste the same to me!"

It lunged for Boyd, but like magic, Boyd could feel himself kick into action. The silk robe that had been given to him by Bird and Goldfish was enchanted and gave him the powers of a Shaolin warrior. This proved to be the case, for with one fluid movement, he did a back flip, and kicked his feet into the air to propel the werewolf straight over his head. It slammed into the rock wall, head first, and with a whimper, it fell to the ground unconscious.

Boyd popped back to his feet without any effort to face the second werewolf. This time, the suit led him into a more kung-fu-like position, with his hands cocked, ready to take on the other foe. With his hands in the air, he exposed the other werewolf to the Armicons on his wrists, and it, too, fell to the ground, taken out of the game.

This is going to be too easy, Boyd thought.

"This way!"

A snarling sound echoed through the cave and soon he saw five werewolves galloping at incredible speeds towards him. *Uh-oh,* he thought, but before he even had the chance to get scared, the robe had him reach over to retrieve a wooden pole holding up one of the lanterns, and soon he was spinning the pole with a precision and grace that he never imagined. *Cool,* he thought.

He began to systematically twirl, kick, lunge, and flip his way around the werewolves, avoiding their snapping jaws and swiping claws by mere millimeters. Boyd spun of the way of one pair of jaws, only to trail the hard end of the pole behind him, so that he could deliver a blow so hard that it left its victim temporarily cross-eyed. Another snarling beast bounded across the tunnel, trying to pounce on him by surprise, but Boyd anticipated the move and pole vault out of the way, making sure that the werewolf landed on the less-pleasant end of the pole. He sent the creature flailing into the canal beside them. The small path was soon filled with equal amounts of both snarls of rage and howls of pain, as each werewolf tried and failed to take Boyd down. Unfortunately for them, his skills were too sharp now that he was wearing the Shaolin robe, and each werewolf met a more punishing fate than the last.

Soon, Boyd found himself standing in the middle of a pile of unconscious werewolves, breathing heavily, but still agile as a cat. He was sure that it was a combination of the hard blows and the Armicons keeping them down, and that the sounds of the battle would soon bring more of Mr. Fang's cronies his way.

His prediction was made real when he heard the sound of two slimy, wet fins clapping together. "Bravo, Mr. McCloyd," said a sarcastic, gurgling voice. "Bra-vo!"

Boyd looked to see Hedley standing on the marble path across the water from him. "What have you done with my friends?" he said.

"Your friends?" Hedley asked, waddling across the path to look Boyd in the eye. "Why, your friends could be *anywhere!* What makes you think they're *here?* They could be safe at home eating TV dinners, or they could actually *be* TV dinners right now. Those werewolves get mighty hungry, you know."

"Where do you come up with this third-rate, villain dialog?" Boyd asked, looking at Hedley like he was an idiot. "It's terrible."

For a second or two, Hedley was taken aback by Boyd's insult. "You don't really think you stand a chance, do you?" he snarled. "You'd best just give up now, because you've already lost! This isn't one of those video games where you can start over if you get killed. This is real."

"Real?" Boyd asked. "I'm talking to a swordfish and wearing a Chinese silk robe. How real is that?'

"Good point," Hedley said, thinking about it. He then gave him the Staredown and said, "You were defeated from the start, Boyd. Look at you! You're just a thirteen-year old loser. What in the world makes you think that you even stand a chance against incredibly powerful killing machines such as myself? We eat pimply faced teens like you as midnight snacks!"

"Hmm," Boyd said, rubbing his chin as if he were really thinking about what Hedley was saying. "Gee, maybe you're right. Maybe I should just go tuck my head under the covers and hide."

"That would be a fine idea," Hedley said with a smirk.

Boyd smiled at him and said, "But if you *are* right, wouldn't it be horribly embarrassing to get your butt kicked by a pimply faced teenager? You could never show your face at the office again."

"I don't think that's going to happen," Hedley said with a huff.

"Well, we'll just have to see, won't we?" Boyd asked.

"I guess we will," Hedley said.

"Fine," Boyd said.

"Oh, this is nonsense," Hedley said. "Come on out, boys..."

The biggest and burliest of the werewolves and panjas began to emerge from around the corners, every nook and cranny soon held some sort of dangerous creature. They all snarled and scratched at the floor as their low growls echoed in the cave. Boyd realized that he was now facing the prospect of fighting a battle that he very well may lose.

"So which is it, Boyd?" Hedley asked. "All of us at once? Or one at a time?"

"I won't waste your time," Boyd said. "Why don't you *all* take a shot?"

"As you wish," Hedley said. "Kill him at your leisure, friends. Make sure to make him suffer."

Although he seemed confident on the outside, in his heart Boyd felt sick with despair. The werewolves and panjas were all moving closer for the kill and he was sure that they would see the fear in his eyes. Something in his soul wanted to give up before he even started. Then he caught the eye of one, single werewolf, and in that werewolf's eyes, he saw something he'd never seen before when anyone was looking at him: *Fear.*

Yes, that werewolf standing across from him was *afraid,* and as soon as Boyd was able to spot *The Fear* in one, he could spot *The Fear* in the others. *That* panja was afraid, and so was *that* one. For some odd reason (perhaps because of the pile of unconscious werewolves lying all around him), Hedley's lackeys were terrified of him, and this was something new to Boyd. He'd never instilled a sense of fear in anyone. Now, he was standing in a cave in front of the toughest, seediest, meanest characters he'd ever seen, and they were afraid. He started to think that he actually had a chance.

One of the more aggressive werewolves crouched, then pounced towards Boyd, ready to devour him. Boyd's suit sent a surge of strength through his body, and with lightning speed, his arms cut through the air, building power for a hard blow. He swung his arm around and landed the palm of his hand right on the werewolf's nose, bringing all three-hundred pounds of the werewolf to a dead halt, midair. The poor beast fell to the ground, as limp as a stuffed animal. Boyd had knocked the werewolf unconscious with one shot.

An audible gasp rang out in the cave, as the panjas and werewolves reeled back in shock, watching their brethren taken out of the game. They didn't know what to think of what had befallen their comrade. Boyd was filled with a surge of energy and adopted a hardcore, kung-fu pose, as he looked around at the others and said, "Who wants some?"

"Don't just stand there, you morons!" Hedley yelled. "Take him out!"

If it were possible for werewolves to look sheepish, this was the moment, as neither they nor the panjas were eager to take on Boyd. Then, they all collectively held their breath and made their assault. With skill and dexterity, Boyd fended off each of them, not so much putting them out of commission as much as keeping them from gaining any ground. As one would approach, a swift kick to the head would send the beast scurrying back to safety. As another would near, Boyd would twirl his pole in an intimidating manner to keep it back.

"How long do you think you can keep this up, Boyd?" Hedley yelled from the safety of the path across the water. "You can't keep us away forever."

"I don't have to keep it up forever," Boyd said as he smacked a werewolf across the nose with his pole. "Not when I have back-up."

He pulled a tiny ginger jar, a fourth of the size of the jars they'd seen at the museum, from his pocket and threw it on the ground as hard as he could. It shattered into a million pieces, exploding into a puff of white smoke. Goldfish had told him to use it if he got into a pinch. "Remember what happened with the ginger jars at the museum?" he said in the teashop as he handed him the jar. "If you ever get in a rough spot, just smash this and help will come."

Boyd stood there, looking at the busted jar on the ground, waiting for something to happen. The werewolves and panjas were also staring at the pieces of the jar, waiting, and for a few seconds, a silence filled the cave.

"What are you waiting on?" Hedley yelled. "Get him!" Despite Hedley's pleas, nobody moved.

Then *they* appeared.

At first, a few of them scurried out of a couple of holes, making their way through the cracks in the rock, but within seconds, millions upon millions upon millions of cockroaches began to flood into the room, swarming the werewolves and panjas, pushing them back the way they came as they formed a protective bubble around Boyd. Cockroaches were swarming everywhere and the werewolves and panjas were doing everything they could to get them off.

"Come on," Hedley yelled as he threw up his hands in frustration. "Don't run, you idiots! They're just cockroaches. Eat them!" True to his word, Hedley began to devour every roach that crawled on his body as if he was enjoying some strange delicacy. Yet, his constant mowing down of the roaches failed to keep them from overtaking him, and soon he was enveloped in a mass of the squirming insects. A panic set in and he began to struggle to free himself. "Retreat!" he yelled, trying to keep the roaches off his head. "Fall back!"

He needn't have yelled such a thing, for the werewolves and panjas were already in full retreat. They hadn't even paused to listen for Hedley's orders. They started running away in desperation, hoping to avoid the itchy, crawling legs of the millions of insects filling the cave.

Boyd stood in the middle of the tunnel, surrounded by shimmering walls of insects as he watched his adversaries run off. The roaches then cleared a path for him through the cave and he began to make his way further on towards where Hedley and his cronies had retreated. "Thanks, roaches," Boyd said, but he felt stupid talking to them.

As Boyd ran up the trail, he could see a light ahead, with shadows dancing all around it, as if there was a lot of activity going on there. He rounded the corner as the roaches began to thin out and found himself standing on a cliff that overlooked a vast area lit by giant floodlights. Boyd was standing on the balcony of a giant cavern decorated with polished stone. At both ends of the balcony were stairs that led down to a large open space on the floor that was divided by a lagoon churning in the center of the cavern.

The canal that had led all the way from the entrance to the cave ended in this lagoon and the whole space must have been six or seven stories high, with balconies and entrances carved into every available space. The opposite end of the lagoon was the central focus of the room, with a seven-story stone carving of a Chinese dragon in the center of two sets of stairs that led to the top, where several doors stood in wait. Sitting in the water in front of the staircases was a large, luxury yacht.

Yet as much as Boyd stared in awe at the strange temple, he couldn't help but notice the hundreds of werewolves, men, and panjas that stood waiting on the floor of the cavern. Each one was looking up at Boyd in silence, scowls and grimaces pasted across their faces, as though they could barely wait to chow down upon him.

"Ah, you finally made it!" a voice echoed through the cave. "And you brought your friends, the roaches. How lovely."

Boyd looked to see where the voice was coming from and saw a large, chunky man standing on the deck of the yacht. He had a glass of champagne in his hand, and looked relaxed, as if he was expecting a big party. "You must be Mr. Fang," Boyd said.

"And you must be that stupid kid who's been causing me so much trouble," Mr. Fang said.

"Where's my family?" Boyd yelled.

"Your family?" Mr. Fang asked. "Why, they're safe and sound." He turned over his shoulder to say, "Bring that annoying kid his family, Hedley."

From below deck, Hedley walked up, pulling Cindy and Ho Yin, who had been pieced together with tape and wire. "Here they are!" Hedley said.

"Get out of here, Boyd!" Cindy yelled. It's a trap!"

"Oh, shut up," Hedley said, throwing a dead fish at her head. "Of *course* it's a trap! You think he doesn't *know* that?"

"Are *they* what you're looking for?" Mr. Fang yelled. "No? What about *these* guys?" He pointed over to another side of the cave, where a group of werewolves were standing next to Reggie, Smelts, and Bjorn, who were all chained together on the floor. "What about them?" Mr. Fang yelled. "Are they your family, too? No? Well, what about these two?"

He pointed to the top of the cave, where Boyd could see his mother and father being lowered a couple of hundred feet above the water in a giant fishing net. It was weighted down with lead weights tied to the bottom. Boyd felt his breath taken away at the sight of his mother and father in danger. "Mom? Dad?" he yelled.

"Boyd?" his mother said, peeking her head through the holes in the net. "Are you okay? What in the world are you wearing?"

"I'm okay," Boyd yelled.

"Son, we're fine," his father said. "Don't worry about us!"

"Quite a predicament, eh, Boyd?" Mr. Fang yelled. "Three groups of very important people, all in dangerous positions. The *first* thing I'm going to do is cut the rope and watch your mother and father fall into lagoon to drown. Those weights on the net will take them right to the bottom. Then, mommy and daddy go bye-bye. You could save them if you want. Or, you could save that big, ugly yeti and his two loser sidekicks, because when I give the order, the werewolves are going to have a feast. A yeti and alligator and polar bear feast."

"I resent that," Smelts yelled. "I'm a *crocodile!*"

"Or you could save your sister and that stupid robot, Ho Yin," Mr. Fang continued. "Because I'm going to tell Hedley to kill them at the same time." Mr. Fang and Hedley looked at each other and laughed. "So which is it, Boyd? Who are you going to save? Because while you're saving these losers, I'm going to be getting the Jade Key."

In that split-second of time, Boyd had no clue what to do. He couldn't save everybody, even if he tried. There were too many werewolves, too many panjas, and too many men.

"What's it gonna be, Boyd?" Mr. Fang yelled. "Don't make me give you ten-seconds to decide. Ten...nine...eight..."

With a blur of motion, Boyd popped off one of the Armicons and threw it straight towards Reggie, Smelts, and Bjorn. At first, the werewolves surrounding them didn't know what to think, until they began to feel the pain that the Armicons caused, and they soon scattered away, giving Reggie and crew just a few more seconds to live as the gleaming silver Armicon rolled to a stop at their feet.

The glow of the silver bracelet seemed to stop everyone in their tracks, giving Boyd just the time he needed to bound off the cliff, where, with the power of the Shaolin robe, he was able to run across the tops of the werewolves' and panjas' heads, each foot landing on an upturned face, a perked ear, or a broad back. He bounded across the cave at a breakneck pace, heading towards the lagoon.

Mr. Fang was temporarily distracted by the commotion near Reggie and Smelts, and didn't see Boyd until he was halfway across the room. As Boyd ran towards him, he was filled with panic and turned to Hedley, yelling, "Get rid of them!" He then ran down a plank, into a small boat tied to the yacht.

"My pleasure," Hedley said, as he turned to Cindy and Ho Yin, pointing his razor-sharp nose at them in the most threatening of ways.

"Wait!" Cindy said. "Can't we talk about this?"

"Uh, no," Hedley smiled as he reared back to jab at the net.

A sound unlike anything anyone had ever heard erupted in the center of the cavern, drawing all eyes towards it. Hedley wheeled around to see that the sound was a deafening roar emanating from Reggie, who had somehow, despite the heavy steel chains wrapped around him, managed to make it to his feet.

Reggie's face was filled with determination as he began to unleash a horrible, yeti-growl that was so loud, it caused everyone to cover their ears with their hands. All eyes were fixed on him, and soon, the chains that had held him in place began to strain, then bulge, then bend, and in a moment of raw fury, Reggie snapped the steel. The chains fell to the ground in a pile, leaving him standing alone in the center of the cave (looking ten times bigger than before) as he breathed heavily, surveying the werewolves cowering around him.

"I don't think Boyd should have to fight this one alone," he said.

"Yo, mate," Smelts said, his powerful jaws wrapped tightly by the chains. "Bjorn and I would love to give you a hand, but we need a little help."

Knowing that he was unable to do it on his own, Reggie turned to Smelts and began trying to free him. "Thanks for ruining my heroic entrance, Smelts," he muttered.

"Ow!" Smelts yelled. "You're pulling too tight!"

"How do you think I got out?" Reggie said, annoyed.

Meanwhile, Hedley knew that it wouldn't be long before he had to make a quick exit, and he turned back to Cindy and Ho Yin to say, "So long, suckers!" He jabbed at the net with his nose a few times, but Cindy and Ho Yin had just enough leverage to move out of the way.

"Hey, fish-face!"

Hedley spun around just in time to receive a crack across the face from Boyd, which sent him flying all the way across the deck, sliding to a stop against the rail of the boat. "Don't mess with my sister, punk!" he said, once again adopting a cool, kung-fu pose.

Hedley rose to his feet, looking angry; his long nose somewhat askew after Boyd had smacked him. "You don't know when to quit, do you?" he gurgled. "You're beat, kid!"

He charged Boyd and began to poke and stab at him in an effort to put an end to Boyd's quest, but the Shaolin robe gave Boyd the dexterity to dodge Hedley's advances, and despite the swordfish's years of training himself to be fast as lightning and deadly as a bullet, he could not hit Boyd. Hedley would thrust and Boyd would dodge him. He would jab and Boyd would do a back flip. Simply put, Boyd was unstoppable as they did their dance of death across the deck of the boat.

As Boyd and Hedley fought, Reggie was having a spot of trouble freeing Bjorn and Smelts. "Aaa!" Smelts yelled. "Too hard! Too hard!"

"Look, I can't break the chains if you're constantly crying about it," Reggie said.

"Well, wherever you pull, it tightens the chains someplace else!"

"What in the world am I supposed to do?"

"Find the key!" Smelts said.

"Oh, just let me look for it on the floor!" Reggie said, rolling his eyes.

Sensing something was amiss, Reggie turned to see that although the werewolves were keeping their distance, the Armicon lying on the ground seemed to have no effect on the panjas that were now inching their way closer. "Uh-oh," he muttered.

Without batting an eye, Reggie reached out and grabbed one of the panjas, swinging all five hundred pounds of the creature around by the leg, taking out a few of its colleagues in the process before tossing the beast halfway across the cave into the lagoon. "Anyone else want a sampling of what I've got?" he yelled, baring his fangs.

"You don't stand a chance, McCloyd," Hedley said as he trapped Boyd against the edge of the yacht. "You're sunk, your friend the yeti is about to be a three-course meal, and old Fang over there is going to get the key." Boyd looked over and saw Mr. Fang climbing a stone staircase that led to the four ornate doors that stood above the water. Behind him were several werewolves, keeping a close eye on his safety. "You fought a good fight, you little runt, but this time your luck's run out!"

A wind rose up in the otherwise still cave, blowing in from the tunnel that led to the outside. As it began to howl through the narrow tunnel, all eyes in the cave focused on the noise. A fog began to seep in from the outside, spreading across the rippling waters of the lagoon and covering the entrance.

A ship emerged from the fog; the very same old Chinese junk, whose tattered sails and rotten wood brought Boyd to the island, and there, on the deck of the ship, stood hundreds upon hundreds of dead, rotting, skeletons and corpses. Leading the charge at the bow of the ship was a familiar sight to Boyd. It was Xiao, the dead taxi driver.

"Onwards to battle!" Xiao yelled in Cantonese, as he dove from the ship onto the floor of the cave. "Take them all down, men!"

The old junk rammed into the shoreline with a crash and the Dead began to pile off the ship by the truckload to attack the panjas, werewolves, and Mr. Fang's men, all of whom were standing there, dumbfounded. There were dead bodies of all shapes, sizes, and smells amongst the group. Some were little more than skeletons with bits of rags that were once their clothes flapping from their bodies, while others looked freshly deceased, with only the paleness of their skin marking the difference between the living and the dead. Some were missing limbs, as if the years of decay had caused their arms and legs (and sometimes heads) to fall off like colored leaves from a tree, while others had horrible pus and maggot-filled wounds or injuries that were enough to make even those with the strongest of stomachs take pause.

With the arrival of the Dead, there was also the stench that accompanied them; a foul, bitter, smell that was worse than a giant garbage dump full of rotting meat. The smell alone was their single, greatest weapon, for the werewolves' keen sense of smell was overwhelmed by the rotting bodies even more than the Armicons. Xiao was leading the charge against the creatures as the battle raged.

"Undying loyalty!" Xiao yelled at Boyd. "Get it? Un-dying!" The Dead swept into the cavern, fighting swiftly and mercilessly, for they had no fear of injury (being that they were already dead). They swarmed groups of werewolves and panjas like a small army, with bony arms, half-rotten legs, and maggoty torsos flailing all over the place. Werewolves swiped at the corpses, sending limbs flying across the cave, but it would have no effect on the dead, for they didn't need their arms or legs. Some panjas would try all sorts of karate moves on a withered skeleton, but the skeleton would just shrug them off and continue pounding away at them. The loss of an appendage would fail to stop the dead person, and they would keep coming for their adversaries relentlessly, even until they had no limbs whatsoever.

The werewolves, who were already incapacitated by the stench, had also lost their main battle technique: They dared not bite into a dead person, for fear of what it might taste like. The panjas were doing their best to swipe, punch, and kick their foes, but were running into the same trouble as the werewolves. Mr. Fang's cronies were losing the battle.

Meanwhile, Hedley had turned away from Boyd, waddling towards the back of the yacht, muttering the whole way. This gave Boyd the chance to run over to free his sister and Ho Yin from the net. "Nice work, Boyd," Ho Yin said.

Boyd could not help but examine the patchwork state of Ho Yin's body. "You're a *robot?*" he asked.

"Boyd, you've got to stop Mr. Fang!" Cindy said. "If he gets that key, we're doomed!"

In all the chaos and confusion, he'd forgotten about Mr. Fang's quest for the Jade Key. He looked over to see that Mr. Fang was now halfway up the flight of stairs, towards the doors, and only his hefty bulk was stopping him from reaching the top more quickly.

All of his concerns about Mr. Fang were superceded by the arrival of Hedley from around the corner of the boat, carrying a speargun. "Like Fang said, McCloyd," he said with a gurgle, "you can't save them all!"

He lifted the spear gun towards the top of the cave and fired a single spear at the net where Boyd's mother and father were suspended above the water. The spear was aimed perfectly, and it tore through the rope that held them in place, sending Boyd's parents crashing down into the water and sinking into the depths.

"Mom! Dad!" Boyd yelled as Hedley cackled.

Without hesitation, Boyd ran to the side of the boat and dove into the cool, green water, swimming for the bottom where his mother and father were struggling to get out. However, Boyd's skills from the Shaolin robe failed to help him under the surface, and he found that he could swim no faster than he could before donning the garment. His parents were too far away to be saved.

Looking behind him, he saw Hedley dive into the water, his natural habitat, as he sped straight towards Boyd, nose first, with the intent to kill him. Just as he was about to run Boyd through with his nose, he was blindsided by another foreign object under the water.

It was Smelts!

Smelts knocked Hedley just off course enough to make him miss Boyd, and then kept on going, swimming all the way to the bottom, where Boyd's mother and father were trapped. With his powerful jaws, he ripped a great hole in the net, grabbed Boyd's parents, and pulled them up to the surface.

"Thank you," Mr. McCloyd said when they reached the surface, stunned by the fact that he had been rescued by a crocodile.

"No worries, mate," Smelts said.

Boyd surfaced just long enough to gasp for air, but was pulled under by Hedley, who dragged him below the water and began to stab at him with his nose. Boyd had just enough agility to dodge each thrust, but he was running out of air with each passing second. Hedley was, too, and they both surfaced for a gasp, but just as quickly, Hedley pulled Boyd below the surface. He tried jabbing him a few more times, but missed again. On his last attempt, Boyd landed a lucky kick to his stomach, which knocked the breath out of him and sent him back to the surface, gasping for air. Boyd burst from the water and began to swim for the yacht.

On the shore, Reggie and Bjorn were now leading the army of dead people in their rout of Mr. Fang's henchmen. At this point, most of the werewolves and panjas had fled, along with the majority of Mr. Fang's men, and those who had decided to stick around were getting trounced. One werewolf made a swipe at a dead man, sending his head flying across the cave to land at Reggie's feet. The head looked up at Reggie and said, "Put me to good use, man!" Sure enough, Reggie picked it up, saying, "Sorry about this!" before hurtling the head towards the werewolf like a baseball, knocking the beast flat on its back.

Meanwhile, Bjorn was having a heyday, romping back and forth across the cave, ramming and swiping and head-butting as many of his enemies as he could, before jumping in the water to swim over to the yacht to see Cindy and Ho Yin. He pulled his massive bulk onto the back deck of the boat, shook the water from his fur, and ran over to give Cindy a major bear hug, almost crushing her small frame in his massive arms.

"Okay, okay," Cindy said with a giggle, before she was quieted by the lapping of his wet tongue against her face. "Eew!" she said, smiling.

"Where's Boyd?" Ho Yin asked as he tried to rewire his leg back together.

Cindy scanned the horizon, looking for her brother in the water, but saw nothing. "I don't see him!" she said.

Bjorn began to grunt and growl, pointing at the stone staircase that led to the top of the cave. Cindy and Ho Yin looked over to see Boyd running up the stairs in pursuit of Mr. Fang. "There he is!" she said.

Mr. Fang was now standing on the edge of the cliff, looking at the four doors before him and breathing heavily from his long march to the top. He looked down to see Boyd climbing the steps after him and said to his werewolves, "Don't let that little brat get past you!" He turned to yell down at Boyd, "It's pointless for you, kid! I'm at the top now and there ain't no way any of you can stop me. The machine is going to be mine! I'm going to be the most powerful man in the world!"

Mr. Fang was focused so intently on Boyd below him that he failed to see the dead man's head flying through the air, missing his face by inches. The head sailed past him, hit the wall, and rolled to a stop on the floor at his feet, staring up at him. He yelled, "You missed, Reggie!"

"Darn!" Reggie said.

The head on the ground focused on Mr. Fang and narrowed its eyes. "You just wait till my body gets up here!" it said. "You'll be joining us before you know it!"

"I beg to differ," Mr. Fang said as he casually booted the head off the cliff, into the water.

"Fang, don't go after the key!" Ho Yin yelled. "You're going to kill us all!"

"Blah, blah, blah," Mr. Fang yelled. "Shut up!"

Mr. Fang kicked open the first door and looked into the blackness before him. He turned over his shoulder to the werewolf standing behind him and said, "Hey, dog, do you think this is the right door?"

The werewolf smoldered under his fur, saying, "I'm not a *dog*, and I have no clue as to which door it is."

"If I pay your bills, you're whatever I say you are," Mr. Fang said.

"Go on a diet, you loon!" the werewolf muttered under his breath.

Mr. Fang ran out to the edge of the cliff to see that Boyd was now about halfway up the staircase, and he felt his nerves kick into high gear. "Nobody told me about *four* doors," he said, slamming his fist into his hand. "Why does this have to be so hard?"

He ran to the second door and opened it, spying inside. To him, it was just another dark corridor, leading off into the abyss. When he ran to the third door, it was the same, as was the fourth. There was no simple answer to this dilemma.

"Hey, werewolf," he said. "You go first."

"Oh, fine," the werewolf said, and he marched headlong into the third door. Mr. Fang waited for a couple of seconds, before he heard a click, a snap, and the sound of metal scraping against metal, all of which was followed by the sound of a werewolf howl disappearing off into nothingness as the poor beast took a long fall into parts unknown.

Mr. Fang turned to the other werewolves and they looked at him with a bit of fear in their eyes. "Guess that's not the right door," he smiled. "Come on. Let's try the next one."

The next door they tried seemed to be booby-trap-free, and Mr. Fang forced all the werewolves in front of him, so that they might suffer whatever cruel fate lay in wait before he did. They scrambled inside and shut the doors behind them, so as to confuse Boyd when he reached the top.

As Boyd got to the top of the cliff, he was followed by Smelts, who had been tagging along behind him. "I hate stairs," Smelts said, trying to catch his breath.

"Tell me about it," Boyd said, bent over and sucking in as much air as he could.

"Great rescuing, by the way," Smelts said. "And that's a nifty outfit you're wearing."

"Thanks," Boyd said. He began examining the doors in front of him. "Which one do you think they took?"

"Beats me," he said. "Odds are they're all booby-trapped, though."

"True," Boyd said.

"Let's just try one," Smelts said. Boyd shrugged his shoulders as if to say, *Why not?* and they went in the first door on the right.

As they walked a few feet into the stone tunnel, the door swung shut behind them and all the torches on the wall magically came to life, lighting their way. Cobwebs lined the walls of the tunnel, which had been there so long that tree roots had grown down between the cracks in the ornate wall carvings. They stepped over each root gingerly, looking for some sort of unforeseen danger.

"So far, so good," Smelts said, but just as he did, an arrow whipped by his head, sticking to the wall, mere inches from his face. "Whoa," he muttered.

"Smelts, look," Boyd said, pointing to the round, jade stone that was embedded into the floor under his feet.

The pathway was littered with the stones, which looked to be some sort of trigger for the arrows that shot out of the walls. "I think I saw this in the movies," he said. He lifted his foot from the stone, whereupon they heard a snap and the sound of ropes straining under the weight of something extremely heavy.

"Duck!" Boyd yelled, and just as he pushed Smelts to the ground, a large, square stone fell from the rafters, right where they'd been standing, sealing them off from the entrance.

"Thanks, mate," Smelts said. He looked over at Boyd to see him looking up at the ten arrows that had flown past them into the wall. "Uh-oh."

"We're lying on the jade stones," Boyd said. "If we move, the whole roof is going to collapse on us."

Smelts looked up to see the large, stone blocks dangling precariously above them. "Well, that stinks," he said. "What do we do now?"

Boyd looked further up the tunnel to see a door around sixteen or seventeen feet ahead of them, with lion statues on each side. "Can we make it to the door?" he asked.

"The minute we move, those stones are coming down," Smelts said. "That is, if the arrows, which I assume are poisoned, don't get us first."

"Well, we could just lay here until someone helps us," Boyd said. "But that could be a while."

"Yeah, and I have to pee," Smelts said.

"Looks like we'll have to go for it." Boyd said. "On three?"

"Sure, why not?"

"One..." Boyd said.

"Two..." Smelts said, but it was too late. He'd shifted his weight from the jade just a tiny bit too much and they heard the snap of the rope breaking above them.

"Three!" Boyd yelled. Smelts grabbed him by the shirt and jerked him off the ground as they began a mad dash for the doorway, milliseconds ahead of the whizzing arrows and falling rocks. With a great burst of energy, they dove for the door, rolling to a stop just inside as the final stone fell from the ceiling, smashing the lion statues into dust as it blocked the doorway.

"I wish I could say that was fun," Smelts said. "But it wasn't."

CHAPTER 37

MR. FANG AND THE JADE KEY

Mr. Fang was standing in front of a giant chasm that had a large, steel pendulum swinging back and forth over the abyss below. He was filled with rage as he watched the werewolves jump for the pendulum and miss, falling to their doom in the bottomless pit underneath them. "Come on!" he yelled as the fourth werewolf fell to his death. "I only have five of you guys left! Can't one of you noodleheads do it?"

In order to make it to the other side of the chasm, one had to jump upon the pendulum, swing across, and then jump onto the small cliff on the opposite side. There were four pendulums across the chasm, each one for a different door, all swinging at different intervals. "Jump, you idiots!" Mr. Fang yelled.

"Forget that!" said one werewolf. "I ain't riskin' me neck for you anymore!" He turned to go back the way he came, but just as he walked back into the blackness, the others heard a click and a snap and the sound of metal scraping against metal, which was followed by another werewolf howl disappearing into nothingness.

"See?" Mr. Fang yelled. "You've got no choice! You can't go back. Now, there's only four of you left, so let's get me on that swinging thing."

The pendulums had the sound of low, heavy wind as they swung back and forth. At the bottom was a tiny ledge, just big enough for two people to jump on. "All right, all right," one of the werewolves said. "I'll do it."

He walked over to the edge, judging the distance as the giant pendulum slowly swung forward and backward. On the third swing, he jumped out into the air and grabbed onto the pendulum for dear life, clinging to the giant, rusty chain that held it. "Okay, now what?" he yelled, as he regained his footing on the base.

"You catch me, now!" Mr. Fang said, and as the pendulum swung back towards him, he had no qualms about leaping for it. While soaring through the air, he latched onto the werewolf's hand and pulled himself up on the base, but he was so bulky that as soon as he grabbed onto the chain, his large gut knocked the werewolf right off the pendulum and down into the chasm. "Whoops," he said, watching the werewolf fall below him. "I gotta lose some weight."

As he swung back and forth, trying to judge the distance to the far cliff, he saw Boyd and Smelts emerge from one of the adjacent doors, in front of their own pendulum. "There he is," Boyd yelled, pointing at Mr. Fang.

"You stupidheads!" Mr. Fang yelled from the pendulum. "That key is mine!" Filled with anger, he jumped for the far cliff, but misjudged the distance. Only the top half of his body landed on the cliff, and he scrambled with all of his might to hold on to the edge.

"This might be over before we know it," Smelts said, watching as Mr. Fang struggled to keep from falling to his death.

But like a cockroach scrambling for safety, so, too, did Mr. Fang scramble up from his predicament. He pulled his fat body over the side of the cliff, rolling like a giant barrel to the safety of the far wall. He was breathing heavily and his tailored, gray suit was covered with sweat, muck, and dirt. "Ha!" he yelled, still trying to catch his breath. "You thought I was going to die! But you were wrong!"

"You win some, you lose some," Smelts yelled.

"Come on, you stupid werewolves!" Mr. Fang yelled, motioning for the remaining three werewolves that were standing on the far cliff. "If *I* can do it, you can do it."

"No, thanks, mate," said one werewolf, taking a seat and dangling his feet over the cliff. "You're on your own."

"I ain't riskin' me life for the likes of you," said the other.

"Good luck on your quest for world domination," said the last. "Send me a postcard."

"Ooo, you stupid dogs!" Mr. Fang yelled, shaking his fist at them. "I'm going to get you when this is all over."

"Oh, I'm shakin' in me boots," said one, dripping with sarcasm.

"He's *so* cruel!" said the other, and they all laughed.

"Give up yet, Fang?" Boyd yelled from across the way.

"No!" he yelled, struggling to get to his feet. He watched as Boyd and Smelts easily made the jump to the pendulum and swung across. They were now but ten meters from him. He ran through the doorway to see that all four doors converged into one tunnel, at the far end of which was another door. He took off for the door, running as fast as his chubby legs could take him, and as he got closer, he saw that the far door was filled with light. Behind him, he heard Boyd and Smelts round the corner and start running. "Fang, stop!" Boyd yelled. "It's too dangerous!"

"Not now," Mr. Fang yelled. "I'm too close to victory!"

As he reached the lighted entrance, a large, caged door slammed to the ground behind him, sealing him off from Boyd and Smelts just before they reached him. Smelts reached his hands through the bars, but couldn't get to Fang. As he reached out, he paused, looking through the bars at the large chamber in which Mr. Fang had found himself. The ceiling was hundreds of feet high, with a small hole in the top where rain was falling through onto the ground. On the floor of the chamber were thousands upon thousands of statues of soldiers, all arranged in perfect formation, guarding a large, marble platform in the middle of the room. On top of the platform was a stone coffin that seemed to be glowing.

"These are Terra Cotta Warriors," Smelts said, staring in awe at the thousands of brightly painted statues that stood below them.

Boyd looked around to see that there were several entrances with steel doors lining the rim of the chamber, as if there were hundreds of ways in and out of the room. "I thought the Terra Cotta Warriors were in Xian," he said.

"Everyone thought that Xian was where Qin Shihuangdi was buried," Smelts said. "But judging by these statues, I think he's really buried here!"

Directly in front of Mr. Fang was a polished marble bridge that arched across the tops of the Terra Cotta Warriors, to the stone island in the center of the room. He began to laugh with excitement, trying to catch his breath and wiping the sweat from his brow as he turned to Boyd and Smelts behind the steel bars. "Whew!" he said, still trying to suppress his giggles. "That was close!"

"Mr. Fang, don't do it," Boyd said. "There's something not right about this."

"Shut up, kid!" he yelled, kicking at the bars. "You've cost me enough, already. If I had a stick, I'd poke you through the bars with it."

"Not much for threats, is he?" Smelts asked, looking sideways at Boyd.

"It's too late for you," Mr. Fang said. "The Jade Key is going to be mine, now! I'm going to be the most powerful man in the world and nobody will stop me. Not you, not the Conspiricetti...nobody! Because I *deserve* it!" He turned his back to Boyd and Smelts and began to make his way across the bridge, towards the coffin, muttering the whole way. "This thing has turned into a big mess. I'm going to get this key and go home and eat a big, fat bowl of noodles."

"This can't be good," Smelts said.

"I would agree," said Boyd.

Mr. Fang walked up to the coffin and looked at it. The Jade Key was there in front of him, embedded in the stone of the coffin. The coffin had elaborate designs of dragons and traditional Chinese pictures on the front to signify that this was the tomb of a very important person. The key was bigger than Mr. Fang thought it would be, a skeleton key that was about the size of his forearm and as cool green as anything he'd seen in his life. "This is a lot of fuss for a stupid key," he said, reaching out for it.

But when he touched it, something strange happened. The whole cave began to rumble, as if there was a large earthquake happening. The ground shook so violently that Mr. Fang lost his balance and rolled to the side of the island, almost tumbling off before regaining his balance. He dropped the key on the ground, only now it was glowing even brighter. With the ground shaking, large rocks began to fall from the ceiling, smashing several of the statues below and causing general chaos in the chamber.

"What's going on?" Boyd asked, looking at the island where Mr. Fang struggled to get to his feet.

The lid of the stone coffin exploded, straight up into the air in a puff of smoke. Mr. Fang looked up in horror as a decayed, mummified hand reached over the side to pull itself up. Then, standing up, he saw a sight that struck fear into his heart.

There before him, Qin Shihuangdi stood in his coffin, back from the dead.

The Emperor said something in Mandarin, his voice booming across the chamber as he looked down with deadened eyes at Mr. Fang lying on the ground.

"Holy moly," Smelts said, his eyes fixed on the coffin.

"Whoa," Boyd said, also shifting his gaze.

"I didn't mean you any harm!" Mr. Fang said, cowering on the ground. "I'll leave you alone, now." He tried to scramble back across the marble bridge, but a low, guttural growl stopped him in his tracks.

Again, the Emperor spoke Mandarin in a most fearsome way. Boyd couldn't understand a word he was saying, but judging by the rumble that filled the room, he knew it wasn't good. As Boyd looked at him, he saw the Emperor was changing, growing bigger right before his eyes, flesh re-materializing on his body, eyes staring at his prey.

The Emperor bent over as he began to grow. Smoke shot out from his coffin, filling the chamber, as a loud roar echoed around the room. By now, the Emperor had disappeared in the thick smoke, and Mr. Fang began to scramble back over the bridge.

Then from the edge of the wall of smoke, the snout of a very large creature emerged. Its muzzle looked like that of a lion, if a lion had gold and green scales. Steam seemed to be coming from its large nostrils, which were ringed by fluorescent, green fur, strands of which hung all the way down to the ground. Soon, its head emerged as well. It was gigantic, with yellow eyes that probed its surroundings with a fearsome intelligence. More of the green fur surrounded its neck.

The creature was a dragon, but it wasn't the kind of dragon that Boyd knew from stories of kings and knights and damsels-in-distress. No, this dragon was quite different; a fact made obvious as the creature emerged from the smoke and was revealed to have a long, scaled, snakelike body. There were no wings on its back, only an incredibly long torso.

It rose high above the marble island, focused on Mr. Fang as he scrambled for safety across the bridge. With its mighty fist, the Dragon shattered the marble bridge into millions of pieces in an attempt to crush Mr. Fang; but he missed his prey, as Mr. Fang dove off, down in between the Terra Cotta Warriors on the ground. Like a cockroach, he scrambled to hide amongst the statues, hoping to avoid the Dragon's gaze. "Do you think I cannot see you, insect?" the Dragon yelled, following Mr. Fang like a snake as he ran away.

"He's in for it now," Smelts said. "That thing speaks English!" The Dragon lifted its long neck up into the air and let out a scream that shook the walls. "Uh-oh," Smelts said as the Dragon spun around to look at both him and Boyd in the tunnel, its face furrowing with rage.

"There are *more?*" the Dragon yelled.

"We're not with him," Smelts said, pointing at Mr. Fang as he scurried away.

"Insolence!" the Dragon yelled, and he swung his tail around with full force, striking the front of the entrance, leaving Boyd and Smelts mere milliseconds to dive back into the tunnel to avoid the falling rocks. The Dragon perched on its back legs like a cobra and surveyed the room. "We are under attack!" it said to the room. "They cannot defile my tomb and expect to go unpunished. They have the Machine, and they are not worthy! Rise my warriors! Rise and recover that which is mine!"

All of a sudden, the Terra Cotta Warriors snapped to attention, coming to life on the floor of the chamber, and with the sound of stone scraping against stone, they began to file out of the room in perfect formation. Boyd and Smelts were digging their way out of the rubble of the collapsed cave when they saw the stone warriors exiting the chamber through the doors on the lower level. The Dragon was unaware of their presence as it watched its soldiers march out of the room. "Aw, man," Boyd whispered, "where do you think *they're* going?"

"I've got a bad feeling about all of this," Smelts said.

They watched as the Dragon spied the last of its warriors exiting the chamber and then it took off from the floor, defying gravity as it shot straight up into the hole in the roof, out into the night air. Both Boyd and Smelts held their breath in anticipation of its return, but nothing happened. The chamber was now silent.

"It just gets worse and worse, doesn't it?" Smelts muttered.

CHAPTER 38

PLEASED TO MAKE YOUR ACQUAINTANCE

Back in the main cave, everyone was trying to recover from the battle. The werewolves and panjas, along with Mr. Fang's cronies, had long since ran away, and the legion of the dead were sorting through the various piles of heads, arms, legs, hands, and feet that were scattered throughout the chamber, each one looking for whatever piece of their body they were missing.

"Come on, folks," Xiao said, motioning to his dead brethren. "We've done our duty here. Time to get back to the coffins, tombs, and shallow graves from whence we came."

Grumbles and groans echoed throughout his friends, for it was quite obvious that battling a group of werewolves and panjas was the most fun these corpses had had in a while. "Fine work, Xiao," Reggie said, handing him the hand he'd lost in the heat of battle.

"Thanks, Reggie," Xiao said. He peeked behind Reggie's bulk to see Boyd's parents standing there, looking a bit shell-shocked. "Are those the parents?" he asked.

As meek as they'd ever been, they both gave a half-smile and a wave to acknowledge the skeleton that was now talking to them. "Uh, hi," Mrs. McCloyd said.

"It's a pleasure," Mr. McCloyd said.

"You've got a real good kid on your hands," Xiao said.

"Thanks," Mrs. McCloyd smiled, but she had trouble looking Xiao in the eye (especially considering the fact that after the battle, he now only had *one*). The last of the dead folks loaded onto the boat and Xiao lifted the plank. "Good work, Reggie," he said. "I hope everything works out for you and the kid. He seems like he's well-suited to fill Ping's shoes."

"Let's hope he is," Reggie said, giving a concerned look over his shoulder at the door that Boyd and Smelts had disappeared into moments earlier.

As Xiao and the junk full of dead people sailed back down the tunnel from which they came, Mrs. McCloyd tapped on Reggie's shoulder warily. "Um, Mister, uh, creature?" she asked.

"You can call me Reggie," he said with a tolerant smile.

"Reggie," she said, "where's my son?"

"Mrs. McCloyd," Reggie said, trying to look sincere, "I'm sure Boyd is okay. I can't imagine him being with a better person than my partner."

"Mom! Dad!"

Mr. and Mrs. McCloyd looked over to see Cindy waving from the yacht in the lagoon. "Cindy?" Mr. McCloyd asked. "Are you okay, honey?"

"Yes!" she said. "Ho Yin's getting the boat ready to go."

Just as she looked back, the roof of the cavern began to rumble, and a small portion of it exploded, sending rock and debris falling into the lagoon. Dust filled the whole cavern as the patter of the rain from the hurricane outside began to filter in. Everyone looked up as the snout of the Dragon emerged from the hole as the dust began to clear.

"What is *that?*" Cindy asked Ho Yin.

"A dragon," he said. He then snapped back to reality, saying, "We've got to get off this boat!"

"What?" she asked.

He grabbed her and pulled her along. "Now!" he yelled.

The Dragon poked its head inside the hole like a snake and let out a horrible scream that made everyone in the cave cover their ears in pain. It scanned the room with its fearsome eyes and then dropped in through the hole, trailing its body across the roof of the cave. It began to circle the room, like a kite on a string, flying low over the water, and then soaring to the top, as if it was checking everything out. The Dragon then focused on the yacht. Emitting a deafening scream, it flew over the boat and then made a dive-bomb, straight into the top with its head, causing an ear-shattering explosion that tore the expensive yacht into a million pieces and created a fireball that filled the cave with smoke. Immediately afterward, the Dragon burst from the water and began to scour the cave again.

Just as before, it focused on the other, smaller boats in the cave and destroyed them in the same way. Reggie dove into the water and swam for Ho Yin to help him get to the shore faster. Cindy rode on Bjorn's back as they made their way toward safe ground. They'd gotten off the boat just in time.

When they made it to shore, Cindy's parents ran over to wrap her in a giant bear hug that rivaled Bjorn's large grasp. "We missed you so much, darling," Mr. McCloyd said. Her mother hugged her and kissed her all over her face.

"Mom," Cindy said, trying to squirm out of her arms, "I love to be hugged, but there's a dragon up there."

"Too right," Reggie said, keeping a wary eye on the creature, "I'm all for sappy reunions, but I think we'd better head for someplace safe before big, bad, and ugly takes a liking to yeti-meat."

Just as he said it, the Dragon swooped down over their heads, as if giving a warning to the group that they were next. "What about Boyd?" Mrs. McCloyd said. "We can't leave without Boyd!"

Reggie grabbed her and looked her in the eye, saying, "Mrs. McCloyd, you're going to have to trust me. Come on!" As they ran for the tunnel, Reggie kept looking over his shoulder at the lagoon, searching for some sign of either Boyd or Smelts emerging from the cave, but he saw nothing. *Come on, Smeltzie,* he thought. *Don't prove me wrong!*

As the group got about halfway to the exit, they saw that the Dragon now had them in its sights. It swooped low over the water and made a beeline for them. Cindy was still holding tight to Bjorn's neck and she was followed by Mr. and Mrs. McCloyd, as Bjorn sprinted on all fours for the exit. It was Reggie and Ho Yin who were left behind, as Reggie kept having to run back and pick up pieces of Ho Yin's body as they fell off. "It's no big deal," Ho Yin kept saying. "Leave it!"

"But it's your *leg!*" Reggie said.

"I'll build a new one!"

Reggie began a full-on sprint for the exit with the Dragon just behind him. Just as he dove for the door, he heard the snap of the Dragon's powerful jaws. The entrance to the cave wasn't quite big enough for its head, but it didn't stop the creature from trying to get at them as its jaws kept snapping at the group, unable to get inside. Everyone stood with their backs against the wall, just inches away from the glistening, razor-sharp teeth that snapped at them.

"This dragon doesn't breathe fire, does it?" Mr. McCloyd asked, looking at their narrow passageway.

"This is a Chinese dragon," Ho Yin said. "They don't breathe fire."

The Dragon pulled its jaws out of the hole and leaned its head up to it, peering inside with its large, yellow eye. "Sushi should be served raw, not cooked!" it said.

"It talks!" Reggie exclaimed.

"It!" the Dragon scoffed. "You dare talk like that to an **Emperor?** You *deserve* to be eaten, you pathetic beast."

"I beg your pardon," Reggie said, offended.

"We didn't mean any harm," Cindy said. "We were trying to stop Mr. Fang!"

"That's a pitiful excuse," the Dragon said. "For your mistakes, you'll pay dearly." It turned from the entrance and spun around, striking it with its tail. Several rocks fell from the ceiling and everyone inside huddled against the walls to avoid the debris. The Dragon whipped its tail around a second time and again, more rocks fell from above the entrance. This time, everyone took refuge under Reggie's broad shoulders in the hopes that he would prevent the cave from collapsing on top of them.

But that wasn't the Dragon's goal. It only wanted to trap the group, and it did so by sealing the entrance with the rubble. Once the falling rocks had covered the entrance, its job was done, and with a flourish, the Dragon made its way out of the hole, into the typhoon that awaited it outside.

Inside the collapsed cave, Reggie shrugged off the dust and debris and did a head count. "Everybody okay?" he asked.

"We seem to be," Ho Yin said. "Do you hear anything out there?"

Bjorn put his ear to the rocks, then shook his head.

"What happened to Boyd?" Mrs. McCloyd asked. "What in the world is going on?"

"Madam, that explanation might take more time than we have," Reggie said.

"Was that a *dragon?*" Mr. McCloyd asked.

"That was a *green* dragon," Ho Yin said. "One of the more temperamental ones."

"Do you think Boyd's okay?" Cindy asked.

"Boyd is with Smelts," Reggie said, this time sounding less sure of himself. "He couldn't be with a better person."

CHAPTER 39

UP, UP, AND AWAY!

Back in the chamber, Boyd and Smelts made their way through the debris of the collapsed cave, towards the island in the center where the key lay. "Do you see it?" Boyd asked.

Smelts was scanning the room, making sure there was no sign of the Dragon anywhere. "No, mate," he said. "I think it's gone."

They walked in silence to the island, each one climbing the side until they found themselves mere feet from the jade key as it lay on the ground. Boyd approached the key first, with Smelts sheepishly peeking over his shoulder to have a look himself. "What now?" Boyd asked, staring at the glowing prize in front of him.

"Are you gonna take it?" Smelts asked.

"Do you think I should?" Boyd asked.

"Do we even **need** it now?" Smelts asked.

"I don't know," Boyd said, looking up at the hole in the roof. "I don't think I have a choice anymore."

"Sure you do," Smelts said. "We could walk right outta here and forget that this place ever existed. There's no shame in it, mate. Once you take that thing, there's a lot of responsibility that falls on your shoulders, and if you don't think you're up to it, then there's no point in takin' it."

Boyd sighed. He felt like he'd had to make one too many important, Earth-shattering decisions in the past few weeks, and here was yet another one. "Why don't **you** take it, Smelts?" he asked.

Smelts smiled as if he was flattered by the suggestion. "The world ain't ready for a talkin' croc to save it, mate," he said. "This one is your responsibility."

For a second or two, Boyd thought about the fact that this was the moment when his life was going to change for good. Everything up to this point had been a game, but he knew that when he took the key in front of him, nothing would ever be the same again. "Seriously, Boyd," Smelts said, again. "There's no shame in walkin' away. You should only do what you're ready for."

Boyd looked Smelts in the eye and said, "If I don't do this, then someone else will, and that person might not be a good person. How many Mr. Fangs are there out there? If there's one, then there are a hundred." He looked back to the key and said, "No, I **have** to do it."

"I couldn't imagine a better person, then," Smelts said, standing back from him.

Boyd took a deep breath and grabbed the key. He felt a surge of energy roll through his body, unlike anything he'd ever experienced. In fact, the energy was so powerful and so instantaneous that it sent a shock-wave across the room, knocking Smelts back onto the ground and cracking the stones on the walls.

For a few seconds, Boyd became translucent, his body the same texture and hue as the key. A light seemed to emanate from him, so bright that when Smelts looked up, he couldn't look at Boyd directly.

Lightning seemed to go off everywhere at once and the cave began to quake, as if Boyd were drawing energy from everything around him.

Back in the main cave, the quake was so powerful that it shook loose some of the rocks that had trapped Reggie and the rest of the gang, and a bit of light from the outside began to filter its way inside. "What in the world was that?" Mr. McCloyd asked, trying to stay on his feet as the earth shook.

"Let's hope it's not that Dragon," Reggie said. He climbed to the top of the rock pile, and with all of his strength, he pushed a large boulder out of the way, giving them just enough room to crawl out of the hole. He peeked outside, saw that the Dragon was gone, and turned back to everyone. "The coast is clear, kids," he said. "Come on up."

They made their way out of the hole and observed the devastation that the Dragon had wrought while they were trapped. None of the boats had survived its wrath, as what was left of them was now just smoldering debris floating in the lagoon. The cave was empty except for them.

"Where's Boyd?" Mrs. McCloyd asked, tears welling in her eyes. "Boyd isn't here!"

Once again, the cave began to rumble and the lagoon began to bubble and churn, as if something extraordinary was happening below the surface. Then, in an explosion of stone and wood, Boyd burst from the doors above the lagoon like a bullet, rising up to the top of the cave. He was flying! The glow remained with him and wherever he flew, he illuminated the cave. He surveyed the room and saw his friends and family on the shore, every one of them looking up in awe. In fact, they were so awestruck, they failed to notice Smelts walk up to them from the lagoon."

"Quite a sight, eh?" he asked.

"Smeltzie!" Reggie yelled, wrapping his large arms around his comrade. "You're alive!"

Smelts was doing his best to breathe under the pressure of Reggie's strong arms, but managed to mutter, "If you keep hold of me like this, I won't be much longer."

Boyd floated down from the ceiling to hover in front of his friends. He held the Jade Key in his right hand as he said, "You're all okay! I was worried."

His mother's eyes were as big as they'd ever been as she looked at her flying son. "Boyd," she said, "you're...you're..." And with that, she passed right out into Reggie's arms.

"Is she okay?" Boyd asked.

"She's just not used to seeing her son soaring through the air," smiled Ho Yin. "Not to mention the yeti, talking crocodiles, werewolves, and malevolent dragons. She'll be fine."

"You got the key," Cindy said, admiring it in Boyd's hands.

Boyd looked at it for a second. "I can fly," he said, as if he was still in shock at his own abilities. "I can fly!" He then snapped back to reality and looked at his parents as his mother awoke from her short nap. "Are you guys really okay?" he asked.

"We're fine," Mr. McCloyd said, but he looked tired.

Mrs. McCloyd looked up at Boyd and smiled, tears streaming down her cheeks. "I'm so glad you're okay," she said. "I was so worried."

"We were both worried, Boyd," Mr. McCloyd said.

Boyd was so glad to see his parents again that he was on the verge of floating down and giving the two of them a huge hug, but he caught a glimpse of Ho Yin standing behind them with a serious, worried look on his face. In that instant, he knew that his job wasn't done. "Mom, Dad," he said, "I've got to go."

"What?" Mrs. McCloyd asked. "Go? Go where?"

"Boyd, everything is okay now," Mr. McCloyd said. "We're safe."

"No, dad," Boyd said. "Everything's *not* okay. I've got one last job to do." He looked at his parents and smiled. "I love you guys," he said. "I'll meet you back at the mansion."

"Mansion?" Mrs. McCloyd asked. "What mansion?"

"I'll explain everything," Ho Yin said.

Like a bolt of lightning, Boyd shot out into the night air, straight into the heart of the typhoon that hung over Hong Kong. The second he came out of the cave, he was hit by a large gust of wind, yet it didn't affect his flight. He could feel the strong gusts, but they couldn't blow him off course. It was as if his flight was independent of the laws of physics, like he was traveling in some kind of bubble that kept the wind from messing up his hair and the rain from pelting his face.

He also couldn't explain his ability to control his movement while soaring through the skies. He thought about what he wanted to do and he could do it. It was if he had always known how to fly, as if the skills had always been in his brain. It all seemed so natural.

The most amazing part, though, was the sheer exhilaration of traveling at great speeds over the waves below. Lightning flashed off to his left or right, illuminating the black islands in the distance or the large ocean swells below him. He flew just over the surface of the water as the waves whipped beneath his chest. The lower he flew, the faster he seemed to be going.

The storm seemed to be raging at its most powerful and Boyd could feel the bad energy that was focused on the islands ahead. As he moved closer to Hong Kong Island, he started to make out the faint lights of the city. He moved on shore and flew along the tall buildings close to the water, their lights zipping past him in between drenching sheets of rain, as if he was on a high-speed train whipping through the city.

He zoomed past the buildings of Tsing Yi and the large, red cranes of Lai Chi Kok until he shot up into the air over the buildings of Kowloon to see the grand cityscape of Hong Kong rising through the haze of weather. He rose upwards, slowing to a stop as he hovered above the edge of Kowloon, looking across the water for some sign of the Dragon. Something inside him told him that the Dragon was in the city and something inside him told him the Dragon wasn't alone. Something inside him told him that something very bad was going on here.

Hong Kong had seen many typhoons over the years, but the one lashing the island on this particular night was one of the worst ones ever. The winds were strong and constant, whipping street signs back and forth, and permanently bending trees under its oppressive strength. The streets were full of runoff water that was constantly replaced by the never-ending sheets of rain. What was usually a bustling city, filled to the brim with humanity, was now a virtual ghost town, not a shop open, not a soul wandering the streets, and only the odd, insane taxi driver braving the elements to get a fare.

No one was on the street, so no one saw the invasion that lay ahead of them. No one was near the water, so no one saw the first of the heads emerge from the waters of Victoria Harbor, each one stoic and unmoved, not the least bit disturbed by the long journey they'd made on the bottom of the ocean to get there. In lines of twenty, they emerged from the water, onto the shore, rising in perfect formation, clad in rock hard armor and carrying a myriad of ancient weapons at their disposal.

The Terra Cotta Warriors of Qin Shihuangdi's tomb had risen and were marching through the streets of Hong Kong.

The stone soldiers marched with determination, filling the rainy streets from side to side. Each one knew their purpose as they moved towards their final destination. As they marched down a one way street, a lone taxi driver screeched to a halt in front of them, his windshield wipers on high as he peered out to see thousands of the Terra Cotta soldiers marching towards him. This poor soul was a bit too stunned to realize the danger he was in, for when the statues got close enough, they swarmed around the car, rolling it over and over until it was perched upside down against a shop window.

Everything that stood in the way of Qin Shihuangdi's army was destroyed as they marched through the city, ranging from garbage cans, to streetlights, to empty buses. An army of stone warriors was cutting through the streets with one destination in mind: Fang Tower.

Boyd zoomed across the water, past the tankers waiting out the storm in the harbor and the low buildings along the shore, towards Fang Tower. He hovered about twenty feet above the street, looking up at the top of the building. The streets were empty from the storm and the rain seemed to have increased on this side of the water. The sky was starting to grow light gray as the sun came up somewhere behind the heavy masses of clouds, but he couldn't see the top of the tower because of the rain.

The closer Boyd got to Fang Tower, the more he realized that something was horribly wrong. Something had moved through the streets of the city before him and destroyed everything in its path, overturning cars, knocking down trees, and causing a general chaos that was only compounded by the storm. As he rounded a corner to find himself on the main boulevard that led to Fang Tower, he saw that the streets were now filled with the Terra Cotta Warriors, their formations marching on the building.

Boyd was in awe of the statues, for there were more than he could count, marching like a well-trained army below him. What was even more amazing was that they were swarming on Fang's tower, climbing the walls of the structure like ants on an anthill, making their way higher and higher up the tower, ripping it apart as they moved upward. Boyd hovered at the side of the building, unsure of what to do now that he was there.

Then, a giant steel girder came plummeting down from above, landing mere feet from Boyd. Its pointed end drove straight into the concrete of the street, standing upright. It was followed by giant, razor-sharp shards of glass that seemed to rain down all around him. He zipped away from the debris as larger, flaming pieces started to fall to the ground. The building was coming apart a hundred floors above him. *The Dragon is doing this*, he thought.

Using his newfound powers, he flew to the top of the building to observe the smoldering wreckage of what should have been the upper floors of Fang Tower, specifically Mr. Fang's penthouse. Now, there was only a smoking, steel frame that had been violently ripped to shreds. Papers and documents were whipping everywhere in the wind and rain, but there was no sign of the creature that caused all the damage. A thick cloud moved in over the top of the building and everything became foggy. Boyd flew around the building, looking for a sign of the Dragon, but saw nothing.

Then from out of nowhere, he felt a gust of wind, and he flew out of the way just in time to avoid the snapping jaws of the Dragon, who had perched itself like a centipede on the side of Fang Tower. If Boyd was fast, then the Dragon was his equal, for as Boyd flew for safe haven, the Dragon kept up with him and he began to fear for his safety.

"So you've found the jade key," the Dragon yelled over the howling wind. "This was all about *you* then, I take it." It snapped at Boyd a few more times until he took shelter in the burning, steel girders that kept the creature from getting a clear shot at its prey.

"This isn't about me," Boyd shouted.

"A mere child," the Dragon said. "You're nothing but a child."

"Why are you doing this?" Boyd yelled.

"Because I *can*," the Dragon shouted. "Because no one will ever control the Machine. Not while I have anything to say about it."

It reared back its powerful head and rammed straight through the steel of the building, sending giant beams flying in all directions and leaving Boyd exposed. The Dragon was angry, as it chased him all around the building, wrapping its golden, snakelike body around its steel frame as it attempted to get at Boyd.

Boyd was losing ground in his battle, for the Dragon was now only missing him by inches, so he took off, flying straight down the skyscraper, towards the street below, hoping to lead it away so that it would stop destroying the tower. It followed him down to the street, propelling itself like a missile, straight at him.

Having only a split second to dodge the Dragon's charge, Boyd flew out of the way just in time, leaving the Dragon to plow into the concrete street below, its long, golden body disappearing into the subway system. Everything grew quiet for a few seconds, with only the rain pattering around Boyd as he looked at the large, steaming hole in the ground where the Dragon had disappeared. In that brief moment, he allowed himself to think that it was all over, that he was safe, and that this whole debacle was behind him.

But then the Dragon burst from the ground, sending concrete flying in all directions as it tried to devour him. It was even more angry now, as it pursued Boyd. He had no choice but to fly backwards in an attempt to avoid its snapping jaws, but the Dragon was too fast. Boyd had to take off, full-speed, through the streets of the city, with the Dragon in hot pursuit behind him. If it hadn't been so terrifying to have an angry, incredibly fast Dragon pursuing him from behind, Boyd might have felt exhilaration as he flew at mind-boggling speeds through the streets of the city, zipping around corners at razor-sharp angles, dodging the occasional neon sign or clothes wire or tree that appeared from nowhere.

In fact, he became so engrossed with speeding through the city that he failed to notice that the Dragon was no longer behind him. When he did notice, he slowed to a stop, hovering in the street as he searched his surroundings. Except for the wind, the city around him was quiet. No one was on the street and the wind was whipping the trees on the sidewalks back and forth against the buildings.

Then, the Dragon walked out from behind a building, calmly looking at Boyd. It didn't move toward him or try any kind of attack. It just stood there, looking at him. "What have you done to my island?" it asked.

"What?" Boyd yelled over the raging wind.

"What have you done to my island?" it asked. "When I left, this was a beautiful paradise, with green trees and blue ocean. It was my own glorious nirvana. Now, it's practically destroyed."

Boyd had no answer for the Dragon. Perhaps Hong Kong *was* once a paradise. Now, it was a series of canyons made of concrete and glass. Whatever natural beauty that might have existed before this moment was long gone. "I'm sorry," Boyd said.

The Dragon looked around at the city that surrounded him. He said, "When I first came here, this place was a paradise on Earth. Perfection. The sky was clear, the trees were a marvelous shade of green and covered the mountains like a warm blanket. The water was deep blue and teeming with life. It was everything that the Earth should have been. Now, it is but a mockery of what it once was, a perfect example of the greed and indulgence of this race, and a perfect example of why you are not worthy of my machine."

"What do you mean?" Boyd asked.

"I am taking back what is mine," the Dragon said. "You are not ready for an object of such power. You cannot even manage the gifts you are given. How could you expect to manage the Machine?"

"But we need it," Boyd said. "It could change the world!"

"Nonsense," said the Dragon. "You do not need a machine to change the world. The Machine is only a device that would cause trouble and strife, a device that wars would be fought over, that men would do anything to have in order to have power. And that was not my intention in creating it."

Boyd turned to see the terra cotta warriors marching down the street towards him. At the front of the line, several of the warriors were carrying the Perpetual Motion Machine on their shoulders. They marched right past Boyd, down the street, towards Victoria Harbor. "Where are they going?" he asked.

"Back to the island," the Dragon said. "They will take the Machine apart and scatter the pieces around the world again." The Dragon watched silently as his soldiers disappeared into the water. "Someday you will be ready, but now is not the time."

Boyd watched as the last of the warriors marched past him and disappeared beneath the surface. He took the Jade Key and offered it to the Dragon. "I guess you'll be needing this," he said, feeling a twinge of regret at giving away such an incredible gift.

The Dragon reached down with its gargantuan hand and took the key from him. Once he had passed it on to the Dragon, Boyd could again feel the drops of rain on his face and his robe grew soaked as he slowly drifted back to the ground. "You are a good person, Boyd McCloyd," the Dragon said. "You are destined for many great things."

With that, the Dragon raised its large head up towards the sky. It looked like a giant cobra, and its arms were outstretched, spanning the street between the buildings. The wind began to swirl intensely, as if the very center of the typhoon was hovering around him. Boyd had to grab onto a pole to keep from flying away, as the vortex of wind turned the street into chaos. A funnel cloud began to form in the dark clouds above the Dragon and a tornado touched down on the street, enveloping the area.

It was as if the Dragon was drawing all the power of the storm into itself. The clouds changed from a dark gray to a light gray, then to a wispy white, and soon there were no clouds at all. They had disappeared into the Dragon itself.

Boyd had never seen a sky as blue and clear as what now hung over Hong Kong, and as the Dragon drew the last of the storm's energy into itself, the morning sun was revealed and turned the city of glass, concrete, and steel into one of the most fascinating things that Boyd had ever seen. The towers above him reflected the sun almost as brilliantly as if one were staring at it directly. Although there were tree branches, leaves, and paper littering the street, the rain and wind seemed to have washed the city clean of all of its muck and grime. It was as if something had rid the city of the last thirty years of dirt and filth, and uncovered the jewel that was lying beneath it.

And there in the center of it all, stood the Dragon, still perched on its hind legs, four stories tall, taking in the grandeur of his island. He seemed somewhat stunned, as if he'd been so angry when he arrived that he never bothered to look at what he was destroying. He breathed in the fresh air with his loud, powerful lungs, and then moved down to Boyd's level to look at him. "You're a very worthy successor to Confucius Ping," he said.

In the bright, morning sunlight, Boyd had the chance to observe the Dragon in all its glory. His scales seemed to absorb the light of the sun, making him brighter and more glorious than a golden jewel. He was a majestic creature, strong and powerful, but the color on his scales gave him a sense of fragility and loveliness that reminded Boyd of the delicate radiant wisp of a rainbow.

"To think that puny men made all of this," it said, looking around. "To think that their simplistic minds, their lowly, wasted brains would have the vision to create such grandeur."

With an ease that betrayed its size, the Dragon rose from the ground, straight up into the sky. It soared back and forth over the city a couple of times before darting off over the mountains and out of sight.

Boyd stood in the middle of the street, taking in the city while it was still silent. A gentle breeze blew between the buildings and waved the trees back and forth. The people of the city were starting to make their way out onto the streets, each of them looking a bit hesitant, frightened at the chain of events that had taken away the typhoon.

Boyd wanted to fly back to the Mansion, but his powers had been taken away with the key. He wondered about his parents, Cindy, and the rest of the gang, but something in his heart told him that they were fine and now on their way back home. Feeling a heavy weight fall over his body, he thought he'd had enough excitement for one day, probably even for one lifetime, and he started walking down the street, on his way back to Ping Manor.

EPILOGUE

PART I

Mr. Fang looked like he was on the verge of tears as he stood on the street with a crowd of people on that glorious, sunny morning, looking at the skeletal remains of Fang Tower. After the terra cotta warriors had done their business in retrieving the Machine, the building was just a shell, ripped asunder by the stone hands of the warriors.

"My building," he whimpered. "They tore up my building."

At that moment, Mr. Fang looked very much like his building. His clothes were still torn and tattered from everything he'd been through, and his face and hands were full of cuts and scrapes. After his encounter with the Dragon, he'd scrambled out of the cave and onto one of the small speedboats docked on the island, where he went through a harrowing journey across the ocean at the height of the typhoon to get to Hong Kong Island. Now, he was standing in front of the charred remains of his empire and it felt like things couldn't get any worse.

He was wrong.

"Mr. Fang?" a voice called out from behind him. He turned to see two rather large, white men in dark suits and mirrored sunglasses approaching him, followed by no one else but Mr. Davis from the Conspiricetti. "Mr. Fang, might I have a word with you?" Mr. Davis asked.

After all that he'd been through, Mr. Davis was the last person Mr. Fang wanted to see. "What do *you* want?" he said.

"I believe you *know* what we want," Mr. Davis said, a slight smirk on his face.

"Look, can't you see this isn't good time for me?" Mr. Fang said. "I haven't had a very good day so far. I don't have the kid. I don't have the money. And I don't even want to join that stupid club anymore, so leave me alone!"

Mr. Davis cleared his throat, trying to calm himself. "First," he said, "it's not a *club;* it's an *organization.* Furthermore, you have failed to deliver on what you promised. Third, we've come to collect our fee."

"Fee?" Mr. Fang yelled. "*What* fee? I told you I didn't *have* the fee!"

"Men?" Mr. Davis asked, looking at the two large fellows beside him. They grabbed Mr. Fang by the arms and began to lead him towards a black car sitting in an alley.

Struggling to break free the entire way, Mr. Fang yelled, "You can't do this to me! Do you know who I am? I'm Fang!" Just as the men were shoving him in the back of the car, he saw Mrs. Fang standing beside another black car parked behind the first one.

"Honey?" Mr. Fang yelled as they stuffed him into the car. "Honey, call for help! They're kidnapping me!"

Mrs. Fang said nothing.

"Honey? Honey, call for help! They're bad people."

Still, she said nothing. She only looked at him.

"Call for help!" he yelled as they shut the door on him.

Mrs. Fang watched as they drove away with her husband. Mr. Davis approached her. "Well, Mrs. Fang," he said, "I'd like to congratulate you on being the newest member of the Conspiricetti. Welcome to the organization."

"Thank you," she said. "I've waited a long time for this day."

PART 2

Sitting in the damp confines of a large cargo ship headed back to Hong Kong Island, and surrounded by the smell of wet fur from the werewolves sitting beside him, Hedley was filled with anger. "Nice work," he said to Neville, who was sitting beside him. "**Really** nice work. I hire you guys to do a job and you're defeated by a bunch of dead guys! **Real** nice!"

"Oh, shut up," Neville said, looking seasick as the ship rose and fell with each wave. "And just so you know, even though we failed, we **still** get our fees. Don't try to get out of it. It's in the contract."

"Fees?" Hedley said, incredulous. "Yeah, right. You've got to do the job right to earn the money."

"Uh-uh," Neville said, pulling out the very contract from his pocket. "If you'd bothered to read the fine print when you signed this, you'd have realized that we had a 'pay-or-play' clause going. You've got to pay us no matter whether we deliver or not."

"I don't think so," Hedley said. "You'll get paid for this over my dead body."

"That can be arranged," Neville said, and the growls of a host of werewolves could be heard in the cargo hold.

"It's been a while since I ate tuna," said one werewolf.

"Be careful when you eat 'im," said another. "Catfish like 'im got lots of tiny bones that could end up chokin' 'ya!"

"I'm not a catfish," Hedley said, filled with fear.

"That don't much matter to us," Neville said, his teeth glaring with drool.

It would be a long sea voyage for Hedley.

PART 3

It was three weeks later when Ho Yin walked into the library to interrupt Boyd from his reading. Boyd was engrossed in volume twenty-one of Mr. Ping's almanac when Ho Yin interrupted, saying, "Pack your things, Boyd."

"What?" Boyd asked. "Why?"

"We're off," Ho Yin said. "We're leaving tonight."

"Well, this is sudden. Where are we going?"

"Bird and Goldfish just informed me that one of our contacts in Australia has gotten wind of a bit of kangaroo trouble down in Cairns."

"Kangaroo trouble?" Boyd asked. "What kind of kangaroo trouble?"

"It seems that a group of them have taken control of a small town and are holding the townspeople hostage until their ransom demands are met."

"What are the demands?"

"All humans are to leave Australia within a week or they'll take over the whole country by force."

"I never liked them 'roos," Smelts said, walking in the room with a bag slung over his shoulder, ready to go. "They're a shifty lot. Can't trust 'em as far as you can throw 'em."

Within the hour, Boyd was standing in front of Ping Manor beside Ho Yin, Smelts, Cindy, and Bjorn, along with his mother, Mrs. McCloyd, who had elected to stay in Hong Kong while Mr. McCloyd went back to Canada. As Reggie pulled up in the limousine, Boyd felt a swell of excitement inside him. He knew that whatever lay ahead of him, his family, and his friends would be something unique. He was a million light years away from the kid he was just a few months ago, and he wasn't sad to see that part of himself go. He had gone from ordinary to extraordinary, and his life never seemed better.

They stuffed their bags in the trunk and everyone settled inside. From the driver's seat, Reggie leaned back and said, "Everyone ready?" They all smiled as he said, "Good! Let's go kick some kangaroo butt!"

And they drove off to do just that.

THE END

WELCOME to the Appendix for this book. The world of Mr. Ping is vast, weird, and wonderful, and with well-over one hundred volumes of the Almanac of the Twisted & Weird available over the last two centuries, there is a wealth of material that one needs to have access to in order to fully understand this twisted world in which we live.

Thus, the terms on the following pages have been taken from the text of this book. These terms are followed by a page number. On the corresponding pages, you will find information that might give you context and help you understand what it is that you were reading about.

As we said at the beginning of the book, it is not necessary to read this Appendix to understand the book, but it will most certainly add to the flavor of the text, as well as provide clues to future mysteries for Boyd, Cindy, Reggie, et. al.

Thanks for your continued support of Acclimated Spooks, Light, and Power.

THE MANAGEMENT

MR. PING'S
ALMANAC
OF THE
TWISTED & WEIRD

1 THE YETI

The Yeti is a large biped that stands at least eight feet tall and has white fur over the entirety of its body, razor-sharp teeth, and long arms that hang to the ground. The yeti is quite fast for its size and has amazing strength. Found mainly in the Himalayan Mountain range in Asia, but also known to frequent popular golf resorts and yoga retreats throughout the world.

2 NICK LAI AND RAY WONG

Twins separated at birth, Nick Lai and Ray Wong are notorious in the Hong Kong underworld not only as assassins, but also for their martial arts skills. Both Ray and Nick are also known for their penchant for McDougal's hamburgers and Japanese comic books, and have battled both Ho Yin and Mr. Ping several times over the years. Although they are quite skilled, they've always come out on the losing end of these battles, as detailed in the following excerpt from Mr. Ping's Almanac, Vol. 92:

...Nick made the mistake of coming after me too quickly, making the young person's assumption that a man who looked as old as I must not have the fighting skills to take on a young, fit, spry fellow like himself. Because of his generation's failure to have any respect for the elderly, he decided to take me out first.

He also had absolutely no sense of subtlety, for he was attacking me right there on the streets of Wan Chai with a crowd of tourists, locals, and businessmen watching his every move. "Your time is up, old man," he said, holding his fists in a threatening manner as he stood across the road from me. "Time to hand the reigns over to a new generation."

To be quite honest, I had no desire to fight either him or Ray. I just wanted to eat my meal in peace and then go back home to settle in with one of the new books I'd purchased.

Somehow, these two saw fit to attack me during my leisure time.

"Are you prepared to die, old man?" Ray asked. "I hope you're enjoying your meal, because it will be your last."

A crowd had formed around us. I sat at one end of the circle with my splendid curry and pot of tea sitting on the outdoor table in front of me, while Ray and Nick were in defensive poses at the opposite end. "Have the two of you no manners?" I asked. "Can you not pester me when I'm *not* enjoying a meal?"

"Make as many excuses as you like," Nick said. "Today is the day you'll be beaten by the Lai brothers."

"I thought we agreed we were the Wong brothers?" Ray said over his shoulder.

"No," Nick said, perturbed. "We agreed that we were the Lai brothers."

"No, we didn't," Ray said. "We said the Wong brothers."

"Look, can we talk about this later?" Nick hissed.

"Get it right and we wouldn't have this problem," Ray muttered.

"Are you two going to be long?" I asked. "Because if you are, I could finish my meal."

"Shut up!" Ray said.

"Okay," I said, resigning myself to battle. "You two are martial arts experts, I take it?"

"That's right," said Nick. "You've finally met your match."

"No one can match our skills and knowledge of the ancient arts," Ray said.

"Really?" I said, feeling a sudden desire to put these two poor souls in their place. "I'll tell you what...I'm going to teach you boys a lesson right here and now, so that, number one, you'll learn to leave a man alone when he's eating, and number two, so you'll stop bragging about how great you are, because it's really quite embarrassing."

"Try what you want," said Ray. "We hate to hurt old men, but for you, we'll make an exception."

"Yes, yes," I said, brushing aside his ridiculous comment. I narrowed my eyes and put down my chopsticks. I looked at Nick and said, "I'm going to defeat *you* with this piece of baby corn." I held up a floppy piece of baby corn that I'd pulled from my curry. "And I will defeat you," I said to Nick, "with this piece of cauliflower." I held up a piece of cauliflower in my other hand. "*And* I will do all of this without getting up from my chair. Then you will know what a *true* master of the martial arts can do."

"Ha!" said Ray. "I'd like to see you..."

Ray failed to finish his sentence, for I'd flung the baby corn straight at his face, aiming for the perfect angle on his chin that would render him unconscious. Because of my in depth knowledge of acupuncture, I knew that if the baby corn hit just perfectly on the edge of the right side of his chin it would knock the bones of his mandible together in just the right way to strike the nerve that would cause him to lose consciousness. He flopped to the ground, out cold.

Nick looked at his brother on the ground, then looked at me with panic in his eyes. I held up the cauliflower and said, "You're next."

He turned to run, but I sent the cauliflower flying at his feet, knocking one foot behind the other and causing him to trip and fall, his head striking the ground in just the right way so that he, too, was rendered unconscious. Just as I had told them, I had defeated them with a piece of baby corn and cauliflower. The crowd burst into a round of spontaneous applause and I finished off my meal in peace...

3 SNAKE POTION

One of Mr. Ping's arch-enemies was a chemist by the name of Mr. Wu, a man who provided help to a wide variety of Mr. Ping's enemies over the years. Mr. Wu was not actually a chemist as much as he was a master of the Black Arts. He used his knowledge of traditional Chinese medicines to further his own goals, selling his patented "Longevity" Potions, "Kiss-Me-Quick" sprays, "Pox-on-Your-Enemy" seasonings, and "Bigger-Stronger-Better-Looking" drinks to the weak and easily influenced all over Asia.

Mr. Wu dabbled in all sorts of macabre schemes, including using those rare or endangered animals to give his teas and potions extra kick and shaving the heads of small children to use their hair in anti-aging powder. In short, Mr. Wu was not a pleasant man and because of all of his questionable activities, he had several unfortunate encounters with Mr. Ping at various times during his career. The Snake Potion was one of his most famous creations. Consisting of a repulsive mix of snake venom, horse urine, rotten teeth, aged and fermented pig saliva, moldy cheese, twice-chewed noodles, and four-day-old, used toilet water (amongst other, less desirable ingredients), the Snake Potion helped to change its user from human form to snake form at will. The potion was known to last for three days, after which, the user would no longer have the ability to shape-shift.

However, one of the known side-effects of the potion was the unfortunate retention of snake-like characteristics after the potion had worn off. For instance, when a person reverted back to human form, they might still have the reptilian eyes of a snake, or continue to have the forked tongue, or even the fangs. These side effects never disappeared and can be seen even today in several people around Hong Kong. Needless to say, the potion is very volatile and can have different effects on different people.

As for Mr. Wu, he was last seen when Mr. Ping raided his laboratories to rescue famed reporter Amy Chu of the Hong Kong Morning Enquirer, as detailed in the following excerpt from Mr. Ping's Almanac, Vol. 55:

...Amy and I ran as quickly as we could from the old warehouse, knowing that it was a time-bomb waiting to explode. The smell of the Tasmanian Devil Powder was thick in the air, and we were barely able to catch our breath.

"Go on without me, Amy!" I yelled to her. "You have to get out of here before Wu sees us."

"I'm not going without you, Confucius," she said, grabbing my hand and pulling me along behind her.

"I can't risk anything happening to you, Amy," I said. "You must let the world know what you've seen here."

"But Confucius," she said, "There's something I have to tell you..."

"You'll pay for this, Ping!" Mr. Wu shouted from the platform above us. He was ranting and raving back and forth like a madman. His face was red with rage and spittle kept flying from his lips.

"You've pushed it too far, Wu," I yelled over my shoulder. "It's over!" I turned back to Amy and said, "Run! Now!"

"If this is the end, then I'm taking you with me!" Mr. Wu shouted, and out of the corner of my eye, I saw him strap some strange contraption to his back. Immediately, I realized that it was one of his old flamethrowers.

"You'll never get away in time!" He laughed as he raised the muzzle of the flamethrower in my direction.

"No, Wu!" I yelled. "The Tasmanian Devil Powder is highly volatile! This whole place will go up in flames!"

"And take you with it, Ping!" he laughed. He had clearly gone insane. "So long, fools!"

I had stalled him long enough to let Amy run out of the building, and as he pulled the trigger of the flamethrower, I dove under a forklift sitting by some large, tin pipes. Immediately, the entire place went up in flames and the warehouse exploded, sending the flimsy tin walls soaring out in all directions ... Mr. Ping survived the encounter with Mr. Wu and the exploding warehouse, as did Amy Chu. Mr. Wu has not been seen since that day. The authorities believe he perished in the blast, but his remains were never found, leading Mr. Ping to personally speculate that Mr. Wu was not, in fact, killed in the blast. The recent resurgence of Snake Potion in the underworld of Southeast Asia is further proof that Mr. Wu may still be at large.

4 ENGLISH SPECTACULAR FOOTBALL LEAGUE

Although Reggie played goalie for two years in the League, he was eventually forced out of the organization and off of his team after it was discovered that he was, in fact, a yeti, and not an extremely hairy man with an excellent drop kick and unnaturally long arms that helped him be one of the best goalies to ever play the game. His subsequent lawsuit (charging the league with yeti-discrimination) forced the league to change its rules to "humans-only," whereupon it was discovered that there were two kangaroos and an orangutan secretly playing for other teams (all of whom were subsequently removed from play). The "humans-only" rule is widely credited with making play in the league a little bit less exciting.

5 BIGFOOT

Known as the "less intelligent" breed of the yeti, the Bigfoot clan is widely credited amongst the yeti populace as having besmirched the good name of yetis around the world with their backward, attention-getting ways. The distinctions between the Bigfoot clan and those of other yeti breeds, such as the Patagonian Yeti, the

Himalayan Yeti, and the Ural Mountain Yeti, are numerous. Bigfoots prefer rummaging through human waste containers, such as dumpsters or garbage cans, having adapted to life near the big cities, whilst most other yetis prefer to hunt their food for themselves. Bigfoots have been known to court media attention, even going so far as to flirt with the notion of exposing yeti secrets to the world on television shows in the United States such as Timeline 6:30 and The Truthful News Hour with Commercial Interruptions, whilst most other yetis around the world have chosen to keep their existence a closely-guarded secret.

Whereas most yetis around the world have white fur, the Bigfoot's fur is ashy-brown, and though most yetis have at least forty-eight razor-sharp fangs, Bigfoots rarely have any fangs at all, due to their teeth having rotted away from over-exposure to human junk foods (Cupknoots and Winkles being their favorites). Bigfoots rarely bathe and their stench can be smelled for miles. They also enjoy picking boogers from their noses and wiping them on any available surface, making them notoriously easy to track in the wild (as Bigfoot boogers have a purplish hue and are rather large). Bigfoots love to watch television through the front windows of people's houses at night, and have been known to enjoy house cats as midnight snacks.

6 WEREWOLVES

The werewolf's origins are unknown, but werewolfism (as it is officially known in scientific circles) is thought to be caused by some form of mad-jungle-cat disease, whose murky origins have been traced back to Eastern Borneo. The werewolf is covered in thick fur of a variety of colors and stands at varying heights due to the physical stature of the "victim" (i.e. The person who was originally attacked). If the victim is short, then they will be a short werewolf. If the victim is tall,

then they will be a tall werewolf. Normally werewolves, when slumped over in "prowl" or "menace" mode, stand between six and nine feet tall, depending. The fur color of the werewolf also depends on the complexion of the "victim" and can range in hue from dark black to a more reddish-blond werewolf (and even an albino in one case regarding a Mr. T. Terwilliger of Westcott, Pennsylvania in 1964). Yet a common physical characteristic of all werewolves is their glowing, yellow eyes, and mouth full of razor-sharp fangs. The upper torso of the werewolf is thick and muscular; a torso much wider than the short, stubby legs that carry it. In fact, it is those short, stubby legs that seem to make most werewolves want to run on all fours when chasing their subjects.

Physically, a werewolf seems to be a perfect hybrid of both human and canine sensibilities. They can speak or they can howl. They can think or they can use their animal instincts. They can be animalistic enough to chow down on their prey, and yet sensible enough to floss that very prey out of their gums at the end of a meal.

Most modern werewolves are thought to have come from the Balkan region of Europe, and because of the quick transference of lupine abilities between humans, are thought to have easily spread around the world at a rapid pace during the late eighteen-hundreds. It must be known that werewolves might very well have been a dominant species on the planet, surpassing even the human population, were it not for the Great Werewolf Flea Plague of the early 1900s. Due to the generally poor cleanliness of the werewolves, an infestation of the Flea Plague broke out and killed off a great many of the werewolves of this time period. Over the years, the more hardy of the werewolves learned how to bathe, shampoo, and condition, and thus the cleanliness of the werewolf population did an about face.

After that, werewolves abandoned their more "animalistic" sides, and for a time, embraced their cultured side, wearing fine, tailored suits, combing their hair in elaborate and stylish ways, and adopting a refined air of nobility, considering themselves a breed of creature that was a cut above other creatures on the planet Earth. Regardless of their cultured airs, they are capable of great savagery, brutality, and hostility, as demonstrated by the way the werewolf mafia of Great Britain has risen to the top of the organized crime world in the latter half of the twentieth century.

7 CANTONESE

Cantonese is the official dialect of the Southern reaches of China, and mainly spoken in Hong Kong. A little know fact is that Cantonese is the language of the Great Southeast Asian Speaking Toads of Vietnam. Although the toads, which are found in the rain forests of Southern China, do not actually carry on coherent conversations (or at least, any conversation that humans might understand), it has been proved that the toads do, in fact, say Cantonese words instead of the usual croaking, which has disoriented more than a few travelers when they were in the region, as the sound of hundreds of toads speaking Cantonese can prove to be a bit disconcerting.

No one knows how the toads acquired their language skills, but after a study was done (funded by Serious & Earnest Incorporated), it was discovered that although the speaking toads seem to have a vocabulary of over one hundred and twenty words, the most common words spoken were "Feed me insects!" (not in that particular order).

8 "SOMETHING TREMENDOUSLY STRANGE IN THE WOODS OF MANITOBA" taken from Mr. Ping's Almanac, Vol. 33

Mr. Ping was the kind of person one could count on to dive headlong into mystery and danger, but every once in a while, his instincts would sound the alarm and steer him in a different direction. This happened to him on a visit to Manitoba in Canada, while investigating a mysterious patch of land:

...I don't know if it was the gray and blustery day or whether I'd let the locals' superstitions get to me, but standing at the edge of the field, looking into the thick patch of trees that stood in front of me made me a little bit anxious. My logical mind tried to take over, telling me that they were just trees and that there was nothing to fear from a thicket of trees. Yet my emotional side told me something else; that I'd have to be a fool to venture into these woods.

All week long in the small town of Mooseloon, Manitoba, the local townsfolk had done nothing to make me think that anything other than sheer and utter danger lurked in those woods. It seemed as if everyone I talked to had something particularly frightening to say about them.

"I wouldn't go there if I were **you**," the owner of the local hardware store told me when I inquired about them. "I had a cousin, Mortimer was his name, and he went deer hunting in those woods, eh, and he nearly got eaten."

"By a bear?" I asked. "By wolves?"

"No, sir," he said. "He was almost eaten by the *deer*! Red eyes, he said they had, eh. And that they were smart. Hunted in packs, like lions or tigers, with steam comin' out their noses and razor sharp antlers, eh."

Mayella Eubanks at the local hair salon had a different, but equally bizarre story to tell. "My friend, Martha, was driving down the road one night," she said, "And all of a sudden, her car just died, right

there on the highway. No lights, no gas, nothing that would make her car work. It was pitch black out there and she didn't know what to do.

"All of a sudden, her car starts shaking like there were a thousand people rocking it back and forth, and it seemed like several of them were jumping on the roof and hood and everything. She was quite terrified, you know, and screaming at the top of her lungs, when all of a sudden, it all stops and her car starts right back up again. She looks around and there isn't a soul anywhere within fifty yards to be seen."

Bobby Riggs, a schoolteacher, was driving by the woods one day and looked in his rear view mirror to see a man, dressed entirely in black, sitting in his backseat. "When I turned around, though, he was gone!" Susan Jones had the same thing happen to her, as did seven other people I talked to.

"How big are those woods?" I asked the Mayor one afternoon.

"Don't know," he said.

"It hasn't been surveyed?" I asked. "This is farm country. I assume that that was prime cattle grazing land."

"Sure it is," he laughed. "And sure, we tried to get it surveyed, but it changes."

"What do you mean?" I asked. "What changes?"

"I mean the size of the woods change," he said. "One day, we'll count a certain amount of acres, and the next day, it'll be twice that size. Not to mention it makes the instruments malfunction."

Ravenous deer, mysterious strangers, malfunctioning machines, these were the very things that made me want to venture into the woods to see what was lurking there. Not to mention the fact that no food would grow on any of the adjacent land, and all of the surrounding farm houses were empty due to suspected

"hauntings." Yet now that I was standing in front of these woods, I wasn't so sure that I wanted to go inside.

All my life I've been a firm subscriber to the theory of bad places. Sometimes, the magnetic energies of the Earth can converge and fill a place with either good fortune or bad. Though these places are few and far between around the globe, they still exist, and draw their kind to them. Standing in front of the woods, I realized that this was a bad place, and I knew that it would be a bad idea to go inside, **looking** for trouble.

And for only the second time in my entire life, I abandoned my original plans, for no other reason than utter and complete fear. I would not be going into the woods on this day I sensed that the danger was too great, and as I walked back to my car, I felt a great sense of relief. Yet just before I shut the door, I heard laughter, unmistakable and far away. I couldn't tell exactly where, but I knew its reason. The laughter was mocking me because I was afraid.

So be it...

9 FANG'S GOOD FORTUNE NOODLE EMPORIUM

Part of the wildly popular chain of Fang Good Fortune *restaurants (including* Fang's Good Fortune Duck House, Fang's Good Fortune Dim Sum Palace, *and the ever-popular* Fang's Good Fortune Fried Chicken and Ice Cream*) that are found throughout the Hong Kong region,* Fang's Good Fortune Noodle Emporium *was the first in the chain of fine eating establishments. Founded in the late seventies by a young Mr. Fang and his wife, Mrs. Fang,* Good Fortune Noodle Emporium *was popular with the locals for their very unique noodle dishes and hot pot recipes. Although the* Good Fortune Noodle Emporium *was shut down at various times over the* years for a myriad of health and safety reasons, including the discovery of rat meat in one hot pot and a still-uncategorized industrial-strength mold that grew on the walls, a steady stream of bribe money to health officials kept the place in business. Regardless of the rumors about what horrible things are in the food, the locals still come in droves, and even celebrate the horror of what might be lurking in their meals. Some locals even created a small shrine to worship under the horrible green mold on the walls, until local officials discovered the mold was, in fact, radioactive, and had to have a HAZMAT team remove the wall. Specials at Good Fortune Noodle Emporium: *Furry Friends Hot Pot (No. 47), Green Beans and Cricket Heads in Butter (No. 324), and the ever-popular Spicy Noodles and Deep Fried Rat Legs w/Honey Mustard Sauce (No. 128 and recently "re-added" to the menu by Mrs. Fang).*

10 KOWLOON

Also known as Tsim Sha Tsui, Kowloon is a tourist quarter and is filled with shops, karaoke clubs, parks, apartment buildings, and electronics stores, not to mention various forms of scum and villainy that call the place home (and their rivals who, in some cases, live but two blocks away). Kowloon also has world class cultural sights, art galleries, and museums, as well as some of the finest hotels in the world. The district is a haven for backpackers that are either seeing Hong Kong or using it as a port of call for other destinations.

However, what makes Kowloon special is the fact that it happens to sit on what many believe to be an important magnetic nexus point for world geography, specifically, the Yau Ma Tei area and what is known as the Temple Street Night Market. It is widely known that, depending on their strength, magnetic nexus points draw strange and unusual things

to an area (as proven with other magnetic nexus points such as Easter Island, Stonehenge, the Forbidden City, Dealey Plaza, and Tahlequah, Oklahoma in the U.S.A.). Thus, Kowloon has its fair share of bizarre creatures and unexplained happenings. Of certain interest would be the gathering of fortunetellers and Cantonese opera singers at the Night Market, and the telepathic rats that frequent the area (weak minds beware!)

11 THE CONSPIRICETTI

AT THE REQUEST OF THE PUBLISHER, ALL INFORMATION ABOUT THE CONSPIRICETTI HAS BEEN REMOVED FROM REFERENCE IN THIS EDITION. FOR MORE INFORMATION REGARDING THE CONSPIRICETTI, PLEASE CONSULT THE ENTRY FOR TIBERIUS CEASAR OR MR. PING'S ALMANACS, VOL. 28, 35, 37, AND 61.

12 THE OUIJA BOARD

Before the invention of the telephone, the telegraph, and even email, human beings had an excellent, long-range, instantaneous communication device about whose existence few knew. That device was the Ouija Board. Consisting of a board with letters written across the front and a lightweight pointing device, the Ouija Board is used to communicate across the temporal fields and can even work between dimensions. If used properly, the Ouija Board can send telepathic messages to others, speak with those that have long since passed, or communicate with creatures regardless of language barriers (several highly skilled Ouija Boardists are able to communicate quite freely with their pets). Messages are relayed through the Ouija Board by placing the hands on the pointing device and allowing the magnetic waves, prana, and Qi to flow through their bodies, into their hands, and across the board to spell a message.

However, in order to use the Ouija board to its fullest potential, it is highly recommended that the user be specially trained at a licensed and certified school, preferably the Mr. Ping-endorsed "Sanjay Patel School for Ouija Board Mastery and Skill, serving the Ouija board needs in over fifty locations around the globe (check the internet for details)."

Use of a Ouija board without proper training can have unforeseen consequences, most of them bad. Demonic possession in Ouija board novices is quite common, and although it is easily cured and causes very little stress on the possessed, it can be quite disconcerting to those friends and family members around the person being possessed. Improper Ouija board usage has also resulted in a sort of addiction, much like one might become addicted to computer solitaire, in which the user, because they might be picking up meaningful messages, believes that they must continue using the Ouija board until the messages answer all of their questions. NOTE: IMMEDIATELY STOP using a Ouija board if the messages it is delivering seem vague or cryptic. This is usually a sign of a poltergeist or demon playing tricks on the user and could result in a haunting or possession. Ouija board messages are always crystal clear in meaning, and the board should be abandoned immediately if they are not. Lastly, avoid those that are interested in Ouija boards or encourage others to use one, no matter how well one might know them. The odds are that if they are trying to encourage Ouija board use, it means that they are probably suffering from a low-grade possession and could, very well, kill the next person that uses the Ouija board with them (through no fault of their own, mind you). The following excerpt is taken from Mr. Ping's Almanac Vol. 62:

…We sat in the dim light of the attic just as Gertrude put

her hands on the pointer and began to channel the energy of the universe into her board. "This is right well ridiculous, Mr. Ping," Reggie said to me, trying to worm his way out of the moment.

"I think Reggie's just trying to hide his fear by making fun of this whole thing," Smelts laughed. Reggie summarily punched him on the arm. "Ow!"

"That's me hiding my fear using aggression," Reggie said, giving Smelts the Evil Eye.

"Quiet, you two," I told them. "I'd like to get on with this."

By now, Gertrude's hands were pushing the pointer back and forth across the board, as if they were channeling static from the radio airwaves, looking for a frequency in which to tune. Suddenly, the pointer stopped cold, then drifted over to a letter. "H," Smelts said, pulling out a piece of paper to write down the letters. The pointer began to move again.

"E," Reggie said, gazing out of the corner of his eye at the board and looking just as scared as he felt.

"L," I said, also writing the message.

"L!" Smelts said, almost dropping his paper in fear. "H-E-L-L! We're channeling demons! Stop, for pity's sake!"

"O?" Reggie asked as the pointer moved over the final letter. "H-E-L-L-O! Not Hell! Hell - o!"

Smelts tried to play it off by saying, "I knew that."

"Hello," I said. "Gertrude, tell them hello."

Gertrude was deep in concentration on the board, looking every bit the gypsy woman that she was, with her Eastern European nose and dark, deep set eyes. "Ze vibrations are very strong with dis van," she said. "Ze are near."

"You mean, like, in the room?" Reggie asked, his eyes

frantically searching every corner.

"No, not here," Gertrude said. "But close." She focused on the board again and asked, "Who are you?"

The pointer moved a bit more quickly this time from letter to letter, spelling out the word, "Terry."

"It's Terry!" Smelts said, his voice filled with awe. "Can you believe it? It's Terry!"

"Who's Terry?" Reggie asked, sounding skeptical.

"I don't know," Smelts said. "I thought someone else might know."

"Do you know, Mr. Ping?" Reggie asked.

"I don't know anyone named Terry," I said.

"What about you, Madame Gertrude?" he asked.

"Look, babushka," Madame Gertrude said, opening one eye in an annoyed fashion, "If you vant this to vork, you haff to shut up. Do you get it?"

"Oh, yes," Reggie said. "Sorry. Continue."

Madame Gertrude closed her eyes and took a deep breath, once again channeling her energies into the pointer. "Terry," she said, slowly. Then with more dramatic emphasis, she said, "Terry! Tell us about yourself."

Slowly, the pointer moved across the board. "I" was the first letter, then it moved to the number thirteen.

"I-thirteen," Smelts said.

"Unlucky thirteen," Reggie said. "Oh, this is a bad day!"

"Is Terry on the thirteenth level of Hades or something?" Smelts asked.

"No," Gertrude said, still annoyed. "Terry is thirteen years old."

"That must have been when she died," Reggie said. He began to wipe a tear from his eyes, saying, "How sad! The poor girl thinks she is still thirteen years old, even though she's been dead for years."

"Please be quite, yeti," Madame Gertrude said. "I cannot concentrate with ze spirit ven you continue to prattle on like zis."

"Oh, sorry," Reggie said. "Terry," she said. "Terry! Where are you right now?"

The pointer moved across the board, forming new words. "It's an address!" Smelts said, his eyes wide with wonder. "31 Wicket Drive. Hey, that's this street."

"It's the house right next to yours," I said.

Madame Gertrude broke her concentration again. "31 Wicket Drive?" she asked.

"Yep, that's it," I said.

She slapped her hand to her face in frustration and said, "Oh, I knew this would happen."

"What?" Reggie asked.

Madame Gertrude walked over to the attic window and pulled up the shade, peering out into the dark night. She lifted up the window and yelled out into the night air, "Terry, I vill get you for zis!"

"Is she nuts?" Smelts asked. "I don't think there's a ghost out there. It's in here."

"No, no," Madame Gertrude said. "Zere is no ghost here. Ve vere just picking up the brain frequencies of my little neighbor girl. I sink she's a low-grade psychic and she does zis just to annoy Gertrude."

"So we're not channeling a ghost?" Smelts asked.

"No," Madame Gertrude said. I peered out the window beside her to see a rambunctious looking teenager looking up and laughing at us. "I vill **find** you and tell your mother!" Gertrude yelled. "You keep out of my head, you little monster!"

"Nyah, nyah!" the little girl yelled, making a face at us.

"See?" Reggie said. "I told you these stupid things don't work."

"Ve cannot do ze board," Madame Gertrude said, waving

us away. "Not until zat little monster goes to bed!"

I shrugged my shoulders and sighed. I would have to contact my Uncle Lao at a later date...

13 CRYSTAL BALLS

The source of much misinformation in modern times, due to fabulous stories and fairy tales passed down through generations (usually involving haunted houses or gypsies), crystal balls are actually inter-dimensional storage places for information. There has been a long held misconception that crystal balls can be used to contact the dead on other, mysterious planes of reality, but this is not the case. They are actually more like computers. Whereas a computer is a tool that can be used to access information, so, too, is a crystal ball; but where a computer stores said information on a hard drive or disk, a crystal ball stores the information in another dimension.

With the right skills or training, one would best use a crystal ball as a secure storage space for ideas, be it ideas for novels, inventions, or ideas for a self-run business. However, crystal ball usage is not as simple as one might imagine, and there are some unusual aspects to its operation that tend to send most people scrambling for cover. Mr. Ping got his first crystal ball in 1923:

"...And here it is," said Mr. Pablum, unveiling the brand new crystal ball for me. Not that it was brand new, really, for it had taken thousands of years to create it under the geological formations of the Earth. However, it was new in a sense that he'd only recently polished it down, rounded out the edges, and created a useful device for me to use.

"It's beautiful," I said, gingerly taking it into my hands.

"Is this your first crystal ball?" he asked.

"Yes," I said. "I've heard lots of things about them and I've thought about getting one for years, but I've only just now got around to it."

"Well, I think you're going to be very pleased with this one," he said, smiling.

I held it up, looking into its crystal clear center, expecting it to come to life before my very eyes. It was heavy, almost like a bowling ball, and when I looked through it, it turned the world on the other side upside-down.

"I'm going to tell you how to get started so that you'll be prepared for class tomorrow," he said. I'd enrolled in *Basic Principles of Crystal Ball Usage for Beginners* at Atticus Atherly University to help me prepare for using the crystal ball to its fullest advantage, and I was looking forward to a bit of instruction from Mr. Pablum. "Now remember," he said, "Every crystal ball is unique. It warms to its user. At first, it may seem difficult, but after a while, it will become easier and easier. First, you want to make sure it's placed in the right section of your house, based on the basic tenets of Feng Shui."

"Okay," I said.

"What I'd like for you to do tonight is go home and light a candle behind the crystal ball," he continued. "Dim the lights in the rest of the house and relax, sitting cross-legged in front of the ball. Take fifteen minutes with your eyes closed and let your mind wander. Then, once you feel relaxed, open your eyes and concentrate on the flame of the candle through the crystal ball. Take as long as you need. When you feel your mind start to wander freely, jumping from one thought to the next without any effort, you've accessed the crystal ball. Don't try to control it. Just let your mind wander. Spend about thirty minutes there. Once you're done with that, you

should make yourself a nice peanut butter and jelly sandwich, walk up to the roof, and howl at the moon like a crazed, three-toed sloth."

"Excuse me?" I asked.

"A crazed, three-toed sloth," he said, looking at me seriously. "Then, once you've done that, you should go to your kitchen, put two cinnamon sticks up your nose, and say these words: Vesti la Giubba!"

I didn't know what to say. "Are you serious?" I asked.

"You want it to work, don't you?" he said.

"Well, yes," I said.

"Then don't ask questions," he said. "These are time-honored traditions and they are not to be trifled with. You can't change thousands of years of history just because you feel silly. And by the way, here is your costume."

He pulled out a large, black gorilla suit and handed it to me. "Costume?" I asked.

"Yes!" he said, throwing his hands into the air. "Now, do you want it to work or not?"

"Well, yes, but..."

"Well, then, just do it," he said. "Call me in the morning."

And with that, he shuffled me out the door. Something about this whole affair made me feel like the butt of a severe practical joke...

14 "THE BARBARIC CAMEL-MEN OF THE SAHARA" from Mr. Ping's Almanac, Vol. 22

Mr. Ping spent the year 1921 traveling through Africa. During the early part of the year, he traveled with nomads through North Africa, searching for the elusive and mysterious Tutankarachmana Falls. The days he spent traveling through the Sahara were harsh. The stress of trudging across a hot desert under blazing temperatures with no shelter but the turban on his head had a significant effect on Mr. Ping. It was during their second week in the desert that an amazing experience happened that derailed his original intentions for the trip. Late one night, Mr. Ping heard voices; conspiratorial mutterings all around his camp:

...I laid there, daring not to move, thinking that bandits had come into our camp with plans to rob us of all our belongings. I had expected bandits on our journey, just not so soon. I peeked over my blankets to see what they might have been doing. Their language was Arabic, but they spoke Arabic with a strange, guttural accent, and all of their voices were low and bellowing. "Go on!" they said, whispering. "Be free my brothers and sisters, and **please** never let them torment you again!"

I quickly realized that the bandits were trying to steal our camels, **send**ing them off into the desert, and I knew that something had to be done. I jumped up from my resting place, ready to take action against this scourge of the desert. "Unhand my camels, you ruffians!" I shouted in my best Arabic. "Thievery will get you nowhere!"

I glanced around to look for the bandits, but saw nothing but camels...a *significant* amount of camels. We seemed to have gained at least ten more camels than what we had when I'd gone to bed for the night. "Come out and show yourselves, you cowards!" I yelled, but still, no one appeared.

It was at this point that I looked over at my comrades and found that all of my fellow travelers were in a pile on the right of me, each one bound and gagged and looking at me in a desperate manner. "We missed one," I heard a bandit say. Then I realized that the bandits were not what I thought they were. In my naiveté, I had assumed that our assailants were humans, but in the dark of the moonlight, I soon realized that these

"bandits" weren't actually human at all.

They were *camels*.

Large, lumbering beasts, they looked different from the camels that I was used to. Their humps were bigger, their mouths more articulate, and their eyes wielded a fierce, fiery intelligence that radiated anger. "We don't want to hurt you, two-legs," one said to me, as it tentatively approached me. "We just want to free our enslaved brothers and sisters."

I assumed **a** defensive posture; my body language warning the camel not to come any closer, all the while shocked that I was surrounded by camels that could talk. "These camels are ours!" I said. "You will not take them!"

"Listen to the savage!" one camel muttered. "He actually refers to our brethren as *property!* We should kill them all and be done with it."

"Silence!" the biggest camel said. "We knew our mission when we left. We must not stray."

I knew that I was in a great deal of trouble and had no clue how to get out of it. My only hope was to surrender and hope that these strange, speaking camels would use their better judgment and not kill me...

15 "THE BOTTOMLESS PIT OF DEATH" taken from Mr. Ping's Almanac, Vol. 63

The Bottomless Pit of Death was supposedly located in Peru, high in the Andes mountain range on a nondescript hilltop overlooking a fertile green valley. Rumors of the pit had circulated throughout the world; so much so that the hype drew Mr. Ping to its location. After hearing stories about the pit, Mr. Ping expected to see totems or hieroglyphics or some other sort of warning signs along the way telling the wayward traveler that they should stay far away from this horrible place. However, this was not the case. The Pit sat inside of a small, wooden shack that was

barely maintained by a couple of farmers from the valley below. The shack was quaint, but falling apart, and definitely not reminiscent of the grand Incan temple that Mr. Ping had expected to stand on the site:

"This is it?" I asked my guide in Spanish.

"Si, señor," he said, shrugging his shoulders as we stood in the rickety tin shack that stood over the hole.

"There's certainly not a lot to it," I said.

"No, señor," he said.

"Well, then," I said, "What's so legendary about this hole?"

"Es bottomless," he said, once again shrugging his shoulders.

I came to the quick conclusion that my guide knew little more than I did. I leaned down over the hole and peered into its depths, hoping to find an answer, but there was none. It was just a hole in the ground, around four feet wide and three feet thick; its brown rock walls disappearing into parts unknown.

I picked up a rock from the ground and dropped it into the hole in the hopes that it would provide some answers. I heard it ricochet off the walls a couple of times, but never heard it hit the bottom. *I guess it really is bottomless,* I thought.

It was at that moment that I realized something was wrong. I began to put things together in my mind. *What was it that sent me here? What did they want? Why would they send me on a fool's errand?*

I quickly realized what had happened. I had deluded my**self**.

"Come on," I said to my guide. "We've got to get back to Lima!" I pulled him out of the shack as quickly as possible, my heart sick with worry that we were too late. Days later when we arrived in Lima, my suspicions were confirmed.

The Tahitians had taken over the United States...

16 "THE LAST T-REX IN CLEVELAND" taken from Mr. Ping's Almanac, Vol. 17

Mr. Ping's first (and only) encounter with a dinosaur in 1924 was addressed in an Almanac entry from Vol. 17:

...Attending the 1924 Ohio State Exhibition in Cleveland wasn't my original goal in traveling to the United States that year, but my host, Dr. James Worthington, was so proud of his prized pig that it would have been unbelievably rude to refuse his offer. So early one Saturday morning, I helped Dr. Worthington load his massive pig into the back of his truck and set off for the city.

The Ohio State Exhibition was a farm trade show. It brought farmers from all over the region into Cleveland, where companies could show off their latest farming equipment like the newest plows and tractors, and farmers could show and sell their prized livestock. Of course, one must keep the family entertained as well, so while mother and father were looking over the goods, their children were riding the carnival rides set up on the midway or perusing the strange and unusual shows that these sorts of events tended to have. On the main strip, one could ride an exotic elephant, test their stomachs on some sort of spinning contraption, marvel at the bearded lady, or cozy up to their sweetheart on the ferris wheel.

After unloading Martha the Pig (who gave me a nasty bite as I tried to pull her from the back of the truck), Dr. Worthington abandoned me to go look at the animals on display. I decided to have a look at the midway, for this was the first time that I had ever seen a genuine U.S. fair. It was utterly and completely fascinating to me. I had never seen carnival barkers trying to lure people to their booths to win a prize by throwing a baseball at milk jugs. I had never before seen the "Tilt-a-Whirl," although afterward, I was filled with regret with my choice to ride it because my stomach was terribly upset, and the "corn dog" that I ate afterwards did nothing to prevent that queasy feeling.

As the day progressed, I found myself standing in front of a large, multi-colored tent with a giant banner that caught my eye. The banner read, *The Last Tyrannosaurus Rex Left in Captivity,* and I wondered how on Earth they could fake this one. The werewolf man was fake (I'd seen a real one two weeks earlier), the bearded lady was simply a man in a dress, and the two-headed cow was just a stuffed toy. I assumed that the "last" t-rex was going to be an iguana sitting, bored, in its cage under the hot lights and watchful eyes of sullen, bitter children.

I couldn't have been more incorrect.

The tent was dingy and hot, seeming to gather all the heat of the day in one place, and the dust clogged my lungs, for it had been very dry that year in Cleveland, not to mention the fact that the OSE seemed to have been held on the driest patch of land in Ohio. I stood with a variety of people in line, waiting to see the fallacy that was the "last" t-rex. The line was filled with an interesting mix of Americans. There were citified folks from Cleveland, enjoying the more decadent side of life, and there were backwards bumpkins who came out of the hills once a year for the fair and then disappeared back to their barns for the rest of the year.

We all waited in a narrow corridor made from tent flaps that glowed red as the sun shone on top of the shelter. The line extended, single file, all the way down the corridor and then around a corner, where, supposedly, the main attraction lay in wait. Everyone was hot and tired and a wide variety of putrid smells were emanating from the various folks around me.

Finally, after shuffling down the hall for the longest time, we rounded the corner and there, before us, stood what we'd all been waiting to see. I was shocked to find that there in front of me was an actual, living, breathing Tyrannosaurus Rex (although "living" might have been a strong word). Where I assumed that a dinosaur such as this might stand tall, a good twenty feet from the ground, and be prowling back and forth in its captivity, what I saw before me was a sad and pathetic sight.

The poor beast was lying on its stomach, its arms and legs splayed out to its sides and its head at an awkward angle on the ground. Hundreds of feet of chains were racked across the creatures back and head, presumably to keep what I knew to be an extremely powerful and agile creature from munching on the onlookers. In places, the chains had worn into the poor beast's thick, leathery hide, especially around its head. It looked diseased, as white foam slowly crept out of its mouth, and a yellow puss ran from its eye. I was completely and utterly appalled and had to look twice to make sure that this pitiful creature was actually breathing.

A fat, mustached man in a colorful striped suit stepped out from behind a curtain with a large, gold walking stick, looking bored and unhappy to be giving yet another spiel to this audience. "Step right up, ladies and gentlemen," he yelled, "And see the eighth wonder of the world, the last surviving *Tyrannosaurus Rex,* captured at *great peril and expense,* and brought all the way here to Toledo...er... Cleveland...to be observed by the fine folks of the Ohio State Exhibition!" The man began to pace back and forth across the small stage, as if he was letting us, the audience, in on his own little secret. "The creature, so fierce and full of mean-spirited fire and anger, killed not *one*, not *three*, but *thirteen* unlucky men, rest their souls, as it ran rampant through a small island in the South Pacific, gobbling up the infirm, the elderly, and the young alike. Any creature that wasn't fast enough to outrun its deadly chase met a gruesome fate! But capture the creature we did, and we brought it all the way back here for you to see..."

At this point, the T-rex began to stir, a low growl rumbling in its chest, which was quickly met with a whack across its nose by the barker's gold walking stick. This was all I could take, so I raised my hand, saying, "Excuse me..."

The man smiled in a way that said he was just barely tolerating me interrupting his routine, and said, "Yes? The Chinaman has a question."

"If this is the last T-Rex in the world, then what in the world is it doing chained to the floor here in Cleveland?" I asked.

"Excuse me?" he said.

"Shouldn't we be doing everything in our power to keep the poor creature alive? As a miracle of modern science?"

"Ah," the Barker said, smiling at me and revealing his ugly, brown teeth in the process. "A *skeptic*! This beast is used for *scientific purposes*, my friendly Chinaman. We only bring the creature out for special events. The rest of the time she's as happy as a clam in the hallowed halls of Forkington University."

"What are those sores on its back, then?" I asked. "Are those from the chains?"

"Sores are natural on creatures such as this," the Barker said. "They usually occur in the summertime. Part of their mating routine."

"And the puss in its eye?" I asked.

"T-Rex's secrete special chemicals from their eyes to ward off predators," the Barker said, growing annoyed with my line of questioning.

"What kind of predators stalk the biggest predators in the world?" I asked.

"Why, the Giant *Moglasaurus!*" the Barker said, raising his hands high in the air and saying it with great, dramatic flourish. "Or the *Bonbodalasaurus!* A hideous creature that stands *sixty feet high* with teeth as sharps as *nails* and *razor-wire* for fur, and who belches *hydrochloric acid* and whacks its victims with trees it uprooted with its *bare hands!*"

"There's no such creature as a Bonbodalasaurus," I said.

"How do *you* know?" the Barker asked, turning away from me and back to the rest of the audience. "Which one of you delightful children would like to feed the evil T-Rex its dinner?" He held up a live chicken for everyone to see.

I looked at the poor T-Rex one last time and felt a great swell of pity for the creature, for it had to have been a miserable existence. Painfully chained to the ground, day after day, subsisting on a diet of raw chickens fed to it by ungrateful little children. I also felt a twinge of regret stemming from the fact that so little seemed to be known about the creature. *Where did it come from?* Dinosaurs had been extinct for millions of years. *Were there more of them? What did it eat? How did it survive for so long?*

All of these questions would never be answered, especially by someone like that Barker, who probably knew nothing about it anyway. I felt sad for the world in that they would never know about such mysteries.

Of course, these were all theoretical ideas and that line of thinking quickly vanished as I exited the tent into the harsh sunlight of the afternoon, only

to be quickly met by two thick goons wearing dirty overalls and three days worth of stubble on their chins. "Da boss sez you wuz makin' trouble," one of them said.

"We don' like trouble," said the other.

"Yeah, we don't like trouble," said the first.

"Well," I said, trying to leave, "I'm glad that's settled. Now, if you'll excuse me..."

"Nah," said the first goon. "I don't think ya understand. We're askin' ya ta leave an' don't come back."

"Or what?" I asked, sensing a threat on the horizon. I had never taken well to threats or aggression, especially from dimwit individuals whose only purpose was to do other's dirty work.

"You're kinda small," said the first one, looking hesitant. "We don't wanna hafta hurt ya."

"You can trust me when I say that you would be hard pressed to hurt me, friend," I said. "Now, I've got the rest of the fair to enjoy, so if you don't mind, I'd like to be on my way."

The Barker emerged from the tent, just as I was about to teach his subordinates a lesson. He walked up to me in all of his slimy glory and smiled, once again revealing his brown-stained teeth. "We got trouble here, boys?" he asked.

"We's tryin' ta make dis guy see da light," said Goon One. "But he keeps insistin' on getting' hurt."

"Yeah," said the other. "It's almost like he's beggin' for it."

The first goon made a move like he was going to clobber me, but the carnival barker stopped him, a routine, it seems, that they'd done several times before. "Whoa, whoa, whoa, Sully," he said. "We don't want any innocent people to get hurt."

"They won't hurt me," I said, calmly.

"Lemme at 'im!" said Goon Two, reaching over Goon One for me.

"No, no, boys," said the Barker. "Maybe if I speak in plain English, this here foreigner will understand." He turned to me and the smile left his face as he plugged a moist, mealy cigar into his mouth and began to puff away. "Look, son," he said, "You probably mean well by asking them kinda questions you were asking in the tent, but let me tell you...good intentions can get you in a lot of trouble. Understand?"

"No," I said. "Enlighten me."

"You want the facts?" he asked, getting very close to me with his stinky breath and poking me in the chest. "The fact is, I see your skinny little behind near my tent again, I'm liable to turn my men here loose on you. That means you get hurt! That means you don't bother us again. Got it?"

He stared at me under his bushy eyebrows, **stamped** his feet, and tried his best to look intimidating as he waited, I suppose, for me to acknowledge the threat, but I planned to do no such thing. "First," I said, "Let me tell you that your threats don't scare me. Second, your breath is awful, so I would appreciate it if you took a couple of steps backward. And third, I cannot, in good conscience, allow that poor creature in your tent to suffer under your hand any longer, and I will do everything in my power to make sure she doesn't."

I assume that no one had ever stood up to the Barker before, so he was a bit flabbergasted by my terse response. But soon, he realized that I'd insulted him, so he turned to his goons and said, "Teach this guy a lesson, boys."

He tried to walk away as his goons grabbed me by the arms, ready to do damage. "I think you're a little bit too late," I said. "To teach me a lesson, I mean."

He turned to me, snarling. "What do you mean?" he asked.

"I've already done everything I needed to do," I said, as I held up a set of keys in my hand.

His cigar fell out of his mouth in shock. "*My keys,*" he said, almost to himself. "Where did you get my keys?"

I smiled at him and said, "I believe your 'star attraction' might be a little bit angry at the conditions under which she's been living."

"What did you do?" he yelled, and just at that moment, we heard a roar that hadn't been heard in seventy-five million years.

The T-Rex was up.

Panicked carnival-goers began streaming form the tent, screaming bloody murder as they ran for their lives. I knew, good and well, that I had to be on guard for the innocent folks, for it wouldn't take much for a T-Rex who had eaten chickens most of her life to want a little sample of human...

17 "LIEUTENANT CYANIDE AND THE ROCKETWAFTE" taken from Mr. Ping's Almanac, Vol. 45

During the second world war, Mr. Ping served as a special agent for Britain and their allies; his job being to suss out the mysterious weapons programs of the Axis powers around the world. It was during this time that he first encountered his lifelong enemy-to-be in the form of Lieutenant Cyanide:

...I had been held prisoner in the room for three days with nothing more than moldy bread and water to keep me alive, both of which were delivered by a sweaty, unshaven guard who looked bitter that he had to keep an eye on me. His feelings of bitterness were entirely understandable, for the heat was oppressive and unbearable, the lack of moisture from the desert outside leaving my tiny, tin shack, as stale and musty as any place I'd ever known.

I could barely believe that I was in this situation and I knew the person that had given away my identity was none other than Petite Louie back in Cairo. Because of Petite Louie's infernal double-cross at that restaurant, I was now a prisoner of the Nazis, awaiting my fate in the middle of nowhere in the North African desert.

I was *exactly* where I wanted to be.

The walls of the shack were thin and because my days as a prisoner were so monotonous, the arrival of a convoy of trucks outside meant that something big was happening. I heard German voices speaking outside in hushed tones about my capture. Soon, a latch was undone, and my sweaty guard led in a small contingent of Nazi officers, all dressed in immaculately pressed, gray uniforms and looking decidedly large, blond-haired, and blue-eyed. Bringing up the rear was the chief officer, a seven- foot tall, imposing fellow, also with blond hair and blue eyes. He had the rugged, good looks of a movie star and carried himself with an authority that made the soldiers under him willing to serve.

The main officer pulled out a piece of paper, read it, and then looked at me. "Gerald Jones?" he asked, a sarcastic grin pasted across his face.

"That's me," I said, stoic and refusing to look at him.

"You don't look like a *Gerald Jones*," he said. "You look Chinese."

I just stared straight ahead, refusing to make eye contact with him.

"What were you doing in our territory, Chinaman?" the officer asked, leaning over to look me in the eye.

"Germany doesn't control the whole world, sergeant," I said.

"That, my friend, is only a matter of time," he laughed.

"And I am a *lieutenant*. I would prefer that you refer to me in that way, Herr Jones."

"How long are you going to hold me prisoner?" I asked.

"Until we kill you," he said, laughing. "And that could be today or it could be tomorrow. We'll just have to see how well you cooperate."

"Fine," I said.

SMACK!

The Lieutenant slapped me very hard across the face with the back of his hand and said, "You will address me with *respect*, little man. And if it's not to my liking, then I'll take you out back to kill you myself and leave you for the buzzards." He meant business and I didn't have enough information, so I thought I would have to fish it out of him. "Now that you understand my feelings regarding disrespect," he said, "Let me ask you again. What were you doing in our territory?"

I looked up at him seriously and said, "Now that you understand my feelings on intimidation, let me tell you again. Germany doesn't control the whole world. Or *me.*"

At first, murderous rage filled his face and a twitch in his left eye betrayed his resentment. But then, a grudging wave of respect washed over him and he smiled. "You're a brave man, Mr. Jones," he said. "The last person that spoke to me in such a way was never seen again."

"Congratulations," I said. "You must be very proud of yourself."

His reluctant smile vanished and he stood up. "Put him in the truck," he said to his lackeys. "We're taking him with us."

"Yes, sir," they said.

He walked to the door, about to leave the shack, but then stopped midway, as if he just remembered something important. "Wait," he said. He turned back towards me and struck me with the butt of his pistol, knocking me to the floor. "Okay," he said, just before I lost consciousness. "I'm done."

I awoke hours later, bouncing across the dusty desert in the back of an army transport truck. The side of my face was painfully tender from being pistol-whipped and the three soldiers that were guarding me looked as though they were ready to give me the same were I to make a false move. The tan flaps of the truck were rolled up on the sides to let the cooler air in, but it really made no difference. The heat was oppressive in the sun or the shade, and the wind was like a furnace blowing in our faces.

However, because the side flaps were rolled up, I was afforded a perfect view of the road, and where we were headed. At the moment, we were traveling through the craggy rocks of the desert, a lifeless landscape more akin to what I would imagine the moon to be like there. We rounded a corner and I saw that we were driving along the edge of a canyon, and as we moved closer to the canyon's edge, I couldn't believe what I saw.

Below us was what appeared to be a clandestine army base, filling the entirety of the floor of the canyon. Tents, warehouses, and equipment were everywhere, but that wasn't what surprised me. What actually surprised me was what was at the far end of the valley. Standing tall above the canyon floor, with its tip extending just above the lip of the cliffs, was a *rocket*.

It was tall and slender, painted as tan as the desert around it, with a large, German flag painted on its side. In the confirmation of the rocket's existence, the first object of my mission had been fulfilled. Now, all I had to do was get the coordinates of the rocket and I

would be able to report back to the allies and enjoy a nice cup of tea, hopefully in a more hospitable climate.

"Sit down," one of the soldiers said to me when he observed that I was looking at the base. They lowered the flaps and my view of the rocket was obscured. I would have to put my plan into action later.

I was taken to yet another miserably hot tent, whereupon I was tied to yet another miserably uncomfortable chair, and watched by yet another miserably grumpy guard. I sat there for hours. The tent was dark, with very little natural light, so it was hard to tell whether it was day or night. I assumed that it was placed well away from the rest of the camp, for even if I were to concentrate very intensely, I could not hear anything stirring outside. Normally, a person in such a situation would get bored and go a bit stir-crazy, thus making them highly susceptible to the harsh interrogation techniques of their captors, but I had been trained in meditation by a group of Thai monks several years earlier, so I used the time to concentrate on my wounds, willing them to heal, and abandoning the self; being one with the universe around me. It was actually quite pleasant.

However, my guard was getting extremely bored and restless, so much so that I saw him begin to fall asleep, his face leaning on the barrel of the rifle he held over his shoulder. "Excuse me," I asked, snapping him out of his stupor.

He wiped a bit of drool from his chin and angrily looked at me. "What?" he said in German, sounding annoyed and embarrassed at the same time.

"How long are you going to keep me here?" I asked, also speaking German.

"Shut up!" he said, turning away from me.

"You know, you're fighting on the wrong side," I said. "Germany is not going to win this war." He ignored me. "There are thousands of transport ships on their way to North Africa right now. They're going to roll right through the desert and march right up to this base. It will be a complete slaughter. They know about the rocket and they've made it their highest priority to destroy it."

"They know of the rocket?" the soldier asked, sounding concerned.

"*Of course* they know about the rocket," I said, sounding as confident as I could. "Their plans are to infiltrate the base and then wipe the place off the map. That rocket technology is too advanced to let it sit idle. They've got to destroy it."

The guard looked at me, momentarily filled with despair at the thought that he was riding on a sinking ship. But just as quickly, he snapped out of it. "You lie!" he said, spitting at me in anger.

"You want proof?" I asked.

"You have no proof," he said, full of contempt.

"If you want proof, then watch the guard that brings in the food," I said. "He should be arriving any minute now. He's a spy for the allies. Watch the way he delivers the food. Observe the hand signals he gives me. We're in control of the base and it's just a matter of hours before we go to work."

I had timed my conversation with the bored, uncomfortably sweaty guard so that it would coincide with the meal delivery for the day. Like clockwork, the German grunt arrived with the miserable fare that they called food, walked over and sat it down, all under the oppressive gaze of the soldier guarding me.

It should be noted that the food delivery soldier did nothing out of the ordinary. Having watched him deliver several meals before this one, I had observed his facial ticks

and the quirky way in which he held the meal, for his hands had a slight, nervous tremor. It was nothing to the casual observer, but I had planted the seeds of paranoia in my guard and he watched the other soldier like a rat, looking for any sign of the unusual. It only took slight ticks and movements to signal to my guard that this other soldier was working as a spy, and as soon as he left, the guard turned to me with a terrified look on his face.

"How many of you are there?" he asked.

"We have all we need," I said, looking bored. "Did you see his hand?"

"Yes," the guard said.

"He was telling me that we're only about half an hour from Operation Destroy Rocket. There will be no prisoners. There will be no survivors."

My guard was now standing there, nervously trying to figure out what to do. His lips were dry and cracked and my manipulation of him was made much easier by the fact that he was severely dehydrated. "Operation Destroy Rocket," he said to himself.

"I can spare you, Jurgen," I said.

"How did you know my name?" he asked.

In actuality, I had heard the previous guard mention it, but he was too paranoid to realize it. "I know everyone's name," I said with a smug look on my face. "Now, if you'll release me, I can take you to the safe zone that's been designated."

"Safe zone?" Jurgen asked.

"We've not a moment to lose, Jurgen," I said. "You seem like a good man. I'd hate to lose you in the coming carnage."

"Operation Destroy Rocket," he said, staring at the floor.

"Untie me, Jurgen," I said. "Let me help you."

And just as Jurgen was walking towards my bindings, a voice rang out behind me. "Bravo, Mr. Jones," he said. I looked back to see the Lieutenant from earlier standing in the corner, applauding. "Convincing my men of the coming slaughter. Absolutely brilliant."

"Save yourself, Lieutenant," I said. "Join us, for it's only a matter of time."

He walked over and leaned right down in my face, saying, "The slaughter will only be that of the Allies, my friend."

"Sir," the guard said. "The base is overrun!"

"He lies, Herr Friedrichs," the Lieutenant said. "He is a master manipulator and has played you for a fool." He turned to two of his cronies and said, "Take this weakling to the brig. He has betrayed his nation."

"But, sir..." the guard pleaded.

My guard was dragged out of the room, kicking and screaming, protesting his innocence and speaking of the coming carnage at the base. I began to feel guilty at my manipulation of him and vowed that if I were to escape, I would help to free him as well. "So, Mr. Jones," the Lieutenant said, turning his attention back to me, "Would you care to inform me of your real name now, or will I have to torture it out of you?"

"When I am informed of *your* name," I said, "I shall inform you of *mine.*"

"Fine," the Lieutenant said. "Anyway, it *would* be best if you knew the name of the greatest military strategist in the history of the world. Alexander the Great? George Washington? Napoleon? They were all mere simpletons compared to the greatness that is *me.*"

"Hyperbole not withstanding," I said, "Your name, please?"

"I am Lieutenant Stefan Schuster," he said, "Commander of the Rocketwafte mission here in North Africa."

"Lieutenant Cyanide," I said, narrowing my eyes at him. "At last we meet."

A scowl passed over his face at the sound of the nickname he'd acquired from his earlier exploits. He was notorious for acts committed on the battlefield too unspeakable to be explained here. He was an evil, conniving, bitter man who wasn't filled with the slightest bit of mercy or civility. "I would prefer that you call me Lieutenant Schuster!" he said, gritting his teeth.

"Schuster, Cyanide," I said, shrugging my shoulders. "They're both evil."

He smacked me across the face with his leather glove. "Do not besmirch my father's name like that," he said, a tick forming in his eye. "He was a great man."

"Yes, I've heard of him," I said, lying. "It's unfortunate that his son has failed to live up to that name."

He raised his hand to whack me across the face again, but caught himself and softened. "You have not told me your name yet," he said.

"Confucius Ping," I said.

"Confucius Ping?" he asked. "The writer of the almanacs?"

"One and the same," I said.

A look of bemusement passed over his face and he chuckled. "How ironic," he said. "Der Furher is a great fan of your books."

"*Was* a great fan," I said. "I canceled his subscription years ago when I discovered what an uneducated tyrant he was."

He darkened, saying, "Your sarcasm knows no bounds."

"Tell me about the rocket," I said. "No one has such technology yet, and here the Germans are far ahead of the game. How?"

"Really, Mr. Ping," he said, "The Nazi party has simply brought out the best in the average German, including our scientists who have worked very hard to create the ultimate killing machine. Imagine a rocket that can deliver bombs with precision, guided by technology that would enable us to pinpoint specific locations on a map within an inch of their actual location. Imagine our machines orbiting the Earth, watching all of it's activities. The weather could be monitored by these machines, these *satellites*. Photographs could be taken of cities and military bases. Imagine a world where we could use these satellites to communicate *electronically*, sending bits of information all around the world, *instantly*. Almost like mail, but without **envelopes**. *Electronic* mail. I call it *E-mail*."

"All of that which you speak of is impossible," I said. "It will never happen."

"Ah, but it is the reality of the German army right now," he said. "And it's all here at this base. The first satellite is set to launch tomorrow. And it is to be followed by the first man to go into the heavens."

"Pah!" I said. "Space is for the stars. Man does not belong there."

"Oh, but he *does*," he said. "And do you know who is architect of this grand dream? The keeper of the flame? The grand intelligence that has put the wheels of progress in motion for Germany?"

"Uh, could it be you?" I asked.

"Precisely!" he said, his toothy, white smile beaming from ear to ear. "I am the *greatest* mind of the twentieth century and it is from this mind that the future is born. *My* future! A world filled with large, *superhighways* that people can use to travel from town to town; neighborhoods away from the inner cities, where people might escape from the trials and tribulations of the downtown core into housing that we can erect virtually overnight. A world where people drive large cars, filled to the brim with that limitless natural resource: *Gasoline!* Imagine large, industrial factories, using atomic energy to power our homes and offices. But best of all, imagine a device that allows people to communicate like the radio, only with sound and picture. A device I call *television*. *This* is the world I envision for the future."

"Sounds positively dreadful," I said. "I hope it never comes to pass."

"We are closer than you think," he smiled. "*Much* closer." He walked a short circle around me and said, "Would you care to inform me of your mission now? Or should I just kill you?"

"Kill me now, kill me later," I said, "It makes no difference to me. I have already achieved my mission."

"You've already achieved your mission?" he asked, laughing. "It certainly doesn't *look* like you've achieved *anything*. It looks **to** me like you're in quite a predicament."

"Looks can be deceiving," I said.

I jumped to my feet and swung the chair around, striking Lieutenant Cyanide across the head and shattering the chair into pieces. As he fell to the ground, stunned by the surprise blow, I delivered a crushing right to the first guard and a remarkable kick to the other, giving me just enough time to smash their heads together and leave them unconscious.

The Lieutenant was sitting on the floor, unsure as to where he was, when I walked over to him, twirling the ropes that had previously held me captive. "Really," I said, as I tied his hands together behind his back, "You should train your soldiers to tie their knots better. It was almost too easy to escape."

Once the Lieutenant came around enough to understand me, he laughed through his pain. "You dumkoff!" he said. "Where do you think you're going? It's a ten day walk through the desert in any direction. You'll *never* get off of this base alive."

"Oh, well," I said, "If that's the case, I guess I'll just have to see what kind of damage I can cause before they kill me."

"Guards!" he yelled at the top of his lungs.

Knowing when to make a quick exit, I hurried out of the tent, only to round the corner and meet two guards running my way, gun barrels raised. "Stop!" they yelled.

I changed direction and ducked around a corner just in time to dodge a hail of bullets zipping past me. "Stupid guns," I muttered, for I detested guns as the weapons of brutes and savages.

Running through the maze of tents was confusing and everywhere I turned seemed to lead me into a mass of confused and paranoid German soldiers. Finally, I ducked under the flap of a supply tent to try and get my bearings. I had to figure out my next move, for it wouldn't be long before I was found. I had a base to destroy...

18 "THE MOON MEN OF PATAGONIA" taken from Mr. Ping's Almanac, Vol. 47

One of Mr. Ping's first encounters with extra-terrestrial beings was in Argentina in the twentieth century, though it was not what he expected it to be:

...My stay at the lovely residence of the magician Alejandro Garcia Gonzalez in Buenos Aires eventually had to come to an end, so I said my goodbyes to my longtime friend and his lovely wife, Maritza, and boarded the bus northbound into the hinterlands of Patagonia to investigate the strange rumors that had bubbled up amongst the gauchos that roamed the plains just below the Andes mountains. On my way through the European-influenced architecture of the city, I vowed to return to Buenos Aires one day so that I might stay for a more extended period of time and brush up on my Spanish.

Soon, we were out of the city and on the dusty roads, heading north. As we moved inland, further from the coast, the land changed from flat, marshy areas to the rolling hills and grasslands of the Patagonian plains. Something about the cattle-filled countryside made my heart flutter, and although it was not the American West of legend, the place still evoked a *sense* of cowboy adventure. Those feelings were reinforced by the gauchos, Argentina's version of cowboys, who would ride along on their horses, their dusty leather chaps draped over the sides of their magnificent steeds as they herded the cattle through the land.

Unfortunately, I had to rely on my romantic visions of the gauchos as a way to distract me from the horrible conditions that I was subjected to inside the bus. The vehicle which took me from Buenos Aires seemed to be one gearshift away from either falling apart completely or exploding. It was packed to the brim with all sorts of travelers, some carrying luggage, other carrying livestock, all of whom were stuffed three to a seat or left standing in the aisle. I tried not to look at the floorboard, for under my feet the floor had rusted, and in places one could see the dirt road whipping by under the bus. Yet my view from the window robbed the turgid circumstances of their power and I dreamed of the trip that lay ahead of me.

Two days later at approximately **11:06** AM, the bus dropped me off at a ranch with beautiful views of the majestic, snow-capped mountains in the distance. The ranch was known as Rancho Luna and was owned by Hernando Valasquez, a longtime subscriber to my almanacs. It was known as the Moon Ranch because Valasquez purchased the land after spending a few nights camped out on its vast fields and seeing the moon rise high above the surrounding plains. He was so inspired, he named the ranch after it.

Señor Valasquez had written me a letter one month earlier detailing the strange events that had occurred on his ranch. One night, his family and ranch hands were awoken by what sounded like an explosion. Upon exiting the house, they could see what appeared to be a large fire, miles away on top of one of the mountain peaks in the distance. In the letter, he said that he thought it was a meteor of some sort and that the next day, he sent some men towards the mountain in hopes of getting a better look. For seven days, smoke rose from the top of the mountain, and although the ranch hands, continued working, they all kept a wary eye towards the sky, unsure as to what might actually be sitting in the snow above them.

A few days later, the ranch hands had shown up at the ranch from their trek to the foot of the mountain, and they were all now frazzled and speaking gibberish about ghosts that had plagued their camp one night. They returned Señor Valasquez's horses and promptly quit their jobs, intent on moving back home. Señor Valasquez promptly dismissed their "ghost" claims and continued with his work. Yet, it was that very night that the glow first appeared. Just as the sun went down, Señor

Valasquez heard a commotion amongst his hands. Everyone seemed to be pointing at the mountain and whispering to each other in fear. When Hernando looked up, he saw that the top of the mountain was glowing in the moonlight. It wasn't a beautiful, nighttime glow, but more of an eerie, ominous green that seemed to be emanating from just behind the peak.

Because of the stories of ghosts being seen by others at the ranch, the glow from the top of the mountain in the **west** was the last straw. Señor Valasquez's workers began to go back to their villages, filled with fear at the curse that had been placed on the ranch. Soon, Hernando was left with a small core of his most trusted workers and thousands of cattle wandering freely on his land. He could hire no one else, because word had spread about the glow and the ghosts and this newly-invented "curse." The rumors were spinning out of control, including stories of cattle disappearing (true, but they were likely stolen by cattle rustlers seizing the opportunity), then ranch hands disappearing (false, for the hands that "disappeared" had never worked there in the first place), all the way to stories of Señor Valasquez performing animal sacrifices to appease some god of some sort (totally false).

At his wit's end, Señor Valasquez wrote me and asked if I'd investigate. Luckily, I had a window of opportunity in my schedule and caught the first steamer to South America. Now, I was at the infamous Rancho Luna and I could see the effects of what Señor Valasquez had described to me. In just a few months' time, I saw how rundown the ranch had become. The few hands he had were desperately trying to keep the cattle in line and couldn't keep up with the daily tasks that such a large operation entailed.

"Señor Ping," Hernando said to me as he walked to the front gate to meet me with a hearty handshake. "I received your wire a few days ago and was expecting your arrival."

"Señor Valasquez," I said, "It's a pleasure to meet you."

Señor Valasquez was a tall, sturdy man who looked like he'd done his fair share of work in his lifetime. Normally, he did supervision and business administration at the ranch, but since he now had so few helpers, he, too, was dressed like the traditional gaucho, with leather chaps and a hat pulled down over his head. He looked young for his sixty-two years, with the only thing betraying his actual age being his white mustache.

"We were just saddling up to pick up a couple of cows that strayed from the herd last night," he said. "You can stay here and rest from your trip, or if you'd like, you can ride with us."

"I think a ride across your ranch would freshen me up quite nicely," I said.

"Excellent," he said. "I'll have Juan prepare a horse for you."

Riding through the rolling hills and open plains of Argentina with the Andes rising up in the distance was an experience that I don't think I'll ever forget. The sun was high in the sky, making the snow caps in the distance glow with white intensity, and the wind was whipping the grasslands all around us. I galloped up beside Señor Valasquez to chat with him. "You look tired, señor," I said.

"This whole situation has been very hard on me and my family," he said. "I don't know what might be up there on that mountain, but if I don't get to the bottom of the problem soon, this ranch will go under."

"I assume that the glow is still up there on the mountain," I said.

"It is," he said. "And I cannot find anyone to investigate the problem. I would go myself, but I'm too old to be making such a journey to the top of a mountain. On top of that, even my best men are afraid to go. Not that I would blame them." We rode along in silence as we watched his men round up the lost cattle in the distance. "I'm a great admirer of your work, Mr. Ping. Your exploits leave me astounded."

"Well," I said, "Someday soon you'll be reading about my exploits here, Señor Valasquez."

"I hope it has a good ending," he said, staring off into the distance.

The plan, formulated that evening at camp under the millions of stars of the Patagonian plains, was for Señor Valasquez's best men to take me as far as the hiking trail that led to the top of the mountain, from which point I would hike to the far side of the summit so that I might investigate this strange, green glow. I had climbed mountains before and brought along such provisions as the adventure would need.

Hernando wished me luck and I set out with four of his men, three of whom were quiet, lonely riders who looked vaguely ill at the thought of having to go so close the mountain. The fourth rider was a pleasant fellow named Pancho, who was rather hefty and chose to ride a burro rather than a horse. He also sweated profusely. "You're loco," he said, smiling at me from his burro with crumbs of cornbread pasted in his beard.

"Why is that?" I asked.

"Why do you think?" he said, nodding towards the mountain with a goofy smile on his face.

"I don't think I'm as superstitious as others, Pancho," I said. "It is the unknown that scares us the most, and in order to eliminate our fear, we must face our fears."

He laughed at me, taking another large bite of his

cornbread. "You're a philosopher," he said. "Only philosophers speak that way." "I'm no philosopher," I said.

"Aren't you scared of going up there?" he asked.

"Not really," I said. "I've seen much worse than what I would imagine is up there."

"What if it's a ghost?" he asked.

"Ghosts can't hurt you," I said.

"What if it's a monster?" he asked.

"Then I'll outrun it," I said.

He paused and then lowered his voice for dramatic effect. "What if it's the devil?"

"If it's the devil, I'll ask him a few questions about the terrible things he's done."

Pancho laughed again, turning to the other riders to say, "He's loco, all right. He doesn't even fear the devil!" He sat on his burro with a wistful look on his face, lost in thought. "I will go with you," he said.

"Why?" I asked. "No one else is brave enough."

"Oh, I am afraid, señor," he said. "But I cannot ignore your confidence. My mother always told me that a confident man can usually be trusted."

"I hope your mother was right," I said.

As expected, the horsemen led me to the opening of the trail head that led up the mountain, but where I thought I'd be marching up the mountain all by myself, I was actually blessed with Pancho as my partner. He was extremely pleasant company on the easier portions of the hike, informing me about the daily life of being a gaucho on the plains: the monotony, the tediousness, the boredom. He talked of his wife and his mother and his sister, who listened to no advice that was given to her. He talked and talked and talked, about everything and about nothing,

and were it not for the long, steep, uphill portions of our trip in which he spent most of his time gasping for air, I would say that he got on my nerves. But luckily, the climb was more uphill than anything else, so he never drove me crazy.

It was a three day hike to the summit and each day, just before sunset, Pancho and I would look for a hospitable place to set up camp. My preference was always in a place with an open view, where I could look out over the ever-growing landscape that lay below us. There was nothing more wonderful for me than those three days going up the mountain, as I would wake each morning to catch the cold, crisp sun rising over the landscape below me.

But then, as we moved ever higher, the trees began to disappear, and then the shrubbery, and then all plant life, climbing to altitudes inhospitable to such things. We were now high up on the side of the mountain, where snow could be seen between the rocks and covering portions of the trail.

Trying to catch his breath on a particularly rugged portion of the trail, Pancho said, "Señor Ping, this is the highest I have ever been in the mountains. My mother will kill me. She told me never to go up into the mountains. She said only death awaits those who tempt the mountain gods."

"Aren't you a little bit old to be taking orders from your mother, Pancho?" I asked.

"Ha!" he said. "You don't know my mother. If you knew my mother, you would be inclined to listen to her or she would smack you thirty times upside the head. That is what she did to me when I misbehaved as a child. That is what she did to me as a teenager. And whenever I am at her house as an adult, she smacks me upside the head just for good measure."

"Well, it seems to have benefited you greatly," I said.

"Eh," he said, shrugging his shoulders, "Maybe, maybe not. Have you ever been smacked upside the head thirty times? It hurts!"

On our final night before we crossed over the pass that would take us to the summit, we were able to get a good look at the green glow that had enveloped the mountain. It lit up the entirety of the landscape, turning the snow outside our tents an eerie green and leaving the landscape around us as bright as day. Pancho and I stared at the glow in silence late into the night, trying to comprehend what it was we were seeing, but the words escaped us.

I expected to awake early the next day to begin the search for the green glow's source, but that night, after we'd gone to sleep, the green glow's source found us. As I lay in my tent, I noticed it seemed as if the sun was coming up. The ambient light in the tent grew stronger and stronger. At first, I though it was an anomaly, but then I looked around and realized that it was as bright as day outside, only green.

I looked over at Pancho, who was still sleeping right beside me, and tried to nudge him awake, but his sleep was too deep and it only served to make him snore louder. I thought I heard something over the far ridge and soon my suspicions were confirmed as I began to hear the crunch of stones as someone walked towards us. Even through the tent, I could see that the green was coming from whatever it was that was outside my tent. When I opened the front flap of the tent, I couldn't believe my eyes.

There, walking just over the ridge towards me, were aliens!

I had never seen an alien before and certainly had no expectations as to what they should look like, but this creature was unlike anything I'd ever seen. It was short, very short, around three feet tall, with half its height coming from its egg-like head. Its large black eyes were just above its mouth, all of which were located at the bottom of this huge cranium, giving it an extremely large forehead.

The creature wore no clothes, although I'm not sure that clothes would have actually fit its tiny little frame. It had three fingers on each hand, all of which looked like thumbs and the same amount of toes on each foot.

Yet the strangest thing about this pudgy, slow-moving, odd creature was the fact that it was glowing as green as a cactus and lighting up the whole area by itself.

I must have startled the poor thing when I popped my head out of the tent, for its short, stubby leg certainly helped it jump out of the way in time. It scrambled with incredible speed, as it and its comrades scattered and quickly disappeared into the surroundings. However, try as they might to hide form my gaze, their intense green glow gave away their hiding places.

Usually, I trust my instincts, and I felt that these strange little creatures meant me absolutely no harm, so I emerged from the tent. Gradually, they began to peek out from behind the rocks, their large, black eyes peering at me, then at their colleagues, as if each of them were unsure what to do next. I heard them communicating with each other through sounds that can only be described as clicks, chirps, and soft growls, and eventually, one of them slowly walked out from behind its rock, filled with trepidation.

My mind began to race, trying to think of some sort of universal symbol of welcoming that might make the small creature feel okay, as if it was welcome here and that I would

do it no harm. For me, the universal sign of welcoming was a big, broad smile, so I smiled at the creature as it walked towards me.

It was a huge mistake, for my smile frightened the poor beast to death and it was the better part of an hour for me to get him to emerge again. The next time, I made sure not to smile. As the creature came up to me, examining me all over from head to toe, more of the small creatures came out, ever so slowly, to do the same thing. One by one, they emerged until I was completely surrounded by all of them. The glow from the small, green creatures was as bright as day and just as *they* were examining me, *I* was examining them.

Their skin was smooth, not a wrinkle on their bodies, and they were fairly chubby for their size, with thick, gooey arms and large pot bellies. As they chattered away in front of me, one of them was finally brave enough to touch me and as its hand touched my hand, I felt its soft, warm skin. It gave me utter and complete joy to be in contact with such a spectacular creature, and I felt that the creature felt the same way, for as soon as he touched me, he turned to the others and gave a few clicks and grunts. Soon, the others were reaching and pawing at me until I felt a bit overwhelmed.

As one of them grabbed my hand and began to tug me up the mountain, I realized that they were trying to communicate with me. I looked over my shoulder to see a couple of them examine, then abandon, Pancho's sleeping body in the tent, and then I thought, W*hy not?* I let the creatures pull me along, each one trotting below me in a fairly jovial manner. The sun was just beginning to rise as they led me over the summit of the mountain.

It took us a while to reach the other side, but it could have taken days and I would have

paid it no mind, for just to be in the presence of such fantastic beings was enough to keep me going for days. Soon, the bright, crisp sunlight had risen over the horizon and I was able to examine my companions under a different set of circumstances. They were now milky white in the bright sun and looked sensitive, almost fragile in the daylight. Still, they chattered on and on, eventually leading met to a sight that stopped me in my tracks.

As we rounded a small cliff, I saw that a giant crater had been blown out of the side of the mountain, its walls black from a fire. In the center of the crater, I saw the remains of what looked to be a large spaceship, its tail sticking up in the air while its nose was buried deep into the earth below it.

Here, there were several more of the little creatures, all of them busy at various tasks on the hull of the six story tall ship. They worked like little ants to repair the damage that had been caused. The ship was magnificent, but unlike anything I would have imagined. Science fiction movies and stories failed to prepare me for what I saw before me. The ship looked like a giant, well-cut diamond, it's surface as smooth as glass and translucent in the early morning sunlight. Even as the small creatures were preparing the ship on the outside, because the ship was crystal clear, I could see more of the creatures working on the inside.

Yet even on the inside, I saw no visible gears or motors, nothing that I would recognize to make the ship run. It was quite simply perfection in every way, shape, and form, as beautiful as the diamond of a wedding ring or an iceberg rising high above the blue waters of the arctic.

Theories began to form in my mind regarding the creatures' arrival. I quickly assumed that the glow was from the many little beings wandering around on the side of the mountain. I assumed that the streak of light and explosion that Señor Valasquez saw on that fateful night was the aliens' ship crashing to the Earth, and were it not made from a rock-hard, diamond-like substance, I assume that the ship would have disintegrated on impact, but because of its virtual invulnerability, it simply embedded itself into the side of the mountain. Then my worst suspicions were confirmed as we rounded a bend. I saw a makeshift morgue, where there were hundreds of alien bodies from what I assumed to be the crash. Their colleagues had laid them side by side on the ground in long lines across the mountain. I saw that there seemed to be some sort of pattern on the ground.

One of the aliens was chirping and clicking at me the entire time, pointing to the bodies on the ground, then pointing back at the ship. He was trying desperately to communicate something to me, but I wasn't smart enough to figure out what it was. It grabbed my hand and led me to the other side of the ship, where I saw several more of the aliens lying on the ground.

Although they weren't dead, they were most certainly ill, each one looking weak, moving slowly, if they were moving at all. Several of the aliens were tending to those lying on the ground, but the prognosis was grim in my eyes. Those that were on the inside looked like they didn't have long for this world. I looked over a few of them, judging that their poor condition was a result of the crash, but as I looked at them, I saw no bruises, cuts or abrasions, nothing to indicate to me that any of them had suffered any kind of physical trauma. I came to a grim conclusion in those very

minutes. These aliens were not injured. These aliens were sick.

At first, a wave of fear washed over me, and I began to worry about my own health. I wondered what sort of illness these poor creatures had brought to the planet and how soon it would spread through the world's population, but then, my rational mind took over and my desire for self-preservation took a backseat to my empathy for these amazing little creatures that toiled away all around me.

Throughout the day, I tried communicating with them, but it was a worthless endeavor. Their language was filled with clicks, grunts, and growls, sounds so foreign to my ears that I gave up trying. On top of that, I was sure that their world was completely different than ours and that even if we found some minor way of communicating, the information that we would have had to trade back and forth would have taken years to understand.

When I tried to understand by pantomime, I saw that they were probably trying to tell me about the crash and their desire to get the ship working again and off of this planet, but I could never be sure. For all I knew, they could have been plotting or explaining the proper way to roast me during the evening cookout.

After a fruitless few hours, they finally pulled me up and back over to their ship, even bringing me inside the stark, glass-like environment. They pointed back and forth, as they clucked and clicked what I assumed to be directions on how to fly the thing, but it all just passed through my ears as I marveled at the complexity of the machine.

When we arrived back outside from the tour of the ship, I noticed that a member of my "greeting" party was trailing behind the pack, unable

to keep up with us. Not only did this alarm me, it also alarmed its companions and they immediately ran over to him as he collapsed into their arms. A sneaking suspicion told me that there might have been something wrong with Earth's atmosphere for these aliens.

Throughout the day, I felt extremely helpless, unable to understand what these creatures were doing on the planet, unable to understand their language, and unable to understand why these poor souls were dying off by the dozen. As the day wore on, I noticed more and more of the creatures falling ill, more and more unable to work on the ship, more and more unable to even move. My fear was that these poor beasts were fighting a losing battle, and I also feared that my presence among them wasn't helping matters. A scary scenario played out in my head.

After the crash, Señor Valasquez had sent some men up the mountain to check what was wrong. They came back claiming to have seen ghosts. The "ghosts" in question could only have been the aliens. My fear was that Valasquez's men had transferred some sort of virus to the aliens in that brief encounter and that the virus was rapidly spreading through their population. It would not be uncommon. A large percentage of the Native American population had been wiped out because of smallpox brought over from European settlers. These aliens looked to have come from a pristine, antiseptic culture, free from germs and harmful bacteria. Exposure to the grime of Earth could have been a major shock to their system. Still, it was just a theory.

As I sat in the middle of a large group of them that evening, all of whom were examining me and trying to figure me out, one of the aliens came running out of their ship towards their leader. He clicked and grunted excitedly, and soon, he began to tug at me, pulling me towards the ship.

Once inside, they sat me down on a large chair and gathered around. Although I should have been paranoid that they were about to serve me for dinner, I wasn't, and rightly so. One of the aliens got behind some sort of control system that, to me, simply looked like a colorful array of crystals. It hovered its hands over the crystals and brought a holographic image to life. I'd never seen anything like it. It was much more advanced that anything I'd ever imagined here on planet Earth. Floating in front of me was a pristine, three-dimensional planet. It was black, with large, glowing green spots on it. I assumed that the spots were urban centers, where these aliens lived on their home planet.

The alien zoomed out from the planet to reveal a star, much like the sun in our galaxy. Suddenly, the holographic sun sent out a burst of energy and began to swell, growing ever larger until it began to envelop the alien's planet. The image then zoomed in towards the planet to ground level, showing a society in chaos. Cities were crumbling and thousands of the aliens were fleeing in terror.

It cut to a great armada of diamond ships, all of which left the planet at the same time, which I took to be a mass exodus to escape the swelling sun. But then, as the ships were leaving their own solar system, their sun exploded and shattered all of the planets in the area. The resulting asteroid storm looked as though it both destroyed and separated the large contingent of ships, including the very ship that was now embedded in the side of the mountain. I saw an image of an asteroid striking the ship, sending it far off course, whereupon they crashed on

Earth. Then the hologram flickered away.

The aliens were exiles from a dying planet, lost in the far reaches of space and dying off, one by one. These poor creatures were in desperate need of help, but there was nothing I could do. I was just as helpless as they were.

What was I to do? A two day trek down the mountain to get help would have been fruitless. The locals were superstitious enough. Their desire to help a group of dying aliens would probably have been small, even if I could convince them. On top of that, what could they do in the first place? They knew no more than I did, and it would probably cause a scene. To make matters worse, I wasn't even convinced that these poor creatures would live long enough for me to bring the help back, as they all seemed to be growing ill, the numbers of the sick increasing every day.

And so, I became a passive observer. Whereas the aliens took great interest in me in the beginning, once they saw that I could be of no help, they abandoned me, ignoring my existence, paying me little mind as they worked to leave.

It was a fruitless effort.

For three days, I stayed at the top of the mountain with the aliens, with very little food and no water, watching helplessly as these poor, beautiful creatures died off, one by one. They were valiant beings, never letting the hopeless odds stop them from their tasks. When I arrived, there were hundreds of them. Three days later, they were down to ten, and those ten didn't look so well. I abandoned my passive personality and helped the last aliens arrange their dead in their specific pattern.

Their ship loomed massive on the horizon above us. The last few aliens stayed close to me in their final hours, still clicking and chirping away

to me, trying to communicate something. I could do nothing but listen. I thought of the ranch down on the plains below and imagined what they thought of the disappearance of the glow, for once the aliens died, they glowed no more.

Finally, there was only one alien left and it, too, was ill. In its last hour, it crawled in my lap, clicking and growling to me softly, as if it was telling me a lovely story. I imagined that it was telling me how wonderful its heaven was and how things would be better once it had joined its colleagues.

And then, in the deep of the night, the tiny alien in my lap lost its glow. I wept as I placed it with the others, knowing that these poor little creatures would never brighten the lives of others. They seemed to want to do no harm, just go to a safe place. And now, none of them would.

In that moment, I realized that *this* was how alien contact was and always had been. It wasn't like a film, with conquering creatures bent on the destruction of Earth, or creatures that could blend in with our society and function on our level. No, alien contact would be fruitless, two cultures unable to understand each other with the odds of coexistence being slim. In those quiet days on the side of the mountain, I had seen what no other man or woman had seen, and as with a beautiful sunset or a violent thunderstorm, the beauty of the moment was lost to memory.

I stayed there for two more days without the heart to leave my newfound friends, absorbing the magnitude of what I'd experienced. Finally, I forced myself back down the mountain, weak, hungry, thirsty, and not quite sure I was ready to go back to the world of man. Yet no matter the beauty of these small experiences, one must always go back.

I met Pancho on the trail. The ranch was still there, the superstitions still there, and the belief that I had solved the problem was still there. They hailed me as a hero, but in my heart, I knew I was a failure for my inability to save them. I told Señor Valasquez nothing of what happened on the mountain, simply telling him to warn his workers that the top of the mountain was cursed and that they should never touch the sacred ground of the summit.

Señor Valasquez gave me a knowing look and agreed...

19 "THE TERROR PADDLE OF MS. EVELYN CRABTREE" taken from Mr. Ping's Almanac, Vol. 69

Mr. Ping had heard of a school on the outskirts of Boston called Evelyn Crabtree Public School. Apparently, the school district had been having so much trouble with this particular school that they had decided to close it down, blow it to smithereens, and rebuild the place forty feet away from its current location. This would not necessarily have gotten Mr. Ping's attention, as most schools of this day were full of poisons or cancer causing agents of some sort (and that was just from the cafeteria food), but this school was different. It seems that the place was haunted by the very teacher whose name it bore, Ms. Evelyn Crabtree.

Rumors ran rampant about the ghost of Ms. Crabtree and the floating paddle sometimes seen in the hall (replete with holes bored into the wood, so as to whack a student's bottom with less wind resistance), about how the old, discontinued reading books would mysteriously appear in the children's desk each morning with all of the words blacked out on the pages, and about the disembodied cackles that echoed through the building. Needless to say, a ghostly teacher wandering the halls and scaring the pants off of poor, unsuspecting children was not conducive to learning.

A school board member had heard of Mr. Ping and called him in as a last resort before they tore the building down. "Maybe you could save us some money," he said. Mr. Ping agreed to help, feeling that a child's education should not be impeded by the sight of a ghostly old woman with blackened eyes and long, bony fingers who was constantly braying, "You're tardy, Mr. Stevens!"

...I went during the **second** day of my visit and saw nothing strange or unusual, although I did find it peculiar that none of the students were brave enough to go to the restroom by themselves. Each time I saw a child in the hallway, they were being accompanied by an adult. Another odd sign was that all of the teachers locked their classrooms doors while they taught, as if they were keeping something horrible from getting inside their rooms. However, the most striking thing I witnessed was the simple fact that there were so few students; about ten to a classroom. Most of them had been scared off.

Not that the school itself didn't contribute to the sense of foreboding. The place looked as though it might have originally been an insane asylum. It had an old, 1800s brick facade on the outside, giant radiators in each room that clanged and rattled in a jarring way when they were turned on, and vomit-green paint on the walls. There was nothing at all about the environment that was conducive to learning, and I felt pity for those students and teachers who had to be there everyday.

Having seen nothing of substance during my visit , I got permission from the Principal to let me spend the night in the school, and as the sun went down on that cold, November night, I read a book in the main hallway, preparing myself for a long wait. That wait would be much shorter than anticipated,

as it was just after nightfall that I heard the first cackle of Ms. Crabtree.

It came from far off down the hall, around a corner (as ghost cries usually do, so as to lure one to their doom). Naturally, ghost cackles, moans, and piercing screams were old hat to me at this point in my career, so after a few persistent noises, I was able to continue on with my reading (*The Hound of the Baskervilles*, a book I had checked out from the **Tahlequah** Public Library when visiting in **Oklahoma**).

Since Ms. Crabtree's cackles failed to get my attention, I assume she decided to trot out her old bag of tricks, and I must say that some of them were quite effective. She had a tendency to let out an evil hiss at the most startling moments, usually from somewhere behind me, or just around the corner. I'd never really encountered a hissing ghost before. Then, there was also the time when I reached down for my glass of tea to find her gooey, nicotine-stained false teeth resting at the bottom of my mug.

At just around midnight, I caught my first glimpse of her peeking out at me from the door of a classroom down the hall. I quickly ran to that classroom and found nothing inside. However, upon exiting I got a good, long look at her as she stood at the far end of the hall, quietly tap-tap-tapping her paddle in her hand. She was a hideous sight in the cool, blue light of the dark hallway. Her hair was pulled back into a severe, conservative bun, her eyes were dark and black (as is the norm with ghosts) and she had a rather large hump on her back that gave her a striking resemblance to my good friend, Quasimodo. On top of all of that, she wore an old, faded dress that looked similar to the one I'd seen her wearing in an old yearbook.

"Can I see your hall pass?" she said to me, and I can't say that I didn't feel a slight twinge of fear. She seemed to exude some sort of supernatural authority.

"I'm not a student, Mrs. Crabtree," I said.

"*Ms.* Crabtree!" she said. "Get it right, you dirty, stinking pile of mongrel drool!"

"So sorry, ma'am," I said. Suddenly, a hiss burst forth from behind me. I turned to look, but there was nothing there. Then, I turned back down the hallway and she was gone. Without warning, I received a whack with a paddle on my backside. As I rubbed my sore, stinging derrière, I heard her cackle with delight somewhere off in the distance. I didn't see her again that night.

The next day, having hard-proof of the poltergeist that occupied the halls of the school, I decided to do a little bit of research on Ms. Crabtree at the local library. I pulled out every newspaper article that I could find regarding the school, and in every single one, I found that Ms. Crabtree seemed to be the most stern looking woman on the planet. She had a horribly harsh face, one that was just as ugly in life as it was in death, and all of the kids in her class photos looked miserable. She had taught there for thirty-five years, terrorizing the students right up until her death in 1965, when she died in her classroom, one cold, winter morning.

I made my way back to the school to go through its records for the year 1964, specifically those records that had something to do with Ms. Crabtree herself, and an interesting clue jumped out at me. It seemed that the 1964/65 school year had a troublemaker enrolled. He was a young student by the name of Dalton Hogshead Jr., and this fifth grader's homeroom teacher that year was none other than Ms. Crabtree.

Dalton Hogshead Jr., it seemed, was transferred to what was then known as P.S. 749, Ms. Crabtree's school. His file was about seven inches thick and was full of every rule infraction that he had ever made. It started on Dalton's very first day that year, when one of his spit wads flew into the eye of a fellow classmate and sent said classmate to the hospital, for the velocity of the spit wad was enough to force the poor child to wear a patch over his eye for the rest of the year. The next day, there was another incident involving bubble gum in the hair of Sylvia Jones, the most popular girl in school. The day after that, a small fire was discovered burning in a trash can in the hallway, and although it was never proved that Dalton was the culprit, the incident was put in his file anyway.

The list went on and on; fights, bullying, spit wads, failed homework assignments, and more spit wads (his weapon of choice). I began to have my suspicions about Mr. Hogshead and all of those suspicions were confirmed when I found Ms. Crabtree's report card for Dalton for the first two quarters. In the first, I found what seemed to be the writing of a teacher who was at her wit's end:

...Dalton's behavior is disruptive, disenfranchising, distracting, debilitating, but most of all, disturbing. He shows no interest in anything other than harming others, distracting others, and seeking the attention of others. I would very much like to have a word with you as soon as possible...

There was no mention of any parent response to Ms. Crabtree's writings. More discipline reports followed, then the report card from the second quarter appeared, which sounded a bit more desperate than the last:

...Really, I don't think that school is an appropriate place for Dalton. Without being presumptuous, I would recommend something a bit more rigid in its structure; something that would keep him focused and out of harm's way. A juvenile detention center, perhaps?...

I found several letters to the principal from Ms. Crabtree as well, each one more and more desperate in their pleas for help and all of which were requests to have Dalton removed from her classroom, if not the school. I assume that the pleas fell upon deaf ears, as her last report card, sent in February of that year, was the biggest unheeded cry for help I'd ever read:

...Nothing works with the boy and he seems to take a sort of sick, perverse pleasure in seeing others suffer. You have failed as parents, if, indeed, you are his parents, as I secretly suspect that he's not your son at all, but more the spawn of Satan...

Photos of Ms. Crabtree's decline during the year spent with Dalton Hogshead Jr. were visible in the school yearbook. Whereas at the beginning of the year, Ms. Crabtree was a fit and healthy, if a bit angry, sixty-year old woman, the last photo in the yearbook showed a withered and gray person who looked twenty years older than her actual age.

And there, in the photo, standing beside her, was none other than a bespectacled, wiry little fellow with curly red hair by the name of Dalton Hogshead Jr. With his coke-bottle glasses and shock of hair flaming around his face, he looked like, if left alone, he could tear down a concrete building with his bare hands. There wasn't a smile to be seen on his face. He looked as angry as Ms. Crabtree, and his cheeks were filled with freckles that seemed radioactive. If a student could look any more unpleasant, I'd certainly never seen one.

So at that point, I realized that Dalton had led to a startling decline in Ms. Crabtree's health, but I was somewhat surprised to find that he actually caused her death on the school grounds that same year. The details were sketchy, but according to the obituary that I'd obtained from the library, Ms. Crabtree died from a heart attack in the hallway of the school. Dalton Hogshead Jr. was expelled that very same day.

According to Dalton's expulsion record, it seemed that he'd exploded a cherry bomb in the toilet in the boy's washroom, flooding the hallways, then set up an arsenal of spit wads to launch at his buddies as they exited their rooms to evacuate the building. He fired his first, large, gooey wad at the first person out of the room, and that person just so happened to be Ms. Crabtree. It hit her right in the face with such velocity that it knocked her off her feet. Apparently, Dalton started laughing uncontrollably as she slipped and slid on the toilet water-covered floors, trying to regain her footing. Upon reaching Dalton and grabbing him by the arm to lead him to the office, she yelled, "Just what do you have to say for yourself, young man?"

To which he replied, "There's a hair coming out of the mole on your face."

It seemed that no one had ever mentioned her mole, or her ugly mole hair for that matter. It had been there for years, but it had been a taboo subject. No one dared look at Ms. Crabtree, let alone speak of the dreaded two inch mole hair on her cheek. Dalton's statement upset Ms. Crabtree so badly that she keeled over right there in the hallway, dead as a doornail as the toilet water flowed past her limp, lifeless body, and the chunks and flecks of Dalton's spit wad dried on her face.

So there it was. I'd found the answer I was looking for. Dalton Hogshead Jr. had killed Ms. Crabtree. Just thinking it caused the building to creak and moan with the weight of such knowledge, and I thought I heard a cackle in the distance. I knew what I was to do. I had to find Dalton Hogshead Jr. and set things right.

My main question had to do with what had happened to Dalton after the "Ms. Crabtree incident." Upon checking the records, I saw that he had quietly moved away, perhaps to another school, perhaps out of school entirely, a fifth-grade dropout. I began to inquire with the locals as to what they thought might have happened to him. I received several strange looks, and a solid majority of questions back at me as to who I was talking about, but no one knew who, exactly, Dalton Hogshead Jr. was. That is, until I ran into Morton Melvins.

Morton worked for one of the local newspapers and was known throughout the region as the "Keeper of Useless Knowledge." He was a fact checker for the paper and worked out of the vast basement underneath the printing presses, where he sat in dim light all day long with nothing to keep him company but large filing cabinets and mountains of information at his very fingertips. Morton was of indeterminate age and had thick reading glasses. I found him hunched over a light table, squinting as he tried to read a newspaper through a giant magnifying glass.

"You must be Mr. Ping," he said without looking up from his task.

"Yes, Mr. Melvins," I said.

"Call me Morton, please," he said.

"Yes, Morton," I replied, ready to give my spiel, but I was quickly interrupted.

"You're inquiring about facts," he said, still intent on the work before him. "I am the keeper of facts, so if it is facts that you want, then you've come to the right place."

"Yes," I said. "I was looking…"

"Dalton Hogshead Jr., I suppose?" he said, and a chill went up my spine, feeling as if he was almost reading my mind. "Yes, yes, yes, not many people have mentioned that name to me over the last ten years. Obscure, obscure. Dredged from the past and out into the present."

"Well," I said, "I was wondering if…"

"I know all, I see all, Mr. Ping," he said. "Not a fact or statistic can sneak by me without it being absorbed into the vast warehouse that is my brain. I'm full, full, full of information of all kinds."

"Yes, well…"

"Dalton Hogshead Jr. is no more," he said, focusing even more on the page in front of him. "Long gone. Sayonara. Finito."

This depressing news deflated my balloon and I began to feel like it was a pointless endeavor. "So, he's dead?" I asked.

"Dead?" he asked. "No. Never said dead. Said finished. Dalton Hogshead Jr., the name, is finished. No more. Poot! Gone."

"What are you talking about?" I asked.

"Shall I spell it out for you?" he asked. "In bold letters? So the world can see as well as you can?"

"Yes, that would probably be nice," I said, feeling somewhat annoyed.

"Ah, yes," he said, finally looking me in the eye through the thick lenses of his glasses. "Dalton Hogshead Jr., he of the Crabtree incident of long ago. He hoped to have disappeared, vanished from the Earth, and a change of name would have been extremely conducive to such an endeavor. But alas, one can *run* from the past, but one cannot *escape* it. Run, run, run, as fast they can, they will never get away from the stink of the past, which wafts through their clothes like perfume, soiled, stinking..."

"Will you get to the point?" I asked.

Morton paused for a second as I interrupted his moment of reverie, then reached into his desk and pulled out an old newspaper clipping. "The Dalton you seek is no longer with us. There's a new Dalton in town, and his name is George."

I looked at the photo in the news clipping and saw a handsome young man in a graduation gown, receiving an award from no less than the current President of the United States. Failing to understand what I was seeing, I read the caption and saw that the young man receiving the award was named George Pigspitt Jr. "Is this Dalton Hogshead Jr.?" I asked.

Morton quickly raised his hand to stop me in my tracks. "I care not for monetary gifts," he said. "My reward is nothing but the pleasure of sharing pertinent information. Nothing more, nothing less."

"Dalton Hogshead is now *this* fellow?" I asked, pointing to the picture.

"As you can see," Morton said, getting back to his work, "I'm a very busy man, unable to deal with the minutiae of life because of the mammoth task set out before me. Shoo, shoo, shoo." He brushed the air with his hand to make me leave and

I was off on a new quest: to locate George Pigspitt Jr.

I spent a week phoning contacts all over the country until I realized that George, formerly known as Dalton, had not moved halfway across the universe, but merely to the next town over. As I turned up at his school that day, I braced myself for the worst of the worst. What kind of monster would I find? I'd dealt with royalty, billionaires, and cult leaders on a regular basis in my life and not batted an eye, but the thought of meeting a rambunctious teenager filled me with apprehension. I had visions of a chain-smoking, leather-jacket-wearing, mustached teen with a deadly gang affiliation and a predilection for whipping out his switchblade at the drop of a hat to teach me a lesson.

I was completely surprised by what I found. George Pigspitt Jr. was an extremely well-kept, well-behaved sixteen-year old. As he walked into the office, I was under the impression that I was to meet an angry teen, but the reality dictated that I met a well-dressed young man with a high-and-tight flattop haircut and pullover sweater. He still had the shocking dark hair, but instead of the brooding photos I'd seen of him as a child, I now saw an admirable smile and he looked me in the eye when he spoke to me.

"You wanted to see me, sir?" he asked. The look in his eye was genuine and sincere as I led him into the borrowed dean's office. I did notice a slightly sick look in his face, however, as it seemed that he thought he might be in trouble as I sat across from him. After all, it wasn't every day that a strange Chinese man pops up at a kid's school and asks to speak with them.

"My name is Confucius Ping," I said. "I'm very sorry to pull you out of class, George, but I'm doing a bit of research and in order to finish my book,

it's important for me to have a talk with you."

"I'd love to be of service to you, Mr. Ping," he said, brightening, but still nervous. "What type of work do you do?"

"I dabble in the strange and unusual," I said. "And I seem to have hit the mother load just a couple of towns over."

"Strange and unusual?" he asked.

"Yes," I said. "You see, I'm doing some research on one Evelyn Crabtree, a former teacher, and my research has led me to the name Dalton Hogshead Jr."

A black cloud passed over his face, as his eyes shifted from mine to the floor. "Oh," he said.

"Do you know Dalton Hogshead Jr., George?" I asked.

He continued staring at the floor as he stammered. "I, uh, I'm sorry. I...I don't."

"Are you sure?" I asked, knowing that I had him cornered. "You see, it's because I think you *do* know Dalton Hogshead Jr., George. I think you know him *very* well."

"I don't know what you're talking about," he said, fidgeting in his chair.

"Are you sure, Dalton?" I asked.

"Shut up!" he yelled, the fiery temper of his youth surfacing again. "Dalton Hogshead is *dead*! It's George Pigspitt now! *George Pigspitt!*"

"Okay, George," I said, trying to calm him down. "I understand, George."

"It's George Pigspitt," he muttered, over and over again. "George *Pigspitt!*"

"George," I said, "I think it's time we talked about Ms. Crabtree."

George looked at me with his big, green, tear-filled eyes and suddenly burst into tears. After allowing poor George to cry it out on my shoulder, I discovered that after the Crabtree incident, his family had suffered great shame and humiliation at his expense, and because his shallow, cruel mother and father didn't want the Hogshead name to be sullied by a ten-year-old murderer (as if the name Hogshead wasn't sullied enough already), they sent him off to live with his aunt, one town over. From that point, he changed his name and vowed to change his life for the better, to make up for the horrible, cruel things he'd done as a youngster. With the help of his caring aunt, he'd made good on his promise, as now he was class president, made straight A's, and was on the honor roll for the school. Yet try as he might, he could never escape his horrible past cruelties, and I was living proof of that failure.

"George," I said after our long talk, "Would you like to make amends for what you did?"

"What do you mean?" he asked, wiping the tears from his eyes and blowing his nose into a white handkerchief. "I can't make amends. Ms. Crabtree is dead!"

"You're just going to have to trust me on this," I said. "What I am going to show you goes against everything you've seen with your own two eyes, and it's risky. It could be dangerous. I want you to keep that in mind."

"Of course," he said.

"Good," I said. "I want you to meet me at your old school at midnight tomorrow night. Okay?"

"Sure," he said.

The night I met him at the school was a classically creepy evening. It was warm and humid, with a thunderstorm approaching as the sun went down. The wind was blowing the trees back and forth, the blankets of leaves billowing in gusts, and the occasional ball of lightning crashed down from the sky, indicating the fury that was to come. It hadn't started raining yet when George's aunt

dropped him off at the school, but the air was so thick that it could begin any second. I was waiting just at the side entrance of the large, old brick building, and I must have looked somewhat intimidating to his aunt as the flashes of lightning illuminated me, for she didn't even get out of the car.

"Thank you for bringing him, Ms. Pigspitt," I said. "You can wait in the car. This won't take long."

She nodded her approval.

"Are you sure you want to do this?" I asked him as he walked up to me.

"Do we have another option?" George asked. He was obviously terrified and the rolls of thunder behind him probably didn't help.

"Of course we have a choice," I said. "We could both go home, forget this place ever existed, and then leave poor, old Ms. Crabtree to haunt it forever. Or at least until they tear it down."

"No," George said as the first patters of rain began to fall around us. "No, I've got to finish this."

Apparently, George knew exactly what was needed to break curses and hauntings. I'd been prepared to give him the whole spiel about what I'd learned in Germany at the *School for Paranormal Combat and Devilry* some forty years earlier, but I saw that I didn't need to. He was ready.

"Fine, then," I said, as I began to fish through my pants in the rain. "Just let me find my keys and we'll go inside."

"Uh, Mr. Ping," George said, "I think that's already been taken care of."

I looked over to see that the door to the school was standing wide-open of its own free will. Someone, or *something*, was already beckoning us inside. "It looks like someone has rolled out the red carpet," I said. "Shall we?"

The halls were the color of a deep, dark sea in the

blackness of night, illuminated only by the searing flashes of lightning. The white light from the storm outside only gave the barest hint of the menacing walls that surrounded us. Just as we walked inside, the doors behind us slowly shut and I heard them lock. "Neat trick," George said.

"That wasn't a trick," I said. "I'm going to keep the keys ready just in case things get out of hand."

"Good idea," he said.

We wandered the creepy hallways aimlessly for a few minutes, hoping that some purpose to this whole affair would reveal itself. I was growing just a tad bit impatient with the whole process, when I realized that it was just about to turn midnight. I was sure that things would get ugly during the witching hour, and as the clock struck twelve, I heard a door slam down the hallway.

"There she is," I said to George, a smile pasted across my face.

George was white as a sheet, a sight that was visible even in the darkness of the hallway. Normally, these kinds of things wouldn't scare me, but the thought of doors opening and closing of their own free will was just enough to give me a fright. A look of sheer terror was in George's eyes, the kind of terror that only a person who knew they'd caused a terrible mess might have. It was at that point that we heard the slow clack of heels around the corner. Someone was walking, very slowly, down the dark corridor, and from the sound of it, whoever it was seemed to be dragging something along behind them.

I heard George gulp when she appeared in the dim light. It was Ms. Crabtree. Her shoulders were hunched over, as if she was hundreds of years old, and in her right hand, she dragged her long, wooden paddle on the ground. She walked to the center of the hallway and stopped, turning her head towards us without saying a word. An awkward silence ensued.

After a couple of seconds, George leaned over ever so slowly, so as not to disturb the entity at the end of the hall, and whispered, "What do we do now?"

Once again, I was completely at a loss. Every ghost that I had dealt with over the years was a unique creature, each with its own style and predilections. Some ghosts were merely looking for a friend, while others were out for blood. I had no clue as to what Ms. Crabtree wanted, but I knew that George was relying on me to help get him through this ordeal, so I said, "Talk to her," in a low voice, sounding calm and reassured, even though I wasn't.

I must have sounded convincing, for George said, "Ms. Crabtree?"

There was no response form the creature at the end of the hall. She just stared at us.

"Ms. Crabtree? It's Dalton. Dalton Hogshead Jr. Do you remember me?"

"You're...tardy..." she hissed. "I...loathe... tardiness..."

"Ms. Crabtree," he said, "I've come to say I'm sorry. For everything I did."

"You...didn't...do... your...homework," she said with a slight gurgle, as if her throat was full of phlegm.

"I was a really bad student," George said. "I was very unhappy and I just wanted to apologize for...well...for killing you."

"No...talking...in... class," she hissed, like a caged cat.

"Ever since that day, I've tried to live a better life, because I felt guilty," George said. "And I want to say that I'm sincerely sorry."

"No...*talking*...in...*class!*" She hissed again. She turned and began to amble towards us.

"Truly, Ms. Crabtree," George said, shifting back and forth uncomfortably. "I'm very, very sorry."

"N O ... T A L K I N G ... IN...CLASS!" she yelled, and now she was moving faster down the long hallway, towards us. Her paddle was raised over her head like a baseball bat.

"Ghosts bluff," I said, trying to sound confident. "She's just trying to scare us. Keep apologizing. She won't hurt us."

"I'm sorry, Ms. Crabtree," George yelled, but by now, it was too late. She was running full speed towards us, screaming like a banshee. My rational side told me that nothing was going to happen, but my emotional side wanted to run like mad. Still, I decided to stay put so that I might help George.

It was a horrible mistake. As soon as she got close to us, she disappeared, but just as suddenly, she reappeared behind us and with her extra-long paddle and whacked our behinds with such stinging ferocity that I felt like I was going to pass out from the pain. Immediately, George and I spun around to prevent a second blow, but she was gone.

Whack!

We were struck again for she had now reappeared behind us. I knew, in my heart, that I could not take another savage, stinging blow to my backside, and I as I heard her cackle all around me and saw the look of pain and horror on poor George's face, I knew that we had but one option.

"Run!" I yelled.

We bolted down the hallway as the whole school erupted in chaos. Fire alarms rang, lockers and their contents were flung open and thrown onto the hallway floor, and lights flipped on and off, all while the horrible cackling of Ms. Crabtree echoed through the school. I fumbled for the keys in my pocket when we reached the doorway, but just as

I had the correct key on its way to the lock...

WHACK!

Another crippling blow from her paddle sent me to my knees.

WHACK!

I heard George receive the second blow and he screamed out in pain. I turned to see the horrible visage of Ms. Crabtree standing over us, laughing as she stroked her paddle with care. "I'm... holding...you...back...a... grade," she hissed.

It was then that I remembered my secret weapon. On a whim, I'd happened upon it and secretly stuck it in my pocket. For some reason that I was entirely unable to articulate, I'd kept it. It was some strange form of serendipity and I knew it would help us out of this terrible situation.

As the noise of the lockers and bells and doors and chaos echoed all around us, I looked up to see Ms. Crabtree preparing for the final blow. She smiled with her black, rotting teeth, and the blue fire of the underworld seemed to be drifting off the paddle she had cocked over her shoulder. I ignored the pain of my stinging buttocks and reached into my shoulder bag, fishing for the one thing that would save us.

George was huddled on my right, refusing to look up at his enemy and sobbing over and over. It was then that I felt it in my hand. It seemed to be warm, almost burning, as if it was the key to the whole problem. I pulled it from the bag and held it up to Ms. Crabtree's face, yelling with all the power in my body, "BACK, FOUL BEAST! BACK!"

In my hands, I held a handwritten note from George's parents that I'd pulled from his school files. It was a note that excused him from class.

Immediately, Ms. Crabtree shrieked, as if her eyes

burned at the very sight of the note. She put her hands over her face and took a couple of steps backward. "BACK!" I yelled. "BACK TO THE DARK REALM THAT SPAWNED YOU!" I slowly rose to my feet, the note thrust out in front of me towards Ms. Crabtree as she recoiled from me.

"That...note...is... forged!" she hissed as she peeked out from behind her fingers.

"No, it's not!" I yelled. "This note is legitimate and you know it!" I thrust the note at her again. "BACK, CREATURE OF THE NIGHT!"

I followed Ms. Crabtree down the hall until I cornered her against a set of lockers. "That...note...is...forged!" she yelled again, but I knew I had her against the ropes. Of course, I didn't know exactly what to do now that I had the succubus cornered. A devilish portion of my personality told me to see what happened when I touched her with the note, and since I'd never really denied myself that type of curiosity, I thrust it up against her forehead.

Immediately, smoke rose from her brow and the note burst into flames. Ms. Crabtree shrieked in pain and shoved me aside, fleeing down the hallway at warp speed, running back and forth into lockers and causing all types of general chaos. Of course, I felt a bit guilty at being the cause of such misery, but those thoughts quickly passed as I realized that my backside was still numb from her blows.

I then felt the ground shake beneath my feet. At first it was a slight tremor, but it quickly grew and I began to fear for my safety. I heard Ms. Crabtree's voice as if it was all around me at once, as she said, "GO...TO...THE... OFFICE...YOUNG MAN!"

Florescent lights began to fall from the ceiling and dust burst forth from the cracks that were forming in the walls around us. The building shook with such ferocity that I knew we had to leave immediately. I ran down the hallway towards the front door, where George was still standing, terrified. "Out!" I yelled. "Get out of the building!"

I grabbed a trash can and threw it through the glass front doors, and just as the building began to crash down around us, we dove for safety. With a gargantuan rumble, the facade of the school began to fall down in a giant cloud of glass and brick and dust. It was at that moment that I knew the specter of Ms. Crabtree was gone forever.

The rain was just a trickle as the rumble of the collapsed building grew silent. I looked over at George, who was completely shell-shocked. He looked at me for answers, but I had none.

"I guess she didn't think your apology was genuine enough," I said...

74464

20 "THE THREE-EYED BLOODSUCKING TURTLES OF MALI" taken from Mr. Ping's Almanac, Vol. 38

Mr. Ping had traveled to Mali to catch the once-every-hundred-years hatching of the river turtles on the banks of the Niger river, with the intention of traveling on to Timbuktu to check out the mystery of the ancient Muslim warriors whose dead bodies seemed to be defending a mud fort in the middle of the desert. At the time, he wanted nothing more than to see the once-in-a-lifetime birth of several thousand turtles on the banks of the river.

Strangely, most of the locals that he had informed of his journey tried to warn him about seeing the hatching of the turtles. They said that danger lurked on the banks of that river, and that such creatures should be left alone to live their lives in peace. Mr. Ping scoffed at this idea, knowing of his great love of nature and his desire to keep the natural world as pristine as it could be. He meant no harm to the turtles; he simply wanted to see nature at its finest, just as a mountaineer might climb the highest peak or an adventurer might seek the North Pole. The turtles were said to hatch under the warm sand during the third full moon of the year and to do so in the dead of night. They would burst from their shells, burrow up through the sand, then crawl down the riverbank to the water, where their mothers would be waiting on them. For Mr. Ping, it was an opportunity to view the miracle of life firsthand. It was also an invitation to danger:

...We chartered a boat to take us up river with a skeptical captain piloting the ship. "You don't want to go to the turtles," he said. "You're messing with things you should not mess with."

"Yes, yes," Neville, my partner on this journey, told him. Neville was a researcher with the *Global Geographical Society* and had waited his whole life to see the birth of the turtles. He was on his way to meet his research partner, Jones, who had gone ahead earlier to set up some scientific equipment and prepare everything for him. They had been adventurers together for over forty years, documenting the wonders of nature for all to see and were known throughout the world as fine explorers.

"We've been warned thousands of times," Neville said to the captain. "It has no effect on us. No scientist has ever documented the birth of the turtles."

"There a reason for that," the captain said. "The turtles...they are no good. They only bring death."

"Turtles bring death?" Neville asked, laughing. "Turtles bring death! That's rich."

But at that moment, I looked into the eyes of our captain and I saw an earnestness that I hadn't seen previously. He truly believed that the turtles brought death and I could see in his eyes that he knew something we didn't.

It was a fairly uneventful trip, with nothing more than low underbrush lining the barren shores of the muddy Niger. The land was hot and dry, all rose-colored and tan; a land looking as if it was cracking and being blown to dust. After the third day on the boat, we pulled to a stop on a grassy riverbank and our captain pointed up the river. "Up there, you will find the turtles," he said.

"Just ahead?" Neville asked.

"Yes," he said. "Ahead about five miles."

"Five miles?" Neville yelled, coming unglued. "We hired you to take us to the *turtles!* Not to dump us off in the middle of nowhere and tell us to walk. My partner is there, waiting for us!"

"Five miles...that way," the captain said as he unloaded our belongings onto the bank, effectively ignoring Neville's outrage.

"This is *outrageous!*" Neville said. "Isn't this outrageous, Confucius?"

"It's just a bit of a walk," I said. "After all, the captain isn't really leaving us. He's just going to wait here. Right, captain?"

"You won't come back," the captain said. "I'll wait for you, but you won't come back."

"What?" Neville said. "What do you mean?"

"I mean you won't come back," he said. "No one ever comes back from visit with the turtles. I'll wait, but I don't expect your return."

Neville was so out of his element that he began a roaring fit, shouting and cursing and kicking the dirt with rage, acting every bit the aristocrat that he was. He went on an endless diatribe about the lack of professionalism in Africa, about how it was a continent going nowhere, and about how the people were blind to the merits of quality work. The captain just ignored him. I still wanted to get more information.

"Captain," I said, "Is it really that dangerous?"

"Yes," he said, unflinching. "You're making a big mistake."

"If we *do* go," I said, "How will we know where to look for the eggs?"

"Look for skeletons," he said. "Skeletons are everywhere."

"Elephant skeletons?" I asked. "Gazelle? What kind of skeletons?"

"*Human* skeletons," he said. "I'll wait here, but if you're not back in three days, I'll go back to Bamako."

"Yes, yes," I said, and I left him. In retrospect, I don't really know what was worse after we got off the boat: the five mile trip through the desert in blazing temperatures or listening to Neville complain for the entirety of the journey about what a horrible place Africa was. It was so hot that I could barely walk, let alone listen to him, and I began to think that he was superhuman for being able to maintain such a long-winded monologue the entire trip. Most of the banter was about his previous expeditions and how he and his partner, Jones, had done so many great and amazing things, and won so many great and amazing awards, and how Jones had better have a nice pot of tea waiting when we arrived.

As the sun reached its highest point in the sky, I began to wonder whether we knew where we were going, for somehow, we'd lost sight of the actual river. But then, as we crossed over a small hill, I could see the river cutting through the land down below. I could also see what looked to be an area the size of a soccer field full of bleached bones on the sandy banks. "Are those what I think they are?" Neville asked.

I said nothing as we made our way towards the water. Sure enough, the banks of the river were filled with the hard, white bones of several hundred people. They littered the area in every direction. "It appears that our captain might not have been exaggerating," I said.

"This is staggering," Neville said, his mouth wide open in awe at what lay around us. "What could have caused this?"

"Well, if we're to believe the locals, it was the turtles," I said.

"The turtles?" he asked. "You really believe those tall tales?"

"The truth lies all around us," I said, motioning to the remnants that lay on the ground. "If this doesn't convince you, then what will?"

Neville dismissed me and began to look around at the bones with a scientific eye. "The turtles are merely fodder for superstition," he said. "I'm sure that these savages just dug up a graveyard and deposited the bones here to scare people off."

"That is even more ludicrous than the thought of all of this being caused by the turtles," I said.

"I know you're into all of this superstitious mumbo-jumbo, Confucius," he said, "But there's got to be an explanation for all of this, and I very seriously doubt that it has anything to do with death-dealing turtles. I mean, look at it logically. Perhaps this is the way the locals bury their dead. Perhaps they put these bones here to scare off superstitious folks from the secret diamond mine that's hidden somewhere nearby. Any way you look at it, it's going to have a logical explanation."

"We'll just have to wait and see tonight, won't we?" I said.

"That, we will," he said, and he began unpacking his scientific gear right there amongst all of the chalk-colored bones, as if it was no big deal. "Where the devil is Jones?" he muttered. "He should have been here already."

I had to admit that I was scared. Something about the local superstitions was too strong. The remoteness of our location was too obvious. The hundreds of skeletons surrounding us made me uneasy. As the sun began to set over the blistering landscape in the west, I kept a wary eye all around me, for be it deadly turtles or wild villagers intent on keeping their secrets, I was not going to let them take me by surprise.

Night fell and Neville had set up lanterns all along the shoreline amongst the skeletons in the hopes that their faint light would illuminate the baby turtles' journey from the sand to the river. The light of the lanterns was the brightest thing for two-hundred miles and they made me feel like a sitting duck as we waited.

Neville had what seemed to be hundreds of writing utensils at his disposal and several cameras set up low on tripods to help him capture the moment that the turtles emerged from the sand and made their way down to the river. I simply stood over to the side, for I felt myself to be more of an observer than anything else. Then I saw something shining in the lantern light.

I casually walked over to see that it was a pocket watch that was attached to the ribs of one of the skeletons, gleaming silver in the light. I assumed that it was a watch that belonged to that very soul that was lying right in front of me. I lifted the pocket watch and opened it, examining the inscription inside.

"Ping!" Neville yelled behind me. "It's happening!"

The turtles were making their way out of the sand, but I was too concerned about the watch I'd found. "Neville..." I said.

"Ping, you're missing it," he said, snapping pictures and drawing in his notebook almost simultaneously.

"Neville," I said, "What is Jones' first name?"

"Gerald," he said. "What in the world did you ask that for? You're missing the whole point of this expedition!"

He continued snapping photos as I looked at the inscription on the inside of the watch, which read, "To Gerald, Yours forever, Maude." The pocket watch I held in my hand had belonged to Neville's partner, Jones. It was apparent that Jones was no longer walking amongst the living.

"That's the oddest thing I've ever seen," Neville said, pausing from his picture taking.

"What's that?" I asked, my stomach filling with dread.

"These turtles," he said. "They've got three eyes! Every one of them."

I ran over to where he was to see the turtles emerging from the sand. They were tiny things, doing everything within their power to rise to the surface of the sand and then flap their way down towards the water. They were all black, with irregular, yellow stripes and spots all over their shells. Sure enough, they seemed to have three eyes, two where a normal turtle would have eyes, and then one perched right on the top of their heads. They were anything but beautiful, but still an incredible sight to behold.

"Isn't this amazing?" Neville said, his eyes filled with the glory of scientific discovery. "I think we have a problem, Neville," I said.

"What are you talking about?" he asked, barely able to look up from his camera.

"Do you recognize this?" I asked, handing him the silver pocket watch.

He glanced over and froze in his tracks. Slowly, he took the watch from my hands and held it up before him. "That's Jones' watch," he said. "Where did you find this?"

"On a skeleton over there," I said.

"His wife gave that to him on his thirtieth birthday," he said, looking over at the skeleton on the ground as thousands of tiny, black, three-eyed turtles crawled down towards the water at our feet.

Before he could say anything else, we heard a low, guttural growl coming from down by the water. It was deep and sharp, as if something with an enormous set of lungs was warning us of impending doom. Neville and I slowly turned towards the sound, dread filling our hearts at the thought of what kind of horrible creature might have made such a noise.

When we looked down to the water in the light of the full moon, we saw a massive head with a four-foot long neck extended out of the water. The warm, yellow lantern light failed to penetrate the darkness, for all we saw was the creature's silhouette. However, there was no mistaking the sound of the creature, as it continued with it's deep, angry growl.

"What is that?" Neville asked.

"Could it be, perhaps, the mother of these little turtles?" I asked. I soon saw three more heads emerge from the waters around it. "Or...mothers?" I asked.

Like a car, casually driving straight from the sea floor to the shore, so it was with the turtle and its shell as it made its way on land. On the surface, it looked like a regular turtle, with its large shell, clawed feet protruding from the sides and flat stomach, but that was where the similarities ended. The main difference between this turtle and the turtles I knew was the sheer size of the creature. It was as big as a car, and its legs were like tree trunks.

But the strangest part about the giant turtle was the fact that the turtle had three eyes, just like its offspring, and the fact that the turtle had long, razor-sharp fangs protruding out from its mouth. Worst of all was the look in the giant turtle's fiery eyes, for it was the look of a mother that observed something very dangerous standing between her and her offspring, and the three other turtles that followed behind it had very similar looks in their eyes.

"Ping, do you see that?" Neville asked, his voice trembling.

"We should have listened to the captain," I said.

"What do we do?" he asked.

"I think our best bet would be to run," I said. "But let's start by just backing up slowly. The last thing we want to do is hurt any of these turtles under our feet."

Under the watchful eyes of the turtles that were making their way up the bank towards us, we began to slowly back away from the danger, stepping gingerly amongst the thousands of turtles making their way in the opposite direction under our feet. Neville was practically catatonic with fear and I felt much the same way, for these giant turtles stood taller than we did and looked horribly menacing.

I glanced down to make sure that we had sufficient running room on the ground and whispered, "When I count to three, make a break for the rock ridge back behind us."

"Okay," Neville said.

"One, two…three!"

We turned to run as fast as we could, but the most unexpected thing happened. One of the turtles from which we were running raced all the

way around us, moving as quickly as a gazelle before turning to confront us and cut off our path. This went against every bit of logic that I'd ever known, for turtles weren't supposed to be fast. They were supposed to be slow and move with precision. Where I thought we would outrun the beasts, now we were completely surrounded, and the growls from all sides told me that these turtles were *angry*.

"Well, that didn't go well," I said.

"It certainly didn't," Neville said with a sigh, his back against mine as the turtles walked a slow circle around us. "You know," he continued, "'In all of my travels, in all of the adventure, in all of the glory, I never remotely suspected that I would meet my end at the hands of giant, three-eyed, turtles in Mali. And yet, here I am…"

21 ACCLIMATED SPOOKS, LIGHT, AND POWER LIMITED

Acclimated Spooks, Light, and Power Limited was an organization formed by Mr. Ping's predecessor Mr. Pranesh (see entry #74), and Bird and Goldfish (see entry #9). The purpose of ASLPL is to serve as an organization dedicated to the acquisition of mysterious and rare artifacts and to help those without the funds to deal with "extraordinary" problems.

22 "THE MYSTERIOUS MULTIPLYING BEGGING CHILDREN OF THE REMOTE VILLAGES IN THE ANNAPURNA MOUNTAINS" taken from Mr. Ping's Almanac, Vol. 79

While trekking in Nepal, Mr. Ping had heard to avoid the Chakrum Gap, just south of the hardest stretch of the Annapurna Range. It was rumored to be dangerous, but curiosity got the better of him because the route through the Chakrum Gap was the shortest route back to Pokhara, where a nice, warm cup of tea and

a comfortable bed were waiting on him. When his guide saw him diverging from the preordained (and much harder) trail, he quickly began to wave Mr. Ping off, as if he was taking a route that led straight into the gates of Hades:

"No, no," my guide said, somewhat panicked. "Bad route. Bad route." His English was limited, but I did my best to question him. "Bad way," he said, pointing over the horizon. "Very dangerous."

Being the grand adventurer I was, I had no fear of danger, be it pickpockets or perilous gorges, so it was with a hint of arrogance that I brushed my guide's warnings aside and continued on my way. "Bad way?" I asked. "Whatever do you mean?"

He pointed frantically at the horizon again. "That way bad," he said. "Don't go."

"Oh, nonsense," I said. "I'll meet you in Pokhara." I walked away, leaving him standing, dumbfounded, on the side of the mountain.

The children of this area of the Annapurnas had been indoctrinated over the years to foreigners who gave them gifts as they traveled through their lands. A well-intentioned, though misguided, American might be on a long hike, come around a corner, spy a darling Nepalese boy, and offer him a piece of chocolate or a stick of gum, thinking that the child would remember them forever for their generosity. Unfortunately, this shortsightedness created hordes of children who would follow hikers for miles, begging the poor souls for a handout as they spoke the only English word they knew: Candy.

"Candy? Candy? Candy?" they would say, over and over again, until they got something.

This was what I assumed I would encounter in the Chakrum Gap trail, and I was right. Hiking by myself, I came around a corner to find a darling little boy standing in the path, his arm outstretched in a begging way as he asked me the age old question, "Candy?" I had none to offer, but it failed to stop the boy from being persistent. "Candy? Candy?"

I tried explaining that I had none, but he failed to understand, and it wasn't long before another boy appeared from nowhere, asking the very same question. "Candy? Candy?"

They continued to follow, hands outstretched, so I chose to ignore them. I walked on for a while, but I soon realized there were more than two sets of footsteps behind me. When I looked over my shoulder, I found not two kids, but four, all of their arms out towards me. "Candy? Candy?"

That's odd, I thought. *Where did those kids come from?* I kept on walking, but when I looked back again, there were *nine* kids. Something about this seemed unnatural, so I quickened my pace.

Soon, a chorus of "Candy?" became the bray of a small crowd of children, and I quickly lost count of the number of kids following me. I do remember an abject sense of fear that filled my heart, as I was sure that every time I would look away and then look back again, the number of kids would multiply. And this time, they seemed to be gaining on me.

It was when I felt the smack of a rock on the back of my head that I realized the mess I had gotten into that day. The last time I turned to look, I saw well-over a hundred angry children, all reaching down to pick up rocks to hurl in my direction. I turned to run as fast as I could to get away, and it was only through sheer luck that I was able to escape with my life. Still, I had more than a few bruises to show for it.

I finally found my guide again in Pokhara. I must have looked terrible, with bruises all over my face and body, and my backpack in tatters. He just looked at me and said, "I warned you. Very dangerous."

Needless to say, I shall never travel that route again without a healthy supply of bubble gum...

23 "THE WOOLLY MAMMOTH OF LAKE BAKAL" taken from Mr. Ping's Almanac Vol. 33

One of Mr. Ping's goals as a researcher, writer, and archaeologist of the unknown was to explain those things that didn't make sense to the average person; to go in and find out the secrets of this planet upon which we live. Sometimes he achieved his goals, while other times, his goals eluded him and he was left explaining the fact that he couldn't explain something, as in the following tale that took place in Central Asia:

...It was almost dark on the edge of Lake Bakal, the water in front of us tranquil and still as the sun disappeared over the horizon. We were enjoying the remnants of the day in that short, magical window of time before the mosquitoes emerged and we would have to retire to the yurt for the evening. The sky was a metallic blue reflected in the lake, with a band of pink lying over the horizon where the sun had disappeared.

We had a nice evening, peeling away strips of dried goat meat with one of Tuk's particularly sharp knives and eating in the firelight. We were hundreds of miles from anywhere with nothing but the sound of the grassland around us to lull us into a haze, and that was just what I wanted. Tuk said nothing as we stared into the fire. I felt he was enjoying the solitude just as much as I was and both of us were too afraid to ruin the moment by speaking.

The sun had finally gone down and I was preparing a kettle of tea to help me relax before I disappeared into the yurt with a book, a lantern, and a cozy blanket. While I was waiting for the kettle to boil, lazily poking at the orange coals of the fire to keep the flames going, I heard it.

It was a low rumble, something furious enough to shake the ground. I looked around to see if there might be an earthquake happening when I realized that the movement was too rhythmic to be an earthquake. Plus, the vibrations were getting louder and faster, as if whatever was making the sound was also getting closer. "Do you hear that, Tuk?" I asked.

He nodded and I detected a hint of fear in his eyes as he listened intently to the sound drawing nearer and nearer. I thought to myself, *How ironic that I venture all the way out here to get away from it all and end up having some monster show up to mess up my vacation.*

At just the right time to snap me out of my bout of self-pity, the yurt beside us was suddenly ripped from the ground and tossed into the air like a washcloth. I soon realized that a horrible creature with amazing, brute strength had just ripped the yurt from its pins and thrown it back over its shoulder.

In the light of the fire, I saw something that I'd never seen before. Standing twice my height, with curved tusks that were as white as snow, and long, brown hair, was a great, elephant-like creature. Just as quickly, I realized that this wasn't an elephant, it was a *woolly mammoth,* a creature long since extinct throughout the world.

It was tall, taller than any elephant I'd ever seen, and its brown, matted fur hung down over the entirety of its body, giving it a menacing quality that was accented by its fierce eyes and long, white tusks that it shook back and forth. This woolly mammoth was angry. *Very* angry.

Tuk had taken off running across the darkened plains to escape the mammoth and I should have done the same thing, but I didn't. I was standing in front of the creature as the steam puffed from its nose and its eyes stared at me, intent on the kill. I'd never seen a mammoth before and I wasn't about to pass up *this* opportunity.

The mammoth was filled with rage, destroying our supplies for the journey, stomping on boxes and whacking our only furniture out into the lake. It seemed to be focusing more on our *things* as opposed to us, which afforded me extra seconds to sketch a picture in my head of what the creature looked like.

I must have concentrated a bit too hard, for the next thing I knew, the mammoth had whacked me on the side with its tusks, sending me flying across the terrain. With a thud, I landed on the lake's shores. I expected a swift and painful death as it came over to either trample or gore me, but neither happened. I wiped the mud from my eyes to see the mammoth throw the yurt around a couple more times and then run off with a giant bellow into the darkness. I heard the distant thumps as it ran off into the night and soon the sound was gone.

I sat there in the mud, staring at the vacant area where the creature had disappeared and found myself utterly speechless. What in the world had just happened? Had a *woolly mammoth*, a long-extinct animal from the ice age really just destroyed our camp? Did this single creature really just appear from *nowhere* and then disappear? I had so many questions that I couldn't even pull myself up out of the sludge.

"What was *that?*" Tuk asked, running up from the darkness as I tried my best to get rid of the mud that covered my clothes. My ribs were beginning to hurt from the creature's blow.

"You know, Tuk," I said, wincing as I took a deep breath, "I have no idea what that was."

Eventually, we got the yurt erected again, and late that night, we finally settled in. The next morning, when we went looking for the mammoth, we saw nothing and there were no discernible tracks from the creature other than those around the yurt. I was left with a predicament that happened all too often in my life: How was I to explain that which I didn't understand?

24 LUKLABOOMAPH, taken from Mr. Ping's Almanac, Vol. 51

Luklaboomaph is the name of a vanished city. It's a name found in various 19th century maps of the Philippines and a city spoken of often in the travel literature of the time, for its location on the main island of Luzon made it a prime shipping port that attracted travelers from all over the world. However, there was one problem with the biggest city in the Philippines in the 19th century. It seems that after the year 1900, the grand city of Luklaboomaph failed to exist. It vanished, completely disappearing from maps, literature, and any other places it may have been mentioned. Naturally, Mr. Ping wanted to get to the bottom of this strange phenomenon and traveled to the Philippines to investigate:

... The story of Luklaboomaph fascinated me. Like Roanoke, Virginia in the 1700s, how could a city, an establishment full of thousands of people, bustling with life and business, simply disappear from the face of the Earth? And why wasn't this matter investigated further? I'd checked the ship logs of several trading vessels of the time period and found that a certain Finnegan C. Wuffle of the ship Gullspit was the first on record to acknowledge the disappearance:

"...We traveled up and down the coast, a ship without a port, a cargo without a destination, looking for that fair city that might supply us with the things we needed to continue on with our journey, but we found nothing. The crew cursed the navigator and would have killed him for leading us to our doom, had I not given him forty lashes to calm their spirits. It turned out that his navigation skills were quite fine and I'd been mistaken in giving him the lashes. He took the apology in stride and continued to receive treatment for the welts on his back. Nevertheless, our problem was still there. The port was gone, or at least, not where it should have been..."

A Roger P. Muddlesmith of the H.M.S. Dutyfree had this to say about the disappearance of the city:

"...By gum, I was standing in the exact place that I'd been robbed not six months earlier on the city's streets, but there was nothing there. And to my left was where that scurvy pub that gave me a case of the dysentery should have been. But there was nothing in that place either, save for the sharp branches of a palm tree and a monkey that seemed to be giving me the evil eye. How a city could disappear, let alone remove every single trace of it's existence, was beyond me. There was absolutely no sign that anything had ever been there..."

After reading these and several more accounts of the strange disappearance of the city, I trekked to Manila, hired a guide, and set out through the steamy jungles in search of this obscure place. I had plenty of information as to how to locate where it was, for almost all of the shipping logs I'd read gave the exact coordinates, both longitude and latitude, of where the city should have been. My goal was to find something, anything really, that proved that Luklaboomaph actually existed.

We trudged for a few days along the muddy trails under the shadow of Mount Pinatubo rumbling in the distance, but eventually, the trails were swallowed up by the dense undergrowth and our time was more occupied by hacking and slashing and sweating our way through the jungle. Eventually, we reached our destination, the exact latitude and longitude of where the city should have been, but of course, our setting hadn't changed much, for we were still surrounded by the thick canopy of vines, leaves, and roots from earlier. My guide, Jose, shrugged, as if he had no clue as to what I had expected to see. He muttered something sarcastic in Tagalog to his brother and we continued moving forward.

We spent several days scouring the location, looking through the brush, digging in the dirt, sifting through the trees, all in an attempt to verify the fact that the city actually existed, but we found nothing. It had been a week of steady rain, humid, hot air, and creepy rain forest creatures that seemed to find my neck a nice place to have a crawl or stretch their many legs. Just as I was about to give up entirely, Jose came running through the woods shouting with excitement.

"Señor! Señor!" he yelled. "I've found something!"

He pulled me up a hill to a small clearing that had been cut into the landscape. There in front of us was what appeared to be a door frame. It was old, moldy, beaten down from exposure over the years, but it was still standing, and beside it stood a sign that had been hammered into the ground.

"**Please**...what does it say?" I asked, for it was written in Tagalog.

"It says, 'Here is where Luklaboomaph existed!'" he said. "'But now it is gone, never to return. However, if you would like to visit, all you need to do is walk through the door.'" Jose looked at me in a curious manner and shrugged. "This is very strange," he said.

"Yes, it is," I said.

"I will see what happens," he said, and then he turned to walk through the door frame standing there in the grass.

"No! Wait!" I yelled, but I was too late. The minute he stepped into the door jam, he disappeared in a flash of light. He was there and then he was gone. His brother, who was standing beside me, went silent with shock.

"Where did he go?" he asked.

My eyes were just as wide as his, and I stared at the empty space in which he had previously stood. "I don't know," I said. We stared at the door in silence for several minutes, unable to speak. "I think he went to the same place the Luklaboomaph went," I said. "And I think *we're* going to have to go get him..."

25   STAGOPTOK, taken from Mr. Ping's Almanac, Vol. 59

Stagoptok was a small Russian town in Siberia that Mr. Ping was asked to investigate in 1958 after Soviet authorities were unable to figure out what had befallen the place. His discoveries were quite disturbing, as detailed in the following passage:

"...Normally, comrade" Lieutenant Kartovsky told me, "We like to handle matters such as this internally. We are a very capable country, with a solid government and hard-working people. We don't like to bring in outsiders, especially foreigners, to help us solve our problems. However in this case, we make exception."

"Well, I hope I can be of some service," I said, staring out at the dreary, snow-covered flatlands as we chugged our way down the road in an official government Volga.

"You see," Kartovsky continued, "We have sources that tell us you are an expert in matters such as these. They say that you can explain that which cannot be explained. Is this true?"

"I can do what I can do," I said. "No more, no less. You shouldn't expect miracles. I may not be able to do anything at all."

"We shall see," he said, staring off into the distance, the brow of his stern, gray Soviet army hat pulled low over his thick eyebrows. "We shall see."

We came to a road block populated by weary, young Soviet soldiers. The snow was now falling, and as the soldiers moved the blockade in front of us, I got the distinct impression that those poor fellows would have been much happier to be any other place at that moment. They peered into the windows of the car as we drove past, saluting when they saw Lieutenant Kartovsky, and then watched us drive on into the snow. It was at that point that I realized there was no one else to be found past the roadblock. There were farmhouses, small villages, all the signs of life and civilization; just no people. Finally, we rounded a corner to enter the city.

Stagoptok was to be a model Soviet city, with wide boulevards, noble statues, and large, concrete buildings to house the hard-fought workers of a perfect Communist society. It was a city built from the ground up, a model of urban planning created from scratch on the grounds of a former farming community. It was obvious that the Soviets dreamed of Stagoptok as being their new urban center, a city of dreams, where only their best and brightest would reside, living the model communist lifestyle.

It looked like it would have been a magnificent city... if any people were there.

Stagoptok was a ghost town. There were wide boulevards, but no cars to traverse them, only the occasional vehicle left stranded in the middle of the snowy streets. There were massive government buildings, new and noble and exciting, but their doors were wide open to the weather, and the snow that had piled up in front had no tracks through it to signal that someone had used the equipment. There were massive, fifteen and twenty-story apartment buildings, but they were empty and lonely, not a light anywhere to signal their use.

"One million people lived in Stagoptok," Lieutenant Kartovsky said to me. "One million people lived here, worked here, had lives here. They made this a great Soviet city. But now, there is no one. Where did they go? Every single person in Stagoptok has vanished without a trace."

"What?" I asked. "You mean to tell me that one million people from this city disappeared?"

"We can find no trace of them," he said.

He had the driver stop the car and we got out in the main square of the city, an empty expanse that, at one time, might have held massive parades to celebrate communism. "So, Mr. Ping," he said, motioning all around him. "You are the great explainer of the unexplained. Tell me:

Where are all the people of Stagoptok?"

I didn't know the answer...

26 LHASA

Located at over 13,000 feet above sea level in the occupied territory of Tibet, Lhasa is the capital of the region and former home to the spiritual leader of Tibetan Bhuddism, the Dalai Lama (a friend of Mr. Ping's who now lives in exile in India).

It should be noted that the former residence of the Dalai Lama, a grand building overlooking the city known as the Potala Palace was visited by Mr. Ping as a guest several times when the Dalai Lama still lived there. In fact, Mr. Ping was with the Dalai Lama when he made his escape to India. The group had to leave in haste, forcing Mr. Ping to leave several important possessions in the Potala Palace, including a year's worth of writing (for what would have been Almanac number 52), several photo albums, and a large jar of marbles he'd won on the street. Although he wanted his possessions back, he was never afforded the opportunity to return. His things are still in the palace to this day.

27 KATHMANDU, taken from Mr. Ping's Almanac, Vol. 82

Kathmandu is the capital of the country of Nepal. It is a dusty, crowded city full of things both magical and mundane around every corner. Being a favorite destination for backpackers, Kathmandu has an interesting mix of both the historical and tacky, and they usually converge in the strangest of ways. Mr. Ping traveled to Kathmandu several times in his life, both for leisure and for work, and had several interesting adventures in the region, including the following excerpt from his almanac:

...One of the oldest parts of the city is a place called Bhoktapur, which is northeast of the heart of Kathmandu. It is dense with buildings and

crowded with people, having no roads wide enough to drive a car or motorbike through, thus making it the perfect place to have a stroll.

Bhoktapur has old, wooden buildings with intricately carved awnings, interesting windows, and cobblestone streets, as well as tall and elaborate temples, all of which completely distracted me, providing the perfect opportunity to have my bag ripped from my shoulder. Having been a pickpocket in my youth on the streets of Hong Kong, I should have been much more aware of my surroundings and paid greater attention to what was happening, but I suppose I became somewhat enraptured with the unique architecture of the area.

The force of the bag being pulled from my arms unexpectedly almost sent me to the ground, but I quickly regained my footing to see a teenager running in the opposite direction to escape with my belongings. Normally, I would shrug off such an incident, for being a savvy traveler means carrying nothing with you that you would be afraid to lose, but this time it was different, for I'd been carrying a set of my journals around with me for fear of losing them. I had no choice but to pursue my aggressor.

I assume that, because the thief knew the twists and turns of Bhoktapur, he thought he could dodge and weave this way and that and be rid of me to reap the rewards of his thievery. Unfortunately for him, he was wrong, for I knew the tricks of the trade. I knew the well-planned routes that ninety-nine percent of thieves around the world use to escape after robbing someone, and as I casually made my way through the crowd, I rounded a corner to find my thief sitting on the ground, preparing to open my bag and retrieve the contents.

"I think that bag is mine," I said from the far end of the alley. "I'd very much like to have it back."

In that instance, I had my first chance to look into the eyes of the thief, and in that split second, I realized that there was something very different about this fellow. He was a teenager, dark brown in the face and a few inches shorter than I was, but there was a world-weariness in his eyes. He was surprised to see me, but made no sudden moves to flee as a normal pickpocket would, as if he'd seen this type of thing before. His face and body language conveyed that I was more of a nuisance than a threat.

He rose to his feet, pulled the bag onto his shoulders and then did something that took me a few seconds to absorb. Instead of giving the bag back or running in the opposite direction...he jumped. And he jumped again. And then a third and fourth time, bounding upwards along the walls until he was on the roof of a building. Peering down over the side at me, his face was still as expressionless as it had been before.

I was completely stunned. I had expected a scared, inexperienced pickpocket and I'd discovered a teenager that could defy the laws of gravity with his acrobatic skills. He was still peering over the edge of the roof in silence, looking at me as though he expected that display of athletic prowess to scare me away. However, it didn't matter whether I was looking at a teenager or a she-wolf, I was not going to let slip my belongings so easily.

"I want my bag back," I yelled up to him. He looked at me and hissed, revealing a set of what looked to be dangerously long fangs. This gave me pause, for I was unsure what sort of person I was dealing with here, and I wasn't entirely convinced he was human.

But I'd dealt with shape shifters and were-creatures and demon spirits before, and I knew he wouldn't be any more of a threat than those things. As he disappeared back over the roof, I rushed inside one of the buildings, up the dark and creaky stairs, and through a tiny door to find myself on the dusty, cracked tar roof, overlooking the other establishments of the city and the hazy brown mountains in the distance. I scanned the rooftops, looking for my quarry and saw him, once again, perched like a bird on the edge of a roof two buildings over, looking through my bag.

"If you would be so kind as to return my bag," I yelled across the way. This time, the thief was truly startled and hissed at me again. He flung the bag over his shoulder, crouched down, and like a super-powered frog, leaped what I perceived to be at least fifty yards from one roof all the way across to another. I'd never seen a person fly through the air with such precision and grace, and although his landing was fine, the roof upon which he landed wasn't strong enough to hold his weight, and he went crashing through the top in a cloud of dust and wood.

I knew I wouldn't have much time before my bag was truly gone, and that to go back down the stairs would take much too long, so I made the leap across the close rooftops towards the thief. After a couple of jumps and close calls, I found myself standing over the hole the thief had fallen through. I looked down into the dim hole and saw my bag lying on a pile of debris. I lowered myself into the hole and discovered that I was in what appeared to be someone's small, dimly lit living room. The thief was nowhere in sight.

I checked my bag to make sure the contents were all there and then proceeded to find an exit. I quickly felt as if

something wasn't right, but before I could react, the thief leaped from the shadows and tackled me to the floor. Because of my rigorous martial arts training, I instinctively rolled with this tackle and kicked him back over my head, sending him flying into the wall and sliding to the ground. I rolled back to my feet and saw that he had already gotten up. There was a face off in the dusty shafts of sunlight streaming in from the roof and I could see that my assailant was more animal than human, as his deep-throated growl filled the room like a low-grade earthquake.

"I just want my bag back," I said, my arms locked in a defensive position. "I don't want any trouble."

The thief hissed at me again and clawed threateningly at the air in my direction. We circled each other for a few seconds, both of us ready for a fight, until we heard the rattle of keys in the door. The thief instantly leaped up through the hole in the roof to escape, leaving me all alone in the room as a Nepalese family walked through the door, completely surprised at the sight of a Cantonese man standing in a pile of debris in their living room.

"Hello," I said, feeling a bit awkward. The family of four said nothing. They just stared at me in stunned silence. I thought about trying to explain to these people how I was in pursuit of some sort of mysterious creature that had stolen my bag, but I figured it would have been pointless. I pulled a hundred dollar bill from my pocket and placed it in the mother's hands. "For the damages," I said with a smile as I pointed to the hole in the roof. I shook the father's hand and gave their kids some candy that I had in my bag, then walked out the front door.

I spent the rest of the day in search of the thief, but could find no trace of him. I inquired with the locals and although they had heard of such a mysterious figure, no one knew where to find him. I realized that I would never be able to track him down and just chalked the whole thing up to mysterious chance.

Although I will admit that, for the rest of my trip in Nepal, I had the distinct impression that I was being followed, shadow to shadow, rooftop to rooftop, every step of the way...

28 "THE MAD-CRAZY LOONS ATTACK THE MCCLOYD HOUSE" taken from Mr. Ping's Almanac, Vol. 92.

Mr. Ping had befriended the McCloyds soon after Boyd was born, informing them of the significance of Boyd's birth date and the job that he hoped Boyd to have when he grew older. At first, they were skeptical, but as time went on, Mr. Ping offered them more and more education on the matter. They gradually came around to Mr. Ping's point of view.

However, being in cahoots with Mr. Ping was no easy task. The strange and unusual followed him around constantly, and both Mr. and Mrs. McCloyd were not immune to the bizarre events in which Mr. Ping sometimes found himself, as evidenced by the McCloyd's failed introduction to Reggie and Ho Yin, an event upset by a strange series of events:

...As I pulled up to the house, I could see Mr. McCloyd peeking out from the living room window, onto the lawn. His eyes widened at my arrival and he began to frantically motion towards me. It was obvious why. Covering the entirety of his property were more loons than I had ever seen in my life.

They had landed on his roof, they had perched themselves in the bushes, and they were waddling all over his lawn, their black and white bodies changing the look of

their landscaping and making a horrible mess from the droppings that they left. Migrating loons landing in the Frankfurter area were not normally a big deal, but I knew that something strange was happening the minute that I saw them on the McCloyd's lawn, for that was the *only* place they'd landed. There was a clear line separating where the McCloyd's property ended from their neighbors, for no loon waddled over that line with their little, black, webbed feet.

The other signal that something was wrong came from the fact that Mr. McCloyd was frantically waving his arms at me, trying to get my attention. "What in the world is this?" asked Reggie from the driver's seat.

"It appears to be a gathering of loons," I said.

"Do you get paid the big bucks for brilliant observations like that?" Reggie asked, rolling his eyes at me. "I can *see* that it's a gathering of loons, for pity's sake."

"You are so cranky lately," I said, dismissing his mood. "You can be really unpleasant to be around during full moons."

"Yeah, yeah," he said. It was simply a defense mechanism to hide his depression.

"I don't think it's safe here," Ho Yin said, sitting beside me in the backseat. "Mr. McCloyd is certainly trying to tell us something and judging by the way he's waving his arms, it might not be good news."

We all looked over and sure enough, there was Mr. McCloyd, still pantomiming something to us from the front window. He was now joined by Mrs. McCloyd and try as the three of us might, we could not figure out what they were trying to say. Reggie looked all around the car, trying to discern what the danger was. "I don't see anything," he said. "Do you

think they're just scared of all these ugly ducks?"

"They're *loons*, Reggie," Ho Yin said.

"Loons, ducks, they're all the same," he said.

"Actually, they're not," Ho Yin said. "A loon in the national bird of Canada."

"And a parakeet is the national bird of Luba-Luba-Land!" he said. "Who cares?"

"He really *is* cranky lately," Ho Yin said to me.

"Look, are we going to sit in the car all day, or are we going to go in?" Reggie asked. "I can't rightly take sitting in this cramped, stinky rental car all day long."

"Reggie," I said, "It might not be safe."

"Rubbish," Reggie said. "Those silly ducks dangerous? That's the most daft thing I've heard all day! I'm going in."

Reggie got out of the car and began to walk towards the house, and as he did, the McCloyds began to wave him away from inside the window, frantically trying to get his attention. Reggie just silently shrugged his shoulders, giving them a look that said he didn't understand them. Soon, it was quite evident what they were saying.

The minute Reggie stepped from the street to the driveway of the McCloyd house, the thousands of loons in their yard burst from the ground and began to attack him. In milliseconds, Reggie disappeared beneath a giant wad of black and white, flapping feathers, as the loons nipped at him relentlessly. Just as quickly, Reggie did an about-face and ran back to the car. As soon as he stepped off their property, the loons calmed down again and settled on the ground, still not daring to set foot off the McCloyd property.

Reggie jumped in the car, his suit ripped to shreds, and his white fur frizzed and standing on end from the attack. "Those bloody ducks are crazy!" he said, trying to catch his breath.

"They're not ducks," Ho Yin said. "They're loons."

"They almost killed me!" Reggie said.

"I fear the McCloyds might be trapped," I said. "We've got to figure out what's going on and get them out of there."

"But how?" Reggie asked. "Those birds are mad-crazy!"

"I've dealt with this once before," I said. "In Vietnam. And it was a harrowing experience..."

29 LEPRECHAUNS, taken from Mr. Ping's Almanac, Vol. 49

In Irish folklore, leprechauns are a type of elf said to inhabit Ireland. Mr. Ping had several encounters with leprechauns over the years, the most important of which occurred in 1948:

...The rain was pounding the coastline as I drove to see Edward McGullicutty, and I could barely see the road in front of me through the torrent. I knew that I shouldn't have been out on such a blustery night, but Edward was desperate for my help and far be it from me to deny a friend in need.

The road wound along the farmland, back and forth, with not a house or village in sight. I was truly in the middle of nowhere. As I rounded a corner, my eyes caught sight of something in the road in front of me, panicked at the sight of my headlights. I immediately thought it was a child, for it was about three feet tall and trotting along in a bouncy sort of way.

In a panic, I swerved to avoid the tot and ran right off the road into a large ditch, where the front of my automobile wedged itself into the mud. My chest was driven into the steering wheel and my head shattered the windshield, but aside from a very small cut on my forehead, I was fine. My worries, however, were with the poor little child I'd almost run over.

I scrambled from the car, out into the torrential rain, looking for the tot. The rain soaked my clothes as I looked back and forth along the highway. I was *sure* that I saw a child, wasn't I? But if I *had* seen a child, where was it?

"Oooo uhm gunna bee let," cried a voice behind me. I spun around just in time to see something disappear over the side of a cliff. I ran to the car to grab a flashlight and then edged my way off the road, over to the edge. I could hear the crash of the ocean waves on the rocks below me, but the night was too dark for me to see. I shined the light on the jagged cliffs below and for a split second, caught a glimpse of just what I thought it was: a small child making its way down the rock face.

"Hello?" I yelled, just before it disappeared behind a rock. "Hello, little one? I think it's too dangerous for you to be on these rocks." There was no response.

I was left in a quandary. There was a young child below me on the cliffs, and I wasn't sure whether or not that child was in danger. Obviously, they *were* in danger, for these cliffs were quite deadly, especially in a torrential rainstorm like this one, but I was also convinced that there was something wrong with this situation. I'd been around enough spooks and ghouls in my lifetime to know when I was being lured to my doom. After carefully assessing the situation, I came to the conclusion that a child in danger was too great a risk, and if there *was* something waiting on me below, I was well-enough equipped to handle myself, come what may.

Being very careful, I made my way down the rock path on which I'd seen the child. For a few brief minutes, I began to feel a bit foolhardy, for there was hardly a path at all, and I had to lower myself over a few very large stones, the likes of which I wasn't sure I'd be able to get back up and over.

I would peer over the rock face, trying to see below, just to make sure that the child hadn't fallen, but I saw nothing. Occasionally, a little path of mud would lead me onward and the tiny footprints in the muck kept me on the right track.

Eventually, I came to an outcropping, over which I had to lower myself. As I fell to the ground under it, I saw that I was standing in front of a small cave. The outcropping provided shelter from the cold rain and the cave disappeared back into the blackness, so far that even my flashlight could not penetrate it. It was a foreboding place, but the mud below revealed that whatever person I was pursuing had gone inside. *This is ridiculous,* I thought. *You're getting yourself into a world of trouble, Ping.* Still, my inquisitive nature propelled me into the cave, for I'd come much too far to let a little darkness scare me away.

The cave was only about five feet high and I had to stay hunched over as I made my way inside. It was warmer inside the cave and very dry. I must have traveled around fifty meters when I saw firelight in front of me. The depth of my descent into the cave also muted the noise of the storm and ocean outside, and I heard what seemed to be a large amount of activity going on just up ahead.

Slowly, I edged around the corner and couldn't believe what I saw. The cave opened up into a large cavern that seemed to be at least thirty meters across with a large fire in the center. What was even more strange was the fact that there were hundreds upon hundreds of little, red-headed men in green bowler hats, jackets, and shorts, all dancing in a circle around the fire. Ale was being passed back and forth and there was a fair amount of singing happening.

It was at that moment that I knew I'd made a huge mistake: I'd stumbled into a nest of *leprechauns*.

I felt so stupid. To think that I was chasing after a child had to be the most idiotic thing I'd ever done. I was in Ireland. I knew that leprechauns were dangerous. Why hadn't I put two and two together and realized I was being lured to my doom by a little Irish creature? My only recourse from such a situation was to quietly slip out the way I came and hope that none of them saw me, but in my fear, I was awkward and I knocked over a large pile of rocks, causing a general commotion. Every single leprechaun stopped what they were doing and turned in my direction.

They couldn't have asked for a better target: A hapless, rain-soaked fellow that looked like a deer staring down the barrel of a rifle. I'd stumbled right into their lair and I was surely going to have to pay the consequences.

"Geddadafloon!" one of them yelled, and with a roar that sounded like an army of barbarian chipmunks, they rushed for me. Now, most people have never been rushed by hundreds of angry leprechauns, so they might not know what the experience would be like, but having had it happen to me, I must say that it is one of the most panic-inducing experiences one could ever have. I have been trained in Buddhist meditation, in the ways of the Shaolin arts, honed my body to be ready for anything that comes my way, but all that training was for naught when I saw the leprechauns coming for me.

They didn't just run along the floor of the cave. For some reason, they defied gravity entirely, running along the walls, the floor, and the ceiling.

Each one had a fire in their eyes and they seemed to be screaming a litany of Irish obscenities at me, their sharp little teeth raining spittle down in front of them. I tried to run through the cave as fast as I could to escape them, but I'd gone a lot further than I remembered and in my panic, I bumbled along much more than I normally would have.

Unfortunately, the leprechauns were gaining on me, so much so that I realized I'd have to stand my ground. Mere meters from the exit, I turned and took a deep breath, ready for action. I thought that I might try to negotiate with them, but I couldn't have been more naive, for they failed to listen to any of my pleading words. They simply attacked me ferociously, all of them coming at me at once.

Luckily, my defensive instincts kicked into gear, and with a flurry of fists and kicks, I started sending the little Irish beasties back the way they came. My punches were powerful, and the leprechauns so light, that I could send each one a good ten or fifteen yards if I connected well enough. However, the sheer rage of the leprechauns kept them on their feet, even after a few hard blows, so I suspected that my time was limited. They kept gaining and gaining on me, trying to overwhelm me with sheer numbers.

It wasn't until I felt those sharp, leprechaun teeth sink into my calf and the blinding pain burst through my body that I realized I was going to lose this battle. The pain was so intense that my leg gave out underneath me and I fell to the ground. Sure enough, I was dog-piled by a mass of little men in green suits, all of them filled with never-ending fury. They pinched and scratched and bit me and it wasn't long before I lost consciousness entirely.

When I awoke, I was tied down to a stone slab in the

middle of the cave, with a particularly hairy and nasty little leprechaun standing over me, looking quite angry (and a little bit rabid).

"Getyersef innabittufapickul, eh?" he said.

"Excuse me?" I asked, unable to understand him

I felt a sharp pain in my ribs and realized that one of the other leprechauns had kicked me. "Don baktakim," it said.

A round of helium-like laughter filled the room and I thought, *What have you gotten yourself into now, Ping?* I wasn't entirely sure that I was going to get out of this one alive, for it seemed that my little Irish friends had been planning a feast, and *I* was to be the main course...

30 "UNEXPECTED VISITORS AT CHEK LAP KOK AIRPORT" taken from Mr. Ping's Almanac Vol. 101

The opening of the new airport on Lantau Island was a cause for celebration on many fronts in Hong Kong. It was beneficial to have a modern facility through which millions of visitors could pass every year, and it was beneficial for the residents of Kowloon, who no longer had to worry about the planes narrowly passing overhead as they landed mere kilometres from them in Victoria Harbor. The new airport was good for the people, the government, and the businesses of Hong Kong.

However, nothing ever works perfectly when something as large and complex as Chek Lap Kok opens, and the airport had its fair share of incidents, ranging from lost luggage, to flight delays, to general confusion about where to land the planes. However, the biggest headache the air traffic controllers had to deal with was an unexpected flight that happened to touch down one sunny spring morning...

...I was reading the morning paper on the veranda, trying to ignore the smog that hung over the skyline. A ringing phone interrupted my

routine and I heard the frantic voice of Chow Yun Dong, a friend of mine who was the assistant manager of day to day operations at Chek Lap Kok airport. "Confucius?" he said. "I think it's very important that you get down here right away to give us a little help."

I wanted to tell my friend to call me back in an hour after I'd finished reading the paper, but there was an urgency in his voice and I was sure that something had gone terribly wrong there. "What's the problem?" I asked.

"I...uh...don't know if I can explain it," he said. "Just trust me when I say that of *all* the people in Hong Kong, you're the one best suited for the job."

I threw some clothes together and had Reggie take me to the MTR station, so that I could take the train to the airport. When I arrived, I couldn't believe what I saw.

There, parked at the terminal closest to the road, was a spaceship.

It was massive, the size of several aircraft carriers, and took up the majority of the landing area with its bulk. It was round, but looked more like a sandwich, with a smooth, silver top and bottom, and elaborate interior crammed in between, with what looked like several levels. The three legs it had landed upon came out of the bottom portion of the ship and looked like the bases that one might find under a bridge.

Traffic was backed up for miles upon miles, for rumors of the spaceship's landing had already circulated throughout the city, and people of all shapes and sizes were trying to get near it in an attempt to catch a glimpse. Upon exiting the train in the waiting area, I fought my way through the crowds until Chow spotted me. He had two of his security guards wade through the throngs of people, and they pulled me into an area that had been cordoned off to keep the public out.

"Thank you for coming," Chow said, leading me at a speedy pace further into the terminal. "Things are really starting to get out of control."

"There's a spaceship on the landing pad," I said.

"That's quite an understatement," Chow said. "It landed at around ten this morning and things have simply come to a standstill. We need a solution and I hope that you're the one to bring it about."

"Well, I'll see what I can do," I said. "Have these aliens already made contact with you?"

"Contact?" he asked, a desperate laugh bursting from his lips. "Have a look for yourself."

We rounded a corner and I beheld a sight unlike anything I'd ever seen. There before me was an airport terminal filled to the brim with aliens. They were large, standing about eight to nine feet high, with rough, green skin, and three large eyes perched on their neckless heads. They grunted and growled, bearing their massive, white fangs at each other, but it didn't seem to be in an angry manner. If I wasn't mistaken, these aliens seemed to be having a good time, almost as if they were on vacation. They gazed in wonderment at all of the things around them, looking as though they'd never seen anything like what was in the airport.

"Come along, come along," one of the aliens said in English as it led a large group around to various places in the terminal. Slobber was dangling from its lips. "The next thing I'd like to show you is something the humans call a *magazine stand*. Primitive as they are, the humans actually like to read, although it is rare that they read anything of purpose or intellect. Most of the time, they read about fashion and entertainment, and in doing so, waste valuable natural resources in the process; so much so that I don't believe they'll be able to sustain their culture more than twenty or more clicks."

Chow and I watched the aliens in amazement, thinking about what might be going through their heads. "We can't seem to get their attention," Chow said. "I've tried speaking to them several times, but they ignore me, much like we might ignore an annoying fly."

"It's odd that they speak English," I said. "More people speak Mandarin in this world than English."

"Ah, but English is the language of business," one of the aliens said to me. It looked the same as all the rest of the aliens, but had a more pleasant demeanor and less green bile hanging from its lips. "Allow me to introduce myself," it said, extending its large, eight-fingered hand in my direction, "My name is Xetootablooshamo, but please, call me Ted."

"Hello, Ted," I said. Apparently Ted had only the vaguest notion regarding his own strength, for he nearly crushed my hand while shaking it. "I take it Ted is your English name?"

"That's right," he said, giving me a smile filled with sharp, smooth fangs. "I'm the organizer of this tour. And what a tour it's become! Are you the leader?"

"Leader?" I asked.

"Yes," Ted said. "Of your race. You've come to work out the details of the package?"

"Well, Ted," I said. "I really don't think..."

"It's getting on lunchtime," he said. "Is the buffet prepared?"

"Buffet?" I asked.

"We'll be requiring at least one human for each member of our party," he said. "And in the last transmission we received, you mentioned something about your younglings serving as hor'devours. Is that still on?"

Chow emitted a slight whimper as I said, "Ted, I believe you're mistaken. There aren't going to be any buffets today."

"Well, then, you must not be the leader," Ted said with a huff.

"I can assure you..."

"Please let us know when the leader arrives," Ted said. He spun on his heels and went back to mingle with the group, leaving Chow and I to talk amongst ourselves. "Apparently, someone's booked a tour," I said. "And I'd hate to see the commotion they're going to cause when they find out that they're not getting the human buffet for lunch."

"What do we do?" Chow asked, a look of panic freezing over his face.

"Well, we need to get to the bottom of who organized this trip before our 'guests' start eating the spectators," I said.

I walked over to Ted once again, interrupting his speech about aeroplanes. "...And as a further illustration of their stupidity, they rely on a highly unstable liquid, known in their circles as 'jet fuel,' to fly those bulky beasts you see just outside the window. To think that they use fossil fuels when there is so much hydrogen floating all around them..."

"Excuse me," I said. "I'd like to clear things up before it all gets out of hand. If you could just tell me who organized this outing for you, and I'll call the head office to see what's been arranged."

"Excellent," Ted gurgled. "I've been speaking with a Mr. Don Davis. He told me everything would be arranged."

"I'll give him a call right away," I said.

The minute I heard the name of Mr. Davis, it all clicked. It was just like The Conspiricetti to organize something like this, sacrificing

humans for their own gain. I wondered what they were getting in return for booking a tour of aliens to planet Earth.

Of course, as angry as I was with The Conspiricetti, it failed to help me come up with a solution to the dilemma. The aliens wouldn't tolerate being held in the airport much longer, and they all looked famished, a point made clear by the way a few of them looked at me, licking their jowls and narrowing their eyes like wolves on the prowl.

"We're in a bit of a jam," I said to Chow.

"You mean you don't have a solution to this?" Chow asked, looking deflated.

"Actually, no," I said. "I'm used to dealing with more Earth-bound phenomena. Although I've been in contact with aliens at several times in my life, in the grand scheme of things, this is out of my control."

"Well, it gets worse before it gets better," Chow said.

"What do you mean?" I asked.

He pointed out the window. "Look."

I looked up just as the whole place started to rumble, and saw yet another large spaceship landing on the tarmac. The designs were similar to the first one, but it looked sleeker, as if it could fly hundreds of times faster than the one beside it. A boarding ramp slowly lowered underneath and a giant, squid-like creature came out with its tentacles carrying it across the tarmac. It was followed by a floating brain and four other aliens similar to the ones that were currently in the terminal. They all had on uniforms and carried long sticks with large, silver balls on the end.

A wave of panic washed over the crowd of aliens, and I looked to see Ted frantically speaking into some sort of device that looked similar to a walkie-talkie. The squid

creature, the brain, and their cronies entered from a side exit, near where we were standing, and crawled right over to us. "Are you the leader?" the squid asked me.

"Uh, no," I said.

"Can you direct me to the Earth leader?" it asked.

"Well, actually," I said, feeling embarrassed, "There's more than one leader here on Earth."

The squid turned to its underlings and said, "*Now* do you see why we have to do this? They've got more than one leader. Really, their stupidity knows no bounds."

"Can I help you?" I asked.

"Yes, yes," the squid said. "Who is leading this tour of Squaddles?"

"*Squaddles?*" I asked, confused.

"Yes, Squaddles," it said. "That's the name of their race… oh, never mind. Point out the leader for me."

I pointed over to our good friend, Ted, who was cowering in a corner behind some magazines. "He's over there," I said, pointing at him. The squid and the brain looked over and got a good glimpse of Ted, who was unable to hide from his predicament.

"Xetootablooshimo," the squid said, "You've got a lot of explaining to do."

"It's not my fault," Ted said. "I was tricked. Duped! I didn't want to bring these people here!"

"Planet Earth is a Class Seven-A planet," the squid said. "I am placing you under arrest for violation of code 46483573859.34343.5343: unlawful tampering with a Class Seven-A society and destruction of their culture."

"No, wait!" Ted said, looking terrified. "I can explain!"

"Bloopord?" the squid asked, looking at the floating brain beside him. "What's your verdict?"

"Guilty," the brain said, although it communicated this

telepathically, for it had no mouth.

"Xetootablooshimo," the squid said, "The judgment has been rendered and this case is closed." It turned to the four guards standing beside him. "Get to it, men," it said.

The soldiers marched over towards Ted, each one touching the sticks with the silver spheres to Ted's head. Instantly, Ted was evaporated into a fine, green pile of dust on the floor. I was appalled.

"You *killed* him!" I said to the squid. "Right there! You killed him!"

"Please," the squid said, dismissing me. "We're not *human*. We don't kill."

"Well, then, what happened?" I asked.

"We simply evaporated him for reconstruction later on the prison planet," he said. He climbed up on a chair to address the group of aliens gathered around us. "Excuse me, people," he said. "I'm afraid there's been a mistake. We kindly ask that you return to the ship and prepare yourself for departure."

A collective groan was heard from the group as they all shuffled back to the boarding area. "Now, now," the squid said, "No grumbling. You all know the risks of getting caught and now you'll have to pay the fines." The squid turned to the brain and the soldiers who were sweeping up the dust that was, at one time, Ted. "Bloopord, underlings... we must go. They're expecting us on Perseid IV any minute now and we're running late."

They turned to walk back to their ship, but my curiosity got the best of me and I had to ask these creatures a question. "Excuse me," I said. The squid and the brain turned to look at me. "I'm very sorry to bother you. I realize that you must be busy, but would you mind explaining to me what just happened here?"

The squid glanced at the brain, and then turned to walk back to me. "Let me put it as simply as you want it to be," it said. "Your planet is backwards and small, and although it's surrounded by intelligent, sentient life forms, it is not quite ready to be visited by those life forms yet. The organizer of this tour knew that when he brought that group here, but he did it anyway, and for that, he must be punished."

"Aha," I said. "All clear."

The squid and the brain turned and walked back to their ship, and soon, the aliens were back on their way off the planet I now had a lot of work to do in covering up this whole affair...

31 "THE TERRIFYING ENCOUNTER WITH THE PANDAS" taken from Mr. Ping's Almanac, Vol. 67

Mr. Ping was taking a vacation through a bamboo forest, just outside of Kunming, China, when he first encountered the panjas. Knowing that Chairman Mao and his cronies would soon cut off China from the rest of the world, he thought he should take one last tour of the country before it lost contact. One of the stops was in Kunming, where he was hoping to spend some quiet time in the bamboo forests, taking in the beauty of the scenery and meditating on where he would have liked to have gone from that point in his life. A chance encounter with a panja changed his plans:

...As I enjoyed my noodles in the solitude of the forest, listening to the wind whip the tall trees back and forth, writing **letters**, and letting the sun keep me warm as it streamed through the leaves above my head, I heard an unfamiliar noise. It was a bit of a growl and as I waded through the thick bamboo trunks, searching for the source of the noise, I saw something unexpected.

In front of me were two cuddly pandas at play. They

were rolling all over each other in that lazy panda way, mock-biting at each other in the tall grass. In that moment, I felt truly blessed, for I'd never seen pandas in the wild before. I ducked down behind a bush and peered over the top, watching them as they rolled back and forth.

But even as I did, there was a feeling in the air that I couldn't shake. For some reason, which I couldn't explain, it all seemed like a show. Weren't pandas solitary animals? I couldn't get over the feeling that the two of these bears were performing like this for me, almost like it was a distraction.

My hypothesis was proved correct when I heard the crack of a breaking stick behind me and realized that someone was in the vicinity. I spun around to see two other pandas standing on their hind legs behind me. It was an eerie sight, for neither one of them moved or seemed to be swayed by my awareness of their presence. They just stood there, silent and calm as cows, yet undeniably threatening.

I'd never encountered pandas in the wild at such close proximity, so I was a bit unsure as to what I could do. Were they threatening? They certainly didn't *look* threatening, for how could an animal as cute and cuddly as a panda bear seem threatening? Yet, that's exactly how they seemed.

Since pandas aren't necessarily small, I figured that my best approach would be to back away from them. I was sure I could handle myself if one decided to attack, but I didn't want to hurt cuddly creatures like these, no matter how threatening they seemed.

I took a couple of steps backwards, when I realized that there were two more pandas behind me. I assumed they were the pandas I had just seen rolling in the grass, yet they, too, were standing on their hind legs. I was now surrounded by four, upright pandas.

I realized that I was being ambushed. One way or another, these pandas were after something and their threatening manner gave me pause. "I don't know what you want," I said, hoping that they'd understand me, "But I don't want trouble."

One of the pandas approached me very slowly, its arms out in front of it, trying to signal to me that it came in peace, but I knew better. As it moved forward, it pointed to my back pocket and then showed me that it was interested in my wallet.

Not only was I dealing with super-intelligent pandas, I was dealing with super-intelligent pandas that had every intention of *robbing* me!

The panda reached for my wallet and I instinctively gave his arm a whack, re-routing it somewhere else with my kung-fu skills. The panda growled at me, and then took a couple of steps backwards in shock. Simultaneously, all of the pandas began to growl and paw at the air, filled with anger.

I adopted a defensive stance, not really knowing what to expect from my adversaries. Of course, I should have expected the unexpected, for just as I adopted a threatening pose, so did they, and utilizing my vast knowledge of fighting stances from around the world, I quickly surmised that these pandas were trained in Motomuri Jujitsu, an ancient warrior art used primarily by the samurai. Then it hit me what I was up against...

...These were *ninja* pandas. And they were dangerous.

Another panda made a swipe for my wallet, this time ready for my counter-move, for as I swatted him away, he tried to grab my arm. I assume that they thought I was just another slow-witted human, but I was well-schooled in martial arts, and I quickly spun the poor

beast around by the arm, straight onto his back.

The pandas were shocked for a couple of seconds, then moved in for the attack. Jujitsu-trained, ninja pandas attacking me in the forest...It was going to be a long day...

32 TSING YI, KWAI CHUNG, SHIM SHUI PO

*Tsing Yi, Kwai Chung, and Shim Shui Po are different sections of Hong Kong, located at various points along the MTR line to Chek Lap Kok airport. Shim Shui Po is located in Kowloon, and near it is a place called Apliu Street, which is a gargantuan street market used mainly by locals that sells all sorts of strange things and pirated goods. Most of the things for sale here are secondhand electronics. Mr. Ping used to frequent Apliu Street to look for the hidden gems amongst the junk, and on one such trip, he ran into something most unexpected (as **written** in Mr. Ping's Almanac, Vol. 98):*

...I was entranced with the ancient stereo system that sat on the table full of junk in front of me when I heard a familiar voice, speaking with accented English, just down the lane. The crowd was thick, and though I tried to search out the voice to put a face with it, I could not see who it was. The accent was German and whoever was speaking was fairly annoyed with one of the merchants.

"Zis iss an outrage!" the voice called out. "You cannot possibly expekt me to gif you zat amount of money for zis vorthless piece uff junk!"

"If it so worthless," said the merchant, "Then why do you want it so badly?"

A pause, and then, "It iss for mine muzzah! She likes ze old transistor radios. Now, how much?"

"I told you the price," the merchant said.

"Nein! You are supposed to bargain vith me!"

Everything clicked in my head and I knew the obnoxious

person in the market. As I rounded the corner to get a better view and saw the fiery red hair standing straight on end, my suspicions were confirmed: Helmut Frankenstein. I elected to watch him from afar to see what he would do. His being in Hong Kong could only mean trouble.

"I am taking zis radio," he said.

"Not without paying for it," the merchant said.

"Zen how much for it?" he asked, his face as red as his hair and spittle flecked on his lips.

"I told you the price," the merchant said with a slight smirk.

"Fine," Helmut said with a huff. "I tried to play fair, but zat does nut seem to vurk vith you. I am takink ze radio."

He turned, taking the large, wooden radio in his arms, and began to walk away, through the crowd. "Hey!" yelled the merchant. "Get back here!" Helmut ignored him and kept walking. Suddenly, the shopkeeper put his fingers to his mouth and let out a piercing whistle.

Almost immediately, two large men appeared from a doorway and went after Helmut. I tried to keep my distance as I followed the three of them, and soon, the two men grabbed Helmut by the arms to stop him. "You didn't pay for that," said one of the thugs.

Helmut turned to the man and looked at him with icy eyes. "Take your hand from my arm," he said, smoldering.

"Give us back the radio and nobody gets hurt," said the thug.

"It's too late," Helmut smiled. "Because you are the vons who are goink to get hurt."

"Oh, yeah?"

"Yes."

Gliding silently through a swiftly parting crowd, I saw his help. It was Frankenstein's monster, and it looked just as it had when I'd seen it many years earlier. Its eyes were still dead to the world and it looked as if it had been cobbled together from various dead bodies, but it moved with the speed of a living being. When it grabbed Frankenstein's abductors and tossed them fifty meters down the street, I knew that this creature was trouble. I could no longer be a passive observer.

Helmut was looking glib in the middle of the street with his monster standing behind him silently. "Never touch a Frankenstein," he yelled at the two men as they struggled to their feet. Everyone was staring at him as he turned back to the merchant. "As I said," he boasted, "I'm taking the radio at my *own* price: free!"

"I think you should give that back to him," I said. He was about to walk away when he heard the sound of my voice, but then he turned back to me, every so slowly, as if he knew I'd been there all along.

"I vas vondering ven you'd show up, Pink," he said, a wicked grin on his face. "I thought I vas goink to haff to just call you directly."

"What are you doing in Hong Kong, Helmut?" I asked.

"That's *Doctor Frankenstein* to you, Pink," he said. "And my business here iss vith you!"

"So you're buying lunch?" I asked. "It will be nice to catch up with you. You'll have to get me up to date on how you escaped from prison."

"The details uff my escape are inconsequential," he said. "Vat matters iss dat ven I vas in prison, all I could think about vas the man who put me there und how I vanted refenge."

"I'm sorry I put you in prison," I said. "Still, when you try to blow up the Brandenburg gate, you can't really expect to be let go gingerly, can you?"

"Enuff uff your sarcasm, Pink," he yelled. Now zat I haff lured you into my trap, I can finally fulfill my dreams uff refenge!"

As he spoke, I saw them. It was just out of the corner of my eye and the crowd began to panic. Every previous time that I'd done battle with Helmut Frankenstein, he'd always been partnered with only one monster. Now, I saw no less than six monsters emerge from the shadows, each one cobbled together from the parts of dead people, each one with dull, white eyes, and each one as mindless as the first. They all seemed to have one goal in mind: Kill Confucius Ping.

"You are surrounded, Mr. Pink," Helmut said, laughing. "Vat vill you do now?"

I thought about it for a second and said, "I guess I'll just have to ably defend myself and then take you to the proper authorities, Helmut. Outnumbered though I may be, you're still going to jail."

He looked furious and yelled, "Kill him, my creatures! Kill him!"

And the creatures moved in towards me...

33 CENTRAL PLAZA

One of the tallest buildings in Hong Kong, Central Plaza is notorious for the lights that change color on its sides at night. The building has seventy-eight stories and is three hundred and seventy-four meters tall. It houses businesses from all over the world, one of which is that of The World Society of the Global Geographic Necessity and Permit Bureaus of the World (W.S.G.G.N.P.B.W. for short). Very early in his career, Mr. Ping heard mention of the W.S.G.G.N.P.B.W. by several colleagues and the benefits of being a member from several people throughout the world:

"...You're not a member of the W.S.G.G.N.P.B.W.?" Nigel asked me, somewhat shocked.

"No, actually," I said. "In fact, I don't think I've even heard of it."

"Oh, you really should become a member, Confucius," he said. "It really is the organization for you. The benefits of membership are numerous. You can always get a table at the finest restaurants without a reservation, you get special rates at the best hotels around the world, and there's an excellent newsletter with writing by some of the finest literary geniuses alive today."

"Really?" I asked.

"Oh, yes," Nigel said. "It's truly an elite organization and it actively seeks out people like you as members."

"Are you a member?" I asked.

"No," he said.

"Well, how do you know all of this?" I asked.

"Well, it's just what I heard..."

At the time, Mr. Ping was sure that Nigel was all hot-air and he dismissed all talk of the W.S.G.G.N.P.B.W., but then he ran into another fellow at a dinner party a few years later and the subject was broached again:

"...Yes," Mr. Swahili was saying as I approached his small group, "I spent all bloody day at those offices, but thankfully, I've gotten the last of the paperwork in."

"Ah, Confucius," Lady Nottingham said to me, giving me a peck on the cheek. "It's nice of you to join us."

"It's nice to be here," I said.

"Mr. Swahili here was just informing us of the dreadful day he's had," she said.

"Dreadful day?" I asked.

"Yes," he said. "Spent the whole day waiting in line."

"Whatever for?" I asked.

"I was turning in my membership forms for the W.S.G.G.N.P.B.W.," he said.

"The what?" I asked.

"The *World Society of Global Geographic Necessity and Permit Bureau of the World*," he said.

"Ah, yes," I said. "Someone mentioned that

organization to me once. What was it, again, that they did?"

"It's not what they *do*," Mr. Swahili said, "It's what they can *offer* you. You can always get a table at the finest restaurants without a reservation. You get special rates at the best hotels around the world. And they publish a wonderful newsletter with writing by some of the finest literary geniuses alive today."

"So I've heard," I said. "But you're not a member?"

"Oh, no," he said. "Not yet, anyway. But I've turned in all of the forms and I expect to hear back from them any day now."

In the subsequent months, Mr. Ping ran into Mr. Swahili on several occasions, and each time Mr. Ping would inquire as to how his application was going:

"...Oh, not well," he said to me when I asked him. "Really, I've had to resubmit the forms several times."

"Resubmit the forms?" I asked. "Whatever for?"

"For some reason," he said, looking off into the distance as if he was absolutely perplexed by the whole matter, "I can't seem to supply them with the right information."

"Really?" I asked. "What do you mean?"

"I don't really know," he said, utterly confused. "I can't say I understand what it is that they want. And then there are numbers. Forms. Statistics. It's quite maddening."

Naturally, Mr. Ping was intrigued, but his interest peaked when he realized that over the course of two years, he ran into seventeen people who were each trying to get into the W.S.G.G.N.P.B.W., all of whom had applications pending. With each person, he tried to get more information:

"...It sounds like a scam," I said to Ms. Gleason when she informed me that her application had been sent back for corrections. "They're probably making a fortune on application fees alone."

"Oh, no," she said. "There is no application fee."

"There isn't?" I asked.

He found out more information from Rafael in Sao Paulo in 1936:

"Well, what was incorrect on your application?" I asked.

"It's very strange," Rafael told me. "You see, the first time, I'd forgotten to fill in a section. That was no big deal, so I filled it out and returned it. This is no small feat, because they only accept applications in person."

"You mean an **applicant** has to deliver it by hand?" I asked. "You can't mail it?"

"They won't accept it by mail," he said, as if it was no big deal. "Anyway, the next time there was some other thing wrong with the application. There are so many pages, you see, so it gets confusing. Finally, after seventeen applications, I got mine rejected again. This time, it was because I spelled my name wrong. How could I have done that?"

Mr. Ping asked Jake Burgermeister about his application while visiting Los Angeles that same year:

"...Application for what?" Jake asked. "What are you talking about?"

"Your application for the W.S.G.G.N.P.B.W.," I said.

"Oh, that," he said. "No, I, uh, wasn't allowed to join." He was clearly embarrassed.

"You weren't?" I asked. "A person of your outstanding quality? Why that's preposterous."

"Something about me not having a tuxedo," he said, looking confused.

"They asked you if you had a *tuxedo?*" I said.

"Of course," he said. "It's on the application."

"Why would they ask that?"

"Well...I...I don't know," he said.

Of all of the people that Mr. Ping spoke with about this ever secretive organization, only a few of them had finalized their applications, and those that had had all been rejected. Never one to shy away from a challenge, Mr. Ping decided that he needed to be a member of the W.S.G.G.N.P.B.W. He set out to contact one of their local offices, but he couldn't find one.

...I asked around and no one had heard of it. I searched the business directories, the phone books, everywhere that I could think of, but no one had any mention of the W.S.G.G.N.P.B.W. I was starting to think that I was out of luck, when I walked right past the W.S.G.G.N.P.B.W. Offices located three blocks from Victoria Harbor. I was sure that I'd walked by this place a thousand times and nothing had been there. Yet there it was, seeming to appear from out of nowhere. I walked right in and got an application, the sight of which shocked me. It was seventy-two pages, front and back. When I arrived home to thumb through it, I realized how difficult it was. Lots of intricate questions about finance, geography, history, and politics, plus strange things like drawing a picture on certain pages based on a subject given. Still, I had nothing of particular importance to do that afternoon, so I set about filling out the application. A week later, I finished...

Mr. Ping took the application into the W.S.G.G.N.P.B.W. Offices on January 27th, 1936 and forgot about it entirely. It wasn't until 1947 that he received a notice back from them telling him he'd filled out his application incorrectly, and had to resubmit it in its entirety. He filled out a new one and sent it, only to receive a letter back from them three months later, informing him that it was still incorrect.

...It would have been easy for me to simply give up, to forget about the whole organization and be done with it, but that was not my style. Every six months for the last fifty years, I have received a notice from them informing me that my application was incorrect and that they needed more information. I was going to keep submitting the application until I was either dead or the organization no longer existed. I was not going to let them beat me...

On December 28th, 1999, sixty-three years after submitting his first application, Mr. Ping received a letter from the W.S.G.G.N.P.B.W.'s offices in Hong Kong, located in Central Plaza, detailing that he had finally been accepted into the group and that he was to come to their offices to pick up his membership package. The letter read:

Dear Confucius Ping: Congratulations on earning a membership with the World Society of the Global Geographic Necessity and Permit Bureaus of the World. As a member of the World Society of the Global Geographic Necessity and Permit Bureaus of the World, you'll be entitled to all kinds of benefits that you won't find anywhere else. You'll get a table at the finest restaurants without even needing a reservation, you'll get special rates at some of the finest hotels around the world, and you'll receive our newsletter with writing by some of the finest literary geniuses alive today. Please stop by our offices located in Central Plaza in Wan Chai to sign your membership forms and pick up your membership card. Sincerely, Boris Boris President, World Society of the Global Geographic Necessity

and Permit Bureaus of the World.

Feeling excited about finally receiving his membership, Mr. Ping rushed down to Central Plaza to get his card, but was dismayed to see that the offices were, in fact, closed for the holidays. He would have to continue his wait.

34 THE PEAK

Also known as Victoria Peak, The Peak is the highest point on Hong Kong Island. Offering spectacular views of the city on one side and an endless ocean view on the other, The Peak is the place Mr. Ping has called home since the twenties. Ping Manor rests atop a small plot of land overlooking Victoria Harbor and houses most of the artifacts that Mr. Ping has collected over the years. The value of the land that Ping Manor rests upon is extremely high due to the prime real estate overlooking the harbor and the scarcity of land on the island in general. Because of this, wealthy investors and land developers have consistently pestered Mr. Ping about selling the property, as detailed in the following excerpt taken from Mr. Ping's Almanac Vol. 96:

...I first ran into Malcolm Tan while taking my morning constitutional through Plantation Road on a bright, crisp, spring day. As I was now getting on in years, I could no longer take the long jogs up and down the old Peak Road, so I chose to spend my mornings taking a brisk walk along the old roads and trails at the top of the mountain.

As I rounded the bushy corner on my way back to the mansion, I saw three sleek black limousines parked in front of my gate, with several men in business suits all following one particular fellow back and forth as he strode up and down the concrete wall, peering through my fence as often as he could. I sighed, knowing exactly who this fellow probably was and

what an ordeal it would be just to get back inside my house.

"Yes, yes," the man said to the others that were following him around, one of which was dutifully taking notes. "Yes, this is it. This is what I've been looking for. Make the calls, Chow. Make the calls."

"Yes, Mr. Tan," said one man. I assumed he was Chow as he pulled a phone from his pocket and began to make some calls.

"Is there anything we can do to make this easier for you, Mr. Tan?" asked another fellow.

"Well, it's irrelevant when it comes to my desire to purchase the property, but it would be nice to make sure the demolition company is ready to rip the house down before the end of the week. That reminds me. Call the architect and have him flown up here immediately to start working on plans for the new house. Tell him to cancel all his other projects. He's working for me now."

As I walked up towards the gate, I was stopped by a couple of burly fellows. "I'm sorry," one said, his hand holding me back. "You're not allowed through here."

"I beg to differ, young man," I said, "But this is *my* house and I believe I am allowed through here."

The burly men exchanged looks and simultaneously pulled out their phones. "Yes," one said. "There's someone here..."

"He looks suspicious..." said the other.

"Claims to own the house..." said the first.

"We can take care of him if you like..." said the other.

"No need, no need," said Chow, who was talking to them on the phone even though he was only ten feet away. He hung up his phone and approached me with a pleasant smile. "Mr. Ping, I presume?" he asked, shaking my hand.

"That's right," I said.

"It's a real pleasure to meet you," he said. "I am

Chow Woo. I represent Malcolm Tan's legal affairs. I was just trying to get in touch with you."

"Were you, now?" I asked. I never liked dealing with lawyers like Chow. They were always duplicitous and conniving and willing to sell a person out to the highest bidder.

"Yes, I was," he said. "Mr. Tan is currently evaluating properties for purchase here on the Peak and we were quite impressed with your space."

"Mr. Tan?" I asked.

"Malcolm Tan," he said. "He's a real estate developer. Tan Tower? The Golden Lotus Building? Uptown Plaza? These are just a few of Mr. Tan's properties."

"I'm sorry, but I've never heard of him."

"Never heard of him?" he asked, looking genuinely shocked. "Perhaps you've seen Mr. Tan in such magazines as *Savvy Billionaire? Super-Mega-Corporation Monthly?* Or *Business Corporation Investor Weekly?*"

"I don't really read those types of magazines," I said.

"Really?" he asked, completely at a loss for words (probably a first for a lawyer such as himself). He quickly snapped out of it and said, "Nevertheless, we'd like to make an offer on the property."

"Oh, I'm very sorry," I said, having given the same speech to hundreds of rich investors over the years. "The property is not for sale."

"Well, I'm sure that once you see our initial offer, you'll be more than willing to..."

"It was a pleasure to meet you, Mr. Woo," I said, walking past him. "Perhaps we'll meet again someday."

"But Mr. Ping," he said, "I think you'll be very interested in our offer."

"No, I won't," I said over my shoulder. "Good day to you."

I tried to make it to the gate, but I knew that my journey would be much harder than that, and Mr. Chow Woo was not the kind of person that could be easily dismissed. "Mr. Ping," he said, catching up with me, "Surely you'll just entertain an offer."

"I don't think so," I said. "This property is mine and it is not for sale. End of story."

"But Mr. Ping, you'd be foolish not to listen to..."

"No, Mr. Woo," I said, interrupting him, "You'd be foolish to keep trying to buy this land after I've given you my answer. Goodbye."

Mr. Woo was left a bit dumbfounded, for I'm sure he'd never before encountered someone who wasn't willing to sell out. Though my confrontation with *him* was complete, a new adversary appeared on the horizon in the form of Mr. Tan, himself. He approached me filled with the cocksure swagger of a man who *always* got what he wanted, and his voice was brimming with the arrogance of money.

"You must be Mr. Ping," he said, extending his hand to shake mine. "Malcolm Tan."

"Hello," I said, trying to get past him. "If you'll excuse me..."

"Mr. Ping, I am very interested in your property," he said, standing in my way.

"I know you are," I said. "But it's not for sale."

"I'm willing to offer you an extraordinary sum of money..." he said, but I interrupted him.

"Let me emphasize again, Mr. Tan, that this property is not for sale."

Mr. Tan laughed at the thought, confident in his abilities. "Mr. Ping, I like a man who knows how to play hardball. You're a savvy businessman. I like that."

"It's not for sale," I said.

"Name your price," he said.

"It's not for sale," I said.

"*Everything's* for sale if the price is right," he said, winking at me.

"Goodbye, Mr. Tan," I said.

"Ping," he said, looking at me grimly, "I don't think you understand who I am..."

"Of course I understand who you are," I said. "You're a man with too much money and privilege. You're a man who thinks that it's your birthright to own what you want, treat people how you please, and do whatever you want to do. You're a man who worships at the altar of money and will step over any unfortunate soul who might impede your progress to what you believe is your destiny. You are a man whose sole emotion is greed, an emotion that is never satisfied and never ending. I have politely informed both you and your lawyer that this property is *not* for sale. All of your offers, deals, and threats will fall upon deaf ears, for I have no interest in selling my house."

Because he was a man of privilege, surrounded by yes-men and those sycophants who would tell him anything he wanted to hear to remain in his good graces, Mr. Tan smoldered in his place, filled with anger at my insolence. It was the same look that I'd seen on the faces of every single person who wanted to buy my property, as it was impossible for them to understand the fact that I had no desire to sell my land. "You're making a huge mistake," he said, approaching me in an intimidating manner. "I don't think you know who you're dealing with."

"Unless you're secretly a shape shifting alien from the planet Xauron Five, I think you're *exactly* who I think you are," I said. "Good day, sir."

I turned to walk away, but he grabbed me by the shoulder and spun me around. "No one turns their back on Malcolm Tan," he said.

Suddenly, Mr. Tan rose from the ground, his face filled with surprise as Reggie lifted him up with one hand. He turned Mr. Tan back and forth as if he was observing some strange insect and trying to decide on the best way to eat it.

"I was just out for my morning constitutional, Confucius. Is there a problem?" Reggie asked, his voice low, husky, and threatening.

"I don't know," I said. "Is there a problem, Mr. Tan?"

"No!" Mr. Tan said, his face filled with the fear at the sight of Reggie's sharp fangs.

"What do we usually say to pushy real estate developers, Reggie?" I asked.

Reggie lifted Mr. Tan up to his face, close enough to get a good whiff of yeti-breath, and said, "The house is not for sale."

He gently put Mr. Tan back down on the ground and Mr. Tan scrambled back to his car, followed by his entourage. "You haven't heard the last of me, Ping," he yelled. "This place will be mine!"

"It was nice to meet you, too," I said, as I watched them drive away.

"Say hello to yet another thorn in your side, Confucius," Reggie said.

"Sad but true," I said. "I'm sure that this won't be the last time we hear from Mr. Malcolm Tan."

"He had bad breath," Reggie said.

"Most billionaires do," I said, and we went back to the mansion for a cup of tea...

35   MR. PU'S AUCTION HOUSE

One of the premier antiquities dealers in Hong Kong, Mr. Pu also runs the world famous Mr. Pu's Auction House, a business that deals only with the finest things for which the world's wealthy elite are willing to bid. Located in Wan Chai, Mr. Pu's Auction House specializes in toys and trinkets for the wealthy. Some of the most notable items they've sold in the last ten years were diamond-encrusted nose hair clippers, jade toilet seats, and original paintings by Xao Lu, the

nine-year old son of Cynthia Lu, hotel magnate and founder of the chain of Luxury Hotels and Spas *around the world.*
Every Friday night, the Rolls Royces and Mercedes stretch around the block, waiting to drop off their high-caliber clientèle at the Auction House, and credit must be given to Mr. Pu for making his auctions more of an "event" than a business. Tabloids regularly publish pictures of the most notable clients at the auctions, and it has truly become the place to be "seen." Mr. Pu spares no expense when hosting his clients, and the after-auction Friday night parties have also become notorious for the well-to-do.
But even as the wealthy flock to Mr. Pu's business, the dark underbelly of his practices are concealed from their view (or so one would believe). To the average person on the street, Mr. Pu would seem to be a harmless antiquities dealer with a savvy business sense, and would pose a threat to no one. He smiles for the camera, donates money to local charities, and coddles his clients; but beneath that cheerful facade lies the cold, black heart of a ruthless businessman, one who has always been willing to do anything to be the best of the best and the number one antiquities dealer in the world.
He will send his underlings to the most dark and dangerous places to search for antiques, regardless of the danger it may pose to them; he'll steal from museums and personal collections just to add antiques to his own collections; and he'll swindle governments out of millions of dollars to get the better deal on certain items. He'd even kill to get certain people out of the way of his empire.
An example of his remorseless crimes would be when he sent a dive team to go in and steal the treasure of the Tiburon lying at the bottom of the Atlantic Ocean while the real, cash-strapped salvage team slept. There was also the time when he swindled young Billy Weaver out of his

inheritance of Spectacular Comics number one, a comic book worth over half a million dollars, by telling the poor nine year old that it was a fake. And of course, there is the alleged, but never proved, story of how he romanced eighty-eight year old Agatha Mills out of her centuries-old family jewels by getting her to sign them over to him on her deathbed.
Mr. Pu has stated clearly that there is nothing he wouldn't do to be the greatest in his business. Yet, there is one thing that has been a thorn in his side over the years, and that is the existence of Mr. Ping, whose own, personal antiquities collection far outrivaled Mr. Pu's in value, eccentricity, and historical significance. Because of this, Mr. Ping has been Mr. Pu's sworn enemy for decades.

36   MR. PING VS MR. PU, taken from Mr. Ping's Almanac, Vol. 38

Mr. Pu's jealousy over Mr. Ping's wealth and antique collection has known no bounds over the years, and it is because of this jealousy that Mr. Pu has done everything within his power to end Mr. Ping's life in the hope that he might get at the vast fortune located inside Ping Manor. Mr. Pu has sent numerous teams of cat burglars into the manor, hoping to steal some of the goodies, but all of those teams were thwarted. He's hired werewolves and manta rays to kill Mr. Ping, but none have been able to do the job. He's tried bribing politicians and police officers to arrest Mr. Ping, but none of it worked. He even tried to bribe Reggie with a steak at one time, unaware that almost all yetis are vegetarians. The two common threads in all of these campaigns are the facts that all of them failed, and all of them were idiotic.
Both Mr. Pu and Mr. Ping had known each other ever since they were both young relic hunters, the difference being that Mr. Pu was out in search of things of monetary value, while Mr. Ping was simply looking for the unusual, with

acquisition of antiques being a nice byproduct of his searches. *Their true rivalry began in the jungles of what is now Vietnam (then known as French-Indochina), where Mr. Ping was on a quest for the Holy Stones of Nak.*

While there, he encountered Mr. Pu in a small cafe located in a small coastal town called Hoi An. Mr. Ping had just had a particularly wild adventure locating the stones and was beaten and bruised from battling the Rock Creatures of Nak that guarded the stones. Little did Mr. Ping know that he'd been followed the entire time by Mr. Pu and his team of henchmen, and while Mr. Ping had a relaxing cup of tea that day, Mr. Pu decided to get what he thought was rightfully his:

...Well, well, well," a voice said over my shoulder. I would have turned to look at him, but my neck was incredibly sore, so I simply stared straight ahead and drank my tea. "If it isn't the infamous Confucius Ping."

A man of well means came and sat across from me at my table. His suit was entirely white, with a matching fedora that he wore cocked over his forehead. "Do I know you, sir?" I asked. It hurt to talk.

"I don't believe so," he said. "My name is Pu. Felix Pu. I'm an antiquities dealer from Hong Kong."

Mr. Pu had a rat-like smile that filled my instincts with wariness. He seemed good natured on the surface, but there were definitely dire motives underlining this fellow's actions. I had only to wait for them. "Can I help you, Mr. Pu?" I asked.

"I realize that you don't know me, Mr. Ping," he said, "But I most certainly know you. In fact, in my line of work, yours is almost a household name. And to think, at only the age of twenty-five."

"My reputation precedes me," I said. "That's not always a good thing."

"Ah, but that's where you're wrong," he said, smiling like a jackal. "You see, we've been watching you since you left Hong Kong, Confucius."

"You have?" I asked.

"Yes, we have," he said. "We'd heard rumors that you had set out on a quest for the Stones of Nak."

"Um-hmm," I said, ready to leave.

"And apparently you've located them, haven't you?" he asked.

"Yes, I have," I said.

He glanced down at my bag like a glutton gazing at a chocolate cake. "Are they...in there?" he asked, his voice trembling. Sweat was forming on his brow and his lips seemed dry.

"They might be," I said. "**Why** do you ask?"

He snapped back to reality and looked me in the eye. "Mr. Ping," he said, "The Stones of Nak are priceless. The fact that you've recovered them is remarkable."

"Well, it certainly wasn't easy," I said, gently nudging my loose tooth back and forth with my tongue. "Unless you call battling a ten foot rock creature easy. Which, if that's the case, you could call it easy."

"That's very funny," he said, but he was concentrating too hard on my bag to laugh.

"Can I help you with something, Mr. Pu?" I asked.

He looked at me again and said, "Mr. Ping, I'm prepared to offer you one million dollars for those stones."

"Pardon me?" I asked.

"All right, two million," he said. "You drive a hard bargain."

"But..."

"Three million and that's my final offer." He looked exasperated, as if he'd never been in such a hard negotiation.

"Mr. Pu," I said, "The stones are not for sale."

"Ha," he said, ignoring me. "What else would you

like? A house? Land? Please tell me."

"Mr. Pu," I said. "The stones are not for sale."

"Nonsense," he said with a smirk. "Everything's for sale."

"These stones aren't," I said. "I went through great hardships to acquire them."

"Yes, yes, that's why I'm offering you the money," he said.

"And I had a specific purpose in acquiring them," I said.

"Who?" he asked, pulling out a piece of paper to write down the name. "Who hired you? What did they pay you? I'll double it."

"There's not..."

"I'll triple it."

"But..."

"Quadruple it."

"You don't..."

"What do you want? I'll give it to you," he yelled. "I need those stones."

I looked at this desperate man in a cold manner and said, "I'm not giving the stones to you." A tick formed in his eye as he grew silent. "You need to understand that I would never give them to someone like you," I said. "Now, if you don't mind, I would very much like to finish my tea. Good day, Mr. Pu."

Mr. Pu was so angry that he began to tremble. The brim of his hat vibrated and his fists were white with rage as he rose from the table to look at me. "Fool," he said. "I tried to negotiate, but you are a fool. I suspected you might be obstinate, so I made some arrangements." He leaned his head over his shoulder and whistled.

Five large hired men emerged from the alley and surrounded the table, each one doing their best to be intimidating as they invaded my personal space. "Oh, no," I said, sounding bored, "Five burly men meant to intimidate me. Whatever shall I do?"

"I gave you the chance," Mr. Pu said. "The time for negotiations is over."

One of the goons grabbed my arm to lift me from my seat, and although I didn't want to hurt him, I had no choice. As a defensive maneuver, I grabbed his hand, specifically his pinky, and twisted it around so as to catch the right nerves. If one is to hit those nerves in just the right way, it will send a flash of pain so intense through the victim that it will render them unconscious. As my assailant fell to the ground, the other four goons' jaws fell open in shock.

One has to understand that most fights can be won in the first few seconds, and if those first seconds are done correctly, it will intimidate your opponent, giving you an advantage. The fact that I knocked out one of Mr. Pu's henchmen by grabbing his pinky with a minimum of movement left the rest of his cronies completely flabbergasted. To follow up on my bold move, I narrowed my eyes and looked around at the rest of them, virtually daring them to try me.

"Don't just stand there," Mr. Pu yelled. "Take him out!"

His men paused for a couple of seconds, still intimidated, but then worked up the nerve to make a move on me. I quickly flipped over the table to block the advance of the first two, and then sent a solid fist into the solar plexus of another. This left me with a couple of seconds to take out the last one. He threw two, wild punches, leaving himself open to a stiff finger to the small of his throat, which cut off his wind pipe. He fell to the ground, gasping for air, as the other three came for me.

Another one swung at me and I used his momentum to jump up and scissor kick him into a table. But the move left me open and I was grabbed from behind by one of them, his arms through my arms. His partner ran over to wallop on

me while I was incapacitated. Yet, he was so angry, his punches were wild, and every fist he threw would land on his partner behind me when I ducked out of the way. After five solid punches to the face by his partner, my captor grew weak enough to let me escape his grasp, just in time to dodge the last punch, which landed squarely on his face. He fell, unconscious, to the ground.

The last goon was filled with murderous rage and threw his punches in a flurry of anger, which made them all the more easy to dodge. It took only one judo chop to the neck to drop him and it wasn't even a hard chop at that. He fell to the ground like a sack of potatoes and as I looked up to see Mr. Pu running away down the street. The bag containing the stones was wrapped around his shoulders and he was a good thirty meters ahead of me. He was moving at a good clip and I knew that I couldn't catch him, so I grabbed a coconut from a nearby fruit stand, judged the distance, his speed, and the wind, and lobbed the coconut up into the air.

Two seconds later, it fell squarely upon the back of Mr. Pu's head and he collapsed to the ground. I ran up to him, took my bag back, walked back to the fruit stand, and paid for the coconut. Then I settled my bill at the restaurant, paying for any broken dishes and property as Mr. Pu's goons struggled in vain to get back to their feet.

And as I walked home on that beautiful afternoon, I made a mental note, knowing that in the span of that five minutes, I had made an enemy for life. My neck, of course, was no better.

Oh, well, I thought...

37 THE STAREDOWN

The Staredown is an art form practiced throughout the world in many different cultures and by many different species. It can range from a "simple" Staredown

between a dominant male gorilla and another gorilla looking for its place in the gorilla hierarchy, to two gunfighters facing off in the old west, to a mother giving "the look" to her child before that child does something that they know is wrong.

The first known instance of the Staredown came as a result of a man by the name of Renaldo the Bloodletter of Spain in the 1400s. Renaldo was such an intimidating force on the battlefield that it was rumored that he'd slayed an entire army before lunch and then conquered a whole country before dinner. Renaldo's reputation was so fearsome that whole armies would turn tail and run at the sight of him, as described in the following ancient text located by Mr. Ping in France while doing research:

...And lo, the soldiers of the armies of the King of Spain did forthwith march unto the battlefields, intent on spilling the blood of the French heathens to proclaim their rightful ownership of the land. And lo, but the French heathens were fierce with their weapons, and full of righteous anger and venom, and they would not fall to the Earth with ease. And lo, then a trumpet did sound, heralding the arrival of one that be great; the one that would hold the line and surely proclaim Spain the victor on this day. And lo, the soldiers of the Spanish army did fall back, a sea of armor parting the way for one that they all held in reverence. And lo, riding a white steed through the parted warriors was he, the one of greatness and courage, the one they called Renaldo the Bloodletter.

And lo, did a gasp rise up from the mouths of the French heathens, as Renaldo the Bloodletter lifted the mask of his helmet.

And lo, did the French heathens begin to step backward as Renaldo the Bloodletter looked at them with his grim and determined visage.

And lo, did the French heathens retreat from the battlefield as Renaldo the Bloodletter stared at them with the courage of a million Spaniards.

And lo, did Renaldo the Bloodletter claim victory over the French heathens without raising his sword or shedding blood, for Renaldo the Bloodletter had defeated the French heathens with the Stare...

The Staredown spread throughout the world with the Crusades, and even became somewhat fashionable during certain battles in the Middle East, where Christian and Muslim armies would shed no blood, but simply give each other the Staredown across the battlefield, with an honor system in place for those that weakened in the face of such quiet force. However, this system of "fighting" proved ineffective when some armies would "ignore" the Staredown and slaughter the other armies, mid-stare.

As time passed, so the Staredown changed as well. It became, over the years, a more subtle form of intimidation, designed to inflict a psychological advantage over one's opponent. In fact, it is believed in

some circles to be a battle between two souls on an unseen, astral plane.

How to perform a Staredown: The rules for a Staredown are very clear and consist of one person focusing in on another person's eyes, never blinking, never wavering from their gaze. The eyes should be considered "locked" and must remain that way until their opponent surrenders. Once a person gives in to the Staredown, their opponent has the advantage, and can either inflict physical harm (a pummeling) or psychological harm (name-calling) on the other.

What to do if a Staredown happens to you: If you look up to see someone giving you the Staredown, do not look away. Most Staredowns are lost within the first two seconds. If someone is staring at you, look back at them to try to discern their meaning. Perhaps they think you're an old friend, or have some sort of romantic interest in you. However, if they are giving you the Staredown, you must continue to reflect the Stare back at them. Blinking IS allowed! However, it must be done slowly, as if the person doing the blinking is bored to tears. Quick blinks are a sign of fear or nervousness and can automatically disqualify a person. Regardless, do not break the Stare and continue until your "attacker" breaks their gaze. That way, you will not lose face.

The Staredown can be intimidating. However, as long as a person knows how to handle themselves in such situations, there is nothing to worry about.

38   PESTO, GNOCCHI, AND   TOMATO SANDWICHES

REGGIE'S RECIPE:
INGREDIENTS: 2 ½ potatoes, peeled, 1 ¾ cups of flower, pinch of salt, 6 sprigs parsley, 1/3 cup pomerola, garlic clove, olive oil

DIRECTIONS: Steam the potatoes (don't boil them, you bloomin' fool!) for around 40-45 minutes or until you can stick a fork in 'em without encountering any resistance. Then mash the little buggers while they're still hot. Knead the salt and the flower into your big hump of potatoes so that it forms a dough. Make little nasty snakes, about as thick as a finger (not a yeti finger...a human finger), then cut the snakes into one inch pieces. Score the pieces crossways with a fork.

Then you cook the gnocchi (and it's called "nee-okkee," not "notchee"!) in boiling salt water till they rise to the surface. Take 'em out.

Meanwhile, take six sprigs of parsley and heat them with 1/8 cup pomerola and crushed garlic in 2-3 tablespoons of olive oil. Simmer, then remove that vampire-killin' garlic. Work it all into the gnocchi, dunk in helpings of pesto, slap it between some Italian flat bread and chow down like there's no tomorrow. Mmm-tasty!

39   See   Appendix on Kathmandu

40   PAPPAW THE LION

The statue over the dinner table in the dining room of Ping Manor happens to be that of a longtime friend of Mr. Ping, Pappaw the Talking Lion. Mr. Ping met Pappaw in 1923 while on safari in Africa. The following excerpt is from Mr. Ping's Almanac, vol. 24, in which he details his first encounter with this mighty and majestic lion:

...Whereas most foreigners in this country were intent on killing wild game to add to their trophy collection, I had no desire to do such a thing, for to kill another creature for sport seemed petty, appealing to the baser nature of mankind. I was intent on simply seeing the wildlife and since this was my first trip to Africa, it seemed like the most appropriate thing to do. We were in the bush, crouched down amongst the tall grass of the savanna, just two-hundred meters from a herd of gazelle, watching the pride of lions as they stalked the gazelles. Little did we know that we, too, were being stalked. Our guide was intent on the lions, his eyes dark, his brow furrowed, as he peeked through the grass. The look on his ebony face was one of caution, as if he expected the worst, being so close to such wild game. His look said that he knew of the dangers of our situation and was very conscious of our safety, both his and mine.

"They've disappeared," he said.

"Who?" I asked. "The gazelle?"

"No," he said. "The lions." He scanned back and forth across the horizon, looking for some sort of sign about what had happened. "This is very unusual," he said, pulling me backwards. "We must leave this place now."

"Are we in danger?" I asked, following his crawl through the tall, brown grass.

"Every minute we are on the savanna, we are in danger," he said.

We made our way through the grass quickly, desperate to escape from the unseen danger that lurked around us, but just as we reached a clearing, our luck had run out. "We must run through this clearing to the other side, and then make our way to the river," he said. "Run as quickly as possible."

Mwembe ran first, moving quickly and scanning the horizon for danger, his red robe flowing in the twilight. I took a deep breath and took off, but just as I did, a large, male lion ran out from the grass and stopped, dead-center in front of me. I ground to a halt in the dust, my heart racing, my breathing accelerated, and sweat pouring from my brow.

The lion just stared at me, its amber eyes looking fierce, and its stance taut, ready to leap on me at any time. I was cornered. "You want a trophy?" the lion roared. "Here I am! Take your best shot!"

I was speechless. I didn't know that lions could *speak*. I'd seen other animals speak in my lifetime, but all under extraordinary circumstances. The last thing I expected on this safari was to run into a *talking lion*, let alone one that spoke *English*.

"I said, 'Take your best shot!', animal killer!" the lion said. He pawed at the ground in a menacing fashion.

"Excuse me?" I asked.

"Where are your guns, human?" it said. "You're just flesh and blood, like all the rest of them without your weapons. Weak and worthless."

"I have no weapons," I said. How I managed to say anything, I'll never know. My whole body was trembling with fear.

"You have no weapons?" the lion laughed. "Ha! I at least wanted a challenge!"

"I believe you've mistaken me for a hunter," I said, holding up my hands in an attempt to calm his anger. "I am not a hunter. I have no desire to kill any animals."

"If there's one thing I've learned," the lion said, "It's that humans are not to be trusted in any way, shape, or form. Come on out, my friends!"

At the lion's cue, several more lions emerged from the grass. I was completely surrounded and feeling hopelessly intimidated. "Nice work, Pappaw," said one lion.

"Are there any others?" asked another.

"Just the guide," Pappaw said. "Don't worry. I know where his camp is. We'll go for him later."

"Mwembe means you no harm either," I said, trying to watch all of the lions simultaneously. "We're simply

out here to celebrate the glories of the natural world."

The lion looked at me seriously for a couple of seconds before a slight grin washed over his face. Soon, the grin turned to a smile, and the smile turned to a giggle, and suddenly, the whole pride of lions was laughing at me. "Beauty of the natural world?" Pappaw said, barely able to breathe between laughs. "That's rich! Oh, that's really funny."

I couldn't help but be offended by their laughter, and when in situations like this, I tend to speak my mind. "What I said is true," I said. "And I don't particularly find your amusement at my love of nature to be pleasing."

The lion tried to suppress his giggles and said, "You know what? We're not going to kill you tonight. You're no hunter. You're just an odd, odd man. Love of nature? Ha!" The lion turned away from me and casually strolled back into the grass. "Come along, fellows," he said, before turning back to me. "If I see you with a gun in these parts," he muttered, "You'll be dead before you even know I'm there..."

Pappaw was part of a rare pride of lions known for their ability to talk, a tribe that was hunted to virtual extinction in the thirties. Eventually, Mr. Ping became a crusader for the pride, winning the grudging respect of Pappaw and his followers. Both Mr. Ping and Pappaw had several adventures throughout Africa in the following years, including their battles with the supernatural female lions known as the Ghost and the Darkness, the British Colonial Army Zombies, and the dreaded Ape City Invasion of 1962...

..."Make a break for it, Ping," Pappaw roared. "These apes take no prisoners!"

Everywhere I seemed to look in the jungle, I could see the black bodies of the gorillas shuffling quickly through the forest. They moved with such precision, like a well-trained army, so as to take the camp by storm. I heard Pappaw's roars back behind me and the screech of injured gorillas in his wake. I assume that he aimed to take out as many of the creatures as he could before they reached the camp.

I ran as fast as I could through the thick undergrowth, sweat pouring from my brow, my clothes heavy and damp from the jungle humidity. Try as I might, I was too slow to stay ahead of the apes, and I knew that they would reach the camp before me. Like a miracle, Pappaw emerged from the brush, running beside me in the jungle.

"Jump on my back!" he yelled, and without hesitation, I grabbed onto his wiry mane and held on for dear life as he darted through the forest. I could feel his strong muscles underneath my body as he moved with grace through the thick foliage.

"What's happening, Pappaw?" I asked.

"An invasion," he said between breaths. "Ape City has long felt threatened by human encroachment and now I guess they're no longer being passive players. They're going to take out your team's camp, and I fear they may have even more ambitious plans."

"You mean we're being invaded by the apes?" I asked.

"That's right," Pappaw said...

Throughout the years, Mr. Ping and Pappaw stayed in touch. Pappaw survived the plundering of the savanna and the severe decline of wildlife on the continent, with thanks being given to Mr. Ping, who personally purchased huge tracts of land, which helped him to establish a game reserve upon which the last of Pappaw's pride could live in freedom. Eventually, age caught up with Pappaw, and during his final days, he spoke with Mr. Ping about his life:

"...I've lived a good life for a lion," he told me. He gazed out over the grasslands of the savanna, thinking, perhaps, of his youth, when he was able to travel for days across the land that he called home. "Perhaps too good of a life," he continued. "My brothers and sisters out there have suffered untold injustices at the hands of man, while my pride lived in relative luxury on this grassy plain."

"But don't forget what you told me," I said. "'This game reserve is a prison,' you said. You were quite bitter about being forced to stay here."

"True," Pappaw said. "But I was unable to see the wisdom behind it all. Because you had us come here, you have ensured the survival of my pride, where we would have almost certainly been extinct by now if we hadn't come. For that, Confucius, I thank you."

"You don't have to thank me, Pappaw," I said. Then I took a moment to look at my friend, to see the map of age that had been etched across his aging face. For a lion who had lived as long as he had, and seen the things he'd seen, he was still remarkably fit. His muscles were strong and powerful, and his brow was noble and full of wisdom. It was the tired look in his eyes that betrayed his age, along with the scars and the flecks of gray in his bountiful mane. He was a lion that was truly as noble as his species' reputation, and in that moment, I was very proud that he was my friend...

Pappaw passed away shortly after their final meeting, leaving his son, Patrice, in charge of the pride. Patrice is still their leader to this day, and had remained close friends with Mr. Ping. The statue in the dining room is a marble recreation that Mr. Ping had created by a sculptor to celebrate the life of Pappaw and the good that he brought to the world. Two sculptures were created, one for Ping Manor and the other for the entrance to the

Pappaw Memorial Game Reserve in Tanzania.

41 COLONEL SAVAGE AND THE RE-ENACTORS, taken from Mr. Ping's Almanac, Vol. 84

The recreation of famous Civil War battles in the United States is a very popular pastime amongst historians and at various times of the year, men and women from all over the country (and sometimes the world) converge on certain historic battlefields, decked out in authentic clothing from the years 1860-1864, doing their best to faithfully recreate the battles of the American Civil War. These re-enactors are quite meticulous in their detail, using the same rifles, costumes, and even language that was used at the time period, and they take their pastime quite seriously. In the late 1980s, Mr. Ping traveled to the United States to witness one of these recreations and encountered something he never expected.

Michael Savage was a high school teacher from Sticklyville, Indiana who took these recreations quite seriously. He had an old, Confederate uniform made from the actual fabric of the time period, a genuine, Confederacy-issued rifle, and an encyclopedic knowledge of the players and battles of this terrible time in history. The U.S. Civil War was his livelihood and he went to all of the major recreations every year.

One of his favorite things to do was scour the battlefields with a metal detector, searching for bullets, belt-buckles, or buttons from the time period that might have been buried under the ground, waiting to be discovered by a collector. On the night before a major recreation, he made a major discovery in a far corner of the battlefield. Excited at his find, he quickly uncovered the sword of a Confederate officer still in its sheath and in pristine condition after over a hundred years of being buried. But instead of turning the sword over to the U.S. Parks Department as he should have, greed overwhelmed him and he kept the sword for himself, wanting to use it the next day in the recreations. What he didn't know was that it wasn't so much that he found the sword as the sword found him, for the shining piece of metal held a deep, dark, dangerous secret that would play out the next day...

...The weather that day couldn't have been better to sit out on an open field and enjoy a historical recreation of a famous battle of the Civil War. The sun was at a bright, early morning angle in a perfectly blue sky, and the field was a fresh, deep green. I had spent a great deal of time over the last few months researching the Civil War, so I expected a lot from the recreation that was about to take place.

To bide time before the big battle, I wandered amongst the participants, making casual conversation about what they felt their role was in the battle and admiring them for their knowledge and love of history. It was around this time that my eye was drawn to a particularly twitchy-looking fellow standing by himself at one end of a wooden fence. His face was drenched in sweat and he had very dark circles under his eyes. I took it that he was either quite ill or very tired. "Are you okay, sir?" I asked.

"What?" he asked, looking at me as if he was greatly annoyed that I would dare to talk to him. He was a member of the Confederate army, with his gray suit and cap, and he clutched the sword on his hip as one might clutch their wallet in a crowded, dangerous place. It certainly wasn't my place to judge this fellow, but I'd seen enough erratic behavior over the years to know that something was wrong with him.

"Well, I don't mean to pry. It's just that you look a bit queasy and I wanted to make sure you were okay."

"I'm fine," he said with a huff. I shrugged my shoulders as he walked away.

I had to keep telling myself that I'd come there as a tourist and not as an investigator, so I went back to the side of the battlefield and resumed my comfortable seat in the shade, a place well-suited to watch the fictional blood and gore that was soon to be spilled in front of me.

At just past noon, the battle began and I started to get a good sense of the scope of this recreation. I'd only mingled with a few of the re-enactors that were encamped near me, but there were many more that I didn't see. As the mock-battle began, I realized that this was a serious recreation and that there were thousands of men on this battlefield. I also realized that it wasn't all fun and games, for as the battle took place, these men did their best to convey the horrors of warfare in whatever way they could.

After a couple of minutes, the group of re-enactors closest to my viewing area entered the battle and I realized something was wrong. They looked confused and disoriented. Every other group on the field knew exactly what they were doing, but this group seemed lost, as though they didn't know where they were.

It was at that moment that I saw the twitchy fellow again. He rode up behind his men on a large, beautiful white steed, carrying his gleaming silver sword above his head. The sword was practically glowing. I knew that something was amiss, and because of prior experience, I was convinced that glowing swords always spelled trouble.

All of the re-enactors' eyes were fixed on the fellow on the horse and his glowing, white sword, as he rode back and forth in front of them. It was almost as if they were all hypnotized.

"Over a hundred years ago," he yelled. His eyes were passionate, full of life, and simply listening to the warm, powerful timbre of his voice seemed oddly convincing. "A hard and proud group of men, not unlike yourselves, fought great battles to separate from the Union and keep the government's nose out of their business. They lost that war to the Union. But times have changed. We have changed. It is time to rectify the misdeeds of the past and create the Confederacy that great men like Robert E. Lee and Andrew Davis had in mind." He narrowed his gaze, looking deep into the eyes of his subordinates. "But there's only one way to do it," he said. "And that way is to use sheer force. Can we do it?"

"Yeah!" cried the men, each of them fired up by the speech.

A burst of light came forth from the sword, a pulse so powerful that it knocked down everyone within a hundred yard radius to the ground. That is, everyone except the soldiers closest to the twitchy fellow. As I climbed back to my feet after the concussive blast, I saw that all of the soldiers looked energized. They had created a perfect battle formation and each of the men in their gray suits looked hardened and angry, ready for battle.

"Are you ready, men?" the man on the horse yelled.

"Sir, yes, sir!" they yelled. Their voices were hoarse and full of fire.

"Then by all that is glorious in the south," he yelled, "Prove that you are worthy to be citizens of the Confederacy!"

The men turned, and with hearty battle cries, they ran towards the other soldiers on the battlefield, But they ran not just for the Union soldiers in blue, but also for their comrades in gray.

"Form a line," yelled the man on the horse. "Form a line."

By now, the other participants in the reenactment had stopped, all of them staring in wonder at the hundred or so Confederate soldiers that were standing across the field from them, forming a perfectly straight firing line and aiming their muskets at their adversaries. "What are they doin'?" asked one man.

"Somebody's always gotta go and mess things up," said another, shaking his head.

A wave of panic washed over me as I watched the Confederate soldiers load their rifles, ready to take aim. I could not sit idly by and watch this horror unfold, so I took off as fast as I could, running for a magnificent brown horse that was tethered to a nearby tree. I mounted the horse, kicked it hard, and took off in the direction of the soldiers.

"Run!" I yelled, catching the attention of the threatening Confederates. "There's something wrong! Run for your lives!"

Apparently, the Confederate soldiers' leader took notice of me and quickened his pace. "Ready!" he yelled.

"Run!" I yelled, heading straight for their leader.

"Aim!" he yelled. "Fire!"

An explosion of smoke and flint roared forth from their guns and suddenly, the other re-enactors on the field knew exactly what the trouble was, for they heard the whiz of the metal musket balls fly by their heads. "That was a warning," the man on the horse yelled. "Next time, we shoot to kill."

"They're usin' real bullets," one of the other soldiers said.

"This is crazy!" said another, backing away.

"Reload!" the Confederate leader yelled.

"They're firin' again," said a re-enactor. "Let's get outta

here." Soon all of the soldiers on the field were running for their lives, everyone fleeing from their positions in a panic.

"Ready! Aim!" yelled their leader, but he was too late, for I was on the scene. I rode my horse straight into the heart of his firing line, sending Confederate soldiers in every direction, running for safety, and disrupting their murderous ways.

"What are you doing?" I yelled as the soldiers tried to regroup away from me and my horse. "You could kill somebody using live rounds."

Unfortunately, the Confederate soldiers were the least of my concern, as I saw their leader riding for me, full speed, with his sword raised above his head, ready to swipe. A nosedive from the horse was the only thing that saved my head from being lopped off. I jumped to my feet and turned towards their leader.

"Nice move," the man said, "But you're just wasting your time."

"I believe you're mistaken," I said. "Who are you and what in the world do you think you're doing?"

"My name is Colonel Michael Savage and I am a decorated member of the Confederate Army, under the command of General Robert E. Lee and the leadership of our honorable President Andrew Davis."

"Huh?" I asked.

"I am fighting to secede from the United States of America and the federal government that insists on stepping on the rights of the individual."

"Uh, I think you're taking this reenactment a little bit too far," I said. "Robert E. Lee and Andrew Davis have been dead for over a hundred years, now. And the Confederacy lost the war."

Colonel Savage smiled at me and said, "Oh, no. The war was never lost. You see, we

were only biding our time. For us, the war never ended."

I looked into his eyes and saw a deadened quality about them, the same mindless look that most of his troops had, and I realized that this Colonel Savage fellow was suffering from some sort of hypnosis.

"Mr. Savage," I said.

"Colonel Savage," he said, sneering at me. "I am an officer and you will refer to me with respect, or I will have you shot."

"I'm sorry, Mr. Savage," I said, "But I don't believe you're a Colonel from the Confederacy. You look more like a janitor from Toledo."

A fiery rage boiled under his skin and he turned to his soldiers, saying, "Form a firing line!"

As his troops moved into position across from me, forming two perfectly straight rows, with the group in front kneeling below the back row, I said, "This is the 1980s, Mr. Sausage. Not 1863."

"Ready!"

"You've got some sort of problem, Mr. Savage," I said. "Let me help you."

"Aim!"

It was then that I realized my luck may have run out, for I was standing across from over a hundred men dressed as Confederate soldiers that had been hypnotized and deluded, all of whom were aiming their rifles at me. *This can't be good,* I thought...

42 "THE STRANGE AND MYSTERIOUS BAT CREATURE OF NEW YORK CITY" taken from Mr. Ping's Almanac, Vol. 56

When he looked at the headlines in the New York Tribune on December 14th, 1954, Mr. Ping knew that his time in New York City would be anything but relaxing: "Mysterious Bat Creature Strikes Again." Over the previous six weeks, there had been a series of crimes being stopped throughout the city; robberies, burglaries, and kidnappings, all brought to a sudden end by the appearance of a strange, bat-like being that removed these criminals off the street.

This creature inspired both fear and adulation in the people of the city. Most people were terrified that a giant bat was running around the city at night, while just as many people were quite *happy that someone, or something*, was taking a stand against the criminals. Reading the descriptions of the creature indicated that he was between six and nine feet tall (depending upon who one spoke with) and had a wingspan of almost thirty feet, which it used to swoop down from the sky to stop the crimes. *"Its eyes," said one criminal, "Dey wuz, like, glowin' yellow or somethin'!"* Another victim of the bat-creature informed the paper that his assailant had claws on its hands and feet, and let out a screech so horrible that it could shatter windows for miles around. There was no way that Mr. Ping was going to turn down an adventure like this, much to the dismay of Reggie, who had just come from doing battle with The Director and was looking to relax:

"We're *what?*" Reggie asked as we walked into my hotel room.

"We're going to go try to find the Bat Creature," I said, taking a sip from my tea.

"Wow," Smelts said, examining my room. "Check out these digs. You got yourself a mighty nice suite here, Confucius."

"Really, Mr. Ping," Reggie said, "We've got a table for three reserved at Le Maison Bleu et la Steak y Frites. It's the hottest restaurant in town. It took me *months* to make these reservations."

"You don't have to cancel the reservation, Reginald. I can go out by myself," I said.

"No, no," Smelts said. "We'll go."

"Smelts!" Reggie said, his hands on his hips in an annoyed manner.

"Really, I can't take another visit to one of those frou-frou restaurants," he said before turning to me to say, "Reggie's been on this fine dining kick ever since we got to the U.S."

"It's so rare that we come here," Reggie said, pleading his case. "I wanted to sample the *cuisine.*"

"Yeah, yeah," Smelts said. He picked up the paper and examined the headline. "Bat creature, eh? You think this is for real?"

"There's only one way to find out," I said.

Of course, having said such a thing, I had absolutely no way of knowing how, exactly, to find this creature. After all, how does one lure a reclusive, vigilante-like Bat Creature out of hiding so as to ascertain the reality of its existence? I didn't know.

We tried wandering through crime-addled neighborhoods, but it seemed that no criminal had any intention of making victims of an eight-foot tall yeti and a crocodile that walked upright. We tried simply staking out a rooftop in the boroughs in which the Bat Creature had been seen, but this idea merely provided us with overwhelming tedium and boredom. After six days of wasting our precious vacation time looking for the Bat Creature that prowled the night, we eventually decided that it was time to give up the search.

"It doesn't exist, Confucius," Reggie said. We were having dinner that evening on the veranda of the hotel overlooking Central Park as the sun went down. "It's just a figment of some reporter's imagination. It's got no basis in reality."

"I beg to differ," I said to him between bites. "I think that this creature *is* real and I think it's a *man*, not a bat."

"A man?" Smelts asked. "A man with a thirty-foot wingspan? You know, sometimes I think you've gone a little cock-a-doodle-doo after that time you spent in the Congo, young man."

"Perhaps," I said, but even as I said it, we heard a familiar sound. It was the sound of struggle and we looked over the railing of the veranda below us to see a man being shoved to the ground as a petty thief smacked him across the face to steal his wife's purse. The man quickly fled off down the street to escape the scene of the crime.

The rich patrons of the restaurant scoffed at what was happening, but did nothing to help the young couple. "Look at what this city has become," one person said, shaking his head.

"Criminals are everywhere nowadays," said another.

"Somebody should do something about that," added a third, but it was the last voice that I heard, for I was already climbing down the fire escape to catch up with both Reggie and Smelts, who had jumped over the side of the veranda. We were on our way to stop this criminal, the three of us running at full speed through the busy, nighttime streets of the city.

"He hung a right," Reggie yelled to Smelts, who quickly ducked down an alley to help apprehend the man.

I struggled to keep up with Reggie, whose large legs could carry him a lot faster than mine could, and I was about twenty meters behind him when a shadow fell over me from above. I looked up to see it swoop down from the sky, gliding above the street swiftly as it moved past us, bent on the same target that we were after: the purse snatcher.

"What in the world is that?" Reggie yelled from up the street as he saw it glide over him.

"It's the Bat!" I yelled, and that was truly what it looked like. Its giant wings spread almost the width of the street and it flew gracefully until it came to a stop and the wings retracted themselves.

By now, the thief was running as fast as he could, for the giant bat had put the *fear* into him, but contrary to what I though would happen, the Bat just stood there in the street. The light was poor and I was unable to make out anything about the creature until it jerked in place a couple of times. I saw some gleaming piece of silver fly out from under its wings, straight at the thief, who was now almost thirty meters ahead of it.

The silver projectiles whizzed straight towards the criminal's head, spinning around and around as they flew through the air before slamming into his cap, rendering the thief unconscious. Then the Bat just stood there. Reggie approached the creature before I did, walking up to it gingerly and saying, "Nice bat. Take it easy, bat-guy."

The bat-creature simply sat there, slumped over, with two large, bat-ears sticking out from the top of its head. Yet as soon as Reggie got close, it shifted its position and turned to him. It was then that I realized that the large wings were actually plastic and formed some sort of drooping, protective shield.

Reggie approached the Bat as calmly as he could, hoping not to alarm it, but it was in vain, for as he approached, the Bat's eyes suddenly glowed yellow and it sprang from the ground like a frog, all the way across the street to a fire escape on the side of a building. I saw that when it jumped, it trailed it's plastic "wings" behind it, almost as if they were not wings at all, but more of a cape.

"What'll we do, Ping?" Reggie asked, looking at the Bat, covered in shadow and perched on the fire escape, observing us.

"Follow it, Reggie," I said.

Apparently, the Bat didn't realize that I was there, for its yellow eyes quickly turned towards me. Realizing it was outnumbered, it began climbing the fire escape and it was in that moment that part of the secret was revealed.

The Bat wasn't a *bat* at all. The Bat was a *man*.

What I'd believed to be wings was a cape, and he had hidden in shadows to avoid being perceived as anything but a menacing bat creature. Yet as he ran up the fire escape to get away from us, I saw, plainly, that it was a man running away from us and not some mysterious, supernatural.

I feared that we were going to lose him, for he had the great advantage of distance over us as he climbed ever upwards, but just as he reached the top of the building, he raised his arm, and with a powerful overhand throw, tossed a sort of bat-shaped boomerang straight over to another building and attached a rope line to it. We were halfway up the building when he swung from the fire escape, around the corner of the other building.

A swinging Bat failed to sway Reggie from his task, for he simply jumped over the side of the fire escape, falling three stories to the ground, and renewing his chase after him. I, of course, had to climb down the more traditional way.

I rounded the corner to see Reggie at the other end of the alley, with the Bat swinging above him, trailed by his long, black cape. He suddenly swung to the ground and stood, facing Reggie. Reggie slowed his pace and began to approach the Bat very cautiously. "Look, mate," he said. "We don't wanna hurt you."

The Bat didn't move. It just stared at Reggie with its glowing, yellow eyes.

"We're just trying to find out what, exactly, you are," I said, approaching behind Reggie.

"I am justice," the Bat said in a deep, husky voice.

"Okay, I get it," Reggie said. "You're justice. That works. And here, I thought you were just a guy running around in a Bat suit."

The Bat didn't respond. It simply stood at the end of the alley, observing us. "And who are you?" it asked. "Or should I say, *what* are you?"

By this time, I'd reached Reggie and was standing beside him in the face off with the Bat. "My name is Confucius Ping," I said, trying to sound calm and soothing. "We were simply trying to get some facts about you."

"Confucius Ping?" the Bat asked. "You write the almanacs."

"Yes, that's correct," I said.

"You've got an impressive body of work," it said. "And I assume that your partner here is the yeti?"

"How do you know me?" Reggie asked.

"Oh, I've read the almanacs," the Bat said. "And if Mr. Ping is here, and the yeti is here, then I would assume the crocodile is here as well..."

Suddenly, Smelts jumped the Bat from behind, tackling him to the ground by putting all of his massive weight into his dive. "Gotcha, Bat-Thing!" he yelled, but the Bat was too well-trained to go down that easily.

With a graceful twist and a kick of his legs, the Bat rolled and sent his crocodile **subject** flying into a pile of garbage cans that were at the side of the alley. It quickly regained its footing and turned to look at us without saying a word. Then, just as quickly, it threw something to the ground, causing a flash of light to blind us and a wall of smoke to explode into the air.

"He's making a break for it," Reggie yelled, running for the smoke.

I followed and as we ran through the wall of smoke, we saw that our mystery man had disappeared. We searched the rooftops and all of the alleys that night, but failed to locate our prey, eventually giving up.

"I think I speak for everyone by saying that Smelts has messed up again," Reggie said as we walked back to the hotel.

"Excuse me?" Smelts asked, offended.

"If you hadn't jumped him, we might have been able to capture him," Reggie said with a huff.

"Hey, you had plenty of chances before I came along," Smelts said. "And anyway, I though it was a giant bat, and that I could wrestle it's wings to the ground. I didn't know it was a man!"

"Leap before you look," Reggie said. "That's you!"

"A big, stinking, banana-loving monkey!" Smelts said. "That's you!"

"Is not!"

"Is, too!"

"Is not!"

"Is, too!"

"Gentlemen," I said, "I would love to stay and listen to your witty bickering all night long, but alas, I must be going."

"See you in the morning for a game of tennis in the park?" Reggie asked.

"Sounds good," I said, and I was off to my room to retire for the evening.

It was late that night in my room when I awoke to a strange feeling. Something was wrong. It was a feeling that some sort of hijinks were happening. I reached for the light when I heard a voice call out, saying, "Don't waste your time."

My eyes quickly scanned the room, just in time to see the two yellow eyes of a figure standing in the dark corner of my suite. It was the Bat.

"Excuse me?" I asked, feeling a bit vulnerable, having been caught in bed.

"Don't waste your time turning on the lights," he said, still in shadows. "I've unplugged them all."

"How did you get in here?" I asked.

"Never leave a fifteenth story window open," he said. "You never know who or what might climb inside." He sat down in the chair by the balcony and said, "I have some questions for you, Mr. Ping."

"And I, for you," I said.

"*I'll* be the one asking the questions," he said. "And *you* will answer them."

Even late at night, taking orders from someone else perturbed me, especially when the person issuing the orders was dressed like a bat. "Do not forget," I said, "That you are in my room now, and as a common courtesy, should not speak to me in such terms."

"You're absolutely right," he said. "I apologize. Now, tell me why you're in New York City. Is there something going on here that I should know about?"

"And if there was," I said, "What makes it your business?'

"This is *my* city," he said. "If there's trouble, I should know about it."

"You should?" I asked. "Why?"

"Because I am its protector," he said. "Because I strike fear into the hearts of criminals who prey on the weak and innocent. I've had enough of the crime here and I'm doing something about it."

"A noble pursuit," I said. "But don't you think it's wrong to take the law into your own hands?"

"If I don't, who will?" he asked. "The crime rate here in the city has already dropped by sixty percent since I made my first appearance. The sight of a giant bat dropping down from the sky to stop these common thugs is enough to make most

of them change their ways. Now, I ask you again, before we end this conversation: is there trouble in New York City that I should know about?"

"No," I said. "I was passing through the city and, having seen you pasted all over the papers, I thought I'd do my best to find out what your angle was."

"Good," he said, getting up to leave the room.

"Just a moment, sir," I said. "You seem to know a lot about me, and I still know very little about you. What in the world possesses you to dress as a bat and fight crime?"

"I have my reasons," he said. "And my reasons are none of your concern."

"Fair enough," I said, before warning him. "I hope that our paths do not cross again, sir. You seem to be on the side of good with what you're doing, but there's a thin line between good and evil when a person takes the law into their own hands."

The Bat said nothing as he opened the balcony doors and dove over the side, disappearing into the night. I was sure our paths would cross again.

Our final night in New York City had us attending a grand gala of the Global Society of New York City, a club that had many branches all over the world, with memberships that had to do with providing aid in non-profit work. I was receiving an award for my work with orphans and Reggie and Smelts were to join me as guests of honor. Sharing our table on this grand evening was the mayor of New York, his lovely wife, and a good portion of the city council.

The evening was a splendid affair in a grand ballroom at my hotel, filled with black tuxedos and striking evening gowns that complimented the warm ambiance of the room. Glittering chandeliers hung from the ceiling and the centerpieces on each table were a rainbow of muted maroons and blues. I was having a great time speaking with the mayor and his wife, but Reggie and Smelts felt a bit perturbed at the whole affair and the way the "elite" of New York went out of their way to avoid the yeti and talking crocodile.

"Bloody upper-crust stooges," Reggie muttered halfway through dinner. "Did you see that woman pretend to faint when she saw me? She actually *pretended* to faint!"

"I believe she was looking at me when that happened," Smelts said.

"Oh, no," Reggie said. "She was clearly looking at me. She acts as if she's never seen a yeti in a tux before. I'm sure she has."

"And a mighty fine tux it is, if I do say so myself," Smelts said. "Is it new?"

"Oh, yes," Reggie said, straightening his bow tie as if he was quite proud of his outfit. "I had it specially tailored for this event. It's not every day that I get to go out on the town like this."

"Give me the phone number of your tailor," Smelts said, straightening his coat. "I believe I've put on weight. I must get this jacket refitted."

"So how do you feel about this 'bat' fellow?" I asked the mayor between bites.

The mayor rolled his eyes. "He's a menace," he said. "I'll acknowledge that the crime rate has gone down, but it's giving people the impression that the police aren't doing their job. Fighting crime is a major task and it won't be long before the criminals start venturing out into the world again, because they will eventually lose their fear of the Man-Bat creature."

I was about to ask the mayor how the police chief felt when a crash was heard above us and several men slid down

through the skylight, guns a blazing, all the way to the floor at the bottom of the ballroom. A panic ensued and everyone burst from their seats to run for the exits, but all the doors to the ballroom were blocked by still more of the men, all of whom were dressed in black and held machine guns. They had a complete lack of fear.

Reggie and Smelts were both ready to strike in an instant, but the danger to the average person was too great, and I waved them off, hoping to get time to reevaluate the situation. I quickly counted sixteen well-armed men holding what appeared to be well over three hundred hostages, and I assumed that the police that had been hired for the evening had already been subdued.

Just as I was calculating the best way to take out these thugs, a grand series of trumpets echoed through the hall, as if introducing a king to the throne. The ornate doors at the far end of the ballroom opened and in walked two men carrying large machine guns. They walked in formation, goose-stepping along with great precision before parting to the side to let the "guest of honor" into the room.

Behind them walked a most hideous fellow, decked out in a red and black tuxedo that was so garish and bright that it almost made my eyes hurt. His skin was pale, almost white, and he had flaming, orange hair, covered by the hat of a medieval fool in a king's court. His cheeks were painted red and his mascara-covered eyes had an insane look about them that made me fear for the safety of everyone in the room.

"Who's this chump?" Reggie muttered. "Happy the Clown?"

"He's going to be *Un*happy the Clown when we're finished with him," Smelts said.

"Greetings to the elite of New York City," the clownfellow yelled as he climbed up

on top of one of the large, round dinner tables. He moved in a flamboyant, stagy manner, as if he was a vaudeville performer playing to the back row of the theater. "It's my unfortunate duty to inform each of you that you have now been taken hostage. My name is *The Jester,* and I will be making the ransom demands for the night. Really, it's a *pleasure* to be in control of you this evening and I hope that my demands are *quickly* met, for I'm sure that there's *more* than one of you that needs a pottybreak."

"Now, see here," the mayor said, rising from his chair. "You can't just barge into this place and start making demands! I'm the mayor of New York City!"

The Jester whipped out a large, red, plastic gun from his jacket and pointed it at the mayor, who instantly froze in his tracks. "Bang, bang," the Jester said, and as he pulled the trigger, a tiny flag popped out of the barrel that said the same thing.

Just as the mayor breathed a sigh of relief, the Jester pulled the trigger again, but this time, it actually fired. A bullet flew straight over the top of the mayor's head, removing the toupee he had pasted there. The mayor tried in vain to cover his bald head, but it was no use. The toupee was long gone. "Well, well, well," the Jester said, blowing smoke from his gun, "It looks as if the mayor isn't naturally curly after all, is he?" Most of the thugs laughed at the joke in classic henchmen fashion. "Any others want to play the big shot?" the Jester asked. "Because I've got *plenty* of bullets and flags in my gun. Plenty!"

I leaned over to Reggie and muttered, "I'm going to go out on a limb here and say that we're dealing with a madman here."

"That's stating the obvious," Smelts said.

"We're going to make our move, ASAP," I said. "Smelts takes the left, Reggie takes the right, and I'll go after this 'Jester' fellow."

"Right-o," Smelts said, smiling.

"Gotcha," Reggie said, rubbing his hands together with excitement.

"On three," I said. "One, two…"

Suddenly, a loud crash echoed through the ballroom and we all looked to the roof to see *The Bat!*

He moved like lightning, using the element of surprise to drop to the floor. With great precision, he whipped several of his silver, bat-shaped boomerangs at as many of the guards as possible, rendering a fair portion of them unconscious, but he was unable to hit them all, for a panic ensued and everyone began scrambling for the exits amid a cacophony of screams, overturned furniture, and breaking glass.

"Reggie, Smelts," I yelled over the noise, "Try to get as many of these people to safety as possible."

"Right, chief," Smelts said.

"Let's go!" said Reggie.

I looked over to see the Jester observing the Bat under his brow, as if he was horribly angry at him for ruining his evening. Still, he seemed far from intimidated and immediately pointed at him, yelling, "Take out the man in the cape! The *man-bat!* And do it *before* I lose all of my mirth!"

Immediately, those thugs that were still standing took aim at the Bat and, without a bit of care for the fleeing crowd, fired their machine guns across the room at him, whipping up a mess of broken dishes, shattered glass, and shredded centerpieces. I assume that the Bat realized that people's lives were in danger, so instead of dodging

the bullets, he raised an odd shaped gun he'd pulled from his belt up to the sky and fired. An arrow with a rope attached embedded itself in the ceiling and suddenly retracted, lifting him up towards the roof quite quickly. The gunfire followed him up as he swung around and landed on a balcony overlooking the room.

"A *bat!*" the Jester proclaimed. "I'm being upstaged by a man who dresses like a *bat!* Where is the *justice* in this world?" Paying no attention to the gun battle and hail of bullets ricocheting off of the walls, he simply walked around in circles, oblivious to the goings on around him, looking as if he was lost in his own, bizarre little world.

Meanwhile, I had taken out at least three of the gunners and had my sights on a fourth, when I saw the Bat throw a smoke grenade into the center of the room, filling a large swath of the ballroom with thick, black smoke, and just before the visibility was reduced to near zero, he threw yet another of his silver boomerangs at the light fixtures, wrapping a wire around them and bringing them crashing to the ground with one hard tug. The room was suddenly dark.

Judging by his past antics, I assumed that the Bat worked better under the cover of darkness, and with the chaos and gunfire and smoke filling the room, I could barely see my hand in front of my face. "You're making it too *easy!*" the Jester yelled into the nothingness. "Take the man *out!* He's dressed like a *bat* for pity's sake! What kind of grown man dresses like a *bat?*"

I kept a wary eye as I ducked to the ground. Bullets were whizzing all around me, as most of the Jester's goons were simply firing blindly in hopes of hitting something, but as time dragged on, the gunfire grew more random, more

sporadic, until it eventually stopped altogether. The Bat had single-handedly taken out the rest of the Jester's goons.

"What is *this?*" the Jester yelled into the darkness. "All of you morons have been incapacitated *already?* I hired you because you're professional assassins! You're certainly not getting a bonus from *me!*"

"It'll be hard to write bonus checks from jail," I said, standing behind him.

"Who in the blue blazes are *you?*" he asked. Up close, his clown-like appearance was even scarier and his crazed eyes darted all over the place as if he could barely focus his attention on me.

"I'm Confucius Ping," I said. "And you're about to surrender."

He pulled his red gun from a side-holster and pointed it at me. "Bang, bang," he said. "It's all it takes to stop you, noodlehead!"

"You can't stop both of us," the Bat said. The Jester spun around to aim the gun at him.

"Oh, this isn't fair," the Jester said. "I'm a stickler for planning and yet nothing is working according to *plan!* I should have factored in being confronted by a Chinese guy and a man dressed as a bat! Of all the luck!"

He pretended to cry, putting his arm to his face as if he was filled with unspeakable woe, but it was only a ruse, for he quickly spun around and fired three shots at the Bat before turning the gun on me. Yet even though he was quick, he wasn't as quick as either of us, and we both easily ducked out of the way. He fired until the click of his gun signaled that the chamber was empty and then he threw the gun to the ground in disgust.

"Well, well," he said. "It's certainly been nice chatting with you, but I really *must* be going."

He turned to run, but the Bat pulled a whip from under his cape and cracked it around the Jester's feet, sending him flailing, face first, onto the ground. He spun the whip up over a beam and jerked it upwards, leaving the Jester hanging upside-down. "You can't do this to me!" the Jester yelled. "I'm an American *citizen!* I have *rights!*"

"Yes," said the Bat. "And the first right you have is to remain silent." He tied a cloth over the Jester's mouth to shut him up.

"Now, look here, Mr. Man-Bat!" the mayor yelled. He was walking through the smoke-filled room with a rather large contingent of police officers and was focused on our Bat-friend. "What makes you think you can just barge in here like this? Do you realize the property damage you've caused?"

The Bat just ignored him, finishing the task of tying the Jester's hands with rope.

"You're under arrest, boyo," the chief of police said, whipping out his handcuffs. "You won't be dressin' like a bat where we're takin' ya!"

I was completely at a loss. Most times, I like to consider myself on the right side of the law, but I felt strongly that the mayor and the chief of police were making a major mistake. Yet, the Bat operated outside of the law, which wasn't to be tolerated either.

Then I had a sudden realization: Perhaps there weren't enough people acting outside of the boundaries of life. Most people followed the rules and did exactly what they were told, never questioning the establishment, never stepping over the line, never believing in an issue so much that they would risk every part of themselves to make it right.

The Bat was clearly out to do good, and if he stepped outside of the norm to get the job done, then that was fine by

me. The police, after all, had always been in the city, as had been crime. If a man wanted to get dressed up as a bat and fight crime in his own way, who was I to stop him, so long as he never hurt the innocent?

So, with a new attitude, I stepped between the police chief and the Bat before trouble happened. "I'm sorry, chief," I said, "But I can't let you do that."

"Ping," he said, sticking his finger in my face, "You ought ta know better than to get in my way, after the las' time you rolled through this city. Yer lucky I don' arrest you yerself!"

"Until this man actually commits a crime, I'm going to have to stand between you," I said. "This isn't a p.r. move that's going to happen while I'm here."

Suddenly, the two exit doors at the back of the ballroom burst open and two more of the Jester's thugs came flying through, only this time, they were completely unconscious and the barrels of their guns were bent around their necks. They flopped to the ground and were quickly followed by Reggie and Smelts, both looking rather chipper after having blown off a little steam. "Greetings, all," Reggie said. All eyes in the room were on him and the talking crocodile, and they both looked rather embarrassed at the attention.

"Look," the chief said, turning back to me, "Either I arrest *him* or I arrest the both... huh?"

The chief went silent, looking behind me. As I turned around, I realized that the Bat was gone, nowhere in sight. He'd used Reggie's entrance as a cover to escape. Try as we might to find him, we couldn't. "I'm gonna remember this, Ping," the chief said. "The day *you* let the vigilante get away."

"You were standing right in front of me," I said. "I'd say that it's both of our faults."

"Don't push me!" the chief said, walking away to supervise his men as they took the criminals away.

As Reggie, Smelts, and I walked down the nighttime streets of New York City later that evening, we spoke of many things, including the strange events that had just transpired. "I, personally, think he's quite mad," Reggie said, speaking of the Bat.

"Mad?" Smelts asked.

"Why, the bozo is completely *daft!*"

"What do *you* think, Mr. Ping?" Reggie asked.

"Yeah, Confucius," Smelts said. "What do you think?"

"I think that people are too quick to judge others and the two of you should *know* that," I said. "If something is different, one shouldn't ostracize it like it's a monster. One should welcome it and make it feel comfortable. At least, until we figure out what its angle is."

"Well, well, well," Reggie said to Smelts. "Looks like we've got a little grumpy gus, here." They were laughing at my lecture.

"Thanks for the warning, *mom*," Smelts said, and they continued laughing. And so, the first of our many run-ins with the Bat concluded. I was sure we'd see him again..

43 TIBERIUS CAESAR
THE ENTRY FOR TIBERIUS CAESAR HAS BEEN REMOVED FROM THIS BOOK. PLEASE CONSULT *ACCLIMATED SPOOKS, LIGHT, & POWER* FOR FURTHER INFORMATION REGARDING THIS SUBJECT.

44 MADAME HOOKWORM
One of the more dangerous and dastardly of Mr. Ping's arch-enemies, Madame Hookworm was, and still is, wanted around the world for a wide variety of crimes, including her most famous

act, the theft and ransom of the Eiffel Tower in Paris. Although Mr. Ping managed to thwart a great deal of her evil endeavors, he was never able to bring her to the proper authorities for arrest, and she remains at large to this day.

Having been taunted and teased almost all of her life because of her strange appearance, Madame Hookworm, then known as Mamie Hookworm, grew to hate all of mankind and made it her life's goal to rob the world of its beauty, just as the world had robbed her of her own. Most of the crimes she has committed, aside form the more obvious ones of embezzlement, theft, and extortion, have involved the defacing of some sort of public landmark. The theft of the Eiffel Tower being the most obvious of her many crimes, she has also made attempts to dye the waters of the Great Barrier Reef in Australia a dull green (a plan thwarted by Smelts early in his career), tried to burn down the great Sequoias of Redwood National Forest in California, and tried to cover the Empire State Building in New York City with a fresh layer of gooey concrete, amongst others. One of the most memorable things about Madame Hookworm is her looks. She is a tall, thin woman, who although quite wealthy, wears clothes that look cheap and hang lifelessly from her skeletal frame. Stricken with a rare jungle disease in the early 1930s when she was living with her British parents in Africa, her skin has remained moist and thin to this day. The veins just below the surface of her face are visible in most places, due to her almost translucent skin tone and she has a tendency to be riddled with pussy, red blisters and pimples. The virus also made the pigment in her eyes translucent, so instead of having blue, brown, or green irises like most people, her eyes are black, and although she can see quite fine, the deep indigo of her eyes can be unsettling for even the most hearty of souls.

But a discussion about Madame Hookworm cannot proceed without noting the very reason that she is one of the most dangerous villains around, for when she fell ill as a child with her dreaded disease, she also acquired a power. For some reason, still unexplained, when she was bitten by a tsetse fly, she inherited the ability to telepathically control animals. It should be noted that her ability to control these animals did not extend to your average dogs, cats, lions, tigers, or bears. No, her ability to control animals extended to a single category of creatures: carrion feeders. She was only able to control the animals that ate other dead animals. The scavengers of the planet were at her beck and call, including things like earthworms, maggots, and flies, and other, larger, animals, like vultures and hyenas. If a particular animal's main diet was dead things on the side of the road, then that animal was her friend, even going so far as to have the ability to control the very germs that lived on dead animals (an ability discovered by Mr. Ping himself, when he fell ill while confronting her). The bottom line is that Madame Hookworm is one of the most dangerous people on the planet. Her methods are obscure and her reasons are mysterious, and it was one of Mr. Ping's biggest regrets that he failed to bring her to justice in his life. One of his closest attempts was the Eiffel Tower Theft of 1962, as detailed in the following passage from his almanac:

...There it was, on top of one of the highest mountains in Switzerland. It was a sight that I would never forget, seeing the Eiffel Tower, in all of its glory, sitting on top of a snowy mountain, the gale force winds whipping at its sides, and snow from the gusts caking on its sides. And as I stood there, looking up at one of the greatest architectural achievements of the twentieth century in the least likely of places, all I could think of was: How? How did she manage to steal the Eiffel Tower? How did she manage to take it apart? How did she manage to transport it hundreds of kilometers across Europe and then reconstruct it on the side of a mountain? As evil as she was, I couldn't help but admire her audacity, her innovation, and her determination.

"That's a sight you don't see every day, eh?" Reggie said as he climbed up the rocky trail behind me. "This Hookworm lass is one serious person, isn't she?"

"She certainly is," I said, putting my goggles back on. We were lucky to have found the Tower, for she'd placed it in one of the more remote regions of the Alps, and a terrible winter had settled over Europe that year, leaving most of the mountains hidden behind cloudy storms.

I had climbed many mountains in my life, and Reggie was certainly in his element, treating our trip up the trails as more of a vacation than a job, but poor Smelts was completely out of sorts. Being a crocodile from the warm climate of Australia, he was miserable the whole way up the mountain. Even for one who walked on their hind legs, the trip up the mountain was difficult, let alone totally unsuited for reptiles like him.

"You okay, Smelts?" Reggie asked as he finally made it up the slope. By now, the blizzard was moving in with a vengeance and our vision was limited.

Smelts looked up at the Tower on the side of the mountain. "Can we go home now?" he said.

"Go home?" Reggie asked. "Are you *serious*? This is like a holiday!"

"Maybe for you, furpants, but I'm downright miserable," he said. "My tail's gonna freeze off here in a few minutes, and I ain't no gecko that can grow it back if it does."

"Oh, complain, complain," Reggie said, dismissing him.

"Look," I said, spying something towards the top of the tower. "It's a light."

Both Reggie and Smelts looked up and saw it as well. Someone was up in the top of the tower. "Do ya think she's up there?" Smelts asked.

"It's probably a trap," I said.

"Wouldn't that be a surprise," Reggie said.

We walked further on until we came to the base of the tower, where we found a most unusual surprise. The lights were on and one of the elevators was waiting on us, doors open. It was starting to get dark and we'd come too far up the mountain to go back the way we came, so we were at a crossroads.

"Well, this is ominous, isn't it?" Reggie asked.

"It certainly is," I said.

"Ominous or not," Smelts said, "I'll bet it's a whole heck of a lot warmer up there than it is down here. I'm going up."

Smelts walked right into the amber light of the elevator and turned to look at us impatiently. "Well?" he asked. "Are you two going to pitch your tents here in the freezing cold, or are you gonna come with me and get this over with?"

"He's got a point," Reggie said.

We walked into the elevator car and the doors closed automatically. Then the car began to rise from the ground, heading towards the top of the tower. "So, I've never dealt with this bird before," Smelts said to me. "Any particular thing you'd like to prepare me for?"

"Be prepared for anything," I said. "And prepare to be disturbed by what you see up there. I always find it a bit unnerving."

"Unnerving like that?" Reggie asked, pointing to the seams of the elevator walls, where little, white maggots were beginning to crawl through the cracks.

We looked around and saw that the elevator was filling with the little creatures as they made their wriggly ways through every nook and cranny. "This is gross," Reggie said as he flicked a few off of his shoulder that had dropped from the ceiling.

"Yeah, Confucius," Smelts said, looking closely at a maggot that had fallen onto his snout. "Why can't you battle villains like 'Flowerpot Man' or 'The Cheeseburger Bandit' or something like that? This Hookworm and Cyanide and Taboo stuff really makes me think I deserve some sort of hazard pay."

"You probably do," I said, observing the centipedes and ants that were now coming in the cart.

"Who does this girl think she's foolin'?" Reggie asked. "What? Does she think we're scared of a bunch of worms and bugs?"

"I can see how some people might find it upsetting," Smelts said, casually observing a horsefly buzzing around his head. "Do horseflies bite?" he asked.

"Yes, they do," I said.

"I see," he said, and he then smashed it on his nose. "So much for him, eh?"

The doors of the elevator opened onto the observation deck of the tower, where the powerful winds whipped the stinging snow into our faces. We could barely see where we were because there was so much of the white stuff, and it was much colder at this exposed altitude than I thought it would be, as the gusts howled through the air.

"Split up and meet me at , the souvenir shop on the other side," I yelled over the wind. "Watch yourselves."

As we each moved in separate directions, I noticed the vultures perched on the guard rails, all huddled together and observing me in their unique, indifferent way. They seemed to be sizing me up for their next meal. Later, I was sure I saw ghost-like visages of short, stocky dogs darting through the snow around me, which I assumed to be hyenas. Madame Hookworm had her defenses well-positioned.

"See anything?" Reggie asked as Smelts and I met him on the other side.

"Vultures," I said. "Hyenas."

"Vultures," Smelts said with a disgusted look on his face. "Can't trust them things, I tell ya. I've a right mind to walk over there and give 'em a good walloping."

We now stood in front of the entrance to the inner part of the tower, and through the frosted windows, we could see, once again, the amber light inside and what appeared to be movement. "Are you ready?" I asked.

"As long as it's warmer inside," Smelts muttered.

"Let's go," Reggie said.

With his powerful, stocky leg, Reggie kicked in the door . Immediately, a swarm of flies flew out, so many that it was like a black cloud had descended on us. The whipping wind soon rid us of that problem, as they were blown off into the snowy abyss. We came inside to see that whatever had once existed in this atrium had been replaced by the ooze and muck and filth of something rotten. It was humid inside and the smell of rotten things was enough to give a person pause. Flies were perched on every available space, worms oozed their way across the floor, roaches and centipedes and other hideous-looking insects flitted every which way and muck seemed to be dripping from the ceiling, as well as the requisite hyenas and iguanas and vultures lying around, lazing everywhere.

And there in the center of the room, lounging on a throne of some sort of brown, dried material, was Madame Hookworm herself, not at all alarmed by the invasion of her lair. She looked worse than usual, which I attributed to the cold weather. Her face was still translucent and veiny, but was blotchy and red in certain places, with an abnormal amount of whiteheads peppering her skeletal visage. I assumed that she was looking right at us, but it was hard to tell with her blackened eyes.

"Ah, Confucius Ping," she said, her voice low and tired. "Right on time."

Ever wary of the vulnerable position we were in, I kept my stance a defensive one. "Madame Hookworm," I said, "You've certainly outdone yourself this time."

"Yes," she said with a wicked laugh. "Were I the sentimental type, I'd almost say that placing the Eiffel Tower on the side of a mountain in the Swiss Alps was somewhat beautiful. Alas, no one will take in such a grand sight but you, and unfortunately, you're not going to live to tell about it. Unless..."

"The government of France has refused to pay your ransom, Hookworm," I said. "They will not negotiate."

She laughed again, lifting her skeletal frame from her chair. "Well, that's certainly a pity," she said. "It's a shame to have to destroy the pride and joy of France, but one must do what one must do." A hyena and a vulture approached her and walked by her side as she made her way towards us. "You know, Mr. Ping," she said, "There wouldn't be problems between the two of us if I could simply get what I want."

"And what's that?" I asked.

"Oh, you know *exactly* what I want," she said, and the tone of her voice, the hatred lodged inside her throat, sent a chill down my spine far worse than the plummeting temperatures outside could have. "And if you aren't ready to give it to me," she said, "Then I must be going."

She began to walk past us to the door, when I turned to her and said, "You know, we can't let you walk out that door, don't you?"

She leaned over her shoulder and said, "You have no choice, Mr. Ping," and then continued, walking

"Reggie?" I said.

"I'm on it," he said, but just as he began walking towards he, he was tackled by a group of growling hyenas and it was everything he could do to keep them off of him.

"Smelts!" I yelled.

"Right-o!" Smelts said, but even as he moved towards her, yet another black cloud of flies swarmed him and he literally disappeared in the creatures.

"Don't you see, Confucius?" Madame Hookworm said from the open door, yelling over the howling wind outside. "You'll never win. No matter how hard you try, no matter what you do."

"That won't stop me from trying," I said, and with all of my strength, I ran towards her.

The vulture at her side flew for me, its sharp talons out in front of it, ready to rip me to shreds. However, I was ready for it, and rolled to my right, swinging my heel around to drive the poor bird, head first, down into the floor.

The hyena was on me next and it was a short, stout, fierce creature. It tried to go for my legs, but I was too light on my feet for it to catch me. Its jaws snapped at me and its guttural growl was meant to intimidate, but this dog failed to have the fighting skills that I had, and when it made the wrong move, I brought my elbow down on top of its head, rendering it unconscious.

Just as I looked up, I saw Madame Hookworm disappear around the corner outside, and I turned back to Reggie. "Are you okay?" I asked.

"Just fine," Reggie said. He had one of the hyenas by the hind legs and was swatting away the others with it."

"Smelts?" I asked, looking at the black cloud in the corner.

"I'm fine," he yelled over the buzz of the flies. "They're not hurting me as much as they're annoying me. I can't see a thing. Anyway, flies are tasty. Go get the goods."

Reassured that my partners were fine, I ran outside just in time to see Madame Hookworm climb up the guardrails of the tower, leaning over the edge. "You fight a good fight," she yelled over the wind.

"Don't jump, Madame," I yelled. "It's not worth it. We can help you with your condition. There is no need to kill yourself."

"Oh, Confucius," she said with a laugh. "You have such a good heart, trying to talk the woman who just tried to kill you out of committing suicide. How noble. How idiotic."

"We can work this out," I said.

"We can't work this out," she laughed. "Especially here, because this tower is going to blow sky high any minute now. And as for killing myself? You just have to be the *stupidest* man alive. Ha!"

With those final words, she stepped from the railing, off into the thin air, plummeting towards the ground below. I ran, desperately, to help her, but was too late. Almost as quickly, I felt foolish, for as I watched her fall, I saw two large vultures swoop down, pick her up with their feet to fly away from us. Once again, she had escaped my grasp.

There was no time for regret, for there was a bomb in

the tower and I had to get my friends to safety. I ran back to the atrium to find a pile of unconscious hyenas piled into a corner, and Reggie and Smelts bent over something in a corner, working diligently.

"Reggie! Smelts!" I yelled. "We've got to get out of here. There's a..."

"A bomb?" Reggie said. "Yes, we know. We're working on it."

I ran over to find that Smelts was busy trying to defuse the bomb. There were only thirty seconds left on the timer. "How did you...?"

"Shh!" Smelts said. "I'm trying to concentrate."

"He's almost done," Reggie said, trying to be reassuring.

We watched as the clock ticked to twenty seconds, then ten, then five, then zero, and nothing happened.

"What's going on?" Reggie asked. "Why hasn't it blown?"

Smelts looked up at us over his reading glasses. "Look," he said, "I defuse *bombs*, not *timers*. And you can consider this one de-fused."

"Where's Hookworm?" Reggie asked.

"She got away," I said.

"How're we gonna tell the President of France that the Eiffel Tower is on the side of a mountain in Switzerland?" Smelts asked.

"Yeah," added Reggie. "And how are we gonna tell him that the inside of it smells like a sewer and has fourteen unconscious hyenas as watchdogs?"

"Yeah, Confucius," Smelts laughed. "How are we going to do that?"

"One thing at a time," I said. "One thing at a time..."

45 PROFESSOR BLANK'S MAN-MADE BLACK HOLE

Invented in the late fifties by a mad scientist by the name of Rupert T. Holmes, but known throughout the world as Professor Blank, the man-made black hole was invented as a deadly weapon to power the rise of Lieutenant Cyanide, now working out of Paraguay. Cyanide, having been defeated in his previous attempts to take over the world by Mr. Ping, had amassed a small army and a core group of Nazi scientists to help advance his cause, and in a preemptive move, had kidnapped Mr. Ping to keep him from interfering. The following excerpt has been taken from Mr. Ping's almanac, Vol. 61:

"...Let me show you my latest creation, Confucius," Lt. Cyanide said, his glorious white teeth seeming to shimmer in the light as he smiled proudly at his work. "Wheel it in, men," he said.

As his comrades wheeled in what looked to be a large, wooden crate covered in a red-velvet blanket, I had the opportunity to examine my surroundings. I was in some sort of laboratory, immaculately clean and white, every surface shimmering and offering a mirror perfect reflection of everything around it. At the far end of the room were very high windows, through which I could see what appeared to be the capitol building in Washington D.C. We were right in the heart of the capitol of the United States.

"What do you have there?" I asked the Lieutenant, nodding over to the covered crate. I was trying to untie the rope that bound my hands, but this time, the knots were too tight.

"That, *herr Ping*," he said, "Is what will make me the most powerful man on the planet. A weapon *so* powerful and destructive that nations will bow down, cringe at the sound of my voice, and be stricken blind by the mere sight of me." He ripped the curtain away, saying, "This is my *man-made black hole!*"

"Your *what?*" I asked.

I guess I failed to be impressed enough to meet his standards, for a very familiar tick began to form in his eye and he had to take a deep breath to help him calm down enough to answer me. "As I said, it is my *man-made black hole,*" he continued.

I heard footsteps behind me and a voice called out, "I'm disappointed, Confucius. I thought you would have been able to recognize my work."

I turned to see that the speaker was none other than Rupert T. Holmes, better known as Professor Blank. He looked the same as he had five years earlier during our previous encounter, only a bit old, graying at the temples. "I should have known," I said, rolling my eyes at him.

"*You should have known?*" Lt. Cyanide asked. "You should have known *what?* That your two worst enemies would eventually team up to see you destroyed? That we would stop at nothing until you were dead? Oh, Confucius, I agree. You *should* have known that."

"No," I said, trying to sound condescending, "I should have known that only the two of you could come up with such a lame-brained idea as a man-made black hole."

"*Please,* Lieutenant," Professor Bank yelled, walking towards me with his hands ready to choke the life out of me, "*Please* let me kill him *now!*"

"*Nein,* Professor," Lt. Cyanide said, stepping in front of him to stop his advance. "He will be dead and gone in mere moments. Don't spoil the fun."

Professor Blank continued to stare at me with crazed eyes that spoke volumes about the ways in which he'd like to kill me, but eventually, he calmed down enough to breathe easier. "Oh, how I hate you, Ping," he muttered.

"Hate is a waste of energy and time," I said. "You should practice loving kindness. So says the Buddha."

"*Anyway,*" Lt. Cyanide said, "As I was *saying,* the black

hole will enable me to conquer the civilized world in record time. Much faster than any army. And once I have done that, I can continue on my quest to create a utopia."

"The utopia-thing again?" I asked, feeling skeptical.

"That's right," he said, his eyes looking off into the distance as if he could see the world he hoped to create. "Imagine a world where *everyone* on the planet could watch the same movies or television shows. Imagine *millions* of television stations, offering news, sports, and entertainment *twenty-four hours a day*, programming beamed down from *satellites* orbiting high above the Earth, making geography and time *irrelevant*. Imagine a world where you would no longer have to cook your own food, where, if you wanted a meal, you could get in a car and drive down the street to a restaurant that served you any tasty, hot food that you wanted, as soon as you walked in the door! It wouldn't be cooked in the slow, usual way. It would be cooked *faster*. *Fast food*, is what I'd call it. But why stop there? Imagine not even having to leave the comfort of your luxury automobile to get your food. You could just *drive* up to a window, *order* what you wanted, and it would be *given to you!* You could drive *through* the restaurant to get your food. A *drive-through!*"

"Why that sounds positively *dreadful*," I said. "Your 'utopia' will never come to pass."

"We'll see," he said. "You just don't have *vision*, Confucius. No *vision*."

"So what about this 'black hole'?" I asked.

"It is what I said it is," Professor Blank piped in. "A man-made black hole. Nothing escapes it. Not even light."

"Well, how in the world can you keep it in a box?" I asked.

"I cannot give away the secrets of my trade," the Professor said, looking down at me over his glasses. "Nor would I *want* to."

"This is the prototype of the black hole weapon we will use," Lt. Cyanide said. "It's gravity is so strong that it will draw everything into it, crushing it all into its dense center. Once we unleash the power of this machine, all of Washington D.C. will be destroyed."

"Yes!" Professor Blank said, rubbing his hands together with glee. "Nothing will escape the power of my black hole. Stone, brick, steel, the marble monuments of Washington will be obliterated, all of them sucked into its powerful gravitational field. Nothing will survive."

"But eventually, wouldn't it just suck up the whole country? And then the *world?* Once you unleash such power, how can it be stopped?" I asked.

Professor Blank looked at me as though I was a fool. "Do you really think I haven't *thought* of that?" he asked. "We are tampering with nature, here, Ping. And if we are to tamper with *nature*, we must first learn to *control* nature. *We* control the black hole. *We* leave it on as long as *we* need to, and then we shut it off."

"Therefore," continued Lt. Cyanide, "We shall leave the black hole on *just* long enough to destroy Washington D.C., then shut it off. Thus, we will have made our point to the world and they can surrender to our greatness."

"And how do *I* fit into all of this?" I asked.

"Well," Professor Blank said, "We thought that since you were going to be the first victim of the machine, you should know how you were going to die."

"Oh, well, thank you," I said.

"I guess we must be going," Lt. Cyanide said. "But not before wishing you the worst of luck when you die."

"Yes, yes," I said. "The worst of luck. I've heard it all before."

Professor Blank came over to kneel beside me, motioning to the box with the black hole inside. "Once we are safely out of this room," he said, "We will switch on the black hole. It is not an instantaneous machine. It takes *time* for the gravity effect to work. At first, you will feel a slight pull in its direction. Then, the pull will get stronger, until you are drawn inside it like everything else. At some point, you will be crushed to death, slowly suffocating under the intense gravity."

"Sounds pleasant," I said.

"Oh, it will be far from pleasant," he smiled, rising to his feet again. "In fact, it should be horrible and excruciating. Good luck!"

As Lt. Cyanide and Professor Blank walked out of the room, cackling like villains form a dime-store novel, I yelled, "Wait! If you're leaving Washington, where will you go?"

"Back to our base in Argentina to plan our further conquest of the globe," Lt. Cyanide said. "After all, we have an army in wait on us there, so we must catch the three o'clock flight to Buenos Aires."

"Fine," I said, having extracted enough information from them.

"Have a nice death," Professor Blank said with a wave as they left the building.

I was in quite a predicament. As soon as they left the room, I heard a beeping sound, and a low hum filled the room. It came from the direction of the box and I could feel a strange energy around me as the gravity shifted towards me. *Well,* I thought, *I guess they weren't lying about the black hole-thing.*

I struggled with the ropes on my hands, trying to get free, but the knots were too well-tied. Meanwhile, all of this was happening as I watched the curtains slowly rise, as the gravity of the black hole kept them from falling limply to the ground. The wooden crate that contained the weapon began to quietly creak from the strain of the gravity inside of it and I watched my tie rise up into mid-air, the end pointing straight towards the box.

I struggled harder with my ropes in a desperate attempt to free my hands, but couldn't free myself as the creaks from the box turned into snaps and cracks, and the sides began to bow inward. The box was slowly collapsing in upon itself. I could feel the gravity now, growing stronger by the second, subtly pulling the skin on my face forward.

I noticed that objects throughout the room were starting to move towards the box, light things at first, like paper clips and pencils and balls of dust from the floor, but then bigger things began to move forward, like boxes, trash cans, and shelving units. I, too, could feel the effects of the gravity and it hurt. It was as if my brain were being sucked out of my nose.

When the wooden crate collapsed in upon itself, I began to lose hope. The wood compressed itself against the black hole harder and harder, virtually shrinking as it splintered into lots of different pieces under the high gravitational field. In that brief moment, I caught a glimpse of the device. It looked like a gum ball machine, with a large, black orb sitting on top of it. In the brief second that I looked at it, a sharp pain appeared in my eyeballs, as if the black hole was sucking the very light out of them.

As I looked away, I noticed my lucky break sliding across the floor. A pair of scissors from the counter had slipped across the floor and I stamped on them as they moved past. Unfortunately, I couldn't reach them and had to use my feet to lift them towards my hands. This was no simple task, as I almost lost them to gravity's pull a couple of times. Luckily, I managed to get them to my hands just as my chair began to edge, ever-so-slightly, towards the black hole.

The movement of my chair unleashed a new panic inside me, as I noticed the things at the black hole that had already been sucked towards it. They were all compressing on top of themselves as the black hole's gravity grew. I worked hard, trying to cut my bonds while the black hole moved me towards it. By now, my chair, with all of my weight up on it, was sliding across the floor, towards the hole, as were several tables in the room and a chalkboard that was upon a set of rolling wheels.

I struggled with the scissors, trying to ignore the effects of the gravity on things like my clothes and the skin on my face. It took all of my concentration, but I managed to cut myself free.

But as I tried to get to my feet, I fell forward onto my face and began sliding towards the hole. I only managed to stop myself by grabbing onto a table that was built into the floor. The gravity was growing stronger by the second and I was running out of time, for the Earth's gravity no longer seemed to have any effect. In that split second, I noticed a couple of birds and lots of leaves from trees outside stuck to the windows, as now gravity was beginning to affect things outside of the building.

Knowing that I was not strong enough to hold out much longer, I decided to make my move. I only had one chance, so with the scissors in hand, I dove for the black hole, and just as the power of the machine rammed my head into its blackness, I used my momentum to jam the pair of scissors straight into the heart of the machine below.

A strong electric shock surged through my body and my head pounded from the device's gravitational pull, but I landed the scissors in the right place and the machine instantly shut down. Things grew calm almost instantly. I took several full, deep breaths, trying to let my lungs adjust to the freedom of the Earth's normal gravitational pull. In that moment, I realized that Professor Blank's invention was indeed a horrible weapon with the potential to destroy the planet. I knew that if he and Lt. Cyanide were allowed to continue their devious ways, we would be living in an oppressive, intolerant world.

The Professor and Lt. Cyanide said they were headed to Argentina. The reality was that they were about to have a rendezvous with *me* at the airport...

46 THE EYE PYRAMID

The Eye Pyramid in Mr. Ping's hallway is a mystery to this day. It was discovered while Mr. Ping was doing an investigation into the ghosts of minutemen soldiers in Vermont in the mid-seventies. The ghosts of the minutemen are another story entirely, but while Mr. Ping was investigating an old, abandoned farm house from around 1778, he found the Eye Pyramid in a hidden compartment in the back of a stone fireplace.

...I opened up the trap door and was shocked at what I found. There before me was a three-foot high stone pyramid with a mysterious eye encased in a smaller, glass pyramid at the top. And what was completely disconcerting about it was the fact that this eye was staring at me. I would move to the right and it would follow. I would move to the left and it would watch me move in that direction as well. It was too heavy to move, so I simply sat there, staring at it for the longest time...

Eventually, Mr. Ping had the Eye Pyramid removed and secretly transported to Hong Kong . He began to see it everywhere: in magazines, books, paintings...it was even on the back of the U.S. Dollar. However, the question still remains: What is it? Mr. Ping never found out what it was or where it came from before he died.

47 "MIRROR, MIRROR, ON THE WALL," taken from Mr. Ping's Almanac Vol. 26

Mr. Ping had long heard rumors of a series of enchanted mirrors located throughout Europe, and in 1925, he went to investigate. While exploring the rooms of a decrepit, dilapidated castle in Germany, a peculiar piece of furniture caught his eye:

...There before me was a mirror, grand and ornate, clear as crystal, with an elaborate gold frame. There was nothing else within the walls of this moldy, old castle. What furniture there was was but piles of cobwebs and rotten wood, sitting in corners and suffering from years of neglect. The rooms of the establishment had long since been abandoned, and I had to climb over several obstacles merely to enter some of them. I had come to the conclusion that there was nothing of value in the place at all.

The mirror, however, was different.

It sat at the very end of one of the upper rooms, a room with no windows. It seemed brighter, more full of life than everything else I'd seen. Whereas everything else in the castle was covered with years of dust, this mirror was in absolute perfect condition, not a speck of dust on the frame nor smudge on the glass. The room in which I found it looked like the inside of a church, but where there might have been religious symbols, a crucifix or stained-glass at the far end,

there was only the mirror, as if someone had once worshiped before it.

I felt a sense of unease as I approached. The mirror seemed to be too enchanting, too alluring. The closer I got to it, the more I wanted to admire myself in it. I could feel a sense of vanity, a sense of pride in my looks that made me want to look at myself in that mirror more and more with every step towards it. It was almost as if the mirror was *calling* me.

The castle grew still and quiet as I approached, and I could feel the room grow darker when I stood in front of it, as if storm clouds had passed over the sun. With apprehension, I looked at my reflection and I couldn't believe what I saw. There I was, only better looking than I remembered myself being.

I had never thought of myself as homely or unattractive, but I certainly never thought of myself as the strikingly good-looking person that was reflected back at me. I was *handsome*. The features on my face were *sharp* and full of *power*. The clothes that I wore fit me better than I remembered. Not only that, they seemed to be sitting on a body that was much more muscular and fit than it had ever been before. My shoulders were broad, my biceps thick, and my legs stocky and powerful. The last thing I noticed was that my hair was *perfect*. It was a perfect *length*, perfect *style*, perfect *color*...everything I could ever hope for it to be.

I had the overwhelming desire to look at myself forever and were it not for a simple twist of fate, I might have. It was only the ear-shattering sound of lightning that snapped me from the daze. I don't know how long I stayed in front of that mirror, posing and preening, and admiring my good looks. When I started, it was daytime, but when I

snapped out of my haze, it was clearly night.

That snap of electrical energy just outside the castle frightened me enough to make me look away for a split-second, and in that time, I realized I'd been in some sort of a trance. Somehow, the mirror in front of me had caused me to lose track of time while admiring my own good looks. I confirmed this by looking at my watch and realizing it had been almost thirty-six hours since I'd discovered the mirror. I was tired, hungry, and thirsty, so much so that I felt weak. I dared not look at the mirror for fear that it might grab hold of me one more time.

Looking down, I notieced what I had failed to see scattered on the ground below me: the dried, skeletal remains of several people, each of them in a position not far from the one I'd been standing in.

I knew at that moment that the mirror had killed them. Each person who wandered into this room and stood in front of the mirror could not look away. Somehow, the mirror reflected what they wanted to see, just as it did with me, and they continued to look at it, unaware of time, until they keeled over dead, probably from starvation or dehydration. I felt none of these things when I looked in the mirror, thus the enchantment. This mirror was dangerous...

48 THE SPRAYING MARBLE FOUNTAIN OF CAPRIZZI, taken from Mr. Ping's Almanac, Vol. 31

An elaborately carved marble fountain located in Mr. Ping's ballroom, the Fountain de la Luna was originally located in a small village just outside Florence, Italy. It is quite large, measuring sixteen feet by sixteen feet, with several immaculate sculptures carved into it, ranging from Roman gods and goddesses, to ornate flowers and greenery. It was rumored that a young Michelangelo was the creator of the fountain, it having been commissioned by the mayor of the small village. The story told of how Michelangelo was so enraged by the pitiful attitude of the townsfolk that once he completed the sculpture, he put a curse on it, vowing that all hypocrites and liars would suffer the wrath of the Roman god Pan for their misdeeds.

...I came into the town, rounding a corner in my tiny car, to find a roundabout in the center of this small, picturesque Italian village. In the center of the roundabout was a large, beautiful marble fountain. This was not so unusual. What was unusual was that there was a crowd gathered around the fountain, looking on as a powerful stream of water seemed to be bombarding some poor fellow holding a sledgehammer in the street. The man struggled and strained to stay on his feet, the sledgehammer poised up over his head in rage, but he couldn't get near the fountain, for the powerful flow of water kept him at bay, no matter what direction he took to get at it.

"What is happening here?" I asked a local, after stepping out of my car and joining the crowd.

"That is the mayor," a bored youth said. It seemed as if he'd seen this type of thing before. "He is trying to destroy the fountain."

"Why is the fountain spraying him?" I asked.

"It does not like the mayor," the boy said.

At that point, the mayor was cursing colorfully in Italian and was soon taken off his feet by a powerful blast of water. The crowd laughed.

"Why would the mayor want to destroy the fountain?" I asked.

"Because it sprays him every time he walks by," said an old woman. "And he surely deserves it."

"Why is that?" I asked.

"Because he is corrupt," she said with a sniff. "I am over eighty-years old and have never seen the fountain spray anyone who was not worthy of getting wet. Liars, cheaters, thieves, and those that will not acknowledge who they truly are are the ones who **would** get sprayed. Not the innocent."

"I see," I said.

"The fountain knows the mayor is corrupt, the police know the mayor is corrupt, everyone knows the mayor is corrupt," the old woman said. "He thinks if he destroys the fountain, it will make it all better."

Another old man approached. "The mayor has passed a city ordinance," he said. "They are going to destroy the fountain."

"But why?" I asked. "It only sprays bad people, right?"

"Yes," said the old woman. "But it does not discriminate. Whether it is a big lie or a small lie, it will spray you just the same. If you steal a small piece of candy or a million lira, you get wet. We are all tired of it."

"But it's a beautiful fountain," I said.

"Beauty does not make up for getting soaked," said the old man. "Plus, no one in this town can ever tell a lie without getting caught and we are tired of it. For instance, if my wife wears an ugly dress and asks me, 'How do I look?' I have to tell her she looks terrible. Otherwise, the next time I walk by the fountain, it will spray me. My wife does not want the *truth*. She wants me to *lie*. It is a *choice*. I either tell the truth and let my wife hate me, or I get wet the next time I walk by the fountain. I want to lie."

"Yes, he is right," said the old woman. "The world needs lies to make it run smoothly. If you are a painter, not every painting you make will be a Mona Lisa. Some of them are terrible. But in this town, we have no artists, because they all gave up after everyone could

not lie to them and encourage them. Musicians, too. They all quit because they heard too much of the cold, hard truth. This fountain is a curse!"

"I see," I said.

I walked over to the Mayor, just as he was about to make another attempt to destroy the fountain, and said, "Mr. Mayor, I'd like to buy this fountain."

He turned to me, water dripping from his face, and said, "You're crazy! Do you not see what this fountain does? It is cursed."

"I realize that," I said. "Still, I want it. How much do you want for it?"

"Money?" he asked. "I'll *pay you!* Just get rid of it."

And so the very next day, I paid some men to box up the fountain and ship it to Hong Kong...

49 TAHITIAN LONGBOAT, taken from Mr. Ping's Almanac, Vol. 51

While investigating an entirely separate affair in the South Pacific ("The Man-Eating, Land-Dwelling Jellyfish Incident" on the Northern Coast of Australia, to be precise), Mr. Ping's plane had an unfortunate accident on the isle of Tatuahuanapooi, a small, very remote island populated solely by males and located around a thousand kilometers east of Tahiti. A bit of engine trouble forced the plane to land on the island. While there, Mr. Ping became a guest of the Tatuahuanapooi islanders, enjoying the luxury of their hospitality as he waited for some sort of rescue boat or plane to arrive. Little did he know what Chief Ooonakanockatoopi had in store for him:

"...Eat well, young Ping," the chief said, slapping me on the back in a hearty manner. One of his tribesmen walked into the far end of the long house, carrying a large plate of grilled fish, surrounded by the most succulent looking fruits I had ever seen.

I was living a dream. To crash land on a tropical paradise like this, the palm trees, the blue ocean, the gorgeous surroundings, was pleasant enough, but to be treated with such sincere hospitality by the Tatuahuanpooians was more than I could ever ask for. It was to be too good to be true.

"You must eat more, Ping," the Chief said. "More. More! Tomorrow is a very important day for you."

It was those words that sent a chill up my spine and I knew that my dream was about to be short-lived. "What happens tomorrow?" I asked.

The Chief smiled at me joyously and said, "Tomorrow you're marrying my daughter and the curse will be broken."

I almost spit out the mango juice that was in my mouth. It seemed that I was always getting myself into these odd tribal rituals, and what was worse was that the results never turned out to be very good. "I can't marry your daughter, Chief," I said. "I'm engaged to be married in my own country."

A dark cloud passed over the Chief's face and the hustle and bustle of the party in the long house came to a stop, with all eyes upon the two of us. "Look, Ping," he said. "I don't care if you've been married fifteen years and have twenty children. Tomorrow, you *will* marry my daughter and break the curse that has befallen this island. I don't care if you love her or not, and I don't care about how you feel. You'll marry her. End of story."

"What curse are you talking about?" I asked, feeling queasy.

I shouldn't have asked. The story was one of the most bizarre ones ever told to me and it answered all of my questions regarding why the island was only filled with men. It seemed that the island witch doctor had put a curse on the women of Tatuahaunapooia after getting the cold shoulder for his romantic advances upon the chief's daughter. The daughter didn't want to marry the witch doctor, so he put a curse on her and all of the women on the island, effectively turning them into monstrous she-beasts, half-panther, half-ravenous-Tasmanian-Devils. Soon, all of the women on the island became dangerous killing machines, frightening off the men. They had since learned that the women-beasts were nocturnal, so the men began to venture outside only during the day, while at night, they locked themselves in the long houses to avoid being eaten by the she-beasts.

According to the chief, the only way to break the curse was to have his daughter marry a foreigner and have her devour the foreigner on their wedding night. Apparently, I was the first foreigner they'd seen in years.

"Chief," I said, "you want me to marry your daughter so that she can eat me and break the curse?"

"That's it," said the Chief. "That's why I think you should eat up, because it's probably going to be your last meal." He laughed in a good-natured way and shrugged his shoulders as if to say the whole problem was out of his hands. "Look, I'm sorry," he said. "Would you like to meet your wife-to-be?"

This was my second mistake. I was not even remotely prepared to meet this woman...this thing...that was to be my wife. Apparently, the Chief had his men set a trap for her to expedite the curse-breaking process. His she-beast daughter was kept in a cage in the woods. There was absolutely no resemblance of the creature in the cage to a human being, at least as far as I could see. All I saw was a horribly aggressive, black-furred creature with what appeared to be four times the amount of teeth that the average panther would have, all of which were razor-sharp and looked deadly. The she-beast had a short snout, like a rottweiler, and thick shoulders. On each of her feet were four-inch-long claws that looked like they could tear through flesh like butter.

"Scary, huh?" the Chief said. At the sound of his voice, his "daughter" dove for him, stopped only by the walls of the cage as she furiously gnawed at the bars, sending frothy drool in every direction. "She's vicious, but I love her," he continued. "After all, she's my daughter."

"Chief," I said, "You can't really expect me to do this, can you? I'm not going to marry that thing...I mean...your daughter."

"I'm afraid you have no choice, Ping," he said, and I felt the spears of his guards pointed in my back. "You're going to marry her at sunset this evening..."

Through his own ingenuity, Mr. Ping managed to escape from the clutches of Chief Tatuahuanapooi, and in a desperate attempt to escape the island, he stole one of the longboats of the tribe. After a protracted chase through the waters of the South Pacific, he managed to avoid their pursuit. He paddled the longboat all the way to New Zealand, and had such an epic journey with it that he eventually had it shipped to Hong Kong. He always feared to go back to Tatuahuanapooi again, and he never knew if the curse was ever broken.

50 BLACK BARRY OF BALTIMORE, taken from Mr. Ping's Almanac, Vol. 74

The dwarf son of two giants from Siberia, Black Barry left his home in the cold plains of Russia because he couldn't stand the ridicule at the hands of the other, much larger, giants. However, even being a dwarf giant still means that he is quite tall, and Black Barry clocks in at well over nine feet, eleven inches. Barry settled in Baltimore, trying to make his living as a janitor at a public school (albeit a very tall janitor). However, the kids at the school teased him relentlessly.

After on particularly vicious series of tauntings as he cleaned up from a cafeteria food fight, Barry lost his cool and started threatening to devour the kids (yet another lesson in where bullying leads). A failed attempt to negotiate the release of the bullying children by the police sent Barry on a destructive rampage in the downtown core of Baltimore and soon the city came to a complete standstill. When word got out in certain circles that Barry was a giant, the U.S. Military came in to put a stop this his rampage. But when they arrived, they found they were powerless, for Black Barry, was seemingly without weakness.

Using jets, tanks, and soldiers, the military tried to stop Black Barry, bombing the very ground he walked on, attacking him from all angles, and leaving a trail of destruction in their wake. Barry would simply march right through their lines, destroying that which was most annoying first, and working his way down from there.

In a moment of desperation, a high-ranking military official (who was familiar with Mr. Ping's almanacs) made a phone call to see if Mr. Ping could offer some sort of help. Mr. Ping had done a small amount of research on giants, especially after his encounter with Bing Bing Click, the Giant of the Australian Outback.

The military managed to pin Black Barry down in an old warehouse and kept him there until Mr. Ping arrived on the scene:

...When I arrived, General Johnson was in a panic, walking back and forth in his tent on the street, barking orders at underlings left and right and generally looking like a man who had absolutely no idea what to do. Airplanes flew overhead and tanks rolled down the main streets of Baltimore, patrolling the area for any signs

of the now infamous Black Barry.

An underling brought me to the general, who had chewed his cigar into a mealy mess in his mouth. "Sir," the soldier said, "This is Mr. Ping. General Watson sent him."

The general looked me over, squinting at me under his hat, as if he couldn't believe that someone such as myself could offer a man of his stature any assistance. "Ping, huh?" he said, his thick, peppery mustache forming a sneer over his large teeth. "All right, Ping, what are you gonna offer me that droppin' an a-bomb on that warehouse won't?"

"I'll offer you an intelligent, informed opinion," I said. "Which is really something your weapons seem to be incapable of doing."

"Oh, a wise guy, eh?" General Johnson said, still squinting at me. "If you think this is a joke..."

"Oh, I don't think this is a joke, General," I said. "I think this is deadly serious. There's a reason that giants haven't had any contacts with humans in hundreds of years, sir, and that's because the last time they nearly hunted us to extinction. Giants, by law, aren't allowed to prey on humans anymore. We're a protected species."

The General looked at me, mouth agape, as if he thought I was the most insane individual he'd ever seen. "Did you really just say that?" he asked.

"Yes, sir," I said.

He looked at me again before yelling out the door. "Get this wacko-nut job out of here!" he yelled.

"Yes, sir," one of the soldiers said.

"Can't believe they waste my time with this..." the General muttered. "I've got situation on my hands and they send this fruitcake."

"General, I assure you..." I said.

"Get him out of here!" he yelled and two soldiers took me

by the arms, trying to force me out of the room.

They were a bit too aggressive for my standards, so I twisted around and whipped both their arms behind their backs, sending them to the ground. "No rough-housing," I said, before turning back to the General. "General Johnson, time is running out."

The General scowled at me and said, "What do you expect me to do, Ping? Should I call Goldilocks and the three bears to deal with this giant? Or Little Red Riding Hood? I hear there's a fellow named Jack that owns a beanstalk and might know how to deal with people like this."

"Your sarcasm is duly noted, General," I said. "But if you will divorce yourself from your tiny little world, perhaps we can defeat this fellow that's causing so much trouble."

"Well, how do you suppose we do that?" he asked.

"I've just the idea," I said, and I began to inform him.

Barry had about a four mile radius around him, inside of which the military was afraid to enter, so in order to enact my plan, I had to parachute into ground zero. General Johnson had arranged for a transport plane to drop me and my equipment into the area, and as I sat in the belly of the plane, parachute strapped to my back, looking at the open door and the long drop below me, for the briefest moment, I though that I'd lost my mind. What was I doing parachuting into a war zone, at the center of which was a giant? What if my plan failed? What if this Black Barry fellow gobbled me up? My doubts were numerous.

A co-pilot peeked out from the cockpit, the wool collar of his leather jacket flapping in the wind, his eyes beady and black through his goggles. He gave me a thumbs up sign to signal that it was safe for me to jump, and without hesitation, I dove from the plane, soaring through the air on the way down to the rooftops of Baltimore, hoping that Black Barry wouldn't see me and place a giant cauldron of boiling water below me. I jerked the ripcord and my parachute burst forth like a huge, wadded up sheet, and I drifted down slowly to the ground, landing on an empty street right behind the warehouse in which Barry was supposedly located.

I removed my parachute and took cover at the side of the building. The sun was going down, bathing the buildings in the glorious oranges and reds of an Indian summer evening, as I hid in the shadows, peering back and forth, looking for the first sign of danger. I circled the building twice, but I couldn't find Black Barry anywhere. He wasn't patrolling the grounds like General Johnson thought he was.

Eventually, I had no choice but to go inside and find this giant myself. I kicked in an old, wooden door on the back side of the building and ducked inside. The only thing stirring in the quiet warehouse were the glowing specks of dust floating in the sunlight that streamed in through the door that I'd just kicked open. I looked around and saw that I was in some sort of old, abandoned reception area that led further into the warehouse. An ominous, dark doorway beckoned me further into the building and I ducked inside, carefully peering around the corners to make sure that my foe was nowhere in sight. I felt fairly safe, for I knew that the part of the building that I'd found myself in was too small for Black Barry to walk through, so I moved with great speed through this wing.

I finally reached an old meeting room with a large, dusty window to one side, which looked out over the floor of the warehouse. I peered through one of the cracked

window panes, but saw no one on the floor. It was empty.

Then, two gargantuan arms burst through the wall behind me and enveloped me in their muscular grasp, jerking me backwards through the wooden supports, drywall, and insulation that separated me from the warehouse floor. Black Barry had me in his grasp and I could barely breathe.

"A SPY, EH?" he said, his hot breath just over my shoulder. "I'M GLAD THEY SENT YOU. I NEED A SNACK."

I quickly regained my bearings as the dust from the wall fell off of me in small clouds. "I'm sorry," I said, "But I'm not your snack."

Using what little leverage I had from the rubble between Black Barry and myself, I wormed my way out of his arms and rolled ten feet away to safety, quickly jumping up to a defensive position. I finally got a good look at him, discovering that he was a bit more imposing than I imagined.

Black Barry was only about ten feet tall, a dwarf by giant standards, but those ten feet were packed to the brim with thick muscle. His pinky, alone, was as big as my wrist, and his chest was as wide as a car. His black hair was thick and bushy, as was his beard, and his cold, blue eyes were practically obscured by the huge eyebrows that sat on his Cro-Magnon forehead. He wasn't a giant, but he was certainly big enough to be intimidating.

"THOUGHT YOU COULD SNEAK UP ON BARRY, DIDN'T YA?" he said. His voice had the chest vibrating density of a tiger growl.

"You're in a lot of trouble, Barry," I said. "The code of the giants forbids you from being here."

"WHAT DO YOU KNOW ABOUT THE CODE OF THE GIANTS?"

he asked, his scowl growing more fierce.

"I know all about that 'Jack' fellow and the incident with the beanstalk," I said. "And I know that because of all the trouble that sprung forth from that incident, giants are no longer allowed to mingle with humans."

"WELL, IN CASE YOU HADN'T NOTICED," he said, putting his hands on his hips indignantly, "I AIN'T NO GIANT. I'M TOO SMALL."

"You're a giant through and through, Barry," I said. "And if the other giants knew you were doing this, they wouldn't be pleased."

"I COULDN'T CARE LESS ABOUT THOSE BOZOS," he said. "BLACK BARRY DOES WHAT BLACK BARRY WANTS AND RIGHT NOW, BLACK BARRY WANTS A SNACK."

With alarming speed, he ran to grab me, but I easily rolled out of the way. He went for me again, his large arms swiping the air as he reached for me. Over and over again, he tried to grab me, but I dodged his advances each time. This only served to enrage him and soon, he began to smash whatever was in his way and toss the remnants of it at me, which meant that whatever old, rusty factory equipment was lying unused in the warehouse was being thrown in my direction.

"COME HERE, YA LITTLE RAT!" he yelled, tossing what looked to be a giant, burnt-orange piece of machinery at me. "ALL I WANTS IS A TASTE."

"Sorry, but no," I said.

I led him around as long as I could, and although I looked like a panicked frog, hopping back and forth on the floor of the building, there was a method to my madness. With every kick, jab, or throw, I was examining Black Barry for the one sign of weakness that all giants have. Each giant is different and have their vulnerable spots located in different places, like birthmarks. I always thought of it as Mother Nature's way of keeping them from being all-powerful. Yet for all of my searching, I could not find Black Barry's point of vulnerability, and since there was no visible sign of weakness, I had to resort to Plan B.

"YER A QUICK ONE, RUNT," he yelled, cornering me like a tiger might corner its prey, never taking his eyes off of me. "WHATS DO YA TASTE LIKE? I JUST WANTS TO KNOW."

"You won't find out today, Barry," I said. I found myself somewhat safe behind a facade of rusted steel girders that had, at one time, supported a rather large piece of machinery. This afforded me enough time to reach into my backpack to pull out my secret weapon.

Although Barry was strong, he couldn't pull the rusted steel apart, so he simply swiped his massive arms at me through the bars, my safe zone just out of his reach. "WHAT ARE YOU DOIN', RUNT?" he muttered. "COME ON OVER HERE AND LET'S GET THIS OVER WITH."

"Fine," I said. "Let's get it over with."

In my hands was an experimental steel cable, one that had been developed for use on suspension bridges in places with extremely violent weather. It had been discontinued once builders realized that although it was strong and flexible, it was much too expensive. Long ago, I'd purchased the remaining inventory of the cable and it was a good thing, for I was finally able to put it to use.

Scurrying like a mouse, I took the heavy lasso of steel cable and ducked out of the safety of the girders. I moved too fast for Black Barry to keep up with me, but he was still in hot pursuit. "SLOW DOWN, MR. APPETIZER," he yelled. "OR ARE YA TRYIN' TO GET ME APPETITE WORKED UP?"

I said nothing. I tossed a pink smoke bomb on the floor in front of him and the whole area was enveloped in the acrid smelling fog. I used this cover to slip close to Black Barry. So close, in fact, that I actually ducked under Barry's legs without him even realizing it. But that was the advantage I needed, for it was then that I strung the steel cord under his legs and around his ankles.

"WHADDYA THINK YER DOIN', RUNT?" he yelled. By this time, I had taken a deep breath and jumped on his back, riding his shoulders like a cowboy might ride a bucking bronco. By now, the smoke had cleared and I had a full view of what was happening. "GET OFFA ME!"

Holding on tightly, I wrapped the steel cable around his arms, wrists, and chest, whipping the gleaming silver of the steel around like a lariat, all while a befuddled Black Barry wondered what was happening.

My task complete, I did a back flip off of his shoulders, keeping the loose end of the steel cable in my hands. I stood up as Barry tried in vain to get the cable off of his body. "WHAT HAVE YA DONE?" he asked.

"Your reign of terror ends today," I said.

"NOT FOR YOU," he yelled, and he took off towards me. But even before he'd taken three steps, he fell to the ground as the steel cables tightened around his ankles.

"That's a Canterbury knot in the cable," I said. "The more you struggle, the tighter it gets."

Sure enough, Black Barry struggled on the ground, trying to free his feet, but every movement pulled the slack of the cables, and soon he found himself in a decidedly uncomfortable position. "I'LL GET OUTTA THIS, RUNT," he muttered, sounding quiet and determined. "AND WHEN I DO, YOU'RE GONNA BE FIRST!"

"Well, then, let's hope you don't get out," I said, and I turned to run for the warehouse doors, pulling the remaining cable behind me. I pulled a walkie-talkie from my pocket and said, "He's caught, sir." Then the doors at the far end burst open, revealing two, large tanks, lights blazing, engines roaring. They sped across the floor of the warehouse, straight towards me. A young soldier mounting the machine gun turret looked down at me as they pulled up. "That him, sir?" he yelled over the engine.

"Yes," I said, attaching the other end of the steel cable to a hook on the back of the tank. "Remember, full speed. Don't stop until he's hooked up."

"Yes, sir," the soldier said, and the tank roared to life, turning back the way it came and going out the doors as fast as it could.

Being dragged behind the tank, twisted in the knot of steel cables, was Black Barry. He was filled with murderous rage as he yelled, "GET ME OUTTA THIS THING! YER DEAD! I'M GONNA EAT YA ALL!"

A jeep sped up and I jumped in beside General Johnson. "Nice work, Ping," he said, as we sped behind the tanks dragging Black Barry through the streets of Baltimore. "I have to admit, I had my doubts."

"Well, let's just hope that those cables hold till he gets to the airport," I said, slightly worried.

"I guess you didn't find his weak spot, eh?" he said.

"No," I said. "And that isn't good. I will, though. I'm sure this won't be the last we see of him."

And so, Black Barry was dragged all the way through Baltimore, to the airport, where the wire was strapped to the back of a B-52 bomber. The bomber took off, Barry in tow, first dragging him across the runway, then through thin air. The pilot's orders were to drop Barry on an island, far away from human beings, until I could do more research.

Although he yelled and screamed with rage as he was dragged up into the air, I knew that he was invulnerable and that the only thing that would be hurt was his pride. The last I heard, Barry was deposited on a nice, uninhabited tropical island in the South Pacific. Black Barry of Baltimore would not take this lightly...

51 THE VENGEFUL FIRE ANTS OF MADRID, taken from Mr. Ping's Almanac, Vol. 28

While traveling through Spain during a blisteringly hot summer in 1925, Mr. Ping encountered something very unusual in the desert-like environment around Madrid. He was on his way to see Dr. Gordo at his home in the mountains and was walking along a footpath when something very unfortunate befell him:

...The path was rocky at the foothills of the mountain and the blistering temperature did nothing to make the trip any more pleasant. The heat seemed to be reflecting off of the white hot rocks and I would have been drenched with sweat were it not so incredibly hot that the intense heat managed to instantly evaporate whatever moisture was on my body.

I made my way through the shimmering landscape until I noticed something peculiar. Every time I'd been to Dr. Gordo's house, the dirt path had been clearly marked, but as I rounded the corner, I saw that where I'd thought the path should have curved around a large rock, there was no path. It looked like where the path should have been, but it seemed to be damaged, as if a flash flood had rushed through, washing dirt and debris over it.

And strangely, there was a new path that veered off from the one upon which I was traveling. A new path would be nothing particularly extraordinary in most cases, but I'd been to Dr. Gordo's home several times in my life and it wasn't really like him to go to all the work of creating a brand new path to his house. Without thinking twice, I took the "new" path and marched right around the large rock in the absolute opposite direction that I should have gone.

I would pay a dear price for it. I meandered along the path for a few meters until I came to a crevasse with loose gravel running through it. The crevasse was small, only a few feet wide, and it was clear that the path continued on the other side, so without hesitation, I walked right into it.

Before I realized what was happening, the loose gravel below my feet gave way and I sunk in, first up to my knees, then my waist, then my chest, and before I knew had the time to react, I had sunk into the gravel like quicksand up to my neck. I tried to move, but all of the tiny rocks had fallen in upon themselves, which created a vice-like grip on my arms. I was stuck.

Furious for getting caught in such an obvious trap, I began to run through a list of my sworn villains in my head, wondering who would have created this contraption. Was it the Duke of Death? The Communist? Señor Hidalgo de Guadalupe? The list was too large to narrow. My only choice was to wait and see who would pull me from this pit.

I'm not sure how long I sat there, buried neck-deep in the gravel, but I was starting to feel dehydrated from the intense heat. Luckily, I was shaded from the direct sunlight by the cliffs on either side of the crevasse, but sun or no sun, I was suffering. Just as I realized that this might be a very dire situation, I saw it.

An ant was making its way across the rocks towards me. My low proximity to the ground gave me an excellent view of the creature as it crawled up and over each of the rocks, making a beeline for me. This small, determined ant crawled all the way over to me and scrambled its way to the rock just below my chin, where it stopped and waved its small antennae in my direction, apparently getting my scent. It looked no different than any ant I'd seen before, aside from the flaming orange color of its body, and I thought that it might have been out for a stroll from the nest.

But the question was: was I watching this *ant*, or was this ant watching *me*? I continued my observations until the ant scurried down below my chin, out of view. Then I felt it trickle up my neck, and then my cheek, all the way until it came into view on my nose. Then it crawled right up onto my forehead, between my eyes, where it then stopped and continued to observe me.

I was totally and completely unprepared for the intense pain of its sting. It felt like a thousand, red-hot needles poking into me at once. After it stung me, the place between my eyes began to itch so intensely that I thought I might go crazy. As the ant crawled down my face, back the way it came, I could feel a lump forming where it had stung me.

I had experienced many painful things in my life, but this was one of the most intense. I could feel the pulse of my heartbeat in the sting and it burned like fire. Tears of intensity were streaming down my face. I tried to catch my breath in the hot air, but nothing decreased the pain.

My heart sank when I saw the other ants coming for me. They were moving in a long, burnt-orange line towards me from a crack in the rock walls. They moved with precision, one coming over the rocks, followed by another and another, all in a perfect line. I soon realized the gravity of the situation.

These were the dreaded *Fire Ants of Madrid*. I'd read about them many years ago, but their existence slipped my mind. The Fire Ants of Madrid were insects that trapped their prey and then devoured them. The whole colony would swarm their captives and have a marvelous feast, eating for days on their immobile victims. But the biggest things that I'd heard of them capturing were lizards or frogs, never anything the size of a human.

Yet here I was.

The trail diversion had to have been their doing, as was the pit in which I'd found myself trapped. These weren't just ants, they were *super-intelligent* ants, and they had laid the perfect trap to catch me. As the pain of the first ant's sting throbbed in my head, I watched as the army of its comrades slowly made their way down from above, millions of the creatures on the move. The line of ants had to have been fifty feet long and they all slowly got closer and closer, ready to devour their next meal: me...

52 "DR. ABSOLUTE ZERO AND THE LATE FREEZE OF 1981" from Mr. Ping's Almanac, Vol. 84

An advocate for climate change...severe climate change...Dr. Absolute Zero was an insane scientist from the 1950s whose goal was to turn the entire planet into a ball of ice. Luckily, Mr. Ping was there to thwart him on several occasions, including the time he tried to freeze the Baltic Sea, and the late freeze of 1981, a portion of which is included here:

...I had never been so cold in all of my life. My bones were chilled, my toes were numb and my beard had frozen like a long icicle on my chin.

The closer one got to Dr. Absolute Zero, the more the temperature dropped, and though I was wearing my extra durable sub-Arctic jumpsuit and my endo-thermal helmet, it did me little good as I got closer and closer to my nemesis.

What had once been the pride and joy of London, Big Ben, was now nothing more than a giant, white crag of ice jutting upwards from the ground towards the sky. That is, of course, if one could have seen it, as there was so much snow flying that during the more powerful wind gusts, one could not see much more than a few feet and that was *indoors*. The strangest part of all was that this was *August 4th!* Luckily, I had my Temperature Epicenter Indicator (TEI) from my previous battles, and all indications were that Dr. Absolute Zero was dead center in Buckingham Palace.

The TEI was right, for as I rounded the corner from the hallway, I saw that the dining room was now an ice-blue cave of despair. There was Dr. Absolute Zero, directing his white weasels to dig through the thick layers of rock hard ice to get at the crown jewels.

"Faster, my ravenous minions!" he yelled. "Faster!" He cracked a white whip above his head. Because he was immune to the cold, he wore a rather classy, white suit with a red tie over his ice blue skin, and his bald head was gleaming from the lamplight overhead.

"I think it's time we called it a day," I yelled into the microphone in my helmet.

He spun around to face me, virtually spitting anger as he spoke. "Ping!" he yelled. "But *you* should have been crushed under the weight of the frozen Thames River! How?"

Knowing that if I were to reveal my secrets (like I did the last time), he would use them against me, I gave him no hints. "You're not walking away with

the pride and joy of Britannia this time, Zero."

"I beg to differ, you simpering fool!" he yelled. "Ice weasels! *Attack!*"

With that, I found myself surrounded by his growling, abnormally large minions, all of which were ready to pounce. Knowing that I had very little time, I pulled my molecular agitator from my belt, extended the metal rod from the bottom, and plunged the sharp end into the ice below my feet until I hit solid ground. "Your crime filled days are over, Zero!" I yelled.

"No!" he yelled, running to stop me, but with the flick of a switch, the molecular agitator began to vibrate every molecule within three hundred yards, causing the building to grow warmer and warmer. Almost instantly, the temperature in the cavern of ice began to rise, and the walls began to melt. I ducked to the side, just in time to keep a large chunk of ice from crushing me as it fell to the floor. Several ice weasels weren't so lucky.

"I'll get you for this, Ping!" I heard him yell. "If it's the last thing I ever do!"

The last I saw of my opponent, he was buried beneath the large sheets of ice that were falling from the ceiling. Later that month, when all of the ice had finally melted, we were able to account for all of the crown jewels, but Dr. Absolute Zero was nowhere to be found...

53 THE WICKED WEATHER KING, taken from Mr. Ping's Almanac, Vol. 88

Born Darryl Custer of Hominy, Oklahoma, the man who would be the Wicked Weather King became famous throughout the region as a local weatherman. Known for his uncanny, spot-on predictions of the weather, Darryl's dream was to take his meteorology degree to the national level on the popular morning television program "Morning." Alas, it was not meant to be, but it wasn't Dave's weather predicting skills that proved his downfall. It was his looks. When KPPP, the station he worked for, was purchased by a major news network, Darryl, because of his thinning hair and portliness, was let go by the network and replaced by a young, bubbly, fresh-faced blond whom the camera loved. To make matters worse, her major in university was not "meteorology", but "aerobics."

Bitter because of being judged not by his skills, but by his looks, Darryl hired a local Cherokee medicine man to give him the power to manipulate the weather, vowing that Chantelle Taggert (the woman who replaced him) would never get the weather right and subsequently be fired. When she would predict rain, Darryl would cause it to be sunny. When she would predict sun, Dave would make it snow. Even in July.

He was sure that she'd be fired, but it wasn't the case. In fact, Chantelle's goofy weather predictions only made her more popular, and soon she had won a spot on the national news, doing the weather for the "Morning" program, the very place Darryl had always dreamed of.

Naturally, this infuriated Darryl, who now dubbed himself the Wicked Weather King, and he soon vowed to destroy all weather broadcasters on television, thus making him the only one left. The first of many assaults came on KPPP, as he planned to end the Chantelle Taggert-era for good by causing a powerful tornado to rip through the station. Luckily, Mr. Ping was there to put a stop to his plans:

...I had never seen a storm so violent hanging over the city, and Tulsa's streets were knee high in muddy rainwater. Cars were being washed into the gutters, along with trees, mailboxes, and anything else that wasn't firmly attached to the ground.

Still, the flash-flooding wasn't as terrifying as the constant lightning. It was virtually as bright as day as the white light of the bolts sparked on all sides of the horizon. The wind was whipping back and forth, spraying sheets of rain onto the windshield of my car as I pulled into the parking lot of KPPP.

I was surprised at what I found. The television station, a lone, beige, four story building surrounded by strip malls and fast food restaurants, looked like a castle under siege. Lightning struck the large satellite dishes at the top endlessly, rain lashed the walls, and trees had been blown up against the sides of the building.

Exiting my car, I fought my way into the storm, through the shattered glass of the front doors, into the foyer, where frantic employees of the TV station were running back and forth, trying to take shelter from the barrage taking place outside. "What are you doing here?" one man asked, his business suit soaked from the rain. "Get out of here! You're putting yourself in horrible danger!"

"I'm looking for Chantelle Taggert," I yelled over the chaos.

"The basement," he yelled. An ear-shattering burst of thunder sent him cowering to the corner.

I ran down to the basement to find the manager of the TV station trying desperately to hold Chantelle back. "Chantelle," he said, trying to stop her. "If you go up there, you're liable to be killed by that blamed fool. Now, will you calm down?"

"I ain't' calmin' down for nothin'," Chantelle yelled. "I put up with that guy's nonsense for way too long." She looked up and saw me coming down the stairs. "Confucius!"

"Hello, Chantelle," I said with a smile.

I suspected that Chantelle had always had a small crush on me and I can't say that I didn't think she was attractive, but I never let romance get in the way of professionalism. "What are you doin' here?" she asked.

"When I heard that Mr. Custer had escaped from prison, I took the first flight here," I said. "Looks like I made the right choice."

"That Dave is a moron," she said, a sour look passing over her face. "Can't he just let the whole thing go? I mean, it's been *six years!*"

"Jealousy is one of the hardest emotions to surrender," I said. "Dave is jealous of you. You have what he wants."

"Yeah, yeah," she said, dismissing my analysis.

"He's almost here!" a man yelled, poking his head outside the door of one of the basement offices.

We ran over to the office to see that he was monitoring a bank of computer screens with weather radar readouts on them. Showing the northeastern section of Oklahoma, the screen looked like a giant hurricane was passing through, with the clear eye of the storm headed directly for where we were located.

"See that clear spot?" the man said, pointing at the screen. "That's where we think he is."

"And he's headed right for us?" I asked.

"Yep," he said.

Chantelle immediately started walking upstairs. "I'm gonna tell that guy what he can do with his meteorology degree!" she said with a huff.

"Chantelle, no," the station manager said, rushing to stop her.

"He's gotten more powerful," I said, taking one last glance at the screen before I went after her as well...

54 "THE WOEFUL ENCOUNTER WITH BARONESS VON STRONHEIM" taken from Mr. Ping's Almanac, Vol. 31

One encounter was all it took for Mr. Ping to fall madly in love with the infamous Baroness Von Stronheim, and though they were bitter enemies at various points in their lives, their love for one another overpowered their hatred. Sadly, it ended tragically. The following excerpt is from their first encounter:

"...And why are you here in Austria?" the Baroness asked me. I couldn't help but admit that I found her alluring. Her eyes were dark, with long eyelashes, and she had a demure smile that she sometimes hid behind the lovely locks of brown hair that hung down on each side of her head.

"I'm doing research," I said. It was a beautiful, late-summer day in Vienna, and I couldn't imagine a more peaceful setting. We were at a café, sitting under an umbrella at a table for two surrounded by the gorgeous architecture of the city. The Baroness had requested my presence at the hotel and I had obliged her.

"What kind of research are you doing here?" she asked. "Art history? Music? I'm intrigued." I was so enamored with her that I felt like I could talk to her all day, but I hesitated, for I was still new at what I was doing and I felt that no matter how comely and intriguing this woman was, I shouldn't reveal my real purpose for being in Austria.

"I'm doing some research on architecture," I said as I glanced at the buildings around me. "In China, we're fascinated with European architecture, so I've taken a scholarly trip to learn everything I can." I was lying, but I felt like I had to do it.

"Perhaps I could help you," she said. "Which period are you studying?"

"Oh, it's not important," I said, trying to dodge her bullet. In reality, I knew next to nothing about architecture. "Would you mind if I asked you a personal question?"

"Of course not," she said.

"Can you tell me what it is, exactly, that a Baroness does?"

She laughed in a relaxed way and leaned back in her chair. We spoke for most of the afternoon at that café, under the watchful eye of her bodyguard, Klaus. In the course of the next two hours, I fell in love with her. She was charming in every possible way; the sound of her voice, her shy smile, her interests, the way she would laugh at my jokes. I had never before been so enamored with someone so quickly in all of my life.

I was so naive.

Well into the second hour of our conversation, she broached the subject again. "Tell me again why you're here in Austria," she said.

"I'm studying art history," I said, but just as the words came out of my mouth, I knew I'd made a mistake. "I mean architecture. Art history, architecture, it's easy to get them mixed up."

"That's true," she said. She had the calm manner of a cat stalking her prey, and for the first time, I felt alarmed. "I'm very impressed with your abilities, Confucius."

"Abilities?" I asked, finishing off the last of my tomato juice. "What do you mean?"

"Your powers," she said. "I've been trying to read your mind for almost two hours and I can't seem to break through."

"Read my mind?" I said, almost spitting up my drink.

"Who did you train with?" she asked.

"Train?" I asked, trying to remain innocent.

"There's really no need to play games," she said. "I know why you're here. I've been watching you since you arrived, yet I couldn't easily track your brainwaves, because of the blocks you've got up in your head. Where did you learn your skills?"

"I trained in Thailand," I said, feeling as though I should

stop playing naive. "Under the Buddhist monks of Chiang Mai."

"Hmm," she said, putting her finger to her chin to think. "I've never heard of them."

"The monks taught me an ancient, meditative technique to keep others out of my head. It's quite simple, but quite effective. You're a telepath?" I asked.

"Amongst other things," she said with a sly smile. "Your brain waves stuck out like a sore thumb in this city, so I felt I had to investigate."

"You're good," I said. "I had no idea you were even trying to read my mind."

"Subtlety is an art," she said. "It allows me to remain anonymous."

"I see," I said.

Now that I knew the Baroness was a telepath, I was trying to stay on guard. Telepaths can be extremely dangerous with their manipulative abilities, making you do things that you might not normally do, ranging from simple things such as dancing like a chicken on a crowded street, or the dangerous, such as revealing secret information that could get you killed. I had encountered telepaths before, but never one so powerful as the Baroness. My problem, however, was that although I was watchful, I still failed to see the Baroness as a threat, probably because I was too focused on her incredible good looks. My light-headed feeling should have snapped me out of my fog, but it didn't.

"I find you to be quite charming, Confucius," she said. "It's a shame."

"A shame?" I asked, slurring my words. Something was wrong.

"A shame that we had to meet under such circumstances," she said, drinking the last of her drink.

"What circumstances?" I asked. My head was growing heavy and I was unable to focus my eyes.

"You're my enemy," she said. "And I must deal with my enemies. I can't have you running around the kingdom now, can I?"

I suddenly realized that I couldn't move. Every muscle in my body was paralyzed and as I looked at my empty glass on the table, I could see the thin, white powder floating at the bottom. "You've drugged me," I said, just as my head crashed into the table.

"Men," she said, shaking her head sadly. "So easy to control."

Before I blacked out completely, the Baroness rose from her chair and walked over to her bodyguard to say, "Bring him back to the castle. If I can't read his mind to find out why he's here, then we'll just have to torture it out of him."

Klaus nodded and began to walk towards me. It was the last thing I remembered...

55 H E L M U T FRANKENSTEIN, taken from Mr. Ping's Almanac, Vol. 8

One of Mr. Ping's most bitter enemies, Helmut Frankenstein, was a constant thorn in his side. The roots of Frankenstein's utter hatred go all the way back to when Mr. Ping was a boy on his first adventure with Mr. Pranesh:

Through some of the locals, Mr. Pranesh had heard rumors of an island just off the coast of China, upon which lived a man from Germany. Apparently, this man was a scientist, a mad scientist one might say, and they said that he performed strange and unusual experiments on the island.

To my fourteen-year old ears, these seemed like tall tales, fantastic stories designed to scare away the locals, and it must be said that the locals did a good job of embellishing the facts. I dismissed most of this information as hearsay and elaborate fiction, but this certainly wasn't the case with Mr. Pranesh. Mr. Pranesh would listen to everyone's stories with devout attention, taking notes and asking pertinent questions in an attempt to separate the fact from fiction and to find common threads in people's tales.

"Mr. Pranesh," I said that night at dinner, "You don't actually believe those stories, do you?"

"Of course, I do," he said. "You've read my books, Confucius. How do you think I had all of those grand adventures? You'll get nowhere sitting around, waiting for things to happen. You have to go out and make those things happen. And part of making those things happen is listening to what others have to say."

"But it can't be true," I said. "A mad scientist on that island? It's the most ridiculous thing I've ever heard."

"Look at it this way," Mr. Pranesh said. "If it's not true, what do we have to lose? We go to the island, there's nothing there. What harm will come of that?"

"Nothing," I said.

"That's right," he continued. "But if we go to the island and actually find this mad scientist fellow, think of what he might offer to society. Perhaps he's working on a cure for malaria or dysentery. Perhaps he's doing something good for the world and needs to be encouraged to share his work."

Then a horrible thought creeped into my mind. What if he *wasn't* doing something good for the world? What if he was on that island for a *reason?* I was a bit apprehensive. Soon we were to be at sea, across the waters, back to my home in China. I was very fearful of going back, thinking that simply being near the orphanage where I was raised would cause me to get caught and go to jail. Or worse, back to the orphanage. Yet, when I arrived, no one paid me any mind.

We began to inquire with the locals about the island and we found no shortage of weird and twisted tales that seemed designed to scare people from going there. There were tales of horrible, banshee-like screams being heard all the way across the water, although Mr. Pranesh was quick to assure me that this couldn't possibly be true, because the weather here wasn't right for banshees. He'd seen them before and the weather where we were was much too humid.

Then we heard other stories about a sea monster that was loyal to this German scientist and that would protect him from intruders. Mr. Pranesh also countered this idea, telling me that every sea monster he'd ever seen wasn't bright enough to be "tamed." He said they happened to be one of the stupidest creatures in the sea and he said that because of that stupidity, he wouldn't be surprised if they were already extinct. He surmised that if ships were, in fact, sinking, then there had to be some kind of heretofore unknown reef that was sinking them.

The last rumor that we heard was one of zombies walking the island and about how the German kept a slave army of the dead to keep him safe and do his manual labor. "This one is interesting to me," Mr. Pranesh told me. "Because if I recall, there was a doctor in Europe, maybe ten or fifteen years ago, who was performing regenerative experiments with dead people, but when he presented his findings, he was laughed out of the place. He disappeared soon after that. In fact, I actually knew the old chap. He was Doctor... Doctor...Oh, his name escapes me."

"Do you think that this is him?" I asked, intrigued.

"I don't know," he said. "But there's only one way to find out, isn't there?"

We tried in vain to find a local boat to take us to the island, but everyone was too superstitious. Mr. Pranesh was finally forced to buy an old junk himself, and we set sail for the island the next morning.

Because of heavy winds, it took us most of the day to sail across the straight, and just as the sun was going down, we saw the sunken ships about which the other had warned us. There was, indeed, a reef there in the water, but it looked more man-made than natural. I had time to look, because our boat ran into it as well and began to take on water.

Having no choice, Mr. Pranesh and I were forced to take to the choppy waters and try, desperately, to swim to shore. We both attached ourselves to a gang plank and swam onward, arriving on the island just as the sun was going down.

What astounded me the most was how nonchalant Mr. Pranesh was about this whole endeavor. When we'd encountered locals who warned us not to go to the island, it only seemed to fuel his excitement. When we passed the sunken ships near the reef, I couldn't help but notice a smile on his face, and when our ship was torn to splinters on that very same reef, I actually heard him laugh with glee. Now, we were trapped on an island to which no local would dare go, with no way back to the mainland, and he was as giddy as a school girl as we made camp.

That night, the camp that Mr. Pranesh made with just rudimentary materials was like luxury compared to the place I slept in Hong Kong. It seemed as if he'd made this type of camp hundreds of times before, and by the time he was done, we had a fire, shelter, a soft bed made of banana leaves, and a nice meal of roasted mangoes and fish cooking for the evening.

"One must always be prepared, Confucius," he said. "No one can put you in a situation that will conquer you if you're well educated."

I believed him because everything I'd seen him do seemed second nature to him. That night as we settled in, came the first event that made my blood run cold and made me doubt the situation into which we'd been thrust. It was a moonless night, with a million stars shining in the sky and I had just begun to drift off when I heard it.

It seemed that the locals were not lying after all. The most horrible wail I have ever heard echoed throughout the island, a sound so raw and piercing that I had to cover my ears for fear my eardrums would burst. Although I wasn't sure what an actual banshee might sound like, I thought that of all the sounds that I'd ever heard, this might be a close approximation. I quickly burst from the makeshift shelter that Mr. Pranesh had made for me and ran for cover.

As I peeked out from behind a rather large, tropical tree, I saw Mr. Pranesh standing outside his shelter, looking calm, and in fact, refreshed and happy, with his magic rucksack in tow over his shoulder. Even in the dark of the night, he turned, knowing exactly where I was and smiled. "Come along, Confucius," he said. "The siren's song is calling us."

Trying to keep up with him, I ran to my tent to put on my shoes and followed him into the thicket of jungle mass that served as a barrier to the interior of the island. He moved quickly, like a jaguar, through the leaves and vines and I struggled to keep up with him as he moved onwards, towards the intermittent wail of the siren.

Just as the humidity of the tropical air was about to drown me in perspiration and the bugs were crawling in every nook and cranny on my wiry frame, we came to a rather large clearing, in the center of which was a castle built from granite. It was a magnificent structure, built only high enough to keep it hidden behind the trees and invisible from the mainland. Inside, there were lights. Electricity had somehow made its way to the island and was glowing brightly in the ornate windows of the castle.

I continued to stand there, staring in dumbfound wonderment at what lay before me, but Mr. Pranesh was already making his way up to what appeared to be a large, Oak door that served as the entrance to the place, and without a worry or care, he proceeded to knock using the large, black metal ring bolted to its center.

After a few seconds, the large door was unlatched and it slowly opened to reveal the first of many horrific sights I would see in my lifetime. Before us stood a man in a butler's uniform. But this was no ordinary man. He had to have been seven feet tall, and disfigured in a most grotesque way that made it seem as if he was all odd angles and mismatched limbs. His face was pale and lifeless and had spots of gangrene on his cheeks, and his eyes were misshapen as well, as if he had an Asian face with two large, different-colored eyes bulging out of the sockets. There was also a stitched scar running across his forehead and two metal bolts protruding out of his neck.

I would have screamed, but the butler slowly stepped aside to reveal a short, bearded man with long, frizzy hair and thick glasses, wearing an apron over a button down shirt. He observed the two of us for a second before focusing on Mr. Pranesh.

"Vat in da vorld? Vidia!" he said, a smile passing over his face.

"Ha!" Mr. Pranesh said. "I *knew* it was you!"

The two of them embraced like old school chums, reunited after years apart, laughing and slapping each other's back. "Vat in da vorld are you doink here?" the man asked.

I might ask you the same question," Mr. Pranesh said before turning to me. "Confucius, I would like to introduce you to Helmut Von Frankenstein. *Doctor Frankenstein*, this is my apprentice, Confucius."

At the time, I had no clue as to the significance of Doctor Frankenstein, as Mary Shelly's book hadn't really become popular in China yet. In fact, I paid little mind to Doctor Frankenstein himself, because I was too focused on his "butler," the grotesque man who opened the door and who had an odd way of staring off into space, as if he was there, but not *really* there.

Mr. Pranesh and Doctor Frankenstein wandered into the castle, catching up on the last few years and I followed. It seemed that Doctor Frankenstein had heard of our coming through his "informants" on the mainland and had prepared rooms for us in the castle, so as to make our stay much more comfortable. As we walked down the hallway towards our rooms, I couldn't help but keep an eye on the ghastly figure at the door. He stood there for a few seconds, looking tired, as he watched us walk down the hall. Then he turned and disappeared down another corridor.

That night, we joined Doctor Frankenstein for a grand dinner, in a large dining room at the center of the castle. It was one of the most sumptuous meals I'd ever had, a regal affair with candles and

different courses, each of which was more delectable than the last. However try as I might, I couldn't enjoy my meal, for my mind was always on the deformed fellow serving us our meal. I made mental observations: his hands didn't match. One looked like the hand of a woman, while the other looked like the hand of a farmer, rough and callused from manual labor. His different colored eyes seemed to move independently of each other, which enabled him to watch you and the person at the other end of the table simultaneously. And then there was the odd way in which Doctor Frankenstein communicated with the creature, through some sort of sign language that was subtle and silent and would only be noticed through close observation.

"Vat brings you to my island, Vidia?" Doctor Frankenstein asked. "Looking for more of ze *unusual* for your almanac?" There was a vague hint of sarcasm in his voice, but it was slight.

"Of course," Mr. Pranesh replied. "And I certainly think I've found it. I suppose I might ask you the same question, Helmut."

"Isn't it obvious?" he said, dismissing the notion with a wave of his hand.

"Well," Mr. Pranesh said, "I certainly have my opinion, but I'd love to hear your interpretation of why you're here."

"Vell, you might have heard rumors," he said. "So I suppose I should start vith zose."

"You mean the rumors about grave robbing and your experiments with the dead?" Mr. Pranesh asked.

"*Pah!*" Doctor Frankenstein said, taking a large bite from his plate. "You're just like *them*, Vidia. Comparing my life's vork, my most *important* endeavor, to a common criminal act. Vat I do

is *much* more important zan zat. Ya, I did dig up a few corpses vith vhich I could perform my experiments, but zey vere *dead*. And I paid zeir families handsomely for ze bodies. Everything vas legitimate." A dark cloud passed over his face as he remembered something, saying, more to himself than anyone else, "It vasn't until *he* got loose and terrorized zat village that the government officials began to take notice of me."

"Who was this that got loose?" Mr. Pranesh asked.

"Ze monster," Doctor Frankenstein said, before waving the whole notion off. "Oh, it's not really important. Vat is important is zat I moved here to ze South Pacific and zat I can now perform my experiments in peace, *vithout* zose nosy observers and bureaucrats who sink zey know everything and can place moral judgment upon me."

Doctor Frankenstein had a tendency to get really worked up over this issue and behind his thick beard, frizzy hair and thick glasses, his face was as red as a tomato. I made a mental note to avoid bringing up this subject again, but it seemed that Mr. Pranesh did not. "But you *were* performing experiments with dead bodies, correct?" he asked.

"Of *course*, I vas," he said.

"Sometimes science, *true* science, *progressive* science, might frighten ze laypeople because zey don't *understand* it. Zis vas ze case for me in Germany. Just because a few people might have seen zeir dead husbands or dead children or dead grandparents valking mindlessly through ze village after they'd been buried for a few months, zey get horribly upset and vant to take it out on *me!* But zat's just pointless. I'm making advances in ze name of science, Vidia. In science, people *have* to make sacrifices."

"You mean to say that you were bringing dead people back

to *life?* And *then* letting them walk around the village?"

"Vell, they really weren't supposed to be out and about," Doctor Frankenstein said, smiling and a little embarrassed. "Zey managed to get the key and zen zey vere off. It took me a vile to round zem up, and ven I did, ze villagers were quite upset."

"What happened when they escaped?" Mr. Pranesh asked. "Did they go home? Back to their families?"

"Vell, no," Doctor Frankenstein said, looking uncomfortable. "You see, ven I bring zem back...I prefer to call it reanimation...zey seem to have no memories of zeir past lives. In fact, zey have few memories at all. Zey're more or less a blank slate, unable to even retain language skills. I have to teach zem sign language in order to get zem to communicate. Anyway, vunce zey'd gotten out, zey just vandered into ze village and stood around, not doing anything in particular. Needless to say, zis vasn't pleasant for ze villagers."

"And then the monster got loose?" Mr. Pranesh asked.

"Yes, he got loose," Doctor Frankenstein said. "Set fire to a few zings. Caused a general commotion. I'd really like to put it all behind me. Zat's vhy I'm here."

After all of this talk about dead people and monster rampages, I found myself in a bit of an agitated state, so I excused myself and returned to my room with the intent of getting a good night's rest, but knowing full well that the odds were stacked against me for fear of what horrible things my dreams might interpret from all of this. I was awoken by a thunderstorm raging outside the castle in the deep of the night. Yet it wasn't simply the thunderstorm, it was also something else. A presence, one might say. Something that filled me with anxiety. I curled up in my bed, pulling the sheets close up over my nose and with each flash of lightning, I scanned my room for what it was that made me feel uneasy.

And then, with one bright, powerful flash, I saw it. Standing in the corner of my room, observing me, was a little boy. Goosepimples raced across my skin and I held my breath. I knew that the boy was staring at me, but my room was so dark in between lightning flashes that I couldn't make out the details. When the next bolt of lightning struck, the boy was gone. Was it my imagination playing tricks on me? Did I *really* see a young boy standing in the corner of my room? I dared not move.

Then, with another flash of lightning, I realized that the boy was now standing right beside the bed, still staring at me in that lifeless way. He was younger than me, pale and ghostly, with light blond hair and eyes that not so much looked at you, as looked *through* you. I couldn't move.

With the next flash of lightning, I saw that he held a piece of paper in his outstretched hand. I felt him place it on the bed next to me, and then as the storm began to recede, a final white-hot flash of lightning revealed that he was no longer there. Yet, the piece of paper was.

I reached down with trembling hands and lifted the paper. Even in the dark, I could read the childlike scrawl of words. It said, *Help us.*

Needless to say, I slept very little for the rest of the night, a subject that Mr. Pranesh remarked upon the next morning. "You're looking particularly pale," he said. "Are you feeling okay, Confucius?"

"Yes, sir," I said, but I was tired.

"You didn't sleep well with the storm?" he asked.

"No, sir," I said. As I spoke, I clutched the note in my pocket, wondering if the dead boy could hear our conversation.

"Doctor Frankenstein is going to show me his electric generating plant," he said. "Would you like to join us?"

"No, thank you, sir," I said. Although I lived in fear of the castle, there was something inside me that made me want to get to the bottom of this mystery. I knew that Doctor Frankenstein probably considered me harmless because of my age, and I suspected that Mr. Pranesh would think it was just the boy in me who had no interest in seeing power generation.

Of course, these thoughts proved wrong as Doctor Frankenstein approached, wearing khaki trousers and a white shirt, followed closely by his tall, deformed companion. "Shall ve be off?" he asked.

"Little Confucius, here, has got a touch of the dysentery," Mr. Pranesh said. "Do you mind if he stays here?"

Doctor Frankenstein rubbed my head in an endearing way and spoke to me as if I was about half my actual age, saying, "Does he have dysentery? Poor sink. You'll feel better tomorrow." He turned to a trail leading up the side of the mountain and said, "Come Vidia! Zere is a lot to see and very little time."

Before turning to follow Doctor Frankenstein, Mr. Pranesh turned to me in a confidential way and said, "I know why you didn't sleep. Make note of anything unusual that you observe." Then, he was off up the hill.

Fear is a strange thing. I was very perplexed by the ghostly vision of the little boy in my room and I wondered what the note could have meant. Who was the boy? Why would he need help? Was Doctor Frankenstein holding the boy as a prisoner on the island? What were Doctor Frankenstein's evil motives? There was no shortage of intrigue for me and the castle, I felt, held all the answers.

I explored every nook and cranny of the place that afternoon, from the dining room to the library to the bathrooms, and found absolutely nothing that answered any of my questions. Everything was normal, nothing out of the ordinary existed in the place. It was then that I noticed the fireplace in the main living area. There was something a bit strange. If I wasn't mistaken, there seemed to be a set of fingerprints rubbed into the ash on the back edge of the brick, as if someone had used it for leverage. In fact, there was *more than one* set of fingerprints back there.

Upon closer inspection, I discovered the latch that opened the secret door in the fireplace, an imposing structure, whose heavy stone swung inward with the sound of granite grinding against granite. I flipped a lever on the wall and a set of lights leading down a long stairwell burst to life. Making sure no one was following me, I made my way down the stairs.

The stairs led farther and father down into a stone basement that looked like some mad scientist laboratory that was well ahead of its time. Electrical equipment was everywhere in the moist, dingy room, wires and connections strewn all over the place, all of it large and cumbersome, and ready to roar to life at Doctor Frankenstein's beck and call. While the upstairs part of the castle catered to the exotic, South Pacific way of life with large windows and tropical plants growing both inside and outside of the residence, the laboratory in the basement was another story entirely. Everything about the lab, from the darkness of being in an underground facility, to the thick, fuzz of mold and moss growing between the bricks in the walls, was the exact opposite.

I looked around for things to document, but couldn't not tell hide nor hair of what any of the equipment was. If I'd had more knowledge of science or some related field, I probably would have been able to surmise what, exactly, all of this was, but I had no such knowledge and I knew that my limited English would not do justice to what was there if I just wrote it down. Therefore, I did the next best thing and drew the equipment.

I must have lost track of time, for soon I realized that I'd been down in the labs for almost an hour. Then I heard the noise. My first panicked thought was that Doctor Frankenstein or his horrible minion had returned, but considering I didn't hear either the shuffling feet of Doctor Frankenstein or the mindless thump, thump of Jeeves, I figured that something else was happening.

Hiding behind what I took to be one of the large, electric generators that powered the castle, I sat in acute observation of the room, trying to figure out who, or what, was following me. Being ever so careful, I peeked out from behind the scene to see who it was walking down the stairs, and when I finally saw the same little boy from the night before standing there, a chill ran through my body. He was staring right at me in that ghostly way, his face as pale as the moon, and his eyes as dark as the empty space surrounding it.

I tried to pretend that I wasn't there, but the little boy just continued to stare at me in a most disturbing way, so I finally said, "Hello?" There was no answer from him, so I asked again, "Hello? Can you hear me?"

The little boy nodded.

"Are you okay?" I asked. The boy had tears well up in his deep set eyes, as he shook his head to indicate no. He looked scared and confused, as if he couldn't believe that he hadn't been caught or accused of doing something wrong.

I began to approach him, but he backed away from me like a dog that feared its master would strike him. "It's okay," I said. "I can help you."

He looked at me as if he was struggling to find the right words and said, "He vill be very angry vith me eef he knows I ham talkink to you."

"He's not here," I said.

"What's the matter?"

The little boy fell to his knees and began to sob into his hands. "He keepsh us prisoner here," he said. "All day und all night. Ve can nevah leaf. Et's torture."

"Who keeps you prisoner?" I asked.

"Here *doktorr,*" he said. "All uff us. Ve vant to go home, but he vill not let us. Not oontil he iss finisht."

"Finished with what?" I asked.

"Hees horrible experiments," he said, wiping away his tears. "He vants to do horrible tings to us. Terrible, horrible tinks. I cannot bear to tink about it."

Suddenly a noise was heard upstairs and the little boy turned to look, filled with terror. "I must go," he said and he quickly turned to run, but not before telling me, "He must know nossink about our visit! Please help us!"

I had no idea of what should be done. This young boy seemed awfully desperate and considering what I knew of Doctor Frankenstein's history, I could only imagine what this Doctor Frankenstein fellow might have in store for this poor little boy and his companions. I vowed to help the boy in whatever way I could.

"You're very quiet tonight, Confucius," Mr. Pranesh said to me during dinner. Indeed, I was quite solemn, lost in the memory of the afternoon.

"I'm just tired, sir," I said. Mr. Pranesh gave me a look that said he knew I was lying, but he was tolerant of my behavior. This wasn't the first time that I felt as if I was being tested in some way, as if Mr. Pranesh was simply looking for the important signs of my being his successor. I felt as if he was documenting my every move to see if I made the right decisions.

That night, just as I suspected, the little boy appeared in my room, just at the stroke of midnight. Only this time, I was ready. I stood in the corner of the room and saw the secret entrance built into the wall's paneling. He walked towards my bed with something that I couldn't see in his hand, and before it could be revealed, I startled the young fellow when I appeared behind him. He looked terrified and yet relieved when he saw that it was only me. "You must come quickly," he said.

He opened the secret panel door and led me inside where there was a lantern hanging on the wall. In silence, we walked down a narrow set of stone steps, ever downward, until we came to an intersection, with dank stone corridors leading off to both the left and right. Unseen and creepy, tropical creatures lurked down the halls, their eyes reflecting yellow in the lamp light. "Dis vay!" he said.

He led me down one of the halls, towards a thick, wooden door, where he undid the latch. I found that we were, once again, back in the elaborate laboratory that I'd found earlier in the day. "Dis is vere ze horror happens," he said.

"Who are you?" I asked. "How did you get here?"

"My name is Helmut," he said as he fiddled with some of the equipment. Why he knew how to work the equipment was beyond me, but he seemed to know exactly what he was doing. Why he wanted to use the equipment was also a bit hazy for me. "I come from Germany. I vas kidnapped by herr Frankenstein and brought here against my vill, so that he could perform his vile experiments."

"He kidnapped you?" I asked, watching him rev up the machinery.

"Yes," he said. "He iss an eefil, eefil man."

"What are you doing?" I asked. He was so intent on his business with the machinery that it was almost as if I wasn't there.

"Nosink!" he snapped, turning towards me like a rabid wolverine. Then, his face softened and he said, "I am simply making my equipment not vork so that he can no longer continue vith his horrible experiments!"

"Where are the other people we're supposed to help?" I asked, a feeling of suspicion washing over me in an instant.

He wagged his finger in an indeterminate direction and said, "Dey are ofer dere. Now leaf me alone vile I finish dis."

He ran around to the other side of the large machine, disappearing from my view. Because of my intense suspicion, I slowly made my way around the corner, fearing to let this boy out of my sight. "Where are you, Helmut?" I asked.

I heard him step out from behind me as he said, "I'm right here."

I turned to see that he was wearing something that looked like a cooking apron, two large, black, rubber gloves and a pair of goggles to protect his eyes. In his hands were two metal rods that, when brought close together, had a stream of blue lightning zap to life between them. I was instantly alarmed and I began to back away from him slowly.

"What are those?" I asked, trying to hide the fear in my voice.

"Dese?" he asked in a sadistically playful way. "Dese are nosink." He lifted them up a bit closer towards me and I backed away. "Vat is da matter?" he asked. "Do I scare you?"

"Those things look dangerous," I said. There was something different about him now. What had seemed like a terrified, innocent little boy now had the look of a depraved maniac that was filled with joy watching others suffer.

"Oh, zay can be dangerous," he said. "But zee jolt from zese vill only cause a little pain. Mostly, zey just knock zee person unconscious." He zapped them together a couple of times, as the blue lightning sizzled and cracked, just enough to intimidate me.

"What are you planning to do with those?" I asked.

"Nosink," he said, and then whap! He thrust them towards me and ten thousand volts of electricity surged through my body, knocking me to the ground. As I lay there, Helmut stood over me with a sadistic grin on his face. I began to lose consciousness, but not before I heard him say, "You make it so easy."

When I awoke, I found myself strapped to a large, stone tablet, spread eagle on the diagonal surface. Both my hands and feet were bound with leather shackles that were pulled tightly and locked with tiny padlocks. I had an awful headache from the jolt that Helmut had given me and had trouble focusing my eyes. I was still in the laboratory, only this time, all of the equipment was humming with life.

"Hello?" I asked, but there was no answer. I struggled for a few minutes to break free from my bonds, but it was no use. "Hello?" I yelled, this time a bit louder.

"I heard you da first time," Helmut said as he walked out from behind a large, humming machine. He was still dressed in the same clothes, only now they were dirtier, covered in grease that made him look like he'd been working on an engine of some sort.

"What have you done to me?" I asked.

"Very simply," he said, "I haff tied you to a table so that I might perform my experiments on you. Does zatt answer your question?"

I thought about it for a second or two and said, "Yes, actually. It does."

"Good," he said. "Now, if you vill excuse me, I cannot perform my experiments if I do not fix da third turbine in a timely manner. Good day."

He ducked around the corner again and I heard the clang and rattle of his work going on in the background. Knowing that I was in a hopeless situation, I realized that I had to think of some way to get out of it. I would never have been a good thief in Hong Kong if I didn't have a bag of tricks to get me out of hairy situations, so I began to devise a plan.

"Have you been working long?" I asked, trying to sound innocent. "When you zapped me with that electric device, I lost track of time."

"No," he said. "You vould have been dead from my torture long ago, had I had zis infernal machine vorking on time. Now, please, leaf me be to concentrate. I cannot stand distractions, und you are not **vorthy** uff my time."

Ah, but distracting Helmut was my goal, as it afforded me time to wriggle my wristwatch down my arm, just where I could bend my fingers down to the latch. "I must say," I said, "I find it rather impressive how you tricked me into thinking that you needed help and then double-crossed me. A fine ploy, if I might say so."

Helmut peeked around the machine with a smug smile on his face. "Ja!" he said. "You are so stupid! It vas almost too easy."

"I can't really say that I understand your motives, however," I said, as he disappeared back behind the machine and I continued unhooking my watch.

"Motiffs?" he asked. "Depravity and efil haff no motiffs! You ver an innocent bird und I vas bored. Vat better motiff cant there be zan zat?"

"Ah, yes," I said. My watch finally came free and with the skill of my light and agile pickpocket hands, I swung my watch around into my palm. I maneuvered it around, so that the thin, metal latch was now between my fingers. "Doesn't it seem a bit wasteful?" I asked.

"Vat?" Helmut asked, still tinkering away.

"Well," I said, as I began picking the lock on my wrist binding, "How many people come along to this island? Probably very few. If you kill me quickly, won't you simply be bored again? Wouldn't it be better to torture me slowly, so that you could keep me alive for further torturing later?"

I heard the clanging and rattling stop. I'm sure he was pondering such a glorious idea, but then the noise started anew as he said, "Zat vould be vonderful, but it cannot be done. I haff to kill you now."

Suddenly, my wrist was free and I began to pick the other locks, first freeing my other hand, and then my feet. Just as I was about to pick the last lock, I looked up to see Helmut standing there with a look of horror on his face. "Vat are you doink?" he yelled.

I began to frantically fiddle with the lock, the urgency of the situation causing my hands to shake. I looked up to see Helmut emerge from around the corner with a giant machine that had two handles, like a gun, only on the end was a giant buzz saw. He pulled a trigger and the machine he had been working on fired to life as the gleaming silver of the saw

began spinning furiously. "Let me help you vith dat last lock!" he yelled, walking towards me with his horrible contraption.

With great luck, the last lock came free and I jumped from the slab just as the sparks flew from the buzz saw as it ripped into the place I was lying. Helmut whipped around to confront me, his infernal machine humming with menace. "Sorry to cause problems," I said, "But I don't really feel like losing any limbs today."

My mocking words seemed to fill him with rage. He dove for me again, but I easily dodged his advances as he was too angry to even think. "I sink you should giff up now," he yelled, "Or I vill make your pain one hundred times vorse."

He was easy to dodge, for all he knew how to do was thrust the saw in my general direction. It was much too cumbersome for him to run with and it seemed to be attached to the machine by a long, black cable. I saw that I had him at a disadvantage now.

"Do you consider yourself to be some sort of evil genius?" I asked as I ducked around his machine. "Because if I just escaped your trap, then that genius part might not be appropriate."

As he chased after me, I found the source of the black cable and saw that it was plugged into the machine, so I jerked the cable away and heard the huge, lumbering metal box grind to a stop. "Vat are you doink?" he yelled.

"Just making it a fair fight," I said, and I quickly spun around to kick his legs out from under him. He fell to the ground, flat on his back, and I jumped on top of him like a monkey, pinning his arms to the ground. "Now tell me," I said. "Who are you?"

"Ach!" he said. "Get off uff me, you giant chickenhead!"

"Not until you tell me who you are."

"Never!" he yelled. "HELMUT!"

Both of us looked over to the stairwell leading into the laboratory and saw Doctor Frankenstein standing in a nightshirt, holding up his lantern. Behind him, stood Mr. Pranesh. "Helmut," he said, "Vat are you doink?"

"Fathah!" Helmut yelled, and he suddenly had the strength to squirm from my grip to stand up. He looked terrified.

"Vat are you doink in here?" Doctor Frankenstein yelled. "You know you're not allowed in this place!"

"I'm sorry, fathah," Helmut said, staring at the ground, his head bowed in shame.

"Confucius?" Mr. Pranesh asked. "Might I inquire what is happening here?"

"He tricked me!" Helmut said, pointing an accusing finger at me. "He said he vould hurt me iff I did not show him da laboratory."

"That's not true!" I said in protest. "*He* tricked *me!*"

"I am very sorry," Doctor Frankenstein said as he turned to Mr. Pranesh. "My Helmut has a bad streak running through him."

"No, fathah!" Helmut said. "He *tricked* me!"

"Silence!" Doctor Frankenstein yelled at Helmut. "I vill no longer tolerate your insolence!" Helmut instantly went silent, like a child who knew that he'd gone too far. Doctor Frankenstein began to look at the machine that Helmut had been working on, his face growing more and more red with anger. "Vat haff you done to my Onomatic Regular Converter? Ach! Eet's ruined!"

Helmut began to quietly edge his way toward the door, as if he could make a grand escape, but Dr. Frankenstein's creepy assistant appeared from nowhere and snagged him by the shirt. It lifted Helmut off the ground to prevent his

escape. "Let go uff me, you giant sack uff rotting flesch!" Helmut yelled. I couldn't help but remark about what a little pistol Helmut was, all wired energy and unfocused anger.

"Jeeves," Doctor Frankenstein said, "Take Helmut to his room. Lock the door on the way out."

Jeeves dutifully grunted and carried little Helmut up the stairs and out of the laboratory. The whole time, Helmut was yelling with rage, his little face as red as a hot pepper beneath his glowing, blond hair. "You vill pay for dis, Confucius Ping!" he yelled. "I vill haff my revenge!"

"You'll haff no revenge, for you vill be grounded!" Doctor Frankenstein yelled after him.

"No, fathah! Don't ground me!"

"Ve vill talk about zis later!" Doctor Frankenstein yelled. He quickly turned his attention back to us. "His muzzah spoils him," he said, clearly embarrassed. "I don't know vat I vould have done vith him if ve did not have zis island."

"What do you mean?" asked Mr. Pranesh.

"Ven I said zee monster vas terrorizing ze German town?" he said. "Vell, I vas not referring to my creature. I vas refferrink to Helmut! He ran away one night and tried to blow up the government buildings. Zee German government forced us to move."

Mr. Pranesh and I watched as Doctor Frankenstein walked back up the stairs, looking tired from having dealt with his son year after year. "I zuppose I have brought zis upon myself by bringing him back to life. Oh, vell…"

And with that, he left the laboratory.

"Bringing him back to life?" I asked, looking at Mr. Pranesh. "What did he mean?"

"It's a long story," Mr. Pranesh smiled, as he led me

back up the stairs. "Off to bed with you."

"But…"

"I'll explain later," he said. "Go!"

And thus, my first adventure on Frankenstein's island was complete. Little did I know, it would not be my last…

56 "THE TAJ MAHAL BANDIT PUTS ME IN A ROUGH SPOT" taken from Mr. Ping's Almanac, Vol. 51

Mr. Ping had many adventures with the Taj Mahal Bandit, each one more dangerous than the last. His first encounter with this villain occurred in 1963:

…Dangling from one of the giant, white minarets of the Taj Mahal isn't the most pleasant place one might find themselves, and I was firmly convinced that this was soon to be a most unfortunate end to my little visit to India. In the movies, when the hero dangles from a rope over a cliff, they can hold on with one hand, and they barely break a sweat. Alas, the movies aren't exactly real life, and as I was suspended, hundreds of feet above the ground, holding onto nothing but a rope, I couldn't help but think how unrealistic films actually were. I could barely hold onto the rope, and it took every ounce of energy I had to maintain my grip, not to mention the fact that the rope was a bit like razor-wire, digging into my hands and burning as I would slide down and lose my footing.

Needless to say, just dangling from a rope on one of the greatest architectural achievements in the world was bad enough, but considering Sanjay Patel, the infamous Taj Mahal Bandit, was standing above me with a wicked smile pasted across his face, things were actually worse than that. "As you fall to your doom, Mr. Ping," he said, "I want you to consider what a horrible mistake you've made in coming here and interfering with my business."

I wanted to dismiss him as a crackpot and a fool, and make fun of his ridiculous, florescent rajah outfit that was bestowed with pointed shoes, a turban, and glitter that shone in the beautiful, midday sun, but I was too worried about falling to let loose with one of my pithy comments. "If I fall and die," I shouted, "You'll be in a lot more trouble."

"True," the Bandit said, "But none of that will matter, for I'll have the *Gem of the Maharajah* and I'll be the most powerful man in the world! Nothing will stop me."

"I'm trying to warn you, Sanjay," I said. "You're out of your element. The *Gem of the Maharajah* is too powerful for you. You could kill us all."

It was true. The Bandit was a small-time thief, used to preying on innocent travelers and oblivious natives. He'd happened upon the map to the *Gem of the Maharajah* and was now having delusions of grandeur. In his uneducated hands, it could very well destroy the world, when all he actually wanted to do was make a quick buck. If I'd have known the trouble I'd be in while trying to deal with him, I'd have given him the money in the first place.

"You're saying I'm not good enough?" he yelled. "We'll see who's not good enough." He whipped a knife from his belt and began frantically sawing at my rope. The knife was surprisingly sharp and I felt a swell of dread at how quickly it cut through my lifeline. "Say goodbye, Ping!" he yelled. "And just remember the face of the man who finally defeated you!"

I sighed, thinking, *How in the world do I keep ending up in situations like this?*

57 "THE AMAZON PIRATES, PART I" taken

from Mr. Ping's Almanac, Vol. 52

Mr. Ping's adventures with the Amazon Pirates was one of the wildest affairs in which he had ever been involved, and this excerpt from Almanac 52 details the beginning of a series of extraordinary events for our intrepid traveler:

...Our boat was surprisingly fast, as they'd cobbled together some sort of old, rusty engine from various spare part that had washed ashore over the years. Unfortunately, they were quickly gaining on our riverboat and I knew that if they were to capture us, it would be the end. "I *told* you we shouldn't have come this way!" Neville yelled, but I knew that I was getting exactly what I wanted.

It seemed that all of the rumors were true. When I looked behind me on the river, I saw what appeared to be a large, Spanish galleon, its towering white sails tucked away for lack of strong wind and its bow strong and majestic. Though it looked old, the ship still seemed to be very well maintained. And lo and behold, flying high above the deck, just above the crow's nest, was the skull and crossbones, as the black Jolly Roger flew in the steamy Brazilian sun. The long rumored Pirates of the Amazon were chasing us.

I was having a marvelous time watching this ship approach from the back of the riverboat when I heard the whiz of a bullet rip past my face. "Was that a *bullet?*" Neville screamed, falling to the deck.

"Yes, I believe it was," I said, quietly ducking in the door to the wheelhouse to take cover.

"I'm going to *die* on this awful river! I know it!" Neville said, curling his legs up to his chest in a fetal position and pulling his khaki hat over his ears.

The pirates were definitely aiming for us, as each time I'd peek my head out of the door jamb, a bullet would fly into the wall, sending splinters and shards of wood in all directions. "They seem to have rather advanced weapons," I yelled to Neville over the roar of the engine. I turned to our captain, Javier. "Javier, where did you say...?"

My question was cut short as Captain Javier had abandoned his own ship. I looked out the window to see him swimming for shore in the muddy waters. "Save yourself!" I heard him yell in Portuguese. "There's no hope!"

I ran to the wheel of the ship and took control. "Who *are* these people?" Neville asked, as he army crawled into the wheelhouse.

"They're the descendants of Portuguese pirates form the 1800s," I said. "It's rumored that they took refuge in the tributaries of the Amazon and ended up staying, along with their treasure. They kill anyone who comes this way."

"*What?*" Neville yelled.

I glanced out the back window just in time to see them ready the cannon, and before I could say duck, a ten-pound cannonball burst forth and sliced through the wheelhouse, just narrowly missing us, but striking the controls of the riverboat dead on, ripping the dash into a million pieces. The pirate ship was now close enough so that I could hear them. "Fuego!" screamed a voice, and this time, the cannonball tore through the center of the boat. Soon, the waters of the river began to creep up through the floor as our boat began to dip further into the Amazon.

"We're sinking!" Neville yelled.

"That appears to be true," I said, and as I figured out my options, I heard the clop of a wooden plank hit our deck and a series of footsteps come across. The pirates had boarded our ship...

58 THE CYCLOPS OF WESTERN BORNEO, taken from Mr. Ping's Almanac, Vol. 18

One of Mr. Ping's first adventures was a trip to Borneo, which is now in present day Malaysia, in search of a Cyclops that was rumored to reside there. The story of the Cyclops was one shared by sea traders throughout Southeast Asia and the legends were so embellished that it was impossible to know whether any of them were true. Some people claimed to have seen the Cyclops, a creature thirty-feet tall, with razor-sharp teeth, and claws that could cut down entire trees with one swipe. These people said the creature looked human, but moved like a panther on all fours.

Of course, there were others who claimed that the Cyclops was a rather erudite fellow of refined tastes who lived in an elaborate mansion built by orangutans deep in the tropical jungle. Others said that the Cyclops was actually as big as a mountain and ate humans as one might eat candy. There were so many wild stories it was impossible to know the truth, and those stories were just from the people who claimed to have seen him. Those that had heard about the Cyclops through friends and friends of friends told even wilder tales, most of which were easy to dismiss from their sheer stupidity.

Naturally, tales like these sparked Mr. Ping's interest, so as a young man in search of adventure, he ventured to the region, hitching a ride on a British cargo ship from Hong Kong to Singapore, hoping to catch a glimpse of this elusive being. Mr. Ping camped out in the jungle for almost four weeks. This was not a particular hardship for him, as he'd trained for years with the famous adventurer Atticus Weathertop during his years in Africa.

However, his wait was ended by a most peculiar sight during his twenty-third day in the jungle. While foraging for dinner one

night, he noticed an orangutan observing him through the thick canopy of leaves...

...There was something odd about this creature. It looked like a normal orangutan in every way, shape, and form, but it didn't move like an orangutan. It moved like an intelligent creature, very deliberate and precise, carefully treading through the jungle in an attempt to see what I was doing. I suspected I might be able to use this to my advantage.

Assuming that an intelligent creature might have lost its instinctual edge, I waited for the chance to duck out of the creature's view. I ran through the forest, coming up behind it before it was aware I was gone and just as I got close, I jumped from the bushes to confront it.

I startled the poor beast half to death and it leaped from its comfortable position on a log, straight into the forest like a bullet. It seems that when a creature like that is frightened, they get their instinctual edge back quite quickly. I wanted to pursue the orangutan to see where it would go, but I was immediately distracted by what flew from its hands as it jumped away from me in fear.

When I went to investigate, I found a very peculiar sight. There in the bush was a notebook, and in that notebook were notes, all of which were written in English and were about me. The orangutan was making notes about my behavior.

I was shocked. Everything the orangutan had written was in extraordinary penmanship, and the creature had been very thorough in documenting my every day existence here, writing about when I had awoken, what food I had eaten, even when I went to the bathroom. It was all there, like some scientific study.

I knew that this wasn't the end of my encounter with the orangutan, and as I settled

into my makeshift shelter for the night, I suspected I'd be visited by my friend again...

Mr. Ping was absolutely correct in his assumption, for that night, he was awoken by a gag being wrapped around his mouth and the paws of eight other orangutans tying his hands and feet. They worked silently, with only their heavy breathing filling the night air. He tried to escape their grasp, but it was a fruitless effort, and they ended up carting him through the jungle to a cave that contained a single torch:

...Something was strange about this cave and as the orangutans took me deeper and deeper into its dark recesses, I began to to get the feeling that this journey might not end well. We traveled several hundred meters into the dark cavern, always along the dry, flat floor, until we came to what appeared to be a large door that looked like the entrance to an ancient castle. The wood was thick and old, and giant iron bolts held the large pieces of wood together.

It was hard to see with the light of only one torch, but one of the orangutans knocked on the massive structure and soon, the lumbering door swung open and we were taken inside. I was not prepared for what we found.

Inside was what appeared to be the interior of a home. But this was no ordinary home. No, this was a home for a giant, a vast space that filled the entirety of the cavern with things that were over-sized to compensate for the extraordinary size of its resident. We stood on a balcony overlooking what seemed to be a five-story high space that filled the gaping chasm below us. The level we found ourselves upon was what appeared to be the "library" level, and its walls were lined with gargantuan books, most of which were taller than I was. Below the library level was what looked to be an "office" level, and below that was a "living" level.

The orangutans dutifully carried me down a massive spiral staircase with steps so tall that they had to "climb" down them as opposed to walk (and in doing so, they managed to thump my head on several steps). When we reached the bottom level, we were in what appeared to be a kitchen area and I was filled with dread almost immediately. One of the orangutans lumbered over to a long rope and pulled it, ringing a large bell that was hidden somewhere in the upper portion of the cave. It echoed over and over.

The orangutans sat me down on the rocks and began to mill about the kitchen, taking care of the more menial chores of sweeping, cleaning the counters, and other daily tasks. The two orangutans that pulled out a large, flat piece of wood and two knives were the ones I was worried about most.

Then I heard it: a low thump, thump, thump that echoed through the cave and shook the ground. It drew closer and closer until a sight rounded the corner that I never expected to see in my lifetime. There before me was a thirty-foot high man dressed in an elegant brown suit and tie, his hair parted perfectly to the side and his beard neatly trimmed. There was only one problem, though, aside from his height: This man only had one eye.

I had found him, the Cyclops of Western Borneo, but what I'd expected to see was not the reality. I expected a large, caveman-like creature that ambled about like a gorilla, wore bearskins, and carried a tree for a club in his hairy hands. What stood before me was an erudite fellow that walked with a refined air and wore an impeccably tailored suit, and the only things that signaled the fact that he was a cyclops were his immense size

and the single eye perched on his forehead.

He approached me with a bemused grin on his face and leaned down to get a better look at me. "Well, well, well," he said, speaking Greek (a language I had picked up two years earlier, thankfully). "Look at what we have here." It was a bit disconcerting to have a giant eye staring at me. I did my best to try to get him to remove the gag from my mouth. "Nickles...Andronicus," he said. "Remove the human's gag." Two of the orangutans came over and pulled the cloth away. "What do you have to say, human?"

"I have a lot to say," I said in Greek. "I have a million questions for you."

"You speak Greek," he said, slightly amused. "I have not heard my native tongue in these parts in centuries."

"I've come looking for you," I said. "I had to confirm whether or not the rumors were true."

"You mean the rumors of my existence?" he asked. His breath in my face was like short explosions of air. "Yes, I do exist. You have managed to find the Cyclops of Western Borneo, human. Or rather, the Cyclops of Western Borneo has managed to find *you*. And he is quite lucky in that regard."

"What do you mean?" I asked.

He rose to his feet and pulled a giant, white cloth tarp from the wall. I soon realized that this wasn't a tarp. It was an apron.

"Well, I'm lucky to have found you for *several* reasons," he said. "One of which is the fact that were I not to have found you, you might have continued to perpetuate the rumors of my existence and I would have had many more humans such as yourself coming here to pester and annoy me." He walked over to the counter and picked up one of the large kitchen knives that

the orangutans had brought to him. "The most *important* reason, however, is simply that it's been ages since I've had a proper meal."

He smiled at me, revealing his large, sharp fangs, and my heart sank. I was going to be his dinner that night...

59 BJORN'S X-500

Invented by Bjorn as a lark, the X-500 is a programmable robot the size of a box of matches and works very much like a robotic beagle. All one has to do is program the robot to "smell" something and it will seek out its target and return it. This proved to be a bit of a nuisance after Bjorn accidentally programmed the X-500 to seek out Reggie's eyebrow hairs. Unfortunately, he couldn't make it stop. In fact, Reggie went without eyebrows for six months after the X-500 plucked every single one of them one night while he was sleeping. In a fit of rage, Reggie swallowed the X-500 to get rid of it, but the tiny robot managed to crawl right out of his stomach while he was sleeping (he snores loudly, thus leaving his mouth wide open), and continued plucking his eyebrows. Bjorn soon realized that he had to keep his robot in a container when not being used.

60 PASCAL, THE MAN-EATING FLOWER, taken from Mr. Ping's Almanac, Vol. 58

Discovered by Mr. Ping in the late 1950s, Pascal is a mutant breed of the Hippeastrum sp. flower (also known as amaryllis), one of only a few left in the world. His natural habitat is the tropical jungles of the South American Amazon rain forest, where it feeds off of large mammals that walk through the thick undergrowth. Mr. Ping was on an expedition, looking for the lost jungle tribe of the Papootees when he stumbled upon Pascal:

...We were hacking and slashing our way through the thick vines when we came upon a large, open space beneath a canopy of leaves in the treetops above us. The fact that there was any type of clearing in this jungle astounded me, but what was even more surprising was what sat in the middle of this clearing.

There before us was a giant flower. The leaves at its base were twice the size of a fully-grown person and standing at attention directly in the center was one of the most beautiful flowers I'd ever seen. The flower's stalk was deep green and as thick as a tree, and at the top, the petals of this amazing creature were a brilliant yellow, each one the size of the hood of a car. I'd never seen a gigantic flower before and I was sure that it had never been listed in any guidebooks that I'd seen.

I turned to Professor Moynahan, who was walking behind me, covered in mud and sweat from our trek. "What's this?" I asked.

The Professor removed his hat and glasses to get a better look at the flower. The expression on his face was that of sheer disbelief and excitement as he approached the plant. "I've never *seen* this before," he said. "Not in any of the books."

"But yer a plant guy," said Rocco coming up behind him, his smelly cigar ruining the cool scent of the forest. "You outta know what that thing is."

"I don't," he said. "This is an entirely new discovery." He ripped off his backpack, fished out his notebook, and began to furiously scribble notes and rip off some of the plant's smaller leaves. "Wait until the men back at the university hear about this."

"Aw, man," Rocco said, sitting on a large root protruding from the ground. "We're gonna be here all day with this reach."

I couldn't help but take notice of the fact that Rocco had been a royal pain for the last couple of days. His already

disagreeable personality had grown worse with time, almost as if the deeper we went into the rain forest, the more irritable and impatient he became. I began to wonder about whether or not we could trust him. However, all of those thoughts quickly vanished when one of the local guides screamed in terror, pointing at the flower.

I looked over to see that Professor Moynahan had disappeared, and then I looked up to the top of the flower to see the Professor's legs flailing. The plant was swallowing him.

"What the blue blazes?" Rocco yelled.

"The plant is eating him," shouted Suzette Pleshette, the reporter from the New York Tribune.

Without hesitation, I ran for the plant to try to retrieve the Professor, but as I approached, the flower, which was once as stiff and straight as a pine, suddenly swung around and walloped me in the side, sending me flying off into the bushes. Then it spit Professor Moynahan out and turned towards the rest of the party. Rocco, who had a machete in hand, was its first target and it swung around with lightning speed, also knocking him off into the forest.

"Professor," I said, approaching him as I tried to catch my breath. "Are you okay?"

"What happened?" he asked. He was covered in some sort of slimy substance that dripped from his body, and he apparently didn't know where he was.

I looked over to see that our entire expedition had fled into the woods, running as far away from the flower as possible. "Come on, Professor," I said, pulling him to his feet. "We have to get out of that thing's reach."

I knew that its stem was only so long and that we'd be safe if we moved away, but even as we reached safety, it suddenly

uprooted itself from the ground and began moving towards us, using its roots for feet. "It's coming for us," the Professor said.

Uh-oh, I thought...

61 ANTI-GRAVITY MARBLES, taken from Mr. Ping's Almanac, Vol. 63

The anti-gravity marbles were discovered by Mr. Ping in 1935 hovering above a large, round rock in the middle of California's Joshua Tree National Park. He was going for a stroll one afternoon through the unique desert landscape of the area when he saw the peculiar sight of nine, gray, glass-like spheres floating in mid-air above a large rock. While experimenting with them, he discovered that putting these objects in close proximity to each other caused gravity to "disappear" (an event that almost proved costly that afternoon, for he was well-over a hundred feet off the ground before he figured out how to diminish their power). Yet, no matter how much research he did, Mr. Ping could not figure out where the marbles came from or how they worked. He developed several theories over the years, some of which included the thought that the marbles were magical, that some bizarre wizard with incredibly bushy eyebrows and a miserable scowl had created the marbles to do some sort of dirty deed. He also hypothesized that it could have been some sort of bizarre geological process that created them and that most of the others, if any, had floated out into space. His final thought was that it was waste from a spaceship that had fallen to Earth. The ship's engines needed to recharge, so they dumped the marbles on Earth, like one might throw away old batteries into a trash can. Still, even though Mr. Ping developed all of these theories, he never got to the bottom of the mystery.

Because the anti-gravity marbles were a source of fascination for Mr. Ping, they were also a source of fascination to many other less savory characters who heard about them, one of which was Felix Featherstone, a thief from Bath, England, who planned to use the marbles as the ultimate theft utensil. *Mr. Ping and Mr. Featherstone had their last encounter on Big Ben, overlooking the Thames in London:*

...When I let go of the marbles, they began to rise up in the air, moving very slowly, not much faster than the speed of a person walking. "You fool!" Felix said. "They're floating to the top of the tower. They'll be lost forever."

"That seems to worry *you* a little bit more than it worries *me,*" I said, trying to squirm out of his headlock. He let go and started jumping in the air, trying his best to grab at the marbles, but they were well out of his reach. We were on the street in front of Big Ben as evening set over London and the magnificent tower began to light up. There were very few people around and had I not been in a battle with Featherstone, I would have thought it was a lovely evening.

However, I couldn't dawdle, for he had already rushed inside the tower, heading for the stairs. I was hot on his trail.

When Felix Featherstone wanted something, he *wanted* something, and although I was in pretty good shape, I couldn't catch him and found myself wheezing like a seventy-year old soccer coach with a penchant for cheeseburgers. I was sure that Felix felt much the same way, but he had too much of a lead on me to care.

Once I arrived in the clockworks portion of the tower with all its gears and whistles and industrial noise, I searched for Felix everywhere. I circled the place several times until I came to an open service door and carefully made my way out onto a railing, where I saw Featherstone at the far end, focused intently on the marbles as they rose up, straight towards him.

"Give it up, Felix," I said. "I'm not going to let you out of here with those marbles."

He scowled at me, baring his yellow, crooked teeth as he said, "Curse you, Ping! You don't know how much these things are *worth* to me." He leaned over the side to look for the marbles and it was suddenly obvious that they were too far out of his reach, so he climbed the railing and dove off the side of the clock tower, his hands outstretched.

"Featherstone, no!" I yelled, but it was too late.

Lucky for him, he grabbed just the right marbles, his fists clenched around them as he floated in mid-air, right in front of the yellow clock face of Big Ben. Felix's weight served as a counterbalance, so the marbles were no longer rising upward.

"Ha!" he yelled over at me. He seemed to be floating, as if the air around him was holding up his body. "You'll never win against Felix Featherstone, Ping!" he said. "You're completely out of your league with someone as smart, brilliant, and intelligent as myself."

"Yes, yes," I said. "You're an evil genius. That's right."

"Ah, but it's true," he said. "And now, with a clever bit of arranging, I shall take my leave of you." He changed the position of the marbles and began to float away from the tower. I couldn't let this happen.

"Is this flight first class?" I asked, and without hesitation, I jumped from the railing, out into thin air, grabbing onto his feet.

"Let go of my, you fool," he yelled. "You'll get us both killed."

I looked down to see the evening streets of London several hundred feet below me and said, "You're not getting away, Felix..."

62   TEMPLE STREET NIGHT MARKET

Located along Yau Ma Tei's Temple Street, the Night Market is where one goes to acquire cheap goods, like clothes, shoes, pirated music, and every other bit of junk that one might imagine. It is also where Chinese opera singers perform on the street, fortune tellers reveal secrets about the future, and where the occasional Dai Pai Dong can be found, where one can purchase such wonderful snacks as fish balls and their pick of mystery meats.

The Temple Street Nigh Market is also known, amongst select circles, as a magnetic nexus point, where the magnetic waves of the Earth converge. There are several magnetic nexus points throughout this part of Asia, but those that occur at the Night Market tend to be stronger than most, and because of this, a wide range of strange and unusual things are drawn to the area, including Bird and Goldfish, Tony Tang, and Alexander the Talking Car. Although most tourists are too oblivious to notice such things, it's not uncommon to see the walking dead strolling through the market, buying goods, or the occasional Fish-Man, Giant Slug, or pack of intelligent, telepathic rats having lunch. To people who frequent the market, these things are commonplace. To the occasional traveler, these things are hard to find.

Still, when traveling to Temple Street, one must always be on guard for pickpockets, unsavory kiosk owners, and sewer beasts that survive on a steady diet of tennis shoes that they rip off of people's feet (sometimes with the foot still in them).

63 FANG TOWER

The crowning achievement of Mr. Fang's success, Fang Tower is a monument to the greed and arrogance of the fattest, most duplicitous man in Hong Kong. Built on the back of cheap labor and money made in shady (and probably highly-illegal) ways, Fang Tower is notorious throughout the city as being the center for bad karma on the island, and the rumors about it might actually be true.

Mr. Fang had the place constructed to emanate bad vibrations in all directions according to the basic tenants of Feng Shui. Unfortunately, Mr. Fang wasn't smart enough to realize that all of the people surrounding his tower would make special arrangements to send that bad Feng Shui back at him. Thus, almost all of the buildings surrounding Fang Tower retrofitted their windows with mirrored glass, sending all of the bad vibrations right back at it. The Feng Shui of his building actually became more of a pain for Mr. Fang than anything else, for the residents around Fang Tower used to secretly try to sabotage the building. On any given morning during the first year of its existence, the tenants would enter the building, passing by bizarre shrines and totems that had been placed there overnight to counter the bad energy. One time, Mr. Fang came to the tower to find a ten-foot high shrine of candles just outside his front door (left by a local political **candidate** with offices next door). Another time, he found a Jamaican witch doctor doing a voodoo dance outside the rear entrance. One Chinese New Year, during the year of the monkey, someone let two hundred monkeys loose in the lobby to wreak havoc on the building, which frightened everyone half to death, for they were not nice monkeys at all, but mean ones that threw poo, spit loogies, and scratched the security guards (all of whom got some strange sort of monkey flu afterward).

Due to all of these hijinks, Mr. Fang has had to double security at the building and has had a consistent problem with keeping tenants. Most businesses that move into the building fail, and those that haven't failed have had to spend enormous amounts of money calling in Feng Shui, voodoo, and exorcism experts to rid their areas of bad karma.

Also of note is the fact that Fang Tower is currently the tallest building the world, although it only retains that title because of a ramshackle, precariously-placed television tower at the top (that, coincidentally, doesn't work). Although protests have poured in from architects around the globe (the main part of the tower is some two-hundred feet shorter than Kuala Lumpur's Petronas Towers), Spagle's Book of World Records, the preeminent record keepers from around the globe, have officially recognized Fang Tower. Rumors that Mr. Fang bribed the nominating committee have abounded since then, but no one has been able to prove anything so far, other than the notable fact that every member of the nominating committee was flown by private jet to Hong Kong during the process and on their return home, each of them seemed to be handcuffed to a large, black briefcase with padlocks.

64 "THE INCREDIBLE HULKING TEENAGER FROM McDOUGAL'S" taken from Mr. Ping's Almanac, Vol. 74

Mr. Ping had heard bad things about the dangerous deep fryers in McDougal's restaurants through several sources. Through the 1970s, the corporation had been installing them all over the United States and Canada as a "revolutionary" way to cook food. They held the patent to the fryer, known as the McDougal Maker, for the last year and kept the McDougal Maker's inner workings a closely guarded secret. This was all well and good for the average person and they happily believed the McDougal's restaurant chain's tales about how they were innovators and about their dedication to creating the best products so that they might offer the best service to their customers. This, of course, was easy to believe because their spokesperson was the always charming and kid-friendly McDougal the Puppet.

But Mr. Ping knew the truth. McDougal's was run by former government scientists and defense contractors who were bent on finding new ways to control people. Their goals had been formulated by a former five-star general that had been fired by the government for his radical, anti-freedom views. He had openly stated that your average human being was not much more intelligent that a cow and thought that if they could get the populace addicted to cheap, tasty food, then they would have a population that was easy to control, for over time, they would become unable to take care of themselves and be forced to rely on others for their most basic needs.

Mr. Ping had inside sources in the McDougal's organization. He knew that they had their nasty little fingers in all sorts of nasty little schemes.

There was the secret ingredient in their burgers: a genetically engineered soybean that made people more susceptible to mind control. There was their replacement of beef with kangaroo meat when cattle prices got too high. There was also the fact that the deep fryer used to make French fries was not filled with oil, but with human sweat, which gave the fries that "special" McDougal's flavor.

The problem with the McDougal Maker was its power source. Rumors within the organization said that the military had shot down some sort of meteorite, whose chunks seemed to be made of a strange, volatile, energy producing material. Each little chunk of the meteorite was enough to power a small home. Even little chunks, no bigger than a millimeter in size, were able to power small machines. Hence, the former military men decided to "commandeer" a few chunks so that they might put it to good use, specifically as an alternative power source to help it keep costs down at their restaurants.

What this all boiled down to was the fact that McDougal's was using some sort of unknown, radioactive power source to cook their hamburgers, and on this *particular night, one of them had exploded...*

....I arrived at the scene of the McDougal's restaurant just after seven PM and found a wasteland caused by the explosion. Hamburger patties were everywhere, littering the ground, covering cars, hanging from trees, and all of them sizzling and charred from the heat of the blast. The only thing more plentiful than hamburger patties were French fries, some of which had been blasted from the building with such velocity that they had punctured the metal bodies of some cars, while others were stuck into trees at a perfect 90 degree angle to the ground.

The fire chief was working with her men to help contain the blaze when I asked, "What could have done this, madame?"

"They were using some sort of experimental deep fryer," she said. "Blew the whole place to smithereens."

"Is everyone okay?" I asked.

"Seems everybody got out except the cook," she said. "Some teenager. Zit-faced kid working the deep fryer. Go ahead and go in while you have the chance, Mr. Ping."

"Thanks," I said.

The firefighters were ensuring that everyone kept a safe distance from the smoldering embers of the restaurant, but I didn't let that stop me for a second. While everyone was focused on a secondary fire raging in a burned out car in the parking lot, I made my way into the smoking ruins of the building. The smell of burnt burgers was more powerful than the smoke of the fire and I had to cover my nose to enter the place. Everywhere I looked, there were tell-tale signs that this was a McDougal's, ranging from the melted wax statue of McDougal the Clown in the lobby, his features melted into a horrible, rainbow grimace, to

the steaming remains of what were once the plastic toys from their *Good Times Kid's Meal.*

I was after one thing and one thing only: to get the source of the deep fryer's power, so that I might study it and analyze it in case the McDougal corporation ever decided to use their power in a destructive way. I climbed my way into the kitchen and found the flattened, tin shell that was once the McDougal Maker. It looked as if a very powerful blast had happened inside, as all four of its silver sides were now flattened like a flower that had been stepped on. And there, in the center of the oven, was a small, glowing purple rock that lit up the whole room. Since I was already wearing my lead-lined suit from my meeting with *Kildare Sinclair* at the *Mansion LaRoche*, I simply put on my radiation mask to take the rock away for safe-keeping.

I took the meteorite and put it in a lead-lined box to protect myself from whatever radiation might be emanating from it and then quickly exited the smoldering remains of the building and gave the thumbs-up sign to the chief. "Did you find what you were looking for?" she asked.

"Yes," I said. "Have you heard any more about what might have happened to that fry cook?" I asked.

"Nothing," she said. "We figure he's been blasted to smithereens or he just up and skipped out of work early. We're not going to know until we go through the place with a fine-toothed comb."

"Thanks for your help, Chief," I said, and I went on about my business. I had what I was looking for now and had gotten it with a minimal amount of fuss.

But there was something wrong with the picture. As I drove away, my thoughts kept returning to that teenage fry cook. That poor, pimple-faced teen with a minimum-wage

job, was forced to slave over a hot stove every night for hours on end, all in an effort to please the perpetually unsatisfied fast-food customer. Now this young lad had been blasted into oblivion by the very white hot stove whose visage he hated to see every single day. That the poor soul had been blown to tiny pieces instantly seemed too simple.

Back at the hotel, I made some phone calls to the McDougal's head office in an effort to ascertain the names of the employees at this particular restaurant, all under the guise of being a newspaper reporter out to cover the story of the explosion and the tragedy that ensued. "Yes, yes," I was saying over the phone, "And what was the name of that poor, young teen who was killed in the explosion? The pimply-faced one?"

"I'm sorry, Mr., uh…" said the operator, a bit baffled by my line of questioning.

"Pence," I lied. "Percival Pence of the Pigspitt Times."

"I'm sorry, Mr. Pence," the operator said, "But no one was killed in the accident."

"That can't be right," I said. "When I spoke to the fire chief, she said that the cook was unaccounted for."

"That was true at the time," the operator said. "But they found him a little while ago."

"They did?"

"Yes," she said. "He was a bit shaken, but they found him at home. Not a scratch on him. It was a miracle."

A miracle? To survive a point blank explosion without a scratch to show for it? Sure, it might have been a miracle, but it was probably much more than that. I'd seen the damage from the explosion. I knew that no one could have survived such a devastating blast. I also knew that I had to investigate this strange turn of events.

I discovered that the name of the teen was none

other than Robert Banyon Junior, a senior at the local high school. I quickly deduced that somewhere out there, there had to be a Robert Banyon *Senior*, and after a quick scan of the local phone book, I found just who I was looking for. I tried calling the family home to arrange a visit, but the line was busy all evening, probably filled with folks trying to check on poor Robert's well-being. Having nothing better to do, I decided to simply pay the family a visit to check on Robert myself.

It should be noted that upon exiting my hotel room, I couldn't help but notice the presence of The Conspiricetti's henchmen doing their grunt work. Three of them, each in their trench-coats, mirrored-sunglasses and fedora hats, were surrounding the hotel, standing on each of the three corners that I could see, watching and waiting, documenting my every move. If I'd had the time or inclination, I'd have shown them the error of their ways with a bit of Shang-Fu, but I had much more pressing concerns.

I couldn't shake the feeling that I was reacting to this chain of events a few minutes too late, and as I drove through the suburbs of town, my worst fears were realized. It looked as if a tornado had passed through the city, devastating houses on both sides of the street, leaving nothing but yellow, wooden splinters both large and small, where the houses used to stand. Something horrible had moved through the area, and I had a sneaking suspicion that the McDougal's incident might be the cause of it.

I arrived at the Banyon home to discover that it was the epicenter of the destruction. Where once a beautiful, coral-colored house had stood, now there was only a vague shell of a family home. Clothes hung in trees that were cracked in half, furniture was strewn

everywhere, wallpaper and insulation littered the lawns in all directions, all while frantic and confused neighbors wandered the streets, trying to make sense of what had just happened to them. In the distance, I could hear the sounds of rescue trucks and because of this, I knew that I had little time.

Standing in the yard of the Banyon home was a man I assumed to be Robert Banyon Sr., a conservative-looking fellow wearing an undershirt, trousers, and large, black-rimmed glasses. He was accompanied by what looked to be his wife, who was wearing a pink robe and had her hair in curlers. Their young daughter, a girl of around nine who clutched her teddy bear as a protector, was quietly gathering up all of her toys that had been strewn about the yard. Each one had the look of sheer terror in their eyes. Robert Banyon Jr. was nowhere to be seen.

"Excuse me," I asked. "Are you Mr. Banyon?"

"Uh, yes," he said. He didn't look at me. He just stared at what used to be his house.

"Sir, I'm Percival Pence of the Pigspitt Press, and I was…"

"It happened so quickly," he muttered. "He just…It happened so quickly…"

"What happened, sir?" I asked. "Where is your son?"

"Our son is gone," the mother said.

"Gone?" I asked.

"My husband was arguing about something with Junior," she said. "Robert told Junior that he didn't care about him surviving the explosion, that he still had to get out there and mow the lawn."

Mr. Banyon said, "He said he didn't have to mow the lawn and that I couldn't tell him what to do. I said as long as he lived in my house, I could tell him what to do. He said when he turned eighteen he was out of here. I said that he could either mow the lawn or

he could be grounded this weekend. He yelled something about hating me. I don't remember much after that."

"Now, he's gone," the mother said. "We don't know where he is. Our house is destroyed."

"Does your son have any places he likes to hang out in?" I asked, feeling a sense of urgency. "A pool hall? A restaurant of some sort? A friend's house?"

"Sometimes he goes down to Al's Arcade on Arbutus," his father said. "Hangs out with those ungrateful, no-good, teenage friends of his. That's the only place that I could think of."

I turned them towards me and looked them in the eye. "I'm going to bring your son back," I said. "If he comes back before I do, I want you to stay away from him. Do you understand?"

"Why?" the mother asked. "He's our son!"

"He's much more than that, now, ma'am," I said. "Just remember what I said."

I turned to leave and felt Mr. Banyon's hand on my shoulder. "Wait!" he said. "Who are you?"

I turned to him with a confident look in my eye and said, "I'm Superman!" before running off down the street. Now, I must note that I am not, in reality, Superman, but I'd always wanted to say something like that at such a time, and when I did, I checked off yet another box on my life's "to-do" list.

Al's Arcade was a typical hole in the wall storefront, nondescript in every way, save for the spray-painted, stenciled sign that hung crooked over the door. The building was just a square box, with grass growing through the cracks in the unused parking lot out front. Though the place looked lifeless on the outside, it was far from lifeless on the inside. Through the hazy neon and roar of pinball machines and video games, I discovered that almost every teenage boy in the city had congregated at the place, some lurking in the corners, while others were crowded around a single machine in the corner, whose player was about to beat the high scoring record. Upon closer examination, I saw that the center of the attention was a pimply-faced teenager in a McDougal's uniform. I'd found Robert Banyon Jr.

"Excuse me," I asked over his shoulder, "But are you Robert Banyon Jr.?"

Never breaking his gaze from the plate glass of the machine in front of him, he muttered, "Who wants to know?" in the most sarcastic way possible.

"I'm Percival Pence of the Pigspitt Press," I said. "I'd like to ask you a few questions about what happened tonight."

"Big explosion," he muttered. "I survived. End of story. Now, beat it!"

As I spoke with him, I couldn't help but notice several big whiteheads on his face and the perverse side of my personality wanted to jab my fingernail into the especially big one on the end of his nose, just to put it out of its misery, but I controlled my impulses. "I'm not talking about McDougal's, Robert," I said. "I'm talking about what happened at your house."

In the split-second that Robert paused to absorb what I'd just said to him, the shiny, silver ball of the pinball machine rolled straight through his paddles, ending his run at the title by a mere two points. "You made me lose, man!" he said.

"I'm very sorry about that," I said. "Look, I think it's important that you come with me. You're in a lot of trouble and I'd like to help."

"I ain't goin' nowhere with you, man!" he yelled. "You guys just think it's groovy to tell us what to do. You, my dad, everybody! Well, ain't nobody

gonna tell me what to do anymore!"

"I'm only trying to help," I said, working to calm him down. I could feel the prying eyes of the whole place on my shoulders, as all of the young, teenage boys with their average haircuts, pubescent pimples, and latent desire to follow the leader had put their eyes upon me, waiting to see what Robert would do.

"You ain't tryin' to help me," he yelled. "You're just tryin' to help yourself!"

"Robert, why don't we go outside to talk," I said. It was then that I noticed something was wrong.

"I don't need no adult telling me what to do," he yelled. Right before my very eyes, Robert had grown what seemed to be a foot taller. Whereas before, he had been shorter than I was, now he was taller, and his McDougal's outfit was starting to tighten on his lanky frame.

"Robert," I said. "Do you realize what's happening?"

"Yeah, I realize what's happening," he said. His voice had grown deeper and his face wider. "You're tryin' to tell me what to do! You can't tell me what to do! *Nobody* can! Adults think they know everything. They're always tryin' to give me advice. Go to university! Don't read comic books! Do your chores! Mow the lawn! They don't want to let me led my own life! I just want to live my own life. I... want...lead...own...life!"

Robert had been growing from a teenage boy to some large, hulking beast. His muscles grew thick and solid, the McDougal's outfit that he wore stretched thin over his skin before ripping at the seams, and his forehead grew large and began to hang over his eyes like Frankenstein's monster. Strangest of all was the fact that his skin began to change color, going from a healthy pink to a dull gray.

Where once a teenager stood before me, I was now faced with a mammoth, muscular, gray creature with torn clothes and a one-note mentality.

"You...big...people... act...stupid!" he said. His voice was deeper and full of anger, and he could no longer put words together to say what he was thinking. "You...no... tell...me...what...do!"

Most of the young boys in the arcade were running around in a panic, trying to get out of the way as Robert's anger filled them with fear. I had no idea as to what to do, but I stood my ground, refusing to be cowed by this giant, brooding, angry, monosyllabic teenager trying to intimidate me. "Robert," I said, "You need to calm down. Something has happened to you."

"Robert...is...calm," he yelled, but I could see in his eyes that he wasn't. "Stop... telling...Robert...what...to... do!"

In that instant, I knew what had happened. Somehow, the radiation from the fryer had mutated Robert, so that whenever Robert got angry, he became a walking, gigantic creature that was just the barest essence of a human being and more of the purest form of adolescence there could possibly be: a giant, angry teenager bent on not being told what to do.

"Robert," I said, "I'm only trying to help."

"ROBERT...NO... WANT...HELP!" he yelled. Were it not for my cat-like reflexes, I would have been dead, as Robert swung his gigantic arm to swat me away. I dodged the oncoming blow as he used his power to smash one of the pinball machines into a pile of glass, metal, and plastic. I quickly deduced that now Robert also had great strength.

He was also fast, for just as I'd regained my footing, he came after me again, leaving me only enough time to run as he destroyed yet another machine in an attempt to pulverize me. "ROBERT SMASH!" he yelled. "YOU NO TELL ROBERT WHAT TO DO!"

I ran out of the arcade, trying to stay two steps ahead of the creature whilst also trying to figure out a way to deal with the problem. Inside the arcade, I could hear the sound of an establishment being destroyed from the inside out, and as I tried to figure out what to do, one of the pinball machines came flying through the wall, missing my head by only a couple of feet. I looked to see Robert stick his gray head out of the hole to scowl at me. "ROBERT *SMASH!*" he yelled.

With nothing but brute force, he literally walked through the wall, intent on seizing me with his massive hands. As I ran away, it all became perfectly clear. I knew what I had to do to stop this lad. I could easily out pace him as he continued to get distracted by bright and shiny things. Even as a mutated creature, Robert still had the attention span of a teenager. Luckily, most of the shops and businesses were closed that evening, or there might have been more damage and loss of life as Robert tossed street lights, cars, and mailboxes in an attempt to, as he put it, "smash" me.

I ran to Elmer's Electronics Outlet, which was a small store I'd seen as I was driving to the arcade. It was closed, so I used the methods I'd learned from my months spent as a theif on the streets of Hong Kong to unlock the door and rush inside. From the safety of the store, I could hear Robert make his way down the street, getting louder and louder as the sounds of breaking glass and crunching concrete echoed through the streets. All the while, he continued to shout, "ROBERT SMASH!"

Then silence ensued as I listened for a sign. Even

through the walls, I could hear his heavy breath as he tried, in his own simple way, to figure out where I'd gone. Then I heard the sound of the front doors of the shop being ripped off, and as the noise settled, I heard the thump of his big, bare feet walking into the building. "ROBERT SMASH PUNY ADULT!" he said, his attention already shifting focus. He seemed more calm now, but he did, occasionally, knock over a cash register or stereo in an attempt to intimidate me. "Where…is…stupid…adult?" he muttered.

"I'm over here," I said, just loud enough for him to hear me, but still well out of his view.

The sound of my voice must have made him angry again, as he began to break things and tear the place apart. "RAHRR!" he yelled. "PUNY ADULT THINK ROBERT STUPID! ROBERT WILL FIND PUNY ADULT!"

Just as I expected, he made his way right to me. I stood in the middle of the television section of the store, surrounded by TVs, both large and small. He walked right up to me and lifted his arms high above his head, as if he was going to drive me into the ground. "ROBERT SMASH!" he yelled. "ROBERT SMASH PUNY ADULT!"

And then, magically, I flipped on the first television with the remote control hidden behind my back. Robert paused, looking up at the TV show in front of him, examining the screen with curiosity. His arms lowered for a split-second, and then, he refocused on me, as angry as ever. "ROBERT NOT STUPID!" he said. "ROBERT SMASH!"

I turned on another television, then another, and still another, until the whole wall behind me was nothing but blaring TVs, each one showing a different program. Robert, who mere seconds

before, had been angry enough to kill me, was now completely engrossed in the drama playing out before him. Hundreds of TVs, hundreds of distractions, and one large, muscular, gray creature standing in front of them, enraptured. In fact, Robert seemed to no longer realize I was even in the room.

I watched his arms lower from above my head, down to his sides, as he looked out from behind that large brow of his and stared at the screens. He stood there for a few seconds, before finally sitting down, cross-legged, in front of the TVs.

I watched as Robert's muscles contracted, growing smaller and smaller as he shrank into his over-stretched clothes. What was once a giant, Mr. Hyde-like creature, was becoming a sullen teenager again. The televisions had done their duty, robbing the teen of his anger and providing a distraction for his angst. When I looked back, Robert Banyon Jr., that incredible, *hulking* teenager, simply became Robert Banyon Jr., teenager.

"Are you okay, Robert?" I asked.

His eyes never left the television screens in front of him as he muttered, "Yeah. Fine."

I had quelled the rage of the savage beast. The monster was no more, only the same bitter, lonely teenager that he was previously, without the least bit of memory about what he'd just done. I heard the wail of ambulances outside and knew that, for now, this ordeal was behind me. Still, there remained many unanswered questions, such as how many more of those infernal machines did McDougal's have in their restaurants across the country? When would this happen again?

I looked at the teenager in front of me calmly watching TV and I was filled with fear. I didn't know the answers…

65 THE WORLD'S LARGEST HAY BALE

Being in a fairly nondescript part of the province of Ontario in Canada, Frankfurter has very little to offer the world, aside from a steady supply of sullen high school graduates. The local Buy-Mart superstore failed to invigorate the town, a new McDougal's restaurant also failed to make an impact, and the recently built strip mall on the edge of town still sits half-empty. It is a town without a future.

However, there was one defining moment in the history of the town, which happened in 1975. Determined to put his town on the map, the mayor, David Flowerpot, vowed to get the city on track by discovering something that could get them into the history books. Mayor Flowerpot talked to several local farmers and scoured the history books and almanacs, before arriving at the notion of creating the World's Largest Hay Bale. He realized that there was a noticeable dearth of world records regarding hay, so he devised one himself.

Working day and night for over a week, the volunteer farmers created a six-story tall, round hay bail on Heddy Johnson's farm, beside her picturesque red barn. Sure enough, Frankfurter got into the history books, but unfortunately, no one thought about what to do with the hay bail once the record was set, so for the next twenty-five years, Heddy Johnson had a giant, stinky, rotting, six-story high monstrosity of hay sitting in her yard. The pulpy remains are still there today.

66 THE GOLDEN MILE

A section of Kowloon (Tsim Sha Tsui) that stretches from the waterfront of Victoria Harbor all the way up Nathan Road, the Golden Mile is a collection of restaurants, tailors, electronic shops, and other, less savory, establishments, all of which bask in the neon glow of the signs high above the street. The area contains some of the most luxurious hotels in the world, but can also be a haven for nasty types who prey on the foolish traveler. At one time, Reggie lived in a penthouse overlooking Kowloon Park on Haiphong Road, but had to move when the owner asked him to leave, citing his inability to rent out any other apartments in the building once word got out that a yeti lived on the top floor. "Look, I'm sorry," said the building manager, "But nobody wants to live under a yeti. They think it's bad luck."

67 TONY TANG'S TEAS

Located in an alley near the Temple Street Night Market, Tony Tang's Teas has been in business for well-over two hundred years, always in or around the same section of Kowloon. Specializing in the strange and unusual in Chinese medicines, Tony, the owner of the shop, has catered not to the general public, but more to those one might consider "in-the-know;" usually people who have advanced knowledge of Chinese medicines, including adventurers, wizards, witches, academics, and so forth. If an adventurer is seeking out gumroot extract to keep from getting malaria in some exotic country, they will go to Tony Tang. If an academic is doing a study or experiment of some kind to try to remove warts from Eastern European noses while using the armpit sweat of the Eastern Javanese Guinea Pig, they'll seek out Tony Tang. And if a witch is looking to put a pox on someone that might have wronged her and she needs goat boogers, the extract of a Walkabee Flower from Polynesia, and a good helping of West African fingernail clippings for her stew to work, she'll seek out Tony Tang.

Tony Tang's Teas has been run by Tony Tang for the entirety of its two-hundred year existence, and the question of Tony's life longevity has been pondered by many people over the years. Tony has only publicly stated that his age can be attributed to a special tea, the recipe for which has been a closely guarded family secret for many years, and that the tea has not and never will be for public consumption because, as he has often stated, "Human beings are too stupid to live forever!"

Because of his location at the magnetic nexus point of Kowloon, Tony's tea shop has attracted a very diverse group of customers, and although Tony is a good person at heart, he has never made judgments on his clientèle, be they good or bad. "It's not my job to be the policeman for the universe," he told Mr. Ping one time. "They come in and they buy something. If they can pay for it, good for them. What they want to do with my medicine when they leave the shop is up to them."

This, of course, has led to a few conflicts with Mr. Ping over the years, as Tony has sold some of his special concoctions to a wide variety of Mr. Ping's rogue's gallery, including Madame Hookworm, Lt. Cyanide, and Helmut Frankenstein. This has sometimes led to problems for Tony himself, as he is currently suffering from a fifteen year witch's curse because he sold a bad batch of Burlysweet flower to a witch from Zimbabwe, which caused her to slap a curse upon him. Tony Tang's Teas has also been home to Bird and Goldfish for over fifty years.

68 YETI-POWDER

An ancient Chinese herbal remedy, yeti powder is rumored to improve the immune system so well that it will cause the user to live forever. Of course, this has never been proved scientifically, but it hasn't stopped those poor souls obsessed with eternal life from using it religiously. The belief in longevity due to yeti powder stems from two well-known facts, one being that yetis never get sick, and the other that yetis have incredibly long life-spans, especially in relation to human life-spans. Thus, a few poor fools took it upon themselves to hunt yetis, grind up their bones, and drink it with some sort of liquid. Yet the first of these supposed yeti-hunters ended up losing their lives. It wasn't because of being mauled or eaten by yetis, though. It was because the type of person inclined to head out to hunt a yeti so as to extend their own lifespan is not inclined to be the brightest bulb in the pack, and most of them ended up being killed doing particularly stupid things. One person died in pursuit of a yeti up the face of Mt. Everest. One person failed to bring enough warm clothes to survive a trek through the region. Countless others fell into crevasses, slipped on ice, or even starved to death, for the Himalayas can be a very cruel environment.

The unfortunate part of this story is that some yeti-hunters actually succeeded in their quest, and because of the cruel indifference of greed and self-centered people, several yetis lost their lives over the years. Although most people think it is a cruel and unusual pastime and that yeti-powder doesn't work, yeti-hunting still occurs to this day, as those greedy souls with no ability to see the stupidity of their actions trek out into the wilds in the idiotic hopes of prolonging their pathetic lives.

69 DUCK WART, taken from Mr. Ping's Almanac, Vol. 23

Very popular in Chinese medicine, but extremely rare, duck wart is said to give people the ability to read other people's minds for a limited time. Duck wart rarity stems from the fact that it is only effective when taken from white ducks who grow a large wart on the middle toe of their left, webbed foot. Once ground into a powder, it is only effective in very, very large quantities, meaning one cup of ground, duck wart powder, consumed when either mixed with tea or juice, can give its user *telepathic abilities for* approximately thirty-six hours.

An unfortunate side-effect of using duck wart is that it often causes mild to severe insanity. Most human minds (especially those greedy and manipulative souls who want to use duck wart) cannot handle three, four, or even

thousands of people's thoughts flooding into their mind at once. Without the ability to hear their own thoughts, the user forgets who they actually are and can rarely remember their own identity afterward.

Nevertheless, duck wart is popular on the black market and its terrible side-effects, high price, and rarity on the market have failed to deter unseemly souls from wanting to acquire it. Some global spy organizations have been known to use it, and several business people have tried it in an attempt to cut better deals in negotiations. However, the most famous practitioner of duck wart is Sally Grindowski, better known through criminal circles as Sally the Scrambler. Mr. Ping first encountered Sally the Scrambler in 1923 while visiting New York City.

...My hands and feet were tied to the chair as I sat in front of the opulent balcony that overlooked Central Park. Someone knew all of my tricks, for the knots on my hands and feet were tied in such a way that I couldn't undo them. I felt groggy, as if someone had slipped something powerful into my drink. To my right and left were two angry looking goons with what appeared to be more muscles than brains, and I began to assess how much of a threat they would be when I broke free.

"I see you've finally awoken," came a voice from behind me. It was a sleepy, low voice, almost seductive in its grogginess. From behind me emerged a beautiful young woman, her black hair curled tightly against her face and her skin pale, almost translucent in her purple flapper dress. But what was most striking about her were her eyes. They were large and brown, with dark, almost black circles under them that betrayed a weariness.

"Sally the Scrambler," I said.

"That's right," she said. "I thought you were going to remain asleep all night long.

Still, you gave me plenty of time to explore the nooks and crannies of your mind. Your psychic defenses are formidable."

"So you're the one plotting to rob the First Centennial Bank tomorrow," I said.

"That's correct," she said. "You almost spoiled our glorious plan. Luckily, we caught you in time."

"Sally, you're making a terrible mistake," I said.

"Am I?" she asked, laughing.

"You're a telepath, Sally," I said. "You have a gift. Why would you want to use it for such worthless endeavors? You could change the world."

She laughed again in a wicked way as she leaned in to look at me, saying, "Worthless endeavors, Confucius? I would hardly say that stealing ten million dollars is a worthless endeavor. I'd say it's a quite profitable one."

She walked over to a bar at the side of the room, where a kettle of piping hot tea was sitting on the counter, and she began to pour two mugs, adding an orange, powdery substance to each one. She brought them over, sat them on a coffee table and then settled into the chair next to mine.

"How do you know I'm a telepath, Confucius?" she asked.

"You have a reputation, Sally," I said. "That's why you've been so successful as a criminal, I suppose, because you always know what your enemy is thinking."

"And yet, not with you, Confucius," she laughed. "Your thoughts are as mysterious as the night sky. Why is it that I can't read your mind?"

"I've had training to keep people like you out," I said.

"And very good training at that," she said. She sounded almost as if she was flirting with me. "Still, although I'm flattered by your thinking of me as a telepath, I believe you are mistaken."

"How so?" I asked.

"Have you ever heard of duck wart, Confucius?"

I paused, for I had heard of it, but only in myths and legends in Asia. "Yes," I said.

"Well, now you know my secret," she smiled.

"But duck wart can't possibly exist," I said.

"It does," she said. "And I've got two mugs of tea right here that are full of it." She rose from her chair and slowly circled me, trailing her index finger along my shoulders as if she were admiring me like a beautiful piece of furniture. "Duck wart allows me to hear the thoughts of others," she said. "Can you imagine what that's like?"

"I can't say that it sounds appealing," I said.

"And you'd be right," she said. "It can be horrible. But I have the gift of focus. If I concentrate, I can turn down the volume of most thoughts, and only hear what I need to hear. So, in that sense, perhaps you're right. Perhaps I am a telepath."

"What does that mean?" I asked.

"Most people, when they consume duck wart, go completely insane," she said. "Very few have the ability to drown out the thoughts of others and over the course of thirty-six hours, they completely lose their minds. Why? Because they've had so many voices in their heads that they completely forget who they were."

"But not you?" I asked.

"Oh, no," she said. "I can control it."

"And how do I fit into this?" I asked.

Sally sat on my lap and draped her arm over my neck, touching my nose in a playful way. "You know about the robbery," she said. "That makes you a liability."

"And?"

"And liabilities have to be eliminated," she said. "So although I like you, I'm going to have to get rid of you. And since I'm not the murderous type, I figured I'd just make you drink a mug of duck wart. You'll basically be rendered a drooling idiot for thirty-six hours as the thoughts of a million people in New York City flood into your head, which of course, gives me time to get my money and leave town before you can identify me. Unfortunately, the whole process will drive you insane, but that's a risk I'm willing to take."

So as I pondered the notion that in mere seconds, I would forget who I was because the floodgates of my mind would be opened to unwanted thoughts, Sally the Scrambler brought the tea over and sat it in front of me. "Bon appetite," she said, drinking deeply from her mug. "Enjoy your insanity..."

70 BIRD AND GOLDFISH

Very little is actually known about Bird and Goldfish other than the fact that they've been a pair of reliable allies to Mr. Ping throughout his life. Working out of the back of Tony Tang's Teas, they have been a go-to source of knowledge for Mr. Ping since the year 1911 and have never wavered from their trustworthiness or honor.

Still, despite their close contact throughout the years, Mr. Ping knew next to nothing about their origins. How was it that a bird and goldfish could talk? How did a bird and a goldfish become partners? How did a bird and a goldfish manage to live as long as these two had? And how in the world did Bird and Goldfish know so much? Mr. Ping tried in vain to find the answers to these questions at several times in his life:

"...And when Napoleon told me the same thing, I laughed and laughed," said Goldfish. "He was certainly a cad."

"Pardon me?" I asked, suddenly perplexed. "Napoleon?"

"Yes," Goldfish said. "He was a cad."

"Napoleon Bonaparte?" I asked. "From France?"

"Yes," he said, annoyed that I didn't get it. "Now about that shroud..."

"Hold on, Goldfish," I said. "You're saying that you spent time with Napoleon?"

"Yes," Bird chirped in. "We both did."

"But...But..." I said, flummoxed. "That would make you old. *Very* old."

"Yes, it would, wouldn't it?" Goldfish said, dismissing me. "Now, about that shroud..."

"Bird," I said, "How old are you?"

"Older than you'd ever imagine," Bird said with a sly smile.

"Now," Goldfish said, interrupting us, "*About that shroud...*"

The more the clues of Bird and Goldfish's origins revealed themselves, the more confusing their history became. The mention of Napoleon gave some indication that the two of them were well over a hundred years old (even at that time), but other clues would be revealed as well, which would only serve to baffle Mr. Ping even more so:

...We could see the Japanese troops marching through Kowloon in a display of sheer bravado, daring us to come out and challenge them. I observed as Goldfish scowled out the window, filled with bitterness towards our invaders.

"I haven't seen savagery like this since the middle ages," he muttered.

It took a couple of seconds for me to register what he'd just said. "Pardon me?" I asked. "Did you just say...?"

"It was nothing," Goldfish said. "Just the ramblings of a crazed goldfish. Pay it no mind..."

It would also behoove people to ignore the fact that Bird and Goldfish seem helpless because they are, in fact, a bird and a goldfish. Just because he is a fish does not , by any means, mean that Goldfish is confined to a fishbowl. He's been seen outside of the bowl several times. "...But I prefer the lovely environs of my bowl more than the cold, remorseless surface world that you people live in," he once told Mr. Ping. "Why anyone would choose to be an air breather is beyond me..."

And Bird is not helpless either. Her flying skills, vision, and sense of smell are unparalleled amongst her species and she is known to use them to great effect, such as the time she apprehended Loose-Tooth Larry as he tried to escape into the Peruvian Andes in 1940.

71 PERPETUAL MOTION

From the Latin *Perptum Movile*, a perpetual motion machine is a hypothetical device that produces energy "from nowhere." That mean that perpetual motion is motion created without energy and that continues indefinitely. A perpetual motion machine, once started, would continue running forever, without use for gas, coal, electricity, or anything else.

Most scientists believe that a perpetual motion machine cannot exist because it would violate the first and second laws of physics. Most claims from scientists (or laypeople) about the creation of a perpetual motion machine are met with disbelief, although there have been rumors and myths about its creation for centuries. One of the most popular rumors of a perpetual motion machine's existence is that of its invention by Qin Shihuangdi, the first emperor of China (the story of which is detailed in this book). Leonardo DaVinci was rumored to have built one, as were 20th century eccentrics Rube Goldberg and Heath Robinson. The latest claim of a perpetual motion machine came from Oklahoma farmer Troy Bullbricker. "Ain't nobody believed me yet," said Mr. Bullbricker to the local paper. "But I knows I made one uh them

there things." Mr. Ping had plans to visit Mr. Bullbricker before he died, but never had the chance.

72 MONGOLS

An ethnic group that number around ten million, the Mongols originated in what is now Russia, China, and Mongolia. At the height of their empire, and under the leadership of Genghis Khan, the Mongols had the largest empire in world history, where they ruled close to 100 million people and over 13 million square miles (which included China, Korea, Afghanistan, Russia, Hungary, and the lands that surround them). Their empire lasted for centuries and during that time, they conquered territories and forced them to trade with their empire. The Mongols conquered northern China in 1200.

73 MONGOLIA

Mongolia is a landlocked country in Asia surrounded by Russia in the north and China in the south. Its capitol is Ulan Bator. The northern parts of Mongolia consist of steppes, which are flat and grassy, while the south is taken up by the Gobi desert. The country is very hot in the summer and cold in the winter.

74 GENGHIS KHAN

Living from 1165-1227, Genghis Khan was a Mongolian emperor and military leader who founded the Mongolian empire by uniting the tribes of the region and conquering lands in Asia and as far west as Eastern Europe. Known as a ruthless and savvy warrior, he laid the foundation for an empire that would last for centuries. Though he has been dead for many centuries, Genghis Khan is rumored to be just as powerful now as he was then, for it is said that his ghost still roams the grassy plains of Mongolia and is awaiting the moment when he can reassemble his army to continue his conquest of the world. The mystery of Genghis Khan's ghost and the army he is building was a high priority for investigation before Mr. Ping

passed away, but he never got the chance to pursue it.

75 MR. PING ACQUIRES THE FIRST PIECE OF THE PERPETUAL MOTION MACHINE, taken from Mr. Ping's Almanac, Vol. 20

Mr. Ping had collected pieces of Emperor Qin Shihuangdi's Perpetual Motion Machine since 1919, when he discovered the very first piece and found out exactly what it was. While visiting the town of Kashgar in western China, he heard rumors of a strange discovery in the middle of the Gobi desert, not far from where he was. Some locals who had traveled through the area had spoken of the shifting sand dunes and how the blowing sand had uncovered a Chinese temple in the middle of nowhere that was sealed shut. Intrigued, Mr. Ping hired the locals to take him to where they thought they had seen the temple. After a blisteringly hot trip through the desert, they finally arrived at their location, which they were lucky to discover, as it was practically buried in sand again, with only the corner sticking out.

...We spent the whole of two days fighting against the relentless wind, trying desperately to dig through some sort of entrance to the temple, and on the beginning of our third morning, we discovered the door. It was ornate and looked to be made of solid gold, with pictures of ancient Chinese soldiers etched in the front. All of the soldiers were guarding some sort of skeleton key that was floating high over a mountain, above which hovered a dragon.

"We are rich!" Ahmed said as he examined the door. "This door is solid gold."

Both he and a couple of his workmen began dancing around in place, celebrating their newfound riches, but I had other things on my mind. "We have to find a way in," I said, examining the seal of the door.

"Yes, yes," Ahmed said. "We have to figure out a way to pry that door from its hinges."

I looked at Ahmed very seriously and I could see that in his eyes he was young and impetuous. The fever lust for what riches lay inside the temple clouded his judgment. "Ahmed," I said, looking at him calmly, "Be careful what you wish for. Riches such as these do not come without a price."

"Yes, yes," he said, having not heard a word that I said.

"Let's try to get the rest of the door uncovered and then we'll figure out how to get inside," I said. I was tired for we'd been digging for hours without a break. I walked over to the camels for a drink of water, leaving Ahmed and his workmen to the task of finishing the excavation.

I should never have left them. I was too young to recognize the look in Ahmed's eyes, and had underestimated their desire for riches and fortune. I should never have left someone like that alone. Instead of continuing the excavation, they set about trying to open the door. Instead of calling me over, Ahmed and two of his men ventured into the temple themselves. It was the last I would see of them.

I must have sat by the camels for a good ten minutes before I realized that I could no longer hear the chattering of Ahmed and his men. Curious, I rose from my shady spot and walked around the side of the temple only to find the golden door pried open and the remaining two men milling about nervously.

"Where's Ahmed?" I asked, looking into the blackened doorway.

They half-heartedly motioned towards the entrance and I knew that things weren't good. With the knowledge that I was making a potentially huge mistake, I ventured just inside the door, where I saw a torch attached to the wall, which lit the dark corridor in front of me. Along walls that had gone untouched for centuries, I saw elaborate Chinese paintings, all of which celebrated a leader with pastorals and drawings of this leader on his throne with thousands of soldiers surrounding him. There were other pictures of the leader imparting his wisdom to a group of students around him. By the look of it, the drawings seemed to have been made around the first or second century B.C. and from that, I surmised that this temple must have been built in honor of Qin Shihuangdi, the first emperor of China. We'd made an amazing archaeological discovery.

But the celebration was tempered, for I found no sign of my friends in that corridor. I walked further into the darkness and called out Ahmed's name, but there was no reply.

The corridor ended at a set of stairs that descended deeper down into the ground, and it was at the bottom of those stairs that I saw the flicker of light from more torches at the bottom. I carefully made my way down, going deeper and deeper into the Earth, where the cooler air was a welcome relief from the oppressive desert heat. As I made my way further, I continued to observe the paintings on the walls with the light of my torch. It never failed that they celebrated Qin Shihuangdi, portraying him not so much as an emperor, but as a god, and I began to think that this emperor might have thought just a bit too much of himself.

At the bottom of the stairs, I found myself in an elaborate room, the walls lined with torches. It was very bright inside, and I was filled with a sense of dread, for I did not see my friends. There were four golden columns in the room to support the roof and hollow places in the walls where elaborately painted statues of old Chinese warriors stood on watch, observing a single, golden pedestal in the center of the room, upon which sat a very curious object.

I paused at the foot of the stairs, a bit too paranoid to go any further inside. Where had my friends gone? There didn't seem to be any exits from this room; this was the end of the temple. The floor was immaculately clean. There was no sand trailed in from any of the others.

I was about to step on the polished floor when I noticed something. It was too clean. After centuries of sitting in the middle of the Gobi desert, amongst the shifting sand dunes, there had to have been a trace of sand on the floor. There was sand everywhere else, including on the walls and around the gold pedestal at the other end of the room. I began to fear for my friends and knew in my heart that they'd met a gruesome fate. I suspected the place to be booby-trapped.

With the bottom of my torch, I pressed down on the floor in front of me and my suspicions were confirmed. Even with the slightest bit of weight, the floor dropped down, spinning like a giant wheel on two hinges. It spun around once and came to a rest just as it was before.

I pushed down on the floor again and saw that below the floor was a large, black hole that went so far down that I couldn't see the bottom, and it was at the bottom of that hole that I suspected my friends had met their demise. I couldn't let the floor deter me, however, for I knew I had to get to the center of the room, to see what was on the pedestal. I scanned the space for a way around the revolving floor and observed that there were two small ledges along the walls, running just below the statues. Hoping that they, too, were not rigged with some horrible device, I made my way over and inched across the room, towards what appeared to be solid ground. I was naive to think that I was home free, for as soon as I put my foot on **the** solid part of the floor, a giant spike crashed through the ceiling, falling inches from my head.

I was at a loss as to what to do or which marble tiles caused the spikes to come down, so I used the torch as a way to trigger the spikes. I carefully pressed down on each tile and it was either solid or would sink into the ground a couple of inches and trigger the steel spike from above. I felt that I was still treading on dangerous ground, for it never ceased to unnerve me when the spikes would burst from the ceiling. Yet that nervousness kept me on edge and it led me safely to the center of the room where the strange object lay on the pedestal.

I stood just a few feet away, observing it, trying to figure out what exactly it was. It looked like a piece of machinery, with a long tube that curled back and forth on itself and few gears and cogs on the side. It seemed to be a part of a greater whole. What I didn't understand was why all of this pomp and circumstance surrounded it. It didn't seem to be made out of gold or silver, or even platinum. There were no diamond-encrusted rings around it or anything of mention embedded in the sides. It was just a piece of machinery.

I assume that in my distraction, I failed to take into account the danger that I was in, and because of this, I absentmindedly reached up and plucked the piece right off of the pedestal. It was a horrible mistake, for as soon as I did, I heard a rumbling and the spikes began to retract back into the ceiling.

I was ready for anything. As I sat on pins and needles,

the temple grew deathly quiet. I expected the roof to collapse or a giant chasm to open up in the ground below me, but neither of these things happened. In fact, nothing happened for almost a full two minutes.

Then I heard it. It sounded like stone grinding against stone. It was quite subtle and had I not been on the edge of my seat in anticipation, I might have missed it, but I zeroed in on the sound. Sure enough I heard it again, only this time, I heard two sounds, one from each side of the room. I spun around to see where it was coming from and then a frightening sight appeared before me.

The stone statues in the walls were coming to life.

They moved stiffly at first, as if every inch that they traveled was a gargantuan effort. They had been standing in the same position for centuries, unblinking, unmoving, guarding their subject with quiet determination. Now, something was threatening that which they were charged to protect and they began to shake off the dust to deal with this "intruder." The only problem was that the intruder was me.

At first, I wasn't very alarmed. I'd seen supernatural events such as this and these statues were moving so slowly, I was sure that they posed no threat. But then, things began to change. I watched the statues and yes, they looked rusty, stiff, and unable to move, but they were simply shaking off the dust. The more they stretched and moved their stone bodies around, the more flexible they became, until in the span of two minutes, they were as agile and spry as I was. They snapped to attention, each one standing straight as a board, their arms at their sides.

I hadn't moved from my position in front of the golden pedestal in the entire time that the statues had come to life.

Now, we all stood frozen, the entire lot of us playing a dangerous game of poker.

Moving as slowly as possible, I turned to look at the statue behind me. the statue turned to look at me. Then, it spun in place with incredible speed and stopped in an aggressive pose, pointing its wooden spear at me. It slowly circled me, its spear pointing at my head all the while, its dead eyes focused like a laser.

With the speed of a cheetah, it thrust the spear towards me and it was everything I could do to avoid being skewered. I was still assessing the threat level, so I didn't fight back. I only dodged the statue's blows.

But I could only remain passive for a few more seconds, because another one of the statues joined its comrade and started thrusting its own spear at me from behind. One, I could handle; two were a threat. So as the one in front of me thrust his weapon one last time, I took the momentum of his blow and pulled him and the spear behind me, straight into his partner. Both statues fell to the ground in a pile of dust and struggled to regain their footing.

It was at this moment that I knew I wasn't going to make it out of this temple alive if I wasn't more aggressive in my actions. As the two other statues struggled to their feet, a silent signal was given and I was rushed by three more of them. I reached down and grabbed a dropped spear and spun it around, sending the blunt end right into the head of one of the first of my aggressors, knocking it to the ground. The other two stopped just feet away from me, giving their fallen comrades time to regain their footing.

Like lions watching their prey, they circled me, spears at the ready. I, too, had taken one of the fallen's spears, and whenever one would make a false move towards me, I would quickly dispatch it with the sharp end of my stick. One ran for me and I dodged him like a bullfighter, using the end of my spear to send him careening onto the revolving floor. The floor did its job well, and bearing the weight of the statue, it flipped over, sending it to its doom at the dark depths of the pit.

Although the other statues thought they had the upper hand by trying to force me towards the revolving floor, it was I who had the advantage. I began to go for them, one by one, using the spear as a pole of sorts with which I could throw my weight around. One would jab at me and I would spin out of the way, only to take out its legs with the spear. Then with a swift kick, I'd send it onto the revolving floor. Another would swing the end of its spear at me and I would duck, sending my spear right into its face, knocking it off balance enough so that I could send it into the pit as well.

With a fair amount of effort, I sent the other two into the pit, and as I breathed heavily, wiping the sweat from my brown, I surveyed the other, motionless statues. I stood there for several seconds, waiting on their advance, but there was none.

"Well, then," I said, taking the machine piece from the pedestal, "I guess that's that."

But even as I took the piece and began to walk away, the whole temple began to rumble like an earthquake. Parts of the ceiling began to fall near me and I knew that the place was about to collapse. Worst of all, all of the other statues had suddenly come to life.

Knowing that I had to make a quick exit, I shoved the piece into my sack, grabbed the spear, and ran for the door. Using the spear as a kind of pole vault, I drove the sharp end into the center of the revolving floor and catapulted myself over it without falling into the pit.

I landed with a thud on the opposite side, just as the columns that held the lower portion of the temple began to collapse. Using every bit of strength I had, I ran up the stairs as chunks of stone fell all around me. When I reached the top, I dove out the door just as the inside collapsed.

I rolled to a stop in the sand, spitting the brown mess out of my mouth and turning to survey the temple. I thanked the stars that I was still alive and took a few deep breaths, but I was filled with false relief, for I wasn't out of danger yet. The underground temple was collapsing in upon itself, creating a giant hole in which all of the surrounding sand was disappearing into. I began a mad scramble away from the hole as I started to sink up to my knees, then to my waist, and then to my chest.

My efforts were fruitless, for the sand swallowed me faster than I could climb out, and everything went black. It was only when I felt a hand grab mine that I became conscious again, and with great effort, I was pulled from the sand into the harsh, desert sunlight.

Coughing and gagging from the mess that I'd inhaled, I looked to see an Urgher farmer standing over me, surrounded by hundreds upon hundreds of goats. He said something with a laugh, but I failed to understand his language. I was very grateful, though, for this nomadic herder wandering through the desert had been in the right place at the right time and saved my life.

As we rode back to Kashgar on the camels with Ahmed's remaining men and the goat herder, I was thankful I was alive. But the more pressing thought in my mind was what it was, exactly, that I'd just taken from the temple. I would have to do some research to find out...

76 JULY 31ST, 1970

July 31st 1970 is a notorious day for many reasons, the main one being that it was the last time that Reggie and Smelts spoke to each other. Because of this conflict, the Himalayan Outback Detective Agency was officially closed, much to the dismay of hundreds of clients throughout Europe, and much to the celebration of hundreds of criminals around the world upon whom the agency had their eye. The offices in Paris were closed on August 1st, the day after the conflict, and everyone that worked there was sent home.

The main problem was that no one knew why.

Something happened on July 31st 1970 between Reggie and Smelts, but there isn't anyone besides the two of them that has any idea what might have gone wrong. They had always been the best of partners and had solved some of the biggest cases in all of Europe, if not the world, including The Great Heist of the Mona Lisa, the Living Pasta Terror of Genoa, and the infamous Disappearance of the Mediterranean Sea in 1949. Plus, they'd brought some of the world's worst criminals to justice, including Petite Louie, Sir Nigel Brickhammer the Hammerer, and the deadly Carrie the Cracker. The demise of the agency left everyone in shock, but the reasons for the demise of the agency left everyone befuddled. How could this have happened? Mr. Ping tried to find out in September of that year, when he tracked Reggie down in the Himalayas:

"...Reggie, what in the world happened?" I asked. "The two of you were inseparable. You worked so well as a team."

Reggie looked at me seriously and said, "Confucius, I will say this and this is all I will say. Smelts did something so truly horrible and wrong and twisted and rotten and despicable that I hope I never see him again. In fact, it was so wrong that I don't think I will ever be able to speak about it again."

"But you were best friends!" I said. "Friends work things out."

"This will never be worked out, Confucius," he said. "Now, if you don't mind, this conversation is upsetting me and I would like to finish my kale and brie sandwich..."

Having no luck with Reggie, Mr. Ping searched through the Australian Outback, looking for Smelts:

"...Do you mind telling me what happened between you and Reggie?" I asked.

"Yes, I do," Smelts said. "I will say that he did something so despicable and rotten and twisted and wrong and truly horrible that I doubt that I will ever talk to him again. In fact, it was so wrong that I don't think I will ever *speak* about it again."

"But..."

"No, Confucius," he said. "It's over..."

Try as he might, Mr. Ping could never get either one of them to open up about what happened and the rift between them remained. However, there were many aspects of their estrangement that troubled Mr. Ping. Both of them only spoke of what a horrible thing that the other had done, but they never spoke about exactly what it was. Yet, when they spoke of this "horrible" thing, they always used the same language, almost verbatim. To Mr. Ping, this was quite strange.

And then there was the mysterious nature of the case that they were working on when their estrangement occurred. The strange part about it was that nobody in the organization knew what the case was and all of the records of what they were doing at that time went missing. Did either one of them destroy the records? They would never say...

...Or perhaps they were unable to say. Regardless, the true

circumstances of their separation remained a mystery right up until Mr. Ping's death. But the question still remains: What happened on July 31st 1970, and why won't either of them talk about it?

77 THE HIMALAYAN OUTBACK DETECTIVE AGENCY

Founded in 1945 after Reggie and Smelts had worked covertly for the Allies during World War II, the Himalayan Outback Detective Agency based itself in Europe as a branch of Acclimated Spooks, Light, and Power Ltd., specializing in the mysterious and unexplained. If someone wanted something strange investigated, something a bit out of the ordinary that your average detective might be apprehensive about getting involved with, then they called on the yeti and the crocodile to do their business. In fact, the Himalayan Outback Detective Agency was responsible for cracking some of the biggest cases in Europe, including The Great Elf Invasion of 1961, The Shroud of Pippin Debacle, and The Incredible Gypsy Plague of Curses that swept through Europe in 1947. They were also responsible for bringing such powerful criminals as Percy the Peddler, Dame Viscous Buxton, and the ever dangerous Cathode Ray and the Xenon Tubes to justice.

But the success of the Himalayan Outback Detective Agency could not survive the events of July 31st, 1970, when a dust-up between Reggie and Smelts ended their successful relationship. The agency was closed shortly afterwards.

78 DEAD ETIQUETTE from Mr. Ping's Almanac, Vol. 63

The following information is an excerpt from Mr. Ping's Almanac Vol. 63, which contains the full 100 rule list of Dead Etiquette. The information was also included in brochures that were distributed in Western Australia during the "Great Zombie Migration" of the

late 50s to help locals deal with their dead brethren:

69. Never ask a dead person how they died more than three times. If a dead person is asked how they died more than three times, they are allowed to ask the questioner three questions. If the questioner gets any of the three questions wrong, said dead person is allowed to trade "vessels" (bodies) with the questioner.

Note: Never warn someone to not ask the dead about how they died more than three times in the presence of said dead person, or the person doing the warning will be forced allow the dead person to trade "vessels" with them.

70. Never offer a dead person a ham, tuna, or smoked turkey sandwich on rye bread. Asking a dead person for any of these sandwiches will automatically enable the dead to switch bodies with the person who asked them the question.

71. Never shake hands with a dead person and say, "How's it going?" This will allow said dead person to take payment of at least three fingers in return for such an insult, for with the dead, it's never "going" well.

72. Never discuss football with any British dead person, for a quirk, or "glitch" in the metaphysical universe forces said dead person to have to follow their conversation partner around for at least seventeen days talking about football nonstop.

This usually produces a certain form of insanity in the listener, usually occurring around day six, although a few have been known to last up to day nine.

73. Never discuss hockey with any Canadian dead person. The results are the same as rule #71.

79 WHALETOOTH/ WIRECAGE

The latest in open source computing programs, Whaletooth and Wirecage were created by world famous programmer Lennox Linus. Coming to him in a religious vision after playing an online role-playing game for six days while only eating chocolate cake and drinking espressos, Linus typed out all thirty-seven thousand lines of code in one sitting before keeling over dead from exhaustion. Those 37,000 lines of code were posted on the internet as his last act and became the source code for two different operating systems which later became known as Whaletooth and Wirecage. In the time since, Linus has also become a legendary cult figure, with several online shrines dedicated to him and his favorite animal, the blue-footed booby. He even inspired a yearly festival in the mountains of Utah, where thousands of computer programmers, hippies, and folks of other ilk come together to drink espressos and eat chocolate cake for three days in tribute to Linus. It is known as the Burning Blue-Footed Booby Festival.

80 See Appendix entry on Whaletooth

81 H-71s

A product of Corporate Conglomerate Corporation Security Corporation, the H-71 sensors are used mainly in banks and high-end museums. The H-71 detects motion in a room, either through stationary lasers or the more refined heat-sensing devices. If the laser is tripped or a foreign heat source is detected, the H-71 emits a potent gas that smells not unlike a combination of rotten eggs, elephant farts, and a shoe that has stepped in a fresh pile of dog poop. This concoction is so powerful and so horrible that it usually renders an intruder unconscious within thirty seconds (thirty of the most agonizing seconds of said intruder's life). The Corporate Conglomerate Corporation Security Corporation (or CCCSC, for short) touts the H-71 as 100% effective against intruders, and even led to the capture of the infamous Taj Mahal Bandit after his attempt to steal the Dutch crown jewels.

82 EXTRAPOLATING P-92 SENSORS

A sensor used in places that contain very valuable items, the P-92 sensors are the top of the line when it comes to security. Created by the Swedish security specialists, Swedenfugen Specialit Corpanhagen, the P-92 sensors are so powerful they can detect and record the movement of a person from the simple act of breathing. The key to the technology is their patented "nose hair" system, which is able to focus in on the specific chemicals produced by human snot, analyze the snot producing area, and then use the vibration of nose hairs to produce an I.D. of a person that is said to be so specific, it even rivals DNA testing for accuracy. However, nose-picking and nose hair advocacy groups have protested the use of P-92s because of their product tests on the nose hairs of orangutans and llamas. Also, it is widely believed that Swedenfugen Specialit Corpanhagen has been keeping what is referred to as a "snot" database of every human on the planet, which some activists decry as an invasion of privacy.

83 YAK BUTTER

Yak butter is milk from cattle (specifically the yak) that has been refined. It is the daily food of Tibetans and known for its pungent smell and yellowish color. Most Tibetans refine the milk in the traditional way. They pour heated milk in a "Xue Dong" which is a large, wooden bucket, then whip the milk up and down hundreds of times to separate the grease from the water. After a while, a light, yellow surface will appear floating on the top. They ladle out that surface and put it in a leather bag to cool. Yak butter is highly nutritious and because Tibetans rarely eat fruits and vegetables, their daily dietary needs are met with this food. Which leads us to the question of why yetis are vegetarians. If there are so few vegetables at the higher altitudes, why in the world would yetis be vegetarian? The answer lies with yak butter. Long, long ago, yetis, too, relied on yak butter for their daily nutritional requirements, but they soon grew tired of its horrible taste and bitter small, and after a meeting of the yeti council, it was decided that they no longer had any interest in yak butter and they chose to rely on vegetables instead. Although this was a tough choice, they managed to eliminate it from their diet altogether. It should be noted that after yak butter was eliminated from yeti diets, the average weight of the yeti dropped from 975lbs to 704lbs.

84 HO YIN, MR. PING, AND THE WEREWOLVES, taken from Mr. Ping's Almanac, Vol. 73

While traveling through London on their way to pay a visit to some friends, Mr. Ping and Ho Yin had an unfortunate encounter with a group of London-based werewolves who had been hired (presumably by the Conspiricetti) to eliminate Mr. Ping. This was in the days when the werewolves were arrogant enough to think they could take him. They were sorely mistaken.

...A rather large werewolf with a pot belly walked around the corner of the dark alley. He wore a lime green suit, a lime green top hat, and carried a

lime green cane. He had the arrogant swagger of a very powerful person and tended to look down his long snout at us.

I assumed this werewolf to be the de facto leader of the fifteen other snarling creatures surrounding us, and I refused to let this intimidating fool have the upper hand, so I spoke first. "My, my," I said. "There must have been a jailbreak at the local kennel." I timed my remark well, for it made all of the werewolves grumble with anger as it is widely known that no werewolf likes to be compared to a dog.

"You're awfully sarcastic for a man who's about to be lunch," the main werewolf said.

"To be quite honest, I really doubt that's going to happen, Fido," I said. "Now are we going to have trouble here, or are you going to call your dogs off?"

"Lemme eat 'im, boss," one of the other werewolves said. "Oh, let me rip 'im limb from limb."

"Yeah," said another. "Let's eat!"

"In due time, boys," said the leader. "In due time."

"Might I ask what you want?" I said.

"I want you dead," he said, his face as calm as a cow.

"Well, there's a noble pursuit, isn't it, Ho Yin?" I said.

"It certainly is, Mr. Ping," he said.

"Look, puppy," I said, barely able to mask my disdain for him and his cronies, "You pretty much have two choices here. One is to turn tail and run back to the dog pound from whence you came, and the second is to try to attack Ho Yin and myself and get yourself into a world of hurt."

"Ee wants us tuh let 'im walk away!" said one werewolf as he doubled over with laughter.

"Wot a bloomin' idgit!" said another.

"Your arrogance is going to be costly, Ping," said the main werewolf. "Samuel?"

A particularly fierce-looking werewolf stepped forward and said, "Yessuh?" He was taller than almost all of the others and drooled a bit more as well. Still, he was impeccably dressed in his bowler hat and neatly shined shoes.

"Samuel," their leader continued, "I would like for you to show Mr. Ping what *true* pain is."

"Yessuh," Samuel said with a smile. Suddenly, he lunged thirty feet towards me, mouth open, claws bared. But even without warning, I was ready for him, for I jumped up into the air, spinning around with a round house kick that landed squarely on his jaw. He tumbled to the ground and whimpered off to the side, holding his face and sounding very much like a dog that had been struck by a car.

"Was Samuel the best you have?" I asked, particularly annoyed at them.

All of the other werewolves had slightly horrified look on their faces that told me that he truly *was* the best they had.

I reached into my pocket and pulled out the handful of change that I'd gotten back in the pub, holding it up in the air so that all of the werewolves could see it. "This," I said, "Is all of the useless change I have in my pocket. It is my weapon of the day."

I spun around and sent one of my smaller coins whizzing through the air, straight at their leader's forehead. I was quite skilled in coin hurling, something I'd picked up in the southern United States many years earlier, and I sent the coin flying at their leader with such force that it took him off his feet, where he landed with a thud on his back. He was out like a light.

"That's two," I said, glaring at the others. "Now, the question is: Who's next?"

None of them seemed very eager to volunteer...

85 HAMSTER RATIONS

A little known fact is that in 1958, a plague befell the hamsters of the world, killing off millions of the poor creatures. The origins of the Great Hamster Plague are still unknown, but it had a major effect on Mr. Ping and company, for Smelts had a pet hamster that grew sick from the plague and died. Smelts was, at this time, inconsolable, and in the month that followed, he devoted himself entirely to ending the scourge that killed his beloved "Poopsie."

"...If I only do one good thing in my life, Confucius," he said to me, "If there's any hope left in this world for hamster owners, then that hope rests with me. We cannot sit idly by and watch as this plague wipes out our beloved pets. We have to get up, take a stand, and fight against the evil forces that have rid so many of their joy. I hear the call, Confucius. I hear the trumpet calling out to rally the troops. And with every bit of decency I have left in me, I will fight this plague. I will fight it until the bitter end. Are you with me?"

What could I do but agree with him? He was so passionate about losing Poopsie that I had no choice. "I'm with you, Smelts," I said.

"And what about you, Reggie?" he asked.

"Yes, of course," Reggie said, not looking up from his morning paper as he ate his cereal.

"And we can win this war on pestilence?" Smelts yelled.

"Yes," I said.

"And we can bring about a cure for this plague?" he yelled.

"Yes!" I said.

"And we can bring our hamster brothers and sisters back from the brink?" he yelled.

"Yes!" we said.

"Good!" he yelled.

"Will you hand me the Sunday funnies before we go save the world?" Reggie asked...

Due to Smelts' dedication, he quickly concocted a hamster plague vaccine and saved the population for another day. The remaining vaccination vials are kept in Mr. Ping's basement in case of another resurgence of the dreaded disease.

Although Smelts didn't win the Nobel Peace Prize as he expected to (though he wasn't even nominated), he did receive a blue ribbon that year for his exemplary work in regard to animal diseases from the European Humane Society, an honor of which he was very, very proud.

86 FLYING LIZARD REPELLENT, taken from Mr. Ping's Almanac, Vol. 57

While vacationing in Hawaii, Mr. Ping ran into a spot of trouble at the expense of one Takashi Sakamomoto, a Japanese researcher doing experiments on one of the more remote islands in the South Pacific. On the surface, it appeared that Professor Sakamomoto chose the secluded island so that he could conduct his experiments on lizards in peace, but his main goal was to keep his experiments away from the prying eyes of others.

Professor Sakamomoto was working to create giant, flying lizards for a secret organization bent on ruling the world, so the farther he was from population centers, the less he had to worry about. But all was not well on the tiny island, for when Big Bertha got loose, things went awry...

...Honolulu was a virtual ghost town, as the whole of its population was trapped in their homes in the fear of what lay outside. It had been like this for a week, and all because of the giant lizards that had plagued the area.

From my hotel room, I had seen them all swooping down upon the area, doing their best to pick off people on the street. Luckily, they weren't as skilled as they should have been, for according to the news reports, no one had been killed. But that was just luck, for the lizards were smart and cunning, and they knew they had only to wait out their prey.

The lizards were of various sizes, ranging from the size of small dogs, all green and scaly with razor-sharp teeth and wings on their arms that flapped like mad to stay aloft, to the biggest one of them all, a large, lumbering creature that was more akin to a giant iguana with wings. Between the smallest of the lizards and the large one that stood silent watch from the top of the tallest building over Honolulu, there were lots of mid-size creatures of different sizes, shapes and abilities.

Aside from the biggest lizard, dubbed Big Bertha by the local papers, most of the creatures kept well out of sight, nesting in the trees of the lush, green mountains that surrounded the city. There, they watched and waited, and with their keen eyes, they would spot any poor soul that ventured out into the open, whereupon they would descend on that person like seagulls going for a hot dog on the beach, swarming and attacking until one of them got the spoils. This would go on until they attracted the attention of Big Bertha, who would swoop down, and with one flap of her gargantuan wings, would blow all the other lizards, off into the distance. This was what had saved most people so far, for Big Bertha was still learning the tricks of being a large, dragon-like predator, and she didn't know how to keep from fanning whatever she was after away from her.

After three days of watching the flying lizards swoop down from the hills in the hundreds, like migrating birds, the locals of Honolulu realized that it probably wasn't the best idea to be out flitting around in the open, so everyone just stayed inside, electing not to make themselves available for the slaughter. Even cars weren't safe, for the lizards would simply rip the metal roofs apart like a pop can with their giant claws. A solution had to be presented.

"Confucius, good to see you," General Hardbrick said, shaking my hand as he met me under cover of darkness at the gates to the local military base.

"Well, hopefully I can be of some help, General," I said. He had called me at my hotel room earlier that day in the hopes that I might have an answer to this problem.

"We're completely at a loss as to what to do," he said, leading me into the fortified building. "And we fear that there might be a food shortage in the city, since people can't get out of their houses."

"Do you have any idea how these creatures got here?" I asked.

He led me to a fellow in a lab coat and very thick glasses. His hair was pasted down on his head and he looked as though he hadn't seen real sunlight in weeks. Behind him were ten or twelve of his scientist companions.

"This is Professor Bardfard," the General said. "He's our resident scientist on the base. He might be able to answer your questions."

"Pleased to meet you, Professor Bardfard," I said.

"Pleased to met you, Mr. Ping," he said. Professor Bardfard was one of those mousy fellows that was so introverted that he could never make eye contact with anyone, despite his astronomical genius.

"Professor," I said, "Do you have any idea how these lizards got here?"

"Well," he said, staring at the floor, "My team and I have developed a probable hypothesis regarding these creatures that we, uh, feel is the most likely scenario for the arrival of the, uh, creatures."

"And that is?"

"Well, uh, after doing some, uh, careful calculations and analysis, we've come to the, uh, conclusion that they were, uh, hatched."

"Yes, hatched," said another scientist from behind him.

"Most probably hatched," added another.

"Hatched?" I asked.

"Yes," said Professor Bardfard. "We've, uh, come to believe that, uh, the lizard eggs have been in, uh, hibernation, so to speak, for millions of years. Probably ever since the Cretaceous period, and have, uh, only recently hatched in the wilderness around, uh, Honolulu."

"Yes, yes," said one scientist from behind him.

"Only recently hatched," said another.

"And then they attacked the city?" I asked.

"By our calculations, the island of, uh, Hawaii, is their, uh, optimal habitat, so they, uh, have reclaimed their, uh, habitat and have, uh, begun to feed in order to grow to their, uh, maximum size, which could be, uh, incalculable," said Professor Bardfard.

"Incalculable," said one scientist behind him.

"Very large," said another.

"It's, uh, only a matter of, uh, time before the, uh, lizards take over the world," said the Professor, looking grim, "And, uh, rule us with an, uh, iron fist, using humans as, uh, snacks."

"Snacks," said one scientist behind him.

"Appetizers," said another.

Feeling somewhat skeptical, I said, "Thank you, Professor. If you don't mind, I'd like to talk to General Hardbrick." I pulled him off to the side in a confidential manner and said, "Are these your best scientists?"

"Well, they usually work in our nuclear development program," he said. "So, they're not biologists, but..."

"There must be a simpler explanation for all of this," I said. "Not to discount their theories, but I seriously doubt that those reptiles were hatched after millions of years. Do you keep records of your radar?" I asked.

"Yes, of course," he said.

"I have a theory," I said. "I'd like to see the records for the day before the lizards appeared."

After several hours examining the radar reports for the whole of the region, I began to notice a pattern. There was a black smudge on the images that followed a line, making its way, very slowly, from what seemed to be an empty space in the middle of the South Pacific. "See this?" I asked, bringing the General into the small room to show him the smudges.

"What about it?" he said.

"These smudges are the lizards," I said.

"Impossible," he said. "Our radar isn't powerful enough to pick up something that small."

"I think it is," I said. "And they've come from here." I pointed to the blank spot in the middle of the Pacific.

"But there's nothing there," said the General. "Are you telling me that these lizards flew hundreds of miles to Honolulu from an empty spot in the Pacific ocean to terrorize people?"

"I don't think that's an empty spot, General," I said. "I need a plane."

"A plane? You're crazy."

"I need to get to that spot, sir," I said. "Otherwise, Honolulu is in big trouble. Especially if there are more of those things out there."

The General rubbed his chin, thoughtfully. "Look, Confucius," he said. "If I get you this plane, you'd better get results. Do you understand?"

"I most certainly do, sir," I said.

"Let me see what I can do."

The leader of the squadron of five soldiers assigned to travel with me was a weathered, craggy sergeant by the name of Mahoney. His entire personality could be summed up by the way he pulled his helmet down over his eyes, the way he squinted when he looked at you, and the well-chewed cigar that always kept him speaking out of the right side of his mouth. "This another one of them certain death missions, General?" he asked, standing at attention in front of his commander.

"It is, Mahoney," the General said.

Mahoney grinned at his commander; his eyes squinting even further and his cigar clenched in his teeth. "Just the way I like it," he said.

Mahoney's team was a tight-knit group of men who seemed to have worked together for so long that they could finish each other's sentences. There was Grizzly, a man practically seven feet tall and half as wide, with an upper lip that constantly quivered as if he was on the verge of lashing out with rage any second for no reason whatsoever. There was Dart, short for Dartmoth, a wiry black fellow with a pleasant smile and one gold tooth. Mahoney informed me that they called him Dart because he was the fastest human alive and could scope out a safe zone in no time flat.

Then there was Jones, a bespectacled, nervous fellow who was in charge of communications and electronics. Jones was our radio man ("And the moron can make a bomb out of two twigs and a stick of bubble gum," Sergeant Mahoney told me. "That's how smart he is. Too bad he ain't got a lick of common sense!"). Lastly, there was The Barber, a good-looking fellow with an impeccable appearance, not a wrinkle on his suit, clean-shaven, and not a hair out of place ("Hey," he said, "Personal hygiene is a high priority in my life.").

"These guys are the best of the best," General Hardbrick said. "We call them The Reliables, because they get the job done right the first time."

"That's us," Mahoney said, smiling and grimacing at the same time. "I been waitin' to get me one of them lizards ever since they ripped off the top of my convertible. As far as I'm concerned, we're having lizard steaks for dinner tonight."

"I only hope it's that easy," I said.

"Lizard steaks," Grizzly mumbled. "Grizzly want lizard steaks." He shoved a clip into his machine gun and growled quietly.

"Sergeant Mahoney, sir?"

"Whaddya want, Jones?" Mahoney growled.

"According to my estimates, we have approximately three minutes to board the plane," Jones said, tapping nervously at his watch.

"All right, all right," Mahoney said, waving him off. "Let's get goin' before Jones here has a conniption fit."

"This is what I'm talking about," Dart said, and soon he was out of the room in a flash.

"Let's go, Barber," Mahoney said.

"Hold on, sir," The Barber said as he examined himself in a mirror. "I gotta clip this nose hair."

"Let's go, prima-donna!"

"Lizard steaks," Grizzly muttered.

General Hardbrick was an efficient man and commissioned a bomber to fly us straight out into the Pacific to look for the source of the lizards' wrath. The plane was prepared in a hanger and we all boarded, waiting for the take-off to see whether we would even get off the ground once the lizards realized we were moving.

The all-clear signal was given, just as the sun was coming up over the horizon. The hanger doors were pulled open and the plane roared to life, slowly making its way out onto the tarmac to take flight. From small port holes on the sides, we could see what looked to be a black cloud rise up over the horizon. "Here they come, boys," Mahoney yelled, manning a machine gun turret.

The plane straightened itself on the runway and was given the go ahead as we began to take off. Still, it wasn't quite fast enough, for the lizards were approaching us at a phenomenal speed, getting so close that they were no longer just a shapeless mass, but a swarm of angry, jaw-snapping beasts. Seeing them fly up beside the plane made me a bit more fearful, for their eyes were angry and their teeth sharp and numerous. I wondered whether we'd even make it off the ground as we heard them thump and bump against the metal fuselage of the plane.

Our transport picked up speed and began to leave the lizards in our wake as we rose from the ground, but that was the least of our worries when a black shadow passed over the window. "Hold on to your hats," said the pilot over the intercom. "We've got company."

Big Bertha was in pursuit.

Almost immediately, machine guns in the front, sides, and back of the bomber rang out, trying to bring the creature down. Yet despite an incredible amount of bullets, everyone was astonished to see the white hot ordinance bounce smoothly off of her leathery skin like raindrops. Bertha was also becoming more adept at maneuvering, for she flitted all about the plane, up over the top, down the sides, and back again. The machine gun fire seemed to be making her angry, and we could hear her piercing hisses and screams even from inside the noisy plane.

"We're gonna try to lose this ol' gal," said the pilot. "So grab onto something, cause it might get rough."

I'd just managed to take hold of a safety bar when the plane banked right with such force that I thought I wouldn't be able to hold on. Then just as quickly, it banked left, leaving me feeling somewhat queasy. Still, the fancy flying failed to confuse Bertha, and she came at us as fierce as ever, even going so far as to ram us a couple of times.

Then, the machine guns went silent and explosions filled the air. We saw the bursts from inside and realized that two fighter planes had been scrambled to take Bertha out. They fired their tiny missiles at her, which seemed to be painful enough to distract her from us. Bertha turned to pursue the jets, leaving us to continue our mission and hope that those two jest made it to safety.

Everyone on the plane looked immensely relieved. "I never envisioned this kind of thing when I signed up for the Marines," the Barber said. "Flying lizards. Who knew?"

"Hey, Grizzly," Dart said. "That lizard kinda looks like your mother!"

"Shut up!" Grizzly said, his upper lip twitching with anger.

We traveled most of the day over the endless blue expanse of the Pacific to destinations unknown. I had asked to be notified when we reached the desired coordinates, and in the late afternoon, Sergeant Mahoney radioed for me to come to the front. "We're in the general vicinity," he said as I leaned in the cockpit. "It's pretty cloudy here, so we're gonna circle a few times at a lower altitude to see if we can spot anything."

"Okay," I said, but he needn't have said anything, for as soon as we ducked below the clouds, we saw it, and we almost saw it too late. There in front of us was a massive black mountain.

"Look out!" Mahoney yelled, and the pilot jerked the stick to the side to avoid a dead on collision with the massive black face of the mountaintop. When he got everything back under control, the pilot said, "How can that be? There's no island on the map."

"Precisely," I said. "It's a volcanic island. That's lava rock."

We began to circle the island to get a better view. The center of the island contained the single, black, volcanic mountain whose summit disappeared into the clouds. It wasn't particularly large, yet it was big enough that one could easily get lost in the thick jungle that lay at the base of the volcano.

"So this is where you think those lizards came from?" Mahoney asked.

"Yes," I said.

"So, what now?" Dart asked.

"We drop to the island," I said.

"That's crazy," Jones said. "If that's where those lizards came from, then there's gotta be hundreds more down there. They'll eat us alive."

"I don't think that's the case," I said, and I pointed down to a tall, white building whose roof jutted just over the canopy of trees. "I think we could find the root of this problem sooner than we think."

"Holy smokes," said Dart.

On the fourth circle around the island, Mahoney directed his men to prepare for the jump, and once the green light came on, all of us filed out the small door, parachuting into the open to land on the shores of the secluded island.

Our landing was clean, and Mahoney's men disappeared into the woods to secure our location. I followed as they moved with predictable military precision through the thick, hot jungle. But we encountered nothing. We

moved through the jungle unobstructed, right up to the door of the white building, where I crouched down behind Sergeant Mahoney.

"What now, Ping?" he asked.

I observed the building for a couple of seconds. Though it was built fairly recently, the jungle mold had begun to creep up its sides, and all sorts of vines and grasses were slowly enveloping the walls. However, there were no windows, and because there were no clues, anything could have been waiting inside.

A flutter was heard behind us; nothing unusual or any different than the birds that flitted about in the jungle canopy above us, but something about it made me paranoid, and when I looked up, I realized that those weren't birds above us. They were tiny, flying lizards.

"Don't move," I said, putting my finger to my lips. I saw Dart and Grizzly look up and spy the lizards. It was no wonder that we'd missed them on our way in towards the building, for they were only about the size of geckos and they blended in perfectly with the canopy above. Plus, when we first arrived, there might have only been one or two of them, but they'd been following us and their numbers had swelled. Now, thousands of these tiny lizards were darting from branch to branch above our heads, and they looked agitated.

As I looked up to observe one that was particularly close to my head, it hissed, and just as it had hissed, all of the lizards hissed together, a sound so loud and unnerving, that I was sure I'd heard Grizzly let out a yelp of fear. "What do we do?" asked The Barber.

"We need to get in that building," I said, turning to Sergeant Mahoney. "I want you and your team to make your way up to that awning, and when I give the signal, I want

you to get in that door as fast as you can. Once the door is open, we're piling in."

"This better work," Mahoney said.

One by one, they made their way up to the awning, until we were all crouched beneath it. The lizards had begun to completely surround us, even landing in front of us on the ground and inching their way forward. Were it one or two of the small creatures, I might have been less paranoid, but there were thousands of them and they looked like they could swarm a cow like piranhas and pick the bones clean with their tiny, razor-sharp teeth.

Grizzly offered to kick the door in, but I waved him off. I was too good at picking locks to let this one slide by, and after a couple of seconds, the door slid open. As the lizards saw the door open, they began to hiss and look even more agitated, so I yelled, "Go! Now!"

Just as they began to rush inside, the small lizards, perhaps sensing that their meal might disappear, began to come for us. They moved as swiftly as cockroaches, and they began to nip at our legs. Luckily, we all made it into the building and slammed the door shut as the thump and knock of the lizards outside echoed in the hall. We could hear their relentless charges and their hisses of anger, and we were quite lucky to have made it inside safely.

We found ourselves in a long hallway that extended off around a corner. Silently, Mahoney signaled to his troops that they were to secure the hall, and without a sound, they made their way down, checking all of the small rooms for danger, one by one, before signaling back to the rest of us that the coast was clear.

I ran down the hall to a corner and crouched beside Dart. We peeked around the corner to see another long hallway, this one dark and foreboding, with other dark corridors that extended off in other directions. About halfway down the hall, there was a room with its lights on. The light could be seen through several rectangular windows on the wall and it looked as if there was movement inside. Mahoney signaled to his men again and they made their way down the hall. Another signal was given and I followed them down the hall and peered in the window. What I saw was a very frazzled-looking Japanese man in a lab coat. He looked like he hadn't bathed or shaved for days, and he had the emaciated look of a man who hadn't eaten anything in a long time. He walked in circles around what appeared to be a small laboratory, muttering to himself behind the soundproof walls.

Then, as if he sensed the presence of someone, he looked up and stared right at us. A look of sheer panic fell over his face and he began to wave his arms frantically, trying to convey something to us.

"What's he saying?" asked The Barber.

"This guy has lost it," said Dart.

"Try the door," Mahoney said.

"It's locked, sir."

"Break it in," he said.

"Wait," I said. "Something's wrong."

By now, the crazed scientist was beating on the window, yelling something to us, but the soundproofing kept us from understanding anything. "He probably went nuts from being locked in that room," laughed Dart.

At that precise moment, we heard a low, rumbling growl that was so alarming that all of the soldiers raised their weapons in defense. "He's not crazy," Jones said. "He's warning us."

With a roar, a lizard twice the size of Grizzly rounded the corner of the far hallway and stopped to look at us. Of all of the reptiles we'd seen so far, this one looked the most fierce, owing its appearance more to that of a dinosaur than to a gecko. It had abnormally large, razor-sharp teeth and an overbite that caused it to drool incessantly. What was worse was its growl, the same low rumble that had alarmed us not seconds earlier. But hadn't the growl come from the other direction?

"What the heck is that?" asked The Barber.

"That's trouble," said Mahoney. "We're not takin' any risks. Take it out, boys."

An eruption of machine gun fire rained down the hall, but the hail of bullets wasn't fast enough to get the creature, for with incredible speed, it ducked back around the corner from which it came.

"We're in a whole heap of trouble," said Jones.

"Radio the plane that we need some back-up," Mahoney said.

"Roger that," Jones said. He tried the radio a couple of times, but there was nothing on the other end. "I can't get contact, sir."

"It's the building," I said. "It must be jamming the frequencies."

"You've lead us into a deathtrap, Ping," Mahoney said. "I love it!" He was genuinely excited.

I looked down the hall and quickly made an assumption. "That creature is a predator," I said. "As are almost all of the reptiles we've seen, so that means it's stalking us." I looked at the Japanese scientist in the room, who was watching us, wide-eyed, as we assessed the situation. "Now," I said, "The man in that room is the key to this problem. We have to get inside."

"That's a steel door," said The Barber. "We'll have to blow it open."

I rolled my eyes. "What is it with your constant insistence on blowing things to smithereens?" I asked. "Leave it to me."

I walked over to the door, pulled out a small toolkit from my belt, and began picking at the lock. To my right, I heard another low, lumbering growl. We looked over to see the lizard watching us a short distance away. "Hey," Dart said, pointing the opposite direction, "Wasn't that thing over there a second ago?"

"It's not the same creature," I said, continuing to pick the lock. "There are two in here."

"Make that three," said Mahoney. We looked down the hall where we'd seen the first one and realized that there were now two making their way towards us. "Grizzly, Dart," he said, "You take the left one. Jones, and Barber, you take the other two."

"Roger that, sir," said The Barber.

"Put your guns down, sergeant," I said, as the large, steel door clicked open. "They'll only make the problem worse." I waved the soldiers into the room, and after checking for the okay with Mahoney, they edged in. "Sergeant?" I asked.

He scowled at me and said, "Please don't question my orders when we're here to protect you."

"I apologize, sergeant," I said. "But at the end of the day, I'd like to see as little violence perpetrated as possible. Now, might I recommend you get inside?" I grabbed him by the collar and ducked in the door just before one of the lizards snapped at him. I slammed the door shut and turned to him, saying, "You don't want to end up as lizard food."

All of the men had their faces pressed to the windows of the lab, observing the large lizards outside, just as the lizards outside were observing them. I walked over to the frazzled, Japanese man in the corner. He cowered as if I was going to hit him.

"My name is Confucius Ping," I said in Japanese. "Can you tell me what's going on here?"

The man sighed and said, "My name is Takashi Sakamomoto. I am the man in charge of this island."

"What's he saying?" asked Mahoney.

"He's in charge of the island," I told him before turning back to Takashi. "We have come from Hawaii, where the city is under siege by giant, flying lizards. We have tracked them back to this island. Can you explain what's happening here?"

Mr. Sakamomoto broke down in tears and crumpled to the ground, saying, "It's all gone wrong. It's all gone wrong."

"What's gone wrong, Mr. Sakamomoto?" I asked.

"They are my creations," he said. "All of the lizards here are my creations. I couldn't control them."

According to Mr. Sakamomoto, the lizards were part of genetic experiments he'd been doing for the Conspiricetti. He said that they had charged him with creating an army of lizards, and he had created several of the creatures over the last few years. But just a few days earlier, a fierce tropical storm had lashed the island, destroying the containment units in which the lizards were held. The creatures had gotten loose and taken over the island, effectively trapping him in the labs, where he'd been without food for several days. He'd been unable to call for help, because of what he referred to as the Iguanasaurs out front. He assumed that the lizards in Honolulu were from his experiments.

"Everything got out of hand," he said. "This wasn't supposed to happen."

"They seem to be impervious to bullets," I said.

"Yes, they've been bred to have bulletproof skin," he said.

"They are the ultimate fighting creatures."

"Well, how are they supposed to be stopped?" I asked. "If bullets don't work, we'd probably have to bomb them, and we can't do that in a civilian center."

"There is one way," he said. "The Conspiricetti wanted to be able to control the creatures, so they had me come up with a deterrent."

"Which is?"

"A spray," he said.

"A spray?" I asked. "What do you mean?"

" A spray," he said. "Like paint in a can. I have created a spray that is allergenic for the lizards. It will stop them and make them weak. It will even kill them if used in large enough quantities."

"Well, why haven't you used it to free yourself?" I asked.

"Because it's all in a storage shed behind the building," he said. "The lizards would have eaten me if I'd ventured outside."

After explaining all of this to Mahoney, he said, "Well, we'd best go get it."

"No, sergeant," I said. "If bullets are ineffective against these creatures, then you and your soldiers are useless. I've been trained for stealth and single-handed combat. I will go get the spray."

"But we've been assigned to protect you," he said.

"With all due respect, sir," I said, "I truly believe that I will be the most effective person for this job. End of story."

With great reluctance, Mahoney agreed, partly because he was deferring to what he perceived as my wisdom on the matters, and partly because I was becoming convinced that he wanted to have no part of those lizards. The rest of the squad settled into the labs and shared their meager rations with a very grateful Professor Sakamomoto.

In the meantime, I devised a plan. Professor Sakamomoto drew a rough map of the facilities on the island, showing me where we were and where the storage shed was in relation to us. It was relatively straightforward. "Except for the last hundred meters," he said.

"What do you mean?" I asked.

"The path from the building to the storage shed is one hundred meters on a curvy path through the jungle. The minute you leave the building, the geckosaurs will know, and they will come for you."

"Geckosaurs?" I asked.

"Half-piranha, half-gecko, half-grasshopper," he said. He looked quite serious.

Doesn't that equal one and a half? I thought, but I kept my sassy comments to myself, for I was sure that the Professor was not mentally balanced at that moment. "How do I get into the storage shed?" I asked.

"There are two pad locks," he said, holding up a key. "This works for both of them. However, you must be quick, for once the geckosaurs have sized you up, they will attack. You're lucky they didn't get you outside the first time." I was about to leave when the Professor grabbed my shoulder, looked me in the eye and said, "How many?"

"How many what?" I asked.

"How many people have they killed?" he asked, tears welling up in his eyes.

"The lizards? None, so far. That's why it's important that this works."

He breathed a visible sigh of relief and sat down on a chair in the corner of the room, putting his head in his hands.

"How you gonna get past those things out there?" asked Mahoney, nodding to the fierce beasts that paced back and forth outside, watching us from the hallway windows.

I looked up at the ceiling and said, "If I can't go through them, then I'll go over them."

The ceiling was hollow, with Styrofoam tiles placed in rows. I pushed one of the tiles out and lifted myself into the crawl-space above the floors. Armed with a flashlight, I began to crawl along the slats of the building frame, towards where I perceived the exit door to be. I knew when I was crawling above the iguanasaurs, for I could hear their breathing below me and I was extra-careful not to make any noise.

As I shimmied across the rafters, I must have shimmied a bit too much, for the nickels and dimes and quarters that I'd had in my pocket came tumbling out, bouncing and rolling across the steel roofing, and making as much racket as possible. I held my breath as the last penny rolled around in a lazy circle, spinning to a stop on the steel beam below. I waited for what seemed to be an eternity for some sign of life below me, but heard nothing

Just as I felt as though it was safe to move again, the tiles below me exploded and I saw the gargantuan teeth of the iguanasaurs. My cover was blown, and considering their massive size, they would soon rip the ceiling apart searching for me.

I crawled along the rafters as fast as I could, but I only made more noise as the iguanasaurs came closer and closer, bursting through the tiles like grenades and rattling my nerves. I soon realized that I could travel faster on foot than I could crawling, so I kicked out a tile below me and jumped to the floor.

I barely had time to get my bearings, for I could hear the sharp claws of their feet clicking on the tile floors as they ran after me, hissing and roaring like mad. As I ran, I made the unfortunate realization that in my panic to get out of the ceiling, I'd lost my sense of direction and was running the wrong way down the hall.

In an effort not to think about the problem, I stopped in the middle of the hall, turned towards the iguanasaurs, and in the blink of an eye, dove towards them. I executed a perfect forward roll, right between the legs of the first creature and rolling to the side of the second one. They both fell in a scrambled mess in an effort to turn around to get me. This was just enough time for me to get past them down the hall.

But once again, in a panic, I hadn't realized that there had only been two iguanasaurs chasing me when there were actually three in the building. I rounded the corner by the last door and was taken by surprise by the third one, which jumped on me from a side doorway, knocking me to the ground as it snapped at my face. I rolled out of the way and avoided a nasty wound from its sharp teeth.

Jumping back to my feet, I had to dodge back and forth as the beast nipped at me. It moved fast and I barely had time to dodge its razor-sharp jaws, but it gave me just enough time to assess its weak spots and as it took one last chomp towards me, I brought my elbow down on top of its nose with all of my might. Just as I suspected, I'd rattled its tiny little brain to the core and it fell to the ground, unconscious.

Without hesitating to examine the beast, I continued my journey down the hallway, coming to the large, painted steel doors that led outside to the path. I turned behind me to make sure that the iguanasaurs weren't following me, then as quietly as possible, I opened the door to peek outside.

Evening was descending on the jungle and I made a mental note about the intense humidity. The sun was setting and the shafts of sunlight penetrating the canopy of leaves above me were as brilliant as anything I'd ever seen. I stepped outside quietly, listening to the sounds of the forest, specifically the sounds of the little lizards coming for me. Yet I heard nothing.

There were no geckosaurs coming in droves at the mere scent of me. There was only the sound of the millions of insects in the vicinity. I stepped out on the walkway and peeked out further from the awning. The trail to the storage shed led off into a dark place in the forest, and feeling like there was no trouble coming, I took off through the woods.

Still, the best laid plans can go awry, and as I jogged down the path, I could hear something rustling in the canopy above. Finally, I saw two of the geckosaurs perched on the leaves above me, staring. They let out a horrible hiss at me, but remained where they were. However, the hiss had an echo, further off. Actually, it had more than one echo, for a chain of hisses erupted from all reaches of the jungle and I suddenly heard what seemed to be a million geckosaurs bounding through the forest at once, presumably towards me.

I knew that I could either stand there and fight them, a battle I stood no chance of wining, or I could run for my life, hoping that I could make it to the storage shed. Looking up, I saw another one of the creatures arrive and it bared its sharp fangs at me as it hissed. I took off running.

Professor Sakamomoto was right. The last hundred meters were the hardest part, for though he informed me of the curvy path, he failed to inform me that the entire hundred meters was uphill, a hill so steep that I had to crawl on my hands and knees in some places. I was making decent time when I felt the first nip of a geckosaur biting into my leg.

I kicked at it and it flew off, but it provided me with a chance to look back and see what I was up against. It wasn't pretty. Millions of the geckosaurs were on the ground, in the trees, and in the air, all of them scrambling over each other to get to me. And every second that I spent looking at them, they got closer. I spun around and climbed the slippery, mossy hill double-time, trying to avoid being lunch.

I could see the storage shed about twenty meters ahead of me on a small gravel path, so I pulled the key from my neck, ready to open the locks. Unfortunately at the same time, about five geckosaurs bit into me and the sudden, sharp pain of their bites caused me to drop the key and it immediately disappeared into one of their mouths. Yet even in such a situation, I couldn't fret. I had no choice but to continue moving forward or be eaten. As I moved closer to the shed, the geckosaurs nipping at me the whole way, I focused in on the two locks, sharpening my senses. Then, I concentrated all of my energy into my arms, filling them with dynamic tension.

When I reached the door, I swung the ball of my hands around with all of my might and sent every bit of my energy into the locks. They snapped like plastic and fell to the floor. I ripped the door open, ran inside, and slammed it shut. The five geckosaurs that were attached to me were quickly removed and placed in a little cage sitting by the door as I heard the overwhelming hiss of their comrades outside.

Turning on a light, I saw in front of me hundreds of metal containers that looked like scuba tanks, and all of them had the words *Flying Lizard Repellent* stenciled on the side. In the corner was a vest into which the tanks fit and a large hose.

Without hesitation, I strapped on a tank, put on the vest, and hooked up the repellent. Once everything was in working order, I squirted a small bit of repellent on the geckosaurs in the cage by the door and they hated it. They tried to escape from their confines, but they had nowhere to go. Although the baser part of my nature wanted to spray the little beasts over and over in response to the stinging welts they'd given me on my leg with their little teeth, I refrained. I had a job to do and torturing a few little geckosaurs for only doing what came naturally to them seemed wrong.

The first thing I did was give myself a light dosing of the lizard repellent, and then I ripped open the front door. Thousands of geckosaurs stood, lying in wait for me, but one whiff of the metallic-scented repellent made them want to run for the high hills. As I silently walked back down the path, the geckosaurs parted like the Red Sea, giving me as wide a berth as possible.

Each step taken in their direction would send them scrambling all over themselves in an attempt to escape. I sprayed some of the repellent on a few of them and it seemed to make them docile, almost sleepy, after the initial squirm of pain.

But although I was safe from the geckosaurs, there was still the iguanasaurs inside. The geckosaurs were small and frightened by the mere scent of the repellent, but I knew that the iguanasaurs would not be so easily defeated.

As I walked back down the trail, the geckosaurs formed a wide berth around me, but I noticed that they followed me nonetheless, hopping and scrambling to see where I was going. They seemed curious, and I deduced that they had been bred for above average intelligence. They were observing me, learning my habits, looking for that moment

when I showed weakness and they could pounce upon me for a quick snack. But the lizard repellent kept me safe and none of them dared get too close to me.

The door inside the laboratories was wide-open and dark when I got back, and the hallway looked quiet and ominous. Considering the intelligence of the geckosaurs, I was sure that the iguanasaurs were there, waiting for me, and I had to think about how to properly defend myself in such a situation.

I quietly stepped inside, repellent at the ready, expecting an attack from any angle. There was nothing; no sounds, no movement, nothing. I inched along further into the halls, but still there was no sign of anything. Finally, I reentered the hallway where I'd jumped from the ceiling and found it still strewn with rubble. I began to grow fearful, wondering what these lizards were plotting, when I rounded the corner to the laboratory where I'd left Professor Sakamomoto and the group of paratroopers. My heart sank.

Peering into the window, I saw the iguanasaurs, all three of them, holding the weaponless soldiers at bay. Mahoney and his men looked terrified and angry at the same time as the iguanasaurs were ready to strike. Without hesitation, I burst into the room, hose at the ready. "Back off, you vile creatures," I said, pointing the hose at them. They turned to me and roared, but they did not move.

"Very impressive, Mr. Ping. Very impressive." I turned to see Professor Sakamomoto standing behind me, a machine gun pointed right at me. "This was almost too easy," he said.

The iguanasaurs hissed and roared, turning to confront me. "What's going on?" I asked.

"Put the lizard repellent down," the Professor said. "You're upsetting my babies."

"What?" I asked, but the lizards roared again, threatening the soldiers. Warily, I eased the tanks from my back and put them down on the floor.

"Now, then, Mr. Ping," Professor Sakamomoto said, keeping the machine gun on me. "You have solved a great deal of my problems, and for that, I thank you. Because of both your generosity and stupidity, I will make your death swift and painless."

"He's double-crossed us, Ping!" yelled the sergeant from the corner. "Those ugly lizards work for him."

"Double-crossed?" I asked.

"That's right, you trusting fool," said the Professor. "Yes, I've been trapped in the labs for seven days, but not because of Sally, Steve, and Stella."

"Those are the names of the iguanasaurs?" I asked.

"That's right," he said. "None of us have been able to get out of here because of all the geckosaurs. They've had us trapped since they got out in that tropical storm. And I had no lizard repellent until you came along. Now, I've suckered you into saving me and sealing your own fates."

"So, the Conspiricetti never held you against your will?" I asked. "You mean you created these lizards on your own?"

"Oh, yes," he said. "And we will rule the world when all of this is over. Especially now that our test case in Honolulu worked so well."

"Wonderful," I said, sighing. "Just another two-bit genius with designs on ruling the world. I had hoped it would have been more than this."

"What do you mean?" he asked.

"Oh, nothing," I said. "You mean something," he yelled, holding the gun

towards me. "What did you mean?"

"What I meant was that if I've seen one demented genius with designs on world domination, I've seen them all. But there's really one secret that is common amongst every single one of them, including you, that they refuse to acknowledge."

"And that is?" asked Professor Sakamomoto, his eye twitching with anger.

"The fact that they're all two-bit hoods, whining about how nobody pays them any attention," I said. "Basically, they're all self-centered nerds who want to be popular."

"Well," he said, looking furious, "That's all very interesting. I'll take your dime-store analysis into consideration as I stand over your grave. And because you saw fit to insult me, I think I'll have to rescind my offer of a painless death for you." He looked over at his iguanasaurs and said, "Kill them, my babies. The feast is yours."

The iguanasaurs looked over at us and growled. "Way to go, Ping," said Mahoney. "Your smart mouth has gotten us into quite a mess."

"And I'm not finished yet," I said, smiling. I'd filled a glass jar full of lizard repellent and placed it in my pocket, and as the iguanasaurs approached us, I pulled it out and threw it at the floor in front of them. It shattered into a million pieces and sent the purple repellent everywhere, including all over the iguanasaurs, which caused them to fall over in pain on the floor and squeal in terror.

"What have you done?" Professor Sakamomoto yelled, watching his babies writhing on the floor in horror.

"The jig is up," I said, and I hurled a test tube towards him, striking his hand and causing him to drop the gun. I turned towards Mahoney and said, "Get the repellent and subdue the lizards."

"Curse you!" Professor Sakamomoto said as he ran out the door to escape.

"Give it up, Professor," I yelled after him. "There's nowhere left to run."

I was almost upon him when he ran straight out the door, into the jungle. "Don't!" I yelled, but it was too late. The next thing I knew was that a million geckosaurs had swarmed him and he disappeared into the chaos of flapping lizard wings...

87 JAPANESE MAN-O-BOT™, taken from Mr. Ping's Almanac, Vol. 68

While visiting world-renowned scientist Yohiro Kanata in Tokyo in 1968, Mr. Ping became involved in a battle in downtown Tokyo between Professor Kanata and his arch nemesis, Saporro Tanpopo. The key difference in this battle was the fact that it took place entirely with giant robots on the streets of the city. Professor Kanata and Mr. Tanpopo were competing to create the ultimate defensive weapon for Japan. Professor Kanata had been working on his giant Man-o-Bot™ for over ten years before Mr. Tanpopo engaged in a bit of corporate espionage and stole his idea, putting his own robot on the fast track to win government contracts. However, Professor Kanata actually won the contract to build the robots, so in a fit of rage, Mr. Tanpopo decided to prove to the government of Japan that his giant robot was superior and he set about to destroy Professor Kanata and the Man-o-Bot™.

The battle raged for forty-five minutes and Mr. Tanpopo had little regard for the safety of the population of Tokyo as he used his robot (and its superior weaponry) to pummel the Man-o-Bot™. But as with all insane billionaires drunk with power, by the end of the battle, Mr. Tanpopo no longer had any interest in simply defeating Professor Kanata and he quickly gained aspirations to control the whole of Japan.

So as the Man-o-Bot™ lay smoldering in the rubble of a collapsed building, no longer able to move, Mr. Ping decided to get involved. Knowing that Mr. Tanpopo's robot had been created to battle large threats, Mr. Ping assumed that consideration had not been given to a lone individual, and he quickly caught up with the robot as it marched towards the Japanese parliament.

...I caught up with the large, lumbering beast as it marched through the streets, crushing cars under its gargantuan feet, knocking over streetlights and road signs, and scraping the concrete facades off of buildings with its wide shoulders. Standing below it as it walked towards me, I was impressed with its actual size. It was a good forty-feet taller than Professor Kanata's Man-o-Bot™ and even after being hit with rockets, pounded by tanks, and doing battle with a robot its equal, it still gleamed silver and maroon in the fading sunlight. It moved just like one would imagine a robot to move, slowly, mechanically, its large, heavy legs parting the air with a low hum and the gears and turbines inside it raging with motion.

I stood below it, right in its path, as it approached. I was much too small for Mr. Tanpopo to take notice of me, so I took my time, aimed my crossbow at a wedge of metal just below its chest and fired.

I hit the mark almost perfectly as my black climbing rope dangled down from its chest. The robot was almost upon me now, so I latched onto the rope and as it walked over me, I pulled myself up off the ground and began the harrowing climb to the top of this massive piece of machinery. It was a hard and grueling climb and the momentum of the monster's legs slammed me around against its metal body several times, almost causing me to lose my grip. After a long slog up the rope, I was able to get a grip in the gaps

between the metal plate on its chest and I slowly began to make my way up the behemoth's chest, towards the head, where I knew that Mr. Tanpopo sat in the control booth.

Something about the idea of creating an eighteen story high robot that looked and acted like a human was kind of ridiculous. Surely there were better designs for robots than modeling them after a human. Humans are lanky, they twist and turn like rubber, folding over, stretching up, spinning and jumping, all the things an eighteen story robot can't do. Their creations could barely move through the streets of Tokyo and although they were tough as nails and able to withstand missile blasts and crumbling architecture, they were slow and dim-witted. The robot moved like molasses and as I hung from its chest, it felt like its balance was off just a hair giving it the ever present feeling of almost falling down (I later found out that this was a natural state and that it would take an extraordinary event to knock down a Man-o-Bot™ because all of its interior gears and gyroscopes maintained the balance).

Thanks to my rock climbing skills, I was able to make my way all the way up to the head of the Man-o-Bot™. Its head was huge, big enough to house the control room where Mr. Tanpopo sat and guided the beast. It had what one would consider a face, with a nose, an exhaust vent for a mouth, and two, yellow, glass eyes, through which the "driver" could see.

And yet, the most fascinating part of it all was the fact that on the back of the robot's head, along an easily traversable walkway, was a small door that led inside. I thought, *Surely this door can't be unlocked,* but as I lifted the latch, it swung right open, much to the dismay of Mr. Tanpopo, who

was strapped into the driver's seat.

"What?" he yelled, struggling to look at me over his shoulder. "What are you doing in *here?*"

"I've come to stop you," I said, a slight smirk on my face at the fact that Mr. Tanpopo was helpless in his base of operations. He brought the robot to a stop in the middle of the street, mere meters from the Japanese parliament building as he struggled and strained to undo the seat belts and buckles that kept him safe.

"You've made a big mistake coming here," he said, trying to sound threatening. His threats rang hollow as one of his belts would not come loose. He started to grow frantic.

I looked over at the wall and saw a large, ten-inch key in an ignition, and thought to myself, *Surely that's not the key to stop this thing, is it?*

I started walking over to the key and Mr. Tanpopo began to go apoplectic. "No!" he yelled. "Don't touch that!"

I turned the key and pulled it out, and soon all of the power systems in the robot went off, leaving this giant machine that had done so much damage to the city of Tokyo as a large, immobile piece of scrap metal. "It's over, Mr. Tanpopo," I said.

Mr. Tanpopo looked very disillusioned and he stopped fiddling with his seatbelt. "I never thought it would end like this," he muttered...

88 NO-SCENT WEREWOLF REPELLENT

One of the biggest challenges in dealing with werewolves is how to avoid the power of their incredibly strong sense of smell. After all, how does an unarmed human battle a werewolf if there is no silver around or no stakes for the heart? A human cannot match a werewolf's strength, the wolf would rip them to shreds, and a human doesn't have the endurance to outrun a werewolf, so fleeing is not an option (and contrary to popular children's stories, werewolves can get into brick houses just as well as they can get into straw and stick houses). Mr. Ping thought long and hard on the subject of how to protect the average person from a werewolf attack, and in the winter of 1978, he came up with the idea of No-Scent Werewolf Repellent, and began selling it in Britain.

No-Scent comes in a spray can, like a deodorant, and comes out in an aerosol spray. The user must spray themselves from head to toe, and once they have done this, their scent "disappears" from their body, meaning a werewolf can't smell a person wearing the product. Werewolves rely on their sense of smell as much, if not more, than their sense of sight, and when a human wears No-Scent, it is the equivalent of putting a blindfold on a human. They cannot smell the person and when taking the spray into account, the odds of a werewolf taking interest are pretty minimal. Werewolves, by instinct, don't take this lightly, and have done their best to try to thwart Mr. Ping in the court system by claiming that the health standards of the No-Scent factory are very poor.

89 WEREWOLF COLLARS

Another deterrent developed by Mr. Ping during the Great Werewolf Explosion of the 1970s, the werewolf collar is simply a modified dog collar with trace amounts of silver embedded inside, which weakens the werewolf. The collars also come with a remote control "shock" system, which will send a good ten thousand volts through said werewolf if it gets out of line. Mr. Ping always felt that the use of the werewolf dog collar was slightly demeaning for the werewolves, and would only use it in very extreme circumstances, like the Werewolf Sit-In of East Brixton in 1978, or the Great Canine Uprising of 1987. It also should be noted that early versions of werewolf collars became legendary in the werewolf community of London. The reason for this is because the collars usually burned away the hair on the werewolves necks.

90 THE DOG WHISTLE GUN

Invented by Mr. Ping and a scientist by the name of Lewis Debenittetti, the Dog Whistle Gun was created as a deterrent for werewolves. Since most canines have hyper-sensitive hearing, well-above the threshold of human beings, Mr. Ping wanted a safe, secure weapon to keep werewolves at bay. Werewolves had become a major problem in the latter half of the twentieth century due to the London werewolf population explosion, and they were becoming much more organized in their efforts (including starting their own temp agency for mob hits and an attempt to unionize themselves to get better wages for their killings and murders). Mr. Ping wanted some sort of weapon that wasn't a weapon in the conventional sense of the word.

The main line of defense against werewolves for the average person was the silver bullet, and considering the fact that Mr. Ping had a great loathing for guns ("Monstrous, evil, and completely without use or merit..."), he felt he had to invent something to keep them at bay. He came up with several devices, including Werewolf Collars, No-Scent Werewolf Repellent, and the infamous Armicons. However, his first invention was the Dog Whistle Gun.

Looking much like a toy gun with a large bullhorn on the front, the Dog Whistle Gun emits an extremely intense, high-pitched sound that can't be heard by human ears but can cause stress for canines. Basically, it incapacitates the werewolf with what humans would think is silence and it has proved very effective for crowd control for the canine set. Werewolf Today, a weekly British magazine that caters to the werewolf population, picked the Dog Whistle Gun as the worst invention of 1979, and several werewolf-centered newspapers warned of the gun and expressed concern about its availability. Basically, the werewolves were afraid that everyone and their neighbor might get a Dog Whistle Gun and because of this, the werewolves would no longer be able to partake in their favorite pastime, which was eating humans.

Mr. Ping's first use of the Dog Whistle Gun was during a trip to the annual Werewolf Governor's Ball in Kent, England. The Werewolf Governor's Ball was a chance for an ever-expanding British werewolf population to thumb their noses at humans and celebrate themselves before going out to snack on the local townsfolk. Each year, they would celebrate in a different city, dancing until late into the night, whereupon they would leave en masse and hunt down the locals. One particular year, Mr. Ping found out the top secret location of the ball and set about to curb the feast:

...I stood on the balcony, unseen by almost all of the clan of werewolves on the floor below. Doing my best to remain downwind from them, I listened to the main speaker delivering his keynote address to all in attendance. The speaker in question was a gray werewolf with very broad shoulders, and he stood hunched over, as if he wasn't as comfortable walking on two legs as he was four. Still, he was a werewolf through and through, with his long, yellow fangs, cold, black nose, glowing eyes, and drool dripping from his chin.

"And once again," he was saying, "We'd like to give a big growl out to Irma and Nigel Zevon for picking the lovely town of Kent for our festivities this year." He motioned over to two shy and demure werewolves with their arms around each other in the corner. They waved to the crowd, who let out a cheer.

"Really good choice, Nigel and Irma. I had an encounter with a vagrant on the street today and let me just say he was *delectable*.

"But really, what would the Werewolf Governor's Ball be without the end of the evening feast?" The crowd of werewolves shouted for joy at the mention of this. "A lot of you have been dancing all night, working up an appetite for the big meal that's headed your way in a few minutes. Just imagine, a whole town of sleepy, defenseless, chewy Brits, all just waiting to be picked clean." The speaker wiped a long string of drool from his chin. "Excuse me," he said, laughing. "I go crazy just thinking about it. Anyway, talk is cheap and actions speak louder than words, so what do you say we go out there and massacre this town?"

Once again, the crowd erupted with joy, and everyone turned for the exits. But there was one thing that was standing in their way: me.

"Excuse me," I said, and every werewolf in the place turned to look at me, "I don't think you'll be massacring anyone tonight."

"A human!" one wolf shouted.

"What's he doing here?" yelled another one.

"He looks tasty," said a third.

"Are you white meat or dark meat?" asked a fourth.

One of the werewolves moved from the floor of the ballroom to the balcony on which I stood. It bared its fangs and prepared to swipe me with its long claws, when I jerked the Dog Whistle Gun from my side and pulled the trigger.

Immediately, the werewolf fell to the ground, clutching its ears in pain. It was rendered totally incapacitated by my invention. An audible gasp burst forth in the room and everyone began to murmur.

"Who's next?" I asked. "Or should *I* be the one to choose?"

No one answered...

91 YETI-PROOF

*Irwin Windsor had a dream and that dream was to get revenge. His father was world-renowned adventurer and explorer Winston Windsor, a man of the world and member of the Global Geographical Society. Winston Windsor met his untimely end high upon the mountain known as K2 in Pakistan, and although the details of his death were sketchy, it was widely rumored amongst the locals that Winston Windsor was killed not from altitude sickness or hypothermia, but by the fierce and nasty-looking creature known throughout the region as "The Ugly, Half-Brother of the Fearsome Himalayan Yeti."
When word of his father's death reached a sixteen-year old Irwin Windsor, he was utterly devastated, and there in the firelight of Mr. Windsor's opulent living room in his opulent apartment in London, young Irwin vowed to get revenge on the creatures that killed his father. He claimed he would not rest until every last yeti had been hunted down and killed. Windsor spent years hunting yetis all over the world, and although he had a vast fortune at his disposal, he failed to kill, wound, or even maim one single yeti. In fact, he failed to even see one.
That is, until he ran into Reggie on the streets of downtown London one rainy afternoon, as detailed in the following excerpt from Mr. Ping's almanac, Vol. 65:*
"...These are the worst fish and chips I think I've ever eaten," Reggie said, spitting the mushy pulp that he'd been chewing onto the sidewalk.
"The key, Reggie," I said to him, "Is that when you eat fish and chips, there has to be *fish* in the batter. You can't get fish and chips without the fish in the batter."
"Well, I can't rightly eat fish when I'm a vegetarian, now, can I?" he asked.

"Your choice is your choice," I said. "But don't complain about the fish and chips when all you're eating is a giant ball of deep fried flower without any fish inside it."

"Fine," he said with a huff.

We were walking down Kensington street on our way to Buckingham Palace for our appointment with the Queen, when right in front of us rose a commotion that sent everyone running in a panic trying to take cover. People were screaming and clamoring all over one another to get out of the way, and cars, taxis, and buses all screeched to a halt to avoid them.

"This can't be good," I said, looking over at Reggie.

Reggie tossed his mushy "fish and chips" in the garbage basket and took off his sport coat, rolling up his sleeves. "I certainly hate to dirty up my suit, but it seems that there might be work to be done."

As the crowd cleared, we saw the source of the commotion, which was a single, well-armed man walking down the center of the road, his gaze fixed upon Reggie. "Who's that?" Reggie asked, examining the fellow for familiarity. He was young, in his early twenties, with curly, black hair. He wore a brown leather trench coat with guns, knives, and even a crossbow attached to it, and he carried a very powerful elephant gun in his hands.

"That's Irwin Windsor," I said. "He's the heir to the Windsor hotel chain."

"A blue-blood, eh?" Reggie said. "Why in the world is he walking towards us?"

"You killed my father, yeti," Irwin yelled from just down the street. He had a grim determination as he raised the gun towards Reggie. "For that, you're going to pay."

"Huh?" Reggie asked. "Who in the world is your father?"

Irwin fired the elephant gun at us, but we ducked out of the way, leaving the pellets to shatter the front window of the candy shop behind us. Reggie and I exchanged looks from the ground, both of us rolling our eyes. Reggie, in particular, looked angry.

"Prepare to die, yeti," Irwin said.

"Shall I take care of this, Mr. Ping?" Reggie asked.

"Feel free," I said, trying to get a stain out of the elbow of my suit from the fall to the ground.

Reggie rose to his feet and began walking towards Irwin, who was reloading the gun. "Look," he said, his voice rough and angry, his yellow teeth bared, and his eyebrows low over his eyes, "I don't know who you think you are, or who your father was, but the fact that you've come to downtown London with all of your stupid little guns strapped to your body, fills me with an anger that makes me want to teach you a very valuable lesson." By now, Reggie was towering over Irwin, who was so terrified that his trembling hands dropped the shotgun shells.

"You k-killed m-my father," he muttered, looking up at Reggie.

"No, I didn't," Reggie said.

"Yes, y-you did."

"No," Reggie said, jerking the elephant gun from his hands and twisting the barrel into a knot, "I didn't."

With a flourish, Reggie ripped the leather trench coat from Irwin's body with one swipe and wadded it up, guns, knives, and all, into the size of a baseball. Then, he leaned into Irwin's face and gave him a good whiff of yeti-breath. "I *loathe* guns," he said with a sneer. Irwin was so scared, he passed out.

When he awoke fifteen minutes later, the London authorities were trying to remove him from a light pole

that Reggie had bent around him in a knot, which of course, wasn't half as embarrassing as the fact that Reggie had left him in his underwear. "I can't really say that I approve of your methods," I told him.

"People who use guns like that deserve this sort of public humiliation," he laughed. He walked over to a police officer and said, "Sorry about the lamp post, sirs. I had to find some way to detain him. I'll pay for the damages..."

Humiliated, Irwin gave up his quest to kill all yetis, but proceeded to start a yeti-proofing business that has achieved remarkable success around the world. He seemed to have tapped into a popular market and his business continues to grow under the motto: "If we can keep a yeti out, we can keep anything out."

Yeti-Proof is one of the most popular security companies in the world, but Reggie still keeps an eye on Irwin Windsor, for the roots of his yeti-hatred run deep. It has always been suspected that Irwin may simply be lying in wait, anticipating the next time he can strike.

92 GINGER JARS

It's unknown where the tradition of booby-trapping ginger jars with magic got started, but the first documented evidence of such a trap was with Sir Harrywith Withmore of Northampton, England in 1876. Sir Withmore was looking for the jewels of a mysterious emperor in a cave in the Yellow Mountains of China, when he stumbled upon a ginger jar:

...When I plucked the lid from the top, I saw the jewels glowing at the bottom of the jar. But as I reached into the jar, the most alarming thing happened....

...My hand fell off.

It happened so quickly; I don't really know what I could have done to save it. It simply fell off. There was no bleeding, no wound. My hand simply fell onto the ground. Yet what was

strange about the whole thing was that I could still move it.

Though my hand was detached from my arm, I could still move it. If I thought about making a fist, the hand laying at the bottom of the jar made a fist. If I wanted to point a finger, it pointed its finger. It was quite disconcerting and I had a feeling that some sort of black magic had bewitched these jewels...

Booby-trapped ginger jars are commonplace and one must be very careful when they approach them. Even if they have nothing inside, it doesn't mean they aren't a trap.

93 THE UNDERWORLD, taken from Mr. Ping's almanac, Vol. 33

Mr. Ping's adventures in the underworld from the year 1932 were some of his more incredible trips. The following details Mr. Ping's first trip to the "other side":

*...*The stranger began to make his way down the plank, towards me. As he moved closer, I could see that underneath the large, straw hat, the man was clearly Asian, but his eyes looked like large, black holes. His skin was more wrinkled than it should have been. The light, pajama-like clothes he wore seemed to be as old as he was. He said nothing to me, only choosing to extend his hand towards me, as if he expected something in return for his help. "Oh!" I said. "The toll!" I fished in my pockets and pulled out a handful of coins, giving them to the boatman.

He looked at the coins for a second, then looked back at me, filling me with horror. "Is that it?" the boatman asked. "Four Hong Kong dollars?"

"It's all I have," I said.

The boatman sighed. "Follow me," he said as he led me up the plank. "You have a lot to learn, young man."

I couldn't help but feel both frightened and strangely comforted by the boatman.

Although his ship was creepy, his presence left me at ease, as if I was in safe hands. "Do you know where Torso Island is?" I asked.

"I'm dead," he said. "There are no secrets for me. I see both the future and the past, as it extends off in all directions, from the first atom to the infinite plains of the multiverse created with every millisecond of decisions made in the world."

"Huh?" I asked, trying to make sense of what he was saying.

"Look, I know everything," the boatman said, annoyed as he walked along the creaking deck towards the back of the boat. "When you know everything, finding a place like Torso Island is simple. Just don't ask me how the universe ends."

"You know how the universe ends?" I asked.

"Of course, I do," he said.

"How does it end?" I asked.

The boatman took the wheel of the ship and turned to me. I was now standing beside him. "If I told you, your brain would explode," he said. "I'm not kidding. It would explode. Literally." He gave me a mean, intimidating smile and suddenly I didn't feel so safe with this boatman after all. "Look, be a friend and pull up that plank, would you?"

After I got my bearings, he walked over and pulled the plank back up on the dock. Slowly, the junk started to drift away from the gravel bank, only the occasional creaks from the hull breaking the calm silence of the cave. I made my way back to the boatman, watching him steer his way into the fog. The fog grew thicker the further we went, and soon I could barely see my hand in front of my face. "How can you see where you're going?" I asked.

"I told you," the boatman said, "I know all. You think navigating in fog is hard, you should try contemplating the moment the sun explodes."

"The sun's going to explode?" I asked, wide-eyed.

"Of course," said the boatman. "Sooner than you think. Of course, that could be thousands of years…or it could be two. Only the dead know…"

94 WITCH CURSES, taken from Mr. Ping's Almanac, Vol. 23

Unlike regular curses, which must always be spoken in Mandarin, witch curses are an entirely different matter. The workings of witches have always been a well-kept secret and try as he might, Mr. Ping never got the truth of their lifestyle or their methods. In fact, of all the horrible, terrible, dangerous things that Mr. Ping encountered over the years, witches were the only things that filled him with genuine fear. His encounters with witches were few and far between, and the ironic part was that he had just as much contact with good witches as bad witches. Unfortunately, his encounters with evil witches were always memorable, and not necessarily in a good way.

What is known about witch curses is simply what Mr. Ping gleamed from hearsay and his own witch curse, which was placed upon him in the winter of 1921. While traveling through rural Virginia on his way to Washington D.C., he stayed over at an old hotel called The Sassafras Inn:

…I don't know why I decided to stay at the Sassafras that night. I was tired and I wanted to get a good night's rest, so the establishment didn't really matter to me. The Sassafras, though not the nicest hotel, was cheap and convenient, being near the train station.

I should have trusted my instincts, but I was too tired. The lobby was dark, with pale green wallpaper and wood that was painted black running midway along it. The entirety of the lobby was lit by the single working bulb in a chandelier that was hanging much too high to be effective. The man behind the counter looked as though he hadn't bathed in a few weeks and seemed to be missing most of his teeth (and those that he did have were broken and scaly).

"You a foreigner?" he asked when I approached the desk with my single suitcase. "You speak English? We don't serve nobody who don't speak no English."

Normally, I would have been annoyed, but I was much too tired. "I assure you, sir, that I speak English quite well. I'd like a room for the night."

"Humph!" he said, somewhat indignant at my indifference to him. "Seven dollars for a room."

"The sign outside says five," I said.

"Foreigner tax," he said, giving me a grimy smile.

I didn't feel like arguing, and there were no other hotels anywhere close, so I gave him the money and went to my room. Unfortunately, the room was not much more hospitable than the lobby. It consisted of what would questionably be called a bed, a wash basin that looked as if it had been used once too often, and a window that had a lovely view of the bricks that had been embedded inside of it when they made an addition to the building.

I was famished, and though I didn't really want to go, I made my way down to the lobby again to search for something to eat. The innkeeper grumbled at the thought of making me dinner, but still shuffled back to the kitchen to prepare a meal for me. He came back with a plate of runny eggs, some mealy bread, and a glass of water that looked as though he'd just pulled it from the creek.

I was midway through my meal when the thunderstorm hit. The wind rose to violent levels outside and lightning cracked with sharp intensity, followed by the thunder to match it. It wasn't long before the sparse lighting of the hotel was taken out by the storm. I ate my meal in silence as the rain pelted the black windows.

"You bring this storm with you, Chinaman?" the clerk asked, his sickly grin illuminated by the flashes of lightning.

I said nothing, enjoying the violence of the storm for a few more minutes before I retired to my room. As I sat back, staring at the window, a flash of lightning illuminated a figure standing outside right in front of me. It was only a flash, but it appeared to be a woman with wet, limp hair hanging down on the sides of her head. It was a bit disconcerting, and with the next flash of lightning, I saw nothing. She was gone.

I looked over to see if the clerk had seen it, but he was too busy burning small pieces of paper in the candle. Another flash of lightning made me look to a window on the opposite side of the building, where in that split second of time, I saw the figure again. I rose from my chair slowly and made my way to where I had seen her. Once again, I saw nothing with the next flash.

I realized something bad was going to happen and when the front door of the hotel blew off its hinges, flying across the room to snap in half on the stairs, I knew it had begun. In the doorway was the woman I'd seen in the windows. She was fairly short and wore a ragged, brown dress. She stood there with a wicked grin on her face, staring at us.

Only this woman wasn't standing. She was floating.

Her black, pointed shoes were hovering almost ten inches off of the ground. Her hair obscured her face, but what I could see wasn't pretty. Her nose was pockmarked and sickly purple in the light of the rapidly diminishing candle.

"Solomon Jonesss?" she said, her voice low and hoarse, as if she'd been screeching and damaged her vocal cords.

Apparently, she was talking to the clerk, who was backed up against the mailboxes behind the counter. "Whaddya want, Beb Proctor?" he asked, his voice trembling.

"You know why I'm here," the mysterious woman hissed. She floated into the lobby and rose high above the counter, dangling limply over the clerk as the thunderstorm raged outside.

"I didn't do it, Beb Proctor," the Clerk yelled. This seemed to have no bearing on Beb Proctor's anger. She made a motion like she was pulling an invisible rope upward, and the clerk slowly rose from the floor, as if he was hanging from the gallows.

I was at a loss. This strange woman was obviously doing something to this man. Regardless of his guilt or innocence in whatever matter they were speaking about, I could not sit idly by and watch a man be killed.

"Let him go," I said.

Suddenly, the clerk fell to the ground and the strange woman spun around in the air to look at me. Her eyes glowed green through her matted strands of hair and she hissed.

"I have no quarrel with you," I said. "But I cannot let you kill that man."

The hairs on the back of my neck stood at attention as she began to slowly float towards me, her head cocked like some animal observing something it didn't understand. Still, her face was fierce and the closer she got, the more I realized how hideous she actually looked. Floating through the air, she moved closer and closer, her face coming within inches of mine.

"You shouldn't be involved with that which you don't understand," she cackled. She lifted her open hand to her mouth and blew some sort of dust in my face. Almost immediately, I started coughing, unable to catch my breath. I fell to the floor, struggling to breathe as this strange woman floated back to the clerk. She jerked upward and the clerk jumped to his feet, moving like a puppet on a string. "There are too many people here," she whispered to him, almost as if she might have been his girlfriend. "Let's go someplace where the two of us can be alone."

She casually floated out the door, pulling on an imaginary leash that dragged the clerk out the door by the hands. As the storm raged outside, the clerk and the strange woman disappeared into the torrent, never to be seen again. I soon caught my breath and checked outside for either of them, but the only thing I saw was the relentless rain. I would not be saving the clerk on this night, regardless of whether he was worth saving in the first place...

Later that night, Mr. Ping discovered that he took home a bit of "baggage" from his first encounter with a witch, for when she blew the dust in his face, she placed a curse upon him (knowledge that he gained later, when the curse was lifted by a "good" witch). He continued coughing all night until, around four in the morning, when he coughed up a small frog that scurried out of his mouth as he lay in bed. Needless to say, coughing up a frog was terribly unnerving. Every night for the next six months, he had a ten minute coughing spell, which always culminated in his coughing up a small, live frog. When the curse was lifted, he discovered that this was the Spell of the Alluvial Moon, a curse native to the eastern coast of the United States. It was only through the good graces of another, equally mysterious witch that the curse was lifted, for she could see that his "aura" had a spell upon it and removed it free of charge.

The Spell of the Alluvial Moon left Mr. Ping quite shaken (as it would anyone who ended up coughing up a frog every night for six months), and he did his best to avoid witches as much as possible after that.

95 GOLDFISH, HEDLEY, AND THE VOLCANO

In one of Mr. Ping's most harrowing adventures from 1983 (the Great Chinese Fireworks Incident that took place in Hawaii), he found himself face-to-face in a battle with Hedley the Swordfish on the side of one of Hawaii's most active volcanoes. Hedley was deadly, and after a protracted, dangerous fight, Mr. Ping found himself at the wrong end of Hedley's sharp nose, a situation that looked most dire. That is, until he found a very unlikely ally:

...At very few points in my life have I tasted the bitter medicine that is defeat, but as I lay on the ground with that horrible, gurgling swordfish's nose threatening my throat, I knew that I'd been beaten. My arm was in too much pain to move and I was sure I'd cracked a few ribs when I fell upon the rocks, so I was useless physically. Plus, there was the fact that this swordfish was much too skilled as a fighter to take him on while injured.

"Not feeling so high and mighty now, are you, Mr. Ping?" he gurgled. His voice had the timbre of a clogged toilet trying to get rid of its contents.

I held onto his sharp nose, hoping to prevent it from jabbing into my throat. "You've got to stop them," I said. "They'll destroy this whole island."

"Oh, really?" the swordfish said. "Is that what they'll do? Look, Mr. Buddha-man, they're paying the bills, not you, so your advice doesn't mean squat to me. In fact, one of the clauses in my contract stipulated that if I didn't kill you, I wouldn't get paid. So I

guess I have to fulfill my obligations, don't I?"

He laughed wickedly and I braced myself for my final moments when a familiar voice rang out. "Set him free!"

The swordfish spun away from me, turning to look back behind him. There, standing on the sharp, black lava rock was no one else but Bird and Goldfish (who, incidentally, was standing on his tail fins). "What in the world is this?" the swordfish asked. "Is somebody playing a joke on me?"

"This is no joke," Bird said, looking at him sternly. "You've picked the wrong side, my friend. This is coming to an end right now."

"Ha!" the swordfish laughed. "Yeah, right. I'll bet you..."

But he was cut off almost instantly, as Bird shot at him like a bullet, her yellow body streaking through the air as she rammed her sharp little beak between his eyes. The speed and momentum of her nosedive sent him flying backwards, straight onto his rump. I could see his eyes trying to regain their focus as he struggled to get up again.

I, too, struggled to get to my feet as Bird came over and landed on my shoulder. "Are you okay, Confucius?" she asked.

"I'll be okay when Maui is safe from him and his thugs," I said.

"RARGH!" the swordfish yelled as he approached us. "No one does that to Hedley and gets away with it!"

Then Goldfish hopped between us, blocking the swordfish's path. "You'll go no further," he said. "This ends here."

Hedley was filled with anger, but couldn't help but snicker at the four-inch tall goldfish standing in front of him. "Oh, this is ridiculous," he said. "Sorry, sir, but you're an appetizer, not an adversary."

"I beg to differ, Hedley," Goldfish said.

The swordfish paused for a second and looked at Goldfish. "Wait a minute," he said. "How do you know my name?"

"I know everything about you," Goldfish said. "You have no secrets with me."

"Oh, really?" Hedley laughed. "And why is that?"

"Because I've watched you for years, Hedley," he said. "I know you."

"What?" Hedley laughed. "What are you? My mother?"

"No," Goldfish said. "I'm not your mother."

"Then who are you?" he asked.

"Hedley," Goldfish said, "I am your *father*."

I had never heard a scream of horror emanate from an air-breathing swordfish before, and after hearing Hedley's reaction to Goldfish's news, I hoped that I'd never have to hear one again...

96 YETI-HUNTING

A sport popular in the 1930s amongst the wealthy elite, yeti-hunting in the Himalayas attracted a wide variety of sportsmen from around the globe, all of which were searching desperately for the prize of a yeti-fur. Although with average people, the existence of the yeti was highly suspect (as it still is today), amongst a certain class of people in both the United States and Europe, the existence of the yeti was taken to be fact, and these wealthy people combed the Himalayas back and forth for several years, looking for the creatures. Ninety-nine point nine percent of these "yeti-hunters" never even came close to seeing a yeti, let alone killing one, and the point-one percent of people that did see a yeti came away traumatized from the experience. Almost all of those that saw the yeti experienced what most yetis refer to as "fang-block." When confronted with a hunter, most yetis use bluster and physicality to scare their predators away, and if

one were to ever experience a
"yeti-charge," it's rumored that
one would never be the same
again. *Reggie was once
confronted by a hunter early in
the century and was none too
pleased with it. The following
excerpt details that experience and
is taken from Reggie's
autobiography entitled,* Yeti Like
Me:

...At first, the chap held
his big, stupid gun up to
me with the fear-fueled
intention to kill me, but
with my lightning fast
reflexes, I quickly
snatched the weapon
right out of his hand.
"Not so tough without
your gun, are you?" I
asked.

He muttered something
in German, his eyes as
bright and as fear-filled
as anything I'd ever
seen. I took the gun
and wrapped it around
his neck, leaving him
just enough room to
breathe. Considering it
was the middle of
nowhere, it would be a
very long time before
he managed to get it
off.

"Guns are for idiots,
idiot," I said and walked
off, leaving the gun
barrel wrapped around
his throat...

97 SMELTS SPILLS FRUIT DRINK

*A sour day in both Reggie and
Smelts' personal histories, the day
Smelts spilled his fruit drink on
Reggie's prized, first-edition copy
of* Harper Lee's To Kill a
Mockingbird *was not a fun day
to be in the offices of the
Himalayan Outback Detective
Agency, as detailed in this excerpt
taken from transcripts of a tape
recorder that Smelts was using to
record an interview with a client:*

SMELTS: (To
client) ...So tell me
again about this
"ghost."

CLIENT: Well, it's
big...and round. I
actually found it to
look rather
frightening, but not
in a way I can easily
describe. It looked
like a giant, yellow
mouse with blue spots
and two beady eyes...
(Reggie enters)
REGGIE: Smelts, did
you do this?
SMELTS: (To client)
Excuse me for one
second. (To Reggie)
I'm with a client
right now, Reginald.
Can this wait?
REGGIE: No, it can't
wait. Did you do
this?
SMELTS: Do what?
REGGIE: This. Did
you spill your drink
on my book?
SMELTS: No.
REGGIE: You looked
away.
SMELTS: So?
REGGIE: So! That's
a sign of guilt. You
looked away.
SMELTS: I did not.
REGGIE: You did it
again!
SMELTS: What are you
getting at?
REGGIE: It's a
classic psychological
technique to find out
if someone is lying.
You watch their eyes.
If they immediately
look to the right,
they're lying. You
looked to the right
all three times...
CLIENT: I could come
back...
SMELTS: No, no, Mr.
Hatch. I'll be right
with you...
REGGIE: Did you do
it?
SMELTS: No.
REGGIE: You're
lying.
SMELTS: How would
you know? I didn't
look to the right or
left that time.
REGGIE: Yeah, but
that time you were
trying too hard.
SMELTS: Could you
please leave? I'm
with a client.
REGGIE: No. You
ruined my book.

SMELTS: It was an
accident.
REGGIE: Were you
going to tell me
about it?
SMELTS: No.
REGGIE: Why not?
SMELTS: Because I
knew you'd get
freaked out like
this.
REGGIE: No, I
wouldn't have.
SMELTS: Yes, you
would have. Look at
the way you're
acting, mate. You're
all googly-goo
because I spilled my
drink on your prized
book.
REGGIE: Well, why
shouldn't I be
googly-goo? You
ruined my book and
didn't tell me.
SMELTS: It was an
accident.
REGGIE: It was an
accident?
SMELTS: Yes, it was
an accident.
REGGIE: How could it
be an accident? It
was on the bookshelf!
SMELTS: Yeah. Sure.
REGGIE: What are you
getting at?
SMELTS: Nothing.
REGGIE: What do you
mean?
SMELTS: Nothing.
REGGIE: What do you
mean?
SMELTS: Well, it was
on the bookshelf,
but...
REGGIE: But, what?
SMELTS: But nothing.
REGGIE: No, but
what?
CLIENT: I really
should...
SMELTS: Please, Mr.
Hatch, this will only
take a second...
REGGIE: What do you
mean it was on the
bookshelf?
SMELTS: I mean it
was on the bookshelf
until I took it off
the bookshelf.
REGGIE: Why did you
take it off the
bookshelf?
SMELTS: I have my
reasons.
REGGIE: What
reasons? You were
reading it? You were

rearranging the shelf? What reasons did you have?
SMELTS: I had reasons. That's all.
REGGIE: What reasons?
SMELTS: I needed it.
REGGIE: Why?
SMELTS: Because.
REGGIE: Because why?
SMELTS: Because I did! Now, I have a client here. Will you please leave?
REGGIE: Not until you tell me what your reasons were.
CLIENT: Look, I really don't...
SMELTS: Please, mate. We'll only be a minute.
CLIENT: But...
SMELTS: Seriously. Just stay put.
REGGIE: What were your reasons, Smelts?
SMELTS: I was reading it.
REGGIE: Liar! You just looked to the right.
SMELTS: I did not.
REGGIE: You did it again.
SMELTS: No, I didn't.
REGGIE: Stop it! Why did you read my book?
SMELTS: I was using it.
REGGIE: Using it for what?
SMELTS: Well, we have that nice wooden table. You know that one?
REGGIE: Yes?
SMELTS: And I was drinking my juice...
REGGIE: Yes?
SMELTS: And there was condensation on the glass...
REGGIE: No!
SMELTS: And I didn't want to set the glass on the nice wooden table because it was so nice...
REGGIE: No!
SMELTS: So I used it.
REGGIE: No!
SMELTS: Yes.
REGGIE: No!
SMELTS: Yes.
REGGIE: You used my prized, first-edition copy of <u>To Kill a</u> <u>Mockingbird</u> as a coaster?
SMELTS: Yes.
REGGIE: No!
SMELTS: Yes.
REGGIE: No! You are...I ought to...If I...Argh!
SMELTS: And then I spilled the juice.
REGGIE: (Unintelligible)
SMELTS: Look, I'm sorry, if that's what you want to hear...
At that point, Reggie walked out of Smelts' office, but he didn't use the door. He walked right through the wall, using his yeti-strength to push a hole through the wood and plaster...

98 SHAOLIN MONK ROBE

Bird and Goldfish acquired the Shaolin Monk Robe from a monk in the Henan province of China many years ago. The robe is said to have been woven from the silky fine hairs of a dragon's chin and have been blessed by the ancient masters of the art of kung fu. Though its origins are hazy, what is known is that when a person wears the Shaolin Monk Robe, they acquire all of the abilities of the best Shaolin kung fu masters that have ever lived. Somehow, the robe imbues its wearer with skills that make he/she a master of the martial arts and virtually unstoppable on the battlefield. Mr. Ping put the robe to use at several times in his career, and although his own skills were quite formidable, the robe was only used when the odds against him seemed insurmountable. It is rumored that the dark masters of Shaolin kung fu created their own robe as a counter to the all powerful robe in Bird and Goldfish's **management***, but its whereabouts have never been known.*

ONE OF THESE PEOPLE WROTE THIS BOOK.
CAN YOU GUESS WHICH ONE?

THE WINNER GETS A PRIZE.

A · B · C

D · E · F

RANDALL P. GIRDNER WAS BORN IN TAHLEQUAH, OKLAHOMA, BUT
STRANGELY ENOUGH, HE IS NOW A CANADIAN CITIZEN AND
SUMMERS IN ORILLIA, ONTARIO.
HE HAS TAUGHT MIDDLE SCHOOL STUDENTS MOST OF HIS
LIFE IN COUNTRIES AROUND THE WORLD, INCLUDING
KAZHUKISTATATAN, BALILAND, THE PEOPLE'S REPUBLIC OF
HOODYHOO, AND POO-POO VILLE.

YOU CAN LEARN MORE INTERESTING FACTS ABOUT
RANDALL P. GIRDNER AT:
HTTP://WWW.BOYDMCCLOYD.COM
HTTP://WWW.GRACELANDWEST.COM